C L A

Setite

KATHLEEN RYAN

author	*kathleen ryan*
cover artist	*john van fleet*
series editors	*john h. steele and stewart wieck*
copyeditor	*anna branscome*
graphic designer	*kathleen ryan*
art director	*richard thomas*

More information and previews available at
white-wolf.com/clannovels

White Wolf Publishing
735 Park North Boulevard, Suite 128
Clarkston, GA 30021
www.white-wolf.com

First Edition: July 1999

10 9 8 7 6 5 4 3 2 1

Printed in Canada.

To my Mom, for her birthday

Setite

part one:
new york

Saturday, 31 July 1999, 12:33 AM
A studio apartment in Red Hook, Brooklyn
New York City, New York

She sat in the exact center of her own apartment, and waited.

The collar of her crisp, white cotton shirt lay open, just as he had left it. The blood on her neck had dried, and the tender skin there itched under the sticky crust. The handcuffs, finally, lay still. Tested, the chains and shackles had held, and she was weary of fighting them.

With the irons, *he* had bound her to and through an old, heavy office chair—solid walnut, too sturdy for her to destroy, even if she wanted to. And, she thought, *he* would have known that she wouldn't. Though the ruddy scratches on her wrists pained her, the knowledge that her struggles had scraped the foul and dirt-encrusted bonds over the polished antique—*uselessly*, by God—hurt almost as badly. Wrist to wood to steel to wood to wrist, the hated things left broad, brick-red stains on her skin, on the shining walnut, and on the center pillar of her home, and there was nothing she could do now but watch, and wait, and remember.

He hadn't left a light burning in the apartment, but through the windows—the enormous, beautiful, north-facing, morning windows she'd rented the loft to have—the city gave her enough light to see by.

The neon, the cars, the streetsigns silhouetted the studio, her workshop, and gave the apartment its own sky-line. There, the easel and its half-cleaned painting, standing tall above the borough. Beside it, a modern sky-scraper, all angles and difficult curves: her quilt stand, stretched with a cavalry flag and draped in mending lin-ens. The workbench, a little apart from the better neighborhood, was a warehouse and factory, the roof busy with neat rows of bottles, cleansers, jars, brushes, boxes of gloves and cotton swabs. The desk, large, straight-lined, imposing, was the—

The desk, dull and dark by streetlight, was real, true cherry. It would glow like copper when the real, true light struck it—when the sun rose, and shone like a god through the beautiful, huge, north windows—

That was the desk, she thought, and remembered.

Monday, 21 June 1999, 11:46 PM
Rutherford House, Upper East Side, Manhattan
New York City, New York

The desk was a wreck. Dusty, dirty, scarred, paint-smeared, neglected, its dovetails were falling to pieces, and the patent mechanisms that had made it "state of the art" before the term was invented had been broken for years. The center lock had, at some long-forgotten date, been sawn through and removed completely. The three side drawers had their locks, but so filthy were the mechanisms that even their right keys could never shut them again. Not that she had the right keys; she wasn't sure, in fact, that the wood around the locks would have survived the experiment. The cabinet side squeaked and rasped when opened, and the swinging table inside sang like a dying elephant if she dared make it emerge.

She wrung a cut-up cotton T-shirt nearly dry of the warm water and wood soap, and began to lift the grime from the desktop. There was too much grit on the surface to risk wiping the rag across it, even along the grain, so she pressed the wet rag flat, and picked the dust up through sheer water tension and the knit of the cloth.

With infinite care, she removed the drawers. The center drawer and one of the side three shimmied in her hands; they would have to be trued-up and pinned solid again. The one cut for storing stationery had been repaired before, horrendously. She shook her head at the huge blobs of wood glue that lined the joints. The fourth drawer, unexpectedly, was sturdy, and all the slats and dividers missing from the others were sliding around inside it. Three were original to the desk, and she smiled over the thin sheets of wood like a child over a cracker-jack prize.

She opened the cabinet side, pulled the table up and out—with a noise, this time, less like an elephant and more like a broken merry-go-round—and crawled half beneath it. She put the bucket and duster aside for the moment, and dug in her hip pocket for a flashlight.

A voice erupted gently behind her, clearing its throat. "Is this," said the voice, "for sale here?"

Startled, the woman dropped the flashlight to the dusty boards. She pulled her head and shoulders out of the cabinet's maw, and looked up with dark-amber eyes. The store was dark, the workroom lamps were facing the wrong way, and the man was standing still further shadowed, in the calm, low light of the stairway leading to the owners' offices.

"No." She slid the grimy bandanna from her long, straight, chestnut hair, embarrassed. "Maybe." With the cleaner side of the kerchief, she wiped the dust from her face and squinted into the landing. "It could be, I guess," she went on, leaning against the comforting bulk of the thing. "It's mine. I'm afraid it's hardly Rutherford House quality..."

"I'm not really looking to buy. I was just curious..." The man's tone left the conversation open.

"I went to a sale with Amy Rutherford and saw it in the odd lot. When she bargained for the pieces she wanted, we brought it in as part of a package deal."

"Why?" And, somehow, the voice was genuinely interested, and she found herself talking on.

"Um...because it wasn't worth anything, really. Because we were really interested in some early Marathi—

sorry, some early Indian brassworks. And of course, if the dealer knew that they were what Amy was after, he might have double-checked his appraisal. As it was, we paid a few dollars too many for the desk, and picked up his 'souvenirs' for pennies. There's one in the niche behind you," she said, gesturing to a display on his right.

"But why all this?" One elegant hand pointed toward the bucket, the cleaners, and the drop cloths.

She smiled, and gestured vaguely with the bandanna. "Because I like it."

The man walked out of the stairwell and into the workroom. He was tall and straight, wearing a charcoal-gray suit that could make a tuxedo look casual—or denim overdressed. He was bald or shaved, but the bones of his skull were beautifully shaped. He wasn't handsome; he didn't have to be; he was complete, and perfectly sculpted, and his dark skin gleamed like candlelit mahogany. He walked into the workroom with the polite diffidence of a guest, picked up the nearest of the glaring lamps, and turned it to shine on the old desk.

"It's good. It's not a bad piece. Why do you say it isn't worth anything?"

"The pull-out," she replied, tapping on the swinging table. "It's built to conveniently store and conceal your typewriter, circa 1920. Patent pending. The estate thought they might be able to sell it to an office-supply place. But hardly anyone wants desks without file drawers, and no one, but no one, uses manual typewriters anymore. Some fool would have taken out the poor creature's guts and drilled holes through him to convert him to the computer age." She stroked the beaded edge of the desktop, murmuring, "And I couldn't let that happen to him."

"To him?"

The woman half-blushed, and put on a more businesslike face. "Sorry. I'm just a little animist. Is there anything I can do for you?"

"You might give me the honor of an introduction."

"Oh." She wiped off her right hand, and gave it to him. Her grip was firm, warm, and confident; his was strong, cool, and dry. "Elizabeth Dimitros. I'm on staff here."

"I'm Hesha Ruhadze. It's a pleasure to meet you."

"The same." She paused, trying to place him. Late visitors weren't uncommon, but she'd never seen this customer before. "Were you here to see Amy?"

"Agnes," he said, naming the senior partner. "She was saving an alabaster figure for me."

"The Old Kingdom ushebti?"

"Yes. You saw it?"

Elizabeth nodded. "I helped authenticate it. It was the best piece the Rutherfords had, this side of the Atlantic." She looked at him, curiously. "Are you interested in Egyptian art?" She stepped out of her sneakers and left them on the drop cloth. With her stocking foot, she touched a power strip, and the blazing workroom lamps flickered out. With her clean hand, she turned up the dimmers that controlled the display system.

The main floor of Rutherford House glowed softly in the lights. The walls of the gallery were the color and texture of eggshell, curved and molded to provide shelves and niches for the treasures they held. The artifacts—few of them were young enough to be merely antique—were masterfully displayed. There was harmony, and tradition, and a feel for Anglican upper-class aesthetics. But there was also a contrast in the groupings that spoke of a more modern hand, one that understood the shock of Zen and the unmindfully disciplined dash of Chinese calligraphy. Ruhadze followed her across the thick, soft carpet to a shelf draped in velvet a shade darker than the walls. A slender collar of lapis and gold beads lay in the hollow.

"This is terribly common of course," she said, "compared to your latest acquisition, but the ibis inlaid in the clasp is the finest carving of the—"

Hesha swayed, suddenly disoriented. There was a bright flash inside his own eyes, and the echo of a waking mind, just beyond his own—with shock he thought he recognized the sensation. *The Eye? Active?* He strained to catch hold of the traces, throwing all his energy into the effort. His body, neglected, began to buckle.

"Sir? Sir!"

He found himself falling against the wall, and the woman sprang to keep his head from cracking open on the shelf. He ignored her completely, and concentrated on following the emanations.

"Are you all right?" Her arms wrestled with the weight of him. She braced her knee behind his back, and turned his unresisting body over. His eyes were closed. "Lie down." He felt her raise his legs and prop them up on something hard, and then a soft, yielding cushion was placed beneath his head. Her hands fluttered at his cheeks and forehead, and he could feel her leave. He was glad; even the slightest distraction made focusing more difficult.

For an instant, the vague and slippery phenomenon held steady in his mental grasp: It was the Eye, he had no doubt now. Somewhere in the world it had been…freed. He had the statue with him in New York; that last-minute decision to bring it with him had been irrational, but thank Set for the omens that brought him to do so. He must go to it as quickly as possible.

A quilted blanket, smelling slightly of attics and moving vans, was spread across him, and his would-be nurse reached for his wrist to take a pulse.

Hesha motioned her away. "I'm all right." He sat up, accepting help he didn't need. Outwardly, he was grateful, and with half a thought spun an effortlessly plausible lie to explain his fall. His inner self was well-masked and racing with questions, analyzing the brief flash of clarity he'd achieved. Elizabeth kept a doubtful watch on him, but his steps were steady and his manner as polished as before the 'faint.' He drew his appreciation to a slow close and checked his watch.

"I really must be getting back to my hotel now," he said. "Thank you again, Mrs. Dimitros."

"Miss," she said, casually. "But call me Liz; everyone does."

He looked into her face thoughtfully. For a moment the mask was set aside and the problem of the Eye left alone. There was a question still unanswered here; the tiny puzzle charmed and tempted him.

"Would you mind," he began, "being Elizabeth to me? I'd hate to blend in with the common herd."

Elizabeth laughed, and her business face dropped away entirely. "Please."

"Would you mind," he asked, "putting that necklace aside for me to look at the next time I come?"

"Of course."

"And would you mind," he said again, "having dinner with me Thursday night?"

"I wouldn't mind at all," she said, laughing in surprise. And after he had gone, and the front door was locked behind him, it was some time before she remembered that the bucket, the rag, and the desk were still waiting.

A black sedan pulled up to Hesha at the curb. The rear right door opened for him automatically, and he slid into the sleek passenger compartment without hesitation.

The car was custom made for him. Its rear windows and the privacy panel were tinted; with the panel raised and the tint made black, the back seat was proof against the noonday sun. It held a laptop and a compact office;

it had phone, fax, a modem, and scramblers for security of all kinds. It was bulletproof, by the driver's insistence—Hesha's own plans were laid to avoid firefights, rather than to protect against them, but he respected the fears of his retainer.

"To Greenwich, Thompson, as fast as you can."

Hesha picked up his phone and dialed the number of his ally, Vegel. The younger Setite was in the position of junior partner in Hesha's quest for the Eye. He would be eager to hear that the Eye was on the move, and as mystified as Hesha that someone else had gotten to the artifact before them...the phone rang for the sixth time, and Hesha began to worry...Vegel would be needed in Baltimore immediately. Hesha was glad he'd sent a full team to Atlanta for this Toreador lunacy; having a Cessna waiting would...the phone rang for the eight time...the ninth...

The phone company informed him that the cellular number he had reached was not responding; the subscriber might be away from his phone or outside the range of their calling area.

Hesha flicked open the laptop and brought up a list of numbers. He punched one into the phone.

Tuesday, 22 June 1999, 12:08 AM
Parking garage, the High Museum of Art
Atlanta, Georgia

"McDonough," said Hesha.

"Sir!" The faintest hint of awe undercut the sharp, professional manner. Vegel's driver had heard the chief's voice before, but not often.

"Vegel's number is down. Find him. Have him call me back."

McDonough sat for a moment, thinking. He tried Vegel's line himself, and when the saccharine voice of the telephone company started its speech, cut the connection and left the vehicle. He double-checked the car's alarms, and walked slowly through the underground garage to the elevator. The eyes of other men and women were locked on him the entire way: guards, drivers, enforcers, playthings, and monsters waiting for their masters to return from the party above. He gave the tight knot of smokers by the exit booths a wide berth and approached the elevator. The doors opened on a heavily built, unsympathetic-looking gentleman in a tuxedo. McDonough kept his hands in sight and steady. His voice was level. "Mr. Vegel has an important call. I need to communicate with him."

"Step in."

The two men rose to the basement level of the High Museum, and McDonough was received by a further eight guards, all in tuxedos. They reminded him of a matched set of knives; sleek, beautiful, deadly.

"Wait here," said the elevator man. Ten minutes later, he returned, holding the door open for a woman—a woman more beautiful and more deadly than any 'knife' in the room. Her dark curls floated around her head as she walked toward him; her plain white, sleeveless gown rippled and flared with each step. She smiled at him, and the rest of the room ceased to exist; she spoke, and he had trouble remembering his own name.

"I'm sorry. Vegel seems to have left my party, Mr...."

"Mc...McDonough."

"You had a message for him?"

"Mr. Ruhadze called. Vegel's phone isn't working. I thought..."

"He isn't here. Let me take the call."

And McDonough pulled a phone from his pocket—too fascinated by the green eyes to notice the guards' hands automatically reaching into their jackets—and called the car in New York.

"Hello," she said, walking to a corner of the room. Her lackeys edged out of earshot.

"Who is this?" asked Hesha, evenly.

"This is Victoria. Victoria Ash."

"It's a pleasure to speak with you, Ms. Ash—"

"Victoria—"

"To what do I owe this unexpected delight?"

"I have your man here…a Mr. McDonough…who came running an errand for you. Of course, Mr. McDonough wasn't welcome above stairs…so as a courtesy to you, I looked for your errant friend myself."

"And?"

"No one's seen Vegel since midnight. A pity; he was a most enchanting conversationalist." She paused. "Is there anything else that I can do for you, Hesha?"

"No," he said, and there was as little emotion in that one flat syllable as there was enticement in hers. "Thank you for your efforts, Victoria. If Vegel should reappear…"

"I'll tell him to call you. He has the number?"

"A great many people seem to have this number. Good night, Victoria."

"Good night, Hesha."

Tuesday, 22 June 1999, 12:50 AM
Near Abingdon Square, Greenwich Village, Manhattan
New York City, New York

Hesha sat cross-legged, stripped of his coat and shirt, gazing intently into an eye of stone. In his hand he held the cord of a hollow bronze amulet. As the flashing, fickle energies twitched at his mind and his muscle, the swinging weight traced a pattern on the paper beneath it. A trickle of fine-ground, burnt powder fell from the pendulum's tip. At last, he broke away from the focus, and looked down at the record of his work.

Five lines radiated from the center. One thin, and terribly short...another locus in New York, perhaps. Another, a third of the way around the compass from the first, was almost as small in length, but the powder there was piled high into a ridge, so strongly and frequently had the string been pulled to that side. A line as thin as the first stretched far, far to the west. The longest, thickest line ran off the paper to the east...the carpet spoiled the tail of it, but it suggested Asia.

The last line, sharp and distinct, led southwest. He would measure the charcoal carefully, later, and find where the longest line ended, if he could—but he knew, with a certainty that drove his fine, elegant hands into fists, that the track south would be roughly a thousand miles long, and that the Eye of Hazimel was loose in Atlanta.

He called for Thompson. Speaking as calmly as could—there was no use putting ideas into the man's head before the facts were available—he commanded, "Thompson, get me a report from your team in Atlanta. I suspect...I want to know where Vegel is."

Tuesday, 22 June 1999, 12:53 AM
Parking garage, the High Museum of Art
Atlanta, Georgia

McDonough heard the shots before he saw anything.

He started the engine.

A handful of guards—the smokers—flew from the exit to their cars, firing at an unseen menace, and they trailed dark ribbons of *something* behind them. The ones that looked back, or tripped, or had to look for their limousines were cut down first—not by guns, but by the ebon tendrils.

Car alarms went off in every direction. Ghouls

stepped from their master's cars and drew weapons on the black mass that streamed unchecked down the ramp.

McDonough watched a gentleman in a pearl-gray suit turn and throw burning smoke into the darkness. The fire disappeared, and he lost sight of the grenadier. Other people—things—began to emerge from cover of the moving night. Vegel was gone…

The driver cursed, put the car in gear, and shot forward. He ran over a teenage girl whose arms were nothing but bone blades and sped through a firefight without giving either side a chance to blink. The exit was blocked, he knew—he pulled into the straight lane that led to the entrance—there were orange and white gates down, but by God, the limo could slam through them…and then McDonough saw a heavy trailer pull up to the curb, completely blocking the way out. It was hauling cement sewer-pipe rings and piles of iron rebar. Swarms of the enemy crawled out of the long gray cocoons. The streetlights behind it disappeared as shadow moved in…

McDonough drew his gun with one hand and reached for the phone with the other. The emergency code: A single button and the transmit command—but he was startled away, cringing as a monster—a boy, a skinny kid with filthy, flimsy clothes—leaped on the hood, firing over and over into the bulletproof glass. It splintered, and the red-fisted child laughed, threw the gun away, and punched a claw into the cracks.

The windshield tore apart, and the other taloned hand reached down.

McDonough was pulled from the car by his hair. The shatter-cubes of glass tore at his eyes and cheeks and hands. Half blind, he shot a full clip into the side of the beast who held him. The maddened vampire shook himself like a dog, and black blood spattered the concrete around them. Then he sank his fangs deep into the mortal neck, drained him dry, and howled.

Inside the remains of the car, the cell phone's faint blue light blinked over and over and over again: "SEND?"

Tuesday, 22 June 1999, 2:36 AM
Near Abingdon Square, Greenwich Village, Manhattan
New York City, New York

The Eye was closed again, and the traces were cut dead. As mystified as Hesha had been to know it open and in another's possession, he was twice as frustrated by the sudden silence. He rested his head on the high back of his chair and listened as Thompson called man after man. No driver—neither agent from the hotel—no pilots waiting at the plane. He called Fulton County police and reported the limousine stolen, and was told there were enough emergencies as it was—or wasn't he watching the news bulletins? Call back tomorrow.

Thompson put his phone down for the last time. "Nothing, sir. I think...I think they're dead." His voice cracked. Ronald Thompson had chosen the team that escorted Vegel to Atlanta. They were his own agents, and some were even friends.

"We won't jump to conclusions, Thompson. No one pushed their panic button?"

"No sir."

"We'll hope, then, that they've gone to ground somewhere." With a keystroke, he put the news page onto the dashboard screen. "Tomorrow they may have time to get word to us," he said. "They may even be on their way out already." Patiently, Hesha let Thompson stay in the room, giving the old cop time and...companionship.

The mortal would need a day or two to adjust to the deaths. In Hesha's own mind Vegel and his team were already six corpses—to be written off and replaced as soon as possible.

Wednesday, 23 June 1999, 2:24 AM
Near Abingdon Square, Greenwich Village, Manhattan
New York City, New York

Hesha turned on his laptop and called up a news site. Atlanta was having, apparently, a terrorist attack.

Historic Charleston lay in arsonous flames. Flare-ups in Savannah were being linked with a militia organization, denied by mayors and police departments, connected to the Atlanta incidents, isolated from the Atlanta incidents—it was a familiar pattern: the Masquerade. By tomorrow morning, the official reports would have settled into human history. He would have to find the truth (or what passed for it among the Cainites) along the grapevine or not at all.

"We're going out, Thompson. When you're ready."

"Baltimore, sir?" asked the driver, hopefully.

"Not yet." The Eye could be anywhere, now, and even the greater faculties available to Hesha in his own haven would be no help in finding it. There were, however, the two short traces close at hand. Somewhere in New York, there was a clue to Hazimel, and Hesha meant to find it. "I have questions for a few friends. Weapons and full jacket, Thompson, just in case. And call the Asp. There will almost certainly be beggars at our door; I want room found for them. Have him join us tomorrow."

Wednesday, 23 June 1999, 7:30 PM
Rutherford House, Upper East Side, Manhattan
New York City, New York

"Miss Dimitros?" the querulous voice of Agnes Rutherford called.

Elizabeth closed the crackling diary before her, stored it neatly in its case, and presented herself at the door of the bindery. "Yes, Miss Rutherford?"

"I am leaving now for London. Call the car around."

Elizabeth obeyed, and looked up from the phone to see her employer still poised in the doorway.

"Mr. Ruhadze's secretary called and asked that you stay to show him the Thoth necklace." Elizabeth nodded her acquiescence, and Agnes went on. "I wouldn't ordinarily leave you alone to deal with one of our most valued clients, but he seems to be willing to settle for an associate on this occasion. Please remember our standards, Miss Dimitros. Your manners and deportment are not always what we could wish for in our staff," she said, looking the younger woman up and down like a statue of particularly dubious provenance, "although I will admit that you do better than most Americans I have employed in the past. And keep those clothes on, Miss Dimitros—"

Elizabeth blushed bright red, eyes wide in indignation.

"I looked over the security tapes from yesterday, and I advise you not to run around tonight in greasy T-shirt and torn dungarees. This is Rutherford House, *not* a jumble sale."

"Yes, ma'am." Liz straightened her shoulders beneath her navy silk dress, and tried to remember whether her plain leather pumps had been polished this week, or the week before. "I brought a smock to work in today, Miss Rutherford."

"Be sure you aren't wearing it when you answer the door, Miss Dimitros."

"Yes, ma'am." Elizabeth escorted her employer to the street door, bid the old lady a polite and properly subservient good night and safe flight, and set the alarm after her.

Delicately, wearing thin cotton gloves, she took the collar from its display and brought it to the viewing table. With care she draped and pinned it on a velvet model of a woman's neck and shoulders, and stepped back to see that the clasp fell correctly, into the hollow of the throat. From the files upstairs she brought the provenance papers—the photographs of the site at which the necklace had been found, copies of reports of its discovery, its sales, the bankruptcies and inheritances, the final auction that brought it to the Rutherfords—and set the House's signature, cream-parchment, gold-embossed folder on the table beside the treasure. At the customer's chair, she laid a jeweler's loupe, calipers, a fountain pen, and a pad of cream-and-gold stationery for notation. Prepared, she turned down the front lights and slipped back through to the workroom. She donned her smock, and set to work on her desk with a home-coming smile.

"Good evening, Mr. Ruhadze. Please, come in."

"Call me Hesha?"

"Whatever you like." Elizabeth reset the door, and turned to her customer. "Miss Agnes wanted me to tell you how sorry she was not to be able to attend to your needs herself." She paused. "If you'd follow me..."

An hour and a half later, Rutherford House's claims for the necklace had proved—so far as could be told by loupe, light, and letter—genuine. The sum agreed to was lower than the first mentioned by Elizabeth, higher than the first suggested by Hesha, and comfortably above the mark Miss Agnes would have been pleased by in person.

They'd passed into companionable conversation, finally. The mutual embarrassment of their last meeting was gone. The assurance was building that the night to come would be, at least, intellectually interesting, and they had discovered considerable tastes in common.

"So, Elizabeth. How did you come to know all this?"

"Oh. It started with a bachelor's degree in art history, which my father promised me would lead nowhere. After I graduated, it looked like he was right, so I hung the first diploma on the wall and went after another."

"Something practical this time?"

"It was supposed to be an M.B.A."

"But it wasn't?"

"My master's thesis was 'The Dissemination from Mesopotamia of Key Motifs in Neolithic Pottery.'" She grinned weakly. "Wall Street expressed no interest. My father had a fit." They watched each other across the table for a moment. "Would you like some coffee?" she asked.

"Never this late, thanks. It'd keep me awake all night. But don't let that stop you."

"In a while. I'll need it to drive home." She tilted her head and returned a cooling question: "How did *you* learn all this, Hesha?"

"I just grew up with it. My family had a rather...eclectic collection of North African household goods from the fifteenth century. Don't ask me how Grandfather came by it all." He thought for a moment. "How is your desk coming along?"

"Fine," she replied, mildly surprised. "Very well, actually. I was just putting it back together when you came."

"May I see?"

Elizabeth blinked, and smiled. "Sure."

The desk stood magnificently, whole once more and polished—where polish could help its scarred hide—to a high sheen. She took the last of her tools and buffers away with the smock, and watched her companion approach the edifice. Hesha Ruhadze slid three fingers across the right side panel. He kneeled to see light on the grain's edge. He rubbed one thumb over the curved saucer of a drawer-pull, and finally slid his dark hands flat across the smooth surface of the restored top.

Elizabeth realized, suddenly, that she was frowning; that she didn't like the way his eyes roamed over the wood. Almost hostilely, she asked, "Why are you so interested in my desk?" It was the first time she'd used the word 'my' aloud for this possession; it was a defense, and she realized it once it was spoken.

"I'm not." He withdrew his touch. "I'm interested in why you care so much about it." Hesha leaned against the wall, and brought out a charming smile. "Why is the desk a he, and not a she, Elizabeth?"

She exhaled, less as a sigh than as an exasperation. Tension fled from her neck to her shoulders. Resignedly, she walked to the cabinet corner, and traced the grain of the old cherry with the index fingers of both hands. "Sleipnir, may I present to you Mr. Hesha Ruhadze. Hesha—Sleipnir." She performed the mock introductions, and paused.

"Sleipnir," said her listener, sardonically.

"This desk, Hesha, has eight legs. Look here—" she pointed to the feet, originally carved to resemble vases on pedestals, "—eight hooves, chipped by steel-wheeled chairs and cloven by his handlers. Someone cared for him properly, once. You can see the difference between the finish by the center drawer and the finish farther away—there was a blotter to protect his hide; you can still tell the dimensions of it by feeling for them.

"But there was a right-handed owner who was sloppy with his coffee. There was a typist who liked their machine facing the same way as the rest of the desk, and who didn't bother to repair the case of their typewriter. Hundreds of lines of ink were tattooed in by the carriage return. Here and here and here—" she struck with her knuckles at dark, ovoid burns on the varnish, "he has seen fire; there were cigarettes left carelessly to die in his company.

"Vandals have pierced him with arrows—God only knows why they wanted to fire nails and screws into the poor thing, but there are the holes to bear witness. There is red paint that spots him like blood, and there is white that flecks him like froth. He is missing parts of himself;

his drawers have been jarred to the very bones and were ready to collapse within him. He has been cut and burned, but he perseveres. He has seen battles and carried the writer through; he has probably survived more enterprises than will survive him.

"He is a war-horse, eight-hooved. Sleipnir."

She finished defiantly, standing between a worklight and the old desk. Her brown eyes flamed clear golden, and her profile was as sharp as the moon's.

Hesha Ruhadze stood watching her, and said nothing. The Eye was in his thoughts, and the death of Vegel and his retinue, and the memory of a daymare: Thoth with a woman by his side who was remembered, later, like the moon in Inundation. He waited, testing the moments before she spoke, or broke, or moved, but silence was no good weapon against her. "You picked up the art of a skald when you studied the Norsemen," he said.

Elizabeth searched his face. He seemed serious. "Thank you," she said, gravely.

"No," he began slowly, "thank you. And please pardon my intrusion into your privacy. I…felt a mystery here, and my particular passion is…detective work. Will you forgive me?"

She waved a vague hand. "For *my* being incredibly silly and melodramatic over a typewriter desk? Of course."

But he could see that it still bothered her, and he considered carefully what next to say to the mortal. If he let it go lightly, the resentment would take root, and a useful tool perhaps be lost. If he took the matter too seriously, she would suspect mockery again, and resent that as well. Hesha took three measured strides to close the gap between them, and looked into the brown eyes of the half-lit woman. "Still. It was an intrusion, and I'm sorry." He paused, as if contemplating the scornful lips tilted up towards his own. "Where will Sleipnir go from here, Elizabeth?" asked Hesha, looking away, returning to a business voice.

"My home."

"Good." He started toward the front of the shop, and held the door to the show floor open for her. "You said the other day that no one uses typewriters anymore. I have to confess that I still use an old one, every now and then. I've nearly worn down the question mark; I'll try," he said, facing her across the table that held the collar, "not to wear you out with questions tomorrow." His black eyes held concern in lightly wrinkled lids. "If you're still available?" She smiled faintly, and nodded. "Meet me at Charles's Fifth at seven?"

She smiled more broadly and replied, "I'll be there."

Hesha settled himself in the back seat of his car. He put the jewelry case and the folder that went with it into a hidden safebox. His driver waited in silence. "Thompson. I have further business in Queens." The black car ceased idling, sliding into traffic like a shark into a school of lesser fish, and began to trace a path south off of Manhattan. "You'll drop me off at a brownstone," and he gave the address. "Take the necklace to our own place here. Have Alex take the shipment down to Baltimore tonight."

"Yes, sir."

"Place a call to the agency. Use one of the corporate names; start a background check on an Elizabeth Dimitros, middle initial 'A,' residing in or around New York, currently employed by Rutherford House Antiques. I'll send a note to Janet later with some details I'd like looked into."

"Yes, sir."

"Be back at the brownstone by three o'clock. I don't expect that you will have to wait very long."

Thursday, 24 June 1999, 10:17 AM
Rutherford House, Upper East Side, Manhattan
New York City, New York

Amy Rutherford walked into the bindery holding a mug of coffee in one hand and the check for the Egyptian collar in the other. "Lizzie?!"

"Yes, Mrs. Rutherford?" asked Elizabeth, glancing up from her silk work on the diary.

Her boss flinched, nearly spilling her morning cup down her dress. "Aunt Agnes is an ocean away, and so is *she*. You call me by my mother-in-law's name again, and I'll have you tarred and feathered. Oh, Lord. You didn't hear that. Do you realize I live in fear of your finding a job somewhere the Rutherford family doesn't demand the royal treatment from their own damn staff? Where the hell was I? The check. The collar! Liz? Have you any idea what you've done?"

Elizabeth looked up in shock. "Wasn't the price high enough?"

"The price? Do you realize you brought it in a quarter percent higher than we've ever gotten out of Ruhadze?" She shook her head. "You're going to have to teach me your sales technique."

Elizabeth stared at the diary for a moment. "I played it by the book, Amy. I swear. I followed Miss Agnes's instructions to the letter."

"Then they worked better for you than they ever did for Aunt Agnes."

"I just...went over the provenance and talked about the workmanship."

"Did he quiz you?"

"Yes," she said, emphatically. "It wasn't an easy sale, Amy. I felt like I was defending my thesis before the board again." She leaned back in her chair. "And then we got to talking about my desk—"

"That reminds me, dear, Antonio and the boys are

making a delivery in your neck of the woods today. Is it ready to go?"

"It's fine. Solid as a rock." Elizabeth made a note on the pad beside the bindery phone. "I'll call the super to let them in. They can pick up the paintings while they're there; the three by the door are cleaned and crated again."

"Wonderful. The desk. Ruhadze was interested in the desk?"

"Sort of." Elizabeth pressed her fingers to her temples. "Amy, what do you know about this guy?"

"Why?"

"I'm having dinner with him tonight."

Amy Rutherford stopped with her mug at her mouth. A lesser woman, a woman who did not have Rutherfords as in-laws, might have choked or spluttered. "You deliberately waited until I had hot coffee in my mouth." She tapped her well-manicured hands on the chair's arms. "Do you mean dinner as in a date?"

"I'm not sure. I think so."

"Oh, Lord. Do you realize—no, of course you don't. Look. We have five clients on our books for whom we will drop anything. Aunt Agnes and my sweet, sweet mother-in-law roll over and play dead for these people. One of them is royalty, three are corporations, and one is Hesha Ruhadze. He's insanely rich, incredibly well-connected, particularly for...well, I hate to sound prejudiced, but, for a black man...and knows more about real antiquities than...than Mother. I think he made his money in the business."

Elizabeth nodded. "But I want to find out about *him*, not his credit rating, Amy."

"He's supposed to be some kind of recluse. At least, he's not showy. There are so many 'celebrities' grabbing the headlines that even the Ford heirs can't make the news without a robbery." She threw her hands into the air. "He's polite. He's charming. I don't think he's married."

"That's always nice to know."

"Yes." Amy shook her head, looking at her employee. She'd always thought of Liz as a plain-Jane, compared to the kind of fashion product New York turned out by the thousands and called beautiful. Bookish and intelligent, a quick learner with a cool head—whether in spite of or due to that bizarre imagination of hers—but that sort of thing seldom led to dinner invitations from millionaires. "Tell me all about it, dear. Oh, Lord. What on earth are you going to wear?"

Thursday, 24 June 1999, 6:58 PM
Charles's Fifth Avenue, Upper East Side, Manhattan
New York City, New York

The taxi lurched to a stop at the awning of Charles's Fifth, and a doorman stepped smartly forward to attend the passenger. A young woman in a long, gunmetal-silver satin evening dress stepped delicately onto the pavement. She leaned into the window to pass a note to the driver. The sun, which was turning New York smog into something like ochre mist, brought out a few strands of copper in her hair, and turned her light tan deep umber. The cab pulled away.

As the glass doors were opened for her, Elizabeth took one last survey of herself. Amy had tried to drag her to some ridiculously couture boutique; Liz put her foot down at the idea of entering anything that couldn't call itself a store or shop and mean it. The gray gown would do, and although Amy had at last admitted it, she informed the younger woman that further dates with Ruhadze would mean that Liz would finally need more than one 'real' dress.

Elizabeth entered the salon, and after a moment's doubt, approached the man at the podium at the end of the room. He snatched upon the hesitation, and began before her: "Miss Dimitros? Mr. Ruhadze's secretary called ahead; Mr. Ruhadze has been detained slightly. He asked me personally to see that you were comfortable." He led her through the crowded restaurant to an alcove with a small, linen-covered table and two luxuriously upholstered chairs. A waiter appeared at his side, holding a tray; the tray held a water glass and a small phone.

"Would you care for something to drink, Miss Dimitros?" asked the patriarchal maître d', as his minion set the water and the phone at her place. "Our wine list—"

"No, thank you. Water will be fine while I wait."

At 8:19 the phone rang, and Elizabeth watched it for a moment as though she had forgotten what phones were for. She swallowed the last of her soda and picked up the tiny handset. "Hello?" she asked the machine.

"Elizabeth? This is Hesha. I'm terribly sorry. I'm at a business meeting. My lawyers have just ordered in and expect me to stay and finish the deal with them. I would walk out now, just to stagger them, but I'd only have to see these buffoons again tomorrow morning if I did. I'm afraid I'll be at least another hour."

"Oh. Well, maybe another time, then."

"No. You must be starving. Please, go ahead and have dinner. I recommend the boeuf bourguignon; it's the house specialty. Enjoy it and pity me with my cardboard Chinese takeout." His voice fell a note. "I won't stand you up, Elizabeth. I promise."

"Good luck with the deal."

"Thank you. I'll see you soon."

"'Bye."

Thursday, 24 June 1999, 8:23 PM
Near Abingdon Square, Greenwich Village, Manhattan
New York City, New York

"Yes, Thompson?"

"Janet calling for you, sir. The agency came through with the report on Miss Dimitros," said Thompson, as the car emerged from the garage to street level. One eye was on the traffic ahead, the other on a blinking light on his console.

"Put her through."

"Good evening, sir. Would you like the highlights, or should I fax it to you?"

"Both, please. Go ahead."

"Full name, Elizabeth Ariadne Dimitros. Born September 28, 1970, to Christopher and Melissa Dimitros. One sibling; an elder brother, Paul Theodore Dimitros. The family is mostly Greek; the Dimitros children are the third or fourth generation in America, depending on which side you count from. 'Dimitros' is the Anglicized version of 'Dimitrouleas'. I'll spare you the rest of the genealogy."

"Thank you."

"Curriculum vita included in the fax; basically, she's an art historian with the practical skills of a museum restorer—she worked as an intern at the Met several summers running—and special interests in anthropology, semiotics, symbolism, and half a dozen other things. Her master's thesis and professional publications are also attached to the report. She's nearly completed her doctorate; her dissertation proposal was not available for copy at time of investigation. She's worked for Rutherford for four years as sales assistant, art restorer, appraiser and buyer. The older generation of Rutherfords seem to think she's still in training; the younger partners regard her as an equal associate—or as near as possible for an outsider. The agency didn't dig too deeply there; I presented the job as a full check for potential employee, current employers not to be alerted. I hope that's all right?"

"Fine."

"Now: There were a few...zingers."

"Zingers, Janet?"

"She has no permanent place of residence. Her mail goes directly to Rutherford House. Her driver's license expired two years ago; the address given on it is now occupied by a jazz musician with three cats and a drinking problem. Her passport was issued at about that time, so the agency expects it to be just as out-of-date.

"Second: Your note mentioned her father's displeasure with her career choice? Brace yourself. He really *did* have a fit. Christopher Dimitros died of a stroke two months after Elizabeth took her master's degree. His wife blamed their daughter for his death, and moved to California to live with her son's family almost immediately after the funeral. Paul Dimitros stays in touch with his sister, but the rest of her relatives won't talk to her—even the ones who still live in New York and Jersey."

"I see." Hesha stretched his legs, and regarded the speaker with calculation. "Other relations?"

Janet cleared her throat, and her employer could see, in his mind's eye, the exact look of disapproval on the woman's face. Janet Lindbergh was an efficient secretary and a model of discretion, but past middle-age, and of a generation that simply hadn't discussed these things over the phone. "She's not seeing anyone at the moment, sir."

"Go on."

"Three serious boyfriends; brief descriptions of the...affairs...are included in the dossier. The last liaison broke off two and a half years ago; the agency suggests a connection between her father's death and her change in habits."

"Thank you, Janet." Hesha tapped his fingernails on the armrest thoughtfully. "Commend the agency on their speed and thoroughness; laser letter on company stationery, but with the puppet president's signature in person. And be sure their investigation halts with this; I want her files and all hard copy removed from their offices."

"Will do." She paused. Just before the connection went cold he heard her mutter, "And have a nice date, sir."

Thursday, 24 June 1999, 9:57 PM
Charles's Fifth, Upper East Side, Manhattan
New York City, New York

"Good evening, Elizabeth." His voice carried clearly through the restaurant's refined din—deep as a river and closer than her heartbeat.

"Good evening, Hesha." She smiled ruefully up at her host. "Won't you join me? They're just bringing dessert."

He sat down in the other chair, and waved a swarm of waiters away. "You look lovely."

"Thank you."

An awkward silence grew, broken by the arrival of the maître d'—himself carrying the tray—with an outrage of chocolate and cup of hot tea for the lady, and a small, steaming, silver liqueur glass for his patron.

"Dinner was wonderful," Elizabeth remarked when the entourage had departed.

"I'm glad to hear it. I wish I could have been here. You weren't too bored?"

"No. It was fun, in a way." He raised an eyebrow, and she continued. "A lady sitting alone in a place like this attracts...attention. I've had four rescue attempts from sympathetic gentlemen shocked to see me stranded. One family party tried to adopt the lonely wallflower. The waiters *would* keep dancing attendance—that was a new experience for me. And half a dozen tourists thought, because of the celebrity treatment, that I was someone they should recognize. They kept sending people past the table to get a better look."

Hesha chuckled lowly. He sipped from the silver cup, and watched as she slipped a fork into the chocolate confection.

"Oh. This is fantastic." Elizabeth closed her eyes and took another bite. She offered the clean teaspoon to her companion, with a flourish that indicated the dessert plate. "Would you like some?"

"Thank you, but the caffeine..."

"Even in chocolate? How terrible for you. I tried to give it up once—" she whittled away at the pastry parts—"but decided that skipping rope was less painful than skipping dessert."

Hesha watched her finish. She relaxed with the teacup into the depths of the comfortable chair, and seemed willing to sit quietly if he cared for it. He let the cup of tea pass by in silence, and when she was done, he rose and offered his arm to her. She knew how to walk escorted, and they made stately progress through Charles's Fifth to the exit. A low, black sedan pulled up to the curb within seconds of Hesha's arrival on the sidewalk, and he smiled down at the woman by his side.

"May I offer you a lift?"

She bit her lip, doubtful. "I don't want to take you out of your way. My house isn't exactly on the beaten path."

"Please," said Hesha, holding the car door open for her, "get in. We'll take you home."

The heat of the June air was enough to give his fingers a little warmth, and so he steadied her shoulder, too, as she nestled into the lush upholstery. Thompson came around to his master's side of the sedan, and Hesha joined his guest in the back seat. Elizabeth gave her address, and the car started off.

Hesha glanced at the driver and pushed a button. Dark glass slid smoothly up to give them privacy, and he gazed at his companion as if distracted before he spoke. "This wasn't quite the evening I had planned, Elizabeth," he said softly, confidentially—though in truth, of course, it was. He had arrived as soon as the summer sun would let him, and had hardly hurried to her side.

She looked at him, and shook her head slightly. "What *did* you have in mind when you asked me?"

"On Monday? Recompense for first aid. You tried to do me a favor. I don't care to be indebted, particularly to strangers." His eyes flickered over her face. "After last night, I was looking forward to the experience. You're a rather unusual person."

Elizabeth let the statement pass without comment, though the tone of his voice suggested a profound compliment. She felt a flush start at her shoulders, and hoped it wouldn't show in the darkness of the car.

"I was also planning to show you a little mystery of my own," he said. She frowned slightly, not understanding, and he continued. "There's a piece I've been working on; a small statue that came into my hands without a great deal of history or background. I have some idea, now, where it might have been carved, but I thought I'd see if you could tell me anything about it."

"I doubt there'd be anything I could see that you couldn't." Elizabeth hesitated. "Amy told me you were something of an expert on antiquities."

Hesha gestured vaguely, modestly. "It was really 'Sleipnir' that convinced me you might have an insight. You might have thought of it as silly, but I was...impressed. What you did was an in-depth *forensic* study of a common typewriter desk.... The point, really, was to let you in on a tantalizing puzzle I thought you might enjoy."

"It sounds like fun. What period is the piece from?"

"That would be telling, wouldn't it?"

"I get no clues?"

"I don't have it with me," he explained, in mild disappointment. "The lawyers took too long."

"Oh."

"I don't suppose...I have more business tomorrow, *and* a formal dinner...would it be too much trouble to ask you to meet me somewhere, around ten or eleven or so? I'll bring the statue with me, and we can talk without all the waiters and tourists and gallants trying to rescue you."

"No trouble at all." Elizabeth swallowed a rush of hope, and brought out some of her business manner to bolster her courage. "But this time," she said, facing him with determination, "I'll be the host. I can't say that my place is anything like so nice as Charles's, but it *is* quiet, and comfortable, and it sounds like I'll need my full arsenal of experts' books behind me to cope with your puzzle.

"And if you're tied up by lawyers again," she finished wickedly, "I'll at least be able to get some work done while I wait for you."

And Hesha, who had had layers of subtle hints ready to persuade her to bring him into her home, allowed himself to be argued into agreeing humbly to her suggestion.

"Thompson? You heard the number and the directions to her door? Arrange to have the apartment searched. Maximum discretion; no traces left to trouble her. In fact, I'd be obliged if you'd see to it yourself."

Thompson kept his eyes on the road, but his attention wavered. "Yes, sir," he said, but his reply had less than its accustomed crispness. "May I say something, sir?"

"If I didn't value your opinion, Thompson, I would have made it clear at the beginning of our association."

"You know I'd never stand in your way, sir, but...she seems like a nice girl."

"I am sure that she is, Thompson." Hesha reflected

for a moment on the tone of his retainer's statement, and went on carefully. "Vegel and all that went with him are dead, Thompson. You are looking for replacements for his team—a driver, a plane, a pilot and crew. *I* am in need of an art historian...as well as a replacement for Vegel's other capacities."

"*Which* other capacities...sir?

"I'm not sure yet, Thompson. There are weaknesses to her; under the right circumstances, they could be made...strengths our organization does not currently possess. But she need know no more of our real business than Alex, or the agency, or Patterson's." They drove in silence for a time, and the master spoke again, speculatively. "For that matter, Thompson, you might wish to consider whether you would care to replace Vegel in that capacity yourself." Thompson said nothing. "Think it over carefully, of course. You have been with me long enough to know that it is hardly an unmixed blessing; and you have seen firsthand what it can do to others. Of course you would have to change the nature of your activities, and I know you enjoy your work at the head of the security team as it is. But do think, and let me know whether and when you might wish it."

"Thank you, sir."

"And soon, Thompson. Keep in mind what happened in Atlanta. We are passing through dangerous times, and a 'living will' might be a good idea."

Friday, 25 June 1999, 11:12 PM
A studio apartment in Red Hook, Brooklyn
New York City, New York

The black sedan glided smoothly to a halt at the entrance to the old warehouse. Streetlights were rare, there was little traffic, and though a few lit windows shone in buildings on both sides of the street, the rooms within were sterile. Blue-tinged fluorescent bulbs burnt late and coldly for janitors and night guards; desk lamps warmed small patches of overtime for corporate slaves.

A tall, broad, grizzled figure in a loose-fitting raincoat left the shadows of a fire escape. He approached the right rear door of the car, waited for the locks to click open, and climbed in without a word. The locks clicked back, and a touch of the tension left his creased, red face.

"Good evening, sir," Thompson said. He nodded acknowledgment to the man behind the wheel, and added, "How're you doing, Asp?"

"Never better, Ron," said the driver.

"Report, Thompson."

Ronald Thompson took a small flip-over notebook from his raincoat pocket. It was a habit, from his time as a cop; from a memory of what an ideal policeman was supposed to be. A younger Ron Thompson had found that, in this world, the reality was less than ideal, and walked away from a dirty job in search of something...cleaner. Now he sat in the back seat of a monster's car and felt no remorse as he laid a young woman's home bare before his master's eyes.

"Here's the layout. Door, a little closet and walk-in space. Open kitchen; counter and stools here—but it doesn't look like she does much entertaining. Library starts here; there's an iron rolling-door behind the bookshelves; probably from the warehouse era, probably why she keeps her books over it. Library runs into office, which runs into living room—there are books everywhere, though. This area is raised up a step, and full of your kind of stuff—antiques, I mean, sir. Her workshop, I assume. Bathroom facilities walled off here. Bedroom curtained off here." He stopped, and said meaningfully, "This entire outer wall is windows, sir."

From the front seat came a sniggering chuckle. "I guess you won't be staying the night, then, boss."

Thompson shot a scornful glare into the rear-view mirror. Hesha ignored the Asp completely, and the detective went on: "Weapons check: Usual assortment of kitchen knives. Further collection of little blades and awls in the workshop. Lots of small, heavy grenadables. No real guns; there's a flintlock in the shop next to a xeroxed article on stabilizing wood found buried in peaty soil. Non-operative.

"There are," he sighed, "a hell of a lot of spray cans and flammables. She's not a smoker, though; no lighters anywhere. Electric stove. Matches, candles and that sort of thing on a bookshelf in the office area, but not many. Fire shouldn't become a problem.

"I found out why she has no address; she sublets the loft from Rutherford House. The paper on the place was a little convoluted. I snapped a photo for Janet, on the off chance you'd be interested."

"Thank you, Thompson."

Hesha flicked the latches open, and as one, the three men left the vehicle. Thompson kept watch on the street; the Asp took a bottle, a package, and a raincoat from the trunk; Hesha accepted the items and turned to go inside the old building.

"Your time is temporarily your own. I anticipate being here at least two hours, but less than five. I will call. If your phone rings, Asp, you both should come back immediately, expecting trouble. If yours rings, Thompson, it's a straight pick-up."

Thompson took the keys and the driver's seat; the Asp took the passenger side. Neither took themselves off guard until the intercom buzzer sounded, the little door to the warehouse opened, and the steel bolts had snapped safely into place behind their master.

Hesha paced slowly along the dimly lit corridor. His steps slowed at each door, and he read the names taped, tacked, or painted on them: Kelvin Photographic; Herlin,

Inc.; Malay Imports; a row of ten doors labeled with the name of a law firm he knew, and marked "File Stores, 7" A-C, D-G, and so on.

He climbed stairs and made turns; he passed by the rest of the law firm's alphabet. At the end of a bare metal catwalk he came to her door. A faded notice on the wall beside it informed him that these premises were owned by Rutherford House, and gave him a number to call in case of emergency or accident. There was no trace of light from within, and no sound. He tested the air before knocking—rust, turpentine, old paint, and grime surrounded him, but through the cracks around the jamb he could detect a trace of smoke. It was good sandalwood and frankincense, complex and not cheaply come by.

He rapped on the door with one knuckle.

On the other side, there was light—warm and relaxing light—and sound—faint strains of something Celtic—and Elizabeth, waiting for him in a dark-blue denim dress and a nervous smile.

She took the wine with thanks and exclamations at the vintage; to his instructions she propped it on the counter to breathe and to settle. She offered him a drink or something to eat; he declined politely, and drifted into what Thompson called the living room. He draped his raincoat strategically—near the center of the loft, easily reached from the sofa or the workshop but out of the way—over an old, walnut office chair, and put the package down on its seat. He made a point of gazing around him, to check his retainer's report, to make his own assay of dangers and exits, and to seem to admire.

The windows that bothered Thompson by day were concealed by night; the same floor-to-ceiling curtains that walled her bedroom rolled down from the joists and kept the bleak city at bay. Hesha tendered his compliments on the apartment, and found opening to ask for a tour.

•

"No, wait." Hesha laughed, and twirled a finger clockwise. "You have it upside down. Now it's only backwards. There."

Elizabeth steadied the package on what felt like its base, and slit open the packing tape with a razor blade. She peeled paper and bubble-wrap away like layers of onion, and was rewarded by a misshapen, unwieldy mystery still swathed in black velvet.

"Close your eyes," said Hesha, and he slipped the shroud away from his prize. "All right, open them."

It was inky-blue, and red, and jet black. It was perhaps sixteen inches tall, and might have been larger had it retained all its limbs, weapons, and trappings over the years. It was fierce, and it seemed to writhe in anger, and it defied with a monstrous grimace those who looked upon it.

Elizabeth stared at it, and Hesha watched her face change as she took in the details. First, there was the frank appreciation of an expert in the presence of the unusual. Her mouth corners twitched as her eyes flickered over the grotesqueries. She reached forward to touch the chipped tip of a broken ax, and her brows furrowed in doubt. Suddenly, her hand darted to the workbench's side. A halogen light blazed into Hesha's eyes, and he flinched away. "Sorry," said the historian, distractedly. She swung the lamp and its attached magnifying lens into position over the raw edge. The Setite blinked back rage—the light stung him, and he lost sight of her face in the red miasma that hovered before his eyes.

Her voice spun through the fiery void: "Is this a trick question?"

He left her there, and walked to the kitchenette. The microwave blinked 12:01 just as he passed it. "No. You were thinking forgery?"

"I wanted to eliminate the possibility." Elizabeth took up a pad, and began making notes. "Particularly after the spectacular build-up you gave the 'puzzle.' One of my professors tried that on me. Bet me lunch over it. I made him pony up steak and cocktails."

Hesha browsed through the cabinets. "Good for you."

"This coloring is amazing." She frowned down at the enlarged ax and arm in the lens. "Made me think it was art glass, to begin with. The carver was a real master."

"And why do you say that?"

"Aside from the fact that the physical surface of the piece is exquisite? Wine glasses are under the island. Rather dusty, I'm afraid. It's the red. Look where he's chosen to leave the red...it's like an optical illusion. Seen from below—the figure is a warrior lording it over the viewer. He's come home from the battlefield absolutely *dripping* blood from weapons, hands, and teeth. Seen from above—it's a demon rising from the fires of hell. His arms and armor ripple with the flame, but the fight hasn't started yet. It's fascinating. And where the black is bluest, that's where he's designed metal trappings. I can't understand how..."

Hesha washed the glasses, and poured for two.

"What are the rules, Professor Ruhadze?"

"The rules?" He set her wine before her, and pressed his own glass to his lips. "For the puzzle...just tell me what you see. Make statements, and I'll tell you if I know them to be true or false. Think of questions I've already looked into, and I'll tell you the answers. Think of questions I haven't looked into...and you get an A for the course."

"It is carved from a solid piece of stone, except for this—" and she pointed to the white of the creature's sole remaining eye. It had begun with three; two empty sockets beneath it attested to their former occupants' existence.

"Yes." Hesha pulled a soft chair into the workshop.

"The stone is chalcedony. Specifically, the kind of agate the jewelers call 'apache flame.'"

"Yes."

She sipped her wine, and said sharply, "It isn't a modern artifact."

"How are you sure?"

"Because," she began, and went on decisively. He granted her the arguments, and the game continued for hours.

"Oh, damn." Elizabeth held her head in her hands, and shook it.

"What's wrong?"

"I had a theory," she moaned, letting him refill her glass. "I had a perfectly lovely theory. And then I went and made putty casts of the sockets. And my theory's ruined. I'm no expert, Hesha. I can't place this blasted thing in a civilization, let alone a time or site."

He put an arm over her shoulders, and pulled his chair closer. "What happened to the casts?"

"Look at this," she said. "I used polymer putty—stable enough to get the shape of the holes and flexible enough to pop out of the sockets without damaging your friend here. And I didn't need to." She handed him half a putty eyeball. There was a small plastic dowel rooted in it as a handle. "Watch this."

With thumb and forefinger, she twisted the remaining cast out of its seating.

"And I'll bet you anything you like," she said, touching the third socket gingerly, "that the last one—yes." She handed him a small, pale stone—the white of the demon's sole preserved eye. There was a hole in the center for the iris, which remained in the statue's head.

"The whites screw into the sockets. There's the stumps of irises broken off in these two. You can see the 'negatives' in the casts. The bases were black; I'd imagine that the 'whites' were red. Yours is the spirit eye; white with a red iris."

She laid her head down on the workbench, cushioned by her left arm, and looked up at the inexplicable marauder.

"Find me a near-Indian civilization with the belief structure to give this thing three eyes and four arms, the warcraft to put those styles of weapons in his hands, the mechanical knowledge of even primitive screw threads like these as *fasteners*, and the tools to work carnelian like *that*—and I'll tell you where he came from. I'm sorry, Hesha. I can't even think of lost civilizations this poor devil could be from. Did the little man who sold him to you come from a spaceship?"

Hesha turned the burning lamp off. "No." He stroked her hair away from her face, and pulled her to her feet.

"Have you had him carbon-dated? There's black grime stuck in his mane and tail."

"You wouldn't believe me if I told you what happened when I tried."

"Inconclusive?" she mumbled, drowsily.

"Something like that."

Elizabeth stumbled down the step into the living room. She leaned heavily against the almond-painted column in the center of the apartment, and began to fall. He caught her, held her, and carried her behind the curtains into her room. Along the way, she tried to speak, and he closed her mouth by kissing her. She kissed back with a kind of sleepy surprise, and then he laid her out on the bed.

He took her sandals off, and untied the sash of the dark-blue dress. She made no noise; the hour and the strong, drug-laced wine had overcome her. Hesha looked down at the quiet body, and studied her intently. After a moment's deliberation, he lifted her up again, turned down the quilt, and covered her with it. Satisfied by the effect, he toed off his own shoes and strode noiselessly back through the apartment.

He took putty and made casts of the demon's

eyesockets for himself. He wrapped the statue into its velvet, plastic, and paper, and set the package by the door.

He went next to her desk—a modern creation of particle-board and laminates, not the heavy antique that stood empty in the studio area—and went through her papers. He pored over her dissertation notes, her address book, her finances. He found a box of old letters, and read with interest the sympathy cards on the death of her father; the venomous words of Elizabeth's mother; the friendly correspondence of brother Paul and his wife, and nodded as the tone grew terse and strained over time. There were what passed for love letters; he gleaned what he could from them as well.

A small silver clock on the desk told him about the sun, and he collected the bottle and glasses. He rinsed the dregs and drugs from them in the sink. He took a flask from his pocket and poured away what little wine he had had to pretend to drink himself.

He found a small blue juice glass in the cabinets; a rubber band, pen, and scrap paper in a drawer; and plastic wrap in a rack on the pantry door. He flexed his left index finger. The claw hidden there slid forward in its scaly sheath, and with it he sliced open the topmost vein of his right wrist. A slow drop of red-black ichor welled up from the cut. Hesha forced his blood forward, and the thin stream filled the little glass quickly. The wound closed over.

He tore a sheet of plastic loose and covered the draught. In fine, small handwriting, he wrote *Hangover cure* on the scrap of paper and snapped it to the glass with the rubber band. He placed his blood on the top shelf of the refrigerator.

From his raincoat, he took a notebook. On a torn-out page he constructed a note, When he had finished, he brought it to the bedroom and propped it against the mirror. Elizabeth lay motionless, in precisely the position he had left her.

Hesha sat on the edge of the low mattress. He took her fingers in his, and watched her face to be sure she knew nothing. He lifted her hand to his lips, and bit.

He drank from her quite slowly. He had hunted earlier, to sate the hunger, but this was better. Her blood coursed gently into him, and the warmth was sweet. He closed his eyes, and let himself enjoy the taste. It was a wonder...the difference in savor between mortals...that the blood should never pall...

The Beast stirred slightly, curiously strong. Hesha had long practice wrestling it, and was well fed—he fought it down. It twisted and turned on him; for an instant the surprise allowed a second duel; rare for the Setite. He knew it was too much to expect truce, but decades of disciplined tending and watchfulness had given him a little slack with the thing. Hesha beat it back again.

Uneasily, he took Elizabeth's life from between his teeth, and licked the tiny wounds closed.

Something light touched his cheek, and his eyes snapped open—it was her other hand, reaching up to caress him. He dropped her wrist, startled, and stared at her as she moved—and kept moving, despite wine, drug, weariness, and the Kiss. She was asleep; she couldn't possibly be conscious. He relaxed as she began to turn. She *was* only moving in her sleep, but she rolled into the sole sliver of light that came through the curtains, and her neck lay bare and pale against her dark hair.

The Beast stretched and roared, and Hesha scrambled to find his shoes in the dark.

He snatched up his overcoat and the statue, slammed the door behind him, and ran down the hall dialing the phone.

"Thompson."

"Sir."

"Baltimore."

"Yes, sir."

Saturday, 26 June 1999, 1:16 PM
A studio apartment in Red Hook, Brooklyn
New York City, New York

Elizabeth woke to the uncomfortable warmth of clothes in bed. Groggily, she threw off the quilt and sat up. Her mouth tasted terrible, her hair hung into her eyes, her dress was twisted around her, and her bra poked into her ribs. She planted both feet on the floor, stood up, and started toward the shower, shucking her dress and the rest of it along the way.

Thirty minutes later she poked her head back out of the bathroom—cautiously. It had occurred to her that she didn't remember the end of the evening. The apartment *felt* empty, sounded empty...she crept to the edge of the curtains, and looked out. No sign of Hesha, she saw with relief. She shrugged into an old, comfortable T-shirt and sweats, and reached for a hair band from a pile on the dresser. The note lay next to them.

Dear Elizabeth—

Good morning—I hope you slept well. The wine was apparently a stronger vintage than expected. I brought you in here—I hope you don't mind—you looked rather crumpled in the living room. I'm afraid you'll feel rather crumpled in the morning, too. My father's secret hangover cure is waiting in the fridge for you. Whatever you do, don't sip it. It tastes worse than it smells.

Thank you for the 'consultation' on the statue. You get the 'A' and I owe you steak dinner and cocktails, if you like. I'm not sure how much longer I'll be in town, but 202-555-7831 will catch up with me eventually, no matter where I go.

Hope to see you again soon.

—Hesha

Elizabeth stuck the note by magnet to the freezer door. She stacked a hangover-friendly breakfast on a tray, added the blue juice glass, and balanced the lot across the room. Sleipnir's broad back took breakfast from her.

She nibbled absent-mindedly at a muffin and started drawing the long curtains up to the ceiling. Her reflection stared back at her, paler and more fey than in her mirror. She cranked open the windows, and the images slanted away, disapproving crookedly of her slothfulness. Elizabeth turned on the fans, plopped down on a stool in the workshop, and turned to her assignment for the day, an American Colonial painting that had been, unfortunately, varnished for its own protection several times.

Most of the afternoon later, picking out another solvent took her past the bench where the putty casts lay, and on the way back she took them with her. She stared at the little eyes, and tried to remember where she had seen their like before. She abandoned the easel to search her office desk. It was a journal article, she was sure now—something the statue had reminded her of—but she couldn't put her finger on the issue or even the year in which she'd read it. She thought of a place in the bedroom shelves that held a bundle of old xeroxed references. She flew to them, and spent half an hour eliminating the possibilities of the shelves, the magazine rack, the bedside table.

"Damn."

Then she saw *it*—just a corner sticking out of a pile of magazines—the cadet-blue paper cover of *The Southern California Archaeological Digest*. Elizabeth leaped for the couch, sent the stack sprawling, and seized the journal.

The article, entitled "Further notes on the Sur-Amech burial site," was 'further' notes because the digs had been disrupted by border wars and travel sanctions to the nation that laid claim to the patch of desert the old necropolis occupied, and because the grave under study was set apart from the main cemetery. Elizabeth looked at the atlas and the dates given for the research—

the author had to have returned to his excavations under threat of fire, if he'd worked when and where he claimed to.

There were photographs of the grave, and diagrams in three angles of the location of each artifact uncovered. Two pieces merited their own diagrams: a beautiful, unbroken example of the pottery native to the time and region, and a carnelian bead the corpse had worn on a thong around her neck.

Elizabeth pored over the writer's description of the little jewel, and walked over to the workbench. She measured the putty casts with calipers, string, and a ruler. The left eye was a perfect match. She grinned, propped her elbow on the bench, and bit her thumb in satisfaction.

Flipping the blue-gray journal over to its cover and contents page, she found the author's name: Dr. Jordan Kettridge, Professor of Archaeology, University of California, Berkeley.

Of course. Kettridge was the kind of man who would rather dig during war than peace; she'd heard of his exploits in Iraq. She'd heard complaints, too, from her own professors and the staff at the museum. Kettridge wouldn't specialize properly. Kettridge wouldn't stay with an expedition, not the way real archaeologists worked the field. Kettridge would waltz in after someone else had been carefully running test trenches and stratification holes for ten years to establish culture and diet and timeline and everything that was *important*, get permission to do a foundation study on some farmer's outhouse, and immediately stumble across the high priests' personal quarters. Some said it was luck, some said it was instinct, but everyone agreed it was goddamn annoying.

Elizabeth found UC-Berkeley on the net, ran through the faculty e-mail to Kettridge, and shot off a query.

Dear Professor Kettridge,

I recently had occasion to review your article on Sur-Amech in the Fall 96 SCAD. I was particularly interested in the pattern of striations found on the carnelian bead from grave d-24. Do they, as they seem to in the diagram on page 138, spiral counterclockwise in relation to the flatter side of the bead?

If so, I believe I have a client interested in purchasing this artifact. The piece is not described as a part of Berkeley's museum collection in the article; I assume that, being a minor item compared to the pottery found during the expedition, it has passed into a private collection. Could you inform me of the final disposition of the bead? Thank you for your time.

Sincerely,
Elizabeth A. Dimitros
Associate, Rutherford House Antiques

That done, she took to the kitchen phone, and punched Hesha's number in from the note he'd left.

"Hello?" It was a machine; eventually it beeped. "Hesha, this is Elizabeth. It's Saturday evening. Thanks for, um, carting me to bed. Anyway. I found something in one of my journals about your statue, I think. Give me a call when you can. Take care. Bye."

She set down the phone, and began scavenging her cupboards for dinner, clearing the remains of breakfast away as she went.

The forgotten contents of the little juice glass went swirling down the sink.

Saturday, 26 June 1999, 9:14 PM
Laurel Ridge Farm
Near Columbia, Maryland

Hesha woke to darkness and the silence of the tomb. Lethargy lifted from him, and he felt the last light of day leave the earth. He wondered if the face of the sun had changed in the centuries since the curse had been laid on him. He wondered if Set fled Ra's glory as he traveled the underworld, or whether the dead god were forced by the curse to attack his grandfather's barge every night, or if Set slept, as Hesha himself did, and fought the curse in the land of the living.

Hesha, childe in the seventh degree from Set, the son of Geb, the son of Ra, stirred in his chamber, and lights hidden in the ceiling glowed dimly at his first movement. They threw the carved walls into deep shadow; shallow relief stood forth like sculpture in the round. Farmers, fishers, hunters, artisans, scribes, priests, nobles, and royalty performed their daily tasks in the friezes. Beneath the arched body of the sky, they marked the hours with ritual, work, prayer, and pleasure. They were copies of the most beautiful art of Egypt, blended into a single masterpiece by modern hands. Hesha ran his night-black fingers over the smooth stone, and traced the outline of the cartouche in the wall to his right: a rope, bound into a loop by thinner cords, filled with the signs of Set's name and the simple title, "Lord of the Northern Skies."

Set's descendant rose and paced the walls, admiring the work. He touched his own cartouche above the lintel of a door, and walked on. In a crooked corner of the irregular cave, he came to the only unfinished section of the work. Chisel, hammer, brush, and charcoal lay neatly in a box at the base of the stone. He picked up the stick of charcoal and drew a last cartouche on the gray rock. Within the oval, he scribed a horned viper, an open tent, a vulture, a man, and an ankh—*VGH'*—Vegel, the artist. His work was over. Hesha chiseled the rock away from the sign and laid the tools down again. The unfinished panel would remain that way forever.

"Thompson," Hesha said into the dimness.

A small speaker among the lights clicked on. "You called, sir?"

"Conference. Half an hour. You and the Asp in person. Have Janet and the doctor call in on secure lines."

Hesha pushed lightly on a papyrus plant carved into the rock, and a door opened to more mundane apartments. He returned clean and clad in a simple robe, the gallahbeyah of his native North Africa. The amulets that had been hidden by western garb swung freely from cords at his neck and waist.

Thompson was waiting for him. A door to the upper areas of the house swung open as he entered, and the Asp made his way into the room. Hesha sat at the foot of the stone bench on which he had spent the day.

"Janet? Doctor? Are you with us?" Hesha asked.

"Yes, sir."

"I'm here, Hesha."

"Let's begin, then. Reports. Thompson?"

"The bodies of Vegel's team are all accounted for, sir. Transportation arrangements are under way; and we've made funeral provisions for their families. I'd like tomorrow and Monday afternoon free to attend services." Hesha nodded approval. "There wasn't much left of the car, but Atlanta police identified it yesterday as a wreck left in Cabbagetown early Tuesday morning. In their opinion, it was stolen for a joyride and then deliberately crashed."

"Probably true," said Hesha, "as far as it goes. Asp?"

"Six of the Family have come to the townhouse looking for shelter—one from D.C., two each from Charleston, Richmond, and Atlanta, all separately, all in a hell of a hurry. I found them crash space here and there, and put them on field rations, per your orders. I gave them your number here; calls have been piling up, but so far they've lain low like good boys and girls."

"That won't last much longer."

"I'm afraid you're right, Hesha," said Doctor Oxenti from her office. "D.C. hospitals and the Red Cross were on our backs for rare types before the riots, and now we're low on everything. Plasma's cleaned out completely; whole blood is in short supply."

"I see." Hesha placed his hands flat on the stone beneath him. "It's going to get worse," he began. "By now you all will have gathered that these riots are Family business. My own branch is neutral, but that won't make a difference to either faction. We support both sides against the middle, and they will take any opportunity they can to use us, to trap us into allegiances we can't afford, or to rend us in the general slaughter.

"Washington, D.C. is now under attack." He drove on, ignoring the expressions on the faces before him, and the gasp—Janet's—that whistled through the speakers. "Assume, based on the war's progress so far, that Baltimore is not only a target, but the *next* target in a line north up the East Coast.

"Our open business and the townhouse are almost certain to be ransacked or firebombed. Begin removing the most valuable and portable pieces, slowly. Fake buys, arrange shoplifting, send things out for recycling, and make small shipments, but don't let it be too obvious that we're withdrawing. Warehouse the goods in the deep country—the Appalachians would be best, I think.

"I want the staff out of the buildings well before sundown every day until further notice. If we don't have more information by autumn, we'll keep later morning hours as the day gets shorter.

"Janet, you're coming out of the city center. Choose whatever files and equipment you want to bring with you, but hurry. You move to new quarters at dawn tomorrow. Asp, you're moving her yourself. We'll pick a safe zone after this meeting, and the location doesn't go beyond the three of us."

"Doctor?"

"Still here, sir."

"Can you leave your research at this time?"

"No." Hesha heard the tapping of Yasmine Oxenti's long, manicured nails on the phone receiver, and then, "A week. I need a week, at least."

"We'll try to give you the week. After that, I want you to take a holiday. Janet, book passage for the doctor to Alaska, one week from tomorrow."

"Alaska?!"

"The sun isn't setting there. I'd send you all if I could afford to do without your aid, but blood banks are particular targets, and you are particularly resistant to efforts by Thompson's people to protect you."

"But—"

"In the meantime, order the usual shipments for the next month. Have your second-in-command coordinate emergency blood drives with the Red Cross. Start at our own open offices, in fact. And put your staff on daylight hours, same as the other businesses."

"How in hell am I going to rationalize that?"

"Convincingly," Hesha frowned, "if you want to save their lives. Should the enemy take the clinic while the staff are still there, our people will be massacred. Understood?"

There was a pause. "Yes, sir."

"And all of you: Cut communications between branches of the organization to a minimum. Close what channels you can. I want our holdings concealed from onlookers as much as possible. I want the four of you speaking to each other as little as possible. Thompson has briefed you all on the emergency procedures; start using them.

"Any questions?" Silence fell. "Further business?"

"Yes, sir." Thompson darted up the stairs and back again, holding several plastic-wrapped bundles on a tray. He wore gloves to handle them. "Family letters for you, and a few others that Mrs. Lindbergh had a feeling about."

"There are messages waiting on your private line, as well," said Janet. "And I show a call from Miss Dimitros's number."

The Asp snickered.

Monday, 28 June 1999, 9:15 AM
Rutherford House, Upper East Side, Manhattan
New York City, New York

Elizabeth let herself in by the alley entrance, and found Amy Rutherford waiting for her on the stairs. She held two cups of coffee and very little patience.

"Good morning, Miss Golightly. Here's your coffee." Amy waited until the younger woman had had a good gulp of the hot, black brew, and then developed a cat-and-canary smile. "Tell Mama all about it."

"About what?" Elizabeth slipped past, hugging the well-wrapped package tightly under one arm. She waggled the package at her boss. "This?"

Amy ran after her, and caught the door to the offices open with a deft foot. "You scamp. You know exactly what I'm talking about. About the *date*."

Liz sat down. "Thursday night didn't go well at all. He had a business meeting beforehand, it dragged on, and he was three hours late." She shrugged. "Dinner was good, though. He and his chauffeur drove me home, and he asked if I could meet him the next night. So he came over Friday after dinner, and we talked antiques and things."

Amy's mouth fell open. "And?"

"What do you mean, 'And?'"

"Good God, Liz. Do you realize you've made fire-irons sound more exciting than that? You sell a cheap Roman bracelet to one of the Miller sisters, and it's all romance and the story of how the glass went from hand to hand along the silk road, and the wedding it was bought for, and the...well, you go on and on, you know you do, and it sells the thing. Here you have not one, but two nights with one of the most interesting men *I've* ever met, and all you have to say about it is, 'He was late. Dinner was good. We drove home. He came over. We talked.'" She ran the sentences together in singsong mockery. "Do you know what I did Friday?"

"You attended an estate sale in Massachusetts." Elizabeth got up and started down the carpeted stairs to the display floor. "How did it go for us?"

"I—well, it went fine. Four good pieces of Philadelphia cabinetry, a nearly complete set of Spode china, a—damn it, you changed the subject. I spent Friday wondering what happened to you Thursday night."

"That was sweet of you, but he was quite the gentleman. Brought me home safe, sound, and with my virtue unassailed."

"Liz—" Amy began seriously, and looked at her. An eight-day clock on the wall beside them chimed the half-hour, galvanizing her into movement. "Oh, Lord. Do you realize we open in thirty minutes? Hurry. The Totiros took the floral, but they also cleaned out all the Nouveau we had in the showroom. We've got to reorganize before ten.... Call Antonio and the boys in to help us with the heavy things, would you, Liz?"

In fifteen minutes, the front room was ready enough to start the day with. The two women tramped upstairs to brush dust from their dresses and jackets, comb Amy's flyaway hair, and make themselves, as Miss Agnes would have put it, "decently presentable." They stole a moment for more coffee and gossip, until the phone rang. Amy reached for it with one hand, but kept her eyes on Liz. "Hold that thought, dear."

"Rutherford House Antiques," she answered, in excruciatingly well-bred tones. "How may I be of assistance to you today? Yes. Yes." Her brows waggled at Elizabeth, and she mouthed 'asking for you.' "She is here with me now, as a matter of fact. Would you like to speak with her?" There was a pause. "In about five minutes. Our hours begin at ten, Mr.... Yes, that is the street. Three blocks from...that is correct. Well, we will see you then, sir."

"Another gentleman caller for you, Lizzie." Amy shrugged and waved away Liz's questions. "Didn't leave his name. Didn't state his business." She glanced at her wristwatch. "Time to unlock."

The elegant smoked-glass-and-chromed-steel doors opened for the first customer of the day. Amy Rutherford drifted unobtrusively forward, neither putting herself in the man's way, nor giving the slightest appearance of neglect, should he be looking for assistance.

His eyes flickered over her, but he said nothing. He started a circuit of the room, examining it silently. From time to time, he would look over at the two women, but his attention seemed absorbed by the antiquities. His hair was a graying ash-blond, his face dark in a way that suggested layers of honest sunburn, not trips to a tanning bed. He wore a wrinkled, khaki button-down shirt with too many pockets, and blue jeans that seemed to have come across the idea of 'threadbare' in ages past and liked it. Neither woman judged him on the clothes; enough VIPs took pride in shabby casuals that he might have been anyone.

"Mrs. Dimitros?" he began at last, addressing Amy. Up close, his carriage seemed younger than the gray hair suggested. His face was a mess of wrinkles, but beneath the lines hid the face of a young man. He could have been thirty-five, she thought...or fifty-five.

"Mrs. Rutherford—I'm Amy Rutherford." Her eyes narrowed as she checked his voice against a memory.

"Good morning, ma'am. My name is Jordan Kettridge."

"Lizzie—" Amy pulled Elizabeth across the room with the tone of her voice. She said to Kettridge, "You called us half an hour ago?"

"Yes, ma'am."

"Jordan Kettridge, Elizabeth," said Amy, informatively. Liz nodded and extended her hand to shake.

"Good morning, Professor Kettridge. I...was hardly expecting to see you here in New York."

"You're Elizabeth Dimitros?" He stared hard at her, and let her hand go a moment later than was entirely comfortable or polite, cocking his head to one side as he studied her. "You don't look like you write." Elizabeth said nothing, but her gaze was as frank and open as the stranger's was blunt and suspicious. Amy glanced from one to the other, and decided to stay close by.

"Well, Ms. Dimitros. The bead in my article does have striations running counterclockwise in relation to the flatter side." His eyes were gray-green and piercing, and they locked with hers. "Though I would have thought, looking at the diagram in *SCAD*," he said sharply, and threw the words down like a challenge, "that it would be impossible to determine that from the angle at which it was drawn."

"Nevertheless," said the young woman smoothly, "I'm glad to hear that the design, at least, matches the bead I'm seeking. Can you tell me who is currently in possession of the bead, Doctor?"

"The artifact is in my private collection, Ms. Dimitros." Kettridge spoke with an inexplicable emphasis—his tone would have suited a death threat better.

Elizabeth kept her shock out of her face, and was glad to see Amy wearing her best Rutherford business expression as a mask.

"I see," Liz said, though she was almost certain that she didn't. "And are you willing to sell?"

"That would depend entirely on the circumstances, Ms. Dimitros." Kettridge rubbed his chin thoughtfully. "Who's the buyer?"

"Rutherford House," said Elizabeth, hoping like hell that Amy's face wouldn't betray surprise and give her the lie.

Kettridge chuckled. "I'm sorry. I don't believe for one minute that you pick your antiques out of archaeological journals at random—who put you up to this?"

Amy broke in. "Doctor Kettridge," she said slowly, "when we represent a client, we do not make a habit of giving their name away to simply anyone who asks for it. Confidentiality is a watchword here. And when the buyer specifically requests us not to divulge their identity, it is a point of honor with us to respect their wishes."

He said, "Honor, is it?" and smiled. His wrinkles wrapped around his mouth and eyes readily enough; the lines had come there smiling in the first place. Elizabeth rallied, and sat on the edge of the center table. "It's far too early, at any rate, to begin discussing terms, Dr. Kettridge. We haven't any idea whether your find is the piece our client wants—we'll need to see your bead to verify that, and match the data on it to the data on the item being sought. After that, we'll contact our client. It is possible, I suppose, that he or she will be willing to make an exception to their confidential status this one time, as a concession to you."

"And just how much data do you have, Ms. Dimitros, on the 'item' being sought?"

Amy cut in. "*Is* the bead for sale, Dr. Kettridge?"

He looked at the two women—Amy Rutherford,

clad in iron-gray, her arms folded, her chin held high—Elizabeth Dimitros, perched on the table's edge, chic and trim in burgundy, following him casually with her eyes—and found his way to the door without quite turning his back on either of them. "I'll think about it," said the professor, and then he left.

Elizabeth let out a sigh, and some of the backbone dropped out of her posture. Behind her, she could hear Amy walk to the viewing table, pick up her coffee cup, and finish it.

"All right," said Amy Rutherford. "What the hell was that all about?"

"I don't know."

"Tell me another one, Lizzie."

"I'll tell you the whole damned story. If it makes any more sense to you than it does to me—I'll—I'll probably die of apoplexy. Look," she said, and told her boss the story of the 'puzzle' Hesha had brought with him. She dug the casts and the journal out of the tote bag she'd brought with her, and the recitation ended with Amy wearing a jeweler's loupe, scrutinizing the tiny bits of putty as if they were the crown jewels of Ruritania.

"I just don't see it," she said, trading the loupe for her bifocals.

"Good. I felt like a blasted idiot. On the other hand, I was hoping you'd know something about the statue, or Kettridge, or Ruhadze that would make that—" Elizabeth gestured toward the display floor with a wild hand "—make some sort of sense."

"And all you did was ask what collection the bead was in?"

"Yes. I signed as Rutherford House staff—you said yourself that Ruhadze was a VIP even to Agnes and your—"

"Don't mention her, please."

"Mrs. Rutherford," finished the younger woman, hopelessly.

They stared at each other across the viewing table.

"So what do we do now?" asked Elizabeth.

"We wait and see if Kettridge comes back, and we wait to hear from your beau. In the meantime…I'll make some phone calls. I always wanted to be a sleuth."

"*Everyone* I know is turning into a detective, these days."

"You mind the store, dear, and don't worry. I can't see how even…Mother…could possibly *blame* you for any of this. It could be a very nice deal. And if we pull it off, I'll see that you get a cut, even if it has to come out of my share." Amy tromped up the stairs, leaving Elizabeth alone in the shop to wonder.

"You have reached 202-555-7831. At the tone, please leave your name, your number, the time you called, and your message."

"Hesha? This is Liz. Look…well…all right. To start with, the article I found was in the *Southern California Archaeological Digest* for Fall 96. If you can't get a copy, I'll fax pages from mine….the article is by Kettridge, Jordan Kettridge; he's a professor at Berkeley. As far as I could make out from the article, he's got one of the missing eyes of your statue. So I e-mailed him to see if he would sell. That was Saturday. He turned up in our showroom this morning, acting as if he was about to…I don't know, start a fight. Punch Amy in the mouth. Damn it. I don't even know why I'm calling. He was hostile, I doubt he'll sell. Do you want Rutherford House to pursue it? Give me a call when you can. Bye."

Tuesday, 29 June 1999, 2:14 AM
A studio apartment in Red Hook, Brooklyn
New York City, New York

Elizabeth staggered through the door and into her apartment. It locked behind her, and she shuffled, exhausted, to the living room and threw herself on the big sofa. For ten minutes, she vegetated in absolute stillness. Only when the standing-up aches from her day at Rutherford House had been replaced by face-down-on-the-couch aches did she move.

Her hand reached out and tapped at a blinking red light, and presently it spoke to her.

"Elizabeth? Hesha. I found the article; I think you're right. You're very quick. Thank you for looking out for me—or at least, gnawing away at my puzzles for me. I'd love to acquire the piece, of course. Put the Rutherfords on the track. They'll finagle it out of him if anyone can. Do look after yourself, though. I've met Kettridge once or twice, and he's a touch...eccentric. The scene today sounds typical of him. I'd hesitate to use the word 'unstable' about such a prominent and capable scholar...." The tinny copy of Hesha's voice slowed, and a note of concern crept into it. "Please, be careful, Elizabeth. I'll talk to you again soon."

Wednesday, 30 June 1999, 11:58 AM
Victor's Authentic Mediterranean Café,
Upper West Side, Manhattan
New York City, New York

Elizabeth sat in a tiny booth of her favorite, very small restaurant, reading a heavy volume on the prehistory of Persia. From time to time, she remembered the salad in front of her, and took a few bites. She turned a page. Without warning, a man slid into the seat facing her. She looked up, ready to scream bloody murder—she was enough of a regular that, even in New York, one of the waitstaff would care—and closed her hand over her keyring on the seat beside her. The tube of pepper spray provided an iota of confidence.

Jordan Kettridge greeted her with an apologetic grimace. "Hi."

She said nothing, but kept her hand on the keys.

"I just wanted to say, I'm sorry about the scene at the gallery yesterday."

Elizabeth, stonyfaced, waited.

"I'd just flown in from Turkey, I was jetlagged, I confess to a terrible temper, and I have been having the weirdest time with this damn bead. There have been some really…strange things happening in connection with it." He smiled ruefully, and the lopsided effect was actually very appealing. Liz still said nothing, but the hand with the pepper relaxed the slightest bit.

"I had a second offer for it, yesterday. Sight unseen," he said, stressing the two words as if they were unspeakable possibilities. "I don't have the faintest idea why." He leaned forward, hands open as though begging her. "Can't you tell me anything about it?"

"Professor Kettridge, I haven't seen the bead," said Elizabeth wearily. "So far as I know, you have a rock with a hole through it."

He nodded. "That's exactly what it looks like. It's not a work of art, it's of no particular archaeological significance, it's not even *made* of anything intrinsically valuable." He searched her face in some desperation. "So why am I being offered ridiculous sums of money to part with it?"

"How ridiculous?" He told her. She put down her book, and stared at him. "Now can you see why I'm worried?"

Elizabeth frowned. "I can see why you're worried today. That's a frightening amount of money for one bead. I still don't understand the scene you caused at Rutherford House, Professor."

"Please, call me Jordan."

"No." She shook her head vigorously. "Why the hell should I?"

"Damn it!" he snarled. "Look I came here—"

"You *followed* me here—it's called stalking, Professor."

"To tell you," he shouted her down, "that I'm willing to consider your client's offer."

Elizabeth waited, and slowly the attention of the staff and other lunchers drifted away from the spectacle.

"I can't say whether he'd be willing to pay such an extravagant price for a lump of rock with a hole through it, Professor."

"The money doesn't matter."

Elizabeth raised both eyebrows, and he relented. His gray-green eyes locked with hers, and he continued levelly.

"The money doesn't matter that much, Ms. Dimitros. But I want to know who I'm dealing with. I don't dig for or sell to thieves, to collectors who deal with thieves, to idiots who want to 'invest' in things they're incapable of appreciating, or to blood-sucking corporate art-buyers." Kettridge was good at reading faces, and he watched the woman across from him carefully as he said each word. On 'blood-sucking,' her expression didn't change in the least.

"Well," said Elizabeth. "I suppose I can thank you for your apology about the scene you made in front of my boss. And I'll remember that you hold a certain code in your dealings; we'll note it in the company's file on the item. If I were you, though, I'd be less concerned about dealing with Rutherford House—which if you know anything about the market, you know is as clean as it gets—than about dealing with someone willing to pay so much, blindly, for your find. Most of our clients are connoisseurs. Sometimes we work for families trying to recover their heritage or build one. As for corporations...well, museums incorporate these days, and corporations build museums. I hope you don't consider building the Getty a sin? We certainly don't deal on the black market. I can't say we check to see whether our clients do; it would be an invasion of privacy."

Kettridge listened. "Ms. Dimitros, I believe in your sincerity. But I'm not sure whether you really know who you're fronting for. Be careful. Be damn careful. There are *dangerous* people mixed up in this business."

"In antiques?"

"No!" He struck the table with a closed fist. "Sorry." He whispered, "In *this*—wrapped up in the bead and whatever goes with it.

"Look." Kettridge stared at the speckled Formica tabletop as if for answers, leaned his head on his hands, and spoke softly. "You read the article. The bead was found in a grave. I excavated that grave from the natural surface down to the cemetery level. As I dug, I found broken pieces of clay with amulet-signs baked into them. They were scattered around in stratum after stratum. The placement suggested that the people of Sur-Amech put one or two a decade onto the grave for *generations* after the body was interred. The writing degenerates after a century or two, but the symbol stays the same.

"When I reached the original surface of the grave, I found the same sign scratched onto a large flat rock, facing downward. When I found the body, it was surrounded by the same kind of stone, with the same rough drawing of the amulet sign—again, facing toward the body. Literally surrounded, Ms. Dimitros—lying on a bed of them, walled in by them, and covered with them. The body was in the worst preservation of any found in the area. We pull desiccated, brittle bones from the sand there.

This was just the dusty outline of a skeleton.

"There's no other grave like it in Sur-Amech.

"And the most interesting thing, Ms. Dimitros, is that the symbol carved into the rocks in that grave is still in use as a protective sign among the nomads who live in the area." He whipped out a pen, took a napkin from the dispenser, and drew a little glyph on the flimsy paper. "It's a ward against the Evil Eye, Ms. Dimitros."

Elizabeth caught the eye of her waitress, and signaled for the check. "Thank you for the lecture, Professor. What's your point?"

"The people of Sur-Amech wouldn't bury this corpse with their own dead. They hauled the body and the stones into virtual wilderness to get rid of it, and they protected themselves against the power of that corpse as well as they could, for as long as they could. They were afraid, Ms. Dimitros. And so am I."

"You believe in curses, Professor?" Elizabeth asked, incredulously. "Is the Smithsonian going to wrack and ruin because the Hope diamond is on display there? Did the Carter expedition really die because they violated Tutankhamen's tomb?" She paid her bill, and stood to leave.

"I wanted to warn you. But I can see that you're blind to it all, Ms. Dimitros. I'm terribly sorry. I hope you'll be all right."

"Thank you." Liz picked up her book and turned toward the door. Kettridge didn't rise. She had to speak to the back of his head. "And the bead?"

"I'll be in touch," said Kettridge.

Wednesday, 30 June 1999, 12:53 PM
Rutherford House, Upper East Side, Manhattan
New York City, New York

Amy found Liz in the bindery. The younger woman was pale, but her eyes weren't red. As she worked, very slowly, but with her usual care and precision, she brushed her hair away from her face, and the hand that moved trembled, just the faintest bit. Amy pushed the door open. "Lizzie?" she asked softly. "What's wrong?"

Elizabeth jumped in her chair. "Sorry, Amy. You scared me."

Amy shut the door behind her. "You were fine two hours ago. Now you're spookier than a cat with its head in a bag. Are you sleeping all right? You aren't walking again?" Starkly suspicious, she asked, "Did your mother call and upset you?" The girl shook her head, and Amy insisted: "Tell me what's happened, dear heart."

"Kettridge…came after me."

"Oh, Lord. What do you mean?"

"I was eating lunch at Victor's, and he sat down at my table. He was trying to…warn me, or threaten me, or something. There's something terribly wrong with this bead, I think…"

In bits and pieces, Amy gleaned the whole story from her friend.

"First thing we do," said Amy seriously, "is insulate you from this whole affair. If Kettridge shows up again, you tell him you're not at liberty to discuss Rutherford business. Tell him to contact the partners. Then you leave as fast as you can, okay?"

Elizabeth nodded.

"Second, I'm calling your Mr. Ruhadze and telling him to do his own negotiations. We'll ask for a finder's fee, but if there's trouble, it's his. Not ours, and certainly not yours, Liz.

"Third, we're going to pin down the mysterious Professor Kettridge. He comes in and out of here without so much as a contact number, fine and dandy. I've been asking after him around our mutual associates already—I'll find out where he's staying, or I'll find him through Berkeley, and I'll get him off your back."

Elizabeth smiled uncertainly.

Amy smiled back. "I'm sure there's a reason for all this. Damned if I can say it'll be a logical one, though. Everyone I talked to Monday said Kettridge was 'a nice guy'—which means nothing, of course—neither 'nice' nor 'good' mean anything nowadays. Kettridge is not supposed to be off his rocker. He can get a little insistent over his favorite theory, but I've never known a scientist who didn't, at least a little. We'll deal with this." She got up and opened the door. "You stick to the diary, Lizzie, and I'll go tackle the madmen."

Wednesday, 30 June 1999, 7:37 PM
Laurel Ridge Farm
Near Columbia, Maryland

Hesha stirred in his sleep.

"Sir?"

Hesha forced his eyes open. He tasted the cool air of the tomb, dusky with the scent of his pets. He was alone...as his mind cleared, he knew the voice. "Janet?"

"Yes, sir. I'm sorry to disturb you so early, but there's been a development I think you should know about."

"Give me a moment." Hesha stood and found his way to the door unerringly. In Vegel's chamber, he let the lights come up. The stone door swung silently shut behind him. "All right."

"We had a call today from Rutherford House...through ordinary channels, but undeniably concerned with your projects there. It seems that Kettridge has seized on Miss Dimitros as a potential source of information. Mrs. Rutherford didn't put it like that, of course."

"Which Mrs. Rutherford?"

"Amaryllis. She expressed concern that you had exposed Miss Dimitros to some sort of danger…and frankly, laid down an ultimatum; if there is trouble between you and the professor, Miss Dimitros must be kept out of it." Janet paused, and speculated, "I got the impression, sir, that she thinks your statue is a stolen item, and that there are black-market forces beneath the mystery."

"That's harmless enough. Don't encourage it, however." Hesha pulled the loose, white eye out of his robes. Ever since the night Elizabeth had discovered how to remove it, he'd kept it on a thong around his neck. He scrutinized it as if for the first time, and made a decision.

"Janet, we're going to take Miss Dimitros out of the professor's way. Start making arrangements for an appropriate Friday flight."

Thursday, 1 July 1999, 11:20 AM
Rutherford House, Upper East Side, Manhattan
New York City, New York

Agnes Rutherford strode stiffly through the front doors of her establishment, and her sharp eyes took in every inch of the display floor with no sign whatever of approval. She looked down at her nephew James's wife—they were nearly the same height, but Agnes could look down at people who were head and shoulders taller than herself without straining.

"Good morning, Aunt Agnes," said Amy. She leaned forward and exchanged dry pecks on the cheek with her elderly relative. "How was your flight?"

"No worse than usual, for this time of year. I look forward to the end of the tourist season, however." The senior partner took a few steps farther into the shop and looked down at Amy from even greater heights than before. "Have we any important appointments scheduled for today? No? A pity, but it will at least leave us time to review the figures for the last week."

Agnes took a moment to view the display again. Her glance came to Elizabeth—and if Amy was dwarfed by the old lady's eyes, Elizabeth was less than an ant. "Miss Dimitros."

"Welcome back, Miss Rutherford."

"Carry on down here." Agnes started for the stairs to the offices, and turned back halfway. "You attended to Mr. Ruhadze last Wednesday? Were you able to sell the collar to him?"

"Yes, ma'am."

Agnes said nothing, but continued up the stairs.

That night, Thompson brought the sedan to a perfect, parallel halt at the curbside. The walls of both tires grazed cement. Between his master's door and the doors of Rutherford House there could be no shorter distance, but he worried anyway. "Careful, sir."

"Relax a little, Thompson. It really is too much to hope that the professor would have staked out the store."

"And if he did?"

"Then you are here, the Asp is...waiting in the wings, and I am not entirely without defenses of my own." Hesha slipped into his suit coat, picked up a shining black alligator briefcase and a brass-topped cane, and stepped out of the car.

Amy Rutherford welcomed him inside. "Good evening, Mr. Ruhadze." He looked at her through earnest eyes, and shook her hand. Her manner was as polished as ever, but beneath the gloss, she was not pleased with him. "Aunt Agnes is waiting for you in her office. Shall we?" She led him through the dim and empty display floor to the office stairs. The workroom was dark. At the end of the corridor, she stopped, knocked once, and ushered him into the throne room, as she thought of it.

"Mr. Ruhadze, Aunt Agnes."

"Punctual as ever, Hesha." Agnes Rutherford looked neither down on him, nor up, but she gave Hesha Ruhadze the gaze of an equal, and half-rose to greet him.

"I would never willingly waste your time, Miss Agnes," he said courteously. "It would be an insult to keep a lady waiting, particularly one with such demanding responsibilities."

Agnes half-smiled. "Sit down, Hesha, and tell us how we can be of assistance to you today."

Amy drew the door shut behind them, and sat respectfully in a corner chair to watch the giants meet. Her aunt—Jim's aunt, she reminded herself, grateful that her own family was less...everything—sat behind a stately, massive desk. Her thin, frail body dwindled in the equally impressive, red leather-upholstered chair.

Ruhadze, on the other hand, fitted the matching seat as if it had been built around him. He was a vision in monochrome—the red leather, in shadow, was the warm, brown-black color of his skin. His suit—of an outdated cut, she realized suddenly, almost contemporary with Agnes's father's days—was the color of coal. The old fabric devoured the light, but his shoes, his bag, the ebon cane he held across his knees, and his bright eyes shone with it.

"I have an unusual request, Miss Agnes." He hesitated, and seemed to pick his words carefully. "I'm afraid that I have inadvertently endangered one of your employees."

Agnes lifted her fine gray brows. "Miss Dimitros," she said quietly. He nodded. "Please explain yourself, Hesha."

"I own a particular item—"

"A statue?" interjected Amy.

"Yes." Hesha half-turned in his chair to include her in the conversation. "It is not, I assure you, 'hot' or 'black market' or anything of the kind. On the other hand, as with many antiquities, the country of its origin disapproves of any entity other than itself possessing the piece. Just as the Greeks want the treasures of Athens returned from England, a certain nation wants my little treasure returned to native soil. I have no more intention of giving it to them than I have of handing the collar I bought last week over to Cairo—less, in fact. Egypt and Greece at least have democracies, museums, and relative peace. They bring their heritage back through treaties, special funds, the United Nations...diplomatic means.

"The government in question, however, has abandoned diplomacy in almost every matter, and is a known haven for terrorists. The ruling party has made it clear that they will hide and back even the most radical of organizations, provided their demands are met and policies adhered to...one of which is the recovery of 'cultural artifacts' that, in fact, they have little claim to.

"I showed Miss Dimitros the statue as a challenge—I wanted to test her skills. Unfortunately for all of us, she was more clever than I could have hoped. Not only did she find some details previous experts had missed, she recognized a piece of the statue in a diagram in a professional publication, and contacted the author."

"Professor Kettridge," murmured Agnes.

"Yes. And Kettridge came to New York to find her."

Amy clicked her tongue against the back of her teeth, and said, "I've looked into Jordan Kettridge's background. He's a fine scholar and no more a terrorist than I am."

"I don't mean to suggest that he is. I suspect that the terrorists recognized the bead, and tried to steal it. They were obviously unsuccessful. From his point of view, I suppose, Elizabeth's message was just another tactic of the thieves. When that failed, there came the extreme bid for the piece...

"I don't know what they may try next, but Kettridge has had two contacts with Elizabeth, and the terrorists are likely to think that she knows more than she does, or can lead them to the professor. For her own safety, I want to take her out of New York and away from Kettridge, the terrorists, and Rutherford House."

Agnes's eyes narrowed. Her thin, pale lips twisted into a speculative frown. "And that's why you asked me to keep her here tonight. Well, Ruhadze, what do you intend to do with our Miss Dimitros?"

Hesha stroked the harsh line of his cheekbone. "My own collection," he began, "is in need of some restoration. From what I've seen of her work, Elizabeth would be the ideal candidate to work on it." He lifted his briefcase to his lap, opened it, and slid a small sheaf of paper across the desk to Agnes. "I would make up your losses, of course, and supplement Miss Dimitros's salary while she was contracted out to me." He waited while the old lady examined the numbers. "These are figured on a week-by-week basis. I doubt that her absence would be prolonged...though there is certainly work enough in Baltimore to keep her busy for months, if need be."

Amy watched her aunt's ice-blue eyes scan the bottom line, and knew what Agnes's answer would be. "Mr. Ruhadze," asked Amy, "Isn't this a matter for the police? Or," she continued sharply, "if all you're suggesting is true, a matter for the CIA *and* the FBI *and* Interpol?"

"It is," said Hesha. "And I have gone to them," he lied. "That's how I came by what information I know. We could arrange to have them take care of her. But Amy," he said, trying to meet her gaze in the shadowy corner, "do you know what the phrase 'protective custody' actually means? It means jail, and isolation, and little hotel rooms with no one to speak to but police officers and nothing to do but wait. I'd rather not inflict that on Elizabeth. She'll be safe in Baltimore, and she will be working at what she likes best. Unless one of *us* tells her about the danger, she won't even need to know it exists until after it's already passed." He looked away again, down at the thick Persian carpet. "I'd offer the same protection to Kettridge, if I could find him."

"Hesha," said Miss Agnes. "I concur with your appraisal of Miss Dimitros's value to us as a shop assistant, but I believe you are underestimating the restoration costs we will be subject to in her absence..."

And Amy listened in vague disbelief as Jim's aunt proceeded to dicker over Elizabeth Dimitros as though she were a French Provincial chair or a Ming vase. Mr. Ruhadze, at least, had the grace to be embarrassed—their eyes met once, as Agnes pulled a rate list of out-of-house fabric workers from the files. He put up very little fight; he seemed genuinely more interested in the merchandise than in the price. At least Lizzie was going where she was...highly valued. Amy stood up, suddenly unable to take any more of the haggling, and Agnes's piercing voice split though the growing headache.

"Amy, where are you going?"

"I need an aspirin, Aunt Agnes. Excuse me."

Amy fled into her own office, downed the aspirin, and sank into her big, overstuffed sofa. She tried to think straight. Terrorists and fugitives and contacts...it sounded like a spy movie, and a poorly constructed one. Ruhadze had explained everything, but...there had to be simpler ways to protect Lizzie. Was he going to all this trouble to protect her because the danger was real and he cared for her? Or was he trying to entice her away for nefarious purposes? *Oh Lord,* she thought, *Lizzie's well over the age of consent....* She argued herself into circles and corners for another half hour or so, until she heard the door open to Agnes's room. Speech spilled into the hallway.

"I'd like to speak with her myself, of course." Hesha's baritone came clearly through the walls.

"Of course," answered Agnes. "She's in the bindery…the third door on your left, Hesha."

Amy left the couch for the door, and opened it just as Ruhadze approached. "Mr. Ruhadze? I have some more questions for you."

He came in and sat.

"Why doesn't Kettridge go to the police? Why shouldn't we simply transfer Elizabeth to our London offices for a month, or a year, or however long this takes? What gives you the idea that there will be an end to it, if terrorists are the enemy? You're moving Elizabeth to Baltimore at a great deal of trouble and expense. Now, if you weren't telling the truth to Aunt Agnes, I doubt you'll tell it to me. Please let me make one thing clear to you. I want you to take good care of Lizzie."

Hesha smiled. He stood up, took her by the hand, and stared deep into her eyes. "Trust me," he told her, overwhelmingly serious, and compassionate, and sure. He waited for the command to sink in. Satisfied that she believed, he released her.

She sighed. "I'm sorry to have gone on like that…but I'm all she has, and I can't just let her disappear. Oh, Lord, do you realize Lizzie's been here since nine? Let's go talk to her, and send her packing. Promise me you'll keep the poor child working only eight-hour days. She'll think it's Christmas. Agnes is just a slave-driver, really."

"I've noticed," said Hesha, as he picked up his things.

She smiled, and led him down the hall to the bindery.

Elizabeth looked up as she came in. "The diary's finished, Amy. If I never read another word about Elizabethan shipping businesses, it will be too soon." She flicked a hand toward the work table with contempt. "I went ahead and started the blasted papyrus—" Hesha followed Amy into the room, and Elizabeth stopped short.

Amy took up her favorite chair, and watched as their visitor came around the table to examine Lizzie's work.

"A tourist piece," he said, and the same contempt filled his voice. "Nineteenth-century souvenir." He leant over the beginnings of the repair work, and nodded approval. "But you know how to restore papyri properly. Good."

"Lizzie, Mr. Ruhadze has asked Rutherford House to lend him one of our most prized assets. How would you like to go to Baltimore and do restoration work on his private collection?"

Elizabeth sat quietly, her hands folded on the desk in front of her. She tried to catch Hesha's gaze, and did, but there was nothing there for her to read. She stared at a beaming Amy, and though the smile was luminous, the eyes were tight and worried. Slowly, the rays of confidence faded in that smile, and the older woman's anxieties revealed themselves in the lines around her mouth, too.

"You don't have to go, of course," said Amy. "And it isn't a permanent post. Your job here will be secure; we'll look after the loft for you. But Mr. Ruhadze needs someone to do the work, and Aunt Agnes is simply putty in his hands. It's all arranged—if you want it."

Elizabeth's glance appealed to Hesha again—and though there was still no sign on his face, his hand grasped her shoulder reassuringly.

"When?"

"Tomorrow afternoon?" he suggested. "You can settle in over the weekend and start work on Monday."

"That's fast."

"I know."

Elizabeth covered the crude cartouche in its protective wrappings. After the papyrus, there would be another diary, perhaps, or deed papers with 'New Amsterdam' at the top instead of 'New York,' or a Renaissance floral with no merit besides age. Hesha's collection would be different. And Hesha himself...but she cut the thought off there.

"I'll go."

Inside the black sedan, it was unsettlingly quiet.

Elizabeth sat with her tote bag at her feet. The tickets to Baltimore were tucked into her sketchbook. She watched the lights of the city speed by, tinted blue-purple by the windows.

Introductions had been made between herself and Ronald Thompson, but Thompson wasn't one to chatter. There were streets to watch, and other cars ever to be suspected of holding the Enemy in one form or another. Hesha sensed, too, that Thompson was unsettled by the 'collection' of Miss Dimitros.

Hesha held his tongue. A kind word to Elizabeth would have soothed her fears and apprehension...but Thompson wasn't ready to hear his master whisper sweet nothings to a 'nice' girl. A curt, businesslike discussion with the girl would have put her in her place as a curator, and nothing more, and satisfied Thompson entirely...but Hesha wasn't ready to relinquish the hold that a feigned romance might have over Elizabeth, and wasn't sure that she would let herself be railroaded to Baltimore with that enticement taken away. He would take a moment with each, separately, soon. If the drive to her apartment was silent as the grave, so much the better for his concentration.

They dropped her off at the old warehouse. She wished them good night, and faded into the darkness of the front door. A loitering figure signaled to Thompson, and the driver confirmed the watchmen's orders. The sedan pulled back onto the main roads, and Thompson looked for Hesha's eye in the rearview mirror.

"Sir..."

"Not now, Thompson. Take us back to Rutherford House. Kettridge has been there recently, and I know now how to find him."

"How well do you know New York?" Hesha asked, unexpectedly.

Thompson considered. "The main roads, the places *you* go, some of those neighborhoods in depth, and a little more, maybe."

"We're going to follow Kettridge with this." said Hesha, dangling the milk-white bead from its cord. "Its power is very low, and I will have to shut out as much of the world as I can while I use it. I will close my eyes and direct you as well as possible. Take turns to follow my line whenever the roads allow. Remember exactly where we are each time I speak to you; if we lose the trail you will have to drive back to that spot as quickly as possible, and we will try again. Do you understand?"

"No," admitted the driver, "but I think I can follow the orders."

Hesha lay down on the back seat, holding the little eye between both hands.

"North from here," he said. Thompson checked for cops, made an illegal U-turn, and drove slowly up the street.

"Stop."

Thompson eased the sedan into place next to a fire hydrant, and waited for the still form in the back seat to say further.

"He spent a long time here...but he isn't here now. Are we near a hotel?"

Thompson blinked in surprise. "We're on the doorstep of a big one."

Hesha felt for the trail through the bead. "Southwest," he said. The car rolled on, and within half a block, he knew the traces were colder than those he'd followed. "Back again. East from the hotel." Again, there was a trail, but a stale one. "Stop. Back again."

"Sir?"

"What is it?" asked Hesha, wearily.

"Let me drive around the block a few times. When you find a good lead, tell me. His 'footprints' are going to be a hell of a mess right in front of where he's staying."

"Do it."

"Stop." Hesha opened his eyes. "He's here."

Thompson looked into the back seat. "Sir, I think maybe you'd better hurry."

Hesha stepped onto the curb, and understood.

They had pulled up outside Grand Central Station.

Hesha very nearly ran to the entrance. He hurtled into the crowds on the main floor, his quick senses devouring the faces of the travelers he brushed past. He scanned the forms of the passengers and pick-ups waiting in the long rows of seats as his footsteps took him instinctively to the walls.

Kettridge was not, now, buying a ticket at the counters or eating at any of the stalls, but he had been to both. He had not, though Hesha's search was taking time, left the building. The Setite drew slowly to a halt. It ill befitted him to run around the platforms and into the subways. He sought the solitude of an empty bank of phones, and pulled his own sleek model from his coat.

Behind him, one of the pay machines rang. He ignored it, and began dialing for Thompson, but it rang and rang until he grabbed it, checked the receiver reflexively, and put it to his ear.

"Hello, Ruhadze. How's death treating you?"

"Professor Kettridge," acknowledged Hesha.

"It's been a long time since Syria, hasn't it?"

"For you."

"Yes," said Kettridge. "for me. You haven't changed, a bit, of course. No scars from that last firefight at Baalbek, I notice. I imagine *I* look like hell, though."

"I couldn't say."

"I don't intend for you to be able to." The mortal's voice held a sharper edge than before, and he continued, "You're getting sloppy in your old age. Using a girl you were seen with so publicly to make the contact—hardly your usual finesse, is it?" Hesha said nothing. "Or were you behind the burglary attempt?"

"That might be a better guess."

"I'll give you credit, though, you weren't behind the high bid."

"I'd double it, if I thought you were interested."

"We both know I'm not.... How about a trade, instead?" Kettridge inquired, thoughtfully.

"What would you take for the bead?"

"I'm not bartering beads today," said the professor. "I'll trade you information."

Hesha considered. "I'm listening."

"I'll tell you where the high bid came from, if you'll tell me why every dead man in the world seems interested in my little lucky charm."

"Not good enough. There are probably five or more intermediaries between you and the bidder."

"No, not this time. Someone was in an awful hurry."

Temptation brushed by Hesha, and she was smiling. "Tell me where the high bid came from, and I'll answer three questions about your bead. Specific questions. How helpful the answers are will depend, of course, on how intelligently you put your questions."

For nearly a full minute—which Hesha spent in efforts to pinpoint Kettridge and his 'lucky charm'—the line gave up nothing but static.

"Harlem. What *is* the bead?"

"It's the eye of a statue."

Kettridge named a street. "Why does it pull me toward Atlanta?"

"It's a subsidiary item to a more powerful artifact. Your eye can locate the main artifact. The main artifact is or was in Atlanta."

"2417A. Basement entrance. How did you find me here tonight?"

"I have another eye of the statue. It can locate your eye. I can follow you anywhere you go, Kettridge," said Hesha, and the mortal could hear the smile in the creature's voice.

The professor, from his own booth deep within the maze of the station, felt a chill run down his spine. He hefted a duffel bag onto his shoulder, and felt the comforting metal lumps of his weapons within. "I wouldn't recommend that, Ruhadze," he said evenly. "I've learned a lot since Baalbek."

"Good. Let me offer you some advice." Hesha whispered into the phone. "Get out of New York as fast as you can. I won't come after you—yet—but if the address you gave me is correct, you have half the hounds of hell on your tail."

"I know. I've singed some. Your kind don't like crowds or fire, do they?"

"Don't assume anything. Don't call *them* my kind," hissed Hesha. "And if you want to rely on crowds for protection, don't go to Atlanta or the other riot zones."

Kettridge looked down at his tickets: Amtrak to Atlanta—through D.C. and Raleigh. He was suddenly afraid. "Damn it, Hesha—your telling me not to is a good reason to go! Why should I trust you? Why warn me? Why all these mindgames? God, I can't believe we're having this conversation—give me a reason why I should believe a single fucking thing you've said, from start to finish?"

"I would rather that you kept the bead, Jordan, than

have it fall into the hands of the high bidder. In the riot zones, they won't care about witnesses. Understand?" He waited. "Jordan?"

The line was dead, and though Hesha quickly found a phone still warm from his rival's hand, he felt the red eye speeding away south. In ten minutes, he could no longer sense it at all.

part two:
maryland

Friday, 2 July 1999, 6:20 PM
Laurel Ridge Farm
Columbia, Maryland

Elizabeth strained to see through the twilight. The woods around them looked much like the woods they'd been traveling through for the past ten minutes, and the road was the same nearly unmarked, two-lane affair it had been. She knew that Columbia was a large, built-up suburb. Logically, there should be houses, shops, lights, and larger streets nearby, but she hadn't seen any since the last stop sign.

The sedan passed a yellow diamond with the most elaborate squiggle on it that Elizabeth had ever seen. She grasped the armrest tightly, and they took a series of curves like a drunken roller coaster. Thompson flicked up the headlights halfway through a sweeping arc, and gray tree-trunks flashed by in a blur. They sped around one last corner and turned up a driveway. It clung to a creekside and then edged its way up the side of a hill, passing a mailbox, unmarked. They bumped gently and slowly over gravelly macadam, crested the shoulder of the hill, and Elizabeth had her first sight of the house of Hesha Ruhadze.

In the center, facing the drive, was a solid massif—a majestically proportioned old house with tall, mullioned windows, grand double-doors under a neoclassical lintel, and perfect symmetry. As the car pulled around, she saw a later addition, tacked on by a lesser architect for a larger family. The back wing tried to echo the front, but it was cluttered with odd side-roofs, long eaves, dormer rooms, and gables that projected at impossible angles. The whole mess was painted white—not recently, and not for the first time. Good red brick showed at the corners, where the winds had had the best chance to knock the flakes away. The roof was verdigris-green copper in excellent repair, and behind a morass of bracken and wildflowers, Elizabeth could see a real fieldstone foundation running underneath it all. It was shabby. It wasn't what she had expected. It did have charm.

Thompson eased the car over the weed-eaten drive and pulled up to a slightly more modern-looking barn. He touched a button on his console and the broad doors slid open. The black sedan rolled gingerly into place beside a car that might have been its twin, and stopped.

Elizabeth stepped onto the clean-swept brick floor. She dragged her carry-on, her purse, and satchel out with her. Thompson walked around, pulled her checked bags from the trunk, and groaned.

"What do you have in here, bricks?"

"They're books. I'm working on my doctorate in Art History. That one rolls, by the way. We can pile everything else on top of it."

"What's your concentration?" he asked, as he swung the lighter suitcase into place and clipped it down.

"It's rather obscure...call it comparative symbology."

"What does that mean?" Thompson began trolling the double-decker baggage along a moss-covered path of slate flagstones.

"Um. Take a bull in a painting—a painting you don't have captions for because you can't read the script the people wrote in. Does it represent fertility? A sacrifice? An amount of goods for barter? A god? If it is a god, which god is it, and why did the painter use the allegory of 'god as bull'? And did it represent that god before or after an invasion from another culture that happened to have a thing for cattle?"

Thompson manhandled the cases up three wooden steps to the porch. "Why can't it just be a bull?" He punched a code into a keypad next to a wasps' nest and opened the door to let her through.

"Sometimes it is. But my specialty is very primitive motifs. The farther back in history you go, the less plain doodling you get, and the more each symbol *means* something important to the person who made it."

Elizabeth turned to look around her. They'd come into the long, narrow kitchen. The appliances were ultra-modern, but the cabinets and table looked, to her experienced eye, as if they were original to the house. She drifted a little into the working end of things, and fiddled idly with a white enamel drawerpull.

"Just set your stuff down here," said Thompson. "You have your choice of rooms, so I'll show you around and let you pick before I take your bag of bricks anywhere. Come on."

He led her through a wide hall into the older half of the building and up a dark and creaking staircase.

"My room is down that way," he said, inclining his graying head to the back of the house. "And the cook's, too, you'll meet him later. The guest rooms are in the front." Thompson leaned into an open doorway, turned a lamp on inside, and stepped away for Elizabeth to have a look. "Or, if you aren't claustrophobic, you can come downstairs. Some people don't like the idea of basements...."

"No, that's fine. I worked under the Met four summers running, and you feel the traffic through the tabletops down there."

The cellar door from the kitchen still led down to the cellar—but where the original inhabitants had left packed earth floors, Hesha Ruhadze had laid shining planks stained nearly black. The fieldstone foundations formed the walls, and support pillars four feet square stood in carefully cut gaps in the dark wood.

The main room was filled with display cases and glass-fronted shelves. Here and there a couch and table, a chair and desk, or stool and workbench were grouped near the exhibits. Several huge tables held binding supplies, pieces of pottery in reconstruction, and other temptations for the historian. Elizabeth dragged her feet past a long, low table full of *things* that needed her ministrations, and only when Thompson cleared his throat and called her could she turn away. On the other side of the long hall—at what she thought must be the outer edge of the house upstairs—he waited at the bottom of short flight of wide, slate steps, holding open a door made in the same style as the floor.

"This was Mr. Vegel's room," he said.

"Mr. Vegel?" The little apartment was richly furnished in a very Victorian, masculine fashion. Three walls were paneled and the fourth was wood only to waist height; above the chair rail it was covered in white satin fabric, and discreet silver pins held papers, photographs, and pieces of fabric to it as if to a huge bulletin board.

"Mr. Ruhadze didn't mention him?" Thompson asked. She shook her head but didn't show much curiosity. He let the subject go. "Books and so forth here," he said, unnecessarily. The entire wall was shelves, not full, but comfortably crowded. He and the Asp had had a rough day going through Vegel's apartment. Hesha's list of items forbidden to the newcomer was long, and there weren't many safe places to store the really dangerous things. After the clean-out, Thompson's practiced hands had massaged the gaps in the shelves. Unless you knew how full Vegel had kept his office, you'd never realize anything was missing. Thompson watched the girl react to the room, her fingers wandering along the rows of rare and expensive editions, and decided that the boss's guess had been correct. It always was.

"Mr. Vegel was the previous curator. He lived down here, mostly. Of course, you're the only guest. You could turn this room into office space, work area, whatever you need, and actually sleep upstairs. The guest rooms do have nice views, particularly in the summer."

"Oh, no," said Elizabeth, looking at the desk and the library. "This will be perfect."

"I'll bring down your things." As he left, Thompson smiled in satisfaction. Trust Hesha to know what was catnip, and for which kitties.... He pressed a code on the kitchen intercom, and spoke into it. "Sir?"

"Yes, Thompson?"

"Miss Dimitros is here. She's chosen Vegel's room. I'll bring her things down in a moment. I've left the impression that you won't be available for at least an hour yet."

"Thank you. I'll see her when Janet and I have finished."

Thompson cut the connection. He picked up Elizabeth's carry-on, and took from the closest drawer an object that manifestly did not belong in a kitchen—a hand-held metal scanner. All the bags were clean.

He looked longingly at the hall leading into the old house. In the space between the walls, there was a hidden elevator. But Elizabeth might not be in her room when the car opened in the first basement, and so he slung her bag full of books over his broad shoulders, and used the stairs. The girl was deep in a book when he brought the luggage in, but she smiled and offered to help.

"No thanks," said Thompson. He put the heavy case in a convenient corner—blocking her off, he hoped, from finding the door hidden there—and in two more trips all her things were with her.

"Well, if you'll excuse me, I have some chores to see to, and business arrangements to make for Mr. Ruhadze's townhouse. If you need anything, there's an intercom here by the door," he said, sliding open a wooden panel. "Just press the green button and speak into it." He closed the tiny cabinet again, walked out, and shut the door softly behind him.

Elizabeth looked up from her unpacking. Was that a

knock? She closed the drawer on her socks, crossed the room—now rather cluttered with open suitcases and boxes of notes—and opened the door.

"Good evening, Elizabeth."

"Hello, Hesha."

They wavered on the threshold. "Come on in," she said, smiling. "I'm still in the messy stages of the explosion, I'm afraid." She backed into the room, and gestured vaguely.

Hesha lowered himself into Vegel's chair, stretched his legs out, and watched her move. She rattled off expressions of gratitude, compliments for Thompson, and amazement at the house. She had questions about the building, and he answered them with his connoisseur's voice and attitude…a stock character, a mask held up for her to look at while he studied her. She was nervous, but comfortable with the surroundings. It was he himself who made her fingers restless and the tiny muscles of her face unsettled. Every time she looked to him, a question was in her eyes, and he made sure to keep all the answers out of his own.

He found himself relieved that the Beast remained calm in her presence…and was shocked to realize that he had been worried unawares. What was it that had given the thing so much strength in her apartment? The statue? His worries about the Sabbat's machinations? Vegel's disappearance? He determined to watch the Beast and his own mind more closely—the weakness could not be allowed to remain.

"Are you tired?" he asked, changing the subject.

Elizabeth stopped in mid-fold. "No."

"But you had to think about it?"

"It's nearly ten, isn't it? I suppose that I should be—I had to be up early to pack—but I'm too excited about the work. I caught a glimpse of some of the pieces coming down here."

He nodded understandingly. "Would you like a tour?"

"Absolutely." Halfway to the door she stopped and faced him earnestly. "Unless *you're* tired. I don't want to keep you from your schedule…."

"I confess that I succumbed to temptation earlier. West Coast lawyers are the worst, I think. I had the cook bring down some coffee…Turkish coffee. I'll be awake all night," he sighed, "but it was the only way I could deal with the fools who were chattering at me. Besides, tomorrow is Saturday. Only my international affiliates will try to get at me, and my secretary can say 'No' in forty languages."

Elizabeth chuckled and followed him out.

"…And the ventilation system is fully labeled…if you have any problems, do let Thompson know," said Hesha. He turned to another corner of the workshop.

"This flat file is full of paper that needs acid-balance treatment. The vertical stores contain ten or twelve paintings that need work of one kind or another, and I have all kinds of stabilization projects, of course. I know that painting restoration is a specialty of yours. If you'll finish just that section during your stay here, I'd be amply compensated for your expenses. However, if you'd like to try your hand at more unusual things…" He paced back into the main room at a businesslike clip. "Here," he said, almost smiling, "is the emperor of all jigsaw puzzles."

It was under glass, on the longest, narrowest table in the entire museum. On smooth fabric lay what once had been a scroll. "Papyrus," said Hesha. "Part of the grave goods of a pharaoh. Thieves robbed the tomb but the left the 'rubbish' behind—baskets, clay pots, food. This was in a plain wooden case, and they ignored it. More literate thieves picked it up later. Unfortunately, it has been shaken and jarred, and some fool tried to unroll it."

He turned and asked of her, "Do you read the hieroglyphs?"

"No."

"Vegel left notes of the script in use at the period," he said, opening a small drawer built into the table. He offered her a sheaf of hand-made sketches. "Also, the tweezers..." He held up a bizarre-looking pair of tongs. "To keep the dust and the air currents from playing havoc with the shards, we had to cover the whole piece with glass. These slip into the gaps at the edges." He demonstrated, setting two halves of a glyph closer together. Gingerly, he tilted the tweezers up and away from the scraps, and slowly drew the tool back out of the danger zone. "You might want to practice with the sections at the top of the scroll first. The damage is less extensive, and the pieces are easier to read."

He whisked her away from the long table, and continued. "Vegel's particular hobby horse—" he led her to an area carpeted in canvas. An unfinished wooden frame ten feet square and one foot high hemmed in the dusty white cloth. On low shelves on three sides, fragments of jars and bowls freed from the matrix reposed in little trays; one half-reconstructed amphora-like vessel stood above the detritus. In the midst of it, a small boulder of dried clay lay at a resentful tilt. Edges of pottery shards stuck out of it from every angle.

"What is it?" asked Elizabeth.

"We—I'm not sure. Vegel collected it from someone; no provenance available." Hesha thought of the haven the thing had originally occupied. They'd never found out why the Malkavian had treasured the boulder, or where it had come from. But Vegel insisted that it hid something unusual, and the elder Setite had agreed—after certain tests and precautions—to let the archaeologist bring the boulder home. "I don't know whether Erich expected to find anything particularly interesting in it. He had been an archaeologist earlier in his career, and I think he simply liked to keep in practice."

Hesha stepped back, regretfully. "That's all for now. If I'm going to sleep in tomorrow, I have to work tonight, and I'm sure you'll want to finish settling yourself. I can spare the time to show you our finished pieces Monday, perhaps."

"Thank you."

He shook his head. "Thank you for coming on such short notice."

She laughed. "Thank you for rescuing me from Aunt Agnes." Her eyes sought out his. Hesha felt the glance coming, avoided it so deftly that she never knew he'd shunned her, and began the walk back to his office. Behind him, her footsteps tapped a trail across the floor—not toward Vegel's room, but to the long table.

"You're not thinking of starting on that tonight, are you?" he asked without looking.

"I thought I'd just go over it to see what's been done so far."

"Well," he said, nodding to himself. "Try not to stay up too late. If you get hungry, there are all kinds of things in the kitchen...just be careful not to wake the cook."

Hesha left his new protégée hard at work, and joined his other servants in the crypt. Even the Asp was shocked to see the smile on their master's face.

Saturday, 3 July 1999, 11:42 AM
Laurel Ridge Farm
Columbia, Maryland

Feeling late and guilty, Elizabeth trundled up the stairs to the kitchen and found herself confronted by a small, unexpected man in an apron, washing dishes. His hair was very dark, and slightly curly. His skin was a shade or two deeper than her own—a clean, tanned, Mediterranean olive color. His rolled-up shirt sleeves exposed arms thick with wiry black hair. He reached for another bowl, and smiled at her.

"Good morning. I'm sorry I'm up so late," Liz said.

"Why are you sorry? It's Saturday, isn't it?"

"I'm sorry for missing breakfast," she began, then hesitated. "Aren't you the cook?"

"Oh. That's just Ron and the Man being polite. I can cook, but mostly I just buy the groceries. Are you hungry? Of course you're hungry. You just woke up, right? Want an omelet?" He gave her no chance to protest. "I was only washing up from breakfast so I could start lunch. We'll call it brunch. I make the best Italian-American French cooking you've ever had." His twinkling black eyes gave her the once-over. "A big omelet. You're too skinny, as my Mamma would've said." He dried a hand on the dishcloth and extended it. They shook vigorously. "I'm Angelo Mercurio. But just call me the Asp; everybody does."

"Elizabeth Dimitros. Liz," she said back. Then, "The Asp?"

"I bite," said Mercurio with a conspiratorial wink, thoroughly enjoying himself in the role of colorful, harmless houseboy. "Anyway. Noon is fine. Ron Thompson's the only early riser I know, and he cheats. Naps from about five to eight. Hesha—Mr. Ruhadze—well, the boss just comes and goes as he pleases. Jetlagged half the time, working himself to a frazzle the other. I can't remember the last time he had anything like a good night's sleep," said the Asp, in total honesty.

"How many other people live here?" asked Liz, watching as the Asp cracked eight eggs into a bowl one-handed.

"Just Ron and the boss and me, since Vegel's gone. House guests, of course. And occasionally the boss will have some of his assistants in for a working party. We're not precisely 'Lifestyles of the Rich and Famous' here."

"What happened to Mr. Vegel?"

The Asp's bright eyes dimmed for a moment. "Heart attack. Very sudden. Just a few weeks ago…and he was a young man, too. Mid-thirties." He picked up a spatula and began to do clever things to the cholesterol-laden omelet. "Maybe we'll have salad for lunch tomorrow, huh?"

Hesha came down the stairs from the kitchen holding a briefcase and a *Wall Street Journal*. He passed the papyrus table on the way to his own study and broke his slightly weary stride to look over Elizabeth's shoulder as he went by. It was only a moment's pause; long enough for the woman to expect comment, short enough that the lack thereof would not seem dismissive or curt. In his study, he laid down the props. In his apartment, he shed the suit and shoes, pulling on khakis and a worn-looking linen shirt. Quick change complete, he stepped back into the basement hall.

"Nice work," he said over his guest's shoulder.

Elizabeth nearly dropped the tweezers into the papyrus. "Lord. You'd think you'd make some noise, walking across a wooden floor, Hesha."

"Sorry."

"Can you take a look at the text near the topmost illustration? I'm sure the painted parts go together, but I can't tell a faded ibis from a faded owl from a faded vulture."

He pulled a chair up the table's edge, and fixed a monocle into his left eye. "Tweezers?" Elizabeth handed him hers and fetched another pair from the drawer. They worked quietly for some time. "It's a falcon," he said eventually.

"That would explain the confusion."

Silence reigned once more, though Hesha could feel

that the woman's attention strayed to his face quite often. He kept his eyes on the text, and his conversation on the work. At length, Hesha peered into the scraps directly beneath him. "I think there's another illustration coming here. See if you can fill that in." He stood up. "But don't wear yourself out. I hear you were up past four last night." Elizabeth smiled, shrugged, and nodded. "Well, do as you choose. But if you find yourself keeping owl's hours, don't blame me." He started to leave.

Reminded, Liz looked up and asked, "Is there an alarm clock I could borrow?"

"You might talk to the Asp or Thompson," said Hesha, watching her. "I don't use one." He added, "Have a nice night," and was pleased to see her distress as she realized he was going for good.

Sunday, 4 July 1999, 7:56 PM
Laurel Ridge Farm
Columbia, Maryland

"Thompson? Report."

"The Asp has two new refugees. Three of the originals have found havens with closer kin under Prince Garlotte. Miss Dimitros took a walk earlier and tripped the perimeter alarm, but otherwise not so much as a raccoon."

"How did she spend her day?"

"She began on one of those modern things...the bluish one...did some more work on the painting she'd already started; some reading in her room; dinner with the Asp and me. I believe she's on the papyrus at the moment."

"Did she get her alarm clock?"

"I lent her mine. It 'mysteriously' shorted out when we plugged it into the socket."

"Good." Hesha thought for a few moments. "Have my car ready."

"*Your* car, sir?"

"Yes. Follow if you like, but I think Miss Dimitros needs a night away from work. Today is a holiday, you know." The old cop looked at him blankly, and he went on. "Independence Day, Thompson. In fact, take the night off. Tell the Asp the same thing."

"Both of them, sir?" Hesha's man's voice was incredulous.

"Yes."

Sunday, 4 July 1999, 10:00 PM
Aboard the sailboat *Lotus*, Baltimore Harbor
Baltimore, Maryland

Over the water, the last strains of 'The Star Spangled Banner' could be heard—confusingly mixed with the orchestral finish that came, a second and a half sooner, over the radio. The diva's voice gave way to the master of ceremonies, and Hesha switched off the channel.

In total silence, the first fireworks went up...and by the time the second round had risen, the popping, crackling noises of the bright red, white, and blue rockets came to Elizabeth's waiting ears. She slid a little deeper into the deck chair, happier at that moment than she could remember being for years...since her father died. Dad had taken her to Atlantic City once, to see the fireworks fly off a decrepit old pier. Her eyes filled with the shooting stars and she forgot her troubles.

Hesha closed his eyes to slits, and enjoyed the flashing colors through the shield of long lashes. But eventually, as at his age, he supposed was inevitable, the charms of the celebration faded. He let his dark eyes roll toward the woman beside him. Elizabeth, still entranced by the spectacle, didn't notice his attention, and he took full advantage of the opportunity to see her in this secret way. The colors above them reflected off of the water around the boat, off the night-pale skin of his guest, in the spheres of her eyes, and from a tear on her cheek, which he didn't understand. Red and gold burst above them, and the water, the girl, and her eyes turned to flame...blue and white and yellow together, and they were tarnished silver...in green and blue, she'd risen from the ocean, and the streaking tears were only seawater falling from the naiad....

The Beast began to stir. Hesha shook himself mentally, and retreated in his mind to the icy core of his nature. This was the opportunity he had looked for to analyze the weakness that had touched him in her loft.

She was not beautiful. That might have tempted what few urges of the flesh remained to him, but in the circles with which the millionaire Ruhadze mingled, beauty—of kine or Cainite or his own kin—was common enough, and had not bothered him in such a way for centuries.

She was not brilliant. Intelligent, yes. Perceptive in an unusual manner, perhaps. But again, he surrounded himself with geniuses of one kind or another—Thompson and the Asp both in their way, Janet a wizard in hers, and Yasmine Oxenti...who *was* beautiful, though he had never considered the fact before except as an asset to her utility.... Vegel had been brilliant. Kettridge was brilliant.

She was not devious. He had a deep admiration for that twist of mind in others, of course.

Was it because he had placed her off limits to the Beast? In the sheer perversity of the thing's instincts, the forbidden nature of the girl—too valuable to be swallowed whole, not yet controlled enough to be kept for food, too unknown to be Embraced—could be enough to drive the creature to frenzy. But again, Doctor Oxenti should be the more tempting. Beautiful, brilliant, devious, and so valuable a retainer that he could never hope to bring her to Set until an equal pawn arose to replace her…if he sought a childe, a victim, a companion, or a—he laughed to himself—a mate, Yasmine should be the kine that took the Beast's attentions.

Elizabeth stirred in her chair, and curled her bare legs beneath her. Her gaze was still on the sparks and the stars, but one hand moved toward her cheeks.

Hesha reached out and wiped the tears away for her. The woman's grateful, troubled face turned to meet his. From within the ice, he directed his face to show a little kindness. He pulled a clean handkerchief from his trouser pocket and handed it to her silently, as though there were genuine sympathy behind the act.

"I'm sorry," she began, but he shook his head. Elizabeth persevered. "No, I really have been enjoying myself. Thank you for bringing me here. It's just…" she started to sob, quite quietly and without losing control.

And Hesha pulled her closer to him, held the shaking girl in his arms—warm arms, in the Baltimore summer—and let her tell him about her father, about everything he'd learned from reading her papers. He listened, and he contemplated cold-bloodedly how best to repair her wounds, and what weaknesses he would leave to control her by, and how soon she could be the equal of the Mercurio twins and Janet Lindbergh and Yasmine Oxenti and Ronald Thompson.

Monday, 5 July 1999, 8:06 PM
Laurel Ridge Farm
Columbia, Maryland

Hesha emerged from his resting place to find Thompson already waiting for him. "Good evening, sir," said the retainer, obviously nervous. "I've…I've made up my mind, sir. About the 'living will' we were discussing." Hesha sat down on the edge of the stone bench. "I would like to become one of the Family, sir."

Hesha nodded, and in his least human tones, asked, "You have decided to become accursed, damned, forbidden the sun, forbidden a heart, bound to the service of Set and through him bound to the service of Apep?"

Thompson faltered. "Sir?"

"You have a purpose in your mind that will fill centuries and drive you forth every night without despair?"

Thompson said nothing. Hesha stood, and advanced on his servant. They stood face to face, within inches of each other, and the mortal could feel the chill of the other's robes—the temperature of the rocks around them—cave-cold.

"You accept the risk that you may lose your mind, like the Cainite we destroyed in Mexico?" Hesha took his man by the jaw. The Setite lifted until the feet no longer touched the ground, and stared golden-irised and slit-pupiled into Thompson's blue-gray eyes. They remained locked together for nearly two minutes...and then Hesha set his servant gently down.

"You have thought about what you know," he said. "Tonight I have told you things you did not know. Think about them. Ask me questions. Consider that your education has begun, and start looking through your men for a replacement for your position. If, after you have learned a little more of the consequences, you still desire Set's blessings, we will need a security man as good as you yourself.

Hesha threw a glance back at the mortal. "And do relax, Thompson. You passed a test just now. There will be others, but if you change your mind at any time, you may turn off the path. There is no *necessity* to 'graduate.'"

"Now," he resumed, in his accustomed tones, "Report, please."

•

Half an hour later, Hesha and Thompson sat at a horseshoe-shaped console, watching the records of the day. In black and white, color, and heat-register, the various views from the farmhouse's security system surrounded the main display. Outside, a stiff wind created a confusion of swaying trees and bracken. The interior shots were calmer. The Asp moved from one screen to the next—leaving the kitchen for the main staircase and his upstairs room. Elizabeth sat in the center of another, motionless except for one hand and arm and the long tweezers they held. Her precise movements went on without hurry or hesitation, but she might have been a statue otherwise.

"Elizabeth Dimitros," murmured Hesha, "is, for all practical purposes, an orphan. You've read her dossier?"

"Of course."

"Good. She needs a family, Thompson. We are going to provide one." He paused, and met the eye of his prospective heir. "It is my intention that she come to see me as a father figure. I would like you to use what talents you possess to put yourself in the role of an older brother or an uncle, whichever you prefer. Consider this your first assignment on your new path. Don't act, but bring the parts of your personality that will be more useful into play. Tell no direct lies, if you can help it. Imply what you will. Less is more, Thompson. Understood?"

"Yes, sir."

"Excellent. Get the car ready. I'll make a token appearance to our guest and join you in the garage in twenty minutes."

Tuesday, 6 July 1999, 3:41 PM
Laurel Ridge Farm
Columbia, Maryland

Ron Thompson loped easily in through the workshop's open door and called out. "Liz? Liz?" He rounded a corner, and found her dabbing slowly at the surface of a painting. "There you are," he said unnecessarily. "Wait—is that the little square thing you started on last week?"

Elizabeth nodded, and carefully brought the cleanser away from the canvas. "The genre painting."

"Genre?" Thompson put a friendly, interested spin on the single word, and was pleased to see her reaction; she smiled and turned the picture to him, explained it in a manner neither patronizing nor dry.

"Norman Rockwell circa 1630. Life as lived by the simple folk in the Benelux."

"Wow." He stepped up to see it better, carefully not looming over her. "That looked just like mud before you came. What are they doing?"

"Farm chores. There'll be more detail tomorrow." She dabbed at it again.

Thompson watched for a while longer, waiting. "I was wondering if you wanted to run some errands with me. I need to do a hardware run for the house and some shopping for myself—I don't know if you need anything, but if you want to give me a list or come along yourself, there's a mall and an art-supply store Vegel used to go to."

"Can you wait half an hour? This is almost done."

"Sure."

Wednesday, 7 July 1999, 2:03 PM
Laurel Ridge Farm
Columbia, Maryland

"Morning, Asp." Elizabeth leaned over the central island of the kitchen, and watched the cook work on some kind of pinky-gray mixture in a steel bowl. She raised an eyebrow.

"Tuna-fish paté," he said. "We're playing 'guess that meal' again. It's breakfast for you, isn't it? The boss is having early lunch—or late lunch, I'm not sure, and good old Ron hasn't made an appearance yet. So the plan is sandwiches."

In the bowl's mirror-like finish, he watched the woman sit down at the table with her book and soda. He concentrated on the ingredients his brother had left ready for lunch. He wished Gabriel had a less professional hand in the kitchen....

"Relish?" he asked, when the bread was sliced and ready.

"Relish what?" she punned shamelessly, but the Asp didn't catch the joke. "Sorry. Yes, please. Sweet relish—provided it's pickles and nothing weird like okra or guava or something."

Raphael laughed again. Elizabeth looked up, startled.

"You have something against nouvelle cuisine?" He frowned into the condiments; he wasn't paying much attention to her.

"Don't you?" she inquired, watching him.

"Well, I'm with Ron. If it's such a bad idea that you have to say it in French, he's against it...with," snickered Raphael, "a *few* exceptions...." He brandished his wide knife over the various mixtures in front of him and began pasting relish onto slices of bread. Elizabeth took the food with a smile, fled down the stairs, and looked back toward the kitchen with something like fear. Silly, she knew, to suddenly shun a man because his laughter was...a little...different. Had she misjudged his sense of humor? She'd come to think of Angelo as a—not yet a friend, but certainly as a potential friend. She was afraid, now that she knew him better, that he would be someone to be tolerated rather than liked.

"Thompson," said Hesha. "Your new assignment?"

The old cop closed his notebook. "Miss Dimitros and I are completely Liz and Ron now, sir. She likes baseball, chocolate, mysteries, and drama. She thinks Vegel had wonderful taste in adventure stories and whodunits, and we dropped in at a bookstore on the way home. She's started me on Shakespeare, and I found a police-procedural series that she wasn't familiar with. She's the little sister I never had—"

"Yes." Hesha said dryly. "Very well. Look to business. I'm intending a long session with her this evening." He walked to his apartment door, disappeared within, and came back out wearing his most elderly-looking spectacles.

"They add ten years, sir."

"Good. I hope that's enough."

During conversation over the papyrus, Hesha turned the subject toward his goal. "What's all this I hear about your dissertation?"

"I'm sorry?"

"Thompson's been going on about bulls and eyes and fish for almost a week now. Somehow," he smiled, "I have the feeling he's gotten things a bit garbled."

Thompson, listening in from the security bunker, snorted. He'd reported the bull story in total accuracy, and understood every word. Still, if it took the boss where they needed to go.... Yes. There she went.

Elizabeth brought out a sturdy manuscript box, and Hesha pointed to the largest empty table. Talking with the speed and enthusiasm displayed only by graduate students in mid-theory, she spread notes, drawings, and timelines across the polished surface. She pulled up a straight-backed chair and sat in it cock-eyed, one leg tucked beneath her, passing diagrams and summaries to Hesha as fast as he could read them. The glasses came out of their case, and his best professorial, fatherly manner came out with them.

Thompson, taking a rest from his own work, turned up the sound on the central screen again. Elizabeth's notes completely covered the surface of the huge table, and there were open books—some of them Vegel's—scattered on top of them. Light blue sticky-notes nearly hid the edges of the largest volume, and he recognized it as one she'd fastened onto the moment she was shown the dead man's room.

"...Good. Strong argument, strong defense." He settled back into the big chair. "But you'll never make a dissertation of it."

Elizabeth went red, and started to speak. Hesha cut her off with an open hand.

"How long have you been trying?" The girl's face grew angry-white. "There's too much here, Elizabeth. You have an entire book, possibly a multiple volume work in this. Take five percent of it, limit the scope, and write that. Take the degree and start publishing pieces in the journals. But this...this is too much."

Relieved, resentful, but generally pleased, Elizabeth relaxed a little into the straight-back. Hesha patted her hand reassuringly.

The debate went on, but Thompson wasn't listening anymore. He'd seen what happened to the girl's eyes when Hesha touched her. Ten-year glasses weren't going to be enough. He hoped that Hesha had noticed the look on Elizabeth's face—and he prayed that Hesha had expected it.

Thursday, 8 July 1999, 9:14 AM
Laurel Ridge Farm
Columbia, Maryland

Ronald Thompson awoke with a jolt.

An alarm—somewhere *inside* the house, by the tone. He threw off the covers and opened a panel by his bed—the perimeter lights were green—the house itself secure, according to the system—but an intruder had made it so far as Vegel's vault. The sun streaming in through the windows reminded him that Hesha would be asleep—sound asleep....

Thompson ran down the hall and jumped most of the stairs to the first floor, bellowing for the Asp as he went. Thank god it was Raphael here—if they had to fight, that murderous little creature was the better of the twins.

He whipped the elevator door aside and took the car down to the second basement as fast as it would go. His stomach objected to the drop, and he cursed Liz for the charade they all had to play. He belonged in his room off the security bunker, not upstairs in that draughty relic of a house. Thompson swore, and snatched one of the guns from the rack by the shaft doors. His eyes scanned the light codes as he ran through the surveillance station, and he swore again. No need to curse Liz. The intruder's entry point was from her room; the damned Cainite would have taken care of her before cracking the door open. Vegel must have been captured, not killed....

The door from Vegel's vault into Hesha's was still closed. Good. There might be time to see who or what had found its way inside. He brought the lights and the camera into full play in the carved stone room, and stopped cold.

Elizabeth Dimitros, clad in light-blue striped pajamas, was stumbling aimlessly around the crypt. The door into her room—Vegel's room—hung ajar behind her. No light shone from the apartment.

Thompson set down his gun. He hit the intercom to his ally, and called the killer off. "It's only Liz, Asp. Looks like she's sleepwalking."

"You're shitting me."

"No. The catch on the door must be faulty. I'll go up and put her back to bed before she knocks her head on a rock and wakes up." Thompson turned the lights in the vault down to a candle's power, replaced the automatic, and set about putting the house in order.

Hesha emerged from his resting place to the outer chamber. He was mildly surprised to see Thompson already in the room, and still more put off by the fact that his servant was not waiting for him. The door to Vegel's apartment was open, and Thompson's hands were busy with the delicate mechanisms that held it shut.

"Thompson?" Hesha lifted an ebon eyebrow, and his man rose to speak.

"The catch was loose, sir." He opened his mouth to go on, but Hesha cut in.

"Where is Elizabeth?"

"I asked her to pick up the mail. It's all right—I set up the box with only the kinds of things she ought to see there. But I had to get her out of the house to work on this."

"And we absolutely must fix this catch today because—?"

Thompson clenched his teeth at the Setite's tone, but answered calmly enough. "Because our Liz sleepwalks, and this morning she stumbled through Vegel's door without realizing it. I thought you'd like the secure areas *secure*, sir."

Hesha nodded. "Of course." He looked at the door's lock edge and scrutinized the work. "Thank you, Thompson."

•

After the sundown conference, Hesha followed Thompson to the bunker, and the mortal pulled the morning's tapes for his employer.

Elizabeth, they saw through the cameras, was working on the boulder, steadily whittling down a previously untouched area of the mud. Hesha dismissed Thompson to double-check all the concealed doors, panels, drop chutes, and caches in the other parts of the house.

Hesha sat down at the console and popped video after video into the machines. He set the counters to start the entire bank of recordings at the same time—roughly an hour before Thompson's frantic morning dash. He waited with the patience of death, and eventually movement began in the view of Vegel's room.

The woman's sleeping form tossed uncomfortably on the massive bed. The sheets tangled around her legs, and her pajama top had slid up until the first button nearly choked her. In another ten minutes, her jerking, unconscious movements had freed her legs, but now they dangled over the side of the mattress. A toe touched the floor, and she sat up. She slipped off the bed and wandered to the closets. Uncertain hands opened a drawer, and she pulled apart a pair of socks. The socks were then set on the bed, and apparently forgotten.

Elizabeth, her eyes half open, shuffled to the desk now. With the eraser end of a pencil, she wrote nothing—partly on the pad of paper that sat cockeyed on the desk, partly on the wood and leather of the desktop. She followed the pin-cushion wall back to the closet end of the room, playing vaguely with the tacked-up notes and articles. Her body hid the spring-latch from the camera's eye, so he couldn't see how the accident happened, but the door opened a crack, and the woman walked through onto the cold stone floor of the crypt.

Hesha observed idly as the other cameras began to

show action—half-clad Thompson running about the house like a jumping jack—the Asp gliding sinuously down the stairs from the kitchen, weapons ready—Thompson in the elevator, in the bunker, in the room with the sleep-walker, plucking her sleeve, closing the door, and nudging her gently toward the bed.

Hesha watched Thompson watching Elizabeth as she slid back into real sleep. The old cop stood still as a statue for eight minutes, then turned and went out by the visible door. For the full eight minutes the Setite watched the mortals captured on camera, and then his finger jabbed the off button.

"Secure?" Hesha asked Thompson, who was just returning from his rounds.

"Yes, sir."

Their eyes leapt at the same moment to the center monitor. With the players off, the settings had reverted to Thompson's last arrangement, and Elizabeth and the boulder were displayed in soundless color. The Asp had just entered the view.

Raphael Mercurio carried a tray—chili, which Thompson knew gratefully was the reheated work of the other twin. Elizabeth smiled politely, but moved to the farthest corner of the work zone.

The Asp dusted off a little table. He set his burden down upon it, just outside the canvas, with a graceful flourish, smile, and jest. Elizabeth smiled again, but her eyes shivered and she stayed where she was. A dusty finger pointed to the mud, and she said something—Hesha leaned forward and called up the sound.

"—This last inch beforehand." Her thin smile came out again. "But thanks for bringing it down. It's very nice of you."

"No, no. It's my job—I got to make sure you don't starve, Liz. You're a pretty girl—you should keep the skin on your bones and the roses in your cheeks, you know?

It's not just me here; you're dealing with generations of Mercurio grandmothers standing over my left shoulder, and they keep going on about it." He laughed, and she tried to smile.

The Asp left Elizabeth to her dinner. She didn't leave the safety of her canvas carpet until his foot was off the top stair cleat, and the relief in her face was patently obvious.

"Holy shit..." whispered Thompson. "She knows?"

Hesha watched his guest wipe her hands clean and sit down to eat. She sniffed at the food suspiciously, and took up the spoon without enthusiasm. "No," said Hesha. "I think not. Merely good instincts. She's afraid of him...and that's interesting." He swiveled in the console chair, and faced his protégé.

"Should I call Gabe in from town?"

"I think that would be for the best. Fear can induce restless sleep. Keep Raphael out of her way until we can make the switch."

"Would you care to do the honors?" asked Elizabeth, steadying a nearly freed fragment of shard and mud between her gloved hands.

"Thank you," Hesha said evenly. He took up the dentist's pick and, with professional skill, scraped away the thin ridges of clay that supported the jug-side and handle in the boulder. In less than a minute, the fragile pottery piece shifted in the matrix, and he took up the receiving tray.

Elizabeth tipped the leaf-shaped fragment gently into the little bin, taking time to select a position that kept the shard's own weight from endangering it. "Down," she said.

"Down," confirmed Hesha, and he set the tray aside.

They leaned back against the canvas steps and regarded their hard-won treasure. Still covered with dirt and dust from its prison, it was an unimpressive, crumbly brown.

"It's not much, is it?" mourned Elizabeth.

Hesha shook his head and smiled. "It's older than we are. That's enough, for the moment. And it may match some of Vegel's shards."

"It's still not much. I'm sorry I dragged you out here for this, but at that last stage...two hands weren't enough, and I couldn't find Ron."

Hesha nodded, but ventured, "Mercurio's in the kitchen...."

Elizabeth turned pink and dove back into the boulder.

Hesha read the flush, keeping Thompson's briefing in mind. It might be fear of the Asp that brought her color up, but he suspected she hadn't even looked for either man...a loose fragment was a fine excuse for seeing him, Hesha, personally. He determined to keep the footing businesslike for the evening. Perching on the edge of the canvas box, he silently examined the progress of the work. The woman had given up entirely on what Vegel had always thought were the most promising sections, and her hands were busy inside a large crater below them.

Elizabeth grimaced inwardly. So the Asp, now that she knew him better, made her back hairs rise and her fists itch—she still should have gone to him, rather than bothering her employer. Self-consciously, she tucked a few loose strands of hair behind her ears. Foolishness had its advantages, however. She confessed to herself she was glad that Hesha had come out of his office. He was sitting not three feet from her. His perfect white shirt-sleeves were rolled up, creased, and dirty from the work; his jetty eyes were smoldering...intent on the rock, completely oblivious to her, of course.

"What are you doing?" Hesha asked. He used the

scholarly voice she'd responded well to over her dissertation. Elizabeth stuffed cloth wadding into the deepest part of the hole and tested the top section with two fingers. She cleared her throat.

"Well, Professor," she began, playing (as he had hoped) the earnest young student, "it occurred to me that the layer Mr. Vegel had exposed was far too cluttered for real progress to go on. I intend to isolate the shard-laden projection and remove it from the body of the excavation. I expect that it will then be easier to separate the shards...working from the rear, as it were."

"Go on, Miss Dimitros."

"That's it." She laughed self-consciously. "If Vegel's guess as to the sedimentation order of this thing is correct, I'm probably going to have to go back to doing it the hard way. But I think he was only mostly right."

Hesha studied the rock. "And the rock is just 'this thing'?" She stared blankly back at him. "It's not a he, or a she, or..." Elizabeth reddened, and Hesha grinned. "What is it?"

"Oh, Lord." She kicked resentfully at the canvas draping. "I tell you a story once...."

"Go on."

"This is an it. This is the rock of Sisyphus. It's big, and bulky, and whenever you get to the goal with it—" she gestured at the leaf-shaped shard in the bin, "—you wind up back where you started, horrendously disappointed that there was nothing beyond the goal but another goal, exactly the same as the first." She scowled into the hole. "How long did Vegel work on this thing?"

Hesha frowned. "A long time."

"And Sisyphus is probably still heaving his misery and guilt and shame up that mountain. He's supposed to have been a smart guy; you'd think he'd do something about it." She caught Hesha's inquisitive gaze, and went on. "There must be other rocks in hell. If he picked up one and gave the boulder a good whack in the same place every time, eventually he'd have a crack started...and one of these millennia, the whole thing would break open as it bounded down the mountain. Sorry; I'm babbling. They probably rolled up his wisdom somewhere in the rock...it's an allegory, after all."

Hesha said nothing, and Elizabeth returned to the crater she was boring into metaphor. *Sisyphus... futility...how appropriate...keep your mind on the job, Lizzie...and keep away from him.* Resolutely, she kept scraping away at the rock. *Best to go home to the Rutherfords without making a fool of yourself. Important client...strong* business *relationship...give you one up on* Miss Agnes*...he wants paintings done, you're damn good with conservation...*

"What next?" Hesha asked.

"Stabilization of the inner surface. It's glazed..." she tapered off, looking at the rock. *And maybe you'll find something decent in this thing...unbroken...or finely decorated...or bones...or even...metal....*

"Your next *project*," Hesha clarified.

"Sorry. I was planning to keep plugging away at this for a few hours more, then begin swabbing down another canvas."

"No papyrus tonight?"

Liz stretched herself, and regarded the huge mass in puzzlement. "I see hieroglyphs in my sleep, at this point. I need a change...and there's just something *satisfying* about digging into this. Put something together over there," she gestured at the long table, "take something apart over here." Elizabeth clicked her tools lightly into one hand, and shrugged a little. "I can work on the papyrus, if that's what you'd prefer?"

"Please, do what you like. The paintings are coming along well enough." He waited, half-expecting her to draw the encounter out longer. For the moment, though, she seemed more interested in Vegel's boulder than in him. *Good*, he thought. Thompson must have been mistaken. He rose abruptly, slapped the dust off of his clothes and skin, and turned to go to his study. Elizabeth didn't even look up, and Hesha stalked out of the room in a perversely dissatisfied mood.

Friday, 9 July 1999, 10:43 PM
Laurel Ridge Farm
Columbia, Maryland

"Hesha?" Liz asked without looking up from the papyrus.

The Setite stopped in surprise, glanced at his silent, stocking feet, and replied, "Yes." He sat down across the table from her, and picked up his own set of tongs. "You're making good progress tonight," he remarked.

"It's an easy section, I think."

Hesha compared her several nights' work—this piece was no simpler than the others; it must be that she had begun to memorize the hieroglyphs. And she'd slept more soundly the night before, though she could hardly be expected to know that. But Elizabeth seemed rather elated—pleased with herself to an incomprehensible degree.

He watched her deftly lay five scraps together to make a single feather sign, and though the next glyph was uncommon, her eyes looked to the notes spread out over the glass for only the briefest instant before finding it. There was something odd about the way she was sitting, as well...he began manipulating shards on his own half to disguise his curiosity.

Chair angle as normal...her hips curved into the seat in the same way...slight twist of her back to keep her long neck and delicate shoulders positioned comfortably over the work...but her shoulders were wrong. Hand with the tweezers—no, the other hand—instead of loose, relaxed fingers flipping through Vegel's transliterations, her fingers were closed in a near-fist, flattened against the table top. Her pulse was quickening the longer he sat with her...what was in her hand? He felt Elizabeth's eyes on him, and bent earnestly over the work.

"I have a present for you," she said eventually. Hesha looked up into the sweetest cat-canary smile he'd ever seen, and the amber lights in her eyes were absolute sparks. "Open your hand, and close your eyes, et cetera, et cetera."

"Pardon?"

"Here."

She turned her left hand over, and lying on the palm was a metal ring. It was a shining dark brown, completely untarnished, and Hesha had never seen it before. He took it warm from her body and peered at the sculpted surface through his old-man glasses.

"It's the crackerjack prize out of Mr. Vegel's rock," said Elizabeth. "The wisdom of Sisyphus, so to speak."

"Ourobouros," whispered Hesha.

"Bronze," she said eagerly, "Though why it hasn't greened away completely I can't imagine. I intend a pH study of the surrounding material."

Hesha hardly heard her.

Bronze, yes, though he had a better guess as to why the metal had been preserved. No inscription...no marks on the interior of any kind. He turned his attention to the design—two snakes, both self-devourers, twined around each other in opposite directions. The heads and tails met together on what must be the top of the piece, and the interweaving bodies formed a tight knot.

"Beautiful," he whispered.

She laughed. "If you like snakes." She leaned back in her chair. "Seriously, though, I agree with you." Elizabeth watched him stare at the little ring and decided to let him alone with it. She reached for her tongs again and began picking at the scattered scraps.

The Setite ran his fingers around and around the outside of the ring.

"Have you tried this on?" he murmured to his companion.

"Yes," she admitted. "Briefly, to see what the approximate size was. I've full measurements and excavation data written down in the 'boulder log' that Mr. Vegel had been keeping."

No traps, then. Still, he would have to examine it more carefully to make sure it was truly safe. He'd keep a close watch on the woman, too...there was a chance the thing was active in some way, and any after-effects would be informative.

"Greek, don't you think?" she said, noticing that his close scan of the prize was finished. "I can't remember any identical designs, but I thought that the two-snake motif might be helpful in tracking down the period and the purpose. Herculean cult object, or perhaps prophetic paraphernalia. Teresias and the snakes in the stable, you know. There's an outside chance of medical symbology, but I think that if the sculptor had meant a caduceus, he'd have made a caduceus."

Hesha slipped the ring into his breast pocket. "Good work," he said abruptly.

"Just luck," replied Elizabeth, modestly.

Hesha wondered.

Saturday, 10 July 1999, 9:28 AM
Laurel Ridge Farm
Columbia, Maryland

Ronald Thompson woke with his jaw clenched tight. Damn good dream, ruined. Didn't dream often. Forgetting it already...

Goddamn alarm.

He flicked open the panel without quite leaving the soft cocoon of his bed. It was an interior breach; Vegel's apartment to Vegel's crypt again. He swore in the foulest language he could think of, and tossed a robe over his grizzled chest. The door was fixed...yes, the door was fixed...she must have subconsciously triggered the actual latch...probably the door had never been loose in the first place...well, this time he'd wedge it shut from the stone side, and no matter how much her sleepy fingers played with the catch, there'd be no more midnight—mid-morning, curse it—alarms.

He pounded down the old house stairs, down the basement stairs, and across the wood floors of the basement rooms. His step grew lighter as he approached Elizabeth's end of the complex, and he laid his hand gently on the knob of her door.

Instantly, the alarm's tone changed. From a persistent, low G, it rose and clamored an octave higher—his earplug throbbed with the shuddering note. He drew back his grasping fingers, as if to stop the noise, but he knew the sound. There had been a second breach somewhere. Hand and knob were coincidence; he threw the door open and found Vegel's apartment abandoned. He switched on the lights, and saw that the door into the crypt was shut.

"Asp," he whispered into Elizabeth's intercom. "Turn on the mike and follow me." Thompson stepped quietly to the secret panel, disengaged the alarm, and opened the way to the crypt. The tone in his ears died completely and unexpectedly.

"Where is she?" he asked the empty room.

"She's not on your damn screens," said his earplug.

Thompson finished looking through the irregular curves and obstacles in the vault, and his stomach turned. There was only one room in the complex that couldn't be seen from the security bunker.

"Run the log back, Asp."

There came a series of keyboard sounds, a low whistle, and Raphael's voice, soft and purring over the circuit. "Her door at 9:28:17. It shut at 9:28:39. She probably...bumped into it. *His* door at 9:29:27. It shut automatically ten seconds later. Sorry, Ron. I know you liked her."

Thompson sat down heavily on the end of the stone bench. "Damn." He looked at his bare feet, his flimsy, plaid flannel robe, and repeated, "Damn. Damn. Asp, pick up the hook, the light, my fire boots, and the kit. Bring 'em down here."

Raphael Mercurio opened his mouth to object, but the sight of Thompson's broad back and clenched jaw on the monitor shut him up. He reached for the kit.

Ronald Thompson stood on the threshold of his master's tomb. He was shod in thick, thigh-high boots. His pajama bottoms were tucked tightly into the boot-tops, and the tightly belted, cut-down remnants of his robe had been tied down around his waist. He held a long, hooked stick in his left hand, and his right index finger was poised above a palette carved in the hands of a scribe. Behind him, the Asp stood ready and silent.

Thompson pressed the latch, and the door to Hesha's sanctum swung open. He pressed a second carving, and the door settled slightly on its hinges. It would stay open now, as it had not for Elizabeth.

The Asp turned on the floodlight. It was curiously baffled and shielded; only dim illumination shone through its cloudy lens. It was enough for the two men watching; their eyes were accustomed by now to the semi-darkness of Vegel's chamber. When the sluggish head of the snake nearest the door began to move, Thompson prodded it gently with the blunt end of the hook, and the viper slithered away into a hole in the wall, seeking its den in sulky temper.

Thompson stepped forward, and the Asp nudged the lamp along behind him. There were two short corridors ahead of them. They took the left, and trod gently along the right edge of it. At the first turn, they passed around a shallow pit, and seven sleepy sets of double-lidded eyes watched them from its depths. At the second turn, for no apparent reason, they waited a full minute, standing close together on the same solid stone.

"Ron," began the Asp, "She's dead by now."

"If she's dead, where is she?"

"In the right-hand passage."

"I didn't hear anything from there. Did you?"

Raphael subsided. He drew forth his own hook-and-loop without comment, and dislodged a curious neighbor from a ledge close by.

They started forward again and arrived safely at the last landing of a narrow, winding stair. The Asp put the lamp into his partner's outstretched hand, and turned to watch the steps behind them. He didn't see into the chamber; the ceiling of the stairs was low and steep, and he was on rear guard before the opening door finished its slow arc.

Thompson saw.

He saw the faint, tall curves of barely lit paintings fading into blackness. He saw the shadows of nearer mysteries, ranged along the walls. He saw, at the edge of the light, the closed sarcophagus. He saw his master's still, night-dark form stretched out upon it, bare to the waist. He saw a woman, draped in folded white cloth that clung tightly to her body. He saw her dark hair, plaited and knotted into a thick headdress. He saw shining gold flash dully at her neck, her wrists, and ankles. The girl—the queen—the goddess—she took up the black hand of the man before her, and wordlessly bid him rise.

Thompson stood in the doorway in shock; it was so much a scene from a painting of Vegel's—and he knew it was a trick of the light. The illusion faded—the chance resemblance died as the woman went on moving, and he saw the truth.

Elizabeth stood over Hesha's dead, cold corpse, holding a lifeless hand to her cheek. She was crying in half-formed sobs, quietly, but as if her heart would break. Her eyes were closed, and if there were words in her mourning Thompson could not hear them.

He took a step down, and the lamp came with him. The linen gown was a plain white nightshirt, wrinkled and twisted until the creases looked like pleats from a distance. Her hair was tangled. As he moved, it looked less and less like the high-born lady's wig and more like fever-locks. Her jewelry was not gold, but living copper....

And the floor was covered—covered so thickly that the light gray stone showed through only in tiny patches—with the same deadly, molten metal: hundreds upon hundreds of copperhead snakes. Thompson looked out across the sea of brazen backs and shuddered. "How many shots are there in the kit, Asp?"

"Two."

"You stay here, then."

"That was *my* plan."

Thompson crept slowly across the stone floor of the crypt, making a clear path before himself with the hook. The Asp moved onto the bottom step and adjusted the lamp to help the walking man—Thompson could sense the assassin's eyes on his back. The light did odd things to the shadows, and the edges of the darkness moved with the bodies of its inhabitants. The old cop could feel, instinctively, the closing of the way behind, and wondered how in hell he could ever bring a body out with him—whether dead, sleeping, or in the panic and shock of snakebite.

"Wait, Ron."

Thompson swiveled through his shoulders, hips, and

knees. He didn't dare move his feet. Uncomfortably, he looked up at his partner. Raphael's hands held a thin cord: the drop line for the lamp. A tiny knife cut it free.

"Here, catch. Tie it to your waist." He knotted his end to the kit and anchored the plastic box behind the door's slack hinges. "I'll bring down stronger rope and some gloves. You're going to need them." And the Asp disappeared up the stairs.

Thompson watched him go resignedly. He made a neat bowline around his hips and concentrated his attention on the floor.

Hook, clear, step. Step.

Hook, nudge, angle, hook again. Clear. Step.

Step. Halfway, now.

Step wide. Hook away the heavy body that blocked the straight way.

Step again. Step—

—and Thompson's boot slipped on an old, flattened, silvery skin. It rasped silkily under the rubber cleats and threw him. He jerked wildly to catch his balance—the hook swung free from his right hand, and it clattered against the stone. The other foot slammed down near the head of a small, skittish creature, and the vibrations of the whole incident traveled throughout the room. When the frantic movements stopped, there were hardly any snakes in sight, but three adults had their bodies coiled ready. Thompson left his feet and the hook where they were, and dropped into breathing that almost wasn't—tight, shallow motions of the ribs that made the head and sides ache but which caused very, *very* little noise. One by one, the challengers relaxed and laid themselves down. Thompson straightened his legs and ankles, raised the hook with the smallest, weakest fingers of his left hand—the only two that had kept the tool from crashing altogether—and began again.

Step.

Step, hook, clear, step.

He was at the sarcophagus. He touched her shoulder, and she muttered something incomprehensible. She slept still, somehow, and her color was healthy—she hadn't been bitten. Thompson hoped the miracle would go on, and prayed that miracles were contagious.

"Ron."

Thompson looked to the stairwell. "Yeah."

"Pull in your line."

Thompson took the straight end of the cord and began to draw it after him. A cardboard box sledged along behind it. More rope trailed from the box. It made a godawful racket, and more snakes fled from the monster. He grinned maniacally as his three opponents struck at and then scattered from the strange and hideous thing that hurt their teeth.

There were gloves in the box, and Thompson put them on. He clipped a strong rope around his waist, and would have hooked Elizabeth into it....

But when Thompson looked down into the eyes of the old, old copperhead that had draped itself around the woman's neck and chest, he knew that the creature would never willingly let him do it. Where his gut had turned before at the danger, his mind turned now at the knowledge that the ancient reptile *thought* and fought in the same idiom that he did.

With one eye on the 'collar,' he reached for the young, slender, gleaming form of a bracelet. In the blink of an eye, he had the little one behind the neck, and he threw it far into the dark places of the tomb. He shuffled his feet to bring himself closer, and the hatchling from her other wrist joined its cousin. The head of the collar turned toward him, and it blinked golden eyes resentfully.

Thompson sighed. He hooked clear a large space on the floor around them, and bent—slowly—to kneel at

Elizabeth's feet. The anklets were larger, older yearlings. He took a deep breath and reached for the left one. Above him, the collar hissed, and he stopped in mid-motion. Nerve lost, he leaned back on his haunches and flexed his hands inside the gloves.

When he—and the collar, too, he hoped—least expected it, his right hand darted out of its own accord. The instinct was good. He could feel the delicate jawbones clamped between his fingers, and he unwound it from her leg in a quick, smooth motion. He leaned back to throw, and the other anklet struck him just beneath the knee.

"Fuck," he cried, and nearly dropped the serpent he was holding. Impatiently, he flicked his wrist and sent the thin body flying into space. He heard it land, too close and audibly angry.

Thompson fairly tore the second anklet away. As he stood, he felt Elizabeth's legs for other snakes, and found one curled like a garter about her thigh. It fled higher, and he had to raise her gown to the level of her hips to catch the thing—it would have bitten her belly, but his thumb got in the way. The leather wasn't thick enough, and this time he could feel the extra sting of venom in the wound.

The collar hissed again. From his awkward crouch, Thompson strained to see what it was doing. His head rose above the level of the sarcophagus just as something struck him in the side—from its markings, he knew it to be the first anklet, the one he hadn't thrown far enough. He stopped cursing. Nothing seemed adequate.

In a frenzy, Thompson hooked the space around them clear again. Without trying to dislodge the giant snake, he took Elizabeth's arm and began leading her away from Hesha. The collar hissed a warning.

Thompson kept walking.

The collar hovered over Elizabeth's jugular, wavering challengingly. Elizabeth herself stumbled. She was still weeping, and the pale streaks ran down her face, her neck, and onto the dull body of the snake.

Thompson took a firmer, higher grip on her arm.

The collar, blindingly quickly, moved to take the open target. Thompson was ready, and he threw himself away from the girl the moment he was sure the copperhead was really coming for him, not for her. Thompson felt the huge, curved fangs enter the meat of his forearm, well above the glove. His arm tore open. Blood flowed freely onto the stones. The old serpent lost a tooth inside its victim, but the momentum of its strike and Thompson's lunge wrested its grip from Elizabeth's neck. Thompson regained his feet, tossed the unconscious woman over his shoulder, and ran headlong for the stairs.

Saturday, 10 July 1999, 7:48 PM
Laurel Ridge Farm
Columbia, Maryland

Hesha woke to a crowded and unexpected press of heavy bodies. The copperheads lay coiled over him in excessive, weighty numbers, and the Eldest had curled protectively around his shoulders. As he began to move, he felt the flickering whisper of the patriarch's tongue on his ear. "Light," he said softly, and the hidden bulbs glowed.

Hesha locked eyes with the old snake, and hissed back.

The Eldest was wounded. He bared his broken fang and arched his neck, the better to display a replacement descending from the roof of his mouth. He complained. He coiled and recoiled, disturbing the lesser snakes. He was fretful. The nest was not safe. The guardians were halved. Those that could had found sanctuary on the body of their ally; those that could not had left for their winter dens in the fields around Laurel Ridge.

Hesha soothed the old and faithful servant. He ran his hands along the slim backs of the copperhead's descendants. In time, they found their necks and bellies secure on the floor again, and the stones did nothing unexpected. The Setite's bare feet slid smoothly among them without causing alarm; he was family, and his scent was theirs.

He satisfied himself that the intrusion had been limited—his treasures and projects were untouched—and made his way, though the center passage, to Vegel's crypt. He noticed with interest that Elizabeth's door was wedged shut with the chisel.

"Thompson."

There was, for the first time in fifteen years, no response.

"Thompson," he said again, with force.

"Sir." It was the Asp's voice. "Sir, Thompson's a little ill just now."

"Ill."

"Yes, sir. Could you—could you come help me with him?"

Thompson's quarters were comfortable but sparsely furnished. They ran to bookshelves full of old magazines, tapes, tattered true-crime case studies, and a fine set of vinyl albums he never listened to. There were a few old certificates on the walls in thin, plain frames. There was one good rug; he'd bought it in Afghanistan. It was beautiful, and it was valuable, but it had attracted him chiefly because the design—though traditional in every other way—had substituted for random decoration the simplified shapes of machine guns and helicopters.

Hesha Ruhadze's chief security man sat in an old, battered recliner with a small trash bin in his lap. His face was unhealthily blue, his eyes swollen half shut. His right arm lay in a jury-rigged basin of newspaper, plastic bags, and blood-soaked towels. Similar wadding covered the lower left half of his ribs.

As Hesha entered the room, the Asp had just come from the bathroom with a double armload of fresh towels. He lifted Thompson's swollen arm and exchanged red cloth for white and beige; the trash bin filled with the dressings, and Mercurio swapped the little can for a mixing bowl. Acidic fumes from the kitchen testified that some receptacle was necessary. The two men looked up at him with weary, resentful, smug expressions. Hesha took the whole scene in in a second, and then wiped the satisfied looks off his men's faces by turning on his heel and slamming the door behind him.

"Mercurio!" he shouted into the intercom.

"Boss, what the hell are you doing?" The Asp followed Hesha into the bunker, angry, annoyed, and afraid all at once. "Ron's sick, goddamn it. He's gonna die, and you just—"

Hesha turned on him. "Wash your hands, you fool!"

Raphael looked from his blood-soaked cuffs and dripping hands to the animal eyes of his master. White with fear, he shrank away.

"Warm four bags and bring them here, quickly."

Raphael scuttled down the hall, running without turning his back on the bunker and the creature inside it.

Hesha sat down at the console to wait. The smell coming from Thompson's quarters was overpowering...old blood, new blood, fear, sickness, venom...fresh blood spilling, wasted on the floor, the cloth, the paper...fresh blood...his eyes drifted to the video display of Thompson's room.

He could not look away, but his hands obeyed his will. The monitor sparked off.

The curse fought him for control of his legs. The man's door was only five feet away. The man was too ill to fight. The man trusted him, and wouldn't flinch from the Beast; wouldn't know the difference between the slave of Apep and the ascetic, thoughtful, rational being that the Setite had fought to construct over the centuries. And the man's choice was made; he was in pain, he would end his life willingly to start the new one now.

Hesha let the waves of persuasion crash against the bastions of his sanity. From the cold center of the storm, he took exercise and amusement in analyzing the onslaught. The Beast surged forward in raw and willful attack, monstrously strong but poorly armed. Hesha thanked Set that his mind was yet clear, and that the voice of the curse spoke in clumsy shreds of logic.

A plastic bag landed in his lap, body-warm and shockingly heavy.

He picked it up and drained it quickly. The curse cried out for more—in perfect concert, Hesha and the Beast lifted their hand—and the Asp tossed them the second bag. The blood streamed down his cold gullet as fast as the first. Hesha braced himself and began to sip, slowly, the third bag. The Beast clamored still, infuriated by the scent of Thompson's life, by the wretched flavor of the bagged blood, by the failure of its fight.... Hesha finished his drink, and the unthinking creature within him seemed to loll over, still angry, but caged...not sated, not too drunk to rage for more supper, but understanding on some level that there would be more soon enough.

"Snakebite," said Hesha.

"Yes, sir." The Asp had retreated down the corridor. One foot was actually inside the elevator. "This morning."

"Antitoxin?"

"Yes, sir. Right after the bite."

"Why is he bleeding?"

"Convulsions, sir. He was puking in the john, and

he just lost it. He broke the mirror when he went down, boss. Then he rolled around in it. I've been pulling glass out of him for over an hour."

"Warm three more bags. Knock before you come in," Hesha directed, moving from his chair, "leave them at the door, and get back out. Understood?"

Raphael nodded. He watched the creature walk into Thompson's rooms, and he fled back to the freezer chamber, glad to have the heavy, insulated doors between himself and his master.

"Thompson." Hesha knelt by his servant's side, clutching the fourth blood bag like a talisman between them.

"Sir." Ron's eyes fought crazily for focus. "Sir, were you here just now?"

"Yes."

"Thank god. Thought I'd imagined it." He leaned over the bowl and was sick in wracking, dry heaves that shook the old chair with him. Hesha patted him on the back, running his fingers along rents in the robe and open wounds in the skin beneath it. No glass was left there. The Asp seemed to have been thorough enough.

The Setite took Thompson's head in his hands, looked into his eyes, and said, "Be calm." The vomiting slowly stopped.

"Is it time, sir?" Ron croaked.

"No," answered Hesha, understanding his man's question perfectly. "Tonight you merely have an unscheduled lesson in the powers of Set's blood." Thompson stared dully at him from swollen eyes. "Let me check your arms, first." Minutes passed with forceps and scalpel. A few shards of mirror were added to the bowl the Asp had started, and from the snakebites came forth a broken fang or two. The bowl and the tools went into the kitchen sink, and Hesha returned from the drainboard with a knife and a large coffee mug in his hands.

"Drink this."

"I haven't been able to keep anything down, sir...."

"Drink *this*."

Thompson took a sip. His eyes flickered to the dark contents in apprehension, and Hesha could see the questions starting.

"Drink it all, Thompson."

When the mug was empty, Hesha filled it again from his wrist. Thompson took it back obediently, and they drank together...mortal from the cup, Setite from the bag. The Asp delivered the rest of the blood as ordered; it flowed into the cold body and trickled from it to fill the mug again.

"Enough." Hesha pulled up a chair opposite the wounded man. "Now burn that. Use it. Don't tell me that you don't know what I mean—keep listening. There is fire in your stomach...like fear..." said the Setite, softly. "Like anger...like adrenaline...like whisky..." his voice went on, hypnotically. "You've done a little drinking in your time, Detective Sergeant Thompson...take the fire, take the whisky, and force it out of your gut. Put it in your arm. The venom you were hit with today...that was fire in the veins, killing you. This is fire in the arteries, destroying the venom. Set your arm on fire...burn the venom away...torch out the glass and the cuts and the bruises.

"Look at your arm, Thompson."

Ronald Thompson moved his head painfully and saw his swollen, discolored limb changing. The streaks of white and red faded; the blue-purple that had begun to fester sweetly turned green-gold, then faint brown, then his own skin-tan. The sickly colors shrank from his fingers, his wrist....

"Concentrate. Don't let it stop."

"What am I doing?!"

"Healing yourself. Set's blood, even diluted, can heal the living. So, I understand, can Caine's...." Hesha looked into Thompson's eyes, lifted the shredded robe from his shoulders, and examined the knotted terrain of his back. "Move it away from your arm. Fix your feet. Then spread the fire to the back. You're still bleeding there." The gashes mended themselves. "Good. You have control over it. Now stand up and be sure every wound is closed."

Thompson stood and tried to obey. He shook his head. "The fire's out, sir."

"Excellent. It was necessary to burn it all. There are side effects. Think about how you felt before and after you drank my blood. With one night's drink, you probably felt gratitude, friendship, nostalgia, tenderness, unreasoning trust...."

Thompson's expression held none of those fine feelings now. Hesha's list was far too accurate.

"Two nights, and you should come almost to love me."

Thompson's still-puffy face took on fear.

"Three nights' drinks form a kind of slavery between the drinker and the one whose blood is taken. It is called the Blood Bond, or the Vinculum, or the Coeur Vrai, or the Oath, or the Coils of Apep, or a hundred other names...and it lasts forever."

As the implications sank in, Hesha's bodyguard turned chalk white. "Forever?"

Hesha stared at the floor. With a long, thin hand, he dismissed *forever*. "Until you die, or until you die again. Long enough. There are said to be seven ways to break it; five are legendary, three are impossible, four are impractical...all of them are difficult, and only one is quick."

Thompson's face lost none of its horror. "So you could...you could use this on any one of us...."

Hesha's eyebrow twitched. "But I do not, obviously." He paused. "Or you wouldn't be in a position to ask the question, Thompson." Without haste, he collected the empty bags, the bloodied knife, the red-stained mug, and took them to the kitchen. He returned with a glass of juice and a new bowl. Setting them in Thompson's hands, he commented, "It is far, far better to *earn* the loyalty of the people you are forced to trust. I find that slaves make unreliable servants. Many of my enemies keep their retainers in bondage—and that, Thompson, is a very useful thing." He sat down again, and his manner changed.

"Lesson over," he said. "Report."

Elizabeth sat atop a tall, thin stool in the studio. She leant on her left elbow, holding a loose bundle of cotton swabs. Her right hand took one up, dipped it into a jar, and rolled it carefully over the fly-specked, smoke-stained surface of the painting. The swab, now a dirty yellow, she flicked into a waste tray by her side. Left hand fed right, the process was repeated, the clean path along the painting's edge growing steadily.

Hesha walked into the room. Where there were shadows, he wrapped himself inside them; where there was light, he merely slipped unnoticed within it. The woman heard nothing. There were new, weary lines around her eyes; the delicate skin was stained the color of old bruises; the lids were red-rimmed. He smelt salt on her cheeks.

Hesha walked back to the door and let the light strike him again.

"Elizabeth."

She looked up in surprise. "Hi." The swabs dropped to the tabletop. "I thought you'd all gone into town until tomorrow. Thompson left a note...."

"It was a lie."

Elizabeth's chin tilted up, her eyes narrowed defensively, and she turned on the stool to face him. She said nothing, but searched his face. It might as well have been carved from marble.

"Come here, please. I would like to talk to you." Hesha stepped back, leaving the way clear for her to go by. After a moment's hesitation, she rose and followed him. "In my study, if you don't mind." The Setite led her to a door she'd never been through. He held it open for her. Hesha paused at the precise distance into the study that would force the wall seat upon his guest, and she took it.

"Tell me about your dream last night," he began.

Elizabeth flushed. "Excuse me?"

"You walked and spoke in your sleep."

Her eyes shuttered against him. "Sleepwalkers don't necessarily remember their dreams, Hesha."

"But you do, Elizabeth, or you would have said: 'I don't remember.'" He almost smiled. "Yours is a very diplomatic dishonesty."

She clenched her jaw and said nothing. Hesha read the lines of her face—anger, caution, resentment, logic. Whatever harm the truth might do her, he had at least put her on her guard.

He went on, softly. "I expect that there are nightmares for you. I want to help." The stern note returned. "In fact, it is absolutely necessary that I intervene."

"I don't understand you."

"I intend to devote the remaining hours before sunrise ensuring that you do." Hesha paused. "Under ordinary circumstances I would never have brought you here. I picked you up in New York as a diversion—" she winced— "from more pressing matters. You were...you are...unique. Contrary. Fascinating. I suspected you had an uncommon gift for observation. I showed you a statue that puzzled me. You put your finger on the crux of the matter in one night. You removed the eye. I was impressed, and I decided that I would visit you often...in New York," he finished heavily.

"Within a day, you had destroyed my plans. There were..." He sought, visibly, for words, and spoke slowly: "...worse things following Kettridge, and I could not, in good conscience, leave you to be found by them. So I brought you here intending to protect you and keep the truth of the danger from troubling you. In time, I would have returned you safely to New York. Or—" his voice lowered. "Or in time, I hoped we might have had a different, less hurried, less disturbing version of this conversation."

"We aren't having a conversation," snapped Elizabeth. "This is a monologue, Hesha."

She takes the truth by the heart, he sighed to himself.

His soft tones and feigned embarrassment dropped away. Curtly, he spelled out the essence of the problem. "In order to keep the reality of the situation from you, the Asp, Thompson, and I have constructed an elaborate charade. The events of this morning prove to me that you, whether you know it consciously or not, have seen through the acting and the stage set. Our little masquerade has put each of us in still greater danger." With the last word, his voice fell, and what came next from Hesha's throat was like thunder.

"Now tell me your dream, Elizabeth, before your gift of perception gets one of us killed."

Elizabeth stared back at him through wide, hard-rimmed eyes. Her face was pale, her mouth shut and voiceless. Her throat was tight with tears and anger, her gut knotted in fear. *He's insane*. Her mind churned frantically, but nothing helpful rose to the surface. *Whatever I'm supposed to have seen, God, why can't I see it now? He doesn't look crazy, he looks...every sentence makes less sense, not more...but he obviously thinks he's explaining something...paralogia...paranoia...but his face...* She turned her eyes away. Whether he was sane or mad, the sight of his face hurt her. His eyes, so near black, guarded by strong brows and cunning smiles...once or twice there had been a gentler look in them, something encouraging and open.... Elizabeth watched his hands instead. The bones were long and beautiful, like a sculpture some god had hidden under flesh...the color of his skin was so rich and deep and mellow a brown...*there isn't a word for it. Like horse chestnuts and old saddles and...he's mad, I think.*

Hesha studied the woman's reaction clinically. Despite himself, he was impressed that she could sit silent after the treatment he'd given her—either she had no will at all, which he knew was not true—or she was stronger than he'd guessed. *Set below,* he thought irritably. *What am I doing guessing?*

He held out his hands. "Come with me," he said.

Elizabeth let him pull her up from the chair, thinking how cold his fingertips were, how impossible he was.

Hesha opened the door to the main hall and drew her behind him. He strode to a full and solid-looking bookcase and slid it aside. The passage beyond was dark and narrow, but the walls were ordinary enough. They turned a corner into lighter, wider space, and a sturdy metal door blocked the way.

"Unlock."

He had kept tight hold of her right hand. As the door swung open, he let go.

Elizabeth walked ahead of him into a long, low room crowded with steel, glass and black plastic. The Asp was there, and the expression on his face was insufferable. Liz took it as astonishment mixed with malice; Hesha knew more of Raphael's moods. He knew the killer was savoring the wreck of the illusion, and why. Hesha smiled, and decided that the Asp was having enough fun. *Pride goeth before a fall,* he thought wickedly, and waited.

Elizabeth had drifted to the security station. The cameras were on—all of them—and the monitors up and working. She took a seat in one of the chairs. She looked at every screen in turn, coldly, and without comment. The front hall. The kitchen. An outdoor scene. The staircase. The front drive. A wall…part of the garage, she remembered. Views of the guest rooms; of Thompson's austere bed, of the Asp's den. A shot of the stairs to the basement. Every possible angle of the museum. Blank corridors. A room she didn't recognize, very messy. Another, rather cleaner. Hesha's study, and the two chairs empty there. Hesha's rooms from another angle, the back of the screen showing behind a large bed, a sliver of neatly kept dressing room to one side. More pictures of the woods, waving gently in night winds. Her own room, she saw without surprise. The bunker—a miniature Asp standing gaping over her shoulder, her own tiny figure motionless in the chair, Hesha looking up at her…into the camera, regretfully. Thompson lying in a chair in a room she didn't know. Stone hallways. Stone walls—carved walls.

Elizabeth leaned closer, staring at the reliefs. The picture was dim and the perspective was wrong, but there was a memory….

"Asp." Hesha's voice rang out. "Introduce yourself to Miss Dimitros."

Liz swiveled the chair. If the cook's face had been stunned before—which she doubted, realizing that anyone in this room would have known precisely who was coming—it was a grotesquely genuine mask of stupefaction now. The small, dark eyes narrowed with anger.

He said nothing, and Hesha filled in the silence. "Elizabeth, this is Raphael Mercurio."

"Not Angelo," she murmured tonelessly.

"There is no Angelo," said the Asp, in a voice clotted with resentment. "Raphael. Gabriel. My brother, my twin, he was here when you arrived. Angelo is...our creation. Our masterwork. The great alibi," he finished, throwing back his head and raising one glossy, defiant eyebrow.

"For what?"

"For everything," said the Asp, menacingly. He glanced at Hesha's face, and backed away. With an air of pride and hatred, he swept out of sight.

Hesha touched Elizabeth lightly on the shoulder. She left the chair, and he steered her through the bunker to a plain, wooden door. Hesha knocked once, but opened it immediately.

"Thompson."

"Sir." Thompson grimaced apologetically. "Hey, Liz." He straightened the recliner, but remained seated. "Sorry about all this."

Hesha allowed no time for pleasantries. "Take off your shirt, Thompson."

Thompson and Elizabeth exchanged glances. He grimaced again. "Yes, sir. I'll need a hand, though. The cuts are closed, but the swelling's gone up...."

"Your right shoulder still?" Hesha frowned. "Help him," he ordered.

Liz bent over the chair and took the loose shirt up and away—gingerly, after she caught sight of the first gauze padding. Beneath the pullover, Thompson was a patchwork of cotton bandages and fresh scars.

"Unwrap his right shoulder. Look at it."

Elizabeth removed the gauze and a cold pack. The flesh of Thompson's arm was puffy and discolored. The fluids trapped within stretched tight two shiny, pink dimples of new skin at the center of the wound. She replaced the dressing with skill and without comment.

Sitting on the edge of the armchair, Elizabeth gazed searchingly into the old cop's eyes.

Thompson returned the stare unhappily. She loved the boss—or had, at least. And she'd trusted her 'friend'

Ron. For the first time in—decades—he was ashamed of something he'd done. And there she went, the gaze broken; finished with him, following Hesha out, walking in his footsteps through the maze. Thompson reached for the mixing bowl, feeling slightly ill.

Elizabeth stood nervously at the door. Light came from the corridor behind her, faint, but enough to throw her shadow far from her feet. Here, on the raised step of the threshold, she could hear Hesha ahead of her in the blackness, making soft noises...hissing, and a fragile rasp like a broom. The sounds stopped, there was a long pause, and then his voice said quietly: "Light."

And Hesha's sanctuary was revealed.

The far wall—all the walls—were covered in painted reliefs. In ochre, dun, black, brick red, and blue as dark as night, three tiers high, each section longer than her own body...there would be twelve sections, she realized. It was the Am Duat—the Book of the Dead for royalty—twelve hours of Ra's journey though the Underworld, each hour divided into three parts, each part depicting an event on the god's trip from dusk to dawn, from death to life. She stepped into the room, and turned to look at the whole:

A bare floor, blue-black walls to waist height, then banded colors: red, black, ochre, black, a strip of dun-colored hieroglyphs, and then drawings done on the bare stone in black. The Ninth Hour covered the wall beside her, and she stared in fascination at the precision of the work. She looked up. Above the highest tier, the artist had reproduced exactly—so far as she could remember from photographs—the decorations that belonged there. For the ceiling, the sky by night; five-pointed, spindly stars covered it in elegant regularity.

The room was enormous. She had felt that from the door. Now she saw that it was nearly empty. Scattered at intervals along the wall lay small chests, low tables and benches made for them, and narrow boxes. Some were golden, some were dusty and worm-eaten. The walls curved with strange irrelevance, as though the masons had chosen to take a walk and the chisel had happened to lead the way. Only the floor and ceiling were parallel to each other. Where the room snaked away, she could see other things, half-hidden behind the living rock.

The largest, most obvious thing to see lay directly before her. Hesha watched in fascination as her gaze fluttered first to everything else in the room.

She was unwilling to notice it.

It was a plain box, simply made. The lid fitted tightly and squarely. It rose from the floor to a height of forty inches. It was forty inches wide, and a little over eight feet long. Elizabeth stared at the thing for a long moment, and at last she walked over to the sarcophagus.

"I was here, in my dream. In this room."

Hesha stayed where he was, and waited.

"But the floor was beaten bronze and there was no ceiling and no sky. The sun shone in, straight down like noon, and there were no shadows."

Her left hand strayed out and brushed the gray surface of the stone coffin with the edge of her palm.

"You were here, lying down. The light was on your face, and the rock and your clothes were brilliant white. I thought that you were asleep. I reached out to…to…" She stared at her hand, as if she didn't recognize it.

"I reached out to tell you something. To show you the sun, I think…but you wouldn't wake up." Her voice, trance-like until now, became a little desperate. "You wouldn't wake up. And I started to feel frost. The metal floor was cold; that was wrong, in the sunshine, and the bed…the mastaba?…was cold, and you were as cold and motionless as the stone.

"And suddenly I knew that you were dead." She

choked back a sob. "You were dead, and I looked down at myself, and I wasn't Elizabeth anymore...."

Visibly, the spell broke. Her hands traced a line over her collarbone, where the Eldest had rested that morning, and her eyes cleared of the memories. Her skin reddened with anger.

"I don't have to tell you, Hesha." Her face was fire; her voice was ice. "You have your cameras and your spies. You can damn well watch my dreams from the outside."

Elizabeth sprinted for the door.

Hesha was three times farther away from the exit; he reached it before she took her third step.

She didn't see him get there; her eyes were open but her mind was too slow to catch the movement. Simply, suddenly, he was in the way, blocking the passage. The message came to her feet too late to stop the headlong rush. Elizabeth dashed into his arms, and the momentum carried her into the space between the monster and the wall. He caught her by the arm and spun her, gathered her in to face him, held her against his body. She didn't scream, and wondered, later, why not.

He said nothing. His vision was tainted red; his fangs slid down from their sheaths and forced his jaw apart; the only sound worth hearing was her heartbeat, her quick, wet breathing, the faint start of a cry in her throat...and his hands, taloned, reached for that throat. His hands buried themselves in her long, dark hair and tilted her face toward him. His head bent to her neck—he lunged for her, she twisted in his grasp at the last possible moment, and his open jaw met her lips, not her jugular. Blood filled his mouth—living blood—and he let it go on; the Beast took Hesha and the woman with him; his last thought was filled with the taste of her.... *It is a deceit; it is an illusion; she is nothing different....*

Elizabeth, shaking and unable to stand under the flames of the kiss, dropped away, and Hesha fell with her, following the blood to the ground. She sprawled on the third step of the tomb; he knelt above her. His hands, supporting her, scraped stone, and the tiny pain brought him—barely—to himself again. He tore his mouth away, wiped her lips clean with his tongue, and sat back. For long seconds he watched her body...at last she breathed...and again...and she opened her eyes and turned her head away from him, struggling to get up.

Hesha rubbed his scraped knuckles and knew in that instant that the Beast had nearly taken her life; that the taking of it would have given him more pleasure than the slaughter of any other living thing; that her murder would have caused him sorrow for the first time in centuries. And part of him wished that it had won.

Elizabeth, her feet not yet obeying her, had still managed to sit up. She pushed herself up to the fourth step with all four limbs, and she did not look toward him.

"Elizabeth. Wait." Hesha swarmed after her and hunted for her hands. He placed her struggling fingers over his wrist. "Take my pulse," he demanded.

She stared up at him in fear. Dark, dark irises in the centers of wide-open white eyes...Hesha heard the roar of the Beast rising again, and he snatched her hands to his neck.

"Feel. Where is my heartbeat, Elizabeth? You won't find it."

She stopped fighting him. Her fingertips searched his jawline, the hollow beneath his ear, the curve of the neck into windpipe. "The first night we met," said Hesha, in a nearly normal voice, "when I fell, you were going to take my pulse. And I stopped you." Comprehension and denial rose in the dark eyes below him. She was trembling now.

"How many nightmares have you had since you met me?" She blinked, and the fighting flush drained from her face. "I think, Elizabeth, that I wasn't fast enough, keeping your fingers from my wrist that night. Without knowing, you knew...just as you knew that one Asp was frightening and the other friendly...as you knew how to reach the ring in the stone...you knew what I was."

"What are you?" she whispered.

Hesha paused. He licked his lips, and his hands tightened, involuntarily, over hers.

"Deathless."

Sunday, 11 July 1999, 4:13 AM
Laurel Ridge Farm
Columbia, Maryland

Ronald Thompson waited angrily. He was sick; he watched the scene in Vegel's apartment through narrowed, puffed-up slits of eyes. He was irritable. Inaction suited him badly; convalescence still worse. Patience he had, and he could have endured the night creditably well—if Hesha hadn't switched tactics in midstream. Thompson was puzzled, and so, instead of lying down and resting (as Janet had pleaded with him by phone to do) he sat at the center of his net and waited.

Hesha came out of Elizabeth's room backwards, bidding the girl good night and better dreams. Thompson nearly choked. As his master turned toward the door of his study, his room, and his sepulcher, Thompson flicked a switch with one swollen finger. Hesha looked up, waited, and then crossed the museum to the bookcase door.

Thompson straightened his abused body in the chair. He shot Hesha an expectant, a *challenging* glare.

Hesha regarded his servant impassively. "Yes, Thompson?"

"Sir," Thompson began. He ground rapidly to a halt. How to go on? "Sir, may I ask you a personal question?"

"You can ask me anything," said Hesha. The Setite's eyes clearly promised no answers.

"What happened," barked Thompson, "to the plan, sir?"

"Which plan?"

"The family plan," said the mortal harshly. Thompson bit his lip, and fought for the right opening—for words civil enough to keep peace with his employer, but strong enough to vent his wrath—and all that would come to him was the blasted, vitriolic curse that had begun the day.

Hesha watched as his prospective heir stumbled over his own ire. The man's eyes hunted the air, and he radiated disapproval. Hesha drew up a chair, sank sinuously into the seat, and said, "Put your thoughts in order, detective. Start again. You object to my handling of the Dimitros situation? Naturally, you have been listening ever since I brought her back to her own room…if you had not caught my performance live, I would have insisted on your review of the recorded version."

Thompson nearly exploded. A shout choked up his chest; his mouth opened—and he saw Hesha's lids twitch, lightly, in amusement. The old cop imploded, instead. So the boss was playing him. *A test,* he realized. *Another test. I wonder if I'm passing it or not.*

"I took her to the place where she felt most comfortable, Thompson. I told her what had really happened to her this morning. I gave you and the Asp hero's laurels, just as you deserve. In a few nights' time, she will recover from the shock of the—" his arcing arm indicated the bank of closed-circuit screens—"security arrangements, and I have no doubt that you and she will be fast friends again in a month or so. In fact, by Tuesday I expect that she will have thanked you for saving her life."

"I'm not talking about that."

"You don't care that she hated you tonight?"

"I do. And you say you've fixed that. And I believe

you, because you're always right about people, and my gut tells me the same thing. But you said last week that we were going to be family to her—that you 'intended her to look on you as a father figure.'" He slammed his fist on the wide arm of the chair. "If you think those were paternal moves you put on her tonight—!"

"I think you have thrown yourself too deeply into the role of 'older brother,'" Hesha interrupted.

"Vampires are all very well, sir, but I wouldn't want my sister to marry one."

"A very Victorian older brother," commented Hesha, in a dangerous voice he had never used on Thompson before. "I am not a vampire, and you've had time enough to learn that. I expect you never to use the word again unless you are referring to Stoker or Hollywood's creations. Do you understand me?"

Thompson nodded warily.

"Furthermore. Elizabeth is *not* your sister, and you'll do well to remember that. Fall too deeply into any role, and you put yourself in danger; fall too deeply into this one and you may get Miss Dimitros killed. She's a target to be guarded, Thompson. Don't let your emotions sway you. Just do your job. As for marriage..." Hesha indulged in near-silent laughter.

"Now. We were discussing my conversation with our guest. I told her she would have many questions. I promised to answer them. There will be answers Thompson; convincing ones. I told her that she was confused, vulnerable. I told her that I cared about her. I told her that I didn't want to say too much tonight, that I didn't want her to leave. I told her that there was more between us than I had realized. I told her that I had never met anyone else like her. I apologized, I confessed, I fell over my feet promising to make it all up to her."

"And did you mean any of that, sir?"

"What would you do if I didn't?" Hesha waited. "Did

you believe it when you heard me say it?"

Thompson uttered "Yes," without tone or emotion.

"Good." Hesha paused and looked at Elizabeth on the monitor. She was getting ready for bed; conscious of the camera, she had decided to change clothes under the covers. "Then I trust that she believed it, too. You know me better. You have doubts. You should."

Drawing breath to speak with, he went out on a tangent. "How many times have you been in Vegel's chamber, Thompson? And in mine?"

"Sir?"

"In Vegel's room there are farmers and hunters and artisans, Thompson. Pharaoh's guards, lords and ladies, scribes, masons. They work at their stations in life, and the river flows past them, and the green fields support them, and the waters cool their thirst, and the fruits of their labor slake their hunger, and the sun beats down on them all, scribe and farmer, master and servant. And that is life.

"In my room, the king is dead, the souls of every man, woman and child are stripped apart and sent to judgment in pieces. They are defenseless as they wander without direction from their tomb to the Place of Ma'at. The world is forever dark, and cold, and once they leave the necropolis there is nothing. The desert is cold and full of monsters. The river cannot give them drink, the fields cannot feed them. Only what the living leave for them can sustain them. And that is death.

"Love can live in the sun. And it is said to flourish in the afterlife. But in the desert between them, Thompson... Neither my kind, nor the Cainites, nor any of the brood of Apep know the meaning of the word after their rebirth. Two of my souls may be here, but my heart lies in the dark underworld, between the jaws of Ammit, the Devourer of the Dead. Understand that. Accept it. And tell me again whether you want to join Set's children."

"*Damn* you, Hesha," whispered Thompson.

"As you say." The creature's voice held nothing.

They sat together in silence for a good five minutes. The main lights went out in Vegel's apartment. Elizabeth lay on her side, reading by the lamp on the bedside table.

"You still," said Thompson, "haven't told me why you changed the plan. I was under the impression, even tonight, that we were going to continue the family game. No changes."

"Miss Dimitros is a very perceptive woman. I knew as soon as I saw her with the Asp that Raphael had no hope of deceiving her. He is limited. Gabriel is much the better actor; that's why I prefer to keep him in the townhouse. My visitors there can look through brick walls, given time...." He trailed off. "Remind me, at sundown, to readjust our arrangements there. I'll need to speak to Janet about the Greywhethers Building."

"But Elizabeth?"

"Let her be. Give her time." He rose. "Gild the cage."

The bunker door shut behind him.

Elizabeth lay in bed, pretending to sleep. Her body remained in the position it had held when she regained consciousness. Her mind was busy taking stock of her situation. She visualized Baltimore on the map, and tried to remember the details of the drive out. She thought about the house, and the cameras, and the woods around the farm. She thought about Hesha, and she acknowledged the blind spot there—she absolutely could not analyze him; could not predict his reactions. She couldn't reach him unless he allowed her to.

But there were other things.

Elizabeth slid out of bed, weakly, and into the desk chair. She reached for the phone, picked it up, and listened. There was a dial tone. She punched in the number for Amy Rutherford's house and waited for the connection. The line opened...and closed with a click. A voice came to her clearly and crisply over far shorter wires.

"Good afternoon, Liz. Do you need something?" It was Thompson.

"I'd like to call New York. How do I get an outside line?" she asked, letting go the fact that she'd needed no extra codes to do so before.

"I'm sorry, Liz." He waited, holding the phone in his room, ready with prepared explanations, excuses, orders from above.

"I think I understand." She replaced the receiver. *Strike one, Dimitros*, she thought. Idly, she turned over the books and tools on her desk—Vegel's desk. One drawer held office supplies: pens, pencils, erasers, staples, cellophane tape.

Elizabeth unplugged the phone, set the roll of tape down thoughtfully, and began—maddeningly slow and inexplicably light-headed—to search her room.

Thompson dropped stiffly into the wide console chair. The lights were green, the cameras on and tracking well. The Asp was long gone, but a litter of crumbs and wrappers testified that he had, in fact, spent the day on duty. Ron swept the trash away, and settled in to make check-up calls on his agents.

He'd finished the last when Elizabeth came out of Vegel's apartment. She was empty-handed, but wearing a light jacket—a kind of photographer's vest—that had several large pockets. With experienced eyes, he determined that she wasn't carrying anything in them.

The girl paused on the edge of the museum floor. She still held the doorknob; nervously, she looked around.

There was no one there, by order of the boss himself, but the little table the Asp had put her dinner on before had been moved to stand beside her door. The tray on top of it held breakfast...lunch by now. She lifted one of the covers away, scrutinized the food on the plate, and dropped the dome back over the sandwiches. After a moment, she lifted the tray and disappeared with it into her room.

Thompson shifted cameras and watched as she put it on the bed. The desktop was empty, he noticed. Why not put the food there?

Elizabeth came back out, closed the door behind her, and walked, with faltering steps, to the studio. She went through the drawers and bins quickly. Thompson put the workshop on the central monitor and zoomed in on her. Aha. That's what the jacket was for. She filled the pockets with her tools—Q-tips, bottles of solvent, masking tape, the discard tray, a magnifying glass, soft brushes, stiff brushes—and picked up the smallest of the paintings under restoration. She left the studio, returned to Vegel's apartment, and spread her loot out on the desk.

Thompson nodded to himself. Good. Work would take her mind off things. He rubbed his eyes, stretched, and went off in search of more of that remedy himself.

"Thompson."

"Sir." Ron stood up; he'd been waiting, not in his customary position by the door, but resting as well as he could on Vegel's stone bench.

"You're looking better."

"I feel better, sir."

"Where is the Asp?"

"On the desk. He's been filling Janet in on the situation."

"Good." Hesha sat down on the bench. "Janet."

"Here, sir. Shall I patch in Mr. Mercurio?"

"Yes, please." More white noise filtered in. "Report."

Thompson began. "The townhouse and the city holdings are secure. The Asp reports no visitors. He says he's bored, sir. Bored and healthy."

Janet Lindbergh cleared her throat. "The last refugee is off our hands, sir. Mr. Vargas departed his safe house this evening with tickets for Seattle. He left a note for you; I'm sending it by courier."

"Good."

His secretary went on: "Dr. Oxenti's clinic has received a small commendation for volunteer services from the local Red Cross. The Doctor would like to return to Baltimore for the ceremony."

"Tell her no." Hesha replied immediately. "And keep an eye on bookings for flights in and out of Anchorage until after the presentation. Freeze her accounts if necessary. Other business?"

"Miss Dimitros tried to call out this morning. New York number—"

"James and Amaryllis Rutherford, 6724 Lake Park Drive," Janet interjected—

"I told her she couldn't. She seemed to take it very well, sir. She took in lunch and one of her paintings at three o'clock; since then she's been quiet as a mouse and twice as well-behaved."

Over the intercom, there came the sound of snorting laughter.

"Asp?"

"You have a comment, Mr. Mercurio?"

The Asp laughed again. "She's taking it well, sir. Oh, she's behaving herself beautifully. Quiet as a mouse. But we're not going to be able to see her being quiet anymore, Ron. She's found all the cameras in Vegel's room, and she's sticking masking tape over every goddamn one of them. Found the microphone, too."

The conference broke up shortly after that.

The Asp lowered his tray onto the table outside Vegel's apartment and knocked once. With the family flair for stealth, he slipped away again.

After a long delay—two minutes, at least—the door to Vegel's room opened a crack. The woman inside peered out. A hand mirror poked through. Its reflection flashed around the basement. The door closed again.

After another five minutes, Elizabeth herself emerged, pale, thin, and nervous. Warily, she took up the tray. She backed into her hole like a badger, and the door shut immediately. The lock clicked after her, and through the thick wood came the sound of something heavy being dragged across the boards.

In his study, the master of the house watched his prisoner's movements.

In the bunker, Thompson saw Liz gather in her dinner, he saw the Asp wolf down his, and he saw Hesha —sitting perfectly, unnaturally still—watch Elizabeth.

Monday, 12 July 3:18 AM
Laurel Ridge Farm
Columbia, Maryland

Elizabeth maneuvered the canvas through the barricade at her door. She set it down on the 'room service' table and then locked the apartment behind her. She picked up the painting, headed for the studio, and puttered around inside the workroom for a few minutes. She pulled another piece, an oil panel, from the flat drawers. With that in hand, she walked back into the main room. Lunch had appeared on the table, but there was no one in sight. *Good*, she thought.

She propped the panel beside the little table and headed for the stairs. She checked the kitchen—empty— and tried the mud-room door. It was locked, and the deadbolt needed a key. She saw why. Even a novice housebreaker like herself could smash the glass above it and turn latches from the outside.

Elizabeth listened. The house was silent. She turned right, into the colonial wing and through the main hall. The front door had no windows set into it; there was just a chance that the bolt was simpler. She turned the knob. No luck. Perhaps she could find a spare key? Of course, this was hardly a house whose inmates would leave their spares lying around. Elizabeth bent to examine the shape of the keyhole and saw that it was parallel to the ground. Hadn't the kitchen door bolt been vertical?

She went back. After a minute, she found the problem; there were three bolts altogether. One turned with the handle and could be set by a spring catch. She'd fixed that. One was near the floor and turned with an odd-shaped knob—she hadn't noticed it the first time. The keyed bolt had been open when she tried it; in an instant the door was open, too. Liz double-checked the snap lock; if she couldn't find civilization in one hike (the word *escape* occurred to her and was promptly dismissed) she didn't want to have to ring the doorbell to get in the house.

The sun shone down through a bleached, thin blanket of clouds. The watery-gray ripples in the cover were moving quickly, but at ground level the air was stultifying: humid, thick, and still.

Elizabeth's eyes stung her. She'd forgotten how dark it was in the house. Through the faint blue afterimage, she set out up the hill. With slick fingers, she pulled open all the vent zippers in her photo jacket. It was bulky and uncomfortably hot inside it; already she was drenched with sweat. Still, she felt better—ludicrously better—knowing that every pocket was stuffed with something useful. The tools she'd gleaned from Vegel's desk and the studio weren't much, but...

In ten minutes she crested the ridge. It was a worn-out mountain, no longer even a foothill, but it was the backbone and a stump or two of rib from an old Appalachian. The granite spine of the giant lay exposed on the hilltop. Elizabeth rounded the curve of it and found a place to climb. The little wall's slope was too steep for the dirt to find much hold, and the blackberry brambles that grew solidly up the other sides were thinner here. She pulled herself up and looked around.

Damn. The landscape was beautiful; it was dark green, rolling country. It was full of trees, and between the contours of the country and the height of the trees, there wasn't much of what she had come to see…not even the house or the drive up to it.

She sat down on the highest point, pulled out a battered brass compass, and found northeast. Baltimore would, or should, lie in that direction anyway, and if she kept her eye out for the broadcast tower as she walked, she'd hit something sooner. She hoped she knew the road to the house well enough to know it if she came to it. The last thing she wanted was Thompson driving up beside her in the sedan just as she reached the mailbox.

Elizabeth set out cross-country.

In a shadowy niche among the brambles, the Eldest watched her go with lazy eyes.

Elizabeth came out of a rhododendron thicket covered in spider webs. She wiped away the strands and dislodged a few hitchhikers. Struggling a little with the thick carpet of old, shiny brown leaves underfoot, she reached out to a wrist-thick sapling for support. It helped her with the descent, and when she had crossed the damp patch at the bottom of the gully, she used the thick roots of the oak above her for a ladder.

The Asp waited on the other side of the tree. He let her pass, and then he broke a dry branch between his hands. It sounded like a shot in the still air.

"Hello, Lizzie." The words were friendly; the tone was not. "Going somewhere?"

Strike two, she thought. "Nice day for a walk," she said aloud.

"Has been." Raphael paused, pursing his lips. "Looks

like a storm coming in now, though. You'd better go back to the house. Don't want you getting caught out in it."

"Thanks." She shifted her weight uphill, and took a step farther away from the Asp, his tree, and the farm behind them. He watched her from half-closed eyes.

"Liz...you don't want to go that way."

She took another step. "I think I do, actually."

Raphael reached out a hand for her wrist. He was quick, but she was jumpy enough to be quicker. She eluded his grasp and they stopped, facing each other, two yards farther from the creek.

"You're supposed to be a smart girl, Lizzie." He lunged again, and this time his trained reflexes won out over her nervous instinct. He pulled her down the slope and onto the slanting trunk of the oak, not gently. "You didn't think it was going to be easy, did you?" He pushed his face up to hers. There was an inch, no more, between them, and the tight, hard gaze of the Asp flickered from eye to eye...left, right...back again. Liz stared back. Her wrist hurt her; he was holding it in a tight twist.

"Come on," he said. "This way."

The pain rotated around her hand. Raphael pushed her easily by the elbow along a path on the edge of the gully. The trees thinned out as they went. They descended into a hollow and began to cross the wetter ground at its base.

"Mercurio!" The shout came from the Asp's shoulder, as far as Liz could tell. "Goddamn it, Asp. Let her go." Static crackled around the voice. It was Thompson. "Let her go this minute. Fuck it, Raf. What if he checks these tapes tonight?"

Raphael released Elizabeth's wrist. She turned and put three yards between them, then stopped, chafing her burned skin. Neither of them displayed any expression. "She was trying to leave, Ron. I got a job to do."

"I know. I'm criticizing your style, not the performance. Hand me over to Liz for a second."

The Asp reached into his shirt pocket and retrieved a very small, flattish, black disc. He tossed it to her. The disc turned out to be a phone. "Hello, Liz," said Thompson's distant voice. "Do me a favor?"

"Maybe," she answered.

He sighed. "You know the path you were coming down? Get back on it and follow it to the drive. I'll pick you up in the car and bring you home."

"To Manhattan?"

Static. Then, "No."

"How far's the walk?"

"Fifteen minutes, twenty, tops."

"See you then."

"Thanks. Give me back to the maverick, there. He and I need to have a talk before the boss wakes up."

"Coffee?"

Elizabeth nodded. "If you're having some."

Thompson clattered around the counter for a few minutes. With the steam rising and the pot filling, he leaned crookedly against the cabinets and watched the girl. She'd taken off her bulging jacket and hung it over the chair back. She sat with both elbows on the table, casually, and her hair was tucked behind her ears. Her hands traced the grain and scars of the battered wooden tabletop, stroking out the same patterns over and over.

Ron pulled two mugs off the rack and set them on a tray. Sugar, milk, the coffeepot, cookie tin. He scooped up the tray in one corrugated fist.

"Mind if we take these down to your room?"

"Why?" she snapped.

"Because I think you might enjoy a little privacy. It's against all my own regs, but hell—if something comes up through the floor, you run and sound the alarm." Liz said nothing. "I'm not kidding, girl. There's a *reason* we've got cameras every five feet. *And* the doors wired so we can keep track of the ones the cameras don't see."

Elizabeth's eyebrows united in disbelief.

Thompson shook his head. "You've seen *him*. Let me start you out easy. Imagine...two of him. Twenty of him. Weaker breeds in six-packs like bad beer. The invisible man sneaking in to steal stuff. God only knows. Now can we go downstairs?"

She led the way. At the steps down to Vegel's apartment, she paused to fish a key out of her jacket. She opened the door and shifted the barricades aside.

"What the hell have you got in there? There wasn't that much loose furniture in the..." Ron ground to a halt. Awestruck, he laughed. "Good job, Liz. Damnation."

Every one of the fancy cabinet doors—some floor-to-ceiling closet pieces, some as small as a medicine chest—had been removed from its hinges and piled up against the entrance. The heavy bathroom door leaned on the secret panel to Vegel's crypt, and its base was reinforced with pieces of the bed frame.

"The tray fits on the desk," Elizabeth directed. "Give me a minute and I'll liberate another chair."

They poured, and mixed, and sipped, and when she'd relaxed enough to explore the contents of Gabriel's cookie tin, he let her get through two chocolate monstrosities before he tried to talk.

Thompson cleared his throat. "Thanks for letting me come in here. I appreciate it."

"Thanks for pretending my carpentry would do a damn bit of good if you decided you wanted in."

"It would slow us down. And it was clever." He hesitated. "But really...I'm glad we're *here*, and not in the kitchen. I've got a few things to say I don't want the Asp—or the boss—listening to later."

Elizabeth gave him steady, stony, sphinx-like attention.

"First—let me say I'm sorry," he began slowly. "I know that doesn't mean a damn thing to you now…but I've got to say it because I do really mean that." He ruffled his grizzled hair, pushing on. "And I want you to know that I…well, I can't say that I—we—haven't all lied to you in one way or another, right from the start. But what I told you about my hometown, about my folks and my high school and why I joined the police and why I left the Force to start my own business—that was all true, every word of it." He paused, and a kind of hopeless look filled his face. "Believe it or not, I like you. And I've got to say I like you even better since this thing blew up in our faces. You've fought it, but you haven't panicked after that first night, and if you're feeling sorry for yourself I can't see it on the surface." He grinned. "Not even the boss was expecting the masking tape, Liz."

The faintest echo of a smile played across her lips. Thompson, uncertain how to keep a good thing going, took a long, hard look into his coffee cup. He shrugged with his hands, and reached for a cookie.

"And I want to apologize for Raphael. He's not a bad guy, once you get to know him, but he resents the boss telling you the Asp's names. The boss thinks—and I think, because I…well, I was watching you over the security system—that you knew the difference between the brothers. Raf doesn't believe it; he's too used to walking around as Angelo and feeling superior because of it. He doesn't know how to act around you, so he's playing the heavy. It'll wear off, I think. Gabe'll bring him around, anyway."

Elizabeth murmured, "You talk as if I'm going to be here a long time."

Thompson flushed a little. "I don't really know," he answered. His mouth twitched as if he'd tasted something rotten in the chocolate. "We're waiting for something on the outside to blow over. The boss is afraid if we let you go now you'd be killed by..."

"Killed by what?" Her voice was hard.

"Things," he finished inadequately. "Other people like him, but different; *other* things; a whole army of things tearing up the eastern seaboard. You saw the reports of riots in Atlanta, in D.C.? They're in the thick of it."

She said nothing, and Thompson could feel doubt pouring out of her.

"Look, Liz. You'll admit that he exists, I hope. If he exists, not breathing, not dying, what else is out there?"

"What else *is* out there?"

"The invisible man. Those six-packs. The late-late-late-show. I wish *I* didn't know," said Thompson, with such finality, with such weariness, that she let the matter rest. He freshened their mugs and took a sip. Minutes went by, and in each one, Ron nearly spoke. In each one, he thought better of it. After a dozen false starts, the words spilled out.

"About him, Liz."

"What about him?"

"About the two of you...don't look at me like that." Elizabeth's jaw had clamped shut. She was clearly unwilling even to listen to this. *Damn*, he thought. *He's really under her skin*. He took a long breath and prepared to risk deeper waters for Hesha's sake.

"Please, Elizabeth. I'm not blind. You're in love with him."

She almost laughed. "No. No, I'm not. I don't know him. You can't love someone you don't know." She set her jaw again. Her lips were abnormally pale and thin. "You can't love someone who locks you up," she said. "Someone who lies to you; someone who spies on you constantly; someone whose hired...guards...throw you around in the name of your own safety—and please don't be offended if I admit I still don't believe in the 'things' you say are waiting for me to set foot out there."

"No offense taken." He struggled to come up with more, and said, "But it sounds like you're working awfully hard to convince somebody."

"You," she insisted. "You're the one with the theory."

"Sure. But you don't have to convince me. You could just say no and stop the conversation. But you're willing—you're eager to keep talking about him, because you really did give a damn, and now he's hurt you. So you want to talk. Therefore—I don't believe you. I don't believe *him* when he denies it, either," he said, and realized that that, at least, was true.

"I've been married twice, Liz. I know the symptoms." He slouched back in his chair. "Let me tell you what's going to happen. Hesha will *not* come to see you. You think he scares you? You scare the hell out of him," said Thompson, crossing his fingers to ward off thunderbolts. Her eyes dropped—she believed that—*God help her*, thought Ron. *And God forgive me*.

"Now, if you don't care, or you can't get past the shock, or you're as scared as he is, you can stay here in this room for as long as the danger lasts, if that's what you really want. And then he'll send you home to New York, and you'll never see him again. But while you wait, each of you will know that the other is just on the other side of the wall—until *he* can't stand it and finds an excuse to run even farther away from you." Thompson, staggered by the size of the lie, foundered and reached for clichÈ. "I know it isn't fair that you have to make the next move." That was better. "What's wrong here is his...fault...because of what he is. But I can't go in there and talk to him like this. So I'm in here. And...I'm asking you." He shook his head. "Because I like you both." He played nervously with his empty coffee cup, and he sounded anything but sure. "Go see him. Talk to him. Maybe even let him try to explain."

Thompson checked his watch and stood up. "I've got to go now. Raf'll be looking for me." He looked over to her, but Liz had her eyes fixed firmly on the carpet. "Please, at least think about what I said. And don't...well, I'd rather you didn't tell the boss I was in here, meddling in his...personal...life..." He picked up the tray and took it out with him. After a few moments the lock clicked to and the sound of shifting barricades came from behind the door.

"Report."

"Miss Dimitros went for a walk this afternoon," said Thompson. "The Asp stopped her short of the interior fence and encouraged her to come back."

Hesha turned from his security chief to look at Raphael. "*Encouraged*," he said evenly.

"Yeah." Raphael sounded slightly defensive even to himself. "I brought her back. And I handed her off to Ron. And then," he said, seeing a way out of his employer's uncomfortable attention, "they disappeared into her room for an hour."

Hesha focused his cool regard on Thompson again. "Into her room?"

"I wanted a look at her arrangements." Ron folded back the cover of his notebook. "The barricade, sir. You can hear her moving it around from the outside, even over the system microphones. As it turned out, she's constructed it from the cabinet fronts of Vegel's storage shelves. I have a sketch here—really, it's no more complicated a construction than a house of cards, but it's reasonably effective and—"

"Resourceful," murmured Hesha, glancing at the piece of paper. He handed it back.

"It didn't take you an hour to look at her room, Ron," interjected the Asp. "What else was going on in there?"

Thompson ignored Raphael's leer and managed—

by slow and careful folding of the sketch as he put it away—not to have to look Hesha directly in the eye, either. "After Raf's 'encouragement'," he began, "I thought she needed a little normality." Ron flicked up the next page of his notebook and met his employer's eyes calmly. "A little metaphorical hand-holding. We had a nice, long talk, sir. Just consider the cage gilded."

Hesha took a long time to speak. "Very well. Other business?"

Elizabeth walked toward Hesha's study.

From the far end of the basement, there came a faint click. Hesha stood in the open doorway.

She held herself together, crossing the space between them at a slow pace that (she prayed) betrayed none of the anxiety she felt. "Good evening, Hesha," she said, taking his favorite greeting away from him. "I was hoping you would be in tonight. Do you have a few minutes to spare me?"

Her host stepped aside and invited her in with a gesture.

Elizabeth smiled. "Actually, if you don't mind..." She pointed with a careless hand toward her own room. "I was thinking of a slightly more private discussion."

Hesha didn't move. "I can override the system, if you wish."

Her upper lip twitched. "But I would have no way of telling whether you really did or not."

His sleek black head inclined toward her. "Very well, then, if you feel safer there."

"Marginally."

When both were seated, Elizabeth smiled as broadly as she could and extended her right hand. "Hello," she said. Hesha took his cue and shook with her. "My name is Elizabeth Dimitros. I was born in Brooklyn; I've lived in New York most of my life. I make my money restoring art for an antique gallery. I'm studying for my doctorate in an incredibly obscure field. I'm single and I'm twenty-nine and I'm not enjoying that very much." She finished with a shrug she'd inherited from her father; flourishing, Greek, and involving the entire arm.

"Twenty-eight," Hesha put in. "Twenty-eight until September."

"Strike three," murmured Elizabeth.

"Pardon?"

"I've never told you my age, let alone my birthday. Not Thompson or the twins, either." A little of her smile disappeared. "I suppose Amy might have mentioned it, but she didn't, did she?"

"No."

"So you know me," she said deliberately, "very well. And I know nothing—nothing, really—about you." She took a deep breath. "And I was wondering if you would care to introduce yourself." Elizabeth swallowed a nervous, choking reflex. "Please."

Hesha put his hands together and gave an odd half-bow with his head and shoulders. "My name is Hesha, truly; it is a milk name that my mother gave me. I have many others. Ruhadze I took from a friend of mine after his death; he had no sons and I wanted to honor his memory. I have been Hesha Abn Yusuf, Hesha Washington, Hesha Abraham....

"I was born between the First and Second Cataracts, in Nubia, that is now Sudan, in a village that no longer exists because of the Aswan Dam, to a people who are disappearing, to a religion that was not supposed to have survived. I have traveled in North Africa, in India, in Europe, and in America. I made my money in antiques, but my current holdings are diverse. I spend most of my time studying old languages and cultures; I try to keep buried dangers from being uncovered by the wrong hands. I am a bachelor by nature," he stressed. "I am considerably older than I look; and until this summer I enjoyed my life a great deal."

"Until this summer," Elizabeth said evenly.

"At solstice, one of the most terrible dangers I sought to confine was exposed. I have no idea who wields it now. At solstice, Erich Vegel, who was my partner and my only...friend," Hesha said, "accepted an invitation to a gala and kept a business appointment there on my behalf. He was killed that night or very soon after, I believe. It is possible that he fell into the hands of our enemies. It is possible that our business associates set him up; that people I trusted are now a threat. At solstice, a night-war started for control of the East Coast. At solstice, I met you. Since then," he said, holding up a finger for each transgression, "you have brought Kettridge back into my circle, disordered my house, invaded my sanctuary, and nearly caused the death of my servant Thompson." With four fingers up, he began another list, in identical tones, and folded down one finger for each item. "You have also discovered how to remove the white eye from the statue, located one of the two missing stones, extracted the ring from Vegel's boulder, and revealed weaknesses in our security system without actually killing anyone under my protection." He finished with his hand closed again.

Elizabeth ventured, "I'm sorry about your friend. And I don't know anything about your danger or your war," she said seriously. Her stomach tightened in painful knots. "As for the last...are you trying to say we're even? Because I don't understand you." She reached for the fist he still held in the air between them. "There's more to this situation than four for four." Her hand closed over his, and Hesha allowed it to remain.

"No. You are correct. I have taken things away. Your liberty and your safety, for example—and I will remain in your debt until such time as I return them to you." His voice, distant and formal, fell on her like icewater, but his eyes found hers and were smoldering hot.

They sat in silence for a long time.

Without words, Hesha opened the hand Elizabeth held. He reached for her other hand, and they went on sitting, saying nothing. The knots in Elizabeth's stomach vanished and were replaced by butterflies—not the ordinary breed born of fear or hope or past loves, but rabid butterflies that hurt and tore her at the same time she felt wonderful. Warm waves of contentment washed down her neck and shoulders to battle with a dreadful chill in her spine. She hoped he would speak. She was terrified of what he might say.

Hesha's hands held the mortal's lightly. His index fingers supported her wrists; he was enraptured by the rhythm of her heartbeat. *Pleasant music*, he thought. He waited patiently while the tempo changed. The matter could not be rushed...when the time was right, he brought out the words he had ready.

"Elizabeth," said the Setite softly, gazing into her eyes. "Don't ask me questions," he hesitated for a finely calculated second, "unless you're absolutely certain," again, a pause, "that you want the answers." He brought her hands together and brushed the knuckles lightly with his lips; he dropped them gently into her lap.

"I have a great deal of work to do tonight," said Hesha, rising. "But I would like to see you tomorrow. If you would care to work on the papyrus tomorrow at ten o'clock?" She nodded gravely, and with as solemn a countenance he slipped through the barricade and away.

Hesha stared at the bag of blood waiting in his apartment.

"Thompson," he said loudly, into the empty air.

A circuit opened. "Sir."

"Have my car ready."

"Your car, sir?"

"Unless you particularly desire to watch me hunt, you will prepare my personal car instead of the chauffeur model."

"Your car, sir," said Thompson, quickly.

The intercom died with a click.

Tuesday, 13 July 1999, 12:31 PM
Laurel Ridge Farm
Columbia, Maryland

Footsteps on the stairs stopped Ron where he stood in the kitchen.

Elizabeth reached the top and found him staring at her.

"Hi," she said.

"Hey, Liz." Thompson answered. "Are you all right?"

"No. But what am I going to do about it?" Thompson kept quiet. "Any chance you could help me put my room back together?" Elizabeth looked up at him, wistfully. "I'm having trouble with the larger doors; I can't hold them up and stick the pins in the hinges at the same time."

"Sure."

"You talked to *him?*"

She nodded.

"Ron...I suppose I should have said this sooner...but thanks." She paused, and Thompson was struck by a fleeting resemblance to his master in the girl's face. "For the advice. And for getting the Asp off my back the other day. And...for pulling me out of there. The snake pit. Someday, Ron, explain to me why there's a room full of snakes in this house. Just not today. Thank you," she finished lamely, "for saving my life." She looked up at him. "God, that sounds so inadequate when you actually come out and say it, doesn't it?"

Thompson smiled and shook his head, but said nothing. He reached for the empty bottle. *Tuesday*, he thought. '*By Tuesday, she will have thanked you for saving her life.' Damn him.*

Raphael rounded the corner from the elevator and slouched against the bunker wall. "What're you doing, Ron?"

"Agency reports. According to these jokers, Kettridge was in St. Louis, Philly, *and* Memphis yesterday. Damn kids. Wouldn't recognize their own mothers in a line-up."

The Asp poured sympathy into his voice. "You need a drink, Ron."

"I have a drink. And I'm not downing any of that paint-stripper you call booze," Ron said, until he saw the bottle Rafael was offering. "Holy shit. Where'd you get that?"

"Present from the boss. For bringing our girl back without breaking her." He shrugged. "I figure I owe you some; I'd probably have at least torn something if you hadn't stepped in." Raphael set a tumbler on the console and filled it with a generous double.

Thompson took a sip, nodded thanks, then picked up his reports again. The Asp plopped himself down in the spare chair and watched the screens. On the center monitor, Elizabeth and Hesha worked at the papyrus table. The sound was turned off, but the sitting figures seemed to be talking companionably enough.

"So." Raphael refilled his own glass contentedly. "Everything back to normal, hey, Ron?"

Elizabeth sighed and put Vegel's notes neatly aside. The manuscript was defeating her. She scooted her chair a foot or two farther down the scroll to a more heavily illustrated portion.

"Tired?" Hesha asked.

"Frustrated." Liz plucked a scrap of vaguely red-tinged papyrus from the side of the table. There was a small black line running across the edge...which failed to match the section she thought it would. "I had such a lucky run on this last Friday."

Her host continued working without comment.

"How old are you, Hesha?" Elizabeth asked suddenly.

"Thirty-three, I think. Perhaps thirty-four," said the Setite, meeting her gaze with an amused, puzzled expression. Elizabeth raised an eyebrow skeptically. "Not counting the years since I failed to die, of course."

"How long ago was that?"

His face hardened. "You want the truth?" Elizabeth nodded. "It may have been 1700 CE; I often suspect that it was earlier. The old calendars don't match each other very well." He watched her. "You're not surprised?"

"No. I was ready for that one; you've dropped enough hints." Liz took up her tongs again, and found a match for the red shard. "Your grandfather's North African household goods from the fifteenth century." She smiled at his reflection in the table. "What does this papyrus say?"

"You think I can read this?"

She laughed. "Yes." She matched two more red pieces together.

His black eyes flickered up at her. "Truth? This is a temple copy of a folk tale about Nepthys. The picture you're working on shows her leaving her brother Set's court, the court of Upper Egypt, to visit their married siblings Osiris and Isis in Lower Egypt. This piece—" he drew her attention to an assembled section—"is a prayer, and this—" another sound fragment—"is a recipe for incense to propitiate the goddess."

"Oh." Elizabeth reached for Vegel's notes and a new piece of paper. She copied down the symbols for the four deities and the two courts and started a search through the scraps for the names.

"How did you meet Professor Kettridge?"

"At a dig in Lebanon. Baalbek. It's a long story."

"Are you going anywhere?" She grinned at him.

"No." Hesha waited, giving her the opportunity, but when Elizabeth neither asked for the truth nor looked for it with her eyes, he went on freely. Jordan Kettridge might not have recognized the events described in the Setite's version, but Hesha made a thrilling story of them. Professor Kettridge shone as an honest archaeologist swept up in international events. Thompson made brave stands against unnamed terrorists; Erich Vegel protected the dig alone, by night, against overwhelming odds; and Hesha (with a fair amount of modesty) took the stage as the linguist, local guide, and quiet man behind the scenes. By the end of the account, Kettridge had discovered Hesha's secret, overreacted, and fled quite plausibly.

"And you haven't spoken to him since?"

The Setite paused. "I suspect I give him the same kind of nightmares I gave you," he looked up at her, "though for different reasons—" and the soft, embarrassed glance in his eyes was a masterwork of misdirection. With a slight, visible effort, he shook off the sentiment. "Kettridge is a scientist. I am...difficult to explain. I don't force the issue on him." Hesha set his tools down on the tabletop. "I think I'm done for the night," he said, stretching. Elizabeth watched his body move under his shirt, found herself staring, and looked quickly away. "You should get some rest, too."

They stood up together. Walking slowly, side by side, they traversed the length of the museum. At the point where Elizabeth would turn toward Vegel's room and Hesha would turn toward his own, she hesitated, and was relieved to find him still standing next to her. His hand reached up to her shoulder.

"Go," said Hesha, hoarsely.

Elizabeth bit her lip. She pulled her key from her

pocket and took the steps down to her door. She listened to his soft footfalls take him farther, to his own threshold, and she turned the key in the lock. For another second she hesitated. *Go to bed, Lizzie. Don't think about it.* She snapped the key out of the wards and opened the door. Against her better judgment, she looked back—

—and saw him lying crumpled on the floor.

"Hesha!"

She screamed and ran at the same time, arrived breathless, and skidded to a stop on her hands and knees.

"Hesha!" Elizabeth's hands shook helplessly. No pulse to take, no breath sounds to listen for. His eyes—his eyes were shut; the lids and irises motionless. She struck the floor with her fist and jumped up again. *The bookshelf*—she flew to it and tried to slide it open. "Thompson! Thompson!" She kicked furiously at the heavy wooden case. "Damn it, Ron!" She whirled around, trying to remember…there were microphones everywhere, but where was the nearest intercom? Her apartment? Hesha's study? "Thompson!" she yelled again.

Elizabeth turned to run to her room. Behind her, the bookshelf slid aside, and Thompson and the Asp dodged around her to reach their master. She was nearly knocked down; she hardly thought about it.

Ron Thompson knelt by Hesha—carefully, without touching him or his clothing—and held the other two off with a gesture. "Sir?"

No one breathed.

"Sir?"

The Setite's left hand crept to his collar. From the cords hung round his neck, at a glacial pace, he selected the newest. "Eye," he said.

Thompson waved Raphael in. "Take his legs." The Asp obeyed, and together they lifted Hesha's unresisting carcass off the ground. "Liz, get the door to his room."

Wednesday, 14 July 1999, 3:56 AM
Laurel Ridge Farm
Columbia, Maryland

"Light," said Thompson. "Sir? We're on the last step. We can't go any farther without..."

The creature in his arms hissed. Sibilant echoes filled the chamber.

"Thank you, sir." Thompson started moving again. "Careful where you step, Raf. They won't bite after he's said the word, but shuffle your feet just to be on the safe side. Turning right, now. Easy."

Elizabeth closed her eyes, took a deep breath, and waded—gently—into the ankle-deep confusion of snakes. The procession passed by the Eighth Hour and the Seventh. Elizabeth had to stop often to find a clear place to rest her feet. She felt as though the stars above moved with them and that the tangle of reptiles had eyes on her.

"Straight shot over to the sandbox, Raf. Liz? Crossing here." They stepped out into the empty center of the tomb. Elizabeth trailed after them, certain now that something was following her.

"Good. Set him down." Thompson laid his master on a long, thin, squat bench—nearly a cot—at the edge of a large, circular patch of white sand. From a tiny chest of drawers beside the circle, he took a bronze amulet on a black cord and a small bag shut tight by a drawstring. He handed them to Hesha without a word, and the Setite's fingers sprang into life.

"What's wrong with him?" Elizabeth whispered.

"Quiet," Thompson ordered. Looking at her face, he relented. "He's all right, he just...concentrating. He doesn't have any energy to spare. Don't distract him." He pulled her up against the wall and cleared space for the two to sit. On the other side of the sand, the Asp did the same.

Hesha's hands stopped. For a moment, nothing happened. Then he sat bolt upright on the bench, stretched his hands out clenched tightly together, and moved his mouth as if he were speaking. The three mortals heard only a faint whistle, like a breeze. Hesha's right arm stuck straight out, steady as stone. Hesha's left arm descended, slowly, holding the bronze figure. The white eye of the statue had been tied into the knot above it. The tip of the amulet touched the sand; the Setite's left arm fell back to his lap, and though his body moved not at all, the pendulum began to sway wildly.

Elizabeth watched, fascinated. The little bob disobeyed half the laws of physics—after a quick whip to one side that stretched the cord to its full length, it zipped back just as fast to the center, changed direction, and swung sluggishly through a short arc. Slow, fast, short, long, making sharp turns, wide angles—*like a magnetic top*, she thought. *Like a toy.* She drew her knees in and braced both hands against the floor, sitting up straighter to see better. Fine black lines appeared on the sand wherever the amulet went—

When it stopped, it stopped suddenly. The eye and the weight made one last desperate pull toward the long line, and stayed there, quivering, dripping dark powder onto the sand. Hesha reached out and grasped the amulet, and the line between his hands went slack.

"Kettridge is in Philadelphia," he said, in a perfectly ordinary voice. "Have the agency provide protection for him. He is not to know the team is there; he is not to be interfered with—but he will need more eyes and firepower than I suspect he can muster on his own. Who saw him there?"

"Pauline Richards, sir. With your permission, I'd like her to head the team. She's one of the candidates I've been considering as a replacement."

"As you will." Hesha opened his eyes. *Kettridge took*

my advice. Interesting. The other red eye remained in New York City. He suspected that a warlock owned it; if true, it was completely inaccessible—but if true, why was it…unattended? There was no presence connected with it. The Eye itself lay in Atlanta. Very well. It could stay where it was, now that he understood the source. Hesha rubbed the white bead between his fingers. He took it off the cord and tied it again around his neck. The long line; the line too faint and too shaky to trace the first night in New York—now he knew where it ended.

He turned to the Asp. "Thank you for your assistance. Can you take the desk while Thompson and I conclude arrangements? Time is short." As an afterthought, he added, "Show her the safe way out, if you would."

"Yes, sir." Raphael danced nimbly away between the copperheads' bodies. Liz hesitated, hovering toward Hesha. "Good night, Elizabeth," said the creature, sternly. Her jaw clenched tight, but she rushed to catch up to her guide and they vanished up the stairs.

"Thompson. The Eye is in Atlanta, but the Eye's source of power lies in Calcutta. We leave for India immediately." The Setite found his feet and made a beeline for the sarcophagus. The snakes opened a path for him. Ron walked in the wake. "Call Janet as soon as you leave me; prepare equipment for yourself and the Asp. Expect the worst. Conference at sundown as usual, but have Miss Dimitros attend."

"Sir? Are we…we *can't* take her with us?!"

"No?" Hesha perched on the edge of his stony couch. "We cannot leave her here alone, Thompson; we cannot send her back to New York until we are sure of her. The doctor is in Alaska. I doubt if her second-in-command would be quite so amenable to our usual storage solution…even if I cared to risk Elizabeth's health by placing her in a coma for the weeks or months of our absence.

We could kill her, of course...but I think we will find her useful in Calcutta.

"Unless you would like me to reconsider, Thompson."

"No." Ron's ruddy face was pale. "No, sir, thank you."

"Leave me," said the monster, lying down. "The sun rises."

Elizabeth appeared—uncertain but poised—in the door between her room and Vegel's carved crypt. Thompson stood, indicated the empty chair beside his own, and smiled reassuringly. He handed a thick stack of documents to Liz, including her own genuine passport, shot records, and university records, which she had left in her apartment in New York. He opened his notebook—a new one, dedicated to Calcutta and nothing else—and sat back with an air of expectation. Raphael took a seat, and after a theatrically appropriate interval, Hesha himself joined the group.

"Good evening," said the Setite, taking his place on the stone bench. "Janet?" He said to the ceiling.

"Here, sir."

Hesha faced Liz and gestured to the disembodied speaker. "Elizabeth Dimitros, Janet Lindbergh. Circumstances forbid a more personal introduction, I'm afraid. Miss Dimitros, we leave for Calcutta this afternoon."

Elizabeth's brows climbed in surprise. Her chin came up sharply, defiantly. The golden glints in her eyes flashed at, through, and beyond the Setite's face, and she withdrew slightly. Still, she said nothing, and Hesha, who had had a quick and quiet speech ready to convince her if it became necessary, set those words aside and went on:

"Thompson and the Asp go with us; Mrs. Lindbergh and the Asp stay here as rear guard. Reports, please. Janet?"

Janet efficiently ticked off the arrangements and assumed identities they'd each be traveling under, including a diplomatic passport for the Asp.

"Diplomatic seal on all his baggage—including you, sir."

"Excellent," said Hesha. "Hotel?"

"The Oberoi Grand. Central, expensive, traditional but refurbished—and with an available suite exceeding Thompson's basic requirements, sir."

Ron spoke up. "We've hedged our bets with rooms under cover at various more appropriate places throughout town. I've got agents en route to take occupancy on schedule and form parts of the guard team. And there will be a H. M. Ruhadze making the appropriate border crossings to account for your public appearance and disappearance as needed."

"Munitions?"

Thompson glanced toward Elizabeth. He and the Asp had their choices ready, but...they were somewhat revealing. Instead of reading the list out loud, he passed his notebook to his employer. Hesha scanned it without expression. He reached toward Thompson without looking, and Ron handed the pencil to him.

"Bring extra supplies of the circled items; we may need them for trade on the black market. If not, we can distribute them for goodwill before we return.

"As for personal belongings: Be ready for anything. Asp, you can pass for local if you don't speak. I want your maximum range of costume ready as soon as we land. The same goes for my kit. We can pick up additional indigenous clothing once we reach the city, but we cannot do it without suspicion unless we blend in before we enter the shops.

"Thompson. Western dress. Tourist gear, business wear, bodyguard for any level from gutter to glitter. If you can pick up the accent we may add an Anglo-Indian range.

"Elizabeth. Pack your bags back up, but don't take all your books. Look over your supposed itinerary and select such volumes as would aid research on your dissertation at those places. Take from Vegel's library as you need, and bring anything we have on Bengali myth. You will study that and the hieroglyphs for most of our stay. As for clothes, I want your own things in your own cases. Thompson, see that she has a tourist, business, and jet-set wardrobe available at the Oberoi Grand when we arrive."

"I don't have jet-set clothes, Hesha," Elizabeth put in. "I suppose your men could steal my suits and things from my apartment—like they have my passport—but my silver dress is the only—"

He cut her off. "We will attend to that."

Elizabeth subsided. Thompson flipped to a new page in his notebook. The master of the house drilled them over baggage claim, shipping crates under separate labels, and the meeting dragged on.

A feeling like nostalgia settled into the old cop's bones. There was Hesha, captain of the expedition, his mind wrapped around every detail. The Asp, murderous but familiar, sleek and silent. Janet, sharp, thorough, thinking of everything almost as quickly as the boss himself. And if Vegel wasn't there to give efficiency a little twisted warmth, at least Elizabeth was finally on the team instead of pulling against it. He could see her, a year from now, working in the museum, chatting with poor lonely Janet, kidding around with the twins, learning from himself how to scan and shoot and run the system at the farm. He glanced down at the sleek, brown head beside him and smiled. *Little sister*, he thought. *Close enough*.

part three: calcutta

Friday, 16 July 1999, 8:06 PM (local time)
The Oberoi Grand Hotel
Calcutta, West Bengal

Hesha woke rapidly. The sun now setting over the Ganges delta had abandoned Baltimore some ten hours earlier; the long journey had taken them into and out of the night an unsettling number of times. Freed from sleep in the cargo compartments of the jets, he had had time to himself. Since the ruin of Atlanta, his prayers to Set had been too rare, his meditations interrupted too often by the Eye and all that came with it. He let his mind dwell a moment on the dreams his god had sent him—painful but promising visions—and the plans now concrete in his thoughts.

Rolling over, the Setite stretched himself. The casket, lined in suede and filled with fire-retardant gel, only gently confined his contortions. In a short time, he had hands, feet, and proper ears again. With a slickly scaled claw, he felt through the darkness. There was a small plug of gel and leather near his head; he pulled it aside and listened.

"Raf? What in hell did you bring *these* for?"

"Black market. They're very hot over here."

"Fine. You stow them. C'mere, Liz."

Hesha opened a tiny hatch that the plug had hidden. The light outside was dim and slightly blue. Satisfied, he prepared to make his appearance.

Thompson's assured baritone continued outside. "Calcutta has no phones worth speaking of, right? We wouldn't use them anyway. Take this. There's a list of numbers you'll need to memorize, I'll give them to you in a second. But the first and last security protocol for our phones is: no names. Ever. Someone dials up and calls you Dimitros, Elizabeth, Liz, Lizzie, anything—or asks you for any of us by name—you hang up. It's a trap call. After we've got the codes beaten into your head, I'll go over whether you leave the phone where it is, call us, call scram, or what. Now. First rule?"

"No names."

"Last rule."

"No names."

Hesha slipped from the aluminum travel-case into blue-curtained dimness. His personal items were strewn convincingly around the room. His truly private bags sat next to the gel-filled casket and had, by order, not been touched. The bedclothes, rumpled, testified to a jetlagged traveler. The bathroom showed enough signs of use; he seemed not to have had a shower before napping. He proceeded to take one now, and in half an hour a clean, rested Hesha, dressed well but lightly, opened the connecting door to the rest of his suite.

"Good evening."

His retainers stopped in their tasks. The Asp set an elaborate machine-gun back into its case. He dropped down beside it on a couch now cluttered with armament. Thompson put down a computer hook-up and found a chair near an empty sideboard. Elizabeth looked up from the central table. Her new phone, a notepad, guide-books and a stack of local newspapers lay piled in heaps around her place.

"Report, please. Thompson?"

"Janet's news is waiting on your laptop. Everything here—so far—has gone without a hitch, sir." He made a short, dismissive gesture with his hands. "We're only half-settled in, of course."

Hesha picked a pistol out of one of the Asp's cases and weighed it in his hands. "Reports at dawn, then." Discarding the weapon, he turned and left them.

Friday, 16 July 1999, 11:27 PM
The Albert Hall Coffee Shop
Calcutta, West Bengal

Hesha walked into the old, smoke-filled café with a book in his hand. It was a worn-out, rebound, foxed and tattered copy of Calcuttan folk tales. The Setite obtained a cup of coffee, a small table, and a straight, slat-back chair. He settled in as though he had all night to read. Through the haze and the variety of lights—none of the bulbs in the lamps seemed to have come from the same country, let alone the same box—Hesha made, without haste, eye contact with a man at the corner table farthest from the door. The Indian was white-haired and bearded, dark-skinned and hollow-eyed. He spoke, smiling pleasantly, to two earnest-looking young students both bearing, in case an onlooker might doubt, university crests and young-people's causes blazoned across their T-shirts, books, and bags. Hesha did not doubt; he was certain these two (whatever their former intentions) would never attend lectures in the sun-lit rooms of Calcutta's classrooms again. He raised his coffee cup to his lips and opened his book to a random page, but he kept one eye on the trio in the corner.

Slowly, courteously, the elder man shooed away his guests. They left, dissatisfied but saving face, without taking notice of the clean-shaven black newcomer who had cut short their audience.

Hesha waited respectfully for a nod from the bearded man, then crossed the tangled, noisy room to join him. Hesha Ruhadze bowed, cleared away some of the detritus left by the students, and companionably took up a seat backing the deep blue-and-green wall of the shop. The old man's view of the café was clear now…and so was Hesha's.

"*Nomoshkar*, Subhas Babu."

"*Nomoshkar*, Hesha Bhai. How have you been, little brother?"

"I do well, Subhas. I do very well. And you?"

"I confess that I bore easily; otherwise my life is sweet." He picked up a coffee, not his own, and Hesha followed suit. They pretended to drink, then set their cups down close to emptier vessels.

"I apologize if my unexpected appearance has caused you to lose friends or business, Subhas. I would have been happy to return later, if you wished it."

"On the contrary, little brother. Those children would chatter all night. I am grateful for the release." The old man brought a colder cup to his lips, set it down, and smiled. "It is funny. The more I insist to them that I have no Family, the more they convince themselves that I am of their own, but ashamed of them."

"Young warriors looking for philosophy in your venerable mind?"

"Rabble looking for a leader, Hesha. Don't flatter them as they flatter themselves. Flatter me all you like, of course." He laughed softly. "Now, what brings you forth, little brother? Surely not the Festival of Snakes; it is too early."

"Conversation with you, Subhas."

"All the way from America? Next time, fly me to your doorstep; I should like to see the land of riches for myself."

Hesha tilted his head toward his companion. "It brings me forth tonight. Calcutta has changed since last I walked its streets...."

"It *has* streets," interrupted the elder.

"And I trust you to know all there is to know about it."

"You honor me." Subhas licked his lips, pushed his chair farther from the table, and crossed his legs. "Make yourself comfortable, little brother. Can you smoke?"

Hesha nodded.

"It is the thing done here, you understand. Accha!" With a wrinkled, spotted hand, he called up an attendant.

"My dear girl," he said into her glazed eyes, "clear this mess away and bring us two lit pipes and two used cups."

When she's left them, Subhas began a catalog of Calcutta night life. "You might say the Camarilla is in possession, little brother. They certainly say it. They have a Prince; they keep court, and the same cast of characters plays out the same little comedy as in...oh, Lisbon, let us say. Ventrue says he wields the power. Tremere witches behind his back. Toreador pretends to rise above it all. Gangrel disdains to need the others. Malkav mystifies everyone, including herself. Brujah shakes a fist at Ventrue. And the Nosferatu watch and say nothing. But in Lisbon, of course, Ravnos is a rare and unwelcome visitor. Here I daresay he outnumbers the Europeans." The girl arrived and handed the empty cups and full, smoldering pipes to her patrons. "Forgive me, little brother. I let my poetry run away from me. This is not what you need.

"The eldest Anglo Kindred keep their lairs in the old White Town. Young leeches sleep anywhere they think is safe. They are often wrong. We have many, many dangerous places here. I will tell you these first. I know," he said, shaking his head at Hesha, "that you will *go* there first, so it may as well be. The Gypsies camp by the river, north of the racecourse, under the workings for the new bridge. Do not go near their homes if you wish to keep your senses and your skin. The Gangrel and the Ravnos keep up a fine little war defending the area from each other. Stay out of Chinatown. This is difficult; there are...maybe seven, maybe eight little neighborhoods that could vie for the title. Since you last left us, strange creatures have moved in from Bangladesh and Tibet. Beware of *them*. There are wizards in the south. I have not heard of attacks by them on our kin for some time—but only for as long as our kin have avoided the temples of Kali. The temple district is...uncertain.

"Sunderban jungle is filled with tigers. I need not

explain myself, I trust?" Both took long, meaningless drags on their pipes and leaned back in their chairs.

"Hunting grounds?" Hesha asked, after a long silence.

"Everywhere. For a newcomer, if you seek crowds after dark, Park Street is good. The hotels are good. The grounds of the Maidan never quite empty, but I should not risk it. Too many trees, not enough masonry."

"Elysium?"

"Ah. You *want* to mingle with the Camarilla? Such poor taste, little brother. Very well. You are in luck, as usual. Tomorrow night the so-called Prince and his court gather to peck at each other. You will find them," he ended, well-bred contempt showing in every line of his face, "at the Bhooter Bari."

Hesha raised an eyebrow. "The Haunted House?" he translated.

"I am afraid so...I believe Malkav's courtier arranges the festivities during Monsoon."

They smoked again, presenting thoughtful faces to the passing mortals. At length, Hesha spoke. "I am greatly obliged to you for your time and wisdom, Subhas Babu."

"May I offer you the opportunity to redeem your debt at once?"

Hesha cast a noncommittal eye over the Calcuttan elder. "Please do, sir. Please do."

"I hear a great many rumors about the situation in the United States. Would you favor me with your considered opinion of events there?"

Hesha nodded, and wreathed himself in pipe smoke. "I speak from the outside, of course," he said, thus reserving the Eye and his own losses from the story, "but the facts as I know them are yours...."

Much later, on the dirty steps of a closed bookshop, in a crooked lane off Albert Street, a dark and ragged figure sat as if asleep. From his urchin's perch, the waiting spy watched a tall, dark, bald stranger stride past him and well away into the rainy night. When the black man was out of sight and hearing, the figure unfolded itself. Short, but taller than he had seemed sitting; poorly dressed, but less tattered than first glance would have shown; dirty and saturnine, but more handsome than the layers of grime would suggest—he flicked his wet hair out of his eyes, turned to an empty space in the air beside the steps, and asked it, "Him?"

Saturday, 17 July 1999, 11:33 PM
Bhagyakul Roy Palace, called Bhooter Bari
Calcutta, West Bengal

Hesha approached the palace from the south. The weeds that choked the pavement had been crushed down by many feet before him; he trod a well-worn path among the enthusiastic vines and grasses. Through the thick, gray veil of rain, he looked up at the old manse. The architect had graced it with cheap copies of classical Greek statues; squatters had added still uglier wire television antennas. The original owners had displayed their wealth in marble and rare stones; time, floods, gentle decay, and encroaching trees had destroyed the mortar and cracked the elegant facade. The windowless walls still stood, the columns and arches were intact, but in the portico where the original family's livery-clad footmen had waited on guests, two dozen shabby, unkempt men crowded close to take shelter from the storm. Smoke rose from pipes and damp cigarettes in their hands. Cheap speakers spewed out a woman's voice: bubble-gum pop with Bengali lyrics.

Hesha glanced back to the treeline and climbed the palace's broken steps. A large man, seated in a position of importance on a column base, rose to greet him.

"*Salaam*, sahib. Members only," he said dully, and prepared to sit down again.

"*Salaam*, bhai," Hesha uttered, in tones of command. The guard stopped moving. "I have a message for one of the members."

"Very good, sahib. You give it to me, I give it to him."

Hesha climbed the final step and faced the poor man down. "I will give it to you," he said, "if you will take it immediately to your lord."

Seriously now, in tones of great respect, the guard placed his hands together over the note. "Very good, sahib." Grateful to go, he scrambled over his fellows and into the shadows beyond.

Half an hour later, the guard returned. He shot commands to the others. They scuttled back into the mansion like rats into holes. The leader himself disappeared, and, onto a clear stage, the Camarilla Court of Calcutta filed into sight.

Hesha waited for them, three steps down, wet but untroubled by it. If his robes were rain-heavy, they were that much harder to see through. If his cane and monocle and bare head glistened unnaturally in the house lights, so much more effective his lone figure would be. As a final touch, he made visible the coiling snake tattooed onto his bare scalp.

A long-faced, blond gentleman in a pale gray suit came to the front of the portico. He and his visitor exchanged long, unhurried silence, and then (clearly to the shock of the Kindred closest to him) he descended gracefully down the broad steps to where Hesha stood.

"Let us walk," said Lord James Abernethie, Prince of Calcutta. "And you will tell me why an openly professed Follower of Set seeks audience with me."

"I am," replied Hesha, "merely presenting myself to you upon arrival in your domain. That is one of your laws, is it not?"

The Prince smiled slightly. "Hardly one I would expect *you* to obey."

"In this case, it is purely a matter of practicality. I am here on legitimate business; I do not wish to alarm you, nor would I care to be attacked in the course of conducting my affairs."

Lord Abernethie drew to a halt. Neither he nor Hesha were inexperienced enough ever to look another Kindred in the eyes unless they were *certain* what they would find there, but the Prince came, in his ire, as close as safety allowed.

"And why in hell should I let one of your kind follow the rules?"

"It is," Hesha began, "*your* Elysium that would be broken. The sympathies of the Court would undoubtedly be behind you; but is it quite safe to have anyone standing," he paused, "*behind* you? As an added consideration, I bring three things. A gift..."

He clapped his hands, and a small, ill-tempered man stepped out of the trees. On a rolling cart, with immense difficulty, the servant pulled a large, olive-and-khaki-colored steel case through the weeds. Hesha pointed, and the Asp brought the cart to a skidding stop half-way to the house.

"Shoulder-to-air missiles. British make, not Russian. And a launcher, of course."

"And why would I need those from you?"

Hesha leaned thoughtfully on his stick. "Eastern problems, perhaps?"

The rain chattered around them, but James Abernethie said nothing for some time. "I accept," the Prince allowed, finally, "pending confirmation that they are as you say, and fully operational. What is the second item?"

"My promise that I do not intend to settle in Calcutta."

Lord Abernethie laughed out loud. "And the third?"

Hesha took from his vest pocket a thin plastic packet. He handed it to the Prince. Lord Abernethie opened the packet, using the envelope to shield the contents from the rain, and read—and recognized—the handwriting on the letters within. His death-pale skin blanched further, and he forgot himself so far as to look the other in the eyebrows.

"Welcome," he said shortly, "to my domain. Won't you come inside?"

"Thank you, your Lordship," said Hesha.

Lord Abernethie, after performing introductions between the visitor and the most distinguished of the guests—their hostess was missing and could not be found—handed his social duties over to one of his childer: the Rani Surama, a dark and dutiful daughter, native to the country (as Lord James was not), wrapped in a flame-orange sari and perfect manners. She took him round to meet each cluster of attendees, then established herself and Hesha in an out-of-the-way corner. Many of his new acquaintances made courtesy calls upon him, but his beautiful escort's discouragement kept the intrusions short, and one o'clock found them deep in conversation.

Surama's long and exquisite hands played lightly along the strings of a zither. It was an antique brought to the palace by her father, and the young Ventrue made use of it for music, for show, and to open a close and probing dialogue on Bengali antiquities. Hesha laughed, smiled, complimented the young lady on her talents and her homeland's treasures. Behind the civil mask, he kept track of the gorgeous creature's attacks and feints as clearly as though she dueled with swords instead of questions. She was checking his story, probably on orders from Lord Abernethie; she was curious on her own account—the waiting court had been given no hint of the Setite's three gifts; she was trying, poor infant, to seduce him.

Eventually, Hesha caught sight of a teenage boy in the crowd. Deferentially, the slim, bony figure made his way to where Hesha and Surama sat. He stared at the floor before him as he spoke. "Rani, your father is looking for you, you know."

"Is he really? Thank you, Michel." The Prince's childe took her leave of Hesha, and wandered away into the party. Michel's eyes followed her longingly; his heart lay in his face. Softly, in archaic Kurdish, he said: "What the hell are you doing, coming in the front like that?" His inflection suggested heartbroken poetry.

"Time is important," Hesha answered in the same language.

"Typhon's pet prophet in a hurry." The old Tremere wizard, a long-time debtor of Hesha's, shook his head. "I don't believe it."

"The Eye of Hazimel is loose in America."

"I'm glad I'm here, then." He paused, and then added: "Just so you know—I am the *greenest* neonate, no more than twenty years dead, sent here by the Chantry in New Delhi. Since my arrival I have become the little Rani's devoted slave."

"I shall do my best to reinforce the idea," said the Setite. "However. The directive force behind the Eye is in Calcutta."

Michel's face took on an even more mournful expression. "You are sure?"

Hesha did not bother to answer, and Michel took up Surama's discarded zither. "What do you want me to do?"

"Pinpoint the source. Then tell me where to find it."

"Mmm." Michel began to play a lovesong. "Hurry, if you are hurrying, and give me the details before she comes back."

"She won't be coming back."

"Why?" The warlock glanced at his companion, but the Setite didn't respond. "Sorry. How could I forget? 'Nothing-for-nothing' Hesha, as always. Let me see.... Lord Abernethie's blood weakness is girls—very young girls."

"Lord Abernethie's daughter, the Rani Surama, is an ambitious young leech with poor taste in friends. I brought proof of her treason with me tonight." Michel stared at him. "I would not make contact with you without providing the good Court something more interesting to watch while we spoke," said the Setite simply.

As the rumors began to fly through the assembled Kindred, Hesha gave the Tremere details enough, and no more. The commotion in the outer rooms grew louder, and the Setite finished:

"You will find me at the Oberoi Grand. I will dine in one of the restaurants each night with a brown-haired white woman as camouflage. Come to our table and talk to me about antiques. It should not compromise your position; I have encouraged half the leeches in town to do the same."

"Then you'll see me tomorrow. If the trace is as strong as you say, this won't take long," said the warlock confidently.

By the time one of Michel's 'friends' came to tell him his lady-love was in danger, the two devils in the corner were ready to act their part. The boy ran, awestruck and anguished, to the Prince's audience chamber. He still clutched Surama's zither in hand. Hesha stood, found a gossiping circle of Cainites to mingle with, and settled in for a long, dramatic, and tedious evening.

Sunday, 18 July 1999, 9:16 PM
Hesha's suite, the Oberoi Grand Hotel
Calcutta, West Bengal

The last closed door to the big room opened, and Hesha came out in a loose, simple black suit that stopped a cut short of a tuxedo. He glanced at the woman waiting, then began filling his pockets with equipment. Phone, cigarette case, lighter...

"Turn, please," he directed.

Elizabeth obeyed. Layers of pale-blue and amber gauze followed leisurely. Thompson scratched his stubbled chin. The Asp leered freely. Hesha inspected her indifferently, and spoke in dull tones: "Janet. Her arms, shoulders, and chest are too bare for Bengal. Are all of your selections along these lines?"

Janet Lindbergh's voice sprang from the phone. "Yes, sir. Jet-set, you said. This is what 'Society' is wearing. Liz—" Elizabeth, no longer smiling, looked toward the phone to wrest her gaze away from Hesha. "Liz, there's a cloth-of-gold wrap in one of the cases. Wear that; I ordered it in case of cooler weather."

"I'll get it," Thompson offered.

"Elizabeth," said Hesha. "We are going to go downstairs and eat. Have you ever had Mughlai food before? Good. Then we will order two sample platters. Offer me things from your plate; I will do the same. In the end you will have eaten most of what is set before us. You are going to pretend to be yourself, one month ago. You know nothing of my house or the security team. You came to Calcutta from Rutherford House at my request, and you are here to assist me in purchasing antiques and transporting them to America.

"I expect that perhaps half-a-dozen people will come to see us tonight. Some of them will be perfectly innocent acquaintances of mine. When I introduce you to them, I will mention Amy Rutherford. Some of them will be less than innocent; I will refer to Agnes Rutherford and you will leave the table, visit the ladies' lounge, and then return to the conversation. If I mention Hermione Rutherford, you will leave the table, visit the lounge, and stay there, pretending to be ill, until you receive further instructions by phone."

Thompson appeared, offering her shawl. "You look lovely," he mouthed. She smiled weakly but stood tall.

"Come along," said Hesha, and she went.

Monday, 19 July 1999, 11:54 PM
La Rotisserie, the Oberoi Grand Hotel
Calcutta, West Bengal

Elizabeth toyed with the last mouthfuls of her coffee. It had been a long evening, full of visits from Hesha's endless stream of acquaintances. Seven times Agnes's name had come up—seven times Elizabeth had had to visit the ladies' room and flutter convincingly to stall, sink, or mirror. The smartly dressed, middle-aged attendant had politely, pointedly, refrained from comment. It would take little acting now to convince the woman that the vain, crazy American tourist was ill, as well.

Liz watched her companion with concern. These two nights—in public—Hesha had been as attentive and charming as when she first met him. He smiled, he laughed with her, his hand reached occasionally for hers...but his eyes were cold. She thought, finally, that she was learning to read him behind the mask. Under the surface, there was not, so far, a tender word for her, nor a sign of the soft and honest glance she hoped for. He was...worried?

Hesha considered, carefully, the personality of his contact. Michel was confident, skillful, and reliable. The Tremere had said that his magecraft would yield results by Sunday night. He had meant this, and Hesha, remembering their efforts together in the Ottoman Empire, had believed it. It might be that the ritual had taken longer than the cocky old boy had anticipated. But Sunday had gone, Monday would come to its end in mere minutes, and there was not only no sign of the warlock, there was no word. It might be that Michel was so new to town that any messenger was risky. But Hesha found it hard to believe that the wily ancient had so few resources.

The restaurant staff were closing the restaurant down around them, and his reverie ended.

"Elizabeth," he said quietly, touching her hand. She looked up at him, waiting for instructions. She was tired; they had been on display here for nearly four hours. She played the part very well, but the strain showed. For an instant, the memory of real smiles on her face came to him, and he noticed what she was wearing —truly noticed—for the first time. Tonight Janet had dressed the girl in strapless, wine-red silk and the Asp had bought a shawl from the bazaars to cover Elizabeth's shoulders. It was a figured brocade of blood-red and jet-black. Hesha began to suspect his servants of exercising their sense of humor at the girl's expense.

"We are leaving," he said. He held her chair and helped her to her feet. With downcast eyes she collected her bag and shawl, and Hesha offered his arm to escort her. "Fortunately, the rain has stopped for now. We can have dessert on the terrace, and gain a little more time."

She kept her chin up, but her shoulders sagged slightly. She leaned a fraction of her weight on his strong arm, and together they set out for the damp, steamy darkness of the café by the pool.

Tuesday, 20 July 1999, 2:16 AM
Five Star Market, Kidderpore
Calcutta, West Bengal

Hesha, dressed in sopping-wet, cheap clothes, leaning heavily on his cane, staggered uneasily down the narrow paths of the bazaar. His retainers would not have recognized him; a dissipated, surly mask hid his face from mortal eyes, his hands were gnarled with disease, he went barefoot through the dirty, stagnating water beginning to gather in the low places of Calcutta. At a rundown, half-height, hole-in-the-wall of a shop, he drew to a halt and wavered back and forth. Hesha looked up at the proprietor. He was a man of fifty, skinny, wizened, and bright-eyed; then he…it…was a near-skeletal creature covered in drooping gray flesh that looked more like wasps' nests than skin.

"All right. I see you, you see me," said a voice like a chainsaw in offal. "What do you want?"

"Information."

"Hah. Well. I have a good deal of that in stock," said the thing sitting in the doorway. "What did you have in mind, old Nag?"

"First, tell me: Are we enemies?"

"I know you, old Nag, and I heard your name in the gutter, but I don't know you that well." The Nosferatu shifted slightly in his seat. "Is there a reason we should be?"

Hesha shook his head. "None…that I know of. I have always regarded your people as the only allies worth having, but I fear your kinsmen have changed their minds toward me." He paused. "I do not look for vendetta, I look for help from you. Do you hear any news from Bombay?"

"I may."

"Bombay can speak for me, if they will. I did them a service some years back."

The gray creature gazed down on him, and slowly spoke. "I'll trade you all I know about your status with my clansmen for all the reasons you think we're on the outs with you."

"Done."

"I'd never heard of you before your visit to the Haunted House." Hesha's face darkened; the Nosferatu held up a crumbling hand. "I know, I know, sounds like a cheap trade. But on my oath, I'll make inquiries and find out whether there's trouble, and why, and give you the information under truce. If we're foes, I warn you first, all right?"

"Now the deal is in my favor, I think."

"No, no, no. I am dying of curiosity; there's a story behind this, I'm sure."

"Your people pressed an invitation on me. To a party in Atlanta, under so-called Elysium. They *insisted.* I had other business; I sent my lieutenant. The party was a death-trap, my cousin was killed in it, and I," admitted Hesha reluctantly, "do not yet know whether your kin meant to catch me in it. There has been no word, one way or the other."

Silence passed heavily between them. The noise of the bazaar at night, the rain on tin roofs, and the shouts and music from the red-light district in the next street surrounded them. The gray creature rustled, then cranked out the question:

"So what's the thing you really want? That we had to settle up truce even to start to talk about?"

"Do you know of a young man named Michel?"

"Wet-behind-the-ears warlock? What about him?"

"We had an appointment. He failed to arrive. I don't care to wait pointlessly; I also feel that it is...unlike him to be less than punctual. I am worried that someone may be interfering with him, and thereby interfering with *me.* I want to find him—or find out what happened to him,"

Hesha finished blackly. "Now tell me," he said in more pleasant tones. "What can I do for you in return?"

"I hear that you're good at bringing things through customs. I need merchandise." Hesha raised an eyebrow. "Banned books, underground newspapers, dirty magazines, that sort of thing," the monster rattled. "I peddle my papers to the kine as well, brother Nag."

The Setite smiled. "I'm conducting business out of the Oberoi Grand. Bring a list with you and I'll have my people ship you as many as you can stock; enough leeches are seeking those kinds of services that you will blend in beautifully."

Wednesday, 21 July 1999, 11:24 PM
The Ming Court Restaurant, the Oberoi Grand Hotel
Calcutta, West Bengal

Michel came in through the front door, exchanged words with the maître d', and started toward Hesha's table. He was dressed well, though his trouser cuffs were darkened with water and mud. Almost naturally, he threaded his way through the crowd of tables and diners—but Hesha, sensitive to the subtlest detail, caught the unnatural: Michel was nervous, almost frightened. The panicky gait put the Setite's teeth on edge.

"Mr. Ruhadze?" said the young man, hopefully.

Hesha stood. "Michel. Have a seat. Can I get you anything?" The Tremere shook his head, and the millionaire waved the waiters away imperiously. "Allow me to introduce you—Elizabeth, may I present Michel Singh. His family runs an excellent investment firm in Bombay; they have turned the younger generation loose to shine in Calcutta. Michel, this is Elizabeth Dimitros, an expert on antiques and antiquities. I was fortunate enough to convince Rutherford House to lend her to me for this trip—you know Hermione Rutherford, perhaps?"

"I'm afraid I haven't had the pleasure," mumbled the bashful boy in the third chair.

"So pleased to make your acquaintance, Michel," Elizabeth rang in, sparklingly.

Michel looked up and made an effort. "Oh, certainly, certainly. I'm charmed, Ms. Dimitros—Elizabeth," he amended, as she opened her mouth to suggest it. For a moment, the whole table smiled.

"Now," said Liz, as if searching her memory, "we were…oh, of course. Michel, I feel terrible running out just as we've met, but I was about to…ah…" she gestured gracefully toward the ladies' room, "powder my nose. Will you excuse me for a moment, gentlemen?"

As soon as the woman was out of earshot, Michel leaned in and began speaking. "I've been followed. I need your help."

Hesha stood immediately. "Come with me." His hands strayed to pockets—he hit the emergency code on the phone, readied weapons—and he maneuvered to put himself between the mass of the room and his companion. Weak. Michel looked tired and hunted, but his boy's face was haggard, and, above all, *weak*.

All this time, Michel talked. "I found what you're looking for, of course. That's why they're here. You were wrong, Hesha—I didn't think I'd live to see it, but you were dead wrong. When the Eye is active, it doesn't draw on Calcutta for power. Calcutta sends power out to it."

Hesha steered the boy toward the kitchen door for safety. The service elevator…fewer crowds…fewer witnesses…they reached the wall, and with half the angles of attack covered, Hesha permitted himself to scan the room, then looked down at Michel in surprise. Michel had lost control—and consciousness—and the print of a small and bloody palm had appeared on his cheek.

Hesha snatched at the air where the invisible hand had rested. Nothing. He forced his eyes to find the stalker...and failed. He grabbed Michel by the waist and shoulders but found the warlock weighed down by another, unseen body. Hesha kept one hand on his contact's shoulders—pulled him up, down, sideways—discovered the opposing force moved too fast for him. Wounds appeared on the boy's skin—double punctures—and the Setite, frustrated, lifted Michel's helpless body over his head. He spun and began running for the doors.

In the corner of his eye, he caught sight of the thing.

She was tiny—no more than eight years old, had she been human—naked as a frog, and twice as fast as dragonflies. Her hair had been hacked off near the roots, her skin was dark, shading to ebon black at the fingertips and toes—and her tiny, delicate jaws were clamped on Michel's dangling arm.

In the moment before she knew she had been seen, Hesha seized her by the neck and broke her. The miniature assassin dropped off and ran. Her steps faltered, her head rocked from side to side, but she twisted through the rising crowds faster than the Setite could follow.

Hesha reached the front door, pushed his way past the confused hotel staff, and found Thompson waiting for him on the other side. Without a word, he thrust Michel's unresisting carcass into the bodyguard's arms and dashed after the child.

Elizabeth emerged from the lounge just in time to see him run past her. She followed without thinking, the emergency tone shrilling from her phone. He was in trouble. She ran, and fought to keep him in sight.

Outside, the monsoon rains poured down. The streets were ankle-deep in water; running feet threw knee-high spray that glittered in the city lights. Over the flood, there was a small shadow—Hesha trailed that. The Assamite could move faster than he, but she couldn't keep it up forever, and his legs were long. If he could keep her in sight.... So long as she stayed on the streets, there would be the splashing footsteps. Hesha swore. The imp's trail turned west, down a narrow alley. He could follow her through that, but her destination must be the park—the Maidan—poorly lit, grassy, spotted with trees, and huge. He called on Set to lend him speed, and kept running.

Elizabeth dove down the dark alley. Hesha was only a silhouette in the downpour before her; there were lights on the next street, at least. She gathered up her skirts, cursed the heavy, water-logged satin, and leapt over the trash and rats. Out, and up the street, and down another crazy lane, across a boulevard, through traffic—and into a morass of vegetation and mud. Hesha was still just visible, heading for a tangled mess of trees, across a triangle of water. Elizabeth kicked her shoes off and sped after him. Her stockings struck gravel and tore, her bare feet hit the mud, and she fell sideways into the pool. When she looked up, Hesha was gone. Thunder rolled across the commons, and she limped painfully out of the dirty water.

The Setite, blinded by the rain and whipping branches, followed the scent of Michel's blood through the trees. On the other side of the thin stand, he caught sight of the girl again. He sprinted, closed the yards she'd won in the wood, and began to close the gap.

Lightning struck.

Hesha shrieked at the flash. His eyes shut down and burned in their sockets, his world blanked away, and the Beast took him running. The curse drove him blindly, colliding into trees, into stones, into bodies, and the life they found the Beast took with them. In control of himself at last, utterly sightless, he fell to four limbs for safety, slipped, and ended in a puddle. Burrowing into the mud, pressing his raw-red lids into the cool water, he waited, face down, for the pain to fade, praying to Set to intercede against the light.

From far away, he heard a high, chiming laugh and, through the ground, footsteps only slightly heavier than the rain pelted away.

Thursday, 22 July 1999, 2:48 AM
The Oberoi Grand Hotel
Calcutta, West Bengal

"Don't bother, Ron. They're nothing." Elizabeth pulled her scratched feet out of the old cop's hands. She tucked her bare legs back under the wreckage of her dress—brass-green watered satin, it had been; crusty, mud-yellow, spoiled and stiff now—and slumped wearily over the sofa's arm.

"Nothing, hell. There's plague rats on the Maidan. Right foot, Liz. And eat your breakfast."

Time crawled by. Elizabeth ate little. Thompson tended the girl's left foot. Both of them watched their phones—as if watching would help—and waited. The Asp, on his, conducted short, whispered, coded conversations with hushed voices in other parts of the city. Twice, Thompson took calls: Janet Lindbergh, worried; Pauline Miles, offering the information that Kettridge had left Philadelphia for Albany.

"Thompson..." Elizabeth began cautiously, "does he *have* to be in by dawn?"

Ron lowered his eyes. "Of course not. He's supposed to check in. But he makes the rules; he can break them. Go take a shower, Liz. Hot water'll make your feet heal faster." He helped her up, and propelled her toward her room.

Thompson and the Asp stayed awake until they were sure, despite the clouds, that the sun had conquered the horizon. Without a word to each other, they sought out their beds. Sleep took hours to come.

•

"Elizabeth Ariadne..." said the man with the moon on his head. "What do you do here?"

Liz looked up from her seat in the lobby of the hotel and let her notebook fall to the ground. It, and the chair, and the ground beneath them faded away. She stood up—one stands, when a god speaks—one stands, also, when one has no chair—and tried to see the figure's face more clearly, but the moon's rays filled her eyes, and the voice was all she knew.

"I...I came to watch the dancers perform. Tonight they were acting out the Curse of the Deer from the Mahabharata."

"Doomed love. I see." The man with the moon on his head turned and walked. Elizabeth, without moving her feet, came with him. They trod on a soft surface, like skin, but it was likewise the cold, hard, night-blue sky. The stars scattered, just as Hesha's snakes scattered when he passed among them.

The moon-god came to a halt and spoke again. "The dancers are too early in the cycle. Tonight begins a different chapter, Elizabeth Ariadne. Look down at my feet."

She obeyed—she could do nothing else—and saw, in a blank space where the other stars would not go—from which the other stars had fled to do the moon his due reverence—a small, dim, red, insolent star that burned her eyes.

"The dance tonight, Elizabeth Ariadne, is taken from the War of the *Rakshasa*. The King Ravana has returned...the Demon Ravana is awake...the *Rakshas* Ravana wages war again." The shining hand of the stranger covered her gaze, and the red star let her go. "Can you remember this?"

Elizabeth shook her head in doubt. "I am dreaming."

"You are dreaming," said the god. "But there will be a way. In your hands, there will be a way—" He stopped suddenly. "They are coming for you, Elizabeth Ariadne. Remember, Elizabeth..."

"Elizabeth...Liz...wake up."

In her seat in the lobby of the Oberoi Grand, Elizabeth opened her eyes and saw Thompson's ruddy face and grizzled brows staring down anxiously.

"He's back," said Thompson. "Meeting in half an hour."

Elizabeth knocked quietly on the door of the suite. The Asp opened it, checked the hallway, pulled her through, shut and bolted the door fast behind her. He brushed past her, left the woman standing in the foyer, and signaled into the common room. Conversation sprang up immediately—hushed, urgent tones, starting in mid-sentence, starting at the exact word they had left off before the knock and the tiny crisis of opening the door.

"...Spent the day in a drainpipe?"

"Better than in the river. Remember it when your time comes."

Unacknowledged and alone, Liz stepped timidly into the conference and sat down.

"Where is Michel?" Hesha asked of Thompson.

"He's dead, sir. He was weak when you handed him over. We took him upstairs, washed the hand print off and tried to...revive him, but before we could do much with him, his body disintegrated." Thompson shook his head. "He wasn't dry, either. He bled, but one of the stains wasn't his blood. I think it was some sort of acid. There were glass fragments on the shirt before the stuff ate it away."

A long, uneasy silence took the room. Hesha, standing straight and solemn by the window, looked out on Calcutta. Huge drops of rain slammed into the glass. Beyond the falling streaks and the gale-tossed deluge, the city lights were dim. Colored neon, traffic signals, garish signs, and bright street lights, all wavered like fountain lamps. Calcutta seemed a city underwater, and the Setite could not see even so far as the horizon.

"Report."

Thompson and the Asp weighed in with the news of the last twenty-four hours. Names of strangers buzzed across Elizabeth's ears: Pauline Miles had lost a man; Das Gupta and Forrest checked in; the team covering the White Town sighted Smith, Jones, and Robinson but had lost track of Tom, Dick, and Harry... Johnson, Jackson, Jameson...Alex, Abigail, and Albert Street. Ramona, Ramana, Ravena, Ravana.... Elizabeth's attention strayed to her notebook, her hieroglyphs, her pen. The stream of information poured down around her like rain.

"What are you doing, Elizabeth?" Hesha's voice, curt and angry, broke into her reverie.

"I came to watch the dancers perform," she replied without thinking. "Tonight they are acting out the Rising of Ravana."

"Elizabeth!" This time, the Setite's tone cut through her, and she jumped. Her eyes met his like a cornered animal's, and she stared. Hesha picked up her papers. The top three sheets were loose, covered in gibberish, shot through with fragments of thoughts in English, and overlaid with line drawings of the three-eyed demon statue. Impulsively, he tore them in half in front of her, then stalked back to the window. "Report, Elizabeth."

Deliberately, Elizabeth Dimitros closed her notebook. She stood, angry-pale and tightly held together, leaning slightly on the glossy edge of the table.

"I will not." Her jaw clamped shut. "I will not call you 'sir,' either. I am not a secret agent. I am not a decoy. So far, the closest I have come to my own profession is browsing the antique shop downstairs. I don't know why you brought me here," she drew a heavy breath, "and by now I cherish no illusions that you will ever tell me the real reason. I was doing what I could on the papyrus from here; I was memorizing Vegel's transliteration notes. I was doing my best to ignore your illegal, impossible, inexplicable—since you never do explain when I ask—activities. You want to stop that, go ahead. I have work of my own I can do." She limped around the chairs to her room. "But I'll be damned if I'll sit here anymore."

The door shut behind her, and the lock turned audibly.

Thompson and the Asp kept quiet. They looked briefly at each other, then kept watch—a fleeting, corner-of-the-eye, nervous watch—on Hesha. With control and precision, he folded the torn papers between his hands. He halved, quartered, and tucked them into the breast pocket of his jacket. Finished, he addressed the open phone as if nothing had happened.

"Janet. Report."

Thursday, 22 July 1999, 4:02 AM
A subterranean grotto
New York City, New York

The dilapidated desk, large as it was, barely accommodated the stacks of books and papers piled all around the old, manual typewriter. The battered lamp nearby performed its duty even less adequately. Darkness threatened to swallow the desk, as well as the misshapen figure behind it.

The occupant, however, seemed to take no notice of its environs other than to prop its sizeable feet on the desk, very nearly shattering the fragile equilibrium of the various stacks. One piece of paper alone—the sheet held by gnarled, grime-encrusted fingers—held the creature's attention.

22 July 1999

Re: Hesha Ruhadze

FILE COPY

Report from Calcutta via Cairo----Hesha arrived and presented himself to Prince Abernethie; one of Prince's childer subsequently terminated; coincidence? Also: H. contacted local Tremere who was then assassinated; Assamite suspected.

Rolph reports from Atlanta----probable Assamite involvement in destruction of Hannah, Tremere regent. Hesha's man Vegel was there at the time.

Hesha allied w/ Assamites?
danger to us?
TRACK MOVEMENTS
as possible

Friday, 23 July 1999, 3:43 AM
The Oberoi Grand Hotel
Calcutta, West Bengal

Late and unannounced, Hesha strode into his suite. Thompson and the Asp, waiting, stood to receive him. With a nod, he dismissed the pair. Gratefully, they secured the area and went off to sleep.

"Good night, sir," said Thompson, leaving.

No, thought Hesha, *it was not*. He stripped his raincoat of equipment, stowed the tools, and hung the dripping trench to dry. Emptying his suit pockets, he glanced at Elizabeth's place at the table. Slowly, he set down two handfuls of tiny supplies. Abandoning shoes and jacket, he selected a thin, crooked piece of steel and stepped over to the woman's door. With an ear and a hand, he listened through the wood, and found no sound but slow, deep breathing and faint, steady heartbeat. The steel drew back the dead bolt, and the Setite opened the door a crack.

Scents spilled out of the room: young woman, old books, ink and new paper, faint fear and anger and tears. Hesha followed the trail; here she had stood in fury, here she had begun to cry, here was terror.... He pulled the darkness safely around him, and crouched by the edge of her bed.

Hesha watched her thoughtfully.

It would be too much to say that he regretted losing his temper with her. His analysis, conducted behind the walls of his self-control, found his own conduct... unsatisfactory. It was unnecessary to bring the woman to the sundown conferences; it might, in fact, be dangerous. She had no need to know the greater picture, even in such limited views as his retainers were given. Elizabeth's duties could be explained just as easily in private, face-to-face. She now lay farther from his influence than ever, across a rift, put there by his own lack of restraint. He had let the masks slip away over a trifle, over nothing. And he could not even put the blame on the curse. It was his own temper; the Beast had simply laid back and laughed at the show. Michel's death was no excuse, no surprise. As he had lain last night in the flooded drainpipe, Hesha had known the Assamite child would finish her mission, one way or another, and had come to terms with all the implications, all the difficulties entailed.

Temper. Plain anger had gotten to him, and after the meeting, as he searched Calcutta, he had both carried it with him and found it everywhere. His Nosferatu contact had not appeared. That he—she?—was unavailable was reasonable, yet Hesha's reaction was unreasoning annoyance. He drifted down to Albert Street and found Subhas holding sway in the coffee-house. The courtesy and deference of the white-haired gentleman slowly disintegrated; Hesha's own civilized face fell, and the two old allies found themselves on the verge of all-out battle. Only the split-second's hesitation, the fighting instinct that sized up the enemy before striking, kept them back. In the dead pause, the experienced, careful pair recognized the false feel of the argument. Hostility quickly turned to mystified calculation—something outside their close-guarded psyches pricked them toward war. Subhas laid his hands on the table, Hesha eased his chair away, and they parted without bloodshed.

As the Setite left the coffee-house, he'd noticed the two students coming in, and the sounds of the young Brujah losing their control—the fleeing patrons of the shop, the howls of the rabble-childer caught by Subhas in a fighting mood, the shattered windows and broken bones—followed Hesha's keen ears down the street.

Seeking more clues, Hesha had waded through the rising water to the bridgeworks. Chaos reigned. The typhoon rained. The gypsy camps were flooding with the rest of the city, but what should have been an accustomed, annual retreat to drier perches was a screaming, surging confusion. A lone Gangrel, furiously calm, turned Hesha back the way he came. The cat-like creature had given out that the tribes were going mad, Bhanjaras and Khana Buddos all together. She blamed the Ravnos, and spat curses on them over her shoulder. Hesha left her before the rage could outweigh her determination to defend her charges.

No longer doubting the *influence* that pervaded Calcutta, the Setite turned to give the curse its due. He hit Park Street and the old cabarets, hunting as clumsily as a night-old Cainite. In his gut grew a fire such as he could not remember; beyond ordinary hunger, beyond the Beast's gluttony—an awkward, unfrenzied, foundering desire. It drove him into a bar. He'd come out with a light-skinned, long-haired girl of Elizabeth's age and build. Hesha pushed her into an alley and drained her dry without remorse. The Beast didn't take him over, didn't even try. Why fight for control when they were of one mind already? Complacent and contented, it curled around Hesha's new anger like a cobra around her eggs. And that made the Setite angrier still. *Unnatural*, he thought. Something deep and sinister was wrong in Calcutta. Hesha, on his guard now, believed he could fight its effects, but he prayed to Set that whatever it was would end soon. He prayed, too, that the elder denizens of the city knew themselves well enough to resist.

Elizabeth kicked slightly, and rolled onto her shoulder. Hesha stared down at her. Sleep had banished her worries...given her peace. Without consulting him, his hand reached out and stroked the hair away from the placid face. Her eyes twitched behind the lids, and her face began to twist into less happy lines. *More nightmares. How does she know?* The creature pulled his hand away, reset the locks, and sought oblivion in his own rest.

•

"Hesha..." said the god in the mask. "Blood of my blood."

"Lord?" Hesha opened his eyes and sat upright. "What do you want of me?" His traveling casket and hotel room were gone; the blackness of dead dreams surrounded him.

"Look upon me."

Hesha turned toward the voice, and made out shapes in the darkness. A vast, serpentine creature with a body like tar filled his vision. The night and the monster's flesh met only at the horizon. Directly beneath him, the figure of a giant with the red mane of a lion, the beak of a bird, and the horns of a ram lay fettered in its coils. As he watched, the god in the mask writhed in his trap, his muscles straining until the veins stood sharply up. The god freed one arm, and the ropy limbs of his opponent flailed about him until they found better purchase on his neck. Freeing his neck, the god sacrificed the arm again, and the fight returned to its starting point.

"My lord," said Hesha, kneeling. His own legs, he saw, were wrapped with the coal-black tendrils of the beast.

"Stand! You cannot afford to bow to me until I am free! Look, instead, upon my companions."

On every side of the god in the mask, there were other figures. Some, lying quietly but with their eyes open, were nearly free of the creature. Others, equally still, were so covered by the tarry scales that nothing showed of their own bodies; the monster had conquered all, and only the shape of the victim remained. A few—very few—wrestled as the giant did.

"And look, now, at what stands behind you." Hesha turned, and found only the empty darkness he had seen on waking. "Look *up*, blood of my blood, and understand."

And Hesha followed the god's commands, and realized that the night in front of him had a shape. It was a twisted pillar formed from the body of the thing below him, and it rose higher than a mountain into the dull sky of the dead. At its peak, wrapped almost entirely in the coils, was a figure the Setite knew well; he possessed a statue carved as its portrait. The demon, four-armed and hung with horrendous weapons, glinted black and blue and dripped red rivers of blood down the column that supported it. *Rivers*, thought Hesha. *The blood of a hundred thousand men...a million...*

"Grandfather sets now," said the god in the mask. Hesha turned back to see his master, and as the dream faded, heard the muffled voice of Set shout from beneath the twining body of Apep: "Remember!"

"Is there something wrong, Thompson?"

Ron's eyebrows shot skyward, and he swallowed hard. "You don't remember, sir?" He perched on the edge of the table, and shook his head. "Hell." He composed himself. "You woke up at sunset, and you shouted something—not in English—so loud the windows rattled. I came in to check on you." His gaze flickered worriedly over his master's face. "You don't remember that? Well...you seemed to be meditating, and you didn't seem to be under attack of any kind, so I left. That was about half an hour ago."

The Setite combed through his memory. There was a dream...something important...gone. He picked last night's suit jacket up off a chair, and sat down. Perhaps if he *did* meditate, the image would return. He doubted, though, whether the angry influence laid over Calcutta would permit calm, studied reflection, and the hotel, noisy with air conditioning and other people's conversation, was a poor seat for contemplation at any time. Some woman was carrying on now, close enough to be heard. Hesha folded the coat between his hands and tried to clear his thoughts. Paper crackled under the cloth. He pulled the folded sheets out of the pocket and turned them over.

Elizabeth had drawn the statue—*The statue was in my dream*. In English, she had written her own name, Hesha's names, 'Dances of India, 6:30 Daily,' rough alphabets, and then 'the red king' seven times and 'the red star' eleven. The printing, carefully formed, looked like scribe's practice. Each iteration of the 'r' in 'red' grew more refined, and the English words trailed off into repetitions of the single letter, which became mixed with a pointed, horizontal oval—the mouth sign that stood for 'r' in hieroglyphs.

Hesha looked back to the gibberish Egyptian. Of course...the woman, memorizing the characters, had practiced writing a language she was comfortable with: English. The writing was not nonsense; it was accidental code. He frowned, and started transliteration. "'Ris'bth" was her own name. "Hsh'" was his, though the symbology chosen was atrocious. "Rwn'" should be "Reauna," but...there was the same pattern, one letter different, "rfn'" which suggested, in India, 'Ravana.' Her consonant shifts tended toward German...with difficulty, he extracted 'red star,' '*rakshasha*,' 'king,' 'Mahabharata,' and 'awake.'

The Setite sat for a moment longer, listening to the echoes of the words in his head. Whatever had been sent to him during the day was lost for good, but he knew, without understanding why, that Elizabeth's notes paralleled the dream.

"Ask Miss Dimitros to step in, if she would."

Thompson grimaced, and began, painfully, "I...I don't think she can, sir." Hesha's eyes pinned him, and he went on, "She's delirious. She slept all day, and when you yelled, she woke up and started ranting about demons and ghosts and kings. I think she caught fever when she ran after you the other night."

The Setite rushed past him and into Elizabeth's room. She was sitting on the bed, trying to talk around the Asp, who was struggling, rather helplessly, to get her to lie down.

"...And the four travelers came to the City of Dreadful Night, to find the Prince of Ra—stop it. Stop it! Hey! But the King of the—let me go, you snake—but the King of the *Rakshash* slept under the heart of the mountain, and he heard the—" She broke off her story long enough to bite Raphael's arm, and the Asp retreated, cursing in Italian. "But the Herald of Ravana sent the Monkey-devil to destroy the accursed wizard...."

"Leave us," commanded Hesha, turning a cold, hard gaze on his minions. "I'll see to her."

Hesha picked his way over to the bed; the woman or the Asp had flung the blankets and sheets to the floor. Elizabeth, left to herself, sat tailor-fashion on the mattress, smoothed down her crooked nightshirt, and began reciting again.

"Once, in the City That Never Slept, there lived a young girl of humble family...."

"Elizabeth." Hesha sat opposite her, and searched her eyes. There seemed to be nothing behind them. "Who sleeps under the heart of the mountain?"

"Ravana, King of *Rakshasa*, slept under the heart of the mountain for ten thousand years, but now he slept no longer. The mountain tore open from root to tip, and the King strode forth to meet the Three from the East."

"Who is the Prince?"

"The Prince of the *Rakshasa*, Hazimel, who turned against his father and sleeps beneath the City of Dreadful Night."

"What is the Red Star?"

Her face contorted nearly into tears. "The red star disobeys the Moon, Hesha. I walked on the floor of your ceiling, and the red star bored into the sky." The empty eyes filled with pain. "Hesha?"

"I'm here with you, Elizabeth, but I can't see very well." He took her hands. "You'll have to tell me where we are."

"We're in the fields outside the Prince's tomb. There's a storm coming, and it's getting darker. The clouds are blotting out the sky."

"Good. The red star will not see us. There should be a building very close by; a temple," suggested the Setite. "It has lotus columns and statues leading to it. You can see the temple, Elizabeth."

"Yes..." she hesitated. "But it wasn't there...."

"It was *always* there, but you had not noticed it. We are going to shelter from the storm inside that temple, Elizabeth. I am walking toward it. Follow me out of the fields."

Her expression changed. "This is a nightmare," she said slowly.

"Come out of it, then. Can you see me? Follow me out of the dream."

Elizabeth came to herself, suddenly, as though she were a rope let loose in a tug-of-war. Hesha kept watching her, wary that the trance would pull her back again. Her eyes cleared completely, and he forgot to look away, wondering what it was that made them light and dark at the same time. Surely, in three hundred years, he had seen eyes like hers before....

"Where have I been?"

He shook his head. "I'm not sure. Thompson thinks you were fevered; I think you were caught in visions. I had something of the same experience myself today." Elizabeth looked down at their hands, still joined together. "Let me apologize for my temper last night. No one is quite themselves in Calcutta anymore." Her gaze rose to his again, and he said, slowly, "I understand you followed me last night, after Michel was attacked. That was very brave of you." He squeezed her hands. "Don't ever do it again," then added, "I want to know that you are safe."

Hesha rose and opened the connecting door. "Thompson, Elizabeth and I are going out to dinner. You and Mercurio are welcome to do whatever you want," he said, without turning to face his bodyguard. "Close your mouth. Calcutta is sufficiently dangerous tonight that you would not be able to protect us even if you had an army—and I think that Calcutta is *in* enough danger that it will leave us alone."

Ron Thompson paced along the Maidan with the slow, rolling gait of a cop on the beat—on his beat, in the rain, on a bad day, after an argument with the sergeant, during a gang war. With one eye, he kept tabs on the Asp in point position. With the other eye, he watched Hesha and Elizabeth strolling ahead of him. They seemed, despite all sense, to be enjoying themselves. Over the open circuit of his phone, he caught a steady stream of muttering curses. Mercurio, not content to express his disgust with mere body language, vented his spleen into the ether.

Hesha Ruhadze walked between his men. He chose to ignore them; he carried a huge golf umbrella with a ridiculous pink-and-white canopy. His attention centered entirely on the girl by his side. She wore a thin black dress and a thin black raincoat. Elizabeth's sandals flowed with the Hooghly's water, but the tears that had threatened since they came to Calcutta were dry at last. They wandered into the Maidan grounds, and the Friday-night carnival air swept around them despite the rain. The snake charmers, beggars, flower sellers, and street performers gave him a thousand scenes to show her, and enough things to talk about that avoided...unpleasantness.

A bead-seller, draped with hundreds of strings of his own wares, approached them, hawking his cheap glass fervently at the lady. The Asp closed in, and Hesha felt Thompson's lingering resentment step nearer. Elizabeth listened to the man's pitch and smiled, but shook her head. "*Na, dhonyabad*."

Hesha chuckled, and moved her along. "Your Bengali pronunciation is very interesting."

"Why doesn't that sound like a compliment?"

"I am sure the man was flattered that you made the attempt. Most Americans don't." They turned, passed out of the little pavilion village, and struck out toward the city lights again. "Didn't you want any souvenirs?"

"Cheap beads? I can buy the same kind in New York...if I ever get back to New York." She frowned up at him.

"You'll go back to New York." Hesha assured her. He switched his grip on the umbrella and clasped her hand. "I promise." Elizabeth, neither satisfied nor seeking to argue about it, let him keep hold of her hand as they walked. "Let's go up to the bazaars and take a look. The shops may be closing, but I'll find you a souvenir worth having. Something nice for your apartment? A rug? A handmade leather desk set for Sleipnir? Do you," he asked seriously, "care at all for brass?"

"Brass?"

"India is very good for brass...." He led her north through a maze of little streets, and they came out on a wider avenue lined with shops. As they went, the Asp scouted ahead of them. Thompson checked their trail to be sure they were not followed. Hesha kept his own eyes open. And Elizabeth, without thinking about them much, noticed two things: First, that the signs over the stores and on the billboards used a little less Sanskrit and English type and more Arabic letters; second, that Hesha, whom she had never seen wearing jewelry anywhere but around his neck, had on a string bracelet. As they walked hand in hand, their wrists rubbed against each other, and the beads knotted into the bracelet chafed her skin.

They made their way up the little bazaar, taking a last look around establishments closing for the night, window-shopping at the Muslim stores that had shut at sundown for the holy day. Then Elizabeth, at first content to follow where her companion led, started choosing their path. To begin with, her side-trips made sense—an antique store, a sari weaver's, a stall parting with the last of its sweet pa'an desserts—but gradually, any little thing could catch her eye and send them down an alley and up the next street without explanation.

Hesha gave her sightseeing full rein, even when the excursions lost reason and Elizabeth seemed to wonder, herself, why this building or that intersection was so interesting. She came to a halt near an old, ill-kept mosque, made a comment on the architecture, and suddenly decided to duck into a tiny passage nearby. The Setite joined her in splashing down the sidewalk—acting, to Elizabeth, as if a wild dash through the dark gap between two old houses was normal. The tiny lane bent halfway through, where the tenements facing one street met, crookedly, the backs of those facing the other way.

And in an instant, Elizabeth felt Hesha's hand leave hers. By the time her eyes could find him again, his arms held writhing darkness. Thompson and the Asp's strangely subdued flashlights drove the shadows back, and Liz saw in horror that Hesha's changing hands clutched a child.

Hesha pinned the tiny girl to a cracked stucco wall, and the skinny, charcoal-colored waif let out a thin cry. Doubling up her little body, the child got her knees beneath her and leaped out. The plaster shattered, but the force of her stick-thin legs was enough to propel herself and the Setite across the alley. They slammed against brick stairs on the other side. The child, her head down and fastened like a tick to Hesha's forearm, pushed away again. The wrestlers swung round against a softer surface—Elizabeth—and hurled the mortal woman into the wreckage of the first wall.

The lights moved in, wavering, and then stopped abruptly. Liz felt the Asp beside her and found a hand reaching down to lift her to her feet. Standing again, she looked toward the battle. The smaller figure, despite the warm lights, was only gray-brown, barely visible. The taller figure stood over his enemy on weirdly jointed legs and struck at her with scaled talons. He tore wounds across the child's naked skin with a whip-like, forked tongue two feet long.

Elizabeth drew breath to scream, but the Asp was faster—his arm curled about her neck and his callused palm covered her mouth before the sound escaped her. She choked, tried to bite him, but stopped. Pressure on her nostrils warned that he could suffocate her as easily as silence. In his other fist, she saw the silhouette of a gun, changing aim with almost mechanical precision as the fighters moved back and forth. When it stopped, when the furious spray from the whirling monsters died down, Mercurio shoved her forward, and Liz saw that the fight was over.

"Gloves," ordered Hesha.

He dropped the body of his enemy into the water beneath him. It twitched, and the Setite walked onto it with his thick-soled sandals. One heel ground the child's chin into the pavement. Elizabeth flinched. The victor rinsed his claws off in the stream, and Thompson stepped forward, snapping latex gloves onto his master's re-forming hands. Hesha immediately threw down his blood-stained raincoat, peeled out of his shirt and trousers and let them fall into the rushing flood. He checked himself over and carefully washed away the red-black ichor from his wounds.

"Clean, sir." Thompson confirmed.

Elizabeth shuddered. Hesha's scaly hide had begun to seal itself; the gashes and bites inflicted by the creature under his foot closed up. None of them had bled. The scales melted away, and with the change in his skin, the odd joints and height disappeared. Ron signaled to the Asp. Raphael took aim on a spot under the water. Thompson slipped out of his own coat, draped it over his boss, and returned to the staircase and a steady, two-fisted grip on his pistol.

Protected by the gloves, Hesha reached down, seized the girl by the forehead and jaw, and pinned her against the brick steps. Her infant muscles worked terribly against the pressure, and half-formed sounds fought their way through clenched teeth. Without warning, the Setite released his grip on her chin and the child's mouth flew open. Faster than the watching mortals could see, his fingers darted in and came out holding a gray, flapping piece of dead tissue: her tongue. He threw it into the gutter, clamped down on her skull again, and looked into her eyes. She shut them quickly.

"Thompson. Give me a gun and silencer. And pry her eyes open." Ron said something beneath his breath, but Hesha caught it. "Cut the lids off, then."

The old cop moved in. He fit the weapon together and laid it on the step below Hesha's hand; he took a small knife from his sleeve and bent over the child's head. The Setite leaned closer to the gray face and spoke short words, commanding words, at the girl. Her lips still formed the beginnings of syllables. He shouted Arabic at her, whispered it, searched the ruined eyes for signs of obedience or uncertainty. "Quiet," he tried in English.

"Hold her head," he said shortly. Again, he let her jaw free. With a crack, the little girl's jaw disintegrated as the bullet passed through, and when the blur of movement stopped, a quarter of her face lay splattered on the plaster wall across the alley. Hesha tried his commands again. Finally, as her captor concentrated on overpowering her will, the small, determined creature on the steps managed to make a sound.

Hesha jabbed at her with a careless, impatient claw. He regretted it instantly—there had not been enough left of the girl to take the ragged cut. She shrieked, shriveled up, and dried to powder on the spot.

In the empty moment afterward, there was hardly any noise in the alley.

The rain rattled and plonked over the wreckage. It had before; it would again. In Calcutta, in July, the sky falls on the city. Rain fell on the dust that had been an Assamite and turned it to mud.

Elizabeth, still the Asp's prisoner, sobbed in terrible, heart-broken gasps. Her breath hurt her; the water on her face was not the rain. Her full and stinging eyes flickered slowly around the circle of light. She feared what lay outside it, and she feared the three men standing in it with her. Hesha moved toward the Asp, and behind him Thompson gathered up the tools of the gruesome surgery. Liz's gaze retreated; she would not look at either of them.

"Let her go," said Hesha. "Let her go."

Released, she staggered, and the monster caught her by the arms. Gently, he turned her down the alley, away from the fast-eroding corpse on the steps, and started the long walk back to the hotel.

Saturday, 24 July 1999, 2:24 AM
The Oberoi Grand Hotel
Calcutta, West Bengal

Elizabeth, bending over the sink, looked up from the drain to the faucet. A dark-brown hand held a wet washcloth out to her—her eyes flickered up to the mirror and saw Hesha standing behind her. She was sick again, and he held her shoulders while her body fought to void an already empty stomach. The acid trickled into the running water. The damp cloth moved coolly across her forehead. Her convulsions stopped, and he waited while the woman rinsed the bile from her mouth.

"Don't touch me!" She wrenched violently away from the creature's unresisting hands.

Hesha stayed where he was and let her put the whole length of the room between them.

"She was just a baby. *A baby!*" Elizabeth shrieked the last word.

"No," said Hesha.

"You killed a little girl," she spat at him, "a child. You tortured a baby girl to death."

"No," repeated the monster, calmly. "This is part of the nightmare you had earlier."

"Goddamn you! Goddamn you, this was real. I saw you do it." She burst into tears. "Why did you *kill* her?!"

Hesha stepped forward, carefully. He stopped at a finely chosen point—exactly the distance she would allow. "This is part of the nightmare. Your Red King under the mountain. The Monkey-woman, sent to kill the wizard. Nothing in the nightmare is what it looks like."

"I *saw* you kill her," Elizabeth whispered dangerously. "And I saw *you*." She swallowed against the churning of her guts, and trembled. "What are you?"

The Setite shook his head. "Another part of the nightmare."

"No!" Her hands, clenched into white fists, beat against her legs in frustration. "Truth! What are you? What are you? *What are you?*"

He closed the space between them and gathered her into his embrace. They stood there for perhaps five minutes—the mortal woman shaking, shrinking from him, arms wrapped tightly around her body to protect herself from him, but crying on his shoulder just the same. Hesha said nothing, yet he held her together against the wracking sobs. They slowed, the anguished cries subsided into weeping, and when he knew she was mistress of herself again, he released her.

Elizabeth tried to retreat without having any place to go. She collapsed onto the carpet in the corner, and said dully, "Leave me alone."

Hesha knelt on the floor, just out of arm's reach. He was aware, suddenly, of the warmth left on his skin by her body and of the hot, damp tears soaked into his shirt. Under the sound of the woman's ragged breath, he began to notice her heartbeat. He shook off the rhythm of her blood and broke the silence.

"I killed that creature," said the Setite evenly, "because she had tasted my blood, and she had endangered my mission and my people, and because she killed Michel." He spaced the words out, let them fall on her slowly.

"Who was Michel to you?"

"The wizard. And she was the Monkey-woman sent to destroy him. She—it—was not a child; not a baby girl for you to cry over. She might have been a child, a century ago. But my enemies took that child, trained her, killed her, and turned her into an assassin under their control." He paused. "A tool for killing."

From where his heart used to be, there came a whisper: *What kind of tool will you turn Elizabeth into?*

"I told you I keep buried dangers from coming into the wrong hands. I came to Calcutta because one of the worst of them is loose in the world. The Red Star that terrifies you in your dreams." He looked at her. She was listening, at least. The mention of the star struck her, and she might be prepared, finally, to believe in what he had come for. "Michel would have found its source for me. Together we could have learned enough, I think, to stop the Eye—the star—if it were being used for harm." His voice hardened. "The assassin put an end to that hope. More people will suffer because of that girl and whoever paid her to kill my friend. They destroyed him to keep him from talking to me." He wondered as he said it if that might even be fact.

Hesha leaned back against the heavy curtains, and stretched his legs. Heavily, sadly, he told her, "But you...you shouldn't have had to see that. It was terrible, and I *am* sorry that you have come so close to the center of this." He studied the bedspread, her night stand, the room beyond. After a precise interval, he looked back to the woman in the corner, and held a hand out to her. "Forgive me, Elizabeth," he pleaded. He shook his head, and said again, "You shouldn't have had to see that." *Lord,* he prayed, *you sent me a seer when you knew I had lost Vegel, and I am grateful. But why this woman? And why did she have to see so much so soon?*

Hesha felt warm fingers clasp his, and he sighed with what breath he had. He looked to her; he followed her glance to their joined hands; he smiled ruefully.

Elizabeth took his hand in both of hers. The cuff of his shirt lay over the wrist, but she thought, underneath...there it was. A bracelet of knotted hemp and polished white beads. The largest hung low, and she pulled the string around to see it better. Without surprise, she recognized the white eye of the statue.

Neither spoke. The room had been peacefully calm a moment earlier. It was dead calm now, charged for a storm.

"You always," said Elizabeth, "wear that on a thong around your neck. Why is it on your wrist tonight?" Before he could answer, she pursued the logic. "You put that on your wrist. You took me walking, and you put it up against my wrist." More slowly, "And after that, I started...going sideways. Going places for no reason." She closed her eyes and pulled her arms back around her knees. "That was why you were nice to me tonight. So you could hold my hand and put that in it. I was just...the string on the pendulum....

"You used me."

Hesha grew a claw and cut the bracelet off. He closed his scaled hands around it.

"Yes," he said.

"To find the girl."

"No. I didn't know what you would take me to." The Setite paused, rubbing the stones in the bracelet against each other. They clicked like the blue prayer beads of his long-lost home. "Given time I could find anything in the world myself. I don't have time, Elizabeth. I am looking for short cuts. I need fast answers. I put you...in circuit...with the eye stone to trace the source. I did not expect to find the assassin; that is the truth."

Very quietly, Elizabeth murmured: "But I am still just the string of the pendulum to you."

"No. The string in the pendulum is any cord, any thread. You are irreplaceable, Elizabeth." And as he designed the lie, he realized that it was true.

"Irreplaceable," she repeated, laughing low in her throat. Hesha started—her tone had changed completely. From high hysterics, she had descended to a cynical, unpredictable level he wasn't sure he could reach.

"Why is that funny?" he asked sharply.

"Please," said Elizabeth, shaking her head. "Go away now. I'm tired."

The phone rang in the next room. Hesha looked toward the door, reluctantly. She laughed again, and climbed onto the bed.

"Go, Hesha. The *rakshasa* are calling you, and someone wants me to sleep."

"Hesha Ruhadze?" It was a man's voice, heavily accented but speaking English well enough.

"Here."

"I need to talk to you in person. Right away. I don't

think my name would mean anything to you. But I talked to Michel a few nights ago, and I think you need to talk me at least as much," said the stranger cockily, "as I need to talk to you." He let that rest for a moment. "I'm in the Pink Elephant, downstairs. Come in the next ten minutes, or don't come at all."

Hesha sidled diffidently into the darkened, music-drowned club. The persistent drumbeat crept up from the wooden floor into the soles of his feet. The smoke and colored, moving lights played tricks on his eyes. He scouted out the bar, called for a whisky and soda, and scanned the room for familiar faces. Relieved to find none, he pretended to sip his drink. With the attitude and expression of a determined late-night drinker, he stalked around the dance floor to a small, empty patch of booths and tables. The Setite sat in the crook of a curved bench, leaned against the wall, and proceeded to make the booze disappear.

After a casual delay, a figure detached itself from a group of girls gyrating in the flashing lights. With swaggering steps, the man approached Hesha's table and swiveled his hips under the table.

"Ruhadze. Nice of you to drop by."

The newcomer was dark-haired and handsome, but slovenly. He wore a wicked-looking, greasy imperial and his jet-black, arched eyebrows seemed as pointed as the mustache and beard. Locks of curling, untamed hair fell over the unnaturally pale brow, and he brushed them back as he smiled. Hesha examined him without comment. Tested by silence, the stranger lost. He hurried on anxiously:

"All right. I'm here to make a deal with you." He scratched at his chin. "You're looking for something. I know where it is. I can take you to it."

"Your name," prompted Hesha.

"Aren't you interested? I thought you were hot to find the..."

"Your name," the Setite ordered.

"Ravana. Khalil Ravana."

"Go on, Khalil. And call me Hesha, if you would." His momentum broken, the stranger with the *rakshash* name hesitated. Hesha filled in the gap. "Why do you believe that I am looking for something?"

"Michel," Khalil replied. "He came to me asking a pack of questions about...about a place I know. He'd had plenty of time to ask before, but he wasn't interested until you showed up. Then he gets killed here, on your doorstep. Word has it he didn't even get to sit down before they got him. So, I figure. You're looking for what he was looking for. And he didn't get the info to you before they got him. Now, I don't know who 'they' are, but I can guess. And I have a feeling that I'm not a *healthy* dead man anymore. I'm here to spill my guts so they can go after you, instead."

"How kind." Hesha steepled his fingers. "And what is it that you want from me?"

"Well, I'm not sure yet. Maybe you can owe me one."

Hesha shook his head. "Name your price."

Khalil shrugged. "Look. I'll show you the merchandise. I'll take you there. If it's what you want, we can work out the deal then. Call this," he seemed to be listening to someone on his left, "a service done in return for...future considerations." He wrinkled his mustache. "For one thing, you can get me the hell out of Calcutta."

"I am capable of doing that," confirmed the Setite.

"Right. So." Khalil nodded. "I'll meet you in here tomorrow, right after sunset, and take you to the spot."

Hesha lifted an eyebrow. "No. Tomorrow, at nine o'clock, we will meet you outside the hotel."

"Who is 'we'?"

"Who *are* we." The Setite folded his hands and stared

the unlucky Ravnos into momentary silence. "That," he said, "is my concern. Meet us outside, next to the bookseller, at nine o'clock."

"I never said anything about—"

"And I did not ask you about other people, either. Still, you will escort me and my followers from the bookseller, not this meat market, at nine o'clock. If you and your friend—" Hesha gestured to Khalil's left side— "wait for me here, you will find yourselves left behind when I leave Calcutta."

"Just one fucking minute, you dirty snake." The Ravnos's temper, magnified by the anger overlying the city, brought him to his feet, shouting. "I don't have to put up with this shit from you. There's no one else can take you to the—I could walk out of here right now, and where the hell would you be?"

"For some reason, Mr. Ravana, I don't think you *can* walk away from this. Inform your employer that I prefer to deal with principals; I will make an exception in this case for his or her sake. There can't be many truly…*expendable* peons at his disposal at a time like this." The Setite stood, bowed mockingly to the man he could see, sincerely to the invisible listener, and departed.

Behind him, mixed with the sounds of the music, he heard Khalil kick the table. It flew across the room, breaking glass and heads along the way, and a stream of curses followed it. When the Setite looked back, the younger monster was surrounded by half-formed shapes and blobs of color that had nothing to do with the club's lights.

Hesha fitted his monocle into place, turned to climb the great Dutch-tile staircase, and permitted himself half a smile.

Saturday, 24 July 1999, 11:03 PM
A back street in Grey Town
Calcutta, West Bengal

Ron Thompson sat, cold and wet, on the backboard of a shuddering donkey cart. His mood was as black as the night around him, which was saying a great deal. The typhoon—a thousand-year storm, by CNN's reckoning—had rolled in at dawn. If the sun had risen, though, Thompson hadn't seen it. The clouds were too thick. Despite having hovered over land for eighteen hours, Typhoon Justin showed no signs of slackening. The Himalayas had trapped the rain and wind on their way north. The gales that drove them could not force the system over the mountains, but neither were they giving up the struggle. The water ran three feet deep over the city. The lights in the more civilized portions of the city flickered and threatened to give out. And in the slums the madman with the reins drove them through, the power was gone completely. Visibility: zero. In disgust, Thompson gave up his sentry-post and hunkered down beside the Asp. The water and floating vegetable mess swirled about his ankles, but the bright green boards of the cart's sides afforded some protection from the wind, at least.

The little green wagon pulled up next to a massive, complicated ruin of an apartment building. Water poured over the cracked walls in sheets, gushed out and around the few rain spouts and tin gutters. Thompson and the Asp waited, looking up at the broken windows, torn awnings, and feeble shutters. When it became clear that the cart had really and truly stopped, they clambered down off the back of it. The Asp took up guard, so far as the rain would allow, and Thompson lent Liz a hand as she jumped into the knee-high brown flood. Hesha stepped out alone, on the opposite side.

Khalil Ravana leapt from the buckboard to the back

of the unfortunate donkey. With quick, practiced fingers, he unhitched the animal from the traces. He kicked her flanks—she refused to move—and he whispered horrors into her ears. Wild and white-eyed, the jenny fled the tiger's roar, up a short flight of stairs and into the half-shelter of an open hallway. He vaulted off, tied the beast to a railing, and turned to hop back down the stairs.

"Aiii!" A high-pitched complaint and a stocky, gesticulating female blocked his path. In Hindustani, she demanded an explanation of the donkey. Khalil snapped his fingers, and a heavily muscled man with an ax crested the stairs behind him. The phantom licked his lips and raised the bloody weapon over his head. "Aiiiiiii!" Twice as loud and three times as shrill, the screaming woman disappeared behind the corner and into a dark doorway.

Khalil turned a smug face to the four waiting in the street. He sauntered down the steps, opened a thick, surprisingly solid-looking door, and picked Hesha out of the little group by eye. "We're here. Come on." All four started toward the open portal. The Ravnos laughed. "No. Just you, Ruhadze."

The Setite stared wordlessly at his guide.

"What? What? You want to go back to the hotel empty-handed? You come alone or you don't come at all. I tried to tell you this last night, you cocky ass."

Hesha stepped closer to the doorway, examining the wood, the crumbling building, and the Ravnos's sneer. "*She* comes with me," said the Setite. His eyes scrutinized every muscle of the younger creature's face. Khalil's lids flickered, and a tic began over his right temple. For a moment, Hesha thought the man might lose control entirely—but as he teetered on the verge, the look the Setite expected came over him. Again, Khalil seemed to listen to someone close by, and his expression cleared.

"All right," he agreed, evidently to his own surprise. "But only her. The others stay here."

Hesha called out: "Give Miss Dimitros a flashlight and a camera."

Thompson and the Asp said nothing…so loudly that Elizabeth caught every word. The boss was nuts. The whole thing was a trap. The girl wasn't ready. The girl, at least, was dressed in jeans and sturdy shoes tonight. The girl wouldn't go. The girl would go. As their constrained, well-trained faces spoke all this, the two men strapped Liz into a web belt hung with tools, slung a rugged old camera—waterproof—around her neck, and clipped a fanny pack full of film under her raincoat. The last thing she read from them before the Asp pushed her forward was a kind of commiseration: not to each other, but identical glances, right at her, that said they had been where she was, and they hadn't liked it, and they wished she were anywhere but there. Oddly comforted, Elizabeth followed Hesha down the passage. She kept her hand on her phone, and repeated Thompson's list of alarm codes to herself keep her calm.

The dimly lit hallway ended in a staircase up. *I am being followed,* thought Liz. *Seven-two-two.* The staircase brought them to a half-balcony, broken at the outer edge. *Someone is in the room with me: eight-three-four.* Khalil led them into an abandoned apartment and over a roof. *The police have arrived: three-zero-six.* The roof came to a broken, twisted fire-escape. *I am wounded: one-one-one.* The guide wrenched a ladder free of the iron wreckage and propped it against a wall. *Hesha is wounded: nine-nine-nine.* They climbed up, walked along a bastion of old brick between two buildings, and paused at a dead end. *Fire: five-two-eight.*

Khalil disappeared into the bricks. His head and hands still stuck out above the baked clay. Hesha took hold of the callused fingers, and stepped into the illusion. He reached back for Elizabeth, and she took hold. Inside the bricks, she could see nothing, and so reached for her flashlight. They were on a spiral staircase with a very low ceiling; it led down into the masonry. The bricks gave way to stone, the stone to brick again, and the steps curled away beyond the stifled lamp's glow. Their feet made little noise on the dusty cleats. Soaked clothing failed to rustle; after a time it stopped dripping, and Elizabeth could hear, very clearly, that hers was the only breath taken in the musty chimney.

I confirm your call, she thought in defense. *Four-nine-four.*

At long last, the descent stopped, and the three crawled along a tunnel. It kept to the horizontal, for the most part, and wound through ruins that had nothing to do with cement, bricks, or the tenements above them. Between stretches of rubble and blank stone, Elizabeth noticed figure carvings and words written in something like Sanskrit. She would have stopped to study them, but the other two set a pace on all fours she found hard to keep up with.

I have lost eye contact: Eight-one-eight.

Suddenly, the elbow-bruising, knee-scraping passage opened out. Liz unbent, stretched, and played her flash over the path ahead. This place, tall enough to stand in, was a quarter-sphere: one flat wall, vertical; a tile floor, almost at right angles to the wall; and breathing-space carved out of the rubble. Behind them, the hole they had entered by. Ahead, the outline of a door. Its history leapt to the eye: sealed with stone, broken into, filled in again with brick and clay, broken a second time, a third—possibly more often. It was open now between shoulder height and the lintel, and Hesha had just climbed up the rubble and through.

Elizabeth set her foot on a stable-looking chunk of debris, held onto the jamb for safety, and gained the top of the broken seal wall. She crouched there for a moment, rearranging her gear. The flashlight, swinging from its clip, played across the curved, vaulted ceiling. The beam bobbed across Khalil's cheerful face and laid-back posture; he reclined easily along the top of a carved balustrade at the other end of the room. Liz aimed the light lower, looking for a spot to jump down to, and screamed—

Corpses covered the floor—some fresh, some skeletal, some in putrescent states of decay—and were covered in turn by rats, unhealthy, hairless, lesion-covered creatures that scurried into empty jaws, hollow ribcages, and festering flesh-tunnels at the sound of her cry. After a second's pause, they showed themselves again. Eyes red in retina-flash turned toward her meaningfully. A handful advanced on her; the rest went back to their feast.

Hesha's voice carried across the claw-clicking scrabbles of the vermin: "Leave her alone," he commanded.

Instantly, the horrors disappeared. Elizabeth shuddered. The bare stone floor lay clear now. She fell gratefully to it. Suspiciously, nervously, she took in her real surroundings. The ceiling remained the same; the walls, revealed, were carved rock, not rat-ridden earth. Khalil still lounged on his railing, but his expression lacked cheer. Disappointment lingered on his face. And Hesha, unseen before, occupied the far right corner of the chamber. His forefinger ran along the painted reliefs, not quite touching them, and his brow furrowed in concentration. Liz crouched by the door, watching him.

Khalil, for a good five minutes, had the patience to do the same. Then the Ravnos cleared his throat. "Good?" he asked brightly.

Hesha stopped and faced the Ravnos. "Good. But this is still not the source."

Khalil clicked his tongue. "Nope." But he showed no signs of moving.

"What do you want?"

"Well," Khalil sat up. "You're hunting for the Eye. It

sticks out all over you." He shrugged his shoulders. "I could be valuable guy to have along for *that* ride. It's our Eye, after all, not yours. So I might know things you'll need later." He scratched his chin. "So. If I show you the last room, you take me out of Calcutta with you. *And* you protect me. *And* you make *nice* to me," he snapped out, losing his genial mask to spite for a moment. "And I'll help you find that Evil old Eye."

Hesha considered for a moment, and then spoke—slowly, in carefully chosen words. "I will take you with me," he intoned, "and protect you," he paused, "as long as you continue to aid me in my quest for the Eye of Hazimel."

"Deal," shouted Khalil. He burst out laughing, and looked up at his new partner in a fit of camaraderie. "Imagine the look on old Abernethie's face—a gypsy and a snake taking each others' word for bond. Well, come on. It's down here." He tapped the floor with his toe, and a pit opened beneath his feet: rock-cut steps, leading down…filled, at the moment, with floodwater. Khalil dropped into it lightly, waist-deep, and grinned at Elizabeth. "Bring your aqualung with you, sweetheart?"

Hesha caught her eye. "Photograph this room. I want details of the murals." She nodded, and he followed Khalil down the hole.

Left by herself, Elizabeth propped her flashlight against one wall and began recording the other on film. When all four were done, she cross-lit and started again. With waterproof pencil and notebook, she made notes on the estimated measurements of the room. She waited nervously with the camera and lamp in her lap. The pool of water lay undisturbed. Eventually, she rose, changed the angle of the light again, and took a third set of portraits, this time with her notebook in each shot for scale. The time crawled by.

Am waiting at rendezvous: Two-seven-one.

Sunday, 25 July, 1999 12:34 AM
The burial chamber of an unmarked tomb
Calcutta, West Bengal

Khalil, bored beyond belief, lay full length on the stone lid of a muddy sarcophagus. His companion's light roved around the chamber like a darting yellow firefly; he himself would rather be back at the disco—better still, loose in New York. *There* was a city of sin for you. The Ravnos folded his hands over his belt and dreamt of America.

Hesha floated from wall to wall, scrutinizing the symbols, the designs, the scenes, and, finally, rows of script carved into the rock. Satisfied at last, he sighed. The burial chamber, even though he suspected it might be a false one, came from the same culture as the *rakshasa* statue—some of the work seemed to be by the identical artist, in fact. The few breaths of air he had held in his lungs for talking bubbled away, and his dead body settled more surely on the slippery floor. He kicked his sandals off to gain better purchase, drew his own camera out, and proceeded to go around the tomb in detail.

On the third wall, near the corner, he found the crucial passage. Instructions. Hesha paused, reading them, and stood stock-still for a moment.... He had sought the Eye for more than a century; the shock of success (though the Setite had always been confident of succeeding *eventually*) gave him pause.

Instructions for the containment, sealing up, and safe transportation of the Eye of Hazimel.

Hesha very nearly laughed. The task was tremendously simple...once you knew the secret. It had taken him more skill to translate the old script than he would need to catch the Eye. It was peasant magic, hedge sorcery, literally child's play—mud pies. Holy river water mixed with earth (*silt from the Ganges*, he thought, *from the Nile*) touched to the orb would close the lid. A thick coating plastered around the Eye would put it to 'sleep.' The dry and hardened clay would protect the artifact from harm...and the magician from the artifact. The scribe went on to detail a story about the rescue of the Eye from thieves, a tale of a mighty *rakshasa* who commanded it wisely, an invocation to Hazimel. The inscription continued below another relief, but the additional text was lost. Directly over a legend about the origin of the Eye, some illiterate hand had taken a chisel to the mural. The shallow scratches described a variation of a Bengali folk tale—the destruction of a demon-queen's heart with a palm-leaf sword. Hesha photographed that section carefully, cursing the graffiti writer. Perhaps he could decipher the broken carvings later. He moved on to the next panel, then the ceiling, and the sides of the sarcophagus itself. He took his time.

Elizabeth loaded another roll of film into the camera. She'd used half the supply already; better, she thought, to save rest of the exposures in case there were more rooms Khalil hadn't bothered to mention yet. If there were an angle of this chamber she hadn't caught, it wasn't for lack of trying. Or time.

She clipped the camera back onto her chest and picked up the light. Curiosity brought her to the first (or last) panel of the series. It was hard to know where the narrative—she was certain the carvings depicted a definite myth, not disjointed scenes—began, but you could start with this corner. Reading left to right, she traced a story in her own mind, at least.

In the first relief, a city fell to invaders. On the left side, it showed tall, beautiful buildings, on the right, the warriors outside the gates. In the second panel, the towers fell, the warriors controlled the streets, and the refugees poured out. Larger than the rest, and so, probably, more important, ran a strange man. Elizabeth studied him carefully. He bore a few of the symbols assigned to demons—*rakshasa* or *asura* or the evil dead—but his eyes were clearly the most important feature in the artist's mind. They didn't match. One was at least three sizes larger than the other, and the remains of the paint showed irises of different colors. In the third scene, the *asura* stood in jungle, surrounded by mountains, and in several poses across the landscape seemed to be commanding the construction of a temple or palace in the distance. In the fourth panel, the demon, large and central, took the left side to fight a band of invaders from the captured city, shown in miniature high in a corner of the design. On the right, he dispensed justice to prisoners tied to columns of his nearly finished building.

In the fifth section, by far the busiest and most difficult to interpret, an army from the distant city came to conquer him. Even understanding that the scene progressed side-to-side, Elizabeth found herself defeated. There was an army; there was the palace of the *asura*; the *asura* fought; but on whose side did the animals battle? If the demon commanded the beasts of the field, why were some of them in aggressive postures *inside* the palace's courtyard? If the creatures fought for the army, why were so many facing away from the *asura* and attacking, apparently, their own?

Unfortunately (Elizabeth listened to the sound of that word, and admitted she was biased against the demon with the mismatched eyes), the last panel showed a clear triumph for the *asura*. In his finished temple, he held court. Behind him, a large (or immensely important—size could mean anything at this level of pictography) demon-god with a hundred heads and arms stood in state. He, or she, or it, Liz concluded, must have sent the animals to help the demon win the battle. At least half its heads weren't human, and she picked out a number of rats, dogs, cats, monkeys, and asses among the crush.

Without warning, Elizabeth found herself flying back from the wall. Sprawled on her back by the steps, she looked around frantically, wondering who'd hit her. She realized, in terror, that the earth itself was moving. The tremors raised dust from the cracks in the floor and pelted the flagstones with grit from the ceiling. Elizabeth crab-walked to the balustrade and grabbed it for support. She braced for the worst. The Lord's Prayer shot to her lips, and 'Hail Mary' followed it. The last shock rolled through the ground as she got to 'now and at the hour of our death.' The vault blocks stayed where they belonged, the floodwater stopped jumping out of the staircase, and the gravel near the broken door lay still.

Her phone beeped, and she jumped. After the angry earth-rumbles, the modern, *friendly*, staccato tone seemed absurd. Elizabeth almost giggled in relief.

"Hello?" Thompson's voice, she thought. The static was so bad it was hard to tell. "Still with us?"

"I'm here," she answered.

"Hello? Hello? Anyone there?" The signal broke up entirely for a second, then: "Circuit's open, just...no one...can't get an answer."

"I'm here!" Liz shouted into the phone. "I'm here. What happened? Can you hear me?"

Thinly, through the noise, the Asp's voice: "Try again...street...."

The line went dead, and Liz stared at the little hand-set in disappointment. She racked her brain for *Have survived earthquake and can hear you. Connection too bad to speak*, but the situation seemed too specific. She sent four-nine-four, then holstered the phone and looked at the pool. The sloshing water revealed nothing of the situation below. She checked her camera for damage, retrieved her light from the corner it had bounced to, then pulled her legs up and sat tailor-fashion on the railing. Adrenaline—the second jolt of it that night—spread out from her stomach.

Elizabeth waited patiently for half an hour or more, just watching the water calm down. At length, she noticed a new ripple on the surface. She felt the railing cautiously for new tremors, found none her fingers could detect, and smiled as the pool moved more dramatically. The other two were returning; in a little while they could be out from under the ruins. She slid off the balustrade onto the flagstones, and walked around the railing to meet Hesha and the gypsy as they came out.

The water surged, and Khalil leapt up from it like a rocket. He shook himself like an animal in the air, flinging spray across the room. Liz shielded her eyes with her hand and kept her attention on the pool. A heavy thud reached her ears—she looked up and saw the guide bashing his body against the door seal. He hauled back and threw his shoulder against it again—he was trying to batter his way out, though the opening was in his arm's reach.

Elizabeth gasped, "What are you do—" and broke off when she caught sight of his face. Khalil's eyes stared out at nothing, so far open that the whites showed all around the iris. Stark, unreasoning terror filled them, and his wild-animal glance returned to the pit over and over again. His mouth hung open like a panting dog's, and his bared teeth were clear enough in the light: The canines, elongated into fangs, glittered cruelly.

"Oh, my god," whispered the mortal woman. She backed away from the monster *and* from the unseen danger down the stairs.

The Ravnos ran against the wall another time, so forcefully that he bounced back and fell howling onto the floor. His eyes began to change—the lids narrowed—now predatory slits, they searched the room for prey, not escape. The creature rushed Elizabeth, picked her up in clawed hands, and threw her into a corner. He pounced on the huddled body, stuck his nose into the crook of her neck, smelt her, pawed her collar half off her shoulders, and licked her bare skin. She scrabbled away along the wall. His face grew puzzled for a moment. Then all expression dropped from it, and the animal came back. Khalil jumped to her side again, seized her shoulder, and—

—a noise came from the pit, and his eyes changed again. He began to turn around.

Instantly, Elizabeth was aware of Hesha as a blur between herself and the monster. The scene froze: Khalil Ravana, spread-eagled on the floor, Elizabeth pressed up against the wall, Hesha in front of her, his hand still holding the blunt end of something pale piercing the other man's breast.

"Don't scream," the Setite said calmly. "The earthquake may have weakened the tunnels. Have you been wounded?"

"Just bruised, I think."

"Good. Now help me with him." Hesha dragged the Ravnos's corpse as far as the door. "Climb over. Now, steady the body as I pass it to you. Don't try to take the weight yourself." Together they manhandled the stiff through the opening, and Hesha began tying nylon cord around the dead man's torso. Elizabeth looked at the weapon in Khalil's chest and confirmed her suspicions.

"He's a vampire," she said, and her tone was so strange that for an instant Hesha stopped what he was doing.

Smoothly, he went on with his knots. Equally smoothly, he told her, "No. He's a *shilmulo*."

"He grew fangs. You staked him and he's dead, Hesha. He's a vampire," she insisted coldly.

"Elizabeth," said the Setite, with a trace of impatience, "if I staked you, would you still move around after the fact? If I pierced your heart, would you survive? Khalil will, *shilmulo* do, humans do not." He tied the rope ends to his own feet, and bent down to enter the tunnel. "Watch the stake. If it shows signs of coming loose, tell me immediately. I would rather not have to repeat the procedure in a more confined space." Liz hesitated, and he caught her eye. "What is it now, Elizabeth?"

"Does he drink blood? And don't go on about mosquitoes or leeches or Maasai. You know what I mean. Truth, Hesha."

Hesha looked down at the gypsy's face. Maverick eyes stared back at him, and flickered hungrily.

"He does," said the Setite, and he crawled into the hole, dragging the paralyzed Ravnos after him.

Sunday, 25 July, 1999 4:45 AM
The Oberoi Grand Hotel
Calcutta, West Bengal

"The room is secure, sir," Thompson's voice came from three earpieces in three different parts of the resort. "Hallway unobserved."

"Bring him around. Transport, watch for opening doors. Distraction, report and delay anyone coming up. I will come by the center route to provide a more attractive target."

Transport, in the form of the Asp, a bellboy's cart, and a suspiciously bulging garment bag, crossed the lobby and entered the service lift safely. Distraction, in the form of Elizabeth, stationed herself by the passenger elevators and played convincingly with camera, watch, notebook, sandal strap, and the morning newspaper. An early hotel maid found herself accosted for directions to a prominent shrine in an unmappable portion of the city. As Hesha passed by, Liz professed her thanks, double-checked a street name, and let the woman go.

"He's in," Ron announced. "Everyone come home."

'Distraction' strolled along the corridor to the suite. The Asp opened the door for her, smiled wearily, and they bolted behind them in unison. Elizabeth moved to the big table and began unstrapping gadget after gadget. She threw the film into the refrigerator, ducked into her room and changed her mud-stained clothes for fresh pajamas, and collapsed onto the couch to watch the others. Khalil, unwrapped but still frozen, lay on the floor in the middle of a bed quilt. Thompson and the Asp counted down, lifted, and carried the body into Hesha's quarters. They took the corner into the sitting room, and Liz picked up the sounds of final adjustments to couch, windows, and *shilmulo*. Thoughtfully, her fingers played over the keys of the little computer in front of her.

"Asp," said Hesha, "our guest will not be in the best of health or temper when sunset comes. Find a blood bank or hospital and steal ten or fifteen units from their stores. Cold supper will serve better than none…."

"Yes, sir." Raphael vanished into his bedroom.

"Thompson—I want you and Janet to find out everything you can about the tremors tonight. I want local coverage here, I want local from the source, if Calcutta was not the center. Full report on BBC, CNN, Voice of America, NPR, Chinese governmental, Russian public and private and pirate stations. Pick up the wire services, as well."

The old cop nodded, picked up his phone, received the laptop from Liz, and walked out, dialing.

Hesha turned, seemed to notice the last member of the team for the first time, and looked at her curiously. "Elizabeth? What do you want?" the Setite asked cautiously.

"You saved my life tonight, didn't you?" Elizabeth said, her voice full of wondering gratitude.

Hesha nodded. He felt better; he was on solid ground again. A thankful attitude opened up vast avenues of control over the girl. He raised one hand in a subtle, nobly deprecating gesture, and stepped closer to the couch. He decided to sit on the cushion beside her. He moved to do so, and she smiled at him. "You nearly got me killed tonight, didn't you?" she said, in an utterly different tone.

Hesha sat down on the coffee table. Warily, he waited for the rest of it.

"I looked *shilmulo* up on the Internet just now. Five

links to various Rom dictionaries…several dozen links to pages devoted to vampires, Hesha."

"There is no such thing as a vampire, Elizabeth. It is a buzz word that incompetent translators to English tack on to any mythological creature that survives by feeding on something in a fashion repugnant. The monster need not even drink blood to qualify for the honor, nor human blood, nor be undead—"

"Stop," Liz said abruptly. "Listen," she asked earnestly, looking into his ebon eyes with her amber-brown ones, "I…I think I may be in love with you." Just as solemnly, with the same serious yet uncertain cadence, she went on: "I think, also, that I would be better dead than feeling this way toward you…that I would rather see you dead, than to feel like this. And I don't understand why, after everything I have seen, I can still feel anything toward you." She took a moment's breath, and the creature in front of her thought of a little blue glass left in a refrigerator in Brooklyn, and thought he knew the answer.

"Please, Hesha…tell me the truth. What are you?"

The Setite paused, weighed the moment carefully, and slowly let his everyday mask slip away. Revealed, his skin was slightly lighter-colored. His bare scalp sported a detailed, coiling snake tattoo in deep black ink that had never faded. Open and unguarded, honest eyes looked out at the woman on the couch, and as he spoke his voice trembled a little.

"I am the dead priest of a dead god. That is the truth."

Elizabeth smiled bitterly. "You give me a different answer every time." A tear rolled down her cheek, and she rose to go.

"They might all be true," he said softly.

She kept walking and did not answer. Hesha stood, caught her door before she shut it, and gazed at her in appeal. "Close your eyes," whispered the Setite, slipping into the girl's room.

In surrender or weariness or hatred or lust or love, her lids dropped, and Hesha leaned down to kiss her lips. After a moment's hesitation, she kissed him back. The Setite felt her mouth move, but felt nothing beneath the surface of his skin. The Beast drove forward, listening hungrily to her heartbeat, thrusting the sound to the forefront of his consciousness. Elizabeth's arms stole up his back, drawing their bodies closer, and the Beast picked out the vibration of her life and savored it—cut off Hesha's connection to the floor, to the feel of her nightshirt under his fingers, even took the simple pressures of holding her, and of the fingers digging into his back. With an immense effort, he drew away—shook the veils from his senses—and took the clear moment to carry her to the bed. The Beast threw itself at his mind, but to the Setite's surprise and relief, the anger over Calcutta was gone. Without that aid, the curse was weaker than himself, and he locked it away.

His hand crept under her shirt. Her heartbeat pulsed through her ribs and flesh and into his palm. Hesha sought the woman's mouth again, and found it soft, warm, and more eager than before. His fangs slid down, and he tore the slightest wounds in her lower lip. She flinched, but he brought blood through the pin-prick holes. He drank slowly, hardly drawing more from the cuts than they bled of their own, and the mortal's gasping, shuddering breath told him the struggle was over. Elizabeth relaxed into his arms, unresisting, still holding him.

Hesha sipped delicately from the veins of his lover; the monster went on devouring his victim. Hesha savored the taste of Elizabeth's strangely sweet, adrenaline-sour blood; the Setite fed off a captive. Hesha felt the pounding of the girl's heart and was glad to know she shared the ecstasy; the calculating coldness of his mind counted the beats and measured their strength. When the steady rhythm broke and fluttered, he licked her lips clean, sealing the cuts.

He looked into her puzzled face, smiled, and whispered sleep to her. Elizabeth curled up under the blanket, and he put an arm over her. She slipped off into dreams, and Hesha looked sluggishly to the window. Dawn...he might make it to his room...but the drapes were closed tight here, the blanket thick...mortal women placed a particular importance on staying after...it might be useful...for controlling her...with his free hand, he pulled the discarded counterpane around himself in double and triple folds and piled the pillows over his head. Ra gained the horizon, and his descendant fell safely into slumber.

Thompson, checking around the suite for the last time before retiring himself, found Hesha's casket open. In dreadful anticipation, he opened the door to Liz's room. He watched her breathing for a moment, then went back and dug a mylar sheet out of the emergency case. With an air of duty done despite better judgment, he made Hesha's burrow sun-proof, and left them together.

Alone, sitting on his own bed, he stared at his hands. If he bent the wrists back and held them up at an angle, Ron could just see the pulse under the skin. He stood up suddenly, opened the curtains, and let the morning light strike him. He lay down and the sun came up, and he fell asleep basking in it.

Sunday, 25 July 1999, 8:32 PM
The Oberoi Grand Hotel
Calcutta, West Bengal

"Khalil? Can you hear me?" Hesha bent delicately over his guest's paralyzed body. "Have you recovered? Look to your left, twice, if you understand me."

The jetty eyes signaled intelligently enough.

"Good. Brace yourself." The Setite put one hand on the gypsy's chest, the other on the stake. He pulled.

Whatever mysterious...compulsion, *aggressive* compulsion, had taken hold of the undead in Calcutta seemed mostly to have abated. Hesha thought Khalil should be harmless enough now.

The Ravnos sprang free, flailing wildly to get away from the older monster. Khalil scurried, ratlike, to the opposite corner of the room, and crouched defensively.

Hesha let him go, backed up a trifle, and sat down on the arm of the couch with his hands in view. "I apologize," he began, "for the manner in which I put an end to your...seizure...last night. You passed very quickly beyond reason, and, having promised to protect you, I could hardly let you run out into Calcutta in such a state." At his feet lay a small blue cooler; he opened it, drew out a blood bag, and tossed it underhand to his guest. "I assure you, none of that is mine."

"Yeah. Right."

Hesha snapped the stake in two and shrugged. "I assume, Khalil, that your employer has you fully bound to his service. You hear his voice from a distance; you obey him when you clearly would prefer not to. I have a great deal to accomplish and no blood to waste where another has gone before me. Drink that and fix your chest. There are more in here." The Setite leaned down and picked up a bag for himself, then pushed the cooler halfway across the room. He sank his teeth into the plastic and winced at the taste. Khalil, after a moment, joined him. The Ravnos was a messy eater. He tossed the empty bag aside, seized the cooler and went through six or seven more before stopping.

"There are fresh clothes hanging in the closet for you, if you would like to dress. And a shower, of course..." Hesha eyed the mud-caked hair and dirty feet of the *shilmulo* pointedly. "It is my custom to hold a meeting among my staff at sunset. If you have anything you care to contribute, you are welcome to attend, provided you mind your manners—I do not allow my retainers to be interfered with, even by allies.

"If you wish to leave, you are free to do so." The Setite caught clearly the flash of panic on the other's face, and let the sentence end itself. Khalil was deathly afraid of something *out*side. Hesha rose to join the mortals in conference. The Ravnos remained in the corner, looking more like a trapped animal than ever.

The Asp, Thompson, and Janet Lindbergh were waiting for him—the first two in chairs at the main table, the last by phone, an open net connection, and a miniature laser printer.

"Good evening," said Hesha. "Report."

"Yes sir," Janet responded promptly. "Ron, the first file for him, please.

"The following facts are undisputed by any sources. First, Typhoon Justin, centered over West Bengal and Bangladesh, lost momentum at last and returned to tropical storm status. Second, Bangladesh suffered massive, deadly mudslides in nearly every corner of the country. Third, Bangladesh was at the epicenter of a considerable earthquake whose effects were felt as far as Rangoon and Delhi."

Hesha contemplated the report before him. Without looking up, he asked, "How are our people?"

"Everyone checked in on time, sir," Thompson answered.

"Elizabeth?" inquired the Setite, in the same detached tone.

"Sleeping. When we try to wake her, she starts talking about Ravana again. I thought it best to let her be, sir." To Thompson's relief, his master remained at the table, and the conference went on without further reference to the girl.

•

Hesha shook the dreaming woman by the shoulder. "Elizabeth? Can you hear me?"

Liz mumbled incomprehensibly.

"Elizabeth!" Hesha said sharply. She stirred. "Good. Talk to me. Tell me about Ravana."

"Ravana...the three overcame Ravana. They tore him down from the mountain, cut him open, and gave his heart to the sun to eat. The Prince of Storms let go his hold on the kingdom...Ravana died in the center of his power, in the midst of his children. They had not come to aid him. He put his curse on them, from the center of his power: They should go mad; they should be no more; and so it was. Their nights will dwindle unto nothing...even *rakshasa* cannot fight the power of three curses at once...murder, calumny, and the madness..." She flickered briefly into a normal voice: "It's a common enough metaphor, Professor. The rebellious children cursed by a grandparent—usually part of a colonization cycle. Campbell makes too much of it, but Graves is sound...." Clarity faded to fairy tale—chapters Hesha had heard before—and decayed further into meaningless murmurs.

Monday, 26 July 1999, 10:02 PM
Unfinished works of the second Hooghly Bridge
Calcutta, West Bengal

Hesha approached the gypsy camps by the same route he had tried on the Friday. He walked to and through the site of his previous encounter, down through the northern half of the camp, and under the bridgework itself without being accosted by the feral guardians. He passed through the center—well south—out through the other side, and no Ravnos called him out or tried to do *anything* to him. It was against all possibility that every *shilmulo* in the settlement could restrain itself when presented such a pretty mark as a serious, public, devout Follower of Set.

Hesha stopped on the southern limits, and looked back thoughtfully. There were, he realized, a great many fires lit among the shacks and tents and wagons—not cookfires, which need not be so large—not drying fires, since the flood-dampened stores weren't hung near them. Hesha had avoided them on the way through as a matter of course. Now he turned his steps back to the nearest, drawing as close to it as his courage would allow, and squinted into the heart of the light.

It was a scrap-wood bonfire, knee-high and not quite four feet across. Piles of fabric lay atop the board-ends and broken crates, charring and melting in the heat—a cardboard suitcase, a broken violin, a pile of books, photographs, a set of hairbrushes, half a dozen decks of cards—as each sheet of paper smoldered through, the ashes peeled away into the wind, and wisps of old cloth drifted with the smoke.

Hesha retreated into more comfortable shadows and watched the people in the vicinity. He was almost certain that the fire was the end of a gypsy wake…the dead man or woman's possessions destroyed by smashing and burning them…but no one grieved at the blaze or in the tents around it. No mourners stood here or at any other open fire he could see—and the passersby averted their eyes from the sight.

Half an hour later, the Setite walked into the Albert Hall Coffee Shop.

Subhas's table was empty.

After a moment's contemplation, Hesha sat down in the old man's usual seat. He placed his hands on the table, and the waitress he remembered Subhas dealing with came over to serve him.

"*Nomoshkar*, sahib. What would you like me to bring to you this evening?"

"Turkish coffee, please." As she started to go, Hesha

cleared his throat. "Pardon me, but could you tell me where my friend, the gentleman who usually sits here, might be?"

The polite, dark-skinned girl shook her head. "Oh, no, sir." She seemed upset, and turned back with plenty of conversation on her face. "It's funny that you should ask that. We have all been worried—he was a very kind and generous gentleman, and no one has seen him since the night of the earthquake." Hesha encouraged her with a nod. "Every night he comes in just as the lights go on, and leaves just as we close the doors. He never misses a night...not until the quake came. And tonight is the second evening he has been gone. I am afraid something might be wrong with him. The owner thinks that the old Babu—pardon me, sir—the old gentleman may have lost family in East Bengal." Her eyes showed more than that; the Setite saw that she feared Subhas had died. "If you see him, sir, do tell him that all of us here are very, very concerned for him. Please ask him to send us word if he is all right."

"I will," said Hesha. "If I see him."

Tuesday, 27 July 1999, 1:02 AM
Five Star Market, Kidderpore
Calcutta, West Bengal

"Old Nag!" The peddler stared in amazement for a moment longer, and then shook his head. "Damned if I'm not glad to see you," the Nosferatu declared wonderingly.

"And I am extraordinarily relieved to see you," Hesha replied.

They regarded each other in silence for what seemed like a long time, even for creatures of their patience. Then the gray-skinned monster rasped out: "About our arrangements..."

"Yes?" Hesha's tone implied a limited bargaining distance, and the face in the little bookshop bobbed nervously.

"You found Michel before I did, I hear. Which renders that deal null and void, I'm afraid. But the other...I won't be able to fulfill your wishes for some months, at least. All my contacts are temporarily unavailable."

"I accept that as an excuse for nonpayment of the debt," Hesha said, and the monster amid the magazines appeared relieved. "Tell me, though, where were you Sunday morning...when the quake hit?"

Warily, the Nosferatu answered: "In a drainage tunnel."

"Underground and underwater?"

With even more caution: "Yes."

"There are no creatures of the night in Calcutta but ourselves, are there?"

After a terrible, rattling sigh: "No. No one. I was on my way to meet some friends that night. I came up to street level, and they were gone. Every one. The Ravnos are gone, the Court is gone, the Prince is dead...." With a hint of hysteria in its voice, the bookseller shouted, "I am the Prince of the City, old Nag!" In a lower tone, he added, "My first act is to abdicate my throne. How about it? Want a city, Prince Hesha? Lord Ruhadze?"

"I'm leaving town, I think. I'll see that you receive at least partial payment for your attempts on my behalf." Hesha leaned on his stick and resumed walking toward the hotel. "If you ever find yourself in a position to tell me what I asked about, the Grand will have a method available; ask after me at the front desk."

The short, gray, spindly creature looked down at him, and the Setite's long strides halted. Trembling, licking its lips, nervous, the Nosferatu leaned in. It asked, "What did you *do* to Calcutta, old Nag?"

Hesha stared at the hideous face for a moment, shook his head, and moved on.

Tuesday, 27 July 1999, 2:51 AM
The Oberoi Grand Hotel
Calcutta, West Bengal

Elizabeth lay swathed in blankets. Her eyes moved like a dreamer's, but her face never relaxed into peaceful sleep. The covers were undisturbed; she could not have moved much since Thompson and his master had checked on her at sundown. She had not eaten since Sunday. She took water only when bullied into it, and even then in small sips. Hesha looked at his pet antiquarian with concern; if the trance were unbroken another day, they would be forced to put her in a hospital to keep her from dying of dehydration.

He pulled her by the shoulders into a sitting position, then propped her up with mounds of pillows. Liz showed no reaction. He called her by name—softly, sharply, commandingly, even (though it took an effort) with tenderness in his voice to bait her. The Setite took her hands—she neither resisted nor clasped back. The expressions on her face reflected things she saw outside the room, not horror or happiness that Hesha was near.

Without guilt—simply as a point of information—he recalled drinking a fair amount from her. Nothing more dangerous than a pint or two, but a weakened body might not protect against the...trance...so well as a healthy one. Hesha went to the washroom and filled a glass with water. Slowly, with a few spills, he persuaded her unconscious mouth to swallow properly. He brought more, managed to give it to the woman without choking her, and sat beside her for a while, holding the empty cup in his hands. A faint clicking sound caught his attention, and he glanced down...his claws, extended, tapped a rhythm on the thin glass. Hesha lanced one wrist with the other thumb and let the blood flow into the cup. He held the reddish-black fluid under Elizabeth's nose, and called her again. Faint signs of recognition rewarded him—he put the glass in her hands and held the rim to her lips.

"Elizabeth? Can you hear me? Try to drink this."

Ron Thompson came into the sickroom quietly, looking for his employer. He found a scene that disturbed him more than anything else he had known in Calcutta: Elizabeth, apparently awake, sitting up, seeing nothing, talking nonsense about kings and monsters and page-boys and demons—amulets draped around her neck—a tape recorder on the bedside table—traces of red on the girl's lips—Hesha sitting at the foot of the bed, listening intently and holding an empty, bloodstained cup.

Hesha caught his driver's eye and signaled silence. He mouthed, "What is it?"

Thompson glared at him like a thundercloud. He beckoned brusquely. Hesha eased off the bed carefully, so as not to disturb the recitation, and joined him on the other side of the door.

"Sir," began Thompson in darkest tones.

Hesha scanned the conference room over Ron's shoulder. Janet's line was open; the Asp and Khalil sat at the main table, playing cards.

"Thompson," Hesha whispered warningly, "you know how deeply I value your opinion. However. This is not the time, the place, or the *company*," his eyes flicked meaningfully toward the Ravnos, "in which I would desire to hear your views. Understood? We will take this up in private, later.

"Now," he said, resuming conversational volume, "what was it you came to see me about?"

Ron hesitated, stumbling over the sudden change in gears. He pulled his notepad from his breast pocket to reassure himself. "Our agents have their exit assignments, sir. We're prepared to close up shop on your word." He turned to the marked pages, but hardly glanced at them. "The 'good-will' items we brought with us have been delivered to the bookseller in the Five Star. The gentleman was rather overwhelmed by the consignment, but we persuaded him to accept."

"So...you progress," said Hesha.

"Yes, sir. But so far...the agents know where they're going, but you haven't given me any information yet to start arrangements for us. What's the next step, sir?"

The Setite stepped away from the wall, seeming to grow taller and more commanding. He approached the table and looked down at the card game in mild disapproval. Thompson, guessing ahead, unobtrusively took his place at the foot of the table. The Asp laid his cards face down and waited respectfully for his employer to speak. Khalil Ravana, sensing the shift in atmosphere, fanned his cards perfectly, and elegantly, and set the hand to one side. He made himself comfortable, relaxing into the soft chair, resting his arms on the padded rests, and letting his quick fingers play amongst the poker stake in front of him.

"Bullets?" Hesha remarked.

Khalil picked up a 45mm round and spun on its point like a top. "He wouldn't play for money."

"I warned him not to."

"And Khalil here didn't want to play with matches," the Asp sneered.

"I see." Hesha seated himself, dialed Janet into the conference, and began: "As you are all aware, my primary project at this time involves tracking down the Eye of Hazimel. Khalil Ravana," he nodded at the Ravnos, "has provided substantial aid in this direction. In return for his services, we will provide transportation and sufficient false papers to allow him to emigrate to the United States.

"What none of you have been told yet is that Calcutta, as a nucleus of Family activity, no longer exists." The Setite regarded his guest reservedly. "Perhaps you need confirmation of this?" The Ravnos shook his head, and Hesha smiled inwardly. There were, as he had thought, at least *four* survivors—the bookseller, himself, this errand-boy, and Khalil's master. Of course, Khalil's master need not have been in the city at the time...Hesha shelved the speculation for later and continued his speech.

"When we concluded the second half of our agreement, Khalil, you implied that your knowledge of the Eye and its properties would make you useful to me as I searched for it. I have called this meeting to discuss our next move toward the artifact, and I would be grateful if you would contribute to that discussion."

Raphael's face twitched slightly at his master's implied invitation to 'discuss' anything.

Thompson, more accustomed to Hesha's tactics with third parties—and more often asked in fact for an opinion, despite the scene over Elizabeth moments before—cleared his throat and started talking. "Well, sir, maybe the time has come to go to Atlanta ourselves. If you knew for certain what had happened to..." he paused, looking for terms to hide behind, "...your associate, you might learn something. Isn't that where the first trace led?"

"That is true," said Hesha.

Thompson snatched at straws to keep going. "California? The professor's notes will be there; you know from Liz that he had relevant info. He probably didn't tell her all of it."

The Asp translated 'discuss' in his head: Play up and play dumb.

"I like the idea of Atlanta," he said slowly. "But I can't help but wonder about the little nest of lines running around New York City. There were traces headed that way we never followed up."

Hesha nodded, and Raphael let his pent-up breath go. He'd taken it—whatever it was—in the right direction. Let Ron pick it up again....

With a sleek and superior air, Khalil held both hands up to stop the conversation. He shook his head condescendingly. "Gentlemen, gentlemen...you're on the wrong track entirely. Professor's notes? Cold killings? You're lucky I'm here. Atlanta is old, old news. And New York is no good; the Eye has never been in the city, whatever you may think." He let his voice lilt up, and his final word rolled off his tongue momentously: "Chicago."

"Chicago?" Hesha inquired evenly.

"Chicago." Khalil smiled.

"You are certain of this?"

"The Eye is in Chicago," said the cocky young gypsy. "I swear. See? I told you I'd be useful. Atlanta, hell..."

Hesha studied his partner. "Very well," he said. "Thompson. Janet. Reservations and security through Chicago." Hesha had no more use for Calcutta. His discovery in the underwater chamber of the tomb had prepared him for this next, and perhaps final, leg of his quest. "I want to be out of India by sundown. Khalil, you have two hours until dawn. Be ready by the time the sun catches us. If you have more things to do than can be accomplished in the time, make a list of them and the team will attend to it."

The Setite rose. "Questions?" No one spoke. "Then I look forward to seeing you all...Wednesday night, I believe."

As the dead filed into the next suite to rest, Hesha clapped a hand on his bodyguard's shoulder, and Ron felt a paper pressed into his palm. After the door closed on them and the sun rose, he sat down at the table to read it.

Thompson,

Ignore Khalil. Find out from Miles where Kettridge is and arrange for our transportation there. If the good professor has gone to ground in Chicago, very well—the Ravnos is telling the truth. Simply be sure that we arrive before him.

Send Khalil to Chicago no matter where we go.

H.

Wednesday, 28 July 1999, 7:27 PM (local time)
Upstate New York

The cabin was small, rough, new, and intended to look both older and more rustic than was plausible. It smelt of disinfectant, detergent, dog, tourist, grass, fish, and dirt. Over 'country' print curtains black duct tape stuck black plastic sheeting to walls and windows. Patches of sunshield on the door and near the ceiling testified to the scrupulous care with which the creature's servants looked after his interests. When Ra released the Setite from sleep, Ron Thompson was there, waiting patiently.

"Good evening, sir. I've brought you breakfast."

"Local bank?"

"Your own vintage, sir. I had it driven up with the car. We're in upstate New York, by the way."

"You've been busy. Report."

"Yes sir. Pauline Miles and her team tracked Kettridge here. Presumably, Chicago was a blind by Khalil, and I hope the left-luggage office opens that skunk's crate in the daytime." Thompson ran a hand through his grizzled hair.

"Pauline's team has been weakened by the losses you already know about. I sent all but the die-hards home for a break. They need it...they saw more than they should have. Kettridge has been amazingly popular these three weeks.

"I kept Pauline here; she's in the know now, for certain, and she's weathered the storm well enough. She's still my top pick to manage the detective work if I buy it, but there's a lot to be said for brute force and the ability to manage that. So I've brought in Matthew Voss for a try-out. He comes from the executive-protection side of the business. His team is fresh and ready to come in, but so far I've kept his people away from what's left of Pauline's squad to minimize the risk of Family rumors spreading. We have a small army of security, a fair-sized arsenal, both the cars, Miles and Voss, the Asp—who has already sighted in half the guns for his own aim—Janet taking care of the baggage difficulties, myself, and you, sir."

"Where is Elizabeth?"

"Awake and in her right mind," said Ron with satisfaction, "having dinner with the others."

Hesha rose, stretched, and selected a map from a pile on the unfinished table. "As your replacement, are you suggesting Miles, Voss, or both?"

"Both, I think."

"I am inclined to agree with you." Hesha pored over the country as represented by contour lines, tree cover, water table, fault zones, stratification, highways, local roads, footpaths, fire breaks, school districts, police jurisdiction, zip code. At last, he picked out an ordinary trail map showing points of natural interest, and sat staring at it. "When the others have finished eating, we will go. Voss's team for back-up. You, the Asp, Pauline, and Elizabeth will travel with me." His shoulders twitched. "I can feel your disapproval, Thompson, but she has proved to be an invaluable sensitive. If there is trouble, she will know; probably before we do.

"Also," said Hesha, "if these two are satisfactory, you might look forward to joining the ranks of Set once the Eye is secured."

Thompson sat very still. "Thank you, sir. I will certainly keep thinking about it."

Elizabeth hiked last along the steep, winding trail. No clouds marred the night. The full moon shone so brightly overhead that none of the hikers had turned on their flashlights. Hesha appeared for a moment, above her, on a switchback of the path. She looked up at him, admiring the figure he cut as he moved—proud, silent, sure-footed—his skin gleaming blue-black and the whites of his eyes glowing like stars. He vanished beyond the curve. Thompson filed into view close behind, and Liz could see every gray hair silvered by the moonlight; she saw, and pitied, the bent back, the tired set of his shoulders. The Asp, lighter-stepping, stealthier, more sly in every movement, passed his partner at the turn. He pulled Ron's pack open, dug something out of it, and stuffed the item into his own gear. The older man marched more easily, and his thick hand reached up to Raphael's shoulder. The Asp pretended not to notice, and moved out of sight.

In front of Elizabeth, Pauline Miles kept steady pace. While it was hard to hear the Asp make his way along the path, it was difficult to see Pauline. She was short, thin, naturally dark, and her dull, dark-blue clothes blended easily with the shadows.

The track widened just after the bend, and the two women matched step for the last few yards. Their three companions had stopped ahead of them in a break between the trees. Pauline and Elizabeth caught up, found places opposite Ron and Raphael, and held their position quietly. Hesha waited, stock-still, for a full minute, and then moved across the meadow in a straight, unfaltering line.

Elizabeth brushed through clusters of some plant that smelled terribly sweet, and picked a branch from one to carry with her. She looked at their destination—another climb, she supposed—a majestic, tumbled mass of stone and forest rising above the shallow valley. Hesha was two-thirds of the way to the foot of it already.

"Liz—watch your laces," Pauline whispered.

Elizabeth stooped to one knee to tie her shoe. For a brief second, she felt a wave of heat. The earth beneath her hands felt more like asphalt than anything else. Liz blinked and saw stars—shook her head, and felt the ground again. Grassy, rooty soil. Her fingers dug in and found a worm, a few pillbugs—she knelt until her cheek nearly touched the dirt, and no scorching sensation came to her face. Liz rose in doubt and walked the rest of the way trying to see out of the corners of her eyes.

•

Hesha approached an opening under a tilted rock, peered inside, and then confidently beckoned to the others. He led them around and to right, pulled himself up and over a sizable boulder, and looked down into a passage the width of a city sidewalk and the height of two men. A wall of rock had, long ago, split in two. The forces that had riven it had forced the pieces closer together at the top, wider apart at the bottom, forming an irregular tunnel sloping down into the earth. The 'floor' was dirt and rubble washed in by water. The walls sported moss and small plants only so far as light might enter the crack.

The Setite observed all this without pausing. He turned on his light and led the others into the hill. One by one, four lamps clicked on behind him.

At the end of the descent, the tunnel opened out into a large, ungainly chamber. The five lights—very small and dim in comparison to the dark expanse they had to contend with—played over the billowing curves of the cave. Elizabeth recognized the smooth, weird shapes of water-cut and water-built limestone. She fanned her flash's beam out as far as it would go, and turned it on the ceiling, which soared to the right past the limit of the light. To her left, it swooped down to within four feet of the floor. A bizarre combination of claustrophobia, agoraphobia, and vertigo washed over her. She looked to her footing, sharpened the focus again, and tried to keep the light on the same level as her eyes. The others stepped out, each taking a slightly different route to avoid the stalagmites and columns jutting up from the floor. Hesha picked his way to a narrow, nearly invisible opening and the team followed—though it was a tight and difficult squeeze for Thompson.

On the other side was a disturbingly familiar chamber. Elizabeth felt as though she had walked into a natural chapel, the cave's roof vaulted like a cathedral's. More stalactites, stalagmites, and columns had formed here than in the first room, and the largest of them formed two uneven lines...like rows of pillars in a ruin. The few formations down the center of the room lay low; pillows, ropecoils, and buttons dotted the gently rolling floor, and the icicles and curtains suspended from the ceiling hung no lower than the tops of the 'pillars' on either side.

"Wait here," said Hesha. His voice echoed. He lowered it, and went on: "The professor will be easier for me to handle by myself. I don't care to have him harmed by one of you," he said, glancing toward the Asp, "even by accident, and I do not want any of you shot or burned by him in an attempt on me."

Elizabeth clambered up and found a damp seat on a stone stump. She watched as Hesha picked through one of the packs, strapped a large and heavy rubberized-canvas sack to his back, and set out across the 'chapel.' He traversed the slippery, rounded terrain without a misstep, selected a deep shadow in the right rear corner of the cave, and headed unswervingly toward it. By the moving shadows, she realized that what she had taken for the 'back wall' of the cathedral must be a free-standing column of enormous size. She squinted to see better.

Hesha reached the side passage he had chosen and turned back to look at the giant pillar himself. His lamp caught the thing in sharp profile, and Elizabeth gasped. For an instant, the sidelit formation had seemed to move; an optical illusion gave it a hundred monstrous faces and distorted limbs. The Setite moved on and darkness settled on the far end of the cavern once more, but Liz dropped off her perch. She knew that ghastly image; she had seen it last in a mural under a tenement in Calcutta. She popped the filter off the powerful lens in her hand, and started running along the 'aisle' of the chapel.

The hot halogen bulb flooded the huge hall with light. It stripped the shadows away from the pillar and threw them into the corners of the room. It picked out dirt and rust imprisoned under the translucent calcite film. But the faces were gone. Elizabeth studied the surface of the hundred-headed demon—of the natural, two-story, stone pillar that must have grown for eons and stood for millennia—and tried desperately to find an angle from which she might see the faces again. The harshest light refused to bring out the contours that could have fooled her eye. The softest light, filtered again, as Hesha's lamp had been, failed to duplicate the conditions. Thompson, confused but willing to help, took the flash and stood where Liz thought their employer had been, and though she returned to the stump and called out directions to him, the faces never reappeared in the stone.

Ron came back, curious and slightly worried. He asked, "What was it?"

"I thought I saw something."

"Moving?" The Asp jumped in.

"No. Just...there."

Elizabeth said nothing more, and Thompson stayed by her while Raphael and Pauline went off to search the room for more practical things, like exits. Their voices ricocheted up and around and back to Ron and Liz's ears, and the girl flinched.

"You've got a feeling about something?" The old cop asked softly.

She grimaced. "No. Its just...the echoes...sounded as though there were more than four people in here. Can we go back to the first cave?"

"Sure," said Thompson, and they jumped down off their stumps together.

Hesha followed the trail of the red eyestone easily—almost smugly, with a full-belly kind of contentment. The bead around his neck seemed to tug him along the track, and the sensation of cool, carved, blood-colored chalcedony hovered like a beacon when his steps aligned with the correct direction.

The Setite savored the potential for triumph. He had nothing, yet, and he knew the danger of assuming victory before the battle had been fought—but by night's end, he might have accomplished his goal. It was *possible* that the Eye would be Set's by daybreak. It was *possible* that his quest would end, and that was an astonishing possibility.

He cherished, too, the confrontation ahead. Hesha could admit to himself that he looked forward to seeing Jordan Kettridge again. The young man—no, not so young, realized the creature—was an unusual specimen. Rarely did Hesha encounter a human so hard-headed, so unshakable. Kettridge could be won over, but not bought. He could be convinced by evidence, but not turned by anything Hesha could find to tempt him. Any mortal could be broken, of course, but they were of so little use afterwards. So for the past sixteen years, Hesha had made Kettridge's career into something of a hobby. The Setite amused himself by funding Jordan's work, supplying him with grants and minor clues to support the archaeologist's theories. He smoothed over governmental difficulties, kept the academic wolves at bay, and used his influence to help the professor obtain any visa to any nation he wished.

Someday, he might tell Jordan all that he had done for the man—but he liked the picture of a dead Kettridge standing before Osiris (if Osiris ever regained proper control of the underworld again), faced with the feather of Ma'at, reciting the list of his deeds, being questioned by the gods about his relationship to a Child of Set called Hesha Ruhadze…and giving, innocently, all the wrong answers.

The red line fell to a level below. Hesha wedged himself into the corners of a ladder-like, easily climbed chimney, and descended carefully to the slick stone beneath.

He found a dead end.

In a den-shaped space the size of a double bed, a man's body lay prostrate on the rock. The Setite braced himself for what might come, and touched the outflung arm of the ragged figure. His fingers gripped flesh as cold as stone, but not rigid. An old corpse? It smelt very dead...but the texture of the skin suggested withering flesh beneath, not the corruption of the grave. A Cainite...dormant...or meeting Final Death in a way Hesha had never seen before.

The Setite swung his light around to examine the carcass. The stick-thin, haggard shape was bare-chested but wore loose trousers, sneakers, and a belt. Filth, caked mud, and dried gore hid the original colors of his clothes and encrusted most of the body. More significantly, to Hesha's mind, an old swath of something paler overlaid the other stains like a sash. The fat-yellow stream began at the man's swollen, ravaged left eyesocket and dripped down his face, neck and shoulder as if a tallow candle had melted out of the blinding wound. Some of it still glistened as if fresh, and new drops of the stuff had fallen onto the cave floor as though the candle had been wrested from the corpse very recently.

Hesha leaned over the body and picked up the red eyestone. He held the bead between his palms and attuned himself to it for a moment, then attached it to the cord that held the white eye and the amulet. He retraced his steps as far as the top of the chimney, turned completely around twice, and realized that he had a new problem. The white stone was as good as a bloodhound for tracking the red ones. The red one around his neck felt the call of the Eye itself, gave a location, and general bearings—but only as the crow flew. In the labyrinths of a limestone cave, Hesha could not walk a straight line toward the source.

The Setite pulled out a compass and his phone.

"Either the professor is being very, very clever," he said to his team, "or we're dealing with someone else altogether. Someone more dangerous. There is a dormant

Cainite here. The prize is gone, but there's no sign of a struggle. How our friend might have managed that, I don't know, but he has the object we are looking for. I want you to have the backup team come up and cover the cave entrance. They are to prevent any other persons from entering the caverns. If our subject tries to leave, allow him to do so, but alert me immediately, have him trailed, and keep him closely guarded. Do not, on any account, fire on him.

"In the meantime," Hesha continued, "you and the others are to split into even groups and begin a search for our friend. His position at the moment is to my southwest, up roughly eighty feet, and half a mile away. From the point at which I left you, I approximate him to be due west, forty feet above you, and just under a mile away. Concentrate in that area and mark everyone's feet before you go. I will contact you again if I scent any of your paths or if our target alters his position."

Thursday, 29 July 1999, 12:41 AM
Upstate New York

Ron Thompson slid warily down a steep incline. It was scattered with loose stones and extremely treacherous. He knew this because he had spent the last half hour climbing carefully up it to see whether the shadow at the top led anywhere.

"Blind alley," he said to his partner. "Let's go back to the junction and try the center."

Liz tried to move like the Asp. She discarded the example and tried moving like Pauline Miles, and felt better. Bare rock to bare rock—loose stone was bad; it slipped under your shoes—avoiding damp places and pools—she could still hear herself, but not so loudly as Thompson's heavy footsteps.

The middle way went nowhere, but quickly. The crevasse at the end of it was too wide and deep for them to cross; logic argued that Kettridge could not have crossed it either, and they returned to the junction. The first of the left-hand holes descended. They believed they were still underneath Kettridge's level, so they took the second. An hour later, mentally exhausted by the vast variety of hiding places in the honeycomb they had just explored, they turned to the down-slope. That, at least, was wide, smooth, and easy to walk along.

It looked as though it would dead end in a pit, but Thompson flashed his light around the bottom of the tunnel, found another shadow he couldn't explain, and the two of them scuttled down into it. The light revealed the shadow as more stream-bed; they crawled beneath the low but narrow, knife-like knee of the ceiling, and stood up in a chimney with a near-perfect ladder wall rising higher than the lights would reach.

Thompson clipped his flash to his chest and started the ascent. He pointed, ordering Elizabeth to another route, not directly beneath his. She took hold of a ledge, got her feet beneath her, and mounted the steep stairs. Reach, step, reach, step...her light bothered her, her fingertips chafed on the rough stone, and her jeans weren't as loose, climbing, as they had seemed while hiking. Liz began to lag behind. She looked over at Ron, realized he had two full lengths on her. While she watched, he stopped moving straight up and started pulling himself forward—he'd reached the top. Elizabeth grinned and picked up the pace. Twelve feet to go, at the most...

Sounds from above:

"K—"

Spang. Thwack. Thud.

Elizabeth froze.

"Shit." A man's voice—familiar, but not Thompson.

"Liz—" Thompson, sounding strange.

She fairly ran the last eight feet to the top, slipping

twice in her haste, pushing her head over the top without thought for the consequences. Thompson lay there, twisted to one side, lying in a curled, half-fetal position. His right hand, speckled with sticky crimson, touched the blunt end of a golden-brown stake in his chest. Liz shoved her light above the edge and saw another man—Jordan Kettridge—running to and kneeling at, the body of her friend.

"You're a rotten shot," said Thompson angrily. "Feels like all lung."

Jordan choked. "I thought he'd come alone. Oh, shit. Ron…I dropped the aim when I saw it was you, I swear to God…but the trigger—"

"Save it, Jordan." Ron coughed, and Elizabeth swarmed up beside him. She held his head off the ground and tried to keep his body still. Tears poured down her face. She fumbled frantically with the buttons of her phone.

"Wait," Ron groaned. "Stop. Don't call him."

Elizabeth misdialed, cleared, and started over. "He might be able to *help* you—" she pleaded. "You told me, he healed you after the snake bites—"

"Maybe he'll heal me. Maybe he'll kill me." Thompson looked up at her, trying to explain. "He wants to replace Vegel." His glance caught Kettridge's, and the younger man looked away. "I thought I wanted that. Since then…" he gasped, and a little more blood spilled from the edge of the wound, "I know that I don't. But I don't think…that Hesha…will just let anyone go…."

His hand closed over Elizabeth's. She let the phone fall into her lap.

"Let me tell you something," he said gently. "You think he cares about you? You haven't seen him lie enough. I thought there was something to him. Then I saw how he manipulated you. I don't believe much of him anymore…I don't want anymore to be like him …." His voice trailed off like a sleepy child's, and his eyes shut for a moment.

Then, wide-eyed and suddenly stronger, he asked, "You love him?" Elizabeth's eyes shifted uneasily. "You don't really love him. His blood—their blood—does things to people. One sip, you care about them. Two, you love them. Three drinks makes a slave out of you. That's how *he* put it, little sister."

"I haven't—"

"You have. *Twice.*" Ron's voice dropped to a harsh whisper. "The hangover cure, that night in New York." She opened her mouth to protest, but the dying man overran her. "Then, in Calcutta, I caught him feeding it to you while you were in that trance, telling stories...two drinks, Liz."

"I've lied to you, too, of course. You start to do that, around him...for the best of reasons. But I'm just a liar, Liz. The Asp is a cat burglar and an assassin. And Hesha's a vampire, no matter what fancy words he puts over it or whose definition you use. *He's* the thing from the late show. So don't call him. Give me a quiet grave, first."

Thompson rolled a little, toward Jordan Kettridge, and his lined, fading face fairly begged. "Get her away from him," he whispered. "Get the hell out of here. Leave the Eye...just don't risk yourself or her...get Liz away...."

His hand pulled Elizabeth down to him, and she wrapped her arms around him tightly. "Ron...please... we'll get an ambulance...."

"They're gonna airlift me out of a cave?" he tried to joke. He coughed again, and this time blood spilled freely from his mouth. "Don't worry, little sister. I'm getting away. Watch me run. Watch me—"

Ronald Thompson ran out of his life smiling, with his eyes fixed on Elizabeth's face.

Kettridge covered the old cop's face, and Elizabeth hung her head, crying bitterly. Jordan walked away and left her alone for a long time.

•

"Miss Dimitros..." Kettridge approached the kneeling woman cautiously.

"Yes," she answered, dully.

"I am sorry. Ron and I...were friends, a long time ago. If he had wanted Hesha—"

Elizabeth turned her head to look at him. "That's easy to say now."

"I mean it." His gray-green eyes locked on hers, and she discovered sincerity there.

"What now?"

"If you will let me, I'll try again for Ruhadze."

"To kill him?"

"Yes." Jordan nodded, adding, "and to destroy the Eye for good. There's a way out uphill from here. If I can stake the vampire, I'll be leaving by it. If I can't, I'm going to die here," he said calmly. "You can go now, if I can trust you not to warn him."

Liz took a deep breath and let go of Thompson's cooling hand. "I want to help you."

"Are you sure?" Elizabeth nodded vigorously, and stood up. She took a gun off Thompson's hip, and Kettridge stepped back, despite himself. "Then call him. Tell him something...convincing."

Liz stared at her phone. Hesha's number—she dialed it in, and waited.

"Yes," answered the rich, deep voice she remembered.

Elizabeth looked down at Thompson. *No names*, she thought. *I could use his name and warn him*— "Hello."

Somewhere in the labyrinth, Hesha paused. For the woman to call was...unusual. "Report," he said guardedly.

"We found a campsite. My partner is looking it over; we think you should take a look. Without the supply you're carrying," she said, thinking of the sack of wet Ganges mud, "he's afraid to go into the bags."

"Why are you making the contact?"

"The phone wouldn't work in the area. There may

be too much rock between you and it—or the object may be there and interfering. He sent me back to the last junction to try." She gave detailed directions and then cut the call off. Kettridge laid a hand on her shoulder, led her around a corner, and set her down by a backpack and rolled-up sleeping bag. A *campsite*, she thought in surprise. *True enough*. Then the professor dragged Thompson's body out of sight of the chimney, cocked and loaded a crossbow, and settled in for a wait.

Sounds from the chimney:

Nothing, for almost an hour.

A faint, scraping footfall.

Kettridge turned, aimed, and fired. *Spang. Thwack. Thud*. He loaded another stake into the bow, then flashed Thompson's bright, unfiltered light at the prone figure by the stair edge. The body lay still. Elizabeth joined him at the corner, checking the color of Hesha's skin. It was fainter and grayer than the tone he affected while waking...it was, in fact, the shade she remembered from the dream of his death, and the night in Calcutta when he let his illusion go. The tattoo stood out in the flash.

Liz crept forward and tried to lift the body. It came up all in one piece, rigid and stiff as a board. Hesha's eyes complained to her, and she looked quickly away.

Jordan Kettridge lowered the crossbow. He brought Hesha into the center of the chamber he'd used as a camp, and from a pack at his waist, he pulled out a clear, zip-lock bag. It bulged with pale goo and an Eye the size of a baseball. He laid it down three feet from Hesha's corpse.

"We're leaving." He shoved Liz back down the passage, threw his backpack on, and started running up a side path. He took a gray metal box with three lights and four buttons from the same pack that had held the artifact, armed it with the first button, pressed a second, and glanced back to see fire and rockfall consume the room behind them. He turned up another corridor, and started running, nudging the girl along whenever she faltered. He pressed one and three, and the passage they had just left collapsed. At the end of the tunnel, a tiny hole led out into moonlight. Liz scrambled through it, Kettridge shoved his pack ahead of him, and fell out headfirst himself.

The slope under them was grassy and steep, and they ran down to the valley floor in minutes. Breathing heavily, falling down under the weight of his bag, Jordan triggered the last charge, and half the hill seemed to shake and fall in on itself.

Later, in a rented car on its way to Manhattan, Jordan kept a close watch on his passenger. She wept some of the time, and she talked about Thompson, trying to arrange for herself the things she thought she knew about the man. She ranted at other moments, and though a fair amount of the anger came at Kettridge himself, she was most bitter and furious at Hesha. *She hates him*, thought the hunter. *She's definitely not still under his control*. With a great deal of relief, Jordan relaxed behind the wheel. Hesha Ruhadze had died for the last time beside his victim, Ron Thompson. Hesha Ruhadze would never haunt antique-shop assistants or obscure Berkeley anthropology professors again.

Friday, 30 July 1999, 2:43 PM
A studio apartment in Red Hook, Brooklyn
New York City, New York

Home again, thought Elizabeth. She stopped for a moment on the threshold—she had never thought to see her rooms again. They were, for that instant, the most beautiful place on Earth. Then she looked down at herself, shuddered, and ran for the bedroom.

Liz stripped off her blood-stiffened clothes, threw

them into the trash, and plunged under the full force of the shower. First it was too cold, then scalding hot—she adjusted the knobs, but she didn't care—Thompson's blood had soaked through her jeans. It was in her hair. It was under her fingernails. She scrubbed away the gore, then washed again, trying to forget that Hesha had ever touched her, anywhere. After forty minutes, she got out, pruny from the water and rubbed raw by the washcloth. She went to her wardrobe, realized that most of it was in Hesha's house…with her dissertation notes…and her favorite dress…and her grandmother's silver jewelry…. Liz pulled on a white dress shirt that she'd bought to give to her sister-in-law and a pair of khakis that had somehow escaped being packed off to Baltimore.

She rambled to the kitchen and started her answering machine. It told her there were forty-seven messages, and she hit PLAY as she opened the refrigerator. An old boyfriend called to see if she still existed, and the fridge was empty. There was a note inside from Amy explaining that she'd had it cleaned out. A series of clicks represented wrong numbers and telemarketers. Liz pulled a cardboard dinner from the freezer and slammed it into the microwave. More clicks. Her brother had called. The museum wanted to know if she could fill in while a permanent staffer took a sabbatical. Liz made juice from a frozen tube of concentrate, poured herself a glass. She snagged her dinner and sat down at the coffee table to sort through her mail. Later, satisfied, somehow, by the ordinariness of the junk, the coupons, the credit-card offers, the sales notices—fur coats and dishwashers had so little to do with dead men in the mountains—she drifted over to her workshop.

Antonio, the delivery foreman at Rutherford House, had left a stack of small pieces and a few notes. Liz looked through them and put the pieces away for later. She saw the eye molds still sitting on her workbench; she threw them out hastily.

Sleipnir caught her eye, and she ran a hand happily over her desk. She sat down on the polished top and gazed out the huge, gorgeous windows. Her thoughts turned to Amy...better to call her tomorrow, when all the things that had happened had settled a little more. She knew, thinking about it, that it would be hard to talk to someone *outside*—and now Amy *was* outside—about everything. Kettridge had offered his phone number; had let her talk. she had needed badly to talk, and Jordan had even listened. After the shock, he understood. He was still intense and a little awkward, but very nice, very kind. Paranoid, too, she realized—trying to give her tips on sunlight and fire and how to get the right weapons if she ever needed them. He was running scared and didn't know how to stop. Elizabeth supposed that a thing like Hesha might do that to a person.

New York settled down under a golden afternoon. People left their buildings and walked to buses; unlocked and un-Clubbed their cars. The locals stepped down to the corner grocers and back, and drifters simply did. Elizabeth watched them all, and a sinister feeling crept up her back. On impulse, she reached for a spray can from the shelves, found a lighter by the candles in the library, and put them together experimentally. A very satisfactory jet of flame rewarded her. She sat for a long time on Sleipnir's broad back, cradling the can to her chest and holding the lighter white-knuckle-tight in her left hand.

The sun began to fade. The warehouse shadow grew longer and longer, and streetlights glimmered on one by one. Suddenly Elizabeth felt called to action. She gathered up all her spray cans, matches, lighters, lamp oil, and candles and set them out strategically. She double-checked the bolts on the (thank god!) inch-thick steel door to her apartment, locked all the windows down tight, and piled a heap of light, noisy junk in front of the swinging pane that led onto the fire escape. She ran down the curtains and retreated to the sofa, keeping her improvised flame-throwers close at hand. At the slightest noise her hand reached for them; she started whenever unexplained silence fell on her. The vampire had taught her to sleep by day—free at last to fix that, exhausted, and bone-weary, Elizabeth realized that she would not shut her eyes until they closed of themselves.

Elizabeth felt her left shoulder tighten up. She flinched and looked back, sure that something had come up behind her. There was nothing—she looked to her right—and suddenly, Hesha's face appeared in front of her own. His eyes were yellow, with inhuman, slit pupils. Her heart jumped as she stared at the apparition. She thought of the fire, but her body had turned to lead and refused to obey her. She could not even look away.

Hesha said nothing.

Liz sat frozen like a statue, in a paralysis so complete her lungs gave her only short, quick breaths—as she panicked, the rhythm quickened, her head grew light. Terror dug deep claws into her, and the vampire's golden eyes bored through her brain. She was dizzy and felt like falling, but her body refused even to collapse.

The monster spoke at last. "Good evening, Elizabeth." He reached out and took the can and lighter from her. "Clever, as always. And you paid attention during our time together. That you failed is not your fault; you cannot fight what you cannot see." He placed his hands on her chest and pushed her unresisting body back on the couch. "Be comfortable."

He knocked the woman's petty arsenal off the coffee table with one sweeping arm. The cans clanged horribly on the floorboards, and the raucous noise echoed down from the rafters. Hesha seated himself on the table, and kept his unblinking eyes on his prisoner.

"It has become necessary for me to kill you. I doubt

that you would appreciate many of the reasons for this. It is not in my nature to explain, and it would not be within your ability to comprehend me should I speak the whole truth to you." He paused. "While you await your death, however, you may desire something to take your mind off your situation, and I invite you to consider this: If you had not allowed Thompson to die—yes, I know about that—I would not be here to kill you now.

"You betrayed me. I understand that, and I fault myself—my handling of you has been flawed from the beginning. I sinned. I almost fell into compassion. I allowed myself and my meditations to be distracted by the Eye. I underestimated a mortal—the same mortal—more than once. I saw clear signs and misunderstood them.

"You killed Thompson, Elizabeth," he murmured, puzzled, "and I had not seen even the shadow of that in you. I see most things...." The golden eyes came closer, until Elizabeth felt she were drowning in them. "Have you anything to say?" His irises deepened slowly to black. "If you sit still, you may whisper."

Elizabeth tried to leap up and scream at the top of her lungs. Hesha seemed disappointed. He raised an eyebrow.

"How did you know about Ron?" She could hardly hear her voice herself.

"I found Kettridge's cave at the same time you did. He believed there were only two entrances. He neglected to consider holes a human body could not squeeze through. I listened to it all."

"Why did you let him die?"

"Why did you?" he asked in a tone of genuine curiosity.

She swallowed hard. "How did you escape?"

"You staked me. I am not a vampire; I am a Child of Set. I have no heart for Kettridge to spear me by, and I am difficult to destroy. No more questions. No more explanations. Do you have anything to *say*?"

Elizabeth thought for a moment. "Kill me quickly."

"No." Hesha's gaze turned gold again.

"You die tonight for Thompson's sake," intoned the Setite. "You die tonight that I may redeem myself in my Lord's grace. You die tonight because alive you are a temptation to me." He began to chant in a language Elizabeth did not know. Then: "You are beyond my control. You are a burden on my will." The strange language flowed through her ears again. His voice rose, repeated one phrase half a dozen times, and fell to silence.

Hesha's fingers traced the line of her jaw. His hand tilted her head back, and his arms snaked around her. Elizabeth watched terrible, sharp fangs like a viper's drop down from behind his canines. She closed her eyes and braced herself for pain, for a torn throat and a severed windpipe; she prayed for unconsciousness to come soon, even if the monster were determined that death should await some plan of his own.

She felt an unexpected softness, a tender kiss, on her mouth, and the shock was worse than a wound. Hesha, pretending to want her, in a room in Calcutta...his lips slid along her cheek, kissed her again beneath the ear, and finally bit into the vein.

Elizabeth screamed for what seemed like an eternity, but was less than a second; the scream never passed her lips. Her breath caught. A gasp escaped her. The worst of the attack wasn't pain, but heart-wrenching, bittersweet ecstasy. She clutched at him desperately, drawing him closer, and forgot everything...she pressed herself against him...her heart ached—it couldn't beat fast enough.... Her cheek rubbed against his, and she felt his skin grow warm with what he stole from her. She flushed for a moment, and felt it fade as more blood left her. Elizabeth lost the strength to hold him, and sagged into the strong cocoon of his arms. Time slowed—or Hesha sipped more delicately—and she seemed to float in a luxurious sea. Bells rang in her ears, and lights danced before her eyes. In a moment, the chimes and colors fell behind her, and there was nothing left but the sea—she couldn't feel the pressure of his hands or the tingling of her own fingertips—there was the sea of ecstasy, darkness, and the faintest memory of a body...somewhere...with a tiny, stinging pain in the side of its throat. She held onto that a minute longer, dizzy and dwindling, thinking not of her life ending, but of the touch of him going away forever...she could remember his arms....

Then there was nothing—just enough of it, for just long enough, for her to know always what nothing was like—

—and a single drop of fire landed in her mouth.

She had a mouth, she had a body. It was a mass of sharp pain and chill, stiff, dull agony. She kicked and clawed at something she couldn't see—it tore back at her, trying to destroy what little there was of her—and the fire came back to her mouth. Wine, pure water, strawberries, acid, thickened passion, mother's milk, bitter gall, vinegar, burning hatred...singing guilt...a power...other men's memories...deliciously and unspeakably wrong to drink, but impossible not to swallow. The stuff filled her heart and coursed through her veins, and the sharp pains went away. It went on flowing, and the agony subsided.

Elizabeth opened her eyes.

She was sitting in her father's old office chair. Hesha's face, devoid of expression, looked into hers. His eyes were gold. His hands held chains and shackles, and while she tried to understand why he hadn't killed her yet, he clamped them on her wrists, through the back of the chair, and around the steel pillar in the center of her apartment.

Hesha left without another word.

Saturday, 31 July 1999, 3:56 AM
A studio apartment in Red Hook, Brooklyn
New York City, New York

Elizabeth Dimitros sat in the exact center of her apartment and waited. She was through remembering. She could not even guess how much light would be too much—twilight, or the glow before dawn, or the full rays of the sun—but she would know, soon, just how much was needed to kill a vampire—how deadly Ra was to the body of an infant Child of Set.

From time to time she listened for footsteps in the hall. If one of the other tenants passed by, she could yell and try to find shelter before sunup. Antonio sometimes started his rounds at five o'clock—would that be too late? If Hesha were going to come back (*Hesha isn't going to come back*, she thought bitterly) he might use the door, as he had in leaving.

The sky grew paler.

Perhaps it was best this way....

Footsteps—coming closer. Elizabeth's heart leapt. Should she call out? No, the walker was already coming to her place—there was nothing else at this end of the hall. She turned herself in the chair and looked desperately at the opening door.

She didn't recognize him at first—she only knew she wasn't seeing Hesha.

The man smiled, looked her up and down, slowly, glanced at the shackles, and licked his curling lips.

"Hello, sweetheart," said Khalil Ravana. He grinned evilly. "Did you miss me?"

About the author

Kathleen Ryan has worked for, with, and around White Wolf Publishing since 1993. Her first fiction pieces, about a young mage named Amanda, appeared as book-openers in **Mage: The Ascension**, first edition. Through cajolery and threats she has managed to get an Amanda piece in every major **Mage** release since then, wrangled all the fun parts of **Tradition Book: Euthanatos** for herself, and snuck most of **Changing Breed Book: Kitsune** into the back of **Hengeyokai: Shapeshifters of the East**. **Clan Novel: Setite** is her first novel-length published work.

The Vampire Clan Novel Series.................

Clan Novel: Toreador
These artists are the most sophisticated of the Kindred.

Clan Novel: Tzimisce
Fleshcrafters, experts of the arcane, and the most cruel of Sabbat vampires.

Clan Novel: Gangrel
Feral shapeshifters distanced from the society of the Kindred.

Clan Novel: Setite
The much-loathed serpentine masters of moral and spiritual corruption.

Clan Novel: Ventrue
The most political of vampires, they lead the Camarilla.

Clan Novel: Lasombra
The leaders of the Sabbat and the most Machiavellian of all Kindred.

Clan Novel: Ravnos
These devilish gypsies are not welcomed by the Camarilla, nor tolerated by the Sabbat.

Clan Novel: Assamite
The most feared clan, for they are assassins of both vampires and mortals.

Clan Novel: Malkavian
Thought insane by other Kindred, they know that within madness lies wisdom.

Clan Novel: Brujah
Street-punks and rebels, they are aggressive and vengeful in defense of their beliefs.

Clan Novel: Giovanni
Still a respected part of the mortal world, this mercantile clan is also home to necromancers.

Clan Novel: Tremere
The most magical of the clans and the most tightly organized.

Clan Novel: Nosferatu
Horrific to behold, these sneaks know more secrets than the other clans—secrets that will only be revealed in this, the last of the **Vampire Clan Novels.**

...........................continues.

The American Camarilla is under siege. The Sabbat offensive is sweeping the East Coast. The Eye of Hazimel, an ancient and disgustingly powerful artifact, has resurfaced and even now wreaks havoc. *Have we got your attention yet?*

There's more to come. Victoria, Vykos, Ramona, Hesha, and others all have greater roles to play. Anyone who *survives* has greater roles to play.

Astute readers may already be putting clues to the mysteries together, but everyone will note that the end date of each book is later than the end date of the prior book...and that the plot thickens the more you know. The series chronologically continues in **Clan Novel: Ventrue** and then **Clan Novel: Lasombra**. Excerpts of these two exciting novels are on the following pages.

CLAN NOVEL: VENTRUE
ISBN 1-56504-805-9
WW# 11104
$5.99 U.S.

CLAN NOVEL: LASOMBRA
ISBN 1-56504-807-5
WW# 11105
$5.99 U.S.

Monday, 12 July 1999, 12:01 AM
Executive suite, The International, Ltd.
Amsterdam, The Netherlands

Jan Pieterzoon leaned far back in the over-stuffed chair and massaged away the tiny red marks on his nose from the wire-rimmed glasses that now rested on his desk. He craved whisky. *Needed* whisky. But it never settled well these nights. He suspected that his stomach had atrophied and shrunken to nothing from the years of disuse. There were, of course, many such stories among the Kindred, but who knew which were mere flights of fancy and which to believe? And to ask an older, more knowledgeable Cainite would be too great an admission of ignorance. For ignorance was weakness, and the weak seldom survived. Not for long.

"Are you all right, Mr. Pieterzoon?"

Jan nodded but neither spoke nor opened his eyes. Marja would still be concerned. She would ask him what she could do for him, and at this moment, the question itself would be enough. Hearing her speak Dutch soothed his nerves. So many of his business contacts were in French, or German, or—God help him—English.

"Can I do anything for you, sir?"

"No thank you, Ms. van Havermaete."

Mr. Pieterzoon. Ms. van Havermaete. Jan allowed the pained smile slowly to spread across his lips. *How long have you served me, Marja?* Still, the formality. And so it would remain. Jan could not allow himself familiarity between them; and as long as he could not, she would not.

He ran his fingers through his short, blond hair, and then rubbed the muscles of his ever-smooth jaw. Each muscle in his entire body seemed to be a reservoir of tension, and unfortunately he had no time to seek out his acupuncturist.

"We leave for the United States very soon," Jan said, opening his eyes.

This was news to Marja. "The States? *How* soon?"

"As soon as possible. Within a few nights."

He watched as she digested the information, made lists of the necessary arrangements in her mind. "Business?" she asked.

"Not technically speaking, no."

She nodded. That would impose another set of criteria on her preparations. A trip to meet investors or deal with labor representatives would have been entirely within her realm of operations. If the trip were related, however, to the shadowy dealings of the Kindred, of which she knew only and exactly what she needed to know, other considerations took precedence.

"Security?"

Jan thought for a moment. "Ton and Herman."

"Assistants for yourself?"

"Yourself and Roel." Roel was capable, personable, a good companion for Marja. Jan chose him for that reason. Neither had the slightest idea of the underlying commonality that tied them to Jan.

"That should do. We can augment personnel later, if necessary," Jan explained briefly. "I don't want to waltz in with a full-fledged entourage. Matters may be...sensitive enough without the appearance of presumption."

Marja made her mental notes. "Destination?"

"Baltimore. We'll be staying at the Lord Baltimore Inn as guests of Alexander Garlotte. Please make the necessary arrangements," he told her more from habit than from need.

Marja turned to leave the office. Her skirt, longer than was the current style, hung almost to her knees. Her simple yet attractive sweater gave Jan the impression of unintentional seductiveness—or would have if he'd gone in for that sort of thing anymore. *Ironic,* he thought. *I sought a victim and found a trusted associate.*

"Ms. Havermaete," he called, just before the door

closed. She stepped back into the office. "The factory in Bonn—it will have to be closed. There won't be time to deal with it properly now."

"That's sixteen hundred workers' jobs, sir."

"I'm quite aware of that," Jan responded matter-of-factly. "There are also the financial interests of sixteen investors. The scales are hardly balanced. See that the paperwork goes out in the morning."

"Yes, sir." Then she left him.

Jan did not begrudge Marja her humanitarian impulses. Several of his corporations were ardent supporters of nonprofit organizations. That was how he'd found her in the first place. His own philanthropic tendencies might be more focused, but they were no less sincere for that. It was one of his few concessions to conscience.

As Marja's footsteps receded, Jan reluctantly turned his thoughts back to the events that had necessitated his upcoming journey.

"Our friends across the Atlantic seem unable to deal with their difficulties," Hardestadt had said. Jan had made the trip down to Nantes, to one of Hardestadt's countless havens, at the behest of the elder Ventrue. Such a personal audience was not typical.

"You are aware of the Sabbat disruptions on the North American continent?" Hardestadt asked as he passed a silver goblet to Jan across the small space between their matching Louis Quinze chairs.

"Yes, my sire." Jan felt so small next to the man. A backdrop of centuries lent additional stature to the elder's strong chin and aristocratic features. The study in which they sat, despite the plush rug, the velvet curtains, and the inviting grain of the mahogany bookshelves, was cold. Sterile. Unchanging. As he raised the goblet to his lips, the mere bouquet of the vitae set Jan's head swimming. Just a sip—the life's blood of elders long ago sent to Final Death—burned his mouth and throat, but the burning danced maddeningly along the thin line between pain and pleasure. Warmth spread throughout Jan's torso, his arms and legs. He felt color rising to his usually colorless face.

"You will have to go over there and straighten out this mess," said Hardestadt.

Jan, dizzy after his second sip from the goblet, thought he must have heard incorrectly. There was much honor to be gained in such an affair, but certain niggling details demanded his increasingly fogged attention. "I am to accompany the military command?" he inquired.

"You *are* the command," Hardestadt said bluntly. "Events elsewhere do not allow for us to expend unlimited resources in assisting our cousins. The Sabbat are delinquent malcontents, have been from the beginning. Return them to their place. And try not to be too long about it."

The significance of the words, the immensity of the task, slowly permeated Jan's reeling mind. Open warfare raged in the streets of America. The Sabbat had somehow achieved a coordination of action at a level that had eluded them for the centuries since their inception. It was a situation worthy of the attentions of a justicar, of a whole *band* of justicars. And Jan was being sent to take care of the matter. By himself.

"Yes, my sire."

Jan took a large draught from the goblet, as large as politely possible. The fire cleansed him from within.

"I know you will not fail me in this," Hardestadt said.

I will not fail you, Jan silently nodded agreement. *I will not fail you...and survive.*

Saturday, 17 July 1999, 11:53 PM
2 Logan Square
Philadelphia, Pennsylvania

Morty had never really understood the meaning of the term "meaty thump" until the very last second of his existence, not that it did him much good. After all, the thump in question was made by his body hitting the concrete of the Dock Street sidewalk, and the meat—well, the less said about that part, the better.

From thirty-seven stories up, Lucita looked over the edge of the building dispassionately, her long black hair dancing in the strong breeze. The wind tugged at her loose sleeves and leggings, but less effectively, and the chill of the air failed to raise goosebumps on her olive skin. Once, a wind like this would have brought tears to her eyes, but no longer. She looked over the edge at the splatter pattern Morty's immortal guts had made on impact and *tsk*ed to herself. It was messy, too messy. She was getting sloppy in her old age.

Morty had been a warm-up, not even a paying job. He'd simply crossed Lucita's path a year or so previously, the last time she'd been in Philadelphia, and had made a profound annoyance out of himself. Lucita prided herself on keeping an even keel these nights (her sire, Satan roast his flabby, scabby soul, had constantly harped on her temper as something that would someday get her killed) but there were still a few ways to get a rise out of the dreaded Monçada's only childe.

One was to call her "babydoll."

Another was to try for a quick grope, though God alone knew why a vampire felt the need.

And a third was to resort to crude insults relating to Lucita's ethnicity.

Morty had gone three for three in the space of thirty seconds, which had to be some sort of record. As a result, he'd gotten himself reclassified, moving from the list of "imbeciles who can be ignored" to "practice."

Two nights back, Lucita had agreed to a new assignment from an old acquaintance. She'd felt rusty. She'd felt unprepared. She'd felt like...she needed practice.

And thus it was that Three-Finger Morty, one of the meanest sons-of-a-bitch ever to run a pack through the streets of Philadelphia, ended up as a bloody smear on the sidewalk outside a brew pub.

Lucita sighed and hugged herself, more out of worry than as a way of warding off the weather. As warm-ups went, dealing with Morty had been barely worth the trouble. She'd be after bigger prey now, more powerful, more intelligent, and certainly more likely to be aware of her *modus operandi* than some street-level thug.

"This one," she said to no one in particular, "looks like it might actually be work." Then, without a backward glance, she opened the door to the stairwell and drifted down in its shadows, on her way to leaving the city behind.

Playtime, like Morty, was over. She had work to do.

next: ventrue

Dan Chaon's short story coll
spread acclaim on publication in the USA, and was a
National Book Award. *You Remind Me of Me* is Chaon's first novel, and his first book to be published in the UK. He lives in Ohio, USA, with his wife and two sons.

Praise for *You Remind Me of Me*

'A mesmerising debut . . . *You Remind Me of Me* imparts a deeply moving empathy for lives gone sorely awry'
The Times

'*You Remind Me of Me* is a beautifully written exploration of the emotional paths chosen by rootless people desperate to hold on'
Literary Review

'A heartbreakingly beautiful look at the architecture of thwarted desire and the rampant destruction that minor incidents can wreak upon the seemingly most ordinary of lives'
The Spectator

'Hypnotic . . . haunting . . . A lovely, insinuating book with a special staying power . . . Chaon's achievement is to rescue his characters from oblivion and make their lives seem as real as our own'
New York Times Book Review

'Remarkable . . . Chaon has written an apparently claustrophobic novel that feels paradoxically large, generous and, ultimately, quite moving'
Washington Post

'A remarkable first novel . . . Not only satisfying but devastating'
Editor's Choice, *Entertainment Weekly*

'What a writer! Dan Chaon is going to have a breathtaking literary career'
Peter Straub

By Dan Chaon

Among the Missing

Fitting Ends

You Remind

You Remind Me of Me

Me of Me

Dan Chaon

John Murray

First published in 2004 in the United States of America by Ballantine Books

First published in Great Britain in 2005 by John Murray (Publishers)
A division of Hodder Headline

Paperback edition 2006

1

A CIP catalogue record for this title is available from the British Library

B-Format ISBN 0 7195 6541 3
A-Format ISBN 0 7195 6861 7

Portions of chapters 3 and 9 are from 'Where Is Your Mind', a story commissioned by Stories on Stage, a live dramatic short story reading series, produced by Chicago Public Radio.

The quotation on p. 104 is from *Ascent to Civilization: The Archeology of Early Man* by John Gowlett (McGraw Hill: New York, 1984).

Typeset in Monotype Garamond

Printed and bound by
Clays Ltd, St Ives plc

Hodder Headline policy is to use papers that are natural, renewable and recyclable products and made from wood grown in sustainable forests. The logging and manufacturing processes are expected to conform to the environmental regulations of the country of origin.

John Murray (Publishers)
338 Euston Road
London NW1 3BH

To Dan Smetanka
&
to my sons,
two good brothers
&
to my wife,
Sheila:
always, everything

PART ONE

PART ONE

1

March 24, 1977

Jonah was dead for a brief time before the paramedics brought him back to life. He never talks about it, but it's on his mind sometimes, and he finds himself thinking that maybe it's the central fact of the rest of his life, maybe it's what set his future into motion. He thinks of the fat cuckoo clock in his grandfather's living room, the hollow thump of weights and the dissonant guitar thrum of springs as the little door opened and the bird popped out; he thinks of his own heart, which was stopped when they got to him and then suddenly lurched forward, no one knew why, it just started again right around the time they were preparing to pronounce him deceased.

This was in late March 1977, in South Dakota, a few days after his sixth birthday.

If his memory were a movie, the camera would begin high in the air. In a movie, he thinks, you would see his grandfather's little house from above, you would see the yellow school bus coming to a stop at the edge of the long gravel road. Jonah had been to school that day. He had learned something, perhaps several things, and he rode home in a school bus. There were papers in his canvas knapsack, handwriting and addition and subtraction tables that the teacher had graded neatly with red ink, and a picture of an Easter egg that he'd colored for his mother. He sat on a green vinyl seat near the front of the bus and didn't even notice that the bus had stopped because he was deeply interested in a hole that someone had cut in the seat with a pocketknife; he was peering into it, into the guts of the seat, which were made of metal springs and stiff white hay.

Outside it was fairly sunny, and the snow had mostly melted. The exhaust from the bus's muffler drifted through the flashing warning lights, and the silent bus driver lady caused the doors to fold open for him. He didn't like the other children on the bus, and he felt that they didn't like him either. He could sense their faces, staring, as he went down the bus steps and stood on the soft, muddy berm.

But in the movie you wouldn't see that. In the movie you would only see him emerging from the bus, a boy running with his backpack dragging through the wet gravel, a red stocking cap, a worn blue ski jacket, stones grinding together beneath his boots, a pleasantly rhythmic noise he was making. And you would be up above everything like a bird, the long gravel road that led from the mailbox to the house, the weeds along the ditches, the telephone poles, barbed-wire fences, railroad tracks. The horizon, the wide plain of dust and wind.

Jonah's grandfather's house was a few miles outside of the small town of Little Bow, where Jonah went to school. It was a narrow, mustard-colored farmhouse with a cottonwood beside it and a spindly chokecherry bush in front. These were the only trees in view, and his grandfather's place was the only house. From time to time a train would pass by on the railroad tracks that ran parallel to the house. Then the windows would hum like the tuning fork their teacher had shown them in school. *This is how sound feels,* their teacher said, and let them hold their fingers near the vibrating tines.

Sometimes it seemed to Jonah that everything was very small. In the center of his grandfather's bare backyard, an empty pint of cream would be the house and a line of matchbook cars, Scotch-taped end to end, would be the train. He didn't know why he liked the game so much, but he remembered playing it over and over, imagining himself and his mother and his grandfather and his grandfather's dog, Elizabeth, all of them inside the little pint container, and himself (another part of himself) leaning over them like a giant or a thundercloud, pushing his makeshift train slowly past.

He didn't call to his grandfather when he came into the house that day. The door banged shut, the furniture sat silently. He could hear the television talking in his grandfather's room, so he knew his grandfather was there, dozing in the little windowless room, an addition to the house, just space enough for his grandfather's bed and a dresser, a small TV and a lamp with curlicues of cigarette smoke around them. His grandfather was propped up against some pillows, drinking beer; an old blanket, pilled cotton, silk edges unraveling, was thrown across his grandfather's middle, an ashtray balanced on it. Tired. His grandfather worked as a janitor, he went to work early in the morning, while it was still dark. Sometimes when Jonah came home from school, his grandfather would come out of his room and tell Jonah stories or jokes, or he would complain about things, about being tired, about Jonah's mother—*What's the problem with her now? Did you do something to get her mad? I didn't do anything to her!*—and he would swear about people that he didn't like, people who had cheated him, or maybe he would smile and call Elizabeth to him, *Babygirl, babygirl, what are you doing there, does a babygirl want a piece of lunch meat does she?* and Elizabeth would come clicking her nails across the floor, her bobbed tail almost vibrating as she wagged it, her eyes full of love as Jonah's grandfather crooned to her.

But Jonah's grandfather didn't come out of his room that day, and Jonah dropped his bookbag to the floor of the kitchen. There was the smell of smoke, and fried eggs, and the old food in the refrigerator. Unwashed dishes in the sink. His grandfather's door was half-closed, and Jonah sat at the kitchen table for a time, eating cereal.

His mother was at work. He didn't know whether he missed her or not, but he thought of her as he sat there in the still kitchen. She worked at a place called Harmony Farm, *packing eggs,* she said, and the tone of her voice made him imagine dark labyrinths with rows of nests, a promenade of sad, dirty workers moving slowly through the passageways.

She wouldn't talk about it when she got home. Often, she wouldn't want to talk at all, wouldn't want to be touched, would make their supper, which she herself wouldn't eat. She would go to her room and listen to old records she'd had since she was in junior high, her eyes open and her hands in a praying shape beneath her cheek, her long hair spread out behind her on the pillow.

He could stand there for a very long time, watching her from the edge of the doorway and she wouldn't move. The needle of the phonograph pulsed like a smooth car along the spiraling track of a record album and her eyes seemed to register the music more than anything else, her blinking coinciding with a pause or a beat.

But he knew that she could see him standing there. They were looking at each other, and it was a sort of game—to try to blink when she blinked, to set his mouth in the same shape as her mouth, to hear what she was hearing. It was a sort of game to see how far he could inch into the room, sliding his feet the way a leaf opens, and sometimes he was almost to the center of the room before she finally spoke.

Get out, she would say, almost dreamily.

And then she would turn her face away from him, toward the wall.

He thought of her as his spoon hovered over his cereal. One day, he thought, she wouldn't come home from work. Or she might disappear in the night. He had awakened a few times: footsteps on the stairs, in the kitchen, the back door opening. From the upstairs window he saw her forcing her arm into the sleeve of her coat as she walked down the driveway. Her face was strange in the pale brightness cast by the floodlights that his grandfather had installed outside the house. Her breath lifted up out of her in the cold and drifted like mist, trailing behind her as she moved into the darkness beyond the circle of porch light.

We won't be staying long, she would tell Jonah sometimes. She would talk about the places where they used to live as if they'd just come to Jonah's grandfather's house for a visit, even though they'd been living there for as long as he could remember—almost three years. He didn't remember much about the other places she talked about. Chicago. Denver. Fresno. Had he been to these cities? He wasn't sure. Sometimes things came in flashes and images, not really memories at all—a staircase leading down, with muddy boots outside of it; a man with a fringed jacket like Davy Crockett, asleep on a couch while Jonah looked inside his open mouth; a lamp with autumn leaves patterned on it; a cement shower stall where he and his mother had washed together. Sometimes he thought he remembered the other baby, the one that had been born before him. *I was very young,* she told him. That was all she would tell. *I was very young. I had to give it away.*

I remember the baby, he said once, when they were sitting together talking, when she was feeling friendly, holding him in her arms, running her fingernails lightly back and forth across his cheek. *I remember the baby,* he said, and her face grew stiff. She took her hand away.

No, you don't, she said. *Don't be stupid. You weren't even born yet.* She sat there for a moment, regarding him, and then she shut her eyes, her teeth tightening against one another as if the sight of him hurt her. *Jesus Christ,* she said. *Why don't you just forget I ever told you anything. I mean, I confide in you with something that's very private, and very important, and you want to play little pretend games? Are you a baby?*

She sat there coldly, frowning, and began to gather and arrange her hair, ignoring him. She had long hair that reached almost to the belt-loops of her jeans. His grandfather said she looked like the country singer Crystal Gayle. *Don't you think she looks pretty, Jonah?* his grandfather would say when he was trying to cheer her up, but she would only smile a little, not really happy. He watched as she shook a cigarette from her pack on the coffee table and lit it.

Don't look at me that way, she said. She took a sip of smoke from her cigarette, and he tried to make his expression settled and neutral, to make his face the way she might want it to be.

Mom? he said.

What?

Where do babies go when you give them away? He wanted to make his voice sound innocent, to talk in the way a child on television might ask about Santa Claus. He wanted to pretend to be a certain type of child, to see if she might believe in it.

But she didn't. *Where do babies go when you give them away?* she repeated, in a high, insipid voice, and she didn't look at him, she didn't think he was cute or forgivable. He watched the rustle of her long hair, her hand as she ran the head of her cigarette against the rim of the ashtray.

They go to live with nice mommies, she said. After a moment she'd shrugged darkly, not liking him anymore, not wanting to talk.

But he did remember the baby, he thought. He and his mother had seen it at the market, being watched by a lady he didn't know. The baby was pink-skinned, and had a tiny head without hair on it and it was inside something—a basket, he thought, a basket like apples came in at the grocery store. The baby was dressed in a green velvet suit with a Santa's head on it, and rested on a red cushion. It moved its hands blindly, as if trying to catch air. *Look,* his mother said. *There's my baby!* And a lady had looked at them, stiffening as his mother bent down to wave her fingers over the baby's line of vision. The lady had looked at them, smiling but also frightened, and she had spoken to Jonah sharply.

Please don't touch, the lady said. *Your hands are dirty.*

He remembered this vividly—not only because of the baby but because of the lady's eyes, the way she looked at him, the sharp sound of her voice. It was the first time he really understood that there was something about him that people didn't like.

He thought of this as he ran through the house that day, swinging a whisk he'd found in one of the kitchen drawers, pretending it was a magic wand he'd stolen. He thought about the baby, about his mother walking on the gravel road in the dark, and he stood at the edge of her bedroom door, looking up at the padlock she had installed there. It was the room that she'd had when she was a little girl, and then a teenager, and she had many beautiful things—there was a music box where she kept her jewelry, with a tiny ballerina that stood on a spring and turned around and around in front of a little mirror; there was a box like a little square suitcase with 45 rpm records in it; there was a photograph of her mother, who had died, in a small gold frame; there were seashells, and dried branches spray-painted silver, and postcards of paintings taped to the wall. Monet. Chagall. Miró. She'd named them for him once.

He had never even touched anything when he went in, but somehow she knew that he had been going into her bedroom while she was at work. She didn't say anything to him, but one day after work she came home with the lock kit, and he watched as she screwed the hasp onto the door frame, as she fitted the shackle of the padlock into the eye of the hasp and clicked it shut, neatly. She turned to him as he stood there watching, her eyes careful and hooded.

There are precious things in my room, she said softly. *I don't want a robber to get them,* she said, and now, standing outside the door, it gave him a lonely feeling.

After a while, he called for Elizabeth. He got a piece of lunch meat from the refrigerator and whistled for her. He called again, and he heard his grandfather's bed creak as she got down from the foot of it, where she had been curled up comfortably, sleeping while his grandfather slept. *Elizabeth!* Jonah said in a high, tempting voice, and she nosed his grandfather's bedroom door open and peered out at him warily, trembling a little, sidling sheepishly as if people were applauding and she were shy. But when he threw the piece of bologna, she caught it in midair.

She was a Doberman pinscher, older than Jonah by quite a few years. She was not just a pet, his grandfather said, she was a guard dog. The world was changing, his grandfather said, you couldn't leave your door unlocked at night like you used to. There was Charles Manson, a killer; there was the hitchhiker who murdered the man who gave him a lift over near Vermillion; there was the uprising at Wounded Knee. You couldn't trust people anymore, his grandfather said, and Elizabeth would chase a stranger's car down the road, she would frighten the Mormon missionaries who wouldn't dare come to their door, and sometimes Elizabeth barked and barked from the kitchen, her voice raspy and wet even when there was nothing outside to be seen. *She's keeping them ghosts away,* his grandfather would tell him.

Years later, Jonah could still re-create the dog in his mind, perhaps even more vividly than he could recall his grandfather, or what his mother had looked like then. He'd spent so much time with the dog, the two of them sometimes just sitting on the couch as he petted her, playing quietly until she struggled to get away.

He knew her better than anyone but himself, he thought. He knew the plump shape of her torso, the particular, mottled pattern of her brown-and-black hair, the sinew and bones of her legs, the long, intelligent, pointed snout. Her head was like a noble bird with a long bill, solid, a dignified Egyptian statue that he liked to shape with his hands. He loved her rubbery black lips with their amphibious, warty nodes nestled near her back teeth, and he liked to make her talk, moving her lips with his fingers so that she told him knock-knock jokes or sang along with the theme songs of cartoons they watched. He loved the polished black of her hooked toenails and the mysterious, marrow-bone white stuff he found inside the shell of each claw; he loved the cracked, sandpaper texture of her footpads, the wiggly, recoiling meat of her tongue when he caught it and stretched it out, the freckled, pale, waxy skin inside her ears, the way she'd flap her head back and forth if he touched the right spot, as if a fly were bothering her. He loved the soft bare gray skin of her stomach, the two rows of nipples, which he would press, pretending they were buttons and knobs on a robot he had built.

Goddamnit, Jonah, his grandfather would call, when Elizabeth yelped. *Quit pestering that damned dog! I hope she bites you someday!*

Maybe there was something inevitable about what happened. When he tries to imagine it in his mind it always seems that there was something still and icy about the entire afternoon, something hushed, a kind of expectation, as if things had been prepared for him.

He remembers up to a certain point. He remembers the game they were playing, the fantasy he was in. They were being chased, and like a king in a cartoon he shouted "Guards! Seize them!" Soldiers with spears were running in small steps, single file, down a corridor lined with torches.

They were hiding in the bathroom, he and Elizabeth, and he feels that sometimes he can see it perfectly: his hand turning the lock on the bathroom door, which he loved more than any other lock he'd ever seen. A skeleton key in a keyhole. A doorknob made of cut glass like a jewel. You could pretend you were a king in a palace.

Once the door was locked, he breathed with satisfaction. Breathed, turned back to look at the dog Elizabeth, who stood uncomfortably next to the bathtub, her bobbed tail tucked down, ears laid flat, eyes wary and doubtful.

They're coming for us, he told Elizabeth, and she looked at him and then away, tiptoeing in an agitated half-circle in the tiny room. *They're going to kill us if they get in,* he told her, and he pressed his face against the door, listening.

It was a small room, not immaculate but tidy, chilly black and white tile on the floor, chilly porcelain tub, sink, toilet. A tall cabinet held towels and washcloths. There was a toilet with a fuzzy blue cover on its lid, like the hair of a puppet; there was the sink, a steady trickling drip from the faucet; a toothbrush holder, a medicine cabinet mirror above it. There was a small square of window with its glass textured like ice, Jack Frost designs. Below was the bathtub, clawfoot, deep-basined, the inside of an egg. An orange rust stain ran from the base of the faucet head to the drain.

It was his idea that this was the best place to hide. He remembers this clearly, too, the determination that they should hunker down inside the bathtub to get away from the soldiers that were hunting for them, but there was some difficulty in getting Elizabeth to join him in this plan. He stood in the bathtub and held Elizabeth by her front paws, so that she stood up on her hind legs. He tried to tug her forward, but she didn't want to come. She pulled away from him, and so he got out of the tub and tried to lift her by her hindquarters, but she was too heavy. He had a hold on the loose skin of her haunches, and he managed to lift her off the ground. *Get in!* he said, and gave her a hard shove. *Hurry, damnit!* And she made a sharp sound as he pushed her, as he fell into the bathtub on top of her.

He doesn't really know what happened next. There was a moment, a kind of wave, a blank spot during which the game fizzled away, during which Elizabeth became not-Elizabeth. The two of them scrabbled against the slick porcelain. Perhaps he was trying to hold her down, perhaps he pushed hard against a tender spot on her belly, perhaps she panicked, upended, disoriented, unable to gain a footing. Her thin legs struggled in the air, and her body twisted, trying to right itself, and she made a sound like she was vomiting up a string of yelps. She snapped with her teeth, twisted, lashed, and Jonah felt a spark in his mind that wasn't really awareness.

The first bite was one of the worst. The long front tooth, the canine, sank into the skin just below Jonah's left eye and tore in a line through his cheek to the edge of his throat. Blood shot up and stippled the window. The bottles of shampoo on the edge of the tub clattered as Jonah's feet kicked in a surprised spasm. When he jerked away from her, Elizabeth bit down on his ear and pulled a piece of it off.

Later he would try to think that Elizabeth had gone crazy. People would say that it might have been the taste of blood, that it might have been the noises he was making, the high-pitched sounds that instinctively made her think he was some kind of prey. People would say that attack dogs like Dobermans can be high-strung, that they can lose control of themselves. He didn't want to believe that she hated him. He didn't want to think that he was her tormentor, that whatever he'd done to her, she'd finally had enough. That she bit him and liked it, thinking *at last*.

But she didn't stop. Her teeth raked through his palms when he held them to his face, trailing through his forearms as he flailed at her, trying to hit. One bite cut through his lower lip as she tried to get to his neck, and another pulled the skin of his torn face into a flap. He remembers trying to press the skin back against his face, like it was a puzzle piece he was trying to fit. When he fell out of the bathtub onto the tile floor, he felt wet. He was aware of Elizabeth's front paws clawing fast against his clothes as if she were trying to dig a hole into him, her jaws, bites on his scalp, his neck, his chest as he curled and rolled and kicked, smearing blood behind him. *I'm sorry,* he said. *Mom, I didn't mean to! It was an accident!*

Maybe he doesn't really remember this. Maybe he only imagines it, looking at his body, his naked skin in the mirror. Most of what happened is outside of his memory. He can recall flashes of heat, of pressure, but not pain, exactly. Most people don't understand what it means to be an animal, to be killed, eaten. A quiet peacefulness settles in. The body relaxes, accepts everything.

That was all there was to it really. At a bar, years later, a woman says, *Tell me something interesting about yourself* and Jonah pauses.

I was dead once, he thinks. That's the first thing he thinks, though he doesn't say it. It sounds too melodramatic, too complicated and inappropriate. She is a smooth thinker, this woman, she will look at him skeptically, she will take a piece of ice from her drink and roll it in her mouth.

Oh, really, she'll say, after a moment. *So what's that like? Being dead?*

And he doesn't know, exactly. He is aware of a feeling of rushing forward. It is not unlike the way it felt on the expressway when suddenly, at sixty-five or seventy-five miles per hour, a pair of semi-trucks framed his car on either side, the rushing walls of their trailers creating a tunnel he was hurtling through. Ahead, a rattling garbage truck drifted into the lane in front of him; behind, a woman in a minivan pushed impatiently toward his bumper, sealing him into a coffin of velocity. Enclosed and yet hurtling forward.

At that moment, he felt a memory spin through his insides. The dog's teeth. The yellow house, the wide plain, seen from above. The skeleton key, the baby in the basket, the lady who said *Please don't touch, your hands are dirty.*

He was dead, or almost dead, when his grandfather broke open the bathroom door. He doesn't remember this, he just knows. He is aware of the blood, his own blood, all over everything. He feels the door splinter and fall open. He hears the sound of his grandfather's raw, smoker-voiced moaning. His grandfather caught Elizabeth by the collar, pulling her away, and then his grandfather began to kick her in the ribs and the head.

In the movie, the bathroom would seem to float in space, white and glowing fluorescently. In the movie, the ambulance men bend over him, the corpse of a small boy laid out on the bathroom's black and white tiles. The men are silent and gentle and godlike. He pictures them as kindly aliens, with round, interchangeable heads and large eyes. His grandfather must be there somewhere, off to the edge of things, but he can't see him. By this time, Elizabeth is dead. He can picture her, not far from where he is lying, Elizabeth on her side, her legs limp, paws turned inward, mouth slightly open, eyes staring as his own eyes are staring. A line could be drawn between their two eyes, his and Elizabeth's—two points, A and B, beginning and end.

Jonah's grandfather used to tease him all the time. It wasn't mean-spirited, he didn't think. Just something his grandfather did to amuse himself. He remembers the day before he died, the day before Elizabeth attacked him, an ordinary after-school afternoon, not long before his mom got home from work, when his grandfather called to him. *Jonah!* he called, in his wry, raspy voice. *Come quick! Come and look!* And Jonah had stood there eagerly as his grandfather pointed out the back window, toward the railroad tracks, where some boxcars were parked. *I see the carnival came through here last night,* he said. *Look at that! They left an elephant!*

Where? Jonah said, and tried to follow his grandfather's finger.

There! Don't you see it?

No.

It's right there—where I'm pointing. You don't see it?

No . . . Jonah said doubtfully, but he craned his neck.

You mean to tell me you don't see an elephant standing there? Jonah's grandfather demanded.

Well . . . Jonah said, not wanting to commit himself. *Well* . . . he said.

Jonah scoped along the lines and shapes outside the window again. He didn't see the elephant, but then, after a time, it seemed that he did. In his memory, there is still the figure of an elephant, standing at the edge of the train tracks. It curls its trunk, languidly, thoughtfully, and brings a piece of hay to its mouth.

2

Spring 1977, Spring 1978

Around the time that Jonah was being brought back to life by the paramedics, Troy Timmens was reclining in a beanbag chair in a trailer house on the outskirts of St. Bonaventure, Nebraska, watching some teenagers smoke marijuana. It was late afternoon, about five o'clock, but with the curtain drawn it could have been any time at all. Troy leaned back, settling more deeply, aware of the satisfying crunch made by the Styrofoam pills inside the beanbag chair as he applied his weight to them. He supposed that he was fairly content.

The trailer house he was sitting in belonged to his cousin Bruce and Bruce's wife, Michelle. Troy had gotten into the habit of stopping by their place after school, staying until dinner or beyond, staying until well past his bedtime. If she asked, he told his mother that he had been baby-sitting for Bruce and Michelle's two-year-old son, Ray, and often that was true. It didn't matter. Troy's parents were engaged in the final stages of falling in hate with each other, a stretch of many months that was leading toward their divorce, and everyone involved was pleased to have Troy elsewhere.

Troy was happy at Bruce's place. It was comfortable and exciting, a world he connected vaguely in his mind with California and rock stars.

He loved the things they owned: the black-light posters with their pictures of wolves and skulls and lightning bolts, the stacks of record albums and tapes, the beaded door that led to the kitchen, the refrigerator with an automatic icemaker built into the door, a possession Troy admired, along with stereo systems and microwaves and Corvette automobiles. They always had the newest kinds of chips and snacks that Troy had seen advertised on television, and he was welcome to eat as much as he liked. And the living room, he thought, was breathtakingly luxurious. There was the smell of incense sticks, drifting up from the glass-topped coffee table, and furniture you could sink into—not only the beanbag chairs but also a big sofa with giant pillow cushions. The living room carpet was a thick, brownish-gold shag that covered not only the floor but the walls as well, all the way up to the ceiling. Best of all was a beautiful fish tank, where dwelled an angel fish and a pair of kissing fish and a tiny frog, along with many, many black and orange mollies that constantly gave birth to amazingly tiny babies—babies that, to Troy's fascinated horror, the kissing fish often ate, breathing them into their large puckered mouths. But his favorite thing in the entire house was the plastic skeleton at the bottom of the fish tank, a sunken pirate who clutched a ship's wheel in his bony hands; beside him, a treasure chest belched out bubbles of air. Troy was the sort of child who spent a lot of his time at school drawing pictures of skeletons on his notebooks and onto desks—skeletons with sunglasses and Afros, skeletons laughing happily as they rose out of cartoon graves, skeletons piloting airplanes or driving cars or wielding machine guns.

He was sitting near the fish tank on that day, staring at the little underwater world, mesmerized by the way the pirate skeleton's arms fluttered in the current of air bubbles. He was pretending to be uninterested in the marijuana smoking, though in fact he was watching surreptitiously as a few older teenagers—friends of Bruce and Michelle—drew smoke into their mouths from the lip of a glass water pipe. They were all listening to a comedy record by Cheech and Chong, which was very funny. Everyone was laughing, and Troy leaned back, a bit shocked by the language the comedians were using. His eyes narrowed in the cloud of smoke that hung in a thin layer above their heads, but he was unobtrusive, smiling shyly. He was ten.

But he was different from most ten-year-olds. People at Bruce and Michelle's place always told him so. They said he was like a teenager—an honorary teenager, someone once said, which made him proud. No one minded having him around. He was never any bother.

And maybe it was true that he was unusually mature. There was an aura about him, Michelle told people, though she couldn't put her finger on it. *Old-souled,* Michelle said, and ran her hand through his hair gravely. Something about him, something in his manner and his face and even the way he carried himself that seemed eerily unchildlike. It was those pale blue, malamute eyes, the oddly alert, wary posture. It was the shy yet somehow wolfish grin he'd beam out sometimes, a grin that those teenaged girls seemed to think of as pre-sexy, imagining that in a few years it would evolve into something horny and devastating. And that deep laugh—a laugh that made the stirred-up girls lift their heads and stare for a moment. Troy didn't laugh often, but when he did, it wasn't like the laughter of any ten-year-old boy they'd encountered. He sounded like he was more experienced than he was—a whisper of male prowess, cockiness tinted at the edges with something like melancholy, and they flicked their eyes at one another, amused and yet uncertain: *Where had he learned to make a sound like that?* They exchanged private looks—suppressed turns of the mouth, slight widening of their eyes, almost imperceptible movement of brows. Troy noticed this, but didn't know what it meant.

There were three of them that day, three high school girls, along with a wiry mustached boy of about nineteen who was their leader, who had brought them to Bruce's place. Troy was aware of the subtle attention the girls were paying him, and it made him even more resolutely quiet. He observed them from his corner by the fish tank, thinking that maybe they were making fun of him for some reason, and he carefully glanced down to make sure his zipper wasn't open. He ran his hand across his hair, stroking it flat, and tried to listen seriously to what the comedians on the record album were saying. They were talking in funny accents about eating shit.

He had met these girls before, in a vague way. There was one named Chrissy, who had straight blond hair and a natural tan that made it seem as if she spent a lot of time on a tropical beach; another, Kim, was very skinny, and wore a tight T-shirt that said "I'm With Stupid," with an arrow that pointed in a general way toward whoever happened to be on her left—in this case a girl named Carla. He had seen this girl at Bruce and Michelle's a few times, and he remembered her: *Carla.* She was sixteen years old, a small, round-faced girl not much taller than Troy himself; she had large blue eyes, thickly surrounded with black eyeliner and mascara, and enormous breasts. She wore a scoop-necked T-shirt, and Troy could see the beginning of her cleavage, a slope of moled and freckled skin. He was aware that there was something about Carla's breasts that made them different from other girls', but he hadn't yet figured out that they looked different because Carla wasn't wearing a bra.

There were a number of important things he hadn't figured out yet, though he would before too much longer. For example, he did not know that his cousin Bruce was a drug dealer, and that these girls were customers. He didn't know that Michelle felt uncomfortable about him being there, watching these transactions, that later she would argue with Bruce about it. He didn't know that Bruce and Michelle were young—both of them twenty-four years old—or that they'd already begun a friendship with cocaine that they would spend a good portion of their later lives trying to escape from. In retrospect, of course, there was the way Bruce was fidgeting, his thumb and forefinger tapping against each other like anxious pincers; there was the nervous, walleyed gaze that Michelle fixed on him.

"Troy, Hon," Michelle said. "Would you do me a favor? Would you go check on Ray and see how he's doing?"

"Oh," Troy said, and straightened up as if he hadn't been paying attention. "Sure," he said, importantly, and clambered out of the beanbag chair as the teenaged girls observed him.

This was his job when he was at Bruce and Michelle's place—he was supposed to watch the two-year-old Ray. He was supposed to make sure Ray was occupied, that his diaper was clean, that he wasn't sticking his fingers into electrical sockets or drinking from the bottle of pine-scented cleaner under the bathroom sink. It wasn't work exactly. Troy liked babies. He liked to take care of them, he liked their little toes and their soft, fleshy cheeks. Besides which, he was still young enough that he enjoyed playing with Ray's toys, the building blocks and the See-and-Say and the plastic yellow school bus with the miniature Weeble children that fit inside it. He still felt warmly toward the Dr. Seuss books that he read aloud to Ray. He didn't mind constructing games of pretend or hiding that Ray would find deeply involving. It was easy.

Nevertheless, Michelle was grateful to have him around. When he left the trailer at nine or ten at night and headed back to his own home, Michelle would often give him money. Five, ten, twenty dollars. "Thanks for coming by, honey," she would say, and as she tucked the bills into his hand, their fingers brushed in a way that made him wish that she were his older sister, or his mother.

The high school girls watched him as he sloughed out of the bean-bag chair he'd melted into, and the older boy made a face. Troy saw the boy raise his eyebrows in a not-quite-friendly way, making an "O" with his mouth as he centered his lips over the bong. *Get lost, kid,* the look said.

But the girl named Chrissy called after him. "Hey," she said, and as he got up he turned to look at her again. "Troy . . . is that your name?" He paused, awkwardly, and nodded.

"You're cute," she said. The other girls shifted their significant glances toward her, smirking as if she had made a mean joke. And then they broke into laughter.

That day was not a particularly important one in Troy's life, but it was part of a series of events that he thought of sometimes, part of the continuum of his life with Carla, those early days in Bruce's trailer when the two of them couldn't have ever known that they would eventually get married, that they would have a child together, that they'd end up years later separated and then divorced and yet, he thought, forever trailing this history behind them.

Twenty years later, when Troy was thirty and trying to decide whether or not he was still in love with her, he thought of that time in Bruce and Michelle's trailer. Carla had left him, was living with another man, their marriage was finished. Nevertheless, he had driven from Nebraska out to Las Vegas at her request, at the prompting of her late-night calls. "I just need you to come," she'd said, and he'd gotten into his car and driven for two days. "Will you please, please, just do this one thing?" she whispered, her voice raw and slurred, and he did as she asked, not least because of those long ago days at Bruce and Michelle's, when he'd stared at her chest.

Carla was not the first girl he kissed. The first girl was actually Carla's friend Chrissy, the permanently tanned blond girl, with her dusky arms and pale, lotioned palms. "She was disgusting," Carla said years later, when he told her about it. She didn't remember her times at Bruce and Michelle's as fondly as he did. "God!" Carla said. "How gross! I always knew there was something really wrong with her. She was just the kind of person who would try to seduce a ten-year-old."

And Troy had nodded—he was always convinced by Carla's vehement dislikes, even later, when he became one of them.

But the truth was somewhat more complicated than that, he thought; more than simple words like *disgusting* and *seduce*, though he didn't know what terms would be better to substitute.

It was all mixed up in his mind, twined up with his memories of that time in his life, with his love for Bruce and Michelle's place, with the history of his life with Carla, with the fact that Chrissy wasn't alive anymore.

It was a lot to process, he thought.

And to be honest, he didn't know what was really going on that day, or how it had come to be that Chrissy kissed him. A year had passed since they first encountered each other, and Troy was now eleven, almost twelve. It was the spring of 1978. He had been spending most of his after-school time at Bruce and Michelle's by that point, sometimes sleeping over on a Friday or Saturday night in a sleeping bag on the floor of Ray's room, falling asleep to the comfortable sounds of laughter and loud talking and partying, and then waking up to the dead silence of aftermath, the door to Bruce and Michelle's sealed tight, a blanket draped over a curtain rod to block the light from entering their room, a straggler or two asleep on the couch or curled up on the rug in front of the fish tank, beer cans stacked on the surfaces and the gray smell of stale smoke lingering in the air.

On that morning he'd wandered into the kitchen around six

o'clock in the morning, hungry because he'd forgotten to eat the night before. Chrissy was sitting there at the counter, and at first he thought she was asleep. She had her head down, cradled in the crook of her elbow, and she didn't move when he got some sweetened cereal out of the cupboard and poured it into a bowl. But when he returned from the refrigerator with a carton of milk, she had raised her head.

"Hungry?" she said brightly, and he held himself still, wary. The pupils of her eyes were enormously dilated, so that the gray-green of the irises were almost swallowed up, a thin aura like the rind of sun around an eclipse. Her mascara was smudged: raccoon eyes, he had heard the other girls call it. But she was looking at him expectantly, and so he nodded. *Yes, I'm hungry.* A few strands of hair adhered to the sticky gloss on her lip, and she used the edge of her pinkie fingernail to dislodge them.

"I'll bet I look like shit," she said, in a musing, almost contented voice, and Troy wasn't sure whether she was addressing herself or him. He shifted as she lit a cigarette. She glanced him over lightly, then turned away to blow a line of smoke into the air above their heads.

"Oh, come on, Troy," she said after a moment. "You should know this. When the girl says, 'I look like shit,' the boy is supposed to say, 'No, you look great!' That's the way it works."

"Oh," he said, and fingered his spoon. The smeared makeup made her eyes inscrutable, and he couldn't gauge her expression. "You look great," he said softly.

"You lie," she said. She smiled secretively, then let forth another stream of smoke, her lips puckered like a child blowing soap bubbles. "You've got to be a better liar if you're ever going to get a girl to kiss you."

"Yeah, right," he said, and frowned. This was a game that people sometimes liked to play with children—"How many girlfriends do you have?" they would ask, or "I'll bet those little girls chase you all around the playground!"—and he didn't have much patience with this kind of teasing. He turned his attention to his cereal, sinking his spoon into the soup of milk and floating apple-flavored O's intently, ignoring her, expecting her to lose interest and move on to another room.

Around them, the trailer was silent. He could hear the hum of the fish tank's bubbler, the insistent awakening chirp of sparrows nested in the eaves and awnings of the trailers, or in the trailer court's single cottonwood tree. He made a slurping sound when he brought his spoon to his lips, just to annoy the quiet, and noticed that Chrissy was still observing him expectantly.

"Can I have a bite of your cereal?" she said at last.

He shrugged. "Okay," he said, but when he started to push the bowl toward her, she did something unnerving. She pushed her hair behind her ears and leaned forward, closing her eyes lightly and opening her mouth. She wanted him to feed her.

It was weird, he thought, and he hesitated. But she sat there with her mouth open, and after a moment he held his spoon out. He watched as she slowly closed her lips over it. Her eyes opened as she swallowed.

"Mmmm," she said. "That tastes good. Thanks."

"Uh-huh," he said. He set the spoon back on the counter, not sure what to do with it now that it had been inside her mouth. He had seen the inside of her lips, which were slick and pink and glistening. And her tongue. He wasn't sure what to think about it.

But she didn't act as if anything unusual had happened. He watched as she lifted her cigarette, blowing on the tip of it so that the ember glowed orange through the gray crust of ash. Then she stubbed it out. She smiled.

"Can I ask you a question?" she said. He just shrugged. Her attention was not particularly welcome, but it was also hypnotic in a way he didn't quite understand.

"I heard from Bruce that you're adopted," she said. "Are you?"

"Yeah," he said. "So?"

"So nothing," she said. "It's just that I was adopted, too, so I thought that was interesting. I mean, you don't meet many other people who are adopted, do you?"

"I guess not."

"You guess not," she repeated. She regarded him steadily for a moment, her expression hooded. Then she smiled. "You're funny," she said. Then: "So what do you think about it? About being adopted?"

"I don't know," he said. The truth was, he *didn't* think about it very much, and certainly never talked about it. He'd always regarded this fact about himself as both unimportant and private, like people's belly buttons. He was adopted. *We adopted each other,* his mother had told him. *God brought us right to you and put us together as a family.* He'd known this from an early age, and he'd been taught that it didn't matter at all, that he was no different from anyone else. His parents—Earl and Dorothy Timmens—were just as real as anyone else's parents. But still, it bothered him that Bruce had told this girl about it, and he felt uncomfortable imagining the two of them discussing him. He shrugged, eyeing her suspiciously. "It's not a big deal," he said. "Nobody cares about it."

"Huh," she said: a short laugh. "Oh, sure they do. You just don't know it yet." She made a wry face, her eyes glancing sideways slyly, as if someone might be listening, and she was going to tell him something secret, or dirty. "Don't *you* think about it? Don't you wonder about your mother?"

"Not really," he said. And what else could he say? He looked down, thoughtfully, tracing the fake wood-grain patterns of the counter's Formica surface. What could he tell her? Could he say that he'd always believed his mother when she told him that he was special—chosen, selected, his mother said. When he was little, he used to listen to a record "How Much Is That Doggy in the Window?" He would play it over and over, and in some ways he supposed that he'd always thought his adoption was something like that—that his parents had wandered through a corridor of glass cases containing babies, and that they'd suddenly halted, struck with certainty, in front of a bassinet that contained his infant self. They'd pointed, and a nurse had brought him bundled in a blanket into their arms, a clean and uncomplicated transaction. He'd never much considered what came before that. He knew about sex, about how babies were born, but the idea of being inside someone's stomach—of being expelled wetly from some woman's body—seemed grotesque and unreal. In his mind, that person was like a skin he'd shed, a cocoon husk he'd left behind.

"I guess," he said, "I guess I always figured that it wasn't very important." And he shrugged, shifting uncertainly. He was aware of the inexplicable and almost oppressive heaviness of her attention. It was an ability some girls had, he recognized, a power they could draw upon simply by focusing themselves on a single person. His skin prickled as she leaned closer, as her forearm brushed lightly against his and he could see the pale hairs just above her wrist, the rosy smell of lotion and moist, soft pressure of skin brushing against skin, the way her hair grazed his shoulder.

"Oh, well," she said. She let the pad of her forefinger touch the back of his hand, briefly, smiling at him in a way that wasn't really a smile at all, but something else—a swallowed sadness, a shudder. "I don't know," she said. "Maybe I'm just weird. I'm, like, probably sort of crazy or something. But . . . I think about it a lot. I think, you know, what is she doing now? Like, maybe she's a singer or a famous actress or something. And what does she look like? And what would have happened if she'd kept me? Do you know what I'm talking about? You could have had this whole other different life, and maybe you'd be different, and, well, *happier*. I mean, I know that I don't belong in the family I'm living in now, that's for sure." She made a face. "Maybe I'm the only one, I don't know. But do you really think your parents wanted to adopt a baby? Don't you think that if they'd had the choice they would have had a real baby? I mean, one of their own."

He didn't know what to say to this, and so he was silent. From the next room came the sound of thick male coughing, a throat cleared of phlegm. "Fuck," a sleepy voice muttered sharply, and her eyes shifted toward the sound.

"I feel sorry for you," she said. "You're a kid. You shouldn't be hanging out in a place like this."

And then, without warning, she kissed him. She tilted her head and pressed her lips against his. He felt her tongue move softly, a little flick along the line of his mouth, and he jerked with surprise. Her hands held his cheeks, and her lips moved against his for a moment before she released him.

"There," she said. "Now you'll remember me."

It was about 7:30 in the morning, Saturday, as he walked home, and he could still taste the dark, smoky pressure of her tongue as he hurried through the underpass with its walls of wet, dripping, rust-stained cement, past the little abandoned grocery store with its windows pasted over with newspaper, past the grade school, toward the rows of small houses that made up the street he lived on. As he walked down Deadwood Avenue, a dog barked at him from behind a fence, and a pickup carrying a thin, ancient man in a cowboy hat pulled slowly by on the street. It had been a dry spring, and the yards of the houses were yellow-green, the tired-looking color of the sod that covered the prairie hills on the outskirts of town. St. Bonaventure was little more than a cluster of houses and stores in the middle of a dry plain of wheat fields, asphalt roads, bare, rocky hills. He didn't think of this often, but he was aware of it at that moment—the great expanse of the world beyond the borders, the woman, the mother he'd once been inside of, out there somewhere. His stomach felt fluttery, and he felt infected by the sadness that Chrissy had given to him with her long, slow look, with the weight of her mouth against his. His heart was still light and quick and hollow in its beating.

Here was his house. Curtains drawn. The screen door with its aluminum curlicue molding.

Inside, his father was asleep on the couch. His parents had been fighting again, and his dad was huddled there under an afghan, curled up, one pale bare foot uncovered, his face severe and drawn and pressed against the arm of the couch, frowning in his dreams. His hair stood up in stiff tufts, and his eyes shifted underneath their lids as Troy tucked the blanket over his exposed foot.

He loved his father. That was what he should have told Chrissy. He loved his mother, who was still asleep in the bedroom. He loved Bruce and Michelle and Ray, all his people, his family. He didn't want another life.

3

January 6, 1966

At the home for unwed mothers, Nora still holds out hope that the baby will stop growing, that it will die. Around her, the stomachs of the girls are swelling, becoming taut, and their souls are deflating. There is a smell of old fruit and eucalyptus, there is a large box television playing a game show, "What's My Line," a dozen expressionless girls staring at the screen, some of them smoking cigarettes or biting on their nails or clasping their hands in their laps. One of them is knitting. Knitting. This girl's hands move steadily and the skein of blanket or sweater or shawl is slowly, line by line, becoming a cloth that shrouds the lump of her belly. Nora wants to kill this girl, whose face is as blank as a rabbit's. Or she wants to kill the happy celebrities that the girl is watching as they tell their jokes. Or she wants to kill herself.

She moves along the hallway, walking, creeping, one hand cupped beneath her belly, the other on the wall. She isn't even showing yet, but still she holds her stomach uncertainly. There is a tickling feeling, like a spider spinning a web inside her, maybe she's only imagining it. The walls are cold, warty plaster, painted smooth, and she runs her hands across them as if they are braille, supporting herself as she goes. Doors lined up. She suspects that the rooms are all identical, though she hasn't seen anyone else's. She knows: a single bed, a night table with a lamp and a Bible, a desk with empty drawers, a closet with identical cheap poly-cotton maternity smocks on hangers, a window with a bare, snowy tree in the center of it.

It is not quite a prison, not quite a hospital. A Home, they call it, in the way they call the repositories for the old and the insane "Homes." *They put her in a Home,* her father had once said about a neighbor woman who had lost her mind when she got old, and now Nora herself is in such a place. Being watched over. Taken care of. You cannot lock the door to your room in such a place, and her door won't even stay closed, she doesn't know why. The air pressure, maybe, the wind, something—she has no way of knowing, but sometimes as she lies in the dark the door will click open like an awakened eye, a shaft of light from the hallway will fall across her face. It happens frequently enough that she has taken to leaning a chair against the doorknob when she goes to sleep.

In the dark, she can't keep herself from thinking that it is a ghost. She doesn't believe in ghosts, exactly, but if they did exist they would thrive in a place such as this. Girls have killed themselves here, she is sure of it. It is a deathly place. Silent. Cold. There is the kind of feeling you might have, walking alone through a park in late autumn, when a single leaf falls from a tree and twists slowly to the ground in front of you.

January 6, 1966. This is her fourth day of residence in the Mrs. Glass House, her fourth day of captivity, and it is beginning to sink in. There is no turning back. She should have accepted that fact a long time ago, but instead she still finds herself bargaining vaguely with her body, with God, thinking that it's possible that a mistake has been made. The long months stretch in front of her, and already it seems that she is losing herself. There is nothing to do here but wait, months upon months tunneled in front of her: June, they said, early June most likely. She sits in a chair by the window, reading her book, *The Collector* by John Fowles. It is inappropriate, she knows: "A brutal tormented man and the beautiful, aristocratic young woman he has taken captive," the back cover proclaims, and the story upsets her. *I hate the way I have changed. I accept too much,* the woman says, and Nora underlines this passage as small glimmering motes of snow pass by outside, as somewhere down the hall a transistor radio is playing AM love songs, the Monkees singing "I'm a Believer!" She reads: "I'm so far from everything. From normality. From light. From where I want to be." She closes the book and sits staring at her fingers, which don't seem like her own fingers. It is exactly the wrong book to be reading at the moment, she thinks, though on second thought, a happy book, an optimistic, escapist book would be even worse. If she's going to read anything at all it ought to be about suffering.

She thinks about things that she will never tell people, ugly memories that make her wince when they enter her mind.

Once, she punched herself in the stomach as hard as she could, hoping it would dislodge.

Once, she put something inside of herself—a knitting needle, which is what she had heard they used. But what, exactly, was she supposed to catch hold of with it? She imagined a floating piece of yarn with a glob of cells and blood at the end of it. Hooking it, pulling it out.

Once, she tasted bleach, but couldn't bring herself to drink it.

Have the others done such things? If so, they don't talk about it. They don't talk about much, these girls, as if they are all spies. Mostly, they glance at one another furtively—the scratch of silverware against plates, the sound of chewing, the television voices, the soft, private moan a girl will make when she walks down the hall. What is there to say?

"This is not a sorority," Mrs. Bibb tells them. "Let's keep our socializing to a minimum, shall we?" It is against the rules for girls to sit in one another's rooms and speak privately. It is requested that the girls do not reveal the names of the towns they come from, and it is best if they avoid speaking of their pasts at all—the fathers of their babies, the mistakes that have been made, the families they've disappointed. It is against the rules for the girls to tell one another their last names, and she suspects that most of the first names are pseudonyms as well. Like the girl who knits, who says her name is Dominique. *Dominique,* like the title of the popular song from grade school, the song by the Singing Nun.

"Oh, really," Nora says. "That's an unusual name." And the knitting girl looks down. She has dark eyebrows that meet in the middle of her face, right above the bridge of her nose, and her chocolate-colored eyes focus on the movement of the needles between her fingers. She is a girl who is used to being made fun of, the sort of girl who clutches her books tightly in front of her and plunges through the hallways of high school like she is walking into a blizzard. Nora knew of a girl like this back in Little Bow, a girl named Alice, which they all thought was funny. A Lice, they called her, and the boys sat behind her and flicked their boogers into her badly permed hair. A man who would make a girl like Alice or Dominique pregnant would have to be entirely evil, Nora decides.

"What are you knitting?" Nora says at last, but the girl keeps her head down stubbornly, as such girls will. Someone, their mother probably, taught them to *suffer silently*, taught them *sticks and stones will hurt my bones, but words will never hurt me,* taught them *a quiet girl is better loved.* Dominique pinches her lips as Nora looks at her.

"Well," Nora says, after the silence extends for a time. "It's pretty, whatever it is."

"It's a blanket," says Dominique, finally. "It's just a blanket. It's cold in this place."

"Yes," Nora says. "It's going to be a long winter!" she says, reminding herself unpleasantly of her father, his cheerful, commonplace chatter. For a minute she hates him, misses him, hates him, misses him, like flipping a coin or plucking petals off a flower.

It will be a long time before she sees her father again. This is another one of the rules: relatives are not allowed to visit the girls at Mrs. Glass House, and she recalls her father's sorrowful, doubtful eyes as the matron, Mrs. Bibb, recited this to him. Mrs. Bibb is one of the horrors in a long list of horrors, with her orange hair and freckles and her cheerful, caustic blandness. A person incapable of either cruelty or kindness, Nora imagined, only an indifferent *nice*. It was terrifying, listening to her sweet voice, but what could be done? Nora was expressionless as her father looked at her shyly, as if she might advise him, as if she could tell him what to say or think. "Well, I suppose," he said, and Nora imagined that he was waiting for her to intervene, to lose her nerve, to cry out, "Daddy, don't leave me in this place!" Mrs. Bibb seemed to be preparing herself silently for just such a scene.

"Honey . . . ?" her father said, but Nora didn't say anything to him. She stared down at the ribbed upholstery of the easy chair she was sitting in. He knew what she thought, he knew what her decision was.

Originally, his own ideas had been quite different. "Just tell me his name," her father had said. "I'll talk to him, he'll do the right thing. I can promise you that."

But she shook her head. "No," she said.

For a while, he'd tried to argue. "It's his responsibility, too," her father said. "Believe me, he'd want to know what's going on. You just have to give him the chance. You think you know everything, Missy, but you know, I think that most men, they think that it's their baby, too. Men are not so different as you might think.

"Did he rape you, is that it?" her father said.

"Are you protecting somebody? He's married, isn't he?" her father said. "If he comes around here, I'll know it's him. I'll know it's him, and I'll kill him, you know that, don't you? I don't care about me, they can put me in prison, but I'll kill him."

"Did he hurt you?" her father said. "Did he threaten you? You don't have to be afraid to tell me."

"Don't do anything you're going to regret," he said. "A life lasts for a long time, you may not know that yet."

Of course, these conversations linger in her mind now that she's alone. Her father says, "Just let me help you, babygirl. You're my daughter. I'll do anything for you."

That is the worst part of it, she thinks sometimes: knowing that she has hurt him perhaps more than she has hurt herself. It aches to think of him, to picture him sitting in the mornings, hunched over his cup of coffee at the kitchen table, licking the lead of his pencil as he fills in the daily crossword in the newspaper, alone in the small house. She knows that he is already thinking of this baby of hers, that he won't let it go, that it will be on his mind for the rest of his life. She knows that the coldness and stubbornness she'd turned toward him will be like a cloak she has put on, which she can never take off.

But she cannot choose what he wants for her. Her father is a lover of babies, of families, of connection and structure, and she is not. She knows his stories, the events of the past that he's turned into little trinkets in his mind, telling them over and over, the same words, the same welling of emotion—wet eyes, constricted voice—at the same precise moments in the telling of his sad, sentimental tales. The orphan train, how they picked him up off the streets of New York City when he was only four years old and sent him all the way across the country to be adopted by a cruel farmer and his wife, who didn't want a child but a slave; how he'd run away at the age of fifteen. Or her mother, so beautiful and young, and him almost twenty years her senior, but they were soul mates from the start, his pretty little brown-eyed Sioux lady, how can he live without her now that she's dead? And Nora herself, his own babygirl, the way she used to follow him around and imitate whatever he did, *she even wanted to put shaving cream on her face and pretend to shave, just like her daddy!*

Oh, these stories—by the time she was fifteen they were almost unbearable. She would feel a smooth airtight window sliding up inside her, impervious to sympathy or pity. "I've heard this before," she'd say softly, but that wouldn't stop him.

Here at Mrs. Glass House, at least there is silence. At least there are no stories, and she is glad, because she can't transform what has happened to her into a romance. The boy, the father, is almost gone from her mind now, lingering only in her awareness of her own stupidity. Soon, the baby will be gone, too.

But until then, there must be punishment. Humiliation.

Here, at Mrs. Glass House, they are herded from place to place. They move, very docile, single file down the stairs to the basement cafeteria; they are preparing to walk down the hill toward town, where they will eat ice cream and see a movie. Mrs. Bibb distributes "wedding rings," cheap gold-painted strips of tin, which they are to wear on their left hand, third finger. The Home is said to be a convalescent house for expectant mothers. No one says words like *unwed*, or *bastard*, or *whore*. Certain aspects are pretended. Nora watches as Dominique is given a ring, watches as Dominique slides the ring on, over the chewed fingernail and ugly, wrinkled hillock of finger joint.

They line up. They will be led down the long winding driveway toward the town, young girls in various stages of pregnancy, ripeness, swollen and swelling girls marching single file from the doorway of this place that looks like a haunted house in movies or dreams—The Mrs. Glass House, with its three-story, turreted facade, with its loose gutters and peeling white paint, the long lawn and spike-tipped, curlicued cast-iron fence. If this were a picture, its caption would be: *Dread*. Its caption would be: *The undead stream forth in an endless torrent from the mouth of hell.*

She covers her mouth at the thought but doesn't laugh. She focuses instead on the steady crunch of Dominique's feet against the gravel, the girl's solemn, gracefully bovine trudge. She focuses on the clot of houses at the bottom of the hill, the tender, dirty nub of a prairie town, with its ice cream parlor and its movie house and its little post office and bank and gas station. There is a satisfaction in knowing that such places are dying their wretched deaths, in knowing that such towns are stumbling, wounded, their young people flowing out and away once they leave high school, draining out of the town like blood. Stupid people, she thinks. What kind of an idiot tries to build a town in the middle of the sandhills, a grassy desert where only sod will grow? These are the same people who would be pleased to act as if the fake rings make some sort of difference, the sort of people who will stare out their windows, deeply content, as the girls drift into their streets. After a moment, Nora slips the tin ring off her finger and lets it fall to the ground. She can imagine a soft "ping" as it hits the gravel driveway. She can picture it rolling down some groove in the ditch, through the dry weeds and mud, off toward some adventure. She thinks of the gingerbread man in the fairy tale. *Run, run, as fast as you can, you can't catch me, I'm the Gingerbread Man.*

If she lives long enough her life will have a story, and the story will begin at this moment. Once upon a time, there was a girl who didn't want to have a baby, but she did. Once upon a time, there was a baby who lived in the body of a girl, and there was nothing that she could do about it. Once upon a time, there was a girl who thought her life would be different.

4

June 4, 1997

A child disappears from his grandmother's backyard on a morning in late spring. He is there one minute—the grandmother glances out the window while she is washing the dishes and she sees him standing by the cyclone fence near the copse of lilac bushes, his hands clasped behind his back, talking to himself, as he likes to do.

And then he is gone.

It is a morning in early June, tranquil and warm, and the town of St. Bonaventure, Nebraska, has reached its greenest moment. By July the prairies that surround the town's clutch of houses and trees will have faded to a grayish-tan, the color of lichen, and even the fields of corn and alfalfa will seem artificial, desperately verdant beneath huge, insectlike irrigation systems that stride over the fields on long metal legs. Dust devils as high as churches will rise up in the stubble fields and churn their way across the roads and highways, right into the walking sprinklers as if attacking. Dust will settle on the crops' damp leaves.

But this particular morning the hot, dry, rainless days still seem far away. It is truly, purely spring. School is out. Children play in yards and ride bikes on the sidewalks. Discount City has set up rows of bright pink and blue kiddie pools, in three sizes, along its outside wall. Farmer's

Co-op displays planters full of seedlings—tomato plants and jalapeño peppers and watermelon vines and garden flowers—spreading them out on folding tables in the sun.

On such a day the grandmother is not particularly concerned that she doesn't see the child when she looks out the kitchen window. He's playing, she thinks. The boy, Loomis, is six years old, and in fact is a kind of miracle of restraint and politeness for a child of the late twentieth century. He's the type of child who still consistently presents himself to her to ask, "Grandma, may I use the rest room?" and who will pause to take note of the time on the plastic wristwatch his father has given him because he likes to be in bed at exactly eight-thirty. When she looks out again and sees that he is no longer by the fence she doesn't think much of it. He is a quiet boy, almost aloof in his elaborate pretend games, and she likes that about him. She respects his sense of privacy.

Another twenty minutes pass. The grandmother, Judy, finishes the breakfast dishes, dries them, puts them away in a cupboard. She is watching—half watching—an old musical on the small television she keeps on the counter for company. *Carousel,* very sad. "You'll Never Walk Alone," a woman sings, and she purses her mouth against a welling of sentimental emotion.

She is tired today; she didn't sleep well. Recently she's been troubled by strange fluctuations of her pulse as she lies down to sleep, and then, once her pulse stops accelerating and she begins to drift off, her heart seems to stop. It is as if the body has suddenly forgotten that it is necessary to keep blood pumping, and she rises with a jolt into consciousness, like a cork from the bottom of a bucket of water. Her whole body tingles for a moment.

This happens irregularly, but it had frightened her badly last night, and she had paced gingerly through the kitchen with a cup of warm Ovaltine. She wondered if something was wrong with her. The doctors would blame her weight, she thought. Her blood pressure, probably—she had escaped it up until now, but she saw ahead a whole series of adjustments: pills, diets, tests. She would begin the slow and futile ritual of staving off her own mortality. She had seen this happen with her own mother—the way the maintenance of health began to occupy more and more of her mother's daily life, until most of her waking hours were consumed in a kind of endless tennis match with her own body. Prevent one thing and the ball would come whizzing back over the net: a cold she couldn't shake, another organ failing, another limb hard to move, or painful. Eventually her mother died from shingles—a ridiculous and almost comical-sounding ailment that had beaten Judy's mother simply by virtue of her weakened immune system.

Judy had been thinking of this, pacing through the darkened house, when a noise came from outside—a rattling, the soft echo of a jar rolling over a hard surface. She heard what at first she thought was a high-pitched, raspy voice—a voice not unlike her mother's in her last years—and she shuddered. Out the window, she saw the raccoon. When she flicked on the porch light, it stood up. It held its front legs against its chest like palsied arms, hunching there, cringing. Its eyes glinted, and when she opened the screen door to holler at it, the creature stared at her like a malevolent and senile old person—like one of those old men who glare from their wheelchairs as you pass them at the nursing home. Abruptly, the raccoon dropped from its standing position and trotted to the corner of the yard. On all fours, the animal looked grotesquely swollen, its wide hindquarters jiggling as it ran. She watched as it smoothly slipped through a gap under the fence, near the lilac bush, and vanished.

It is this image that comes to her when she opens the back door to call Loomis. An image of that creature loping, waddling, into the bushes, like a heavily drugged person trying to crawl quickly. Its body was too slow and casual to express terror, but she could tell that it was actually quite desperate. "Loomis," she says, and for a second she thinks she sees a flash of movement, a tail, a swatch of dark pelt disappearing under the lilac foliage.

This image unnerves her at first. She actually shudders—a shadow passes along the nape of her neck—and then there is the emptiness of the yard. "Loomis?" she says, uncertainly.

The yard behind Judy's house is not a place a person could hide in. It is a simple square, a clean patch of grass with some dandelions and clover in it, enclosed by a metal cyclone fence. In the northwest corner is a lilac bush, near the end of its blooming; to the east, along the wall of the garage, is her small garden plot: two tomato plants, two zucchini, four rows of yellow wax beans, a cantaloupe vine she is experimenting with. There are some hollyhocks along the side of the house. But mostly it is open yard. A few of Loomis's toys are scattered there—a Batman doll, a blue rubber ball with yellow stripes, a plastic bag full of dinosaur figurines and soldiers and matchbook cars.

"Loomis?" she says. There is a moment of disorientation, eyeing the yard again, when she thinks somehow he *must* be here, that there's something wrong with her perception, her vision.

He could have climbed the fence, she supposes, though that seems so unlike him. Maybe he tossed something over the edge by accident and went to retrieve it? The wire of the fence crisscrosses in a diamond pattern, easy enough for him to fit his tennis shoes into the holes and hoist himself over. It seems foolish—he is not a particularly athletic or adventurous child, not liable to run off.

Still, she walks across the yard toward the north end of the fence, her thongs snapping under her bare feet in the warm grass. Here is the narrow alleyway that separates the rears of the houses on her block from the rears of the houses that line the block to the north, just wide enough for the beeping garbage truck to lumber down on Monday mornings. She looks to the right and left—nothing, just trash cans of varying shapes and sizes, plastic and corrugated metal, a few with stuffed garbage bags beside them. Weeds breaking through the cracked cement. Trees and poles, the branches and wire lines interpenetrating. At the far end, where the mouth of the alley opens into a street, a red truck drives past and vanishes. No sign of Loomis.

She is aware, for the first time in many years, of the way the world might look from the point of view of a small child. The largeness of it, the way a common alley might seem to be a mysterious tunnel, the way the back fences and gates of houses have an ancient, abandoned quality. She notices—remembers—the narrow strip of space between the fence and the rear of her garage: another tunnel, but one that doesn't seem maneuverable even for a child, since logs are piled up there—pieces of an old tree that she'd had removed several years ago. For some reason she must have thought the wood would be useful, though now she can't remember why. Now it is spotted with lichen and shelf fungus, wet, rotten, perhaps full of termites or ants.

"Loomis!" she calls, raising her voice for the first time, now not embarrassed for the neighbors to hear her. She lets herself bellow, once: "Loomis! Where are you?" And the dog in the neighbor's backyard to her left begins to bark. He wouldn't have gone there, of course. He hates and fears the dog, a moody and thickly muscled pit bull named Pluto. Nevertheless, she goes to the edge of the fence and peers over, and Pluto runs at her. He is leashed to a clothesline, and the eyelet of the leash makes a hollow sound, like a marble rolling down a pipe, as it passes along the length of the clothesline rope. At the sight of her, Pluto lets out a series of angry, territorial barks, his ears pinned back and eyes bright with outrage.

"Shut up!" Judy says sharply, and claps her hands, a gesture she remembers from childhood, from her mother, when they lived on a farm outside of town and sometimes encountered strange stray dogs. "Git!" she says, and claps her hands again. "Go on now!" And Pluto, impressed, stops barking and watches her warily. The neighbors, the Woodwards, are a childless and cordially unfriendly couple of whom she knows little. They are perhaps in their thirties. The woman, Bonnie, a secretary at the courthouse; the husband, Sherman, a worker at the feedlot outside of town. He is a hunter, and nearly every fall will bring home a deer that he skins and dismembers in the backyard. Beyond this, she knows little about them, and she is glad that they show no interest in her. She is an older divorced lady: *Mrs. Keene,* they call her respectfully. She suspects that they have probably heard some gossip about Loomis and his parents, some version of that unpleasant story, but they have said nothing, and she appreciates that.

She is beginning to get flustered now—somewhere between alarmed and annoyed. Where is Loomis? She is now of the mind that when she finds him she will give him a spanking, though she has never struck the child before. She unlatches the backyard gate—did he climb over it?—and walks into the driveway. The folding garage door is shut, but she peers in through the windows anyway, and then she goes into the garage and looks in the car. She remembers, in a suddenly vivid way, how her daughter Carla used to sit in the driver's seat when she was a child, holding the steering wheel in her small fists and pretending to drive. But Loomis is not in the car. She calls his name, very loudly and angrily now. "Loomis Timmens!" she calls. "If you don't answer me this minute, you're going to get a spanking!" And she strides down the drive toward the sidewalk, her thongs making sharp clacking sounds as she walks. Otherwise, the street is enormously silent.

She *will* spank him, she thinks. She will have to now. He has disobeyed, he has frightened her, and a lesson will have to come out of it. She thinks forward to this: dragging Loomis angrily down the street by his arm, turning him facedown on her lap in the kitchen and bringing the flat of her hand down on his bottom. Ten hard slaps, no more, no less. Sending him to his room without lunch. He may or may not cry—he seldom does, but she hopes that he will this time. Tears will mean that she has been effective, that she has impressed herself upon him and that he has repented. No tears will mean, what? Something to worry about.

That's the fear, she thinks, looking quickly to the right and left. That's the fear. He has been such a good boy, and the idea that this might change makes her heart sink. Loomis's mother, Carla, had been a good child, too, and look how she turned out.

Sometimes Judy tries to pinpoint the exact moment when things had gone wrong with Carla. Maybe it had been a simple moment, like this one with Loomis—willfully running off, without any concern for the consequences, without any concern for the feelings of others. She couldn't remember anything so specific, but she knew that Carla had started out like Loomis: quiet, bright, easily pleased. But then, outside of Judy's control, she had begun to transform. By the time she passed into her teenage years, she had become secretive, vindictive, addictive, in and out of alcohol/drug rehabilitation facilities since she was fourteen.

She pauses on the sidewalk. She has begun to perspire, and she looks up and down her street, Foxglove Road, the small one-story houses with their striped awnings and boxes of petunias and neat, tiny front yards. "Loomis! Loomis!" she calls, and her voice sounds like a parched hen crying for water.

Loomis has been in her care for almost a year now—the only stable year of his life, she thinks. Before that had been a series of trashy catastrophes, starting with his parents' marriage. Judy's daughter—Loomis's mother—Carla, had never been a mature or responsible person. Even at age twenty-eight, Carla was not ready to be married, Judy felt, but her choice of husband was even more ridiculous than Judy could have imagined. The husband's name was Troy Timmens, and he was some six years Carla's junior, twenty-two years old when they married but still an adolescent in Judy's estimation. Troy seemed to have no future plans beyond working as a bartender and turning his late father's home into a partying den on the weekends. When Carla found herself pregnant a year or so later, Judy had tried to tactfully suggest that Carla consider other options, such as abortion. But this had only led to another of their typical arguments—and another period of icy coldness between them.

But Judy was right, of course. Carla was no more prepared for motherhood than she would have been to pilot a jet plane, and Judy found herself called upon to baby-sit for the infant regularly while the nominal parents partied and fought. The marriage had dissolved under the pressures of young parenthood, coupled with a decadent lifestyle. Things grew worse and worse, until at last, when Loomis was three, Carla left town with a man she was having an affair with, taking Loomis with her and this man to Las Vegas, where she proceeded to become involved in drugs again. Troy retrieved Loomis and brought him back home to St. Bonaventure, and then was shortly thereafter himself arrested for possession of marijuana with intent to sell. At which time Loomis came into Judy's custody.

Thinking of these details, she is always surprised at how grotesque and depraved they seem. They are the kinds of things that happen to poor people—to trailer trash, to Indians on the reservations or black people in their ghettos—people whose environments put them at a disadvantage. Carla was raised in a solidly middle-class home. Judy was divorced, it was true, but she was college-educated, an elementary school teacher. Judy's life was supposed to be different. She had been the first person in her family to seek higher education; the first woman who didn't regularly spend her autumn canning food; the first, as far as she knew, who had seen an opera; the first who read literature. She had read Virginia Woolf's novels! And at the same time, she hadn't ignored her family in their times of trouble. She had loaned her brother thousands of dollars. She had spent much of her savings to pay for a nursing home for her mother, who had died with extreme slowness. She had gone into debt to commit her daughter to a decent rehabilitation facility.

Why should it be this way? Why should she have worked so hard to end up with so little, to end up fat and sixty-three, a divorced woman in a flowered shirt and tight shorts and flip-flops, a woman with a heart that palpitated irregularly at night and who was frightened by visions of raccoons? "Loomis!" she cried, and her voice broke, there was the edge of tears in it. There were times when she thought that this child, Loomis, her grandson, would make her life different, when she thought he was the child she should have been given all along, that he was a kind of reward for her hardship.

Why didn't he answer?

She hadn't yet let herself think of the bad things. The grown-up hand and the sack, the things she'd read about. The people who prey on children. The idea of disappearance.

But the more she thought about it, the more she remembered the last time she'd seen Loomis. She'd looked out the window, and he had been standing there by the lilac bush, his hands clasped behind his back, talking to himself, as he always did.

Talking to himself? She felt herself shrinking, even as she paced through the neighborhood, even as she hopefully expected to see him rounding a corner, running out of a bush in a yard, playing together with some group of neighbor children. In the alley, crouched behind a garbage can. In the house, somehow, sitting there and playing Nintendo and wondering where she was.

No, she thought suddenly. And then she could picture it, as if it were a memory. Loomis wasn't talking to himself.

5

1993

After Jonah's mother died, he took the old car and drove to Chicago, the city of his birth. It seemed as good a place as any in which to become a different person. He was twenty-two years old, and his intention was that he would never think of his past again. He would forget his mother, his grandfather, the shacklike yellow house; he'd forget the long humiliating desert of high school and afterward, a job washing dishes in the cafeteria of an old folks' home, a period of months and months and months when he felt certain that he'd finally reached the very bottom of his life.

All that would be erased, he thought. He remembered the way his grandfather had described the death of Jonah's grandmother, years and years before Jonah was born. "Excaping this world," Jonah's grandfather had said with wistful admiration, as if the grandmother's death had involved something masterful and Houdini-like instead of a mere car accident. It was an idea that Jonah felt friendly toward. "Excaping," he murmured under his breath as he crossed the Missouri River into Iowa. And then he corrected himself. "Escaping," he said. "*Es*caping."

He'd made a list of ways that he could improve himself, just to start out with. Grammar, posture. Training himself to say "library" instead of "lieberry," "picture" instead of "pitcher." Straightening his cowardly stoop and squaring his shoulders when he walked. Looking people in the eye when they spoke to him. Smiling. Easy stuff. As he drove along I-80, as glowing green-and-white signs caught his headlights and shimmered with the names of exit numbers and towns, he listened to a tape he had borrowed permanently from the Little Bow Public Library. *Fifteen Steps on the Ladder of Success,* it was called, and as he edged the speedometer up toward eighty, a man with a resonant, vowel-thick voice read aloud. Happiness and Unhappiness were choices that we made, the man said. They were states of mind. "'Problems' have no life of their own," the man explained. "'Problems' are mirages that seem to exist from a low state of mind, and they gain importance only because we choose to give it to them." Jonah listened, running his tongue over his dry lips, the glare of westbound headlights passing over his car, over his face, sliding up the body of the old Mustang like the palm of a hand, his mother's ashes in an urn in the passenger seat beside him. The stuff the man was reading sounded a bit like bullshit to him, but he hoped it wasn't.

Of course there were things he couldn't change about himself, things he couldn't slip loose of. There were, for example, the scars that had been left on him by the dog Elizabeth all those years ago, and every time he walked into a gas station or a wayside cafe, he was aware of the way people lifted their heads, turning their eyes sidelong to observe him, tracing over his skin. He tried to nod firmly at particularly frank gapers—an old farmer in coveralls, sipping his watery coffee, a tattooed motorcycle man, a little boy. He dipped his head, let his bangs fall into his eyes as he walked down the rows of vinyl booths, following a waitress he had flustered by his attempt to smile and make eye contact. There was a flutter among the people, as among grazing animals who sense a predator, and they glance away quickly when he nodded at them. *Jesus Christ,* they thought. *What happened to him?*

The scar they noticed first ran along his cheek from the edge of his eye to his lip. A keloid: a smooth, raised line of healed skin which they might associate with a cesarean section or appendectomy but not with a face. Not in America, not in the twentieth century. It made them think of a pirate, a thug from a pulp novel, a hideous blind beggar in a third-world country, and though there had been several revisions over the years, attempts at plastic surgery, the scar remained Jonah's most prominent feature. He had grown used to certain looks and their variations: the small-mouthed, wide-eyed gaze of frightened, judgmental middle-aged women who associated him with crime; the assessing once-over of macho worker guys who wondered if he'd had harder fights than they; the liberal-benevolent assumptions that he'd had a tragic life, and the subsequent game of pretend, the shifty act of direct eye contact, the ones who tried to make believe they hadn't noticed. But no matter where they looked they couldn't help but see damage: the nick of missing ear, the thin lines that ran along the backs of his hands, and others that pull down the side of his neck and past the collar of his shirt.

He had never known what to say to those looks. Sometimes he said cheerfully "Car accident," or some other lie. Sometimes he just smiled. *Take a good look.*

He hadn't decided what he would say to the wife of the building superintendent when she showed him the apartment. Sometimes it was better to gauge people face-to-face, to study their expressions, get a fix on them. But he knew he'd have to tell her something. He had called her beforehand and was prepared, he thought, for the kind of look she would give him. Even over the telephone there was an abrupt European-accented suspicion in her voice that made him act guilty. "Hello!" she said when she answered the phone, snapping through the receiver in a sharp, alarmed voice, as if addressing a shadowy figure who was slinking out of an alleyway toward her.

Jonah hesitated. He was calling from a pay phone, holding the folded and pen-marked newspaper in his hands while keeping an eye on his illegally parked car. Her voice unnerved him, and he tried to affect a very mild, harmless tone. "Yes," he said, and cleared his throat. *Don't mumble* was one of the items on his list. "I'm calling about the advertisement that was advertised in the *Chicago Reader*. There was an advertisement for furnished . . . eff-efficacies?" He winced. The newspaper actually said "EFFCY'S," which he knew was an abbreviation but he couldn't imagine for what.

"Efficiency?" the woman said in a booming foreign voice.

"Yes," Jonah said quickly. "Efficiency." He tried to imagine why people would use such a word to refer to an apartment, but all he could picture was the manager's office in the old folks' home where he had worked back in Little Bow. He pictured Mrs. Blachley, with her look of perpetual and almost painful delight, with her neatly arranged desk, the aligned display of in/out box, stapler, memo pad, pink paper clips, her hands folded restfully over each other. *Efficiency.* "Of course we're sorry to see you leaving us, Jonah," Mrs. Blachley had said, and beamed brightly, her eyes glassing with the effort of looking directly at him and pretending she didn't notice his scars.

The superintendent's wife, on the other hand, made no such attempt. She was already frowning when she opened the door, a small, thin, bedraggled woman with a mole like the head of an emerging earthworm at the corner of her eyelid and a pelt of gray-black hair on her head. Her jowls and lips were turned down in an exaggerated arc, which nevertheless deepened when she saw him standing there. She stared at him hard, her lower lip protruding and her nostrils widening as if she were furious, as if he were an enemy she were preparing to defend herself against. "Yes?" she exclaimed.

"How do you do?" he said. Despite his determination to the contrary, he found himself starting to adopt that slouching posture he hated so much, hunching, knotting his arms across his chest and tucking his fingers into his armpits. In high school, teachers would always ask him if he was cold, and other students used to imitate him, contorting themselves as if they were in the early stages of multiple sclerosis. "Yes," he said. " I called about the eff-eff-" and then he couldn't get the word out. "Apartments?"

"Efficiencies?" she said, and seemed to glare at the scar on his face. "Furnished efficiencies?"

"Yes, ma'am," Jonah said. He put his arms carefully to his sides, and tried to decide whether he was standing up straight. "I called you this morning," he said, and smiled at her, as he had told himself he would.

The woman paused grimly. Her name, he would later learn, was

Mrs. Marina Orlova, and she had grown up in Siberia. Later, she would tell him that she loathed the American custom of constantly smiling: "They are like chimpanzees," she said, in her bitterly exclamatory voice. She grimaced, baring her teeth grotesquely. "Eee!" she said. "I smile at you! Eee! It is repulsive."

But now she only looked at his smile with a sigh of disapproval, and he felt terribly self-conscious. "You wait," she said, finally. "I will get keys."

The efficiency surprised him. It reminded Jonah a little of a motel room, and he loved it immediately. There was a brown sofa that folded out into a bed, a small two-chair table with a standing lamp beside it, a seashore painting on the wall. In an alcove was a kitchenette with narrow counter space: a sink, a midget refrigerator, a microwave, a half-sized stove, a coffeemaker, some cabinets; and beyond that was a little bathroom, a tiny space not much bigger than a closet into which a toilet, sink, and bathtub had all been compressed. He was taken with the compactness of everything. *Efficiency,* he thought, and turned toward Mrs. Orlova, who stood in the doorway with her arms folded over her breasts.

"This looks great," he said. "Just . . . fantastic." He smiled at her again and looked her in the eye, as *Fifteen Steps on the Ladder of Success* had suggested. "I love it," he said. And he really did. It was the opposite of the house he'd grown up in, with its smoke-stained stacks of clutter, its thick cobwebs and faucets that ran yellowish, sulphuric water. He cleared his throat. "So, well then," he said. "Can I just—? How would I go about . . . reserving one?"

Mrs. Orlova raised her eyebrows, a single dark line that met over the bridge of her nose. "You have references?"

"References?"

"Where you live before?" She tilted her head and shrugged, tossing her hand. "You live somewhere, you have references."

"Oh." With effort, he prevented himself from assuming the submissive posture again. "I'm not sure," he said. "I'm from South Dakota. I'm just moving here."

"South Dakota?" she said, and moved the words in her mouth as if they were a new language. She frowned hard again, deeply and suspiciously, and he shifted from foot to foot. "It's . . . ah . . . west?"

"Yes," he said. "It's over—" and he pointed vaguely, though he didn't know the direction. In the city his mental compass didn't seem to work anymore, and he had no idea which way he was pointing. "Four—" he said, "five hundred miles or so?"

"Hm," she said. She seemed to consider this as if she didn't quite believe it. He watched as her eyes traveled again along the scar on his face, tracing an interstate on a map.

"I was in an accident at a factory," he said. "If you're wondering."

"I wasn't wondering," she said, though her expression softened somewhat. She moved her eyebrows in a complex way. "So what if this place is available? How will you pay?"

"I don't know," he said. "Will you take cash?"

Her face changed again as he took the roll of bills from his jacket pocket, a wad a little bigger than his fist. Her eyes sparked, and her lower lip protruded again as he peeled one-hundred-dollar bills from the stack with shaky fingers. One, two, three, four, five, six, seven.

"There was a settlement. From the accident."

"Ah," she said, and appraised him frankly. "They should have given you a million." She shrugged, considering him for a moment longer, but she seemed to have made a favorable decision.

He'd thought, originally, that the money would last for quite a while. Nearly fifteen thousand dollars, which at the time had seemed like a stunning amount, though he later discovered that houses in most other places, even dilapidated houses, sold for many times that amount. When he left Little Bow, he carried with him 234 twenty-dollar bills, and 100 one-hundred-dollar bills, which he'd tried to hide in various places in the car. A thousand in his wallet, another thousand in the glove compartment, hundred-dollar bills tucked into the pages of books and the pockets of the clothes he'd packed.

This was his inheritance. He had decided, even before his mother's death, that he would get rid of everything when it came time, and that is what he did. He sold the little yellow house in South Dakota, the plot of land, and all the furniture and possessions that he could get money for. Everything else—so many things—he had stuffed into garbage bags and left for the trash man. Gone were most of the photos of his family, letters, papers; gone were his mother's shell collection and worthless knickknacks, his own high school yearbooks and childhood drawings that had been saved, ragged quilts made by his grandmother, his grandfather's collection of Louis L'Amour paperback westerns; gone were piles of newspapers and junk mail and bank statements, canned pears and peas, ten years old at least, that had sat on shelves, never opened; gone were coffee cans full of pinto beans or nails or buttons, a whole closet full of unused cleaning supplies; gone were the horrible accumulations of the last years of his mother's life, when Jonah and his mother both had lost the energy to discard. He found a plastic mug, forgotten on a shelf in the laundry room, with a layer of dead mold floating on the surface of a half-inch of unfinished coffee. Who knew how old it was? It might have been sitting on that shelf for a year or more. He found a twenty-year-old grocery receipt in a desk drawer, along with a huge collection of pencil nubs and pens whose ink had long dried up. Seven-year-old telephone books. Ancient, pre tampon menstrual belts. Keys and key chains. Melted Tupperware. Worthless jewelry.

The auctioneer, Mr. Knotts, shook his head sorrowfully as the two of them picked through the clutter. He cleared his throat when Jonah pitched a packet of photos into the trash can.

"You should go through those," Mr. Knotts said softly, but Jonah ignored him.

"People can be rash when they are in mourning," Mr. Knotts said.

"Yes," Jonah said. He retrieved the pictures and set them back into a pile of things that he meant to keep, but he did this only for Mr. Knotts's benefit—as if he owed the old man something.

Mr. Knotts was a solemn little man with a high-pitched Arkansas accent, and Jonah had originally planned to dislike him. Which was to say that Jonah had not liked the way the man kept calling him "son," on the phone, and he had not liked the man's looks when they'd met to discuss the "auction process," as Knotts had called it—there had been something unpleasantly Christian about Knotts's softly resonant voice, Jonah had thought, and he had grimly noted the various accessories—

the cowboy shirt with its flowery pattern and pearly buttons, the string tie, the silver-tipped size-seven cowboy boots, the blondish toupee—all of which seemed to indicate a certain type of oily, Born Again smarminess.

But this wasn't the case, exactly. "I'm sorry for your loss," Mr. Knotts had said, but nothing else, no sentiment or piety beyond that. "I'm an honest businessman," he had told Jonah, surveying the ramshackle yellow house, "but I'm still a businessman, so I can't promise you much." Then he offered Jonah his hand.

He had a hand that was misshapen in a way that wasn't quite visible until Jonah shook it. Then Jonah realized that the pinkie finger was permanently stiffened, that the other fingers were oddly abbreviated and stubby, so that Jonah felt as if he were closing his hand over an ape's paw or a flipper. Mr. Knotts did not meet Jonah's eye with a serious, significant look; he did not say anything further. He simply let Jonah clasp his malformed hand, and something passed between them. Jonah had felt a rush of warmth for the man, a stranger.

Later Jonah thought it would have been good if Mr. Knotts had been his father. They would have had a steady, quiet, gently melancholic relationship, Jonah imagined. They wouldn't have been close, but he would never have felt unloved. Mr. Knotts would have been the kind of father who hovered, awkwardly tender, at the periphery of a son's life, attentive and formal in a folding chair at a band concert, lingering for a moment before he turned off the light at bedtime, the kind of father who closed his eyelids lightly as he kissed his child's forehead, the kind of father who would clear his throat often and grow misty-eyed. It would have been, what?, *lasting,* Jonah thought.

Mr. Knotts watched as Jonah stowed the urn containing his mother's ashes—her "Cremains," the man at the funeral home had called them—into the passenger seat of the car. Perhaps Mr. Knotts knew that Jonah had not given his mother a funeral. Who would have come to it, after all? There were no relatives, no friends. There was no reason to waste money on a casket and a gravestone and all the rest that the undertakers had tried to sell him.

But he couldn't tell this to Mr. Knotts. "Who doesn't deserve a funeral?" Mr. Knotts would wonder, though he wouldn't say it. Mr. Knotts would identify with Jonah's mother, of course. His eyes would grow gloomy and distant as he reflected upon his own funeral, presided over by his weeping children; his own gravesite, kept neat for years and years by his children and then by his grandchildren. He wouldn't speak of it, but the sight of the urn created an awkward space in the air into which all of these feelings rushed and solidified.

"Is that your momma?" Mr. Knotts said gently, and together he and Jonah stared at the urn that had been balanced on the passenger seat.

"Yes," Jonah said. And he wanted to come up with some sort of explanation. He wanted to say that she wanted her ashes sprinkled over some beautiful landmark, like the Grand Canyon, or the Atlantic Ocean. But he couldn't force the lie into his throat.

"Yes," Jonah said. "That's her."

"God bless her," Mr. Knotts said. "Poor woman."

"Yes," Jonah said.

In the weeks and months after he arrived in Chicago, Jonah found that he remembered that moment frequently—the two of them, he and Mr. Knotts, standing there looking at the urn, at his packed car at the end of the long gravel drive that led to the now empty house.

It could have been a nice memory, he thought, a *conclusive* memory: *God bless her, poor woman.*

But then he would also recall the way he'd stopped the car along the side of the road, only a few hours after he'd left Mr. Knotts behind. His heart was beating furiously, and he'd stumbled out of the car with the urn. He'd dumped the contents out into the weeds in the ditch.

Jesus, he'd think, as he sat in the dining nook of his efficiency, as he walked down a busy Chicago street, as he stood in line at a movie theater. Jesus, why had he done that?

He didn't know. Something had come over him, he guessed. A fear, a panic. He had been driving without thinking for a long while, his hands on the steering wheel and his eyes on the white lines on the road, dashes he was feeding into the body of the car like he was playing a video game. And then he had become aware, for the first time, of the music emanating from the radio. It was a wispy, somnambulant rock song, a high-voiced choir of men sighing disconnected phrases: "Time . . . to the sea . . . good-bye my love . . ." and his skin prickled. He was aware of how light-headed he felt.

The sun came out from the dark clouds with a kind of insistence, almost violent. There were stubble fields lined with barbed-wire fences and telephone poles on both sides of him, and he let the car drift slowly, ten miles per hour, on the berm for a while before he stopped. The tires went kathump, kathump against the uneven gravel shoulder and he thought he might be having a heart attack. There was a soft explosion that radiated from just beneath his breastbone, something like the pins-and-needles sensation of stepping down on a foot that has fallen asleep—only inside him, rippling outward. He felt the sensation wash over his eyes, blinding him for a second, his vision clouded by thousands of vibrating pixels, television static, and then the feeling slipped up his forehead to his hair, a scuttling of insects. A low-level buzzing remained with him as he brought the car to a complete stop, edged crookedly onto the side of the road.

He had remembered something that his mother once told him. "When I die, I want you to bury me under the floorboards," she had said. He'd been something like ten or eleven years old at the time, but even then he had known that this was her idea of a joke. "Cut me up in little pieces and put me in the crawl space," she said. "I want to haunt the shit out of whoever lives in this dump after we do." He remembered sitting there in the dark. She was angry because the power was out, and the tip of her cigarette bobbed. Outside, the rain came down in sheets, and the shadow of the rain and the windblown curtains moved on the wall behind her, a shadow like a giant jellyfish, waving its gentle tentacles.

The ashes sluiced out of the urn and onto the ground. Some of the ash drifted smokily in the air and powdered the leaves of the weeds. Jonah stood there, breathing, then carefully put the empty urn down on the ground beside the pile of ash, and it made a hollow, metallic tunk against the earth, like a coffee can. A single sparrow watched him from a telephone wire. He looked around, trying to identify the place—as if he might, in the future, come back here and try to retrieve the ashes. It was completely anonymous. A breeze rustled down a long field of corn, and he remembered his grandfather telling him once that as a boy he used to wake to the sound of the corn growing. "You could actually hear it growing," his grandfather said. "It made a creaking sound, like a rusty hinge." Jonah picked up the urn and waded through the high sunflower and pigweed toward the fence that surrounded the cornfield, walking cautiously in case of rattlesnakes. He put the urn upside down over the nearest fence post, fitting it over the top of the post like a hat.

No one would remove it, he thought. It would still be there, a marker of sorts, if he ever had to come back.

For a while, during those first months in Chicago, Jonah even considered calling Mr. Knotts to tell him about this. He wanted to explain to someone that he *had* to leave, that he *had* to throw everything away. He wanted to tell someone: *I am going to be a new person,* and to have them answer—

Yes.

Yes, of course you are.

6

Saturday, June 15, 1996

Troy dreams that his child has died, and he wakes up suddenly, suffocating. He wakes because he has stopped breathing. His throat has closed and he sits up abruptly, making a glottal sound like a dog choking on a strip of meat. His hands flail for a moment and he sucks in breath, coughing, disoriented.

It takes him a moment to realize that nothing has happened. This is his house, the house he has always lived in, and his son is not screaming. It is a morning in early summer. He puts his hand to his face, rubbing it dully. He is on the couch in the living room, where he fell asleep the night before, still in his jeans and stockinged feet and unbuttoned white shirt, blinking his eyes under a tent of mid-morning sunlight and lazily drifting dust motes. The television is going, the sound of Saturday morning cartoons, and Little Man is in fact sitting cross-legged on the floor eating dry cereal from a box, completely absorbed. Not screaming. Not dead.

"Shit," Troy says, grimacing, and Little Man turns to look over his shoulder as Troy clears his throat again. Phlegm.

" 'Batman' is on," Little Man says. "It's a new episode. You're missing it."

"Oh, really," Troy says. "Cool." He sits there for a moment, staring slackly at the television as the superheroes and supervillains fight one another. He feels muffled, sluggish, fairly hungover. The long night comes back to him slowly—a party at the tavern where he works as a bartender, the honky-tonk music from the jukebox and the smoke that still clung to his clothes, sitting there drinking with his cousin Ray and some people Ray had just met, a girl from Denver who Troy had kind of liked, who kept covering her mouth with her hand; he remembers spritzing himself with Refreshing Citrus air freshener, trying to disguise the smell of alcohol and marijuana from the teenaged baby-sitter when he came in. He hoped he wasn't too wobbly. He was two hours later than he'd said he'd be, and he knew she was a little irritated as he counted money into her hand—he remembers that much, and then he'd been sitting on the couch after the baby-sitter had left, drinking one last beer and watching a late-night movie, *Vertigo*. He must have simply fallen asleep. He tries to remember. Had Little Man been screaming in the middle of the night? Things have begun to blur together lately: the days, the nightmares, and it takes a moment for the facts of his life to arrange themselves. It is the day after his thirtieth birthday. He is a father, a grown man with responsibilities. His bladder is full, and after a moment he stops casting about for solidifying thoughts and gets up, pads crookedly toward the bathroom.

He feels a little more oriented after he's patted some water onto his face, though he's still a little unnerved. There is something about the dream that lingers. It was as if the dream had been going on for hours before he woke, and it weighs heavily on him, a feeling of grief that weaves its way through his insides as he stares at himself in the mirror. In the dream he had been looking for Little Man, calling for the child through long hallways and rooms full of ominous hums and flutterings, catching glimpses of running shapes. He remembers that in the dream he had stumbled out into the open air. It was the backyard of the house.

This is what Troy recalls most vividly: the small backyard of the house, with its patch of grass, a curled garden hose, a child's shoe near the trunk of the old elm tree. There was a yawning roar of an airplane, a shadow pulling across the ground, and when Troy looked up, startled, he saw that Little Man was sitting at the very top of the old elm tree, perched in the netting of bare boughs. Little Man was crouched on his haunches with his arms around his knees, his feet resting on a thin, quivering branch barely strong enough for a bird. Yet somehow Little Man balanced on it. Somehow, impossibly, it held Little Man's weight, and the child's silhouette hung precariously balanced at the top of the tree. He would fall, Troy knew. Troy could sense that Little Man was already falling even as he tried to run, holding his arms out. Little Man was already plunging through the air, the thin branches snapping and whipping as his son plummeted. There was that awful sound that Little Man was making, a high, fading wail, a falling-scream, a death-scream, which now Troy has in his head and can't shake.

"Shit," Troy says. He gathers up some of the dirty laundry that is spilling out of the overflowing hamper behind the bathroom door and tries to stuff it in. Too full. He puts his foot inside the hamper and steps down hard, compressing, packing it in tighter, so there is enough room to close the lid. He stands there, frowning at it, and his face feels pale and cold with sweat.

He would like to think that things have been going well. He wants to be a good father, that's the thing, even though he doesn't always succeed. Little Man has been living with him for about three months now, and Troy tries not to think of the potential mistakes he's making. It's mostly good, he tells himself. It's mostly happy. They fit together, he thinks, not only as father and son but also as companions. Troy and Little Man, Little Man and Troy.

And really, despite his occasional bad dreams, despite his occasional fuckups and inappropriate behavior, he believes that single fatherhood has come pretty easily to him. Little Man is a quiet, uncomplaining child, and he doesn't seem overly traumatized to be separated from his mother, though of course the child misses her, thinks about her often. "When is Carla supposed to call?" he asks Troy, and "Do you think Carla will come see us this summer?" and he nods grimly when Troy says, "I don't know." He seems to understand, and Troy loves him for that. Troy loves the boy's stern expression, his deep-set, observant eyes, his oddly upright posture. He loves the way Little Man takes things seriously, the way he will sit on the edge of a creek holding a fishing pole, watching the motionless bobber floating in the water with a sharp gaze, seemingly impervious to boredom, the way he appears to enjoy road trips, out to look at cows and horses, his face turned attentively to steadily passing fields and telephone poles and weed-filled ditches. He loves the way Little Man will tell the waitress his order when they eat at the old truck stop out at the interstate oasis, the way he will hold the menu and pick out words he recognizes, like "egg" and "ham." He loves the silent clutch of Little Man's arms as they ride Troy's motorcycle down the thin, rutted cowpath trails that run through the hills north of town, the way Little Man presses his helmeted head against Troy's back. It is even fun to go shopping for groceries, Little Man pushing the cart proudly, despite the fact that it's taller than he is. Troy taking various items off the shelves and holding them up for Little Man's approval, juggling the boxes of macaroni and cheese in the aisle or menacing Little Man with a package of plastic wrapped tripe from the meat section. "Hey, Little Man, how about some of this stuff?" and Little Man frowning thoughtfully, saying, "Dad, I don't think so!"

Little Man's real name is Loomis. Troy had been in favor of the name when the child was born—his ex-wife, Carla, had come up with it, and Troy had thought it was unusual and rugged-sounding, a cowboy name, which was cool. The second choice was Marley, after Bob Marley, the reggae singer. That had been Troy's suggestion, and Carla had said that she thought Marley would sound better on a girl.

But ultimately, Loomis did not seem to stick, not in Troy's mind at least, and he liked it even less when Carla called the boy "Loomy," which for some reason conjured up the image of a slouching, drooling ogre, with one eye bigger than the other. *Loomy.* They had argued about it a little.

"Just don't call him 'Little Man,'" she said irritably. "You're going to give him a complex," and he had frowned at her bossy, judgmental tone of voice. "Why do you have to give everybody a nickname, anyway?" she continued. "It's like, you can't wait to get your hands on people's identities and mold them so you feel superior. I mean, it's like you calling me 'Shorty' all the time, and now he's got to be 'Little Man.' So it's like, what are you? Some sort of giant? Are we supposed to call you *Big Man? Tall Troy?* How about *Humongous?* Maybe we should call you *Humongous.*"

He hadn't said anything. She seemed very hyper—cocaine, he thought, or crank—something like that, where you thought you were clever and your mind seemed sharp and taut as a guitar string. He hadn't wanted an argument, he hadn't wanted to say anything to make her change her mind.

The two of them were sitting in her kitchen, in her apartment, in Las Vegas. Little Man was in the next room, watching television, and her boyfriend, the one she was fucking now—there had been several since they had separated—was out somewhere. Troy didn't ask. The two of them sat at the table and drank coffee and stared out at a tiny desert yard filled with hard gray earth and scattered with dog turds. The cabinets in the kitchen were white, with gold edges around the molding; a gold-painted cupid statue sat on the table, presiding over a bowl of plastic fruit.

After almost a year of being gone, she had called him in the middle of the night. "Listen," she said, and her voice was heavily slurred. "I'm wondering if you could drive out here and pick up Loomis." She had paused, and he could imagine her trying to compose herself, her tongue working thickly. "This is not the right place for a kid," she said. "I was thinking about what you said. About custody and stuff."

"Yeah?" Troy said. "What are you saying?"

"I'm just wondering—don't be an asshole about this—but I'm thinking about whether you were willing to come and get him. Keep him for a few months. Maybe a year. Things are sort of . . . don't start in on me, Troy, but things are not so good here. I think he'd be better off with you." This was about four in the morning, and Troy had the vague idea that maybe everything would change, that eventually Carla and he would get back together, that after a while she'd come back to Nebraska and they'd become a family again, the mess they'd made of their marriage forgotten.

He even imagined this as he sat in her Las Vegas kitchen, as she stared at him grimly, her pupils swelling almost to the edge of her irises, so that it was hard to recall that her eyes were blue. "Look," she said, "if you're going to take him, you can't be dealing anymore. Not even pot, okay? He's a good kid, you know? And one of us has to try to . . . not fuck up, you know?"

"I'm not dealing," he said, which was mostly true. "I'm not even hardly smoking myself," he said, which was not. She laughed.

"Oh, for God's sake, Troy," she said. "Don't lie. You should see your eyes. They're like fucking bloodshot balloons. I wouldn't have even called you if I thought there was any other choice."

Troy thinks of this again, as he and Little Man walk along the dirt road beyond the house, the house that sits at the north edge of the town of St. Bonaventure, the road that leads up into the gray sod-covered hills. They are looking for fossils, which Little Man is very interested in, and Troy bends down to pick up a flat rock, imagining that it will be imprinted with the skeleton of a leaf or a fish, a trilobite. Troy has vague knowledge: At some point in the distant past, this dry plain was covered by a sea, thousands of miles across. Little Man is five years old, and they hold hands as they walk.

"You know what I'm wondering?" Little Man says. "If there was a sea here, what was the name of the sea? And also, were there sharks in it? Was it salt water or fresh water?"

"Hm," says Troy. It sometimes worries him that Little Man will become a genius. And then what will happen? He remembers how Carla used to tease him, when he would sit cross-legged on the living room floor, playing Nintendo with Little Man. "You know, Troy, in a few years he's going to be more mature than you are, and then what are you going to do?" He had grinned at her at the time, but now, remembering the comment, he feels grim.

"Let's see," he says. "I guess that it was probably fresh water, because, you know, there was the Ice Age, and all that? And then it sort of melted and evaporated, and all that was left was the Great Lakes, which are up by Chicago and so on." He thinks for a moment. He doesn't want to end up having the boy think he's an idiot. "Maybe we should go to the library and look it up."

"Okay," Little Man says.

"Do you want to ride on my shoulders?" Troy says. "Are your legs tired?"

And Little Man shrugs. "I wouldn't mind riding on your shoulders," he says, very politic, very formal and dignified as Troy lifts him.

"Uff," Troy says. "Either you're getting heavy or I'm getting old. I turned thirty yesterday, you know. I won't be able to carry you much longer."

"I weigh forty-two pounds," Little Man says, and hooks his heels into Troy's armpits like a jockey gently nudging a horse. "Happy Birthday, Dad," he says.

He's happy, sure. They're both happy, he and Little Man, the two of them together, and Troy knows he should be grateful for that. "Why do you worry about this shit so much?" Troy's cousin Ray asked him recently. "All you do lately is worry, and there's not any point to it."

And when Troy shrugged, Ray gestured expansively at Little Man. "Look at him, Troy. He's content, he's healthy, he's like a midget Einstein in our midst. What more do you want?"

"I don't know," Troy said. The two of them were sitting in the grass at the edge of the park, watching Little Man at play, cautiously passing a joint back and forth. Troy was more paranoid than he used to be, very careful now to pass the joint underhanded, thumb and forefinger, taking a quick hit and just as quickly lowering it. He didn't know why he should feel so uncomfortable. There weren't any other people around, and Little Man was fully focused on the slide he was working out on. Troy watched as Little Man climbed the ladder to the top and sat, hands folded solemnly in his lap, slipping down the metal pathway with the grim, determined expression of an accelerating race car driver. When he reached the bottom, he ran back to the ladder again. He didn't seem to tire of it.

"I need to start thinking about changing jobs," Troy said. "You know? I don't want to be a bartender forever. Besides which, it's a bitch trying to line up people who are going to sit for Little Man until I get off at two or three in the morning. You know, he's going to start school in the fall, and then what am I going to do?"

"Mmmm," Ray said, as if he were trying to sound thoughtful. He drew deeply on the joint and held the smoke in his lungs for a count. He tapped his chest with his palm, one . . . two . . . three . . . four . . . and then exhaled in a stream, his eyes watery and red-rimmed. "Shhhit," he said hoarsely. "What kind of a job are you talking about? Doctor? Lawyer? Senator?"

"Don't be a jerk," Troy said mildly. He was not in the mood for the teasing, affectionately insulting banter that usually passed for conversation when he and Ray were together. "Look," he said. "I'm serious. I thought about maybe going to college somewhere—or a technical school or something. I saw this one thing on TV where you can get a degree in, like, commercial art through correspondence courses."

"What's 'commercial art'?" Ray said, and the way he pronounced it made Troy wish that he hadn't brought it up. Ray was not really the sort of person to talk about making any kind of change. At twenty-three, Ray still spoke grudgingly about high school friends who had gone away to college and never come back. He still had a prescription for Ritalin, which had been prescribed for him when he was a hyper eight-year-old, and which he continued to take faithfully, believing that it helped him concentrate. To Troy, it wasn't clear why such concentration was necessary. Ray worked for the county Department of Roads as a laborer, and moonlighted occasionally for a company that contracted male strippers for bachelorette and birthday parties. It was a great way to meet women and get laid, Ray claimed, and besides smoking pot, his only other interest was working out with weights, an activity that was apparently greatly enhanced by Ritalin. "Commercial art," Ray said again, as if it was a French phrase. "What do you do? Draw pictures for commercials? It seems like you'd have to go to New York or something to get a job."

"I don't really know," Troy said. "It was just a thought." And he listened to the sound of birds in the bushes around them. He didn't feel like being disheartened, which was Ray's general mode of looking at the world, and so he simply shrugged. What else was there to say? He was embarrassed to be thirty years old and still without any clear sense of what most people did for a living. He'd seen a girl he'd known in high school at the grocery store not too long before—she was back in St. Bonaventure visiting her parents, she told him, she was working as an actuary at a company in Omaha.

"Actuary, huh?" he'd said, smiling and nodding. "That sounds interesting." Later, he'd had to go home and look it up in the dictionary.

Which was why the commercial he'd seen had caught his attention. "Tired of being stuck in the same old rut?" the announcer had asked, as on-screen a bedraggled waitress cleared a table of dirty plates with a depressed look on her face. "The Career Learning Center wants to help you discover new opportunities and actualize your potential!" The waitress then looked hopeful as a list of the many degrees you could get scrolled over the screen—computers, drafting, accounting, business. Commercial art was the one that stuck in his mind because art had been his only decent subject in high school. He could still draw fairly well—like the series of dinosaur skeletons he had drawn for Little Man on poster board and pasted on the wall above the child's bed. They were pretty good, he thought, pretty accurate. Even Ray had said so.

"I don't know," Troy said at last. "That was just one idea." Ray had stretched out on the grass and was staring up at the clouds. "It's just like, well, I feel like I need to get my act together. Maybe it's turning thirty."

"Word," said Ray, who sometimes used the slang of the rap musicians he listened to, aping their accents.

"You know what I ought to do?" Troy said. He watched as Little Man ran determinedly from the bottom of the slide back to the ladder again, still intent for the, what?, the twentieth time? Fiftieth? Troy sighed. "I ought to quit smoking pot all the time. And definitely quit dealing the shit."

"Oh, man," Ray said, sleepily. "Come on. What are you talking about? You're not a 'drug dealer.' I mean, how many people do you sell to? Like, twelve or something?"

"More than that."

"Yeah, well," Ray said. "That's stupid. It's not like you're some sort of Al Pacino *Scarface* cutting people's heads off with buzz saws and being evil, you know? I mean, come on. You're *you*. You can't change everything just because you have a birthday and you got a kid hanging out with you. Look, everybody loves you the way you are. Everybody's like, 'That's Troy, he's the man, we love him,' and you're going to be like, 'No, guys, I'm going to be all different now because I turned thirty and I'm having a crisis.' What the fuck is that? That doesn't make any sense."

"Mmm-hmm," Troy said. "Well, if you think everybody loves Troy, you should talk to Carla's mom."

"She's a bitch," Ray said, and stared up at the sky for a while longer before resting his thick, worker-brown hand over his eyes. "You should stay away from her. No way hanging with her is any good for Little Man."

Troy looked at him wryly. "So, what?" he said. "Can you watch him on Saturday night while I'm at work?" And he watched as Ray's slack expression tightened.

"Oh," Ray said. He sat up. "I would, but . . . I think I got a deal that night. Bachelorette party out in Greeley."

They looked at each other. "That's what I'm saying," Troy said. "I'm not so crazy about dealing with Carla's mom either, you know? But she can watch him. She wants to watch him. And I can't find anyone else to do it. That's what I'm saying. I need to make some changes if I'm going to have a kid around." After a moment, he stood up, brushing the grass off the back of his pants. From the top of the slide, Loomis gazed at him and waved, and he waved back.

"You know what," Ray said. "You need to get hooked up with a new woman. *That* is what you need. You don't need a new career. You just need a new squeeze."

"I don't think so," Troy said. He felt strangely heavy, thinking of Carla again, thinking of the old times at Bruce and Michelle's place. Great times. Ray's father, Bruce, was still in prison, serving a sentence for distribution of cocaine, and his mother, Michelle, was in Arizona now, living with an elderly real estate millionaire named Merit Wilkins. In some ways, Ray was still his responsibility, just as he had been back in the long-ago times when Troy used to baby-sit. Just as he had been when Bruce went to jail and Michelle had started dating various old men. During his high school years, Ray had mostly lived with Troy and Carla, crashing on their couch—had more or less become their ward, and maybe still was. That was what this conversation was really about, Troy thought. *Don't leave me,* was what Ray was basically saying, and Troy felt Ray's eyes upon him as he stood up.

"Loomis!" Troy called. "We're getting ready to go!"

He thinks of all this as he drives toward Carla's mom's house with Little Man sitting calmly and silently in the back of the old secondhand Corvette that Troy had once been so excited about but which now suffers from serious health problems. He has to rev the engine at the stoplight to keep it from dying. Maybe something is wrong with the fuel pump. He hears the engine rasping, sputtering like a lung full of bile. He feels guilty and uncertain.

He's making a mistake, probably. Every time he drops Little Man off at Carla's mom's house, he thinks: Of all the ways in which he is probably screwing up as a father this may in fact be the worst. He crosses under the viaduct on Old Oak, turns left on Main toward the park, and turns again into the series of narrow winding streets—Meadow Lane and Sunnyvale, Linden and Foxglove, a little neighborhood on the far end of the park made up of small, pretty, boxy houses, all from the forties and fifties, all nearly identical, and which, when he'd first started dating Carla, he'd thought of as fancy. Sometimes he thinks that he should just turn around and go home, call in sick at work, forget about dropping Little Man off, make some other arrangement. He will see the little white house, with its red trim and shaded windows, with its neat lawn and sidewalk lined with dark petunias, and a stone will sink inside of him.

When he'd left Las Vegas with Little Man, this had been one of Carla's stipulations: "Just don't let him stay with my mom," she'd said. She'd looked at him fiercely. "You know, the minute she hears that Loomis is back in town, she's going to call you up, and she's going to be very nice, and she's going to make you an offer. Just do me a favor. Don't let him anywhere near her. You know what she's like. She can hardly wait to get her hands on him."

As far as he knew, Carla and her mother, Judy, had always hated each other. "Cunt," Carla said when they'd first started dating, when Troy was eighteen and Carla was twenty-four, and Troy had been scandalized that someone would use such a word to describe their own mother. "She's poison," Carla had said. "I don't want to have her anywhere near me!" He learned that Judy had once had Carla committed to a mental institution, that Judy believed Carla had a mental disorder:

borderline personality. And when he and Carla got married, it was a long time before Carla told her mother, arguing vehemently over the phone.

"I wouldn't mind if she were dead," Carla said, and he'd been shocked, just as he'd been shocked when Carla threw away the congratulatory card that Judy sent when Loomis was born; just as he'd been surprised when Judy had called him a "druggie little leech." Just as he'd been awkward when Judy called him to say that she could watch Little Man.

But as for Little Man, he has never complained. That's one thing. In fact, Little Man seems to like his time with Grandmom, and he seems unfazed when Troy drops him off at Judy's house. He runs down the front sidewalk and into the small one-story house, skirting around Judy as she stands on the front stoop with her arms folded over her chest. "Howdy," Troy calls to her, and she lifts her chin slightly in greeting. She is fat but not soft, a little bit over sixty years old, with short silvery-blond hair and leathery skin, bludgeon-thick arms and hands. She has the look of a woman who labors in the fields, in the sun, an old farm woman, though in fact she is a retired elementary school teacher—her look comes not so much from hard work as from relentless bitterness and anger. She squints at him and wrinkles spread out in judgmental rays from the edge of her eyes.

"Hello, Troy," she says, coolly and cordially, and Troy pauses several yards in front of her. Little Man is already inside the house, probably already perched in front of the television, setting up the Nintindo game that they'd decided to leave at Grandmom's house so he had something to do while he was there. Troy hesitates; he had meant to say good-bye to Little Man before he went off to work, but now it's awkward. Judy makes a point of not inviting him into the house.

And so now he just stands there for a moment. "So," he says, as Judy regards him. "Well," he says. "I guess I'll just pick him up in the morning as usual. Around ten or so." He makes a vague gesture with his open palms, but Judy's expression doesn't change.

"Yes," she says. "That sounds fine. I'll expect you."

"Okay," he says, and tries to smile. He clears his throat. Of all the things that he didn't expect from the world, this one perhaps surprises him the most. He has never been prepared to be hated, and maybe this is why he keeps coming back, this is why he smiles at her and offers Loomis up to her three times a week. He can't believe that she'll continue to dislike him forever, and standing there he wants to tell her about his plans for the future, about Commercial Art. He wants to say that he's changing his life. He wants to say that he had a terrible dream, he wants to tell her about Loomis at the top of the tree, getting ready to fall.

But he doesn't. He only clears his throat, politely, hoping that she's disliking him a little less than she did the last time he was standing in front of her. "Loomis!" he calls, vaguely, into the quiet of the house behind her. "I'm headed out, buddy! I'll see you in the morning!"

He shrugs as she stands there, her arms still folded.

"Okay, then," he murmurs.

7

1994

Jonah was better off in Chicago, he thought, better off than he would have been in South Dakota. This was what he told Steve and Holiday, when they had him over for dinner. "Much better off," he said, and he meant it, even though he had been lonely much of the time since he'd arrived. He did not want them to know that he didn't make friends easily, that he had spent much of the past year alone with his own mind, thinking. He didn't want to say that his life in the city so far had been more or less a void.

What did he do with himself? Well . . . He went to the movies a lot, sat at the very rear so he could feel the wall against his back. He watched many movies, film after unmemorable film, tracing the lines on his palm with his fingernail while various banalities played on the screen. He reheated carryout Chinese food in the kitchenette microwave, read various novels—Dickens, Tolstoy, Camus—while spooning up rubbery black mushrooms and tofu from his hot-and-sour soup; he sometimes drank beer at a bar where an extremely intoxicated woman once leaned herself against him and whispered, "Tell me something about yourself." He soaked in the small, efficient bathtub, curled into a space a little larger than a child's coffin—his knees up, filling and refilling it until the hot water was depleted.

He knew this was not what Steve and Holiday wanted to hear. They were a nice young couple, about his own age, spacey with bliss. Holiday had just had a baby, and they were both very excited and proud. Even though they'd had to drop out of college (they were both trying to take classes part-time); even though they seemingly had no more prospects for the future than Jonah did (Steve worked as a waiter at Bruzzone's, where Jonah also worked, but he wanted to be a filmmaker); even though it seemed to Jonah that having a baby would make their lives stressful and difficult—their faces shone with optimism.

So Jonah tried to think of positive things, too. There *were* positive things he could talk about, after all, and he had them all listed in his head as he got off the el train and walked the several blocks to Steve and Holiday's apartment. Good things, he thought. He liked his concise little apartment, and his job as a line cook at Bruzzone's. Boring, but okay. He could mention that he'd begun to take college classes—he registered for them at least, though he didn't always make it very far into the semester before he quit going—Composition 101, The Philosophy of Science, Introduction to Communication Studies. He could legitimately say that he'd sooner or later have a college degree; an associate's degree, at least, anyway. "It's a start," he could say, and shrug. He could tell them that he was saving money, that he was paying his bills ahead of time to develop a good credit rating. He *did* have some ideas about the future: trying to get some decent plastic surgery, for one, he could say. Thinking about different careers. Some kind of normal life: getting married, buying a house. Having kids maybe?

He had these talking points planned out in his mind, but when they were actually sitting there he couldn't bring himself to speak them. They didn't seem like very convincing subjects, really, and he didn't want them to get into the depressing fact that he frequently doubted the possibility of even these simple things. He didn't want them to know that they were the only people he'd had a real conversation with in almost a year. Eventually, he ended up doing imitations of Mrs. Marina Orlova, with her hatred of smiling Americans. He showed them how she grimaced like a chimpanzee and tried out a version of Mrs. Orlova's voice: "I smile at you! Eee! It is repulsive." They laughed and laughed, and Holiday said, "Jonah, why are you so shy? You're blushing. You're so hilarious."

Jonah had noticed Steve before Steve noticed him. He had gotten into the habit of watching other people whom he imagined to be about his own age, just because he was curious. He wanted to know what he should be like. He would walk behind a trim young executive, observing the short haircut, the dark blue squared-off suit and bright red tie, the brisk, purposeful stride; he would linger in a music store to examine a sloe-eyed employee, with pierced nose and tattooed forearms, an attitude of bored, pouting superiority; he would follow two grinning sailors in their anachronistic uniforms, stumbling and laughing loudly as they emerged from a bar. For a moment, he could almost imagine himself into another life. He could exist for a second inside of these people—a flash in which his own skin sloughed off and he turned down a different path, as if he could pass through the membrane of their bodies and suddenly find himself looking out through their eyes.

At first, Steve had just been another vessel he could project himself into. Steve was a waiter—one of those distant, vague figures who moved in and out of the kitchen; a blond, round-faced person with a charmingly earnest demeanor that Jonah vaguely associated with teen idols of the 1970s. There was a way that Steve would widen his eyes and say "Wow!" that seemed to Jonah particularly notable. He tried it out when he got home from work, standing in front of the bathroom mirror. "Wow," he said, and put on an imitation of the sleepy, knowing smile that Steve used. "Cool," Jonah said, in the odd way that Steve did, so that it sounded like: "Coo-el." He and Steve would look very much alike, he thought, if it weren't for the scars. They both had a similar type of straight, blondish-brown hair, a similar round-cheeked boyishness in the face. They were even about the same height—a little under six feet—though Steve's body was better constructed, all smooth lines, like a swimmer. Jonah's own body was more angular, odder—pale-skinned, reddish at the hands and foot soles; broad shoulders and chest and ropy muscled arms, which led to a round, slightly plump belly, and then to narrow legs and long-toed, nobby feet. He was like three different bodies grafted onto one person, he thought, though he also was aware that posture made a difference. He tended to hunch and to let his belly stick out, and if he straightened up and sucked in his gut he looked better. He tried his version of Steve's smile again, looking at himself in the mirror from first one angle, then another, covering up the scar on his face with his hand. *Not bad,* he thought. *Really. Not bad.*

Steve was more present in the kitchen than most of the waitstaff. Mostly, the waiters and waitresses would rush in and out—they would thrust pieces of paper at the cooks, scribbles of food requests, cry "Order!," and then hurry away. And Jonah was even more peripheral than the other cooks—mostly, he was in a corner at a cutting board, chopping mushrooms or celery or carrots, the tips of his fingers at the very edge of the rapid movement of the knife in his other hand.

But Steve had noticed Jonah. Steve was always coming in to chat up the heavyset black woman, Ramona, and the older Mexican man, Alphonso, the two main cooks. Steve would tell them about his pregnant wife, keeping them abreast of the developments, saying "Wow," and "Cool!" to them, and then he brought in photos of the baby's birth, which he passed around in the late afternoon, when the lunch crowd had cleared out and the work had lulled. He was grinning, very pleased with himself, and he gave people cigars as a kind of joke. Even the women.

Jonah watched him with cautious interest. He admired Steve's ease with people, the genial, natural way he would flirt with Ramona, or tell a joke (in Spanish!) to Alphonso, both of them laughing deeply, their eyes narrowed slyly. But it was disconcerting, too, because Steve kept catching Jonah's eye, noticing Jonah's staring before Jonah could drop his gaze. On the day he brought in photos of the newborn, he'd looked directly at Jonah all of a sudden.

"Hey, man," Steve said. "Do you want to see?"

Jonah shrugged awkwardly. "Sure," he said, and Steve came around the divider and passed a few pictures into Jonah's latex-gloved hands. In one photo, a bloody infant, with a body like a skinned squirrel, opened its wide mouth and scrunched its eyes; in another, the infant, now swaddled in a blue blanket, was pressed against the bare breast of an exhausted girl in a hospital gown.

"That's Henry," Steve said. "That's my son!"

"Huh," Jonah said, uncertainly. "Nice."

Steve grinned and extended his hand. "I'm Steve," he said. "I see you looking sometimes, but we never connect."

Jonah started to insert his slick, latex-covered hand into Steve's palm, and then realized how rude and odd it was. "Oh, sorry," Jonah said, and he took off his glove, wiping his damp palm on his shirt.

"I'm Jonah," Jonah said. He felt very self-conscious. *I see you looking at me sometimes,* he thought, and he wasn't sure what else to say. He'd thought his watching of Steve had been quite subtle.

But Steve didn't seem upset about it. "Hi, Jonah," he said. "Nice name."

"Thanks," Jonah said, and he gave Steve the grin he had been practicing, before he realized that Steve might recognize it as an imitation. He looked down at the pictures again, at the wife's expression of wonder as she held the infant—Henry—her face wan and shell-shocked and yet, Jonah thought, quite beautiful. He was embarrassed that he could see her breast, even though the infant's mouth was covering the nipple. "These are nice, really nice pictures," he said, holding the photos out for Steve to take back.

"I've been meaning to introduce myself," Steve said. "I always see you looking over at me, and I'm thinking, 'Wow, I must be getting on that guy's nerves!' You know, coming in here and talking to everybody and kind of like, not talking to you. I must've seemed annoying!"

"Oh," Jonah said. "No, no. Not at all. I didn't mean to . . . give the impression that I was annoyed." He smiled again, and made an effort to look Steve in the eye. "It's probably something about my face. I think my expressions are weird." He cleared his throat, wincing inwardly. Why did he feel the urge to draw attention to his face? It was no wonder he didn't make friends, he thought. He was always making people uncomfortable.

"Actually," he said, "I was just noticing you because you look a lot like someone I know." He didn't know what he was doing, except that he felt the urge to explain his staring. And then, for no reason he could figure out, he said: "You look almost exactly like my brother."

"Oh, really?" Steve said.

"Well," Jonah said. "He's dead now. He was killed in a car accident. But you . . . you look almost exactly like him. I'm sorry for staring."

Steve's eyes widened, and he took the photos Jonah was trying to return to him. "Geez," Steve said. "Wow! How weird!"

"Yeah," Jonah said. "I'm sorry, I didn't mean to say that."

Afterward he was terribly flustered. Why had he said such a thing? He paced his apartment, moving from the kitchen to the bathroom's medicine cabinet mirror; he stood at the window looking down at the empty street, the traffic light at the end of the block blinking yellow in soft breathing beats. It was a very freakish thing to do, he thought, and he sat down on the fold-out sofa and tapped his forehead with the knuckles of his fist, staring grimly down at the carpet. *You look exactly like my dead brother,* he thought. How ridiculous.

But the lie had come to him almost supernaturally, like a premonition, that was the thing. Lies often did. He could actually picture the brother who looked like Steve. He experienced the car accident, a slow-motion slide into a semi-truck on a slick interstate, he pictured the way his brother would throw up his arms in front of his face as the seat in front of him loomed and turned into a thundercloud, an onrushing darkness. He heard his brother's final gasp, which was strangely delicate. "Ah," his brother breathed, and then everything went dark. The whole thing had burst forth with such vividness that it had almost seemed real. He thought of the fairy tale in which one sister is blessed to cough up diamonds, while the other is cursed to spit out toads—that's what it felt like.

Whether this was a diamond or a toad, he wasn't sure. The truth was, the lie had effected exactly what he wanted it to. It had established a connection between them, a bond, and suddenly Steve was interested in becoming his friend. Steve was pleased in some way, flattered that he looked exactly like the brother who had died.

Steve told Holiday about Jonah. Jonah was invited to dinner at their house.

He had been thinking a lot about relatives lately, that was one thing. About the baby his mother had given up for adoption, about his father, who was still out there somewhere, presumably. About his mother and grandfather and Elizabeth. There were times when he thought that his past was more present now than it was when he was living it. He had not kept a single photograph or memento, but memories would constantly float up and create a scrim over his daily life.

He had been thinking about his father, for example. His mother had always been very coy about this—many times she had told him that she didn't know who his father was, and it had always been awkward to ask, since more often than not even a vague hint in that direction would send her into an irrecoverable mood.

"Why do you do this to me?" she would say. "It doesn't matter. Whoever it is, he doesn't care about you anyway. He doesn't even know you exist!" And her teeth would clench together. *"Jesus Christ!"* she would murmur to herself, the plaits of her long hair pulling dully across the surface of the table as she lowered her head.

His grandfather had been more sympathetic. "Son, you know I would tell you if I knew anything about it," his grandfather had said. Jonah had been about twelve then, and had finally gotten up the nerve to speak to his grandfather in private. They sat together, in lawn chairs out behind the house, and his grandfather took a long drink of beer. "I think," his grandfather said carefully, "that it wasn't someone she knew real well. She was living out in Chicago at the time, and I imagine that he was from there, but I really couldn't say."

Not long afterward, on a Saturday, his grandfather had driven him over to the Pine Ridge Reservation, to visit some of Jonah's grandmother's relations. There was Jonah's grandmother's sister, Leona, an enormously fat Sioux woman who stood aside grimly as Jonah and his grandfather sheepishly entered her house. The living room had a cement floor with a thin, faded red rug on it, and they sat there on an old sofa that was draped with an old bedspread, his grandfather and his great aunt Leona smoking cigarettes and saying little. She told them a story about a rattlesnake that had gotten in the window, trapped between the pane and the screen, and how they'd killed it. Some boys who were identified as Jonah's cousins came in to look at them, bronze-skinned, dusty kids, two plump and one narrow, and then they left, ran outside to play, and Jonah didn't follow. He sat there, with his hand across the side of his face, while his aunt observed him heavily. Jonah didn't know why they had never gone back, and when he had asked his mother once she had only shrugged. "That's just what you need," she said, glaring at him. "Go loiter around that dirty Indian reservation. Aren't you close enough to the bottom as it is?" And that, as far as she was concerned, was the end of the discussion.

Jonah's mother *would* talk about his brother sometimes—the baby she had given up for adoption when she was in high school. She would joke sometimes about it. Whenever she saw a lady with an infant, she would say, "Oh, look, there's my baby!" and she would smile at Jonah, as if they were sharing a bitter joke. After Jonah's grandfather died, when she started taking drugs more and more, she would occasionally grow sentimental.

"Don't you wish I'd given you up, Jonah?" she would say, full of slurry self-pity, in a haze of her own angry thoughts. "I'll bet he's a lot happier than you are."

Jonah, a teenager by then, thought about how to respond to this. He sat at the kitchen table considering, watching as his mother's head dipped abruptly, as if her neck muscles suddenly gave out and then recovered. "It doesn't matter," his mother said, and caught her hair in her hands and gave it a sharp tug, testing the strength of her scalp. "Don't even listen to me, just . . . go play somewhere." And she waved her hand vaguely, as if shooing Jonah off toward some carefree existence she imagined he lived. Jonah sat frowning at her. Hating her. Of course he'd have been happier if she'd given him away, he thought, but that wasn't even the point. The point of her obsession, he thought, the reason she kept going over and over it in her mind, was that *she'd* be happier. Her life could have been different, that was the point of everything: the axle around which the dull wheel of their life had turned for as long as he could remember.

He wished he could tell someone these stories. He could imagine telling them to Steve and Holiday at some point, for example, though the lie he had told would make that enormously complicated. He would have to insert the imaginary brother who looked like Steve into the fabric of his past, somehow, in the way that special effects were added to films; he would have to alter or modify certain stories to include his imaginary brother in the action, or at least to explain his absence from the scene.

He thought of this as he sat at the dining table in Steve and Holiday's apartment, but he discreetly avoided mentioning the dead brother again, whose name (he had decided, just in case they asked) was David. "I was glad to get out of South Dakota," he said. They were eating linguine and drinking red wine, Chianti, Steve told him. As he spoke, Holiday leaned her hand against her cheek and smiled, her eyes warm and attentive, as if he were dear to her. "I wanted to . . . find a place with more opportunities. I thought about Omaha, you know, because that's not so far away from Little Bow, but Chicago just seemed, well, more exciting. Sort of like going to New York, but not so . . . scary." And both Steve and Holiday nodded. They were both from Wisconsin, so he guessed they had some idea of what he meant.

"It was brave of you, to set out like that on your own," Holiday said. "Don't you think so, Pie?" she said—she called Steve "Pie" as an endearment—and Steve raised his eyebrows and nodded.

"Absolutely," Steve said. "You'd never been to a city or anything before?"

"Not exactly," Jonah said. "My mother and I lived in Chicago and Denver when I was really little, but I don't really remember it."

"Does your mother still live in South Dakota?" Holiday said.

"Not exactly," Jonah said. He took a small sip of red wine, blushing a little. "She's dead, actually."

"Oh," Holiday said. "I'm so sorry."

"That's okay," Jonah said. He shrugged, feeling himself blushing again. "I'm not . . ." he said, "I'm not sensitive about it."

But there was a respectful silence. There was an awareness that Jonah had experienced tragedy that Steve and Holiday had not, and the two of them looked at him thoughtfully. His brother's name was David, Jonah thought. Maybe his mother had been killed in the same car accident in which David had perished?

They talked about things like movies—which was great, which was fine. One of the things that Jonah had purchased with his newfound wealth was a VCR, and so he had seen both *Carnival of Souls* ("Brilliant!" said Steve) and *Choose Me* ("Highly underrated," said Holiday). Steve talked about the script that he was working on, which was based upon a children's book called *Louis the Fish*, a book Steve had loved as a child and which he thought was a "work of genius."

"It's not going to be a film for children," Steve said. "There are a lot of adult themes that I want to stress. It's going to be kind of surreal and disturbing, but not inaccessible." And when Jonah admitted that he hadn't read or heard of the book, Steve exclaimed enthusiastically, "Jesus, Jonah! You won't believe how incredible it is! I have to give you a copy!" He got up to look for an extra copy of the book, and as he did he gave Holiday a kiss on the side of her face.

"Four hundred and fifty-five!" he exclaimed. He told Jonah that he wanted to give Holiday one thousand kisses before the end of the week, and so he was counting.

Jonah laughed. They were funny together, Steve and Holiday. Delightful. Sometime later, he would realize that they were the kind of people who were at their best when they had an audience. They were happiest when they had someone they could dote on, someone who in turn could bear witness to the way they were in love.

It was not a role he minded playing, of course. Maybe they were interested in him because he had a dead brother, because he had ugly scars and a shy demeanor, a whiff of tragedy. When they talked about other friends, he got a sense of it: Allison, who had been homeless for a while and who was struggling to stay off drugs; Javier, an illegal immigrant from El Salvador who had worked at the restaurant for a time before Jonah got there; Dallas, the bartender they knew who had been divorced twice and hadn't even turned thirty, who once stayed with them for almost a month after his wife kicked him out, sleeping on their couch and rotating through the same three changes of clothing. Listening to the anecdotes they told of these friends, Jonah could imagine himself becoming part of this menagerie, another stray they'd brought home and loved for a while. But he didn't care. All that really mattered to Jonah was that they were interested in him, and their interest—their focused, smiling attention—was wonderful.

After dinner, Jonah and Steve cleared the table and washed the dishes while Holiday sat at the kitchen table, nursing baby Henry. Holiday was a small-boned girl, with short, dark hair and a long face and nose, but her breasts were enormous for such a thin figure. *Of course,* Jonah thought. *They're full of milk.* But he made a conscious effort not to look over at her as she sat, with her blouse lifted. He was drying the dishes, and the first couple of times that Steve handed him a rinsed plate he stupidly said "Thank you!" as if he were being given a gift. Steve and Holiday both thought this was very funny and made a little joke of it: "Here, Jonah. A colander for you!" And Jonah played along. "Thank you so much," he said. "I really appreciate it." In a clownish mood, he did his imitation of Mrs. Orlova for them, and they laughed once again.

"You should be an actor, Jonah," she said. "Have you ever thought about it?"

"Not really," Jonah said. "Not with—" He started to say "Not with my face," but then stopped himself. According to *Fifteen Steps on the Ladder of Success*, one of the signs of a losing mentality was to disparage oneself in front of others.

"I'm surprised," Holiday said. "You didn't even act in high school? You seem like one of those guys who seems shy until they get up on a stage."

"Ha," Jonah said. "Not hardly. High school was like—" And he cleared his throat, accepting the big, dripping pot that Steve handed him. "Well," he said, "let's just say that I wasn't the type to be in plays."

"Were you athletic?" Holiday said.

"No," Jonah said. "I wasn't . . . I wasn't anything really." And he tried to think back. The few friends he'd had were like him, at the bottom of the social ladder: Mark Zaleski, whose IQ didn't quite qualify him as retarded, but who was nevertheless two years older than everyone else in their grade, a friendly but humorless boy who liked to trade comic books and talk about various types of cars; Janine Crow, an intelligent girl, part Sioux like his mother, a girl who developed so early that she looked like a middle-aged woman by the time they were juniors, the sad outline of her bra visible through the dowdy blouses she wore; she was picked on so constantly that she automatically flinched when people spoke to her. And even with these people, he hadn't been close. He was ashamed, sometimes, to realize how little his teenage years had involved anything that other people would recognize as normal rites of passage.

"My brother did a lot of that sort of stuff," Jonah said. "He was in—what do you call it?" He glanced surreptitiously at Steve, trying to imagine what sports Steve might have played. "Track," he said. "And, well, *he* was in a play." He scoped his mind for a minute. *"The Glass Menagerie."*

"Oh, I love that one," Holiday said. "I'll bet he played Jim didn't he? Jim O'Connor, the gentleman caller."

"That's right," Jonah said. He cleared his throat—he would have preferred it if Holiday hadn't been so familiar with the text, which he'd read but didn't remember very well. "How did you know?"

"It's funny," Steve said, wiping his hands on a dish towel. "Actually, *I* played Jim when we were in high school. And Holiday played Laura. The crippled girl."

"That's almost spooky," Holiday said, and Jonah felt his face reddening.

"Well," Jonah said. "He did a lot of things, my brother. He was involved in a lot of stuff." And he was silent as the two of them grew solemn; silence expanded in the kitchen as he continued to wipe the pot that Steve had given him even though it was dry. He wished that he hadn't said anything.

"You must miss him very much," Holiday said, respectfully.

"I do," Jonah said. He averted his eyes as Holiday unplugged Henry from her nipple and lowered her shirt. "We don't have to talk about it, though."

"Oh, no! Of course not!" Holiday said. And when Jonah looked at Steve, Steve was observing Jonah's hands, the thin tooth marks that left scar trails from his wrists to his knuckles. There was a silence, and then Holiday said: "I'll bet Henry would like it if you held him, Jonah."

It was a significant moment, he thought later. It was maybe the first time he'd held a baby. He sat down in the kitchen chair and Holiday lowered Henry into his arms, and he actually felt weirdly shaky. Steve and Holiday smiled benignly, watching, but he almost forgot about them. He was caught up with the amazement of it, the warm, squirming weight that settled into his arms and grew still.

The baby stared at him, steadily gazing. There was a weight of the past. It made him think of the way his grandfather used to sit and look out at the horizon. He thought of his mother's bitter joke: *Oh, look, there's my baby.*

The baby's large eyes settled on him, and though this had been one of his happiest nights in his whole life, it made him melancholy. He had read somewhere that babies are instinctively drawn to faces, that they will fixate even on drawings or abstract, facelike shapes, and round objects with markings that might resemble eye-mouth-nose. It was information that struck him as terribly sad, terribly lonely—to imagine the infants of the world scoping the blurry atmosphere above them for faces the way primitive people scrutinized the stars for patterns, the way castaways stare at the moon, the blinking of a satellite. It made him sad to think of the baby gathering information—a mind, a soul, slowly solidifying around these impressions, coming to understand cause and effect, coming out of a blank or fog into reality. Into *a* reality. The true terror, Jonah thought, the true mystery of life was not that we are all going to die, but that we were all born, that we were all once little babies like this, unknowing and slowly reeling in the world, gathering it loop by loop like a ball of string. The true terror was that we once didn't exist, and then, through no fault of our own, we had to.

8

June 20, 1996

After his fall, Little Man cries for a while. He is going to have a black eye—"A real nice shiner," Troy says—and Little Man touches the swollen area gingerly.

"I can see my cheek," he says, bitterly. "And I'm not even trying to look at it."

He rests his head against Troy's shoulder, nuzzling a bit, sniffling. He seems okay, and Troy tightens his grip around the child's middle. Troy's hands are trembling, and he hopes that Little Man doesn't notice the shuddering of his palm as he presses it against his back. He keeps smelling Little Man's hair as they hurry down the sidewalk.

It freaks him out a little. He thinks of his nightmare, of Little Man falling from the tree. And here Loomis *had*, in fact, fallen from a tree!

"What were you thinking, man?" Troy whispers, soothingly chiding. "Are you going to become a daredevil on me? The Evel Knievel of tree climbing?"

"Those kids lied," Loomis says grimly. "They said there was a bird nest with eggs in it, and I believed them. They boosted me up there, and I fell." He presses the good side of his face against Troy's shirt. "What's Evel Knievel?"

"Oh," says Troy, distractedly. "He was this famous motorcycle guy. He did, uh, daring things." But he isn't thinking about Evel Knievel. He is thinking about the other kids, boosting Loomis up into a tree. "Bastards," Troy says, and his dislike for the other children hardens into something like hatred. Scotty and Davey, little white-trash pieces of shit from down the block. What were they? Eight or nine? Taking advantage of a five-year-old. He had known it when they came running up to the screen door, faces flushed, eyes bright. "Mr. Timmens! Loomis fell! He's hurt! He's crying!" gleeful, he thought, almost shining with excitement. He should have known not to trust them from the beginning, with their ugly shaved heads and their dirty white T-shirts, sockless feet in thrift-store basketball shoes. They'd started coming over to play, to eat his good cookies and potato chips, and when they'd offered to take Little Man over to their house, he'd had a moment of weakness, thinking it would be nice to have an hour or so to himself, he'd do the dishes and wash a load of laundry, stuff he'd been neglecting for several days. He should never have trusted them, he thinks now, and his mood darkens, he bites the inside of his cheek. He tries to think of ways he could scare the crap out of them. Teach them to screw around with his son. *Mr. Timmens! Loomis fell! He's hurt!* Jesus Christ, he had never felt that kind of dread before, running down the block, imagining blood, broken bones. An ambulance.

It wasn't as bad as that. He puts Little Man down in a kitchen chair and holds up three fingers.

"How many fingers am I holding up?" he says, and Little Man looks at him warily, puzzled.

"Three?" he says, and this makes Troy feel a bit better. Troy takes an ice-cube tray from the freezer of the refrigerator and cracks it over a dish towel. He bundles up some chunks of ice into the cloth.

"Here," he says. "Hold that over your eye. It's going to be cold but it will make the swelling go down."

Little Man does as he's told, but winces as he presses the balled, ice-filled dishrag over his eye. "Why will this make the swelling go down?"

"I don't know," Troy says. "Trust me. It just does."

He sinks down into a chair across the table from Little Man, looks him over for a moment. He's okay. Troy reaches into the small glass ashtray that sits in the middle of the table and plucks up the dead marijuana joint, half a finger long, and flicks it toward the sink. Good shot: It lands in the basin where the garbage disposal is, and he leans his forehead against the ham of his hand. He should not be smoking pot in the middle of the day, he thinks, and then he picks up the portable phone, which is also on the table, and puts it to his ear. No sound. He had been sitting there, smoking a joint and talking to Ray on the phone when Scotty and Davey came racing to his screen door, and he supposes that he should call Ray back eventually, just to let him know everything is all right.

But he doesn't feel like it right now. Ray has been in a neurotic mode lately, and they had been talking about Ray's fear that he might have some mental illness, like Tourette's syndrome. "I have these urges," Ray had been saying. "You know? Like, urges to do bad things. I mean, like, suddenly I have the urge to shout profanity in the supermarket. Or, like, I'm at a restaurant, and the waitress is coming down the aisle carrying a load of plates, and I'll have the urge to trip her. I mean, really bad. Like an evil urge. And, you know, I think about exposing myself to, like, old ladies and shit. It's very disturbing."

"Ray," he said. He'd begun to roll a joint automatically, sitting at the table with the phone tucked in the crook of his chin. It's natural to want to get high when he's talking to Ray. "Ray, man, does it ever occur to you that you're just an exhibitionist? I mean," he said, "you're a stripper. You take off your clothes for dozens of women week after week and you think that's, what? Normal?" He drew deeply on the puckered end of the marijuana cigarette, just as the children appeared at his door.

He puts down the phone. Ray has other people to call, other people to complain to. He examines Little Man's black eye again.

"How are you feeling?" he says. "Are you feeling okay?"

"I guess," Little Man says. The area around his eye is black and blue, fairly bad. Falling out of the tree, he'd struck his face against the bark of the trunk. He'd lain there, huddled in the sparse grass, holding his face and crying silently. He is the kind of kid who plays dead when he's hurt. It wasn't until Troy came charging into Scotty and Davey's backyard that Little Man had lifted his head. Jesus Christ, Troy thought.

Where was their mom? No sign of her—the windows of their house were blocked by tacked-up sheets patterned with football logos. A naked engine was sitting on cement blocks near the tree, the grass around it dead from shade and motor oil. *He could've been killed,* Troy thought, and drew breath. He tried to suck the thought back into his brain and out of existence.

"You're really okay?" Troy says now, and Little Man shrugs.

"I'm a little upset," he says.

"Those kids," Troy says. "I'm sorry that they fooled you."

"They didn't know what they were talking about."

"Fucking idiots," Troy says.

Little Man purses his lips and presses the ice against his eye. "I agree," he says.

Troy has been having lifestyle issues, or something. He feels vaguely guilty all day, with Little Man so subdued and quiet. Poor kid, he looks terrible. The side of his face around his eye is bruised brownish-black, and a swollen knot has risen up on his cheek, and he seems very blue.

"I wish I could talk to mom," Loomis says, and Troy actually blushes.

"I'm sorry, kiddo," he says. "You can talk to me, if you want."

But Loomis just turns back to the television. He's been very moody ever since his fall, frowning gloomily at children's programs like "Sesame Street," "Barney," "Mister Rogers' Neighborhood," stuff that usually would have been much too babyish for him. Nevertheless, he sits there, listening as Mr. Rogers sings, "You'll never go down, you'll never go down the drain . . ." holding his old blanket against his face, rubbing the silky lining between his fingers. It's a habit from when he was a toddler, and it worries Troy enough that in the afternoon he calls a nurse he knows, a woman named Shari who is also one of his regular marijuana customers. He has her run over the symptoms for concussion with him: headache, dizziness, confusion, nausea, vomiting, vision change—none of which Loomis is presenting.

"What about tinnitus?" she says. "Ringing in the ears?"

Troy puts his hand over the phone receiver. "Loomis," he calls. "Are you experiencing any ringing in the ears?"

"What?" Loomis says. He mutes the TV.

"Ringing in the ears?" Troy says. "Do you hear any ringing or strange humming?"

Loomis is quiet for a moment, listening attentively. Then he says: "No, I don't think so, " and turns the volume of the television back up.

"Well," Shari says, "keep an eye on him. If he still seems like he's acting funny in the morning, maybe you ought to take him in."

"Yeah? You don't think I should take him to the emergency room or anything?"

"I don't," she says. "It sounds normal." And then she clears her throat. "And how are you doing, Troy? We haven't talked in quite a while."

"I'm okay," Troy says. "Same old, same old."

"Uh-huh," she says. "Well, I haven't been out to visit you in a while, I'll have to do that pretty soon."

"Anytime," Troy says. "You know me. Always present."

And then, after he hangs up, he has the urge to call Carla. Something about Shari's voice, a kind of "wife" voice has reminded him of the ordinary, intimate conversations that men and women have when they live together—even he and Carla had such times, normal mundane stuff that he realizes now is what he misses almost more than sex.

Later, after Little Man is asleep, he tries to call her, and finds that her phone has been disconnected. "The number you have dialed is no longer in service," the computer voice says. "If you feel you have dialed this number in error, please hang up and dial again. If you need help, dial your operator." And then it repeats again, the same message, which he listens to in its entirety.

It's nothing he wouldn't have expected. Of course she'll call when she's ready, when she comes out of whatever new crisis she's found herself in, but he still feels a weird anxiety. A pathway has been severed, one of the last ones, and he curls up on the couch drinking beer, with the phone on the coffee table in front of him, flipping through channels.

He wakes up abruptly from a sound sleep and he is dreaming that he hears a voice from a children's program. Someone like Mr. Rogers says:

No escape for anyone, anywhere.

It scares him for a second. He can see the red light from his digital clock, which says 4:13, and there is a pale, pre-morning color to the darkness. Something inside his stomach makes a trickling sound. Yuck. He can feel himself flooding into his mind, gurgle, gurgle, like water rushing into an empty tub. Now he is hungover but blankly awake, blinking into the dimness, and whatever spirit world he had been touching is gone. He listens, and there is tinnitus, a thin metallic drone in his ear: no escape for anyone, anywhere.

He finds himself thinking about the phone call that came two nights ago, which he somehow associates with Little Man's fall from the tree and with his general anxiety.

Just the usual sort of telemarketing call. "May I speak with Troy Timmens?" the guy said, a woodenly awkward kid who Troy felt a little sorry for, since he seemed to be a lousy salesman.

"Yeah," Troy said. "Present."

"Oh," the guy said, and then wavered. "Oh," he said. It was late in the afternoon, and Loomis was watching cartoons in the next room: Spiderman, which Troy also enjoyed watching. Troy glanced in the direction of the television as the telephone guy got his act together: reading off cue cards, Troy thought.

"I'm speaking to Troy Timmens?" the guy said, at last.

"That's me."

"Oh," the guy said. "Okay." Then he seemed to fumble again. "Well . . . Mr. Timmens, I'm . . . I'm calling today as a . . . as a representative? Of the Mrs. Glass Institute? And we're . . . contacting people who were adopted through the Mrs. Glass House during the years 1965 and 1966. Is it safe to assume? I mean, that you are one of those people? Who was adopted from the Mrs. Glass House during the year 1966?"

"Who is this?" Troy said, and his voice hardened a bit. He didn't like to talk about the adoption thing. It was private information, he thought, and he felt a little uncomfortable to think that this stranger was in possession of some sort of list with his name on it, a file, a record. Stuff he himself didn't know. "Who is this?" he said, gruffly, and then, in his most formal voice: "To what is this concerning?"

"Ahem," said the awkward person. "My name is . . . David. David Smith. And I'm part of a project that's. A project who is interviewing various, various people. And, well. May I assume? That you are in fact *the* Troy Timmens that was adopted from the Mrs. Glass House in July of 1966?"

It was very bothersome. Troy frowned. "Listen, man," he said, "you can *assume* that I'm not liable to talk to someone over the phone about this. You need to send me a letter or something. I'm not going to talk to some guy that calls me up out of the blue."

"Oh!" the person said, now more flustered than ever. "You mean you haven't received a letter from us? A certified letter? It should have. Arrived."

"Never got anything," Troy said, sternly. "So, I don't know, maybe you've got the wrong guy or whatever, but you need to send out your letter again."

"Oh," said the guy. "Are you sure?" His voice sounded strained, as if Troy had somehow hurt his feelings deeply, and he was trying not to cry. God, what was the problem? "Can I . . . verify your address, then?"

"Fine," said Troy. "Look, I'm not trying to be rude. But this adoption stuff is private to me. It's not something I talk about with just some stranger over the phone, okay?"

"Oh," the guy said. "Of course. Of course! We understand completely."

After he hung up, he'd felt weirdly troubled. A little upset, as Loomis would say. And now, at 4:13 in the morning, he feels the same way. It was very uncool of them, he thinks, those adoption people, calling up and bothering folks. It reminds him of a story that his fellow bartender, Crystal, had told him once. One afternoon, an elderly couple had shown up on her doorstep. They were driving through, they said—they lived in Oregon, now, they said, but once, when the old man was a child, he had lived in St. Bonaventure. He had lived in that very house, where Crystal was now living, and he wondered if they might come in just to look around.

"Weird!" Troy said, not sure why he felt so repulsed. "And you let them in?"

Crystal shrugged. "They were just old people," she said. "They were, like, eighty or something. It was cute to think of them driving across the country. They were very sweet."

But once they had been admitted into her house, the old man became emotional. "It's so much the same!" he'd said. "I remember looking out of that window!" And then, when they walked into the living room, he started crying. "Oh!" the old man said. "I can picture mother sitting there in her chair, right there. I haven't thought of that in years." And he'd had to sit down, to get a grip on himself.

"Ugh!" Troy said. "How creepy!" And Crystal looked at him oddly, as if he'd missed the point of her story, or misinterpreted it.

"Not really," she said. "I just thought it was . . . interesting. You know, about the passage of time and all."

"I guess," Troy had said then. But now, thinking of it, he still doesn't think the "passage of time" is interesting. It's invasive and spooky, and he thinks he will tell that to the adoption people if they call him again. "Look," he'll say. "You guys gave up your claim on me a long time ago. Signed, sealed, and delivered. That's the end of the story, as far as I'm concerned."

Sitting at the kitchen table, sleepless, he writes this down on a scratch pad. "Signed Sealed Delivered. End of Story." He draws a cartoon talk bubble around the words, and then frowns, his tongue between his teeth, drawing a skull head, like he used to do when he was a kid. It's a happy skull, and he attaches the talk bubble to its smiling mouth. He gives the skull a bow tie and a porkpie hat. Then he crumples up the paper and throws it away. He gets up and fishes around in a drawer for a particular glass pipe that he likes. He takes his personal stash of marijuana out of the freezer, and sorts a pinch of it free of seeds and branches.

He has done nothing wrong, he thinks, but he feels like a bad person. He feels like *something* is his fault, something that he cannot even name but which sits like a heavy bird in a branch overhanging his mind, and he would know what it was if he only thought about it long enough.

9

March 1966

A girl has disappeared from the Mrs. Glass House. Escaped—that's what people are saying. Nora listens to the muttered bits of gossip in the cafeteria and the television room. She nods as Dominique repeats a version of the rumor, watching Dominique's cold-looking, red-palmed hands at work on her knitting. "I guess they've called her parents," Dominique says softly. "I hope Mrs. Bibb gets fired."

"Mm-hm," Nora says, and glances toward the window. Outside, the snow is knee-deep and dense, the first week of March, and no one seems to be able to explain how the escape was accomplished. They say, for example, that the girl left in the early morning, that her footprints were found in the snow, a soft series of indentations that led to the cast-iron fence, then ended. She must have climbed over the fence, people say—a six-foot fence with arrow-spikes at the top of each metal rail—and then perhaps jumped into the bed of a truck that was waiting for her, idling on the other side. Though there were no tire tracks. And though she was eight months pregnant, huge-bellied, not built for climbing fences and jumping into trucks.

"They don't know how she did it, that's the thing," Dominique says, and Nora can see the way doubt and hope are struggling with each other in Dominique's mind. "She must have been very clever," Dominique says, uncertainly.

Nora is quiet. What is there to say to such stories? They seem ridiculous but beautiful. Who wouldn't want to believe that a girl could plan such a gambit, worthy of a spy? Who wouldn't want to believe that there was a boyfriend out there, an eternally faithful boy perhaps with a flatbed pickup, the exhaust pouring out as you poised yourself over the sharp spines of the fence, the boy calling *Jump! Jump! I love you, baby!* as your legs coiled and you prepared to leap into the crisp snowy air like a horse across an impossible chasm.

Now that a month has passed, Nora finds that she is no longer surprised when she wakes up. There is no momentary gasp of unfamiliarity when she opens her eyes and discovers herself once again in this room, in this place. She lifts her eyelids: The pillow curves away from her vision like a landscape, and when she rolls over, the ceiling spreads out above her, a textured plaster ceiling with blurry yellow smoke stains running across it like the waves of a mirage; a tiny pill of cobweb quivers in an air current. She is no longer sick in the morning, no longer weak with fatigue or sudden gripping hungers. In the low, early-morning light her desk and chair have emerged from the shadows to become solid, and the bare walls are dim but visible. Outside, the blizzard continues unabated—not fierce, but relentless. Fat snowflakes the size of her thumb flatten themselves against the windowpane and pile up against the sill, and she tries to picture that heroic girl trudging determinedly, fleeing in nothing but her smock and a thin autumn coat. It doesn't seem likely.

The girl's name, the missing girl, is Maris. *Maris,* another wishful pseudonym, Nora thinks, the kind of odd, awkwardly lovely name that parents never really give to their children but that girls wish for when they are a certain age, imagining that a name will make them a different person, a princess, an exotic island. It is a good name for a girl who has, supposedly, vanished into the night.

After a while she finds herself drawn to the window. There is the bare tree and the fence beyond, dark charcoal etchings against the undifferentiated whiteness of ground and sky. Her fingers melt the ice at the edge of the glass, and she blinks slowly, thinking of that boy coming to Maris's rescue, his face eager with love, his cheeks ruddy in the cold.

She knows that it didn't happen.

It's more logical, Nora thinks, to believe that Maris committed suicide. Most probably, she has hung herself in her room or taken some well-concealed pills or slit her wrists. Mrs. Bibb and the other authorities have spread the rumor of her disappearance themselves so as not to upset or alarm anyone. They are trying to cover up the poor girl's death by creating a diversion, but the truth is that there is no "Maris," really. There is just another Ann or Kathy or Joyce, a parade of not very bright farm girls who are all in the process of realizing that their futures are sad and pathetic and ugly. They are not "Maris" futures. They are not "Dominique" futures.

Of course that's it, Nora thinks. The girl is dead. But still she has to admire the cleverness of the story, the image of those footprints leading out to the edge of the fence and then ending.

Still, the more she thinks about it, the more she realizes that it's just a myth, just an echo of a local legend that she has heard a number of times. She recalls reading about it in the newspaper one year around Halloween time—a ghost story of sorts that involved the disappearance of a child.

The legend itself is always presented, even in the newspaper, as a "true-life mystery." There are names, dates, places that suggest the sheen of fact. Apparently, for example, this incident took place on December 31, 1899, on a homestead located some seven miles east of Little Bow. The family who lived there was named Ambrose, a young couple with two sons.

On that particular night, a small group of friends had gathered at the Ambrose place to celebrate the coming new year. They sang songs and made toasts while the two boys, aged six and eight, popped corn over the fire. Outside, a heavy snow was accumulating.

At about ten o'clock, Mr. Ambrose asked his elder son, Oliver, to get some water from the well. The snow had stopped falling, and a gibbous moon was visible behind the breaking clouds, casting a pale light over the open yard and the fields beyond. Mrs. Ambrose watched as her son trudged out in his new Christmas overshoes, the silver bucket swinging lightly in one hand.

But the boy had not been gone more than a few minutes when the gathered party heard him cry out for help. "Momma!" he shrieked once, shrilly, as if he were being attacked, and then the sound stopped abruptly.

The adults rushed outdoors, Mr. Ambrose carrying a kerosene lamp, though the whole snow-covered prairie landscape seemed to glow, almost phosphorescent, in the moonlight. There was no sign of the boy, no sound, only the miles of treeless fields and snowdrifts, wafting into shadow. The boy's tracks ended about halfway to the well. There were no other marks of any kind in the fresh snow, only Oliver's footprints, and the bucket, lying there on its side. The wind sent a soft curlicue of powder around it.

According to the newspaper, a subsequent investigation only verified the adults' account of the incident. No further clues were discovered, and eventually the mysterious case was "quietly dropped" for lack of evidence. The last time Nora had seen the story recounted in the newspaper, they'd added a "human interest" element by consulting several experts, who suggested possibilities that ranged from the boy being carried off by eagles to being abducted by a UFO. One man, a private investigator from Denver, debunked the whole thing. He said that perhaps the boy merely made his way to the well in some playful way, so his tracks didn't show—along a fence, maybe—and then had fallen into the well and drowned.

When she was growing up, Nora herself had never thought too carefully beyond the chill left by those clear, abruptly ended footprints. There was an emotional reality to the story, a confirmation of what she'd always secretly felt—that there was something tentative about her own existence, something tenuous. She could remember her father sending her out to do some chore after dark—garbage she'd forgotten to haul, a sprinkler not turned off—and how the thought of that old story would spread across her skin as she hesitated in the doorway, the growing certainty, as she stepped out into the night, that she wouldn't ever come back from her errand.

Even now, sitting alone in her room, thinking of the story gives her an uneasy feeling. She looks at her wristwatch—6:40 in the morning, which is not a time to be superstitious and skittish. But still. The silence suddenly seems uncanny, and she throws back the covers and pads in her nightgown, barefoot, to the door, which is open just enough to be uncomfortable, just enough to feel as if someone could be looking in.

No one is, of course. The hallway is empty; it's still almost an hour until breakfast and the quiet is perhaps even normal. Many of the girls here sleep so much they seem to be barely alive. Twelve, fifteen hours a day, she calculates. There is one girl in particular, "Ursula," whom Nora has taken a vaguely scientific interest in—Ursula appears at lunch and dinner, groggy, eyes pinched, waddling with her enormous belly like a manatee. Nora thinks she is either carrying a grotesquely large infant or twins, but the point is that Ursula seems capable of sleeping anywhere. She sits in the TV room with her fat thighs spread open, her mouth ajar; she sometimes dozes over her food in the cafeteria, nodding with her fork and knife poised on her plate. Once, while they were in line to go out to a movie, Nora had seen Ursula asleep on her feet, waiting to be given her tin ring, her cheek nuzzled against her shoulder, her eyes fitfully closed, even as her feet shuffled forward in response to the other girls' movements. Sometimes Nora wishes that she could be like this girl, that she could accomplish the next dreadful months in a kind of coma.

But it doesn't work like that. Whenever she closes her eyes, there is something circling brightly, in the way that a june bug dive-bombs a lightbulb, swinging in unsteady circles and colliding with the side of the house, falling onto its back, buzzing wildly. There are thoughts of the dying girl in *The Collector*, thoughts of the other girls in the Home, Dominique and Ursula and the lost Maris, thoughts of Nora's own unimaginable future. She sits at the desk in her room and tries to draw faces on a piece of paper, girls with big eyes and bow mouths, modeling contemporary clothing.

Despite herself, she thinks of her father, back in Little Bow. At

6:45, he would surely be up by now, drinking coffee, ready to leave for work.

In 1914, when Nora's father was four years old, he was set aboard the Orphan Train. Nora's grandfather was a beggar who pretended to be blind, and he brought his three sons into the New York Children's Aid Society wearing gunny sacks, shoeless. Her father remembered that clearly: standing in a waiting room, aware of the stink of his own body, aware that the loose sack he was wearing was like a girl's dress. The boys' mother had died, but he didn't know how. Maybe in childbirth, he'd said, musingly, as if she were the forgotten name of a town he had visited. *It all seems like it happened to someone else,* he told her. *It's blurry in my mind.* He remembered, he said, that his father had hoped for money when he brought them to the Children's Aid Society. His father was a crafty, bitter man, and had imagined that his sons might be worth something. He argued for a while with a horrified lady in a heavy blue-gray dress, demanding that the boys show her their muscles, show her they could work! And at last, she gave him some coins and he went away.

The lady had turned to them. "Oh, my poor children," she had said. Nora's father had flinched when she touched his head, but he recalled that her hand had been tender and slow, and that she had brushed back his hair.

"Are you to be my mother?" Nora's father had asked, and one of his brothers had filliped him on the back of his skull.

As a sophomore in high school, Nora found the word *fillip* in *Webster's New World Dictionary, 2nd College Edition.* It was a find that pleased her with its accuracy, a word she hadn't known existed. "Fillip," she said, and thumped her own head like a melon. She sat staring at the dictionary, filled with wonder. It was a word that her history teacher, Mr. Bosley, himself would have to look up. Nora jotted this down. She was doing this as a project for his history class, an extra-credit project that Nora had wanted to do well on, since she had been given a B on the last test. Mr. Bosley was the president of the local historical society, and had offered them a reprieve from his cruel tests if they presented him with well-documented interviews of elderly residents of the community. She had known that her own father's story could help improve her standing in Mr. Bosley's estimation. She was aware that she would need to attain a grade point average of at least 3.5 if she wished to attend the college of her choice. At the time, she was of the notion that her future hung in the balance. She wanted to be a famous and remarkable person—different from the rest of her family.

She wrote:

> Starting in 1854, the New York Children's Aid Society began the "placing out" or "free home" programs to give orphaned and deprived children a chance at a new life in the West. Among these children was my father, Mr. Joseph Doyle. In 1914, at the age of four, he traveled by train to the town of Brussels, Iowa. He had been one of thousands of New York street children which were called "street arabs," but they were actually neglected and abandoned youths who roamed the city. The children made their way in the world by stealing, begging, and working as newsboys or bootblacks or coal shovelers. They spent their nights sleeping in alleys, doorways, and discarded packing boxes.

This is what she had been working on when she found out she was pregnant. The essay remains unfinished, a useless appendage, and she is aware that she will never know how it ends. She will never again interview her father about his experiences, she will never again get the chance to summarize his life and reach a conclusion.

But she knows she will always think about it. She will always wonder whether she would have discovered something about her father's history that explained everything and she will imagine the essay that she could have completed for Mr. Bosley, an A+ essay, she feels. Her mind will pace in a circle around these little mysteries: her father, and the legend of that disappearing Ambrose child, and the girl at Mrs. Glass House—Maris.

Outside it continues to snow. Whatever escaping tracks had been left by Maris would have been covered a long time ago.

10

October 12, 1995

When the packet came in the mail, Jonah didn't open it at first. He glanced over the brown manila envelope, and saw who it was from. *The PeopleSearch Agency* was stamped in smudged black ink in the upper right-hand corner. He saw his own name and address, not even typed, but handwritten in a sloppy, childish cursive, and his heart sank. It didn't look official at all.

He had waited almost nine months for this packet to arrive, long enough to be convinced that the whole thing was a scam. He'd tried calling them once, to check on the "progress" of his, what?, *his account,* he said at last, hesitating, and was immediately put on hold. The phone receiver grew wet against his ear as he waited, listening to crooning soft rock that was played to him through the telephone lines, running his fingernails up across his forehead, up through his hair. At last, after almost twenty minutes, an elderly-sounding woman came on to tell him that his case was still being "investigated."

"We're working on it, honey," she'd said soothingly. "These things can take *years,* I hate to tell you," and he'd nodded politely into the receiver. *Of course,* he said, *I understand,* though he felt his ears heating up, the sound of blood beating, hush, hush, hush. *Three thousand dollars,* he thought. He had given them three thousand dollars, nearly a third of the money he'd been able to save from the sale of his mother's house, the little yellow house where he'd grown up, the furniture—some antiques—and his grandfather's guns and coin collection. He thought to tell the woman this. *I gave you all my money,* he wanted to say. *I should be getting something back for it.* But he didn't. All he said was, "Well!" All he said was, "So! I guess you'll . . . contact me, when you know something?" And the woman had laughed warmly.

"Yes, we surely will," she said. "Just be patient, Mr. Doyle!"

And now, here in his hands was the result of his patience, the result of his savings. A thin nine-by-twelve envelope, not more than a few pages by the weight of it. He put it down on the coffee table, set his little statue of "The Thinker" on top of it. He was a fool.

That day had begun so simply. Jonah had a quick errand to run and he stepped from the foyer of his apartment building into the thick, chilly drizzle of a Chicago autumn day. October 1995: nothing significant happening in the world, or at least not in America, not in this city where Jonah had awakened to find himself alive and existent. Or *sort of* existent. Here he was, Jonah Doyle, aged twenty-five, no known connections, a wanderer in a major U.S. metropolis. Just an ordinary, anonymous person like the others who were moving grayly in the distance along the opposite street. He pulled the hood of his sweatshirt up over his head as droplets of mist speckled his unnecessary sunglasses. He stared down at the movement of his black, square-toed boots on the pavement as he walked. Tough, solid boots, and he was not afraid of stepping on broken glass, or someone's lost, flattened sock, or a bare, hideous chicken bone. Whatever. He crossed over the sad manhole cover that he liked, the manhole cover with grass growing in a ring from its cracks, beautiful baby grass, so new that the green was almost phosphorescent. He admired it again, wondering how it was possible for the grass to survive like that, how long it would last, with the frost coming. He turned up his headphones. The autumn leaves came spinning slowly out of the sky, sharp-edged Technicolor. His life wasn't so bad, he thought. The spike-tipped iron fences at the edges of the sidewalk seemed more vividly black, the three-story brick apartment buildings more solidly three-dimensional. The flap of a wayward newspaper page lifted its broken wing from the sidewalk and flew forward a few paces before settling, and he wasn't disturbed by it. Not really.

He was on his way to buy notecards. He would go to the drugstore and buy the notecards, and then he would go to the library, and then he would go to work, and then he would come home and begin to write the paper that had been assigned to him in his anthropology class. He would try to go to bed by one A.M.

He had been working very hard lately to keep things in order, to be very specific and goal-oriented. He was trying to make each day like a story he was telling about himself. He consulted the planner that he had begun to carry with him—his At-A-Glance calendar, his street map of Chicago, his train and bus schedules, his notes and memoranda. He would find himself shuffling through it even when he knew where he was going, dividing his day into neat segments, detailing it in his mind as he went. As he walked, he projected himself by increments into the future. He could picture the tattoo parlor two blocks away where he would turn left; he could see the aisle of the drugstore where the notecards and other paper products were kept, and the line at the cash register he would stand in. He had an idea of the particular table where he would sit at the library. At exactly one-fifteen, he would leave the library and walk to the el train, and he could visualize a map of the Howard Red Line, a seam that ran along the coastal edge of the city, and he could hear the crackling, murky voice of the train conductor calling out *Roger's Park. North and Clyborn. Loyola.* He could picture the locker room of the restaurant where he worked, his apron and checked cook's pants hanging there in the narrow metal hollow of his locker (#71); he could picture the table where he would stand chopping vegetables while the cheerful, aggressive Spanish of his coworkers passed over his head, and from there he would project himself even farther into the future—imagining his anthropology paper finished, typed neatly, handed in; imagining actually making it through the class to the end of the semester; imagining the college degree he was working toward. He could picture himself as a center point in expanding space—the other cooks moving past him in their hair nets and white aprons, the swoosh of waiters and waitresses passing through, the chatter of diners at their tables, the skyline of the city, the suburbs, the great silent fields that trailed their long emptiness all the way back to Little Bow, South Dakota, where no one who had ever loved him was alive.

And then, lifting his head from these thoughts, he found that he had not even reached the drugstore yet. He had, in fact, walked past it, or made an incorrect turn, or something. He was on an unfamiliar street, and he had to crouch down on the sidewalk at the edge of a building, irritated with himself and a bit shaky, too. He was lost again.

After all this time it should have been easier, he thought. When he first moved to Chicago, he had imagined that he would evolve, step by step, into a new self, a new life. But, though over two years had passed, he was not really a different person. Across the street, seagulls were alighting on discarded food in the Dunkin' Donuts parking lot, and people were hurrying or strolling along the sidewalk toward the el train station. At the end of the block, a bearded man reached toward him—a sun-browned yam of a hand, shaking a Styrofoam cup in which a few coins were lodged. Jonah straightened his sunglasses and moved past the man without speaking, though his back stiffened as the man stared at him.

By now he should know how to deal with these basic things. Most of the time he did. He knew how to avoid a crazy homeless beggar, he knew how to move headlong down the street with his face turned low, with the aura of a person who was busy and on his way to someplace important.

But it didn't come naturally to him. That was what he had been realizing. The pattern of his thinking was constantly being marred by intuition, by his imagination, by stories he told himself that soon metamorphosed into half-truths.

Now, standing on the el train platform, he could remember vividly how the PeopleSearch Agency had seemed like a wonderful solution to his problem. How enticed he'd been by the billboard that showed an elderly woman and a young woman embracing. "Are You Missing Someone?" it said. "We Can Help!" How gladly he'd written out a check after talking to them on the phone.

This had been only nine months ago, a day in late February not long after he'd been to Steve and Holiday's for the last time. Steve had quit his job at Bruzzone's, and the connections between them had become more and more tenuous. Jonah had lost his charm for them—he'd wanted, he realized, to be closer friends with them than they were prepared for.

He remembered once, sitting in their kitchen, playing with Henry while Holiday finished cooking the dinner. Henry was playing a game where he put his hand into Jonah's mouth, and Jonah pretended to eat it up. Henry found this hilarious. His mouth opened broadly, in toothless delight, and he laughed in that strange hiccuping way babies laughed.

"You know," Jonah said to Holiday. "If you guys ever wanted to go out on a date by yourself, or something, I could baby-sit for Henry. If you wanted."

"Oh, Jonah," Holiday said. "That's so nice of you. But . . . we have a really good baby-sitter."

"I'd do it for free," Jonah said. He smiled up at her, and then, when Henry again extended his fingers, he nipped them very lightly. "Arr Arr Arr," Jonah said, and Henry chuckled happily.

"Listen," Jonah said, after they'd played for a little longer. "Does Henry have a godfather? Because, you know, I'd be glad to do it. I mean, like, if you guys died in an accident, or something, I'd be glad to take him in."

Holiday turned from the stove and gave him a long look. Then she tried on a smile. "Well, Jonah," she said. "Both my parents and Steve's parents are still alive. So, I mean, if something were to . . . happen, I suppose he would go to them."

"Oh, of course," Jonah had said. "But they're old! They might not be able to take care of him."

"And I have three sisters. And Steve has a sister and a brother."

"Well, sure," Jonah said. "Right. I was just saying that if . . . it ever came up, I'm available. That's all."

"That's really sweet of you, Jonah," she said. But she'd stared hard as he chattered his teeth against the sour, rubbery flesh of Henry's fingers. "Rrrr," he growled, and her smile tightened, then faded.

Thinking about it later, he was aware that he'd crossed a line that he hadn't realized was there. He'd come on too strong, had tried to settle himself into the closest circle of their life where he wasn't wanted. They didn't say this, of course. But he could tell. They used to invite him places—they went to a festival of animated film, to a farmer's market, to a Korean restaurant where he fell in love with kimchi. But now they didn't call him anymore, and when he tried to telephone them, he always got their answering machine, even though he was certain they were there in their apartment, monitoring their calls. "Hey, guys," he said, awkwardly speaking as he imagined the bland slow turning of a recording tape. "I was just checking in . . . to see what was going on." And then he called an hour later, just in case. One week, he had left them fifteen messages, and not one of them was returned.

He had only been invited to dinner because he had run into Holiday on the street, on Michigan Avenue outside of the Walgreen's, and she'd hugged him and said, "Oh, it's so good to see you! We should get together sometime."

"Okay," Jonah said. "This week is good for me. Any night this week, actually."

"Oh," said Holiday. And then he'd realized that she hadn't meant it, though she immediately came up with a time and date. "It will be so nice to see you again!" she'd said. "We've missed you."

But it was clear, even as he arrived at their apartment, that this was to be the last time. There were silences even as they opened the door, and they would not show him Henry, who was of course asleep, and Steve and Holiday kept exchanging glances as Jonah tried to make conversation.

They used to like hearing him talk. They used to take pleasure in the various things Jonah saw as he wandered through Chicago, they used to say that he was "a brilliant observer." But now, it seemed, they could hardly wait for him to finish. He kept hoping that if he just continued on his observations would become brilliant again. But they didn't. He told a story about Mrs. Orlova, how every time he saw her she said "What's wrong? You look sick!" even when he felt happy. He tried to amuse them with talk about the people he saw from his apartment window, and the neighbors who shared the building with him who were always going in and out. Once, in the middle of the night, a shaggy, drunken young man had taken his trash to the Dumpster wearing only a pair of briefs, tiptoeing barefoot through the light snow with a garbage bag that, when Jonah had later out of curiosity slit it open, contained only beer cans and coffee grounds and grapefruit halves. Once he'd seen a man beating up a woman near the foyer, and the woman had put her hand over her mouth to muffle her own cries. People kissed in doorways, they hurried down the sidewalk or strolled slowly, they called to one another or sang. In the middle of the night, a pair of men had attacked each other, rolling around and gnashing in the street, and one of Jonah's neighbors had opened up a window and yelled at them. "Shut up!" his neighbor had called, throwing a stuffed animal down at them, and the men had both stopped fighting, rising up from their battle to shout angrily at the man who had thrown the toy at them. "Come down, you coward," they called. "Come down, come down. We'll kick your ass!" And they'd both begun to stomp on the toy before, finally, they stalked away together down the middle of the street.

In his mind, this had been a wonderful and hilarious account, one that would please them. But as he talked, he could feel the story faltering, becoming pointless and rambling, and Jonah was aware that they wished he would go home. Holiday was leaning forward as Jonah groped for words. The more painful it became, the more Jonah wanted them to laugh, or nod, or say "Ah!" in the way that they used to.

"I wonder how long we'll know each other," Jonah had said at last, after the pause in the conversation had seemed to settle over them like a layer of soil. He said it cheerfully, trying to sound as if he were just musing, but Holiday looked at him guiltily.

"Oh, Jonah," she said, reproachfully. "We'll always know each other! Once you meet somebody, you don't *unmeet* them."

"Jonah, Jonah," said Steve, as he always did, as if it were an old children's rhyme. "Jonah in the whale." He smiled sleepily, and Jonah thought of the Bible verse that he knew, that had once pleased them.

" 'Take me up and cast me forth into the sea,' " said Jonah. He smiled, speaking sonorously. " 'So shall the sea be calm unto you; for I know that for my sake this great tempest is upon you.' "

"That's so pretty," Holiday said, without enthusiasm, though the first time Jonah had recited it to her, she'd widened her eyes as if he'd performed a magic trick. "Why, Jonah!" she said then. "That's amazing! What is it? Shakespeare?" Jonah had told her that it was from the Bible, from the Book of Jonah. It was the only Bible verse he had ever memorized.

"The Bible is full of great poetry," Steve had reflected. "You've got a really excellent reciting voice, Jonah!"

But now Steve didn't say anything. Even discussion of Jonah's dead brother, David, the imaginary one who looked like Steve, didn't stir their interest anymore.

But Jonah continued to think about it. He had built a brother out of nothing—a brother who had acted in plays and ran track, a brother who had died in a car wreck. *David.* Without even meaning to, talking about it had brought Jonah toward a vague but constant awareness of the real brother who presumably existed out there, the male infant his mother had given up for adoption.

Nevertheless, when he saw the man on the el train, it took him by surprise. The intensity of it. It was the day after he'd been at Steve and Holiday's place for the last time, and he'd woken up late, with a headache from the red wine. *Take me up and cast me forth into the sea,* he thought as he opened his eyes.

He had been late for work that morning, which was unusual for him, and he actually ran the last block to the el platform, full of single-minded anxiety. He pounded up the steps just as the door to the train slid open and the waiting passengers began to funnel their way inside. Usually, he was right at the edge of the ramp as the train pulled up. He had become an expert at gauging the exact spot to stand, so that the doors of the train came to rest directly in front of him and he could be the first one inside. He prided himself on this skill.

But on that day Jonah was the last of the clutch of morning commuters to board. The seats were filled and the aisles were crowded, a thicket of raised arms and solemn faces, so packed that there wasn't even a handrail or support pole to grasp. When the train pitched forward, he stumbled against the bosom of an impassively frowning African woman in a brick-colored scarf. She said something horrible about him in her native language.

But he hardly noticed. For it was at this moment that he caught a glimpse of the man who might have been his brother. Or rather, he saw a face, floating some six or seven heads beyond.

Their eyes met for a moment, and an electric, rippling sensation slid over Jonah's skin. He felt it rise, tingling in his hair, and he was actually dazed.

It was him, Jonah thought. *Jesus Christ! That's him! That's my brother!* They might have been twins. They had the same blondish hair, the same brown eyes and short, blunt nose, the same wide mouth and broad cheeks. And more than that, the same . . . what? That old psychic feeling he'd had as a teenager. An aura, Jonah thought, something like a hallucination. Invisible waves emanated from the person he was looking at.

But the man didn't seem to notice anything. He narrowed his eyes to suspicious slits when he saw Jonah staring at him, then lowered his head deliberately to the paperback he was reading. A person moved, and then another, and then Jonah lost sight of him. Jonah tried to move forward, edging closer to the place where the man was sitting. But before he could even locate the person he'd seen, the train reached the next stop. There was a general, amoeba-like flow of bodies as people poured in one door and out the other. And the person he'd seen was gone.

For weeks after that, perhaps months, Jonah had gone to the el train platform and loitered there, in hopes of catching a glimpse of the person who might have been his brother. He went to the train later than usual and stood behind the waiting crowd, sweeping his eyes across the backs of their heads in his search. He tried to remain unobtrusive, slowly and casually strolling by in his white T-shirt and checked cook's slacks, a baseball cap with the brim low over his eyes. If someone caught him looking, he'd lower his head, staring down at his black scuffed sneakers for a while before resuming.

Maybe this was the child his mother had given up for adoption, he thought. Or maybe it was another child that his biological father had parented, a half sibling that he knew nothing about. Or a cousin. He was aware again of his father—who had lived in Chicago, according to his grandfather. He had never much resembled either his mother or his grandfather, and he considered the possibility that maybe there was a whole tribe of people who resembled him. Who thought like him. Who would welcome him.

But he never found the person he was looking for.

On the day the package came from the PeopleSearch Agency, he had been mulling over a passage from one of his anthropology textbooks, *Ascent to Civilization: The Archaeology of Early Man*. He kept reading it over, trying to make it coherent, to make it fit his thoughts.

"If," he had underlined. "If, as we commonly accept, the lives and values of the most 'primitive' people on earth today are worth as much as any reader of this book, then surely each moment of the past, each person, had equal value. Even in a book like this largely devoted to the Old Stone Age we cannot distinguish the difference between say 150,000 and 140,000 years ago. We do not know what the individuals of those two periods thought, felt, enjoyed, and suffered, or how different they were. But we can at least appreciate that to those people, their lives were as important as ours are to us."

It made him feel sad. Reading this made him feel worse than he had when he'd been reading novels in his literature class, where the characters were full of a purpose and meaning that had embarrassed him. They had motivations, and complexities, and their lives were full of systems of symbolic importance. They represented something. Various things.

The problem with his own life, he thought, was that he had not been born significant. He was like those primitive peoples whose lives left almost nothing—a few bones and flint tools, a charred circle where their fire pit had been. Unlike the characters in great novels, he had no connection to the major world of human endeavor—no relationship to politics, or sociology, or economics, or the great movements of his time. The stuff that would be remembered. What could he say but that his people were the detritus of various empires. Nothings upon nothing. Irish peasants, arriving at Ellis Island and wandering helplessly through the streets of New York; conquered Lakota, nomadic aboriginals, marched to the barren plains of their reservations and corralled there, to wait endlessly. Even the town where he grew up was a nothing town, not a place that an empire really wanted, but only a mile marker, a place that was necessary to own only because it existed in a great blank space in between significant coasts. The great pulse of the world, which throbbed vaguely in Chicago, grew silent as it irradiated out into the plains.

Jonah would not be remembered for anything. That, at least, was a certainty.

He thought of this as he walked home. Maybe his father, or his brother, had more to do with the larger world. Maybe it didn't matter. He didn't have an idea for an anthropology paper, not even a thesis, but only two quotes that circled in his head: *But we can at least appreciate that to those people, their lives were as important as ours are to us.* And *Take me up and cast me forth into the sea; so shall the sea be calm unto you.* There was a great essay in these two thoughts, if only he could bring them together. If only he could articulate it. Mostly, he experienced his thoughts as disconnected, as wobbly planets circled by moons, which were then themselves circled by little asteroids and space junk, all tilting around a central sun, which was himself. His literature teacher said his essays were "ambitious but muddled," and in the margins she wrote repeatedly: "Unclear." "Unclear." Or simply, "Hmmm. . . ."

Mrs. Orlova was outside their apartment building, sweeping the sidewalk with a broom, and he felt a bit better, knowing that she would scoff at everything that troubled him. Loneliness? Significance? Ha! She had grown up in Siberia. He smiled at her as she raised her head from her work to frown at him.

"You look terrible," she said. "Are you sick?"

"No," Jonah said. "Not at all." Even after several years, he was not used to Mrs. Orlova's bluntness—the gloomy exaggeration that was the exact opposite of the midwestern reticence that he'd grown up with.

"You must be depressed," Mrs. Orlova said, and peered at him. "You look sweaty."

"Oh, really?" Jonah said. He passed a hand over his face, which was dry, unperspiring. "No," he said. "It's nothing."

"Whatever you say," Mrs. Orlova said. "I can see with my own eyes that you have been fired from your job!"

"No, I haven't."

"It's worse then," Mrs. Orlova said, looking hard at him. "Someone has broken your heart."

He found the response from the PeopleSearch Agency curled up and crammed ungracefully into the narrow mailbox. It seemed unimportant.

But when he slit open the manila folder, he began to shudder. To actually shudder.

Here was the name of Troy Timmens. Troy's birth certificate. A photocopy of relinquishment papers. The address of the people who had adopted him.

Jonah stood there for a long time, his throat tightening, his breath seeming to harden in his lungs. He looked at the papers.

His life was changing. He could feel it.

11

June 30/July 1, 1996

On the night he was arrested, Troy was thinking that maybe things were okay. He was feeling better than he had in a long time. Pretty good! he thought. Calmed and almost happy, not worrying about anything. There was a little party—Troy and his old high school friend Mike Hawk and Ray. At eleven that night, they were playing Frisbee out in the road in front of Troy's house, under the streetlights. They were a little stoned, and a little drunk, but not so much as to be a nuisance. They kept their voices low, so the neighbors weren't disturbed; they kept their eye out for the infrequent car that might pull down the street; and they politely got out of the way when they saw headlights approaching. It was a friendly game—they didn't stand very far apart, and they passed the Frisbee between them in the same way that a marijuana pipe traveled in a circle from person to person. Troy enjoyed watching the bright green disk hover through the galaxy of insects that accumulated beneath the fluorescence; he enjoyed the minor prowess, the simple athletic movements that were required to snatch the Frisbee out of the air. Nothing special, or competitive: just a toy, passing from hand to hand. Troy, barefoot, in shorts, appreciated the warm, timeless summer air, the intimation of childhood vacation. Loomis was asleep.

Playing Frisbee was also fun because Ray was so notoriously bad at it. "Oh, come on," Ray complained. "Let's play cards or something."

"Cards?" Troy said scornfully. "Ray, how many beautiful summer nights like this are you going to get . . . in your entire life? I mean, if you live to be, say, seventy-five, the number of beautiful summer nights is a very finite number."

"Oh, good," Ray said. "Just what I need for my beautiful summer night. Morbid philosophy from Mr. I-Just-Turned-Thirty!" But he nevertheless followed Troy and Mike outside, and even, after a time, seemed to be enjoying his own lack of competence.

"Okay," he said. "I think I'm getting the hang of it." But the Frisbee, when Ray threw it, wobbled arthritically through the air, or fell on the ground, or spun forcefully in the wrong direction. Once, Troy told Mike Hawk, Ray had thrown a Frisbee and the disk had veered off behind Ray's head, striking an innocent young woman a glancing blow across the ear. It was weird, Troy thought, that Ray could work as a stripper—someone who had such control over his body's shifts and sways and gyrations—and yet he was ultimately so uncoordinated. Ray flung the Frisbee and it sputtered through the air, curving past Mike and landing with a thunk against a tree in Troy's neighbor's yard.

For his part, Ray was still getting a lot of mileage out of riffing on Mike Hawk's name. When they were at the bar, Ray loved to bring girls over just so he could say, "Ladies, I'd like you to meet Mike Hawk." No one thought it was that funny then, but he still kept at it.

"Mike Hawk is really going at it tonight," Ray said, in a sportscaster voice. "Mike Hawk knows when to get hard, and knows how to ease his way in!" This quip delighted him so much that he tripped trying to grab the Frisbee out of the air and fell onto the little patch of lawn between the street and the sidewalk, his long legs scissoring through the air as he fell. For a moment, it looked as if he might have hurt himself, but he bounced back up. "Jesus Christ," he said. "I really suck at this game. Can we light up another joint, please? I don't think I'll ever be able to beat Mike Hawk."

"Hilarity ensues," Troy said, making a wry face and curling his toes against the grass. Things were okay, he thought. Everything was normal. Happy. His life wasn't bad.

He had been feeling a lot of unplaceable anxiety lately. He was upset about Loomis's fall from the tree, and the fact that he couldn't reach Carla, and the call from the guy at the Mrs. Glass House. And just in general. A few days earlier, when Jonathan Sandstrom had shown up at the bar with the latest shipment, he'd been of a mind to refuse it—to quit, once and for all, as he'd told himself he would. He needed to change his life, and after this he thought he would have to start telling his various customers that they'd have to look elsewhere.

It was, relatively, a small delivery. "*Great* to see you, Troy," Jonathan Sandstrom said. He was a blond, glossily handsome guy in his late twenties, with a braying, artificial laugh and an almost disturbingly upbeat demeanor. He gave Troy an elaborate handshake when they met in the parking lot behind the bar. "Troy," he said, and paused dramatically. "You should maybe sit down, because you are going to be so *extremely* happy with the stuff I've got for you, you're not even going to be able to contain yourself."

"Okay, then," Troy said, and gave Sandstrom a quick, hard smile. "I'm glad to hear it." He sat down in the passenger seat of Sandstrom's BMW and opened the small, brightly colored paper tote bag that Sandstrom handed him. "The usual," he said, and grinned confidentially as Troy examined the contents: three large Ziploc bags of fresh, good-smelling Mexican marijuana, a container of hallucinogenic mushrooms, thirty-six tabs of LSD. This would tide him over for a number of months, and after that, maybe he would cut back even further.

"Listen," Sandstrom said. "I know you're not interested in cocaine, and I don't blame you. Very. Difficult. To. Deal. With." He underlined each word with a swipe of his hand. "But I think you really ought to think about Ecstasy. It's a nonaddictive substance. Not dangerous. *Very* popular. I know that some people are not interested in change, and I respect that, but maybe you . . ." and Troy watched as Jonathan Sandstrom built a kind of elaborate structure in the air with his hand gestures, "maybe you want to try a sample, just to test it out."

"I don't think so," Troy said.

"Something different. Just a suggestion."

"This ought to do me," Troy said.

"And that's fine, too," Sandstrom said. "You know what you want, and I respect that." He lowered the window and dropped the cigarette that he had just begun to smoke onto the asphalt. Then took another one out of his chest pocket, lit it, drew deeply.

"Listen," Sandstrom said. "Do you know the way to a little town called Beck? I'm supposed to meet someone there at—" He looked at his watch. "Jesus Christ. At three."

"Yeah," Troy said. "Sure."

They took out a map. Troy fingered the ropes of his tote bag handles, and pointed toward the northwest. He was getting tired, and wasn't thinking about much of anything. There was no way of knowing that the way to Beck would lead Jonathan Sandstrom to a ten-year prison sentence; there was no way of knowing that Sandstrom was being staked out by police, and that Troy was about to be swept up in the wake.

He didn't think of himself as a "drug dealer," exactly. It wasn't as if he hung around outside school yards, tempting children; it wasn't as if he were getting rich off people's addictions. He didn't believe in stuff like crack or heroin, and in fact he basically approved of the so-called War on Drugs, though he also thought that it was long past time that marijuana and other innocuous substances became legal. If the president admitted to trying pot—even if he supposedly "didn't inhale"—was it really such a big deal?

He liked selling marijuana, in the same way that he enjoyed being a bartender. There was a simple, cheerful camaraderie about it. He and the customer would be sitting together at the kitchen table, with the various objects spread out like chessmen in a friendly game—bong, lighter, cigarettes, baggies, the old pharmaceutical scale he used, with its checker-shaped weights stacked in a pyramid. He really did believe that marijuana was basically good for people, that it brought out what was benign in their hearts and heads. He believed the old line—who said it? Bob Marley?—that if only all the world's leaders would get high together, there would soon be peace on earth. Sitting there, talking to someone like the young lawyer Eric Schriffer, or the nurse Shari Hernandez, or Bob Boulder, a guy of about his age who taught tenth-grade history at the high school, or Lonnie Von Vleet, the fifty-year-old hippie guy who supervised the mentally handicapped people at the vocational center and who sat on the city council, it had seemed like he was providing a useful service. He had a place in the world, and at such times the notion that he was engaged in a criminal activity seemed distant and faintly ridiculous. A technicality.

Still, he did want to keep Loomis separate from it, and that was another reason he knew he needed to stop selling. He tried to complete most of his transactions at night, when Loomis was asleep, or, if during the day, when Loomis was out in the backyard, playing. But the time was coming when Loomis would begin to figure things out, if he hadn't begun to already. There had been a night, a few months after Loomis arrived, when the child had awakened and come into the kitchen where Troy and Lonnie Von Vleet were in the process of trying out some of the produce.

"Hi, Dad," Loomis said, standing in the doorway in his Batman underwear, and Troy had taken the bag of marijuana off the table and put it back in the old valise where he kept all his drugs.

"I woke up and I smelled a lot of smoke. I thought the house might be on fire."

"Well, it's not," Troy said. "You should go back to sleep, buddy."

"What's that?" Loomis said, pointing to the bong in the middle of the table.

"Oh," Troy said. "It's nothing. It's a water pipe that Mr. Von Vleet was showing me. That's where the smoke was coming from."

"You were smoking from it?"

"Yes," Troy said. "It was just . . . kind of a dumb thing we were doing."

"It's not very good for you," Loomis said.

"You're right." Troy glanced at Lonnie Von Vleet, who smiled.

"Hey there, Little Man," Von Vleet said. "Do you remember me?"

"Yes," Loomis said, seriously, and he shook Lonnie Von Vleet's hand when Lonnie held it out. "You do magic, right?"

"You've got a great memory, Little Man," Lonnie said, and though he was a bit small-eyed from the samples of produce they'd been smoking, he was still deft. "What's that behind your ear?" he said, and reached out, seemingly pulling a quarter from the shaggy hair that Loomis had tucked behind his ear. He offered it to Loomis, who took it, impressed. Back when Troy and Carla were together, Lonnie Von Vleet had shown a number of sleight-of-hand tricks to Loomis—pushing a pencil in one ear and out the other, making a coin disappear and reappear in his palm—and he seemed pleased that Loomis remembered him.

"You need to go off to bed now," Troy said, after Loomis had taken the quarter and thanked Lonnie Von Vleet. "I'll turn on the fan, so the smoke won't bother you."

"Okay," Loomis said, agreeably, and both Troy and Von Vleet had watched as Loomis disappeared down the hall and into his bedroom.

Troy cleared his throat. "Shit," he said, "I hate being a bad parent," and Lonnie grinned, patting him briskly on the back of his palm.

"What are you talking about?" Lonnie said. "He's a great kid. You must have done something right."

He thought of this again that night, as he and Ray and Mike Hawk sat around the kitchen table. He turned on the exhaust fan in the window above the kitchen sink, and opened the back door, and after they'd smoked a couple of bowls he wandered down the hall to check on Loomis. He felt uncomfortable as he stood in the doorway. Loomis lay there, his arms folded around his chest, a sheet covering the lower half of him. The pictures of dinosaur skeletons that Troy had drawn hung over the bed, as grim as gargoyles. Troy thought about adjusting the covers, but then thought better of it. Loomis was peaceful.

When he came back into the kitchen, Ray and Mike had taken out the old black leather valise that he uses to store his stash—the drugs he'd just bought from Jonathan Sandstrom. The valise was a memento that had once held his father's important papers—deeds, insurance, birth certificates, marriage license, will—all the formalities that made up a person's official life. Seeing Ray and Mike digging through it, he realized that it was probably reprehensible that he had used the valise to store his drugs in.

"Jesus Christ," Ray said, looking up. "Where have you been? We've been sitting here for, like, twenty hours."

"Just checking on the kid."

"You're such a mama," Ray said, and picked up the baggie of mushrooms, holding it up to the light critically. "Do you ever get any Ecstasy?"

"No," Troy said.

"Well, you should. It's a really cool drug."

"I'll take that under advisement." Troy took the bag of mushrooms from Ray's hand and put it back in the valise, then packed the rest of the new drugs on top, leaving only a small black film container full of pot, which Mike was going to take home with him.

"Let's go outside," Troy said. "I'm in the mood to play Frisbee."

It was around midnight when the police showed up. An ambush. Some kind of tip-off, a narc of some sort, and Troy wasn't prepared. He opened the door and three cops were peering back at him, standing broad-chested on the porch under a halo of insects—june bugs, millers, mayflies—that were circling ecstatically around the bare lightbulb. "Troy Timmens?" the first cop said, and Troy began to gesture behind his back at Ray and Mike, who were sitting at the kitchen table. Hopefully, they would recognize the desperation of his hand signals.

"Yes," Troy said to the cop. "Present. That's me. What can I do for you?"

"Mr. Timmens," the cop said, and put a thick hand on the edge of the door, as if to prevent Troy from closing it. "I have a search warrant for this home." He offered forth a folded sheet of paper, like a brochure, and Troy took it gingerly. He could feel himself blushing. He was very stoned, and he knew that the smell of marijuana smoke was rolling sleepily through the half-open door.

"Oh, shit," he whispered. He was aware that the amount of drugs in his house would almost certainly lead to a prison sentence. His chest tightened. There had to be a way out, of course there had to be, and he tried to make his mind move quickly as he stood there staring at the grim faces of the policemen. "Wow," he said. He felt like he could start crying.

Troy thought he knew what it would be like to die, what it would be like in that moment when you heard the retort of a gun someone had pointed at you, when your parachute didn't open, when you sank toward the bottom of the lake with something heavy attached to your foot. Even then, Troy thought, there would be a long, dreamlike pause where you imagined that there was still some way to escape. *Wait,* he thought. His mind moved rapidly through the hallways of a maze. Even as the walls grew narrower, even as the passage sealed in front of him, his mind yearned for that diminishing chink of light, still hoped for mercy, for wild luck, for reprieve or intervention.

"Look," he said, still trying to grasp at that alternate reality that existed before he opened the door, when he might have done something differently, trying to imagine a path into a future in which he might somehow escape. "You guys," he said to the cops standing there. He was aware that his life—the life he had been living, and the life he had been expecting for himself—was disappearing and there was nothing he could think of to do about it.

"Let me think for a minute," he said. But the cops were already pushing past him, with a jingle of keys and handcuffs. Two cops, then three, disappearing into the kitchen and down the darkness of the hallway. There was a clatter of dishes, as cabinets were opened, and one of the men pulled his hands behind his back and put a plastic tie around his wrists, reciting the Miranda rights. In the distance, he could hear one of the policemen shouting: "Come out from under the bed, sir. Come out from under the bed, sir! Sir, I order you to come out from under the bed!" *Ray,* he thought. *What an idiot.* And then he remembered Loomis.

"You guys, wait a minute," he shouted. "That's my kid. That's my kid! Don't hurt him!"

It was the worst moment of his life, and it wasn't until much later that he was able to make sense of the sequence of events, since everything seemed to happen at once.

The first was the sound of Loomis screaming as he was pulled by the leg out from under the bed, where he was hiding. "Loomis," he yelled, and tears sprang to his eyes, his voice cracking. "It's okay, buddy! It's okay, don't be scared!"

The second was the discharge of a pistol, an overanxious young cop, and Troy let out a cry.

And then there was silence. He didn't know at the time that Loomis had fainted at the sound of the shot, had curled up into a ball and gone rigid. He thought Loomis was dead, and the room distorted around him. He was weeping in a way he never remembered having done before, the way Loomis cried when he fell out of the tree: soundless, his contorted mouth trying to suck in air as tears ran down his face and out of his nose. His eyes wide as he tried to choke out words.

Dimly, in the distance, was the noise Ray made as he tumbled over the backyard fence, carrying Troy's valise. *Oof!* Ray grunted loudly, and he and Mike Hawk were running flat-footed up toward the hills behind Troy's house, leaving Loomis's screams, and the ricocheted gunshot, and Troy's weeping far behind them.

12

June 4, 1997

After she has searched for a little over an hour, Judy tries calling some of her neighbors. Her voice is hoarse from yelling, and she is extremely agitated. The presentiment that Loomis has been kidnapped has frightened her badly, and she is aware of a sharp thrum of panic at the edge of her perceptions. Something about her own, ordinary kitchen seems animate and watchful, as if the objects there might suddenly begin to breathe. Her forehead is wet with perspiration.

Nevertheless, her telephone voice remains, in the iron-clad custom of the Great Plains, pleasant and laconic, even as drops of sweat trickle from her forehead into her eyes. "Hi, Dawn?" she says brightly. "This is Judy Keene. How are you? . . . Well, I'm glad to hear it! . . . Listen, Dawn, I seem to have misplaced a youngster over here . . . little brown-haired fellow, six years old. A little small for his age. Wearing a red T-shirt and jeans? . . . No? Well, if you happen to spot him . . . All right . . . Thanks, I will . . . No, I'm sure he's around here someplace. These kids, I'll tell you! . . . Okay, then . . . Well, I'm sure I'll be talking to you soon . . . Yes . . . Okay, then. Good-bye, now . . ."

Her hands are shaking. Of the five neighbors that she is able to reach, none report any sightings. Dorothy Draper says that she heard that dog over at the Woodwards' barking and barking, but of course Judy knows that—she's the Woodwards' neighbor, after all.

"That's Carla's boy, is it?" Mrs. Draper says, and Judy has to suppress the urge to hang up the phone.

"Yes," Judy says. "That's right."

"Well, I haven't seen Carla in so long!" Mrs. Draper says. "How is she doing?"

"Oh," Judy says. "Fine! Just fine!"

"She was always a sweet girl. I remember when she used to come over here to play with Donald. She always had the most unusual games. Very involved. And I'd listen to them and I'd think to myself, 'she ought to be an actress.' Wasn't she in Los Angeles for a while?"

"No," Judy said, and cleared her throat. "Las Vegas."

"Oh," Mrs. Draper said. "Well, it must be good to have her home. Donald is in Saudi Arabia, can you imagine? He's in the navy, and that's where they sent him. I don't understand it, why they have to be over in those places. Has Carla been back in town for long?"

"No, no," Judy said, and pressed her hand to her chest, where another soft firework had erupted. "She's not in town. I'm just watching her boy. He's staying with me. For the summer."

"Is that right?" Mrs. Draper said. "Well, that really must be a treat for you. Do you know, I haven't seen my granddaughter since she was two—and now she's five! And I have said to Donald: Why don't you just send her to stay with her grandma for a few weeks? It would mean the world to me, I tell him. But to fly a child from the Middle East to the United States, and then to Denver, and then for me to drive over there to pick her up. It's very complicated."

"Yes," Judy says. And then she lightly presses down on the lozenge where the earpiece of the phone rests. Disconnecting. She hopes that Mrs. Draper will assume that they have been disconnected accidentally. She has rarely been so rude to another person in her life, but she is certain, at this moment, that she needs to call the police.

The dispatcher, Connie Cruz, answers on the first ring. "Communications," she says, and Judy tells her that she would like to speak to someone about helping her find a little boy.

Connie Cruz takes down the vital statistics. She asks for Judy's name and address, and leads her through a description of the child. "He's got brownish hair and blue eyes," Judy says. "He's wearing a red shirt and blue jeans. About three-foot-five or six. Maybe forty-five pounds."

"And he's a white male?"

"Yes."

"How old?"

"Six."

"Oh," says Connie, who has a six-year-old of her own. "A little guy."

"Yes," Judy says, recalling the repulsive nickname Loomis's father had for him. *Little Man.* "Yes," she says. "He is."

Like the rest of the country, St. Bonaventure had gone through a brief period of "missing child" obsession in the mid-eighties. This was the time when pictures of missing children began appearing on the backs of milk cartons, green-and-white photos of children with their vital statistics printed underneath: name, age, date of birth, hometown, weight, height, hair and eye color, last seen at _____. The photos themselves had a grainy, tabloid quality, the dots that made up the images clearly visible. Judy remembered being unnerved once while shopping, passing the dairy aisle and coming upon rows and rows of these faces staring out at her. Around this time the police department instituted a fingerprinting program in the grade schools, and she recalls the day her second graders had been lined up in front of a table where a sullen, elderly policeman sat with inkpads and thick paper cards. The children were thrilled.

But she herself had thought it was ridiculous. A kind of hysteria. No one she had ever met had actually known of a child who had been abducted. The supposed missing children were always from distant places—California, mostly, Judy noticed—and it was generally assumed that this was a problem in cities. Judy remembered hearing somewhere that ninety-five percent of these children had been taken by one of their own parents, the children mere victims of custody disputes rather than evil-minded strangers. By the time Loomis was born, the urgency of the syndrome had died down. The milk companies no longer printed the photographs, which apparently gave kids nightmares and hurt sales, and the disturbance seemed to fade away. By the time she retired from the elementary school, they were no longer fingerprinting children. Loomis had never been fingerprinted, as far as she knew.

The police car arrives at Judy's house a little more than five minutes after she calls 911. It has been a slow day, and Kevin Onken, the officer who answers the call, has had no reports to file since his shift began at nine A.M.

On a map, the town of St. Bonaventure vaguely resembles a pear or gourd. It is split down the middle by the railroad tracks and the main street that runs parallel. The police department has divided this pear-shaped collection of streets into fairly equal sixths, so that Onken's beat that afternoon is the upper eastern portion. It is primarily a residential area, framed on the south by the main street and to the west by a fairly well-traveled avenue called Old Oak Boulevard. To the north and east, houses trickle like ellipses into the open prairie.

Police Officer Onken, aged twenty-six, listlessly drives in slow concentric circles through this territory. He pulls down his stretch of main street—two gas stations, a motel, Discount Mart. A bit farther down there is a photography studio, a bank, and an old man's bar, The Green Lantern. If he waited outside the bar long enough, one of the patrons would stumble out, blinking in the summer daylight, and clamber unaware into his vehicle. Bam! An easy DUI. But Onken isn't in the mood for waiting. It reminds him, for some reason, of the many unpleasant early-morning autumn weekends he was forced to spend with his father, crouched with their shotguns in chill muddy duck blinds that smelled of dead earthworms and leaf-sludge, his father silently drinking Miller Lite and staring at the sunrise. The men who come out of The Green Lantern—divorced, unemployed, rapidly decaying through their forties and fifties—remind him of his father, and catching them brings him no more pleasure than it did to shoot a duck out of the sky.

And so he merely eyes the bar as he drives past. At the traffic light on the corner of Euclid and Old Oak Boulevard, he turns left and drives past more storefronts, past turn-of-the-century houses that have been converted into insurance and real estate offices and funeral homes, headed west toward the edge of town. He is bored enough that he almost stops to buy lemonade from a pair of little girls who have a stand set up on the sidewalk. They are also selling iced tea and "pretty rocks," which they've apparently picked up out of someone's gravel driveway, and this makes Onken smile. Though he is not married, not even close, he still has hopes to have a lot of children. Five at least. He especially would like to be the father to twin girls, he doesn't know why. He just likes kids, is all.

So when Connie calls in over the radio to report a missing child, the day suddenly seems more interesting. He responds in the affirmative and repeats the address. He imagines himself finding a frightened, weeping kid under a bush somewhere, picking him up, letting the kid wear his cap, letting him ride on his shoulders as he carries him back to his overwrought parents. The kid would hold tightly to him and give him a big hug. He'd be a hero for a moment or two. What other reason is there to be a cop?

Onken turns into the driveway and a heavyset woman in a bright shirt and tight shorts comes hurrying out. She walks quickly over the grass toward him, flip-flops snapping, her face taut, frowning. And then Onken's heart sinks.

It's Old Lady Keene, his second-grade teacher. He feels himself blanching as she lumbers toward him. Second grade had not been the most pleasant time of his life, and even when he does happen to see Mrs. Keene—in the supermarket, or at the county fair, or somewhere accidental—he has always made a point of avoiding her. He doesn't know whether they've actually spoken since he was in elementary school.

But now, here she is. "Hello, Mrs. Keene," he says, stepping out of the car, and she stops to glare at him sharply.

"Hello, Kevin," she says, and gives him her old once-over. It's eerie to hear her say his name. It's the sound of a certain period of childhood: "Kevin," she says, and he is reminded again that he is not particularly bright or appealing, that he shouldn't hope for too much, that he will spend his life not attracting too much attention. She folds her hands behind her back in the way she once did when she was standing over his desk, not even disapproving but simply dismissing him, mildly, as another mediocre child who really wasn't worth her time.

"Kevin," she says, "I'm afraid I need your help."

They go through the usual steps. She has already canvassed the neighborhood, she says, both on foot and by telephone. She says that the child is not "the type" to wander off without telling her. He writes this down in his notebook.

"What about the," he says, "the parents of the child? Have you spoken to them?"

Mrs. Keene looks nonplussed. "My daughter is a drug addict," she says, flatly. "And she is also mentally ill." She clears her throat. "The last I knew was that she was in Las Vegas, but I do not know her current whereabouts."

"I see," Onken says.

"The father lives in town, but he is not the custodial parent. He was arrested about a year ago, and he's currently on probation. I'm the guardian ad litem."

"I see," Onken says. "And have you contacted him? The father?"

"No," she says. "He's . . . under house arrest. Confined to his home."

"His name?"

"Troy Timmens," she says, with soft distaste.

"Oh," Onken says, and he feels an unpleasant weight settle over him. He knows the little boy, he realizes, and he feels inexplicably disturbed. He recalls the botched drug bust, the child's screams as he was pulled out from under the bed; the father, handcuffed in the kitchen, calling "It's okay, Loomis, it's okay," his voice breaking. The father had turned to Onken, his eyes stricken and teary. "Oh, shit, don't do this, please don't do this," he'd whispered, and Onken had said nothing. And then that horrible gunshot, the one that had gotten Ronnie Whitmire suspended, and him standing there, frozen, thinking the worst. Remembering this gives him a bad feeling, and he stands there for a moment, silent.

"So," he says. He looks blankly at his notebook. "Let's see," he says. "Are there any other relatives in town he might have gone off with? Or friends of the family?"

"No," Mrs. Keene says firmly. "Troy Timmens has some cousins or something—Ray, I think that's one of them. Ray Timmens, I assume, but no one *picked him up*. He was in the backyard. He was right in the backyard. He's not the sort of child to—"

"Can you show me the last place you saw him, please, Mrs. Keene?" Onken says. "And then we'll need to go through the house again. I'm assuming the child's room is exactly as it was before he, um, disappeared?"

"Oh, Jesus," Mrs. Keene says. And the part of Onken that still remains in second grade is deeply surprised to see that his teacher has begun to cry.

The last child to disappear from St. Bonaventure was found dead about six hours after he was reported missing. The child was a toddler, a little boy named Joshua Aiken, and there had been a short time when they had been dealing with his case as an abduction. The area had been secured, and a dog handler had come in to evaluate the scene for scents and make scent pads for his trail dog. Things seemed to be going smoothly at first—they had been able to cordon off the scene before family and neighbors had contaminated it too much, and the search was being conducted methodically. They had received tips on several reported sightings when the mother found the child's body.

It was in the basement. Police had searched the area previously but had neglected to look in the one place that, in retrospect, should have been obvious. A chest freezer, a Kenmore Quick Freeze, 24.9 cubic feet, approximately 3 feet high by 6 feet wide. The mother went down the basement stairs and noticed the little stool that was pushed up to the side of the freezer. It was a little three-legged stool that she'd almost forgotten about, which Joshua used to sit on while he watched TV and ate his lunch on the coffee table. *What is that doing down here,* she thought, and then her heart contracted. She put her hand to her mouth.

Later, the coroner determined that the child had suffocated, though it was also possible that he had frozen to death. It appeared that

Joshua had fallen into the freezer while trying to get a Popsicle, and that the lid had struck him a blow to the head, knocking him unconscious. Joshua's corpse lay there, stiffened atop a toppled stack of frozen diet dinners and plastic containers of summer corn and the white-paper-wrapped meat of a recently butchered deer. The child, in shorts and T-shirt and sandals, had already stiffened and begun to solidify in the cold.

Both Kevin Onken and Judy Keene remember this as they watch the dog handler putting his Doberman through its paces. The dog smells an item of Loomis's clothing, and then begins to explore the backyard area where Loomis was last seen, its bobbed tail stiff and quivering, its pointed ears erect.

He's dead, Onken thinks, suddenly. He has read studies. In seventy-four percent of the cases involving children, the child is deceased within three hours of being kidnapped. It's not just the studies though. It's an intuition.

Someone has him, Judy tells herself. Maybe he's with her daughter, who has performed a cruel trick. Maybe he's with Troy Timmens after all; they haven't been able to reach him by phone. Maybe he's simply inside someone's house, a friend, a neighbor, a stranger. But she is certain that he is somewhere. She has never been a superstitious person, but she is certain at this moment she can sense the presence of the child. His little soul. It is a small, steadily blinking pulse, like the light of an airplane moving across the sky at night.

PART TWO

PART TWO

13

April 16, 1993

A week before she died, Nora began to notice activity in the house again. Spirit activity. It was only little things at first: a pulse in the air, a feeling of being quietly observed, a quiver of movement behind her back. Late at night, she opened the door to the refrigerator and a cantaloupe fell out, rolling decisively across the kitchen floor as if guided, perambulating slowly across the tile before coming to a stop at the lip of the living room rug. During the day the telephone would ring and then stop—and not the usual sort of ring either, but strangely extended, the bell mechanism rattling and strangled, like an elderly singer trying to hold a high note for many measures. Of course, it stopped abruptly when she picked up the receiver. She stood there, holding the phone, and the bathroom door clicked open, hesitantly, as if a dog were gingerly nosing at it with her muzzle.

"Elizabeth," she said.

The past had been imposing itself heavily upon her lately, so it didn't seem so improbable that the dog might appear again in some form: a ghost, a presence. Or merely a feeling—tender, female, sad-eyed, tail tucked down with shy shame. Still sorry for what she'd done.

Nora supposed that if she had any decency she would be horrified by such a visitation. If she were a real mother, she would have hated Elizabeth. But all that came was a soft melancholy. "Elizabeth?" she murmured, as the bathroom door swung open. She was prepared.

But there was nothing. Nothing she could see, at least, and she was aware again of the foolishness, the perversity of her feelings. An ache had opened up inside her as she thought of Elizabeth, an overwhelming and unaccountable longing. There was no way to account for love, she thought, or for sorrow, no way to account for the ridiculous thought that in some ways Elizabeth had been her first baby. Her practice baby, she supposed. Even after all these years, she could vividly recall holding Elizabeth in her arms—a shy, lethargic puppy her father had brought home for her on her fifteenth birthday, and she had cradled the dog in her arms until it had gone to sleep, its paws limp and turned inward, the bare pink stomach heaving gently with breath. "Elizabeth" had been the name of a doll she had loved as a child, and also the name that she'd always hoped to christen a future daughter with. "That's not a name for a dog," her father had laughed, but she'd only shrugged.

"Well then, she's not just a dog," Nora said.

"She didn't mean to hurt you," she told Jonah after the accident. She sat by his bedside in the hospital, but she didn't look at his bandaged face, the single uncovered eye that glided vaguely in its socket, scoping the objects in the room indiscriminately. "She was just confused," Nora murmured, as if this would be a comfort to him. He may have heard her voice through the haze of painkillers, but ultimately she knew she was only talking to herself. Mumbling, reassuring herself. Years later, she would see a murderer's mother interviewed on TV, and she recognized that pinched quiver of sorrow and guilt and protective anger. "It was an accident," the woman said. "He'd never . . . on purpose," and Nora understood. She remembered the way her heart had clenched at the thought of her father beating Elizabeth to death, the way she'd sat dully in her chair in Jonah's hospital room, feeling her soul compressing into a wafer, a thin, meaningless cardboard lozenge. Jonah had looked at her—one eye covered, the other, roving aimlessly, raking a blur across her face. "It's locked," he whispered feverishly, and she would never know what he meant, though it ever after felt like an accusation. Her hands wavered over him, but she didn't know where—or if—to touch him.

Did he sense, in those first days that he was in the hospital, that at some level she hoped he would die? Did he know how fiercely she would have loved him if he *had* died, that he would have become a jewel she held inside her? Did he know that she could have endured his death more easily than his survival, his constant, living reminder of her failures as a mother, as a person?

Who knew? Who knew what Jonah was thinking—before or after? He was an eerie child even as a toddler: solemn, slow-blinking, big-eyed. In those few years after his birth when she was well, she was constantly having to reassure people—*No, there's nothing wrong with him. He's just spacey!* Very funny. Everyone laughed. Aged two, he trundled along in the child seat of a supermarket cart, talking to his own hand as if it were another child. A cute little act. He made his hand talk, flexing his fingers so the lifeline crease in his palm opened and closed like a puppet's mouth. People stared at them, smiling, but also a little unnerved. There was something forceful, odd, about his intensity of involvement with this game, and she remembered catching his hand—the hand he was talking to—and pressing it down, holding it tightly. *"Stop it,"* she said, through her teeth. "That's enough." And he hadn't protested. He looked blankly at the hand he had been talking to. "You killed my friend," he said, in his high, clear, toddler's voice, and it had actually made the hairs on the back of her neck prickle. He gazed at her, his eyes expressionless and owlish, and she said again, "Stop it. Right now." She knew it was wrong, but she dug her nails hard into the flesh of his limp hand. If only he had started crying—she would have picked him up, and held him, and stroked his hair, and rocked him against her shoulder. She would have said, "I'm sorry, I'm sorry, Jonah, Mommy didn't mean to hurt you." But he just stared.

"Ow," he said at last. "You're pinching me." And then she stopped. She let her grip relax.

Lately, the more she thought about finding a way to die, the more such memories came stalking her. She watched the bathroom door swing open of its own accord, stood there waiting, expectantly, and after a moment lit a cigarette. Her hands shook, but she managed it: brought the lighter flame to the tip, drew in breath, so that the ash began to glow. She breathed smoke, and that made her feel calmer. She didn't feel calm enough to actually enter the bathroom, but she could stand there, her arm folded across her chest, looking at the dim interior of the room dispassionately. Jonah would be home from his job at the old folks' home by seven-thirty. If he came into the house, the spirit activity would likely cease.

She was aware that she was trembling, shuddering like someone who had been out in the cold for a long time. She was forty-three years old. It was just after five in the afternoon.

Occasionally she tried to pinpoint the moment when she began to lose her mind. The psychiatrists she had talked to had wanted to discuss her mother's death; they had wanted to talk about what happened to her at Mrs. Glass House, but she'd always felt impatient with such conversations. Yes, it was terrible to lose your mother. Yes, it was very traumatic to give up a baby for adoption. But back then she had been doing just fine. For over five years she had managed, she had even been happy.

Look at the years 1966 to 1971. She aged from sixteen to twenty-one without any real problem. They might even be called the best years of her life—those years after she'd left the Home, those years before Jonah was born. It was easy to vanish into the world in those days, when the world was changing so rapidly, everything transformed and made new again. She had been discharged from Mrs. Glass House on a Monday, about a week after the baby was born, and she had known then that she wasn't going back to her father. She was already gone when her father's pickup pulled into the curving driveway of Mrs. Glass House, and when she called him from a pay phone in Omaha a few days later to say that she was okay, she had tried marijuana for the first time and her new friend Maris was standing beside her, the two of them giggling as she pressed her mouth to the receiver.

"You've always got a room here," her father said, earnestly, and she said, "I know, Daddy. Thank you, I know." She'd looked outside the glass wall of the phone booth to where a boy with a shaggy bowl of dark brown hair was leaning against his knapsack, waiting to take them to a place he knew, a communal house where they could stay for free. "I'm just going to be staying with a friend for a while," she told him. The glass of the phone booth was marvelously cool, almost liquid when she touched it, and the boy looked in at her and grinned. A few days later, she and the boy would hitchhike to Denver, and then she would ride with four girls in a blue 1955 Nash to San Francisco, and then she would live in Fresno for a while. She didn't call her father again, after that one time, for almost three years. She sent him postcards, little one-page letters decorated with cartoon flowers in the margins: She was happy, she wasn't thinking of anything, she was getting along fine.

Sometimes she tried to think about those years more specifically. She once collected a stack of notebook paper and tried to write herself a timeline. She wrote "July 1966" at the top of one page, and "August" at the top of the next, and so on. Then she sat there at the kitchen table with all the blank sheets of paper before her, a dozen thin threads tangling and unraveling in her mind. She couldn't put it in order, she realized. And even those things she thought she remembered, she found that she wasn't sure of. She started to remember, for example, that she'd met a girl named Maris in the bus terminal in Omaha, a sleepy-eyed, witty girl with plaited hair, sitting beside an overstuffed knapsack. But then she remembered that "Maris" was the name of the girl who had disappeared from Mrs. Glass House one day in early March. Would there have been two girls named Maris? It didn't seem likely, and yet she was certain that the girl she'd stayed with in the commune in Omaha was Maris. They'd been friends for . . . how long? When had she last seen this girl, what had become of her? She sat, staring at her blank sheets of paper.

It had troubled her all night. She'd been haunted, pacing the house at three in the morning, with the spirits sliding into place like shadows held for a moment under the beam of a flashlight. The house was full of ghosts, and she stood over Jonah's bed and trained her flashlight across his sleeping face.

"Don't . . . don't . . ." he'd mumbled, his eyes pinched, brushing at the light with his hand as if it were a cobweb. "Quit it! I've got to sleep." He didn't know how bad things were.

She could stand it when it was only at night. But now that it was during the day again, she didn't know. She stood outside the bathroom door for a long time, until her cigarette went out. Then she went back into the kitchen, thinking that she would make herself something to eat. She would feel better if she ate something, she thought. Some soup, maybe.

She found a can of soup in the cupboard and put it on the table. Then she found a can opener in a drawer and put it on the table beside the can. Then she found a pot and put that on the table, too. Here were three objects that were real. She didn't look over toward the bathroom, where the door was still open. She didn't hear the soft click of Elizabeth's black nails against the kitchen floor.

"Okay," she said. "Okay." She looked at her palm. She moved her fingers, and the joint creases opened and closed like the chirping mouths of baby birds. A terrible notion. Why should the creases between her fingers remind her of mouths? Why should a thing be like another thing? A word came to her from long-ago days at school—grammar school? Junior high?

Simile, she thought. You use the word *like* or *as*. My love is like a cherry. His cheeks were as red as apples.

It was a kind of craziness, she thought, that there were such echoes everywhere. It made the world indefinite, turning everything into a kind of cruel puzzle.

The handles on the drawer were like eyes.

The tree outside bowed its head like someone who was praying.

The top of a soup can was like a wrinkled, expressionless face.

Was it supposed to mean something? Was there a message in it? To receive these thoughts—similes, metaphors—was to draw closer to the spirit world. At least she hoped so. It was frightening to think that the world was simply a series of echoes, one object mirroring another randomly, emptily, a vast and multiform and mindless series of repetitions. The thought made her shudder, watching as a jellylike cylinder of cream of chicken soup slid into the little pot. She went to the sink and filled the now empty can with water, which she poured over the quivering gel of condensed soup. It eroded a little. There was a mouth she was thinking of, her fingers.

The question was, she thought, when had things started to go wrong? When had she started to lose hold of her mind?

In 1971, when Jonah was born, she had been okay. Twenty-one years old. Five years had passed since the first baby was born, and she was calmer. She was living with Gary Gray by that point, in Chicago. More or less stable. Gary had a job in construction, and they had a little place on the west side. She remembered her swollen belly, the difficulty she had kneeling down to plant petunias in the beds along the side of the house. She had been so big, she remembered, "a whale," she called herself, and that was how they had first come up with the name—as a joke.

"I feel like a whale," she said, and Gary Gray had made a quip about "little Jonah" in her belly. She'd called her father, to tell him that she was going to have a baby, and that she would probably be getting married. She just said this to make him happy. She wanted everyone to be glad for her. She wanted to be glad for herself. Being born, Jonah didn't hurt her nearly as much as the first one had.

14

September 3–4, 1996

Nebraska.

Utter blackness of the nighttime roads, space unraveling beyond the body of Jonah's car, emptiness. His headlights made the road signs glow like the eyes of animals, geometric shapes looming up abruptly.

Daytime wasn't any better, really. There were the towns, one after the other, spaced by a distance of ten or twenty miles, each with its grain elevator, a castle tower rising up out of the prairie. There were the flatlands and pastures that surrounded these outposts—round alfalfa bales like Stonehenge boulders in clean mowed fields; a single bare tree or ramshackle house in a barren lot of dirt-clod stubble; wide expanses of wheat, or corn, or sunflowers, with their thousands of heads turned east toward the sun. Blackbirds alit on the faces of the sunflowers, then rose up, flapping darkly. Bruise-colored clouds bunched up along the horizon that the road wove into, thunderheads with the pale sky above them.

Driving forward, he was aware of himself as a presence, a feeling, a sound track full of dissonance.

If this were his movie, here is where it would begin: foreboding scenery. He rewound the cassette tape over and over again, back to that same song, the distinct, plunking melancholy guitar, accompanied by the bone-notes of a xylophone. When the singer began to sing, he did, too. Staring out through the windshield at the onrushing highway, Jonah entertained himself by pretending that he could see the opening credits superimposed over the horizon.

He thought of his old friend—his former friend—Steve, holding up his palms, thumbs extended, framing the idea of a scene. "The story begins in late summer," Jonah said, imitating the thick, whispery male narrators who spoke in the previews for coming attractions. "It began in September, not quite six months after the boy turned twenty-five." But this didn't sound right, and so he'd gone back to the beginning. "The story begins . . ." he said. He liked the sound of it.

He found himself murmuring the same thing under his breath as he packed stuff into his mother's old car. Some books, clothes, compact discs. "It was September. He was twenty-five. No one knew he was leaving. Or where he was going." He packed some notepads. Some dishes he hated to part with. Clothes. A tent he'd ordered from a catalog.

The rest of his stuff—thrift-store bric-a-brac, winter coat, crappy old RCA radio/cassette/alarm clock, magazines and newspapers, laundry soap, cans of soup, ketchup, and a half-eaten jar of sweet gherkins in the refrigerator—this he left where it was, and he supposed that eventually Mrs. Orlova or her husband would have to clean it out; when they hadn't received a rent check from him in a while, they would open up his furnished room. Perhaps they would half expect to find him there dead, a suicide or a young-man heart attack. Sasha, Mrs. Orlova's husband, would mumble a curse in Russian, pulling at the keys that hung from his belt. Jonah had thought of saying something to Mrs. Orlova, he'd thought about calling his boss at the restaurant, but at the last minute he didn't. Better, he thought, to simply disappear.

And yet, when he woke that morning, he imagined that he was still in Chicago. He imagined the familiar framework of his efficiency, his bed, the dusty lamp and bedside table with its stack of books, the sound of the el train rattling beyond his window, the expectation of the restaurant schedule posted on a corkboard in the dark hallway of the restaurant's basement. The life he'd been leading for more than three years, to no avail.

He was in a tent. He saw a shadow shake against the canvas surface above him, a rustling shape, and after a moment he was aware of the memory of driving, of checking into the campground, a KOA park on the edge of St. Bonaventure. When he unzipped the tent flap and crawled out, the sun was rising low in the sky. There was his car, packed with his belongings; there was a long Winnebago parked across from him. A middle-aged couple—a woman with long brown hair and a fat man with a beard and a Hawaiian shirt—were sitting outside the Winnebago in lawn chairs while their little girl played nearby. They were watching a small portable television and eating peaches, and they waved to him benignly as he looked over, as he limped barefoot over the gravel to his car. He opened his car door and sat down, staring at the road, putting on his shoes and trying to think.

This was not very cinematic. Sitting in the bucket of a car seat with untied shoes, looking at pebbles. The sun hung tentatively over the horizon, gelatinous and shivering like the yolk of an uncooked egg. He could feel an edge of mundane discouragement rising up again, as it often did when he was in Chicago. What now?

He sat there, looking at a map that he had ripped out of a telephone booth phone book, tracing through the puzzle of streets until he found, at last, the one he was looking for—all the way on the other side of town, on the very edge. He reached under the seat and found his pair of binoculars, which he placed on the passenger seat beside him. He listened as the little girl outside the Winnebago sang tunelessly: "Tomorrow, tomorrow, I love you tomorrow," and he watched for a moment as she casually hit her baby doll with a stick in rhythm to the song. He tied his shoes.

For almost a year now, ever since that day in October when the packet came in the mail from the PeopleSearch Agency, he'd been trying to decide what to do. How to proceed. He'd gone over and over the information they sent him, tracing underneath each word, each individual letter with his fingernail, as if there were some encryption buried in it that he could uncover with careful study. Here was a name, an address; a credit report; some court documents.

He'd find himself waking up at night to go through this material, sitting there at the window of his third-floor efficiency, staring out at the empty street below, thumbing through the small sheaf of papers, aware of the strange, floating ache they conjured up, a kind of bottomless feeling. It reminded him of the time he'd found a reproduction of a landscape painting in a book for an art history class, a white house on a jagged seacoast that had struck him with the force of a forgotten memory. *I used to live there once,* he thought, though he also knew that it was impossible. Nevertheless, he could clearly remember walking up the gravel path toward that wooden, red-shingled house, could hear the sound of the waves against the rocks, the calls of gulls. He and his mother must have visited that exact place, he thought, and it was several days before he realized that the painting in the book was the same one his mother had on a postcard that she'd taped on the headboard of her bed. He must have stared into it so deeply that it had lodged in his mind as a memory. Even knowing this, he couldn't shake the feeling that this was a place he'd once been, that he'd walked along that path and into that house, where a friendly blind woman sat in a rocking chair, and the sunlight slanted against the blond wood floors. It wasn't a real memory, he realized, but it felt like one.

That same sensation came over him again as he read through the bare facts of Troy's life. He remembered the baby, the brother that his mother had told him about, her eyes turned sidelong toward him: *I was very young, I had to give it away;* and when he'd asked where the baby had gone when she gave it away, he could see again how her eyes had hardened: *He went to live with a nice mother.*

He had pictured his brother when she said this, very clearly—so clearly that he seemed like someone Jonah had met, a child Jonah had played with, who had perhaps lived in that Winslow Homer shoreline house, with the lighthouse in the distance. He never clearly saw the brother's nice mother and father, though he felt them not far away when he would come to the edge of the green square of lawn where his brother was casually throwing a ball high into the air, holding his hands out to catch it. Just beyond his brother's backyard was a cliff, with the sea below, the high tide lapping hard against the rocks. Jonah had stood there at the edge of the fence, with Elizabeth beside him, her ears pricked up and alert. The boy, his brother, had turned to look at him, and the ball had fallen into his open palms. Their eyes met. The boy had smiled, kindly, mysteriously, and tossed the ball across the fence to Jonah.

Years later, when Jonah and Mr. Knotts had been clearing out the old yellow house, he'd found that ball again, in a box of childhood things. It was deflated, almost flat, fading red with a yellow star in the middle. But it was a real thing. The ball existed, though the land that it had come from, the seaside house and the silent child in the patch of bright green grass, those were only his imagination.

He thought of all this as he drove through St. Bonaventure. He knew, of course, even before he came here that there would be no beautiful coastal house, no bright patch of lawn on a cliff overlooking the sea—none of the things that he'd imagined. And yet he still would never have believed how closely it resembled the place he'd grown up, Little Bow, South Dakota.

Like Little Bow, St. Bonaventure was the kind of town that people passed through on their way to somewhere else. A typical small Plains town. Here were storefronts: drugstore, cafe, barbershop, liquor store, bar. A Pizza Hut, a church. A Safeway supermarket set back from the road, with a half acre of asphalt parking lot in front of it, mostly unoccupied. The town was not quaint, exactly, though the buildings that some of the stores occupied had a turn-of-the-century feel to them, brick and stone, with high fronts like in Westerns. There was no doubt some history attached to the place, it had once been an outpost or way station along some great migration or another, the Oregon Trail, the Union Pacific Transcontinental railroad. Perhaps it was a fort from back in the time when the United States was busy with the project of wresting the land from the native people who had dwelt there—wanting it very badly, but then finding it not very interesting once it was conquered. While the rest of the world was exploding with population, places like

St. Bonaventure were steadily shrinking, fading out. It was the sort of town that Jonah used to talk about bitterly to Steve and Holiday, the kind of town that Jonah had always claimed to have escaped.

He had been wavering now for months, almost a year of rising and falling urgency—an urgency that never went away, but simply tilted back and forth between anticipation and dread.

In the beginning, he'd merely taken pleasure in holding the information in his hands, feeling it take shape in his mind. He read his brother's name over and over: *Troy Earl Timmens.* He spoke it aloud, he read through the home address, *421 Gehrig Avenue, St. Bonaventure, Nebraska 69201*; the place of employment, *Stumble Inn Bar and Grille;* the credit report, basically quite good, a MasterCard and an American Express, a car payment, nothing else. He had a wife, Carla, and a son, Loomis, born December 18, 1990.

Jonah had been especially attracted to the adoption decree, with its odd, archaic language, like some olden-time bill of sale: *"IT IS THEREFORE ORDERED, ADJUDGED AND DECREED that the right to custody of and power and control over said minor child and all claims and interest in and to the wages by said Mrs. Glass Institute shall and do cease and determine from and after this date, and the said Baby Boy Doyle is hereby declared the adopted child of the said Earl Roger Timmens and Dorothy Winnifred Timmens, husband and wife."*

He read this aloud sometimes, too, liking the sound of it. *Baby Boy Doyle,* he pronounced, redolent of some 1930s gangster-movie nickname, faint music of low piano keys and muted trumpet. "Baby Boy Doyle," he said, into the silence of his efficiency. "Troy Earl Timmens." A door thrown open with wind and a scuttle of leaves. Here was the history that moved outside of his mother's knowledge, a pathway tracing its way into the future. *Baby Boy Doyle:* his mother's son. *Troy Earl Timmens:* someone else entirely. The simplicity of it was the thing that stunned him the most. The exchange seemed so easy: a few words, and you were a new person.

At first he thought he was going to write a letter. *Dear Troy Timmens,* he wrote, and then he sat there staring at it for over a month. He wrote: *My name is Jonah Doyle, and I am your brother.* And then he erased it. He wrote, *You may not believe this, but.* He wrote, *I am writing to inform you that I believe that we are related, and I hope that you will be interested in perhaps meeting and.*

And what? The letter was on the table when he got up in the morning, along with a book he'd bought called *The Journey of the Adopted Child.* When he got home from work it would still be there, waiting, mute. A yellow legal pad: He would tear off the top sheet and write the new date at the top—December, January, February—and then he would write *Dear.*

Sometimes, he would get past the greeting, and he would even write the first couple of lines of the opening paragraph. He would open *The Journey of the Adopted Child* and flip through it irritably, looking for some clue about how to proceed. Then he might decide to go out for a walk, to clear his head, to think it over. He might go to a movie, and afterward, sit in the bar on the corner and have a few beers. Then, home again, his head a little fuzzy with alcohol, he'd find himself writing things that he could never send.

Dear Troy Timmens,

Once upon a time there was a woman who had two sons. The first son she gave away when she was a teenager, and she regretted it for the rest of her life. The second son she kept for her own, and she regretted that even more.

Or, even worse:

Dear Brother,

I used to think of you all the time when I was growing up. Our mother would talk about you and she would cry about how she hated herself ever since she gave you away. I'm the kind of woman who would give away her own baby, she would say, and I would sit there and think of you. I used to wonder why she had kept me. Why was I the one who got stuck?

It was not hard to find the street where Troy Timmens lived. He had to stop along the roadside a couple of times to consult his map, but the streets came together with an almost eerie inevitability, the way a wooded trail in dreams led closer and closer toward some unknown, waiting thing. A house, a treasure, a shape rising up with small eyes and bright claws among the dapples of leaves. When he saw the signpost, he slowed his car to a stop, pulled over to the curb.

Without warning, he had begun to tremble, and he held tight to the steering wheel. He was shuddering, as if inside him was a small motor such as powered an old lawn mower, his teeth humming against one another. Up to now, there had been only a steadily growing hollow pit of anticipation in his stomach, but abruptly it had grown huge. It was terror of a sort he couldn't even put his finger on—somewhere at the farthest end of stage fright with its limp-boned, consuming paralysis, and moving from there into something childish and primal, like the pure panic of a light being turned out, a door being closed and locked.

On the edge of Gehrig Avenue, Troy's street, he was momentarily overcome; a thin, thrumming wire stretched taut inside him. He fitted his palms over his face, breathing against his cupped hands.

He didn't know whether he could go through with it.

The first time Jonah had tried to call Troy was on his birthday, in March. He'd begun to realize that the letters he'd been attempting were never going to be finished, he was never going to find the right words that could be sealed up into an envelope and sent out into the empty world, utterly out of his control. Even if he did find the courage to send a letter, he knew that it would be unbearable to wait from a distance, to imagine for days and weeks the moment when the letter would fall into the mailbox, the moment when Troy Timmens would tear it open and—however eloquent Jonah managed to become—scan through the columns of words.

On the night of his twenty-fifth birthday, Jonah had bought a twelve-pack of fancy German beer, to prepare himself. He had drunk three of them when he telephoned Troy's house. It was ten P.M. in Chicago, nine P.M. in St. Bonaventure, Nebraska, and Troy answered on the first ring.

"Y'ello?" Troy said: A deep, country-accented voice, abrupt and thick. Jonah opened his mouth and silence unraveled out.

"Hello?" Troy said again, this time more formal, cautious. And then, after another long pause: "Carla?"

And Jonah had abruptly hung up.

Jonah had called again in late April, and then again in May, and both times it had been the same. Even though he'd written out a script for himself, he couldn't say anything. He would part his lips to speak, but he was only capable of hesitation. He pictured himself stumbling into that brightly lit pause, and his face grew warm with a blush. He would sound like an idiot, he thought. *Hi. My name is Jonah Doyle, and I . . .* He could imagine his hatefully befuddled voice, and his skin tingled with self-loathing. He hung up in April without saying anything. In May, he said, "Is . . . Is this Jonah Doyle?" And Troy said, "I think you have the wrong number."

When he called in June, he'd decided to take a different tactic. He'd decided that it might work better if he pretended to be doing a survey for the Mrs. Glass House Institute, and he'd felt calmer then, pretending to be someone else. But Troy was evasive, irritable in a way that got Jonah flustered. *I'm not liable to talk to someone over the phone about this. You need to send me a letter or something,* Troy said. And Jonah found himself inched into a corner, the conversation that he'd at first imagined was under his control—an interview, for God's sake, how could it go wrong?—had eventually collapsed under the weight of a simple lie: Jonah claimed that the Mrs. Glass Institute had sent a letter, and Troy hadn't received it. It was ridiculous, and he'd made plans to correct it, but he'd never been able to get ahold of Troy on the phone again. Thereafter, though he'd called several times in July and August, all he'd gotten was an answering machine, a hurried, wooden voice: *This is Troy. Sorry I'm not in. Leave a message if you want and I'll get back with you.*

When Jonah had heard this message for the tenth time, he realized what he had to do. He needed to go to St. Bonaventure. Whatever he was going to say, it had to be said in person.

So now here he was. He arrived at last outside the house that, according to all his records and maps, belonged to his brother: Troy Earl Timmens. He parked his car across the street, and hunched down in his seat. *The story begins,* he thought, but the romantic glow had faded from the phrase.

He had been hoping for something a bit better. He had imagined that his brother—with the advantages of a loving family, approved by the Mrs. Glass House and the St. Bonaventure County Court—might have made something more of himself. Even when he'd seen that Troy Timmens worked for a place called the *Stumble Inn Bar and Grille*, he'd thought that maybe it was a fancy place, maybe Troy was a burgeoning restaurateur; he thought Troy was perhaps an artist of some sort, working a bar job to make ends meet while he painted or sculpted or, like Steve, wrote screenplays.

Now, such imaginings seemed less and less likely. Troy's house was a shabby, simple white box, more or less identical to the others on its block—a lower-middle-class neighborhood at the very edge of St. Bonaventure, not far from the barren, hilly prairie that surrounded the town on all sides. It was the kind of home that made Jonah think of a child's drawing: two windows, a door, a triangle roof. Ancient bare branch of television antenna jutting out. There was a faded awning over the picture window in front. The curtains were pulled closed.

An unhappy place, Jonah thought. The unfenced front yard was overgrown—the grass unmowed and going to seed, patches of weeds thriving. There was a dying tree in one corner, half of the branches dry and bare, the others still leafy, but fading. The lot had the look of a property that had been up for sale so long that it could be considered abandoned, but then there was an aging Corvette in the driveway that signaled someone's presence, and there was the simple fact that the mailman delivered letters to this address. Jonah sat up and watched as the mailman, wearing khaki shorts and black socks and shoes, strode up the sidewalk and fit a packet of envelopes into the mailbox. He could imagine the letters that he had considered writing arriving in this way, at this sad house, and it made his heart sink.

The determination that had fortified him during his long drive seemed to leave him like a spirit lifting out of a corpse. All he had to do was walk up the sidewalk himself; all he had to do was summon the courage to stand there at the front door and touch the doorbell with his finger. He tried to project himself into that moment.

Here: Troy Timmens would come to the door, and he would look at Jonah with mild curiosity. They would resemble each other in some surprising way.

"I have some information that you might be interested in," Jonah would say, and he would hand over the packet from the PeopleSearch Agency. "I believe we have the same mother," Jonah would say softly, in a steady voice to buffer Troy Timmens from the shock. "We're half brothers, I think."

And then he would extend his hand for Troy to shake.

"My name is Jonah Doyle," he would say. "I've been wanting to meet you for a long time."

But despite his imagination, Jonah didn't do anything. He sat there, staring at the door, thinking of his mother. "I didn't even look at him," she had told Jonah once. "I didn't even get the chance to look." The nurses had taken the baby away while she was still under anesthesia, and he had pictured her drifting into sleep; he had imagined the thin trail of a baby's crying unraveling down a long blurry hallway while she drifted and dreamed, and then, finally, the infant's wails shrinking away into a dot of silence, blinking out as her mind went white with static.

"I'd be a different person if I'd have kept that baby," she said once, cloudy and blissful, and then her eyes focused and grew stern.

"I should have given you up, too," she said, and Jonah had rested his head against her as she'd stroked his face, tracing the pad of her finger along his scars. "You know that, don't you?" she murmured. "I could have let you be happy."

Even now, this struck him a glancing blow. He saw again the seaside house, the postcard landscape he'd entered as a child. Then he sat up abruptly.

A man had emerged from the house on Gehrig Avenue. He came around from the back, wearing a white button-down shirt and black pants, but Jonah got only a glimpse of him—a broad-shouldered guy, medium height, with a build like a high school wrestler, curly black hair, olive skin. A subtle, steady limp. Then the man was slamming the door of the old Corvette, revving the engine. Jonah was surprised at how calm he felt as he started his own car. Eased out from the curb. *I could have let you be happy,* he thought, and his teeth pressed hard against one another.

In a film, this moment would require some tricky camera work. For a second, the camera would float far above the town of St. Bonaventure with an ambient hum of chords, hovering and then banking down to follow the two cars in motion, almost two-dimensional from above. The red 1981 Corvette, heading toward the center of town and turning left, followed by the boxy, rattling, toylike Ford Festiva, Jonah's mother's old car, white with rust in the creases and cracks. The sky is gray. The leaves on the trees are still green, but it is clearly edging toward autumn. The camera slowly dips as the cars trace their way down the main street, through the few stoplights and finally to a side street—seedy, faded strip of storefronts beyond which the town begins to drift away into aging courtyard motels and trailer parks and fields. At last, the camera's eye settles onto Jonah's face. Troy's car slides into a parallel parking space, and then Troy emerges, unfolding himself from the low-slung bucket seat, limping tenderfooted into a bar that is lit by a blinking neon sign: STUMBLE INN, it says, the letters arranged vertically, and there is the outline of a thin neon cowboy leaning against the words.

In the movie, the camera would hold for a long time on Jonah's face. He would be expressionless, staring, but the music might hint at complex emotions, drifting into a minor key and some slight discord, pulling closer and closer toward his scarred face, toward his eye, with the pupil dilating larger and larger, as if he were moving into a darkened room.

Which he was.

He entered the dim barroom, with its softly damp, gravelike smell and its forlorn jukebox music. It was three o'clock in the afternoon, and the place was quiet. He hovered outside of himself, watching. An older lady, a bartender, busied herself at a chalkboard that listed the food that could be purchased, busily erasing "Chili-Chicken Chimichanga—$4." Two paint-freckled workers sat at the bar, staring at a muted television mounted above the liquor bottles, watching studiously as a beauty whom Jonah didn't recognize was being interviewed on an Entertainment News program. At the other end of the bar, a balding man in a checkered sports jacket poked his finger into his drink and plucked out a piece of ice, which he ate; at the far left, two stout, youngish, red-haired women were playing pool while two red-haired toddlers dangled their legs over the edge of a second, unused pool table and observed, sharing popcorn from a bag. The booths that lined the walls and the tables that were scattered throughout the narrow barroom were otherwise empty.

None of these people looked at Jonah. Entering a place like this, with a face like his, he anticipated the hostile curiosity of townsfolk, but it didn't come. It was as if he was invisible, taking in the atmosphere, trying to locate the person he'd been following. He approached the bar cautiously, and the bartender lady turned.

It was the usual reaction when she saw him—the quick, startled gape and polite swallowing of response, the surreptitious trawl of her glance across his scar, the question: *Jesus Christ, what happened to him?* echoing murmurously against him as she blinked and regained herself.

"Can I help you?" she said, and Jonah cleared his throat.

I'm looking for Troy Timmens, he thought to say. But he just stared for a moment, crossing his arms over his chest. "I was . . . reading the menu," he said, hesitantly. "Is the kitchen still open?"

"Oh, yes," the woman said, and flashed her kindly, silver-edged teeth. She called over her shoulder. "Troy!" she shouted. "What are you doing back there? Will you cook for awhile until Junie gets back? It shouldn't be more than an hour. He had a doctor's appointment!" And a voice, deep and affectless, said, "No problem."

In a movie, the camera would rattle for a moment. It would hover over the outside of the bar, banking through the web of treetops and along the flat tar-paper roof of Zyke's Roller Rink across the street, and then it would begin to gather momentum, speeding up as it plunged toward the Stumble Inn Bar and Grille, until it became the rush of a train as it entered a tunnel—a blur of motion as it barreled through the bar, as the train went straight into the back of Jonah's head and right through him. Here, framed for a moment in the small window through which orders were passed to the kitchen, was the face of his brother, bobbing up and then disappearing. In a movie, there is only the glimpse of the face. Then the film strip breaks off abruptly, snapping and turning around and around in the reel as the projector shines blank light on the screen.

15

September 13, 1996

The parole anklet—the monitoring device—was always the first thing Troy noticed when he woke up. It was not heavy at all: a small black metal box, seemingly hollow, no bigger than a seat-belt buckle, attached to his ankle by a kind of thick plastic watchband. But still he could feel it there, even before he was conscious. It entered his sleeping mind as a discomfort, and then, slowly, his awareness solidified. Here was the anklet's weight against his skin. It was itchy. He reached down and scratched along the circumference of the plastic shackle, afraid to touch the thing, afraid that he would set off the tamper alert, which, he had been told, was extremely sensitive. He could almost feel the thing pulsing, sending out its radio signals to a station where someone sat in a swivel chair before a bank of blinking green and red lights. He was under "house arrest." He had been told that if he moved beyond the perimeter of his yard, an alarm would sound somewhere, and an immediate warrant for his arrest would be issued, and he would be tracked down and sent to prison.

It was sometime in the afternoon. He could feel the dull, steady heat of the sun as strips of it poured through the slats of the blinds, and the unhealthy film of daytime sleep clung to his skin. He stirred, restlessly, and felt a piece of paper crumpled beneath him. It was the T. rex skeleton he'd drawn for Loomis, which must have come untaped from the wall. He sat up and discovered that he had been sleeping in Loomis's bed. He didn't remember why.

In the two and a half months since his arrest, the house had been slowly devolving. It had never been particularly neat, but now as he padded in his underwear through the piles of dirty clothes and unwashed bowls of dried-up ice cream, the stacks of unread junk mail and bills, the jigsaw puzzle that he'd begun to put together as a distraction and then abandoned, the empty plastic bottles of soda—he was aware again that he had been overcome by entropy. "Son of a bitch," he said, as he stepped on the sharp plastic edge of one of Loomis's Legos with his bare foot. He limped into the kitchen and took a cola out of the refrigerator.

He'd been told that he was lucky. He was not in prison, where he would be easy prey for weight-lifting tattooed Nazis and angry Caucasian-hating black men. He had negotiated what was said to be an extremely light sentence—thirteen months of house arrest, with a parole anklet monitor, followed by two years' worth of regular parole. And his parental rights had not been terminated, exactly—though Judy had official custody of Loomis for an indeterminate period. He was still allowed to work as a bartender at the Stumble Inn, though he was subject to random drug and alcohol tests and part of his salary was garnisheed to offset the cost of the probation program.

His lawyer had convinced him that this plea bargain was the most favorable option. His lawyer, Eric Schriffer, had been one of his regular marijuana customers, and he'd assumed that this would mean that Schriffer would look out for his best interests. But now he wasn't so sure. It was true that they had photos of him purchasing drugs from the unfortunate Jonathan Sandstrom, but it was also true that they hadn't been able to accumulate a felony's worth of drugs from his home. Besides which a police officer had discharged a firearm in the direction of a helpless child. Now, thinking about it, he wondered whether a different lawyer, someone from out of town, might have been more aggressive. He might have had a good case to sue the police department.

Sometimes he thought Eric Schriffer had actually betrayed him, leading him into a plea bargain that mostly protected Schriffer himself.

Such ideas occurred to him now, long after he'd signed the myriad of papers, long after the anklet had been pinch-stapled to his bare ankle, long after Schriffer had stopped returning Troy's calls to the office of Goodwin, Goodwin, Schriffer and Associates. He was aware that he'd probably been duped. But what could he do now? Who could he call to complain—the Better Business Bureau? The ACLU? God?

It was over and done with. There was no one who could help him.

On the kitchen table was the black book—his "itinerary," as his parole officer called it. Stamped in gold leaf on the cover it said *Daily Planner* in an italicized, pompous cursive that he found offensive. This was #17 of the many conditions of parole that he'd agreed to: "Offenders will submit detailed hourly itinerary of their activities to parole officer"—and thus *Daily Planner* had become a constant, hated companion through the endless days and weeks of house arrest.

He sat down at the table and flipped it open. Friday the thirteenth: ha, ha. Each hour of the day, from one A.M. to midnight, had several lines next to it where he was to write down his "activities," and he took up his pen and wrote "SLEEP" in capital letters next to one A.M., and then below it SLEEP next to two A.M., and then down the row: SLEEP, SLEEP, SLEEP, SLEEP until he reached two P.M. He glanced at the wall clock, which said it was nearly three in the afternoon, and he was aware that he'd spent more than half his day unconscious.

His parole officer, Lisa Fix, would no doubt take note of this. She commented on patterns that she noticed as she read over the itinerary during their weekly meetings.

"You sleep a lot," she'd said the last time they had met. "Do you think you're depressed?"

"That's a keen insight," Troy said. "You ever thought of becoming a psychiatrist?"

She raised her eyebrows and looked at him over the rim of her glasses. For a bureaucrat, she didn't mind sarcasm all that much, and this was one of the things that made their weekly conferences bearable to him. She was in her mid- or late thirties, he guessed, a plump, freckled-faced, cynical woman with overly permed red hair—divorced, he would assume. She was a type he'd seen frequently in his years as a bartender, the kind of woman he could usually joke with or even flirt with a little as he served drinks, and she didn't seem to mind. She talked to him like she was his begrudging older sister, or a former lover who still liked him a little but knew his ways too well. There was something about her that made him think, for the first time in a long while, of Chrissy, that girl he'd met long ago in Bruce and Michelle's trailer, the girl who had kissed him when he was eleven. Lisa and Chrissy were probably about the same age, he thought.

"Of course I'm depressed," Troy said. "Wouldn't you be, given my situation?"

"Well," Lisa Fix said, "we've talked about various constructive uses for your time. Have you looked any further into the correspondence courses we spoke of?"

"Not really," Troy said. "Not yet." He shrugged. "Hey, listen," he said, "did you go to high school with Chrissy Hart?"

She raised her eyebrows at him. "That girl who committed suicide?" And now it was her turn to shrug. "She was a couple of years older than me, but sure, I knew her. Knew *of* her, at least. We didn't exactly run in the same crowd. Why?"

"I don't know," Troy said. "Just curious."

"A trip down memory lane," Lisa Fix said, and pinched her mouth a bit. "I knew your wife, Carla, too, as a matter of fact. She and Chrissy were seniors when I was a sophomore. I can't say that I remember ever speaking to them. Why? Is something on your mind?"

"I don't know," he said. He looked briefly at her eyes, which were sharply attentive, and then he looked back down. He thought to say *Chrissy was the first girl I ever kissed*, but what would be the point of that? "Just thinking about stuff," he said.

"Well . . ." Lisa said. "Look, Chrissy Hart slit her wrists in her mom's bathtub, and Carla has a serious drug problem and hasn't been heard from in months. I don't see much that's positive that can be gleaned from a discussion of those people." She cleared her throat, and her gaze hooked into him. "Why don't we think about the future instead of the past? Did you fill out that sheet I gave you?"

He grimaced. He still had the mimeographed piece of paper she had given him, onto which he was supposed to write down ten "short-term goals" and ten "long-term goals," but he didn't know where he had put the thing. He hadn't filled it out.

"What about Loomis?" he said. "You said last week that you'd look into seeing if I could talk to him on the phone. That's one short-term goal we can talk about."

Lisa looked at him heavily, as if he were a student who had given the wrong answer, even after she had coached and coached. "Well," she said, "I did look into that. *And.* Loomis's guardian has refused your request. She thinks that it's best if Loomis settles in awhile after . . . his trauma. I can't say that I don't agree."

"Fuck," Troy said, softly. He reddened—he could feel his temper growing, and as he swallowed it his eyes fishbowled with tears of frustration. He sat there, his face impassive, and drew his eyelids down slowly. He lowered his face and pressed his thumbs against his eye ducts for a moment.

"Okay," he said. "Okay. Well then. Let's move on."

At three-thirty he telephoned the headquarters, to let them know that he was traveling to his place of employment. The alarm on his ankle would be turned off for a brief time—ten minutes or so—to allow him to drive the few miles to the bar, to the Stumble Inn. Sitting in his car, he imagined himself as a red blinking dot, stuttering across the screen of someone's computer, watched, monitored. Early on, Lisa Fix had suggested that he think about another job—for example, working for the county's organization for the mentally retarded, for which he would be paid for thirty-five hours, minimum wage, with five hours going to his community service—but he'd stood his ground on this. He had worked as a bartender for years, he said. He was good at his job. It was his livelihood, the one thing he felt confident he did well, and this was the one thing that Eric Schriffer had done for him. They couldn't force him to change jobs. They couldn't completely unmake his life.

"Well then," she said. "I can put you on a cleanup crew for your community service. I was trying to give you a better option."

"I don't want to quit my job," he said. "And I don't like retarded people. What good is minimum wage shit work going to do me?"

"Okay then," Lisa Fix said. She gave him another one of her older sister stares, one that said: *I can't believe you're so stupid.*

Once he was at work, he called the number again, to assure them that he had arrived. He recited his offender number several times, and finally, the man at the other end of the phone said, "Okay. Check. I've entered you into the database."

"Thank you," Troy said, and glanced up to see a middle-aged drunk staring at him. The man had a craggy, oblong face, vaguely like Abraham Lincoln, and his drooping, dim-witted eyes examined Troy for what seemed like a long time. Then Abe smiled, his mouth turned up in a gentle, satisfied bow.

"They got you, huh?" the man said, and widened his grin to show a row of surprisingly large white teeth: dentures. "They really got you now!"

"Yes," Troy said politely, but didn't smile. "They got me."

Crystal was behind the bar, and glanced at him sympathetically as he slid open the cooler and began to count the bottled beer. "Hey, babe," she said. "How're you doing?"

"Mm," he grunted, and wrote on the back of a napkin the numbers of beers that he needed to bring up from the basement. "Slow day?" he said.

She nodded, her hands working in a bus tub of soapy water. "Terrible slow," she said. "For a Friday, especially." She brought up a beer glass and rinsed it under the tap.

"What's the situation with Honest Abe over there?" Troy said. He gestured with his chin toward the man with the dentures, who was sitting by the telephone, staring at it placidly.

"Oh, boy," Crystal said. "I don't know where he came from. He's been here since this morning. He's about eight or nine beers in."

"Well," Troy said. "Ring up his tab before you close out. I'm cutting him off."

She widened her eyes at him, as she always did when she thought he was being harsh or abrupt. She had large blue eyes, and straight, thick hair the color of cedarwood, a round pretty face. She was a nice girl. "The Mormon Chick," Ray used to call her, because her parents were supposedly Mormons from Wyoming. She wasn't religious herself as far as Troy knew—she worked as a bartender, after all—but she exuded a certain kind of goodness. There was a kindhearted innocence to her: She worried about other people's sadness and suffering and wanted to do what was right. She once confided to Troy that she thought people, all people, were basically good at heart, and Troy had looked at her wryly.

"I read that book, too," he said. "You know what? That Anne Frank—the Nazis killed her anyway."

She had argued with him a little back then, but now she said nothing. She cut off President Lincoln without protest, shrugging. "Vivian's here" was all she said, and Troy let out a slow sigh. Vivian was the owner, and she frequently got angry when Troy decided to refuse to serve a customer. "You're not the beer police, Troy," Vivian had said on a number of occasions. "If they're not causing trouble, they can drink until they're passed out on the floor as far as I'm concerned."

Troy slid open the ice cooler to check the status, to see if he needed to bring some more from the ice machine in the basement. "What's she doing here?" he said, frowning. "I thought she was taking the day off."

"She's training a new guy," Crystal said. "She hired a new cook. They're down in the office now, I guess, filling out some forms or something."

"Hm," Troy said. "Is something up with Junie?"

"He's sick again," Crystal said, and pursed her mouth. "I feel so sorry for him!" she said. "He's old. Do you know he's almost seventy? He shouldn't have to be working all the time."

"Oh come on," Troy said. "He likes to work." But the truth was that Junie the cook had been looking worse and worse lately, though he'd never looked exactly healthy. He was a small, wiry Sioux man, with deeply melancholy eyes and a permanent, exaggerated frown, and lately, every time Troy looked at him, Junie seemed to send out waves of pessimism. What if he ended up like Junie, Troy would find himself thinking. Junie, who had been in and out of jail, who smelled of old man b.o., tobacco, and stale beer, was now sick and probably dying. It occurred to him that Junie had once been his age. It occurred to him that a man could live out his last days in a bar like Vivian's Stumble Inn, that you could live for years and years and years with nothing at all, and still exist.

"Geez," Troy said at last, trailing these thoughts. "How sick is he?"

"I don't know. But he's in the hospital," Crystal said. "I might go visit him this weekend. Bring him some flowers or something. Do you want to come?" And then she stopped herself awkwardly. "Sorry," she said.

He was silent. These small, humiliating moments were not the worst thing about his "house arrest," but they were steady and goading, the most constant. He smiled at Crystal, but it felt more like a wince. "I have other plans this weekend," he said, ironically, even as she gazed at him with her large, sympathetic eyes.

"Are you okay, Troy?" she said. "I mean, I know you don't want to talk about it, but . . ." She sighed, made a flustered motion with her hand. "It must hurt you," she said. "You limp."

He felt himself twitch, involuntarily. "No, not really," he said. "It's not tight or anything."

"That's good," she said. She looked down at his pant leg, to where the anklet monitor was discreetly covered. "I just meant, well. Spiritually. It must be painful. It's a very cruel thing for them to do. To put that thing on you."

"Not really," Troy said, and he looked away from her, smiling tightly. The anklet felt warm and heavy. "It's not a big deal," he said. He shut the sliding door of the ice cooler, decisively. "I hardly notice it."

By the time Vivian came upstairs with the new guy, Abraham Lincoln had left peaceably and the bar was empty. Troy was reading the local newspaper, moodily thinking of his own recent appearance on page two. When someone went to jail in St. Bonaventure, everyone was aware of it. "Arrests" were written up on the same page as the obituaries and birth announcements and weddings. The write-up on Troy had been right under a big, grinning picture of a girl he'd gone to high school with. Beneath the descriptions of the girl's bridal gown and her proud parents, Troy had found himself summed up in a few sentences. "Area man. Possession of a controlled substance with intent to distribute.

Court date set." Today, he saw, there was another birth, another death, a drunk-driving arrest.

Vivian came up behind him. She stood there, her chin lifted, watching over his shoulder as he read. He finished the obituary before he looked up.

"Is there something you want me to do?" Troy said.

She made a wave of her hand, as if surprised. "Oh, I wouldn't want to take you away from your newspaper!" she said. She was a raspy-voiced woman in her late fifties, with a blond, steel-wool perm and a stout, shapely figure, which she accented with tight jeans and western blouses. Troy was used to her attitude of resigned suspicion and impatience, as if her main job was to keep him out of trouble, to ensure that he didn't slack off too much or sneak drinks when she wasn't looking. Mostly, he thought, this was just an act. He was a good employee, and she knew it. But it was a role she enjoyed playing, and to please her Troy began to take the liquor bottles off the shelf and dust them.

"I just hired a young guy to work in the kitchen," she said. "He's going to be starting tonight, so you'll have to keep an eye on him. You can manage that, can't you?"

"I hope it doesn't get too busy," Troy said.

Vivian cocked her head. "Well, if it does, it will be a good test for him. He has a lot of experience. He worked in Chicago for years."

"Is that right?" Troy said. Vivian's glasses hung from a beaded chain around her neck, and she lifted them to her face, hovering over the newspaper Troy had been reading, scanning it. "What's he coming *here* for, from Chicago?"

"Fed up with city life, he says," Vivian murmured. "There were some tragic circumstances, I gathered, but I didn't want to pry."

"Mm," Troy said. He continued to run his wipe over the glass bodies of the liquor bottles, frowning. "So what about Junie?" he said.

"Junie had another heart attack," Vivian said irritably, as if Troy were trying to make her feel ashamed. "What do you think I should do? I don't know when, or if, he'll be back. I can't close down the bar to wait and see if he gets well. And I'm damned tired of listening to you bitch every time I ask you to cook for me."

"Okay!" Troy said. "I was just asking." He watched as Vivian lit a cigarette and breathed a stream of smoke down onto the obituary notice.

"Just asking," she muttered. "I don't need you and Crystal guilting me about poor old Junie, that's for sure. I've got enough troubles as it is." She gave him a hard stare, but then they both composed themselves into politeness as the young guy she'd hired came up the stairs.

"Hello, Jonah!" Vivian cried, and Troy watched grimly as she switched into warm-and-friendly mode: the disarming, gold-tipped teeth in her smile, the crinkly eyes, the endearments—"honey," "sweetheart," etcetera. She did this with everyone she hired. For the first week or so, she treated them like she was a kindergarten teacher and they were her prized students. And then they lost their charm. She became a disappointed mother, ironic and long-suffering, tolerating their lack of competence and clucking critically even when she was satisfied with them.

"Hi," the guy said shyly. "I'm Jonah Doyle." He glanced at Vivian, and stood there awkwardly, his long arms limp at his sides before she introduced them. The guy kept his head down, not even looking Troy in the eye, but then when Troy offered his hand, Jonah clasped it in both his palms, squeezing it surprisingly hard. "I'm really pleased to meet you," Jonah said, with a nervous, earnest enthusiasm, as if Troy were someone he had heard of, someone famous.

"Yeah," Troy said. He shifted a bit, uncertainly. A narrow strip of raised scar tissue ran from the edge of the kid's eye, across his cheek. This might have seemed threatening on someone else. But with this guy it just seemed disconcerting. He had a freckled, boyish face, with round cheeks and carefully combed and parted blond-brown hair, and the scar was like an out-of-place appendage—a toe instead of a finger, a misaligned ear, an empty eye socket. It was hard to keep from staring.

"I'm really looking forward to working with you," Jonah said, and Troy nodded slowly, trying to avoid the guy's face. Jonah was dressed up like a churchgoer in a button-up shirt and khaki slacks, but then for some reason he had on heavy black work boots.

"Yeah," Troy said. "I'm looking forward to working with you, too." He glanced over to Vivian, who smiled benignly. If she noticed something strange in the air, her expression didn't betray it.

At least, as it turned out, the guy was competent. When things picked up around 6:30, Troy was fairly amazed at how much more efficient Jonah was than Junie. Troy would thrust an order through the little window that separated the bar from the kitchen and the next time he passed by a plate would have appeared—cheese sticks or Buffalo wings or nachos, arranged neatly and even garnished. He glanced back in the kitchen and watched briefly as Jonah's long, nimble fingers arranged deep-fried jalapeño poppers in a circle over a bed of greens—something Junie would have never bothered with. Junie would have tossed the poppers onto a bare plate once they had cooled off a bit. He certainly wouldn't have fanned them out like petals, or added a little side cup of nacho cheese in the center, as Jonah did. "You're getting fancy, eh?" Doug Lepucki said, grinning as Troy set the plate down on the bar, and Troy shrugged. "New cook," he said, and a popeyed young guy leaning on the bar with a clutched twenty-dollar bill ogled Doug's plate and said, "I'll take one of those things, plus a pitcher."

In his previous life, Troy would have been pleased. People tipped extra on food tabs, and he was under no obligation to share tips with the cook. It was surprisingly busy—the Stumble Inn had never been a particularly popular Friday-night gathering place, but by nine there may have been more than forty patrons packed into the small bar, and he was moving fast, pouring beers and pitchers and fixing drinks, a permanent sheen of sweat on his forehead. He had to empty the tip jar because it got too full.

But the truth was, he felt a little unnerved. It was a rowdy crowd, and the chimes of group laughter, the screams of delighted women, the bellows of asserting men, the general cacophony of drunken voices—the steady rising and falling of human chattering hooked into his spine.

The bar was too full of people for comfort, he thought. Too full of people who knew him, or who knew of him, or who had heard from an acquaintance about his situation. He didn't go out from behind the bar to clear tables of plates or glasses, feeling self-conscious of the monitor beneath his pant leg. A boisterous group of young men in their early twenties, apparently friends of Ray's, were the most troublesome. "Hey, bartender!" they called. "A round of bong hits for the boys over here, bartender!" and a flock of har-har-hars rose up from their table like crows.

What could he say? This was part of his punishment, this humiliation, and all he could do was frown stoically. He thought of Lisa Fix: "I wouldn't say that this is the ideal job for someone in your situation," she had said.

He was aware of Jonah, too. Jonah's eyes on him. He'd turn to look over his shoulder and the prickly feeling on the back of his neck would intensify for a moment. Here was Jonah, his nose and mouth shadowed, peering out from the kitchen as Troy tilted the edge of a glass against the flow of beer. Troy filled the glass, letting the foam fall away and slide down the outside edge of the mug. He looked over his shoulder again, just in time to catch Jonah gazing intently at his back. Jonah smiled, shifted his eyes. "What?" Troy said, but Jonah didn't hear him over the general noise of the bar and Troy was too busy to bother repeating himself.

But it continued to grate on him as the night wore on. Every time he turned to look, there was Jonah, intent in his surveillance, then pretending to glance away as if he hadn't been staring. It made him aware of himself as an object of observation, in general. There were the patrons who knew, watching as he limped along with his hidden parole anklet, turning to their friends to remark, grinning with gossip, as he passed. There was the monitor signal he was emitting, even now. There was the black book, the "itinerary," which Lisa Fix would comment on, prodding the mundane and intimate details of his life, as if it were all typical, as if she could predict the rest of his life with a shrug of her shoulders. All of this settled over him heavily, and when he looked over to see Jonah with his neck craned and his lips parted, scrutinizing Troy's preparation of a round of Jagermeister shots as if it were a magic show, he turned with exasperation to face the guy. *What in the fuck are you staring at,* he started to say.

But it was weird. He wheeled abruptly, irritably, and then said nothing. Jonah was looking at him with a kind of focused, unblinking concentration that seemed almost like a trance. It took him aback.

"Hello?" Troy said, loudly but uncertainly, and Jonah startled slightly, blinking at last as if he'd been asleep with his eyes open. "Hey, man, are you awake or what?" Troy said.

"Oh!" Jonah said. It seemed to take him a moment to lift out of whatever staring rhapsody he'd been in, and Troy shifted a little, uncomfortably. He noticed that there were even more scars etched along the backs of Jonah's hands, trailing along as if something had raked a claw across his skin. *What happened to him?* Troy wondered again, and for a moment a kind of shadow passed over him—something chilly, flapping like a sheet on a clothesline.

"Sorry," Jonah said. "I kind of spaced out for a minute."

"Yeah, well," Troy said. He cleared his throat. "We're kind of busy, if you hadn't noticed. Would you mind getting out there and clearing off the tables? If it's not too much trouble."

"Oh!" Jonah said, and Troy watched as he put on a kind of professional smile, like a mask. "Of course! Sorry!"

What was it? Troy thought. He watched as Jonah loped out onto the floor and began to collect empty glasses. Something was wrong with the kid, something beyond the scars, but he wasn't sure how to pinpoint it. A kind of actory stiffness? Troy had the paranoid idea that maybe Jonah was an undercover agent for the DEA or something, planted here to spy on him. Then he dismissed the thought—he had no connections, nothing worth spying upon, and in any case, whatever this Jonah was, he was no undercover agent. Troy observed as Jonah gathered the dirty beer glasses and arranged them neatly on the end of the bar, lining them up in a careful pyramid, like bowling pins.

"Thanks," Troy said, and Jonah looked him in the eye briefly, then nodded, as if they both knew a secret.

Closing time was approaching and the unexpected crowd began to thin out. The feeling of being watched faded as well, and every time Troy glanced behind him Jonah was busy with something or other. Not staring anymore—and Troy found himself wondering if he'd just overreacted, if he'd just imagined that Jonah had been watching his every move. He'd been feeling so self-conscious lately. He thought he'd get used to the ankle monitor, that it would come to be something he hardly noticed, but instead it seemed like it was worse, day by day, to the point that he sometimes felt like it glowed, or gave off waves of heat or radiation. He looked through the order window and saw that Jonah was dutifully scrubbing the grill with a charcoal pad, his head down, his hand moving like a painter. Troy cleared his throat, but Jonah didn't look up.

Troy leaned against the bar and rested his forehead against the ham of his palm. He heard the door to the bar open and slam shut several times as people left—headed out, headed home—and he didn't even look up. He imagined Loomis, asleep in Judy's house; Carla, somewhere in Las Vegas, tilting her head back as she drained a drink; Ray, opening a forty-ounce beer and tucking it between his legs as he drove home from some bachelorette party, his windows open, angry rap music tub-thumping from his speakers. *My life is ruined,* he thought, distinctly.

By the time two o'clock came around there were only two people in the bar: a man and a woman, French-kissing in a corner near the jukebox, their hands underneath each other's clothing. "Last call!" Troy said loudly in their direction, and the couple lifted their heads like animals surprised from grazing. "Last call!" Troy said, more softly, and the two of them got up and walked out wordlessly.

Troy turned back to look at Jonah.

"I think that's it," he said, remembering the official capacity Vivian had given him, to train Jonah. "Let me lock the door. Then we just finish up the side work, and we're done. Unless you have, like, questions or anything."

Jonah looked up from his sweeping and blinked.

"Questions?" Jonah said, and he had that unnerving, frozen expression again. It was almost like stage fright, Troy thought. His eyes flicked back and forth, like someone who was trying to quickly come up with a good excuse, and his expression tightened. It was as if he were hurriedly scanning for something inside his head, a panicked shuffling through stacks of blank pages on which he'd expected to find words.

"I mean," Troy said. "About the job? Do you have any questions about your . . . duties or whatever?"

"Oh," Jonah said, and Troy watched him hesitate, then relax a little. "No, not really. I think I've got a pretty good grip on it. I'm . . . I'm sorry I spaced out earlier. About clearing the tables."

"No problem," Troy said.

"I get a little . . ." And Troy watched as Jonah gestured, wiggling his fingers at the side of his head. "I space out, sometimes. When I'm nervous. But not, you know, often."

"No worries," Troy said. He gave Jonah an ironic half smile. "I do that sometimes myself."

"Oh, really?" Jonah said, and again there was that silent, disconcerting sense of inner struggle. "We're alike, then, I guess," Jonah said at last, and smiled broadly.

For a moment there was a glimmer of—what?—in Jonah's expression, and Troy hesitated. It was like that itch he got when doing crossword puzzles, that elusive flick of a word in the back of his mind when he couldn't quite think of it. It was like that feeling that is the opposite of a premonition: *Did I forget something? Something important?*

And then it vanished. Jonah turned and began to sweep.

16

September 28, 1996

More than a week had passed since he and Troy officially met, and still Jonah had said nothing.

He thought about it.

He thought about it all the time, in fact. In the morning, pulling a razor through the shaving foam on his face, mowing a shaft along the line of his jaw, he stared into the mirror. *Troy,* he said, watching his lips move, *I have something to tell you.* He sat in the furnished trailer he had rented, sipping coffee, flipping through a textbook from a math class he'd dropped out of. He read: "The Swedish mathematician Helge von Koch hypothesized that an infinitely long line surrounds a finite area."

Troy, he thought. *I need to tell you something.*

And yet he couldn't think of what would come next. He wanted to find the movie of the moments, to see each day as a series of carefully framed scenes, but instead there was only a blank screen. Instead there was a slow drift into daily routine. "Action!" he imagined a director shouting from the sidelines, but he sat still in his car, with his key in the ignition. He closed his eyes briefly.

He arrived at the Stumble Inn that morning before anyone else, read Vivian's menu instructions, and went through the freezer and the refrigerator, checking the stock. Alone in the kitchen in the morning, there was no camera running, only himself, silent, concentrated. *Burgers, Cheese fries, Wings.* He noted the items on the shelves. *Soup—Chili,* Vivian had written, and he began to systematically set out the ingredients—a large can of kidney beans, two containers of tomato juice, some hamburger and pork sausage, some onions, a head of garlic. He found the soup pot in a lower cupboard, uncovered among a clatter of lids and utensils.

I think we are related, he thought, setting the oversized pot upon the stove. *I'd like to show you some information.*

The cans of tomato juice made soft, metallic sighs as he pressed the opener into them, cutting triangular mouths into their tops. He stood there for a moment, staring at them. Breathing.

The chili was on the stove when Troy came in, a little after nine-thirty. Jonah felt his back stiffen when he heard the door open, and he watched as Troy walked past the kitchen without a word, loping quickly, his shoulders hunched, white shirt, black pants, his curly hair still wet from a shower. Troy went directly to the pay phone in the corner near the jukebox and Jonah observed as he scooped up the receiver and punched the numbers, as he reached down, self-consciously, and tugged at the front of his pants, and then, after a pause, mumbled something into the mouthpiece.

Jonah had guessed what this was about already. Vivian had told him little things—about parole, and house arrest, and so on—and so had the other bartender, Crystal. He had overheard conversations as well, things that Troy or Vivian or Crystal had said in passing. He had even, once, caught sight of the parole anklet itself, when Troy had bent down to scratch his calf.

But he wasn't sure if Troy was aware that he knew, and this was awkward. Troy had an almost supernatural ability to sense when he was being watched, and when Jonah saw him sharply lift his head from his phone call, he bent down quickly, back to his duties in the kitchen. He liked to imagine that eventually Troy would confide in him—relating his own version of the events that led to his arrest, etcetera—and Jonah would act surprised. *I'm sure Vivian must have told you,* Troy would say, and Jonah would widen his eyes. *I had no idea!* he would exclaim.

So far Troy had shown no inclination to exchange any personal information. It would take some time, perhaps. They would need to establish some common ground, some shared interests, and Jonah was still waiting for those to emerge. He tried to seem oblivious. He kept his head down, and didn't look up until he heard the soft clack of liquor bottles being examined, the sound of Troy preparing the stock.

"Morning," Troy said, as Jonah peered out through the little window between the bar and the kitchen.

"Good morning," Jonah said cautiously. He was cutting up mushrooms, which he had decided would be an interesting addition to the chili soup, but he didn't need to watch his hands. The movement of his knife, after years of practice, was automatic. He cleared his throat. "It's nice out today, isn't it? Beautiful, um, leaves."

"Uh-huh," Troy said. And then he turned, and Jonah heard his footsteps pound hollowly down the stairs as he went to get ice.

Troy, I have a confession to make, Jonah thought. He tested this several times in his mind, but by the time Troy came up the stairs it sounded ridiculous.

Troy didn't want to be talked to, that was part of the problem. Once he'd gotten his preparations for the day's business settled, he folded himself into a distant and unsocial place, hunching over the surface of the bar with the day's newspaper, emanating silence. Jonah observed as Troy bent toward the headlines and columns of newsprint, tracing his middle finger over line after line. Then he read the comic strips. Then he took a pen from behind his ear and began to work on the daily crossword. After a time, Troy checked his watch and went out to the front of the bar, his keys dangling musically from his clenched hand, to open the door.

"So, well then," Jonah said. But Troy didn't hear, didn't lift his head.

They were clearly related. Jonah knew that, at least. No question.

It was almost unnerving, actually. Looking at Troy, he wasn't sure what to do with the small, circling memories that Troy's physical presence evoked, since in fact Troy had much more in common with the

Doyle family—Jonah's mother, Jonah's grandfather, the various relatives he'd seen in pictures—much more than Jonah himself did. He found himself thinking of the way his mother used to joke about his own pale skin and blond hair. "I can't believe you came out of my body," she used to say, and looking at Troy, he couldn't help but feel that if she were alive, she would find Troy more convincing as her offspring. Here were the black, heavy eyebrows, his mother's very own, and Jonah's grandfather's long, firm-jawed face. There was even a certain kind of heavy, faraway frown that reminded Jonah of those long-ago times when his mother reclined on her bed and listened to records. In Troy, he recognized the distantly gazing gloom that he'd observed as a child. He recalled standing in the doorway, watching her, and how she would lift her head, almost dreamy in her haze of unhappiness. "Get out of my room," she would say, and Troy, glancing up from his crossword puzzle, might be on the verge of saying the exact same thing, with the exact same dull, unwelcoming inflection.

"Did you say something?" Troy said, turning to look over his shoulder, and Jonah raised his eyebrows.

"Oh," Jonah said. He swallowed. "I was just . . . wondering," Jonah said. "Is this considered slow?" he said, at last, after a hesitation. "I mean, in terms of the typical Saturday?" And Troy looked at him wryly.

"I'd consider it slow," Troy said. "Unless you can have customers in the negative numbers, zero is about the worst that it can get."

"I guess so," Jonah said, and chuckled politely. *Say something,* he thought, *say something funny,* but all he managed was a sound in his throat, like phlegm. Troy regarded him curiously for a moment, then turned back to his puzzle.

As anxious as he was for things to move forward, Jonah knew he had to control himself. He was aware that it would be very easy to ruin everything: the wrong words, the wrong moment, the wrong approach, and it would all be over.

I have something to tell you, he thought, and he could picture the very look on Troy's face, the way he would close up, shuttered and inscrutable, the way his eyes would narrow as Jonah relayed his secret.

The more time he spent in Troy's presence, the more he felt sure that he needed a clearer strategy. It wouldn't be enough to simply blurt out the facts and wait for them to sink in. He almost shuddered, thinking back to that moment when he'd been on the verge of walking up to Troy's door: *Hello, my name is Jonah Doyle, and . . .* What a disaster that would have been, he thought, and he looked back with irritation on the person he had been a week ago. How naive, he thought, to imagine that Troy would simply open his arms wide, cheerfully accepting this stranger who claimed to be his half brother.

Looking at Troy now, such an idea was almost laughable. But this had been what he'd honestly imagined: All he had to do was come face-to-face with his brother, and everything would flow smoothly from that moment. *I have some information. I need to talk to you. I want to talk to you, I think I have some information that you'd be interested in, I have something I need to tell you.*

With each opening line that came into his head, he got a clear image of where it would lead. Troy would be blank at first, disbelieving, and then as it slowly settled on him, his face would harden. Jonah could imagine Troy recoiling, his eyes lighting with anger. *You've been watching me all this time?* he would say. *Get away from me, you creepy little sneak,* he would say, outraged. Or even worse, he might simply not care. *So what?* he might shrug. *We have the same mother. Why does that matter? What's the big deal?* And he had no response—nothing to say to Troy's anger, nothing to say to Troy's indifference. That was the biggest problem: Where to begin? How to explain? *An infinitely long line surrounds a finite area,* Jonah thought, and he imagined that in his movie Troy would drift into the distance, as if seen through the wrong end of a telescope: a small, moody silhouette.

Then he lifted his head as the door to the bar opened and light poured into the dimness. The first customers of the day.

By eleven-thirty the Stumble Inn was moderately busy. Jonah's chili was popular, as were the hamburgers, and he found himself working steadily, given over to the immediate tasks at hand. There was a kind of urgency to the simple facts of the job that he had always liked: People need to be fed. They are waiting for their plates to be delivered, waiting to eat.

And Troy liked the simple pressure of waiting customers, too, he could see. They were alike in that way. As the bar filled up, Troy came alive, focused as he hadn't been an hour before, while filling out his crossword puzzle. Now he was alert, brisk, full of sharp-witted banter with the patrons, efficiently moving. And this new energy even extended to Jonah. "Order!" Troy called, and grinned wolfishly as he thrust a check stub into the pickup window.

"Getting lots of compliments on the food," Troy said, and his smile was so good-natured and easy that it seemed, for a single moment, that they really could become friends. An understanding could develop between them, and then when Jonah told him the truth, it wouldn't be a surprise. This all came together in a flash, in a brief exchange of eye contact. Then, as if Jonah had imagined it, the smile was gone; abruptly, Troy turned back to the customers.

For a moment, holding the order slip, Jonah felt that he was in possession of some kind of secret message. Then he looked down at it. "2 CBs w/fry," the note said, in Troy's careful block letters. "1000 isle dress on side." He put the hamburgers on the grill.

If they worked together long enough, he thought, such exchanges would accumulate. They'd become acquaintances, they'd get to know each other, and after a while, a level of trust would develop. A few weeks, a few months, and then, perhaps, it would be easier to say: *I have a confession to make.*

He slipped a spatula under the circles of hamburger, pressing the juice out of them as Troy brought two glasses of beer to a pair of heavyset blond women—twins? Best friends? Jonah wasn't sure, but Troy seemed to know them. Both wore blue jean jackets, and both had been given perms that, now fading, made their hair look brittle and sharp, like fiberglass. Troy put his elbows on the bar and spoke confidentially to the women, and they all laughed together, happily.

When Vivian came up the stairs, Jonah was in the process of arranging the two plates—the hamburgers tucked neatly into buns with crisp lettuce and tomato, the fries spread opposite, the dill pickle between them: simple but aesthetically pleasing, Jonah thought, and Vivian, observing him, seemed to approve. "Order!" Jonah said, setting the plates on the sill of the kitchen window, and Vivian peered out curiously as Troy took up the plates.

"Hi, Rona! Hi, Barb!" she called warmly to the two blond women, and they called back in voices almost distorted by niceness: "Hi, Vivian!"

But when she turned back to Jonah, Vivian made a sour face. "God, I hate those bitches," she said to Jonah, softly. "I wish they'd find some other bar to stink up."

"Oh," Jonah said, wincing a little to hear Vivian use such vulgarity. He paused cautiously. "You don't like them?"

"I hate them," Vivian said decisively. "But I guess that a customer is a customer."

"Yes," Jonah said, but he was a bit taken aback, shocked to see the warmth she had directed toward the two women fall away so quickly when she turned her back. Perhaps he had misjudged her, he thought.

He liked Vivian a great deal. In the beginning, there was a kindliness about her that he had found completely disarming. He had been so nervous—everything about what he was doing seemed fraught with risk and recklessness, but she had greeted him as if he were a dear nephew, as if she had been waiting for his arrival. Sitting in the basement across from her as she looked at his application, he had been surprised by how welcome he felt. She read over the application as if he were a child who had shown her a wonderful report card. "I'm just speechless," she exclaimed, and smiled up at him, looking at his face, at his eyes, and seeming not to notice his scars. She reminded him of the kind of old lady children encountered in books about fantastical adventures: eccentric and wise and gentle. He liked her gilt-edged teeth and the glasses that hung over her large bosom on a beaded chain, the turquoise-and-silver ring on her pinkie. It was easy to feel that she honestly liked him, that she saw something wonderful about him that no one had ever noticed, and when she asked him why he'd wanted to leave Chicago, why he'd want to settle down in "a little hick town" like St. Bonaventure, he'd wanted to open up to her.

"I guess," he said, "I wanted to start a new life." She nodded as if she understood completely, and Jonah felt as if he owed something further to her sympathetic, expectant silence.

"I was in a car accident," Jonah said, almost without hesitation. And then: "It's not something I generally talk about. My wife—" he said, in a soft, steady voice. "She was pregnant, and she died."

"Oh, my lord," said Vivian, and she reached across her desk and put her palm firmly over the back of his hand. "I'm so sorry," she said.

He didn't know why he'd done this, and he'd wished immediately that he could take it back. "I don't like to talk about it," he said. "I shouldn't have said anything—if it could just stay . . . between us, I'd appreciate it."

"Oh, of course," she said. "Just between us," and her eyes rested on him warm and damp and sad, as she patted his hand.

Now some of this fell away: that warm, storybook grandmother quality he'd projected onto her. Now he began to worry that he'd been foolish, and he wished that he hadn't said anything, truthful or not. Vivian seemed to sense his nervousness.

"I'm sorry," she said, and he was aware of that knowing, bright-eyed warmth being turned on, like a switch being flipped. "I don't mean to be mean," she said, confiding gently. Then she whispered: "It's just that there are some people in this town that rub me the wrong way."

"I understand," Jonah said. He thought for a moment, watching as one of the women tucked her hair behind her ears with a quick, nervous stab of her long fingernails. "Are they friends . . . of Troy's?"

"Oh God, no," Vivian said. She looked over her shoulder, back to where Troy was still conversing with Rona and Barb. "I'm sure they'd like to be, but I think even Troy has better sense than to have anything to do with that pair. They're just regulars, and he entertains them," she said. "And he's a good bartender in that way—a good bullshitter."

"Oh," Jonah said.

"I don't mean that as a put-down either," Vivian said, and gave him a soft smile. "Troy's had his problems, but, you know, he's worked for me for a long time. He doesn't have a lot of common sense, I sometimes think, but he's got a good heart, unlike about ninety-nine percent of them out there. I tell you, I've really felt for him lately. It's a shame, that's what I think. Here you have a rare man who really loves his child, is just about dying to be involved in his child's life, and of course! Of course, he's denied visitation rights. Then there's some deadbeat dad like that case over in Cheyenne—he leaves his wife and children and runs off for five years, and then the courts are falling all over themselves to make arrangements to protect his rights as a father. It makes me sick, the way this country is run."

"Yes," Jonah said. He tightened his fingers. She *was* different from what he'd thought. He knew it now, but he also saw that she was a great potential source of information. He knew also that he shouldn't trust her. But if he could just ask the right questions without seeming too eager, too suspiciously curious about Troy, she would be useful.

"So, " he said casually. "I didn't know Troy was married."

"Oh, he's not anymore," Vivian said. She looked over her shoulder again, as if checking to make sure Troy wasn't listening. "Poor guy," she said. "He's separated from the mother—she's out in Las Vegas. Drugs, you know. But they were married once, which is getting to be pretty unusual around this town, I have to say. About half of these girls nowadays have babies with two or three different fathers, and every one of the children a bastard. Of course, they don't use that word anymore, in that sense, like they used to. And I don't think they should—stigmatize the child, I mean. But in my day, girls like that got sent out of town. To homes," she said pointedly.

"Yes," Jonah said, and he thought of the Mrs. Glass House, his mother, pregnant with Troy, sitting in a room. She had never spoken of it directly, except to clench her teeth at the memory. *They took him away, and gave him to a nice mommy and daddy.*

"So," Jonah said. "Where's the child now? What happened to him?"

But Vivian looked at him as if she had drifted in her mind to another conversation entirely. "Who's that?" she said.

"Troy's son. Where is he now?"

"Oh," Vivian said, and shrugged a little, as if she didn't like to gossip. "Loomis? He's with the grandmother now. Why do you ask?"

"No reason," Jonah said casually. He had to be careful, he reminded himself. "I'm just, I don't know, I like kids." He looked down, cutting up limes for the bar, and he hoped that his silence would remind Vivian of his imaginary pregnant wife, who had died in the same car accident that had left him scarred.

It did, he thought. She, too, was silent for a time. "Well," she said, and they both gazed out uncertainly toward where Troy was tending the bar. They watched as he paused and reached down briefly, running his fingers lightly down his calf, touching his anklet.

17

October 8, 1996

On Tuesdays, Troy rode through the streets of St. Bonaventure in a truck. Beautifying things. Sometimes he would be taken to a county-owned facility—the bathroom of a rest stop on the interstate, for example—to scrub the foul, puerile, desperate graffiti off the surface of a stall with a wire brush; or he would walk along the edge of the highway, in a Day-Glo vest, carrying a litter pick and a plastic trash bag. Last week he had spent the day standing on a ladder underneath a railroad bridge, sandblasting a spray-painted declaration: "Jim loves Athena," letter by letter.

This was his "community service" day, his day off from the Stumble Inn. Lisa Fix had arranged for him to have the worst possible job—her revenge for his refusing the Department of Mental Retardation thing she'd offered in the beginning. At seven in the morning he arrived to give a blood and urine sample, and then he stood silently in his vest and coveralls with other men of his ilk—drunk drivers and disorderlies, wife beaters and child abusers, writers of bad checks—all of them waiting to be carried off to their penance. He was grateful, at least, that there was little talk among them. It was like a doctor's waiting room. They stood there in the parking lot in a group, their heads bowed, and a supervisor would pull up. In groups of twos or fours they would be borne away.

His partner that day was a man he knew slightly: J. J. Fowler. They did not exactly acknowledge each other, though there had been a quick, significant exchange of glances as they stood together in the chill morning air, waiting, and there was another when they were selected, together, for the dead truck. For the next eight hours, they would drive around and scoop up the remains of roadkill animals: cats, dogs, squirrels, possums, skunks, raccoons, the occasional deer. It was perhaps the dirtiest job of the lot, but Troy and J.J. said nothing as they got into the truck, where a probation worker sat blandly behind the wheel.

Once upon a time, J.J. had been a regular Friday night customer at the Stumble Inn, and a monthly consumer of Troy's marijuana—and, occasionally, 'shrooms. They used to have pleasant, casual conversations, but as they trundled forward in the truck, Troy said nothing, and J.J. stared ahead through the windshield. Troy didn't know what J.J.'s crime had been—it might be anything, he thought—but they were not the same people they once were. Here was a tabby cat, a tire tread clearly visible down its middle. They got out of the truck, and J.J. used a push broom to slide the stiffened corpse into the large-mouthed shovel that Troy held. J.J. gazed at him elusively but said nothing as Troy dumped the cat into the back of the truck. It was about eight-thirty in the morning.

He had been thinking a lot about Carla lately.

The last time they had heard from her was a day in late April, when she called to talk to Loomis for a minute. It had been almost painful to watch the way the child's face lit up, the bright eyes and wide grin, the shy, soft way he'd said "Hi, Mommy," flushed with pleasure. Troy stood there, leaning against the door frame, listening as Loomis spoke bashfully into the receiver, still not adept at phone conversation. "Yeah," Loomis said, listening intently. "Uh-huh . . . uh-huh . . . okay," and Troy wondered what she was telling him, to make him glow like that.

But when Loomis had finally relinquished the phone back to Troy, her voice was dull and, he thought, a bit slurred. "I'm not going to be able to call again for a while," she said.

"Well," Troy said, "it's not like you've been calling regularly. He misses you, you know."

"Fuck you, Troy," she said. "Don't you think I know that? Don't try to make me feel like an asshole."

"I'm not," he said, and he frowned hard, listening to the sound of people talking loudly in the background—a bar, perhaps, or a party. "Carla," he said. "Listen, I'll send you one of those credit card things—you know, like you get from the phone company? You can charge the frigging calls to my number, I don't care."

She was silent. Over the phone lines, he could hear people near her laughing. Very drunk.

"I'll send you some money," he said. "Do you need money?"

She didn't say anything.

"Give me an address," he said, and after a long pause, she murmured a P.O. box number, a Las Vegas zip code.

"I've got to go," she said, flatly. And then, for a second, her voice softened. "Thank you," she said.

That was six months ago. The check he had sent—three hundred dollars—had been cashed, but the phone card had never been used. In June, he'd sent another check to the P.O. box, this time for only a hundred. Even in the midst of his arrest and parole, he'd kept a close watch on his bank account, waiting for the canceled check with her signature on the back. It never came.

Recently, the thought had begun to come to him that she might be dead. Despite every screwed-up thing she was, he still believed that she loved Loomis, and he found it hard to fathom her silence. She would have called, he thought. She would have called. And then it occurred to him, a cold, misty breath of premonition: She was dead. She was dead, a voice in his mind murmured, and no one had bothered to contact him or her mother. Was that possible? He tried to tell himself that it wasn't, but the thought dogged him, and he found that it returned, unwelcome, at various times during the day. He had even thought to ask Lisa Fix if there were some government agency that might be contacted, some data storehouse that had a record of such things.

But he was afraid to pursue it. He leaned his head against the passenger window of the truck, trying to block the image of her dead face from his mind. Murdered maybe, strangled or bludgeoned. Or, more likely, a drug overdose.

He couldn't help but picture it. Her skin would be gray, of course, unnaturally pale, but still it would be her. Her arms and legs flung out, casually, luxuriously, the way she used to lay when she was in bed beside him. Troy used to love to watch her sleep—the lovely abandon of it. Whereas Troy tended to curl up into a corner, knees pulled up, arms tucked around his chest, Carla liked to sprawl. Her sleeping pose was like a cheerleader, frozen in mid-leap, like someone falling backward into water. She would smile in her sleep, her mouth slightly open. That was what he loved the most, that blissful look she had, the way, when he lightly touched her face, her tongue moved across her lips.

God, he thought, she'd been beautiful.

He was thinking of this as they drove past the street where Judy Keene, and Loomis, lived. He lifted his head and watched regretfully as the green crossroads sign drifted past. They didn't pause, but he felt the street hanging behind him. He imagined for a moment that they would drive past, and Loomis would be standing in the yard, playing. Then he remembered that Loomis was in school. In kindergarten.

He had been working on a letter, since Judy would not allow him phone calls, and he considered this again as they passed her street, driving on. *Dear Mrs. Keene,* he had written.

Dear Mrs. Keene,

I realize there are many good reasons why you have been reluctant to allow Loomis to have contact with me, and I respect that you want to protect him from harm. I know I have done some bad and illegal things in my life. But as Loomis's father, I am writing this note to beg you to find it in your heart to allow me to speak to him, even if this is under your strict supervision. I love Loomis very much, and although I know I have made mistakes I only want what is best for him. Could you find it in your heart to allow me a brief visitation? Or even to talk to him on the phone? There was once a time when Carla didn't want you to have contact with him, and I could have kept you from ever seeing him, but I didn't. If you were to do me the same courtesy, I would be very grateful.

Yours truly,
Troy Timmens

P.S.: I am very worried about Carla, and if you have heard anything about her whereabouts, it would mean a lot to me if you could let me know. If you don't want to contact me directly, you can leave a message with my parole officer, Lisa Fix at 255-9988. Please, Mrs. Keene, I am Loomis's father and I love him. Have mercy on me.

He hadn't sent this letter, though he'd gone over it several times, uncertainly. Did it seem contrite enough? Did it seem unthreatening? Did it seem maudlin, like something a drunk would write? If it were presented in a court of law, as evidence of harassment, how would a jury judge it? He wasn't sure, and so he held on to it, propping the envelope between the salt and pepper shakers on the kitchen table, unsealed and unstamped. Considering.

It couldn't be possible, he thought, that they had the power to separate him permanently from his own child. It couldn't be possible that Judy would have more claim to the boy than Troy, the child's own father, would have. But no one seemed willing to address this—not Lisa Fix, who was noncommittal; not his lawyer, Schriffer, who assured him that everything would work out but who hadn't returned his calls in almost a month; certainly not Judy Keene herself. He suspected that she was the one who had called the police in the first place, even while they were staking out Jonathan Sandstrom. He remembered again the night Loomis had come into the kitchen while he and Lonnie Von Vleet were sitting there, how Loomis had complained of the smell of smoke. He could picture Judy Keene smelling it on his clothes, and Loomis innocently answering her questions, telling her about his dad's water pipe, about the people who came to the house late at night.

Sitting there in the truck, he blushed fiercely. What an idiot he'd been. What an idiot!

At four in the afternoon, when he was released at last from community service, he found himself wondering again if there was enough time to drive past Judy Keene's house.

After he'd called the monitoring service and given them his number, he had ten minutes to get back home. There might be enough time, if barely, to take the long way around.

He had almost done this a couple of times before, but he always lost his nerve. It was extremely dangerous. He would have to drive a little faster than the speed limit, putting him at risk if any cops were waiting, hidden in alleys or behind bushes, in the little speed traps that everyone knew dotted the town, and fed it. He would have to chance the possibility that Judy herself would see him, and report him.

He knew that he would go to jail if he was caught violating the conditions of his parole. The supposed "good deal" that Schriffer had gotten for him would be moot, and the judge would be free to sentence him to prison. Two, even five years. It was a stupid risk to take.

But it was hard to think clearly. He had spent the day brooding about Carla and Loomis and all the ordinary freedoms that he'd once taken for granted. His head was fuzzy with so many thoughts, so many thoughts that led to dead ends and cul-de-sacs.

He pulled out of the County Department of Roads and onto Highway 31, which, at the city limits, became Euclid. He continued east, past the long-bankrupt Bonaventure Motor Lodge, with its old sign that promised LOWEST RATES COLOR TV, past the little side street where the old, abandoned Zike's Roller Rink and the Stumble Inn were facing each other, each moldering in its own way. He made it through the two traffic lights without having to wait, and then came at last to a red light on Old Oak Boulevard, where, if he were going home, he would turn south.

It had been four minutes. He hesitated for a second when the light changed, thinking *no, you shouldn't do this.* And then he accelerated, headed forward, his heart beating fast. He stared at the digital clock on his dashboard, watching the numbers as they pulsed. What did he have in mind? There was the idea that he'd be able to see Loomis, if only briefly, that Loomis would be standing in the yard in front of Judy's house, swinging a stick distractedly, talking to himself as he liked to do, perhaps wandering along the sidewalk, caught up in some pretend game. And at the moment that Troy drove by, he would look up.

And then what? Steal him away? Drive to Canada, to South America, fugitives. He would need to save up some money, he thought. It would take a while for him to find a job, but he would manage it. You could be a bartender anywhere in the world, he thought, and he let the fantasy float up briefly before it began to lose air, like a failed balloon.

There was a pickup in front of him. An old farmer, perhaps mesmerized or comatose, was puttering slowly through town. With excruciating slowness, they passed the Green Lantern bar, the American National Bank, the House of Photography.

Five minutes.

And he saw that it was useless. He would never make it to Judy's house in time, he realized, and it sent a current of electricity through him. Worse than useless. He saw the danger he'd put himself in so clearly that for a second he couldn't breathe. Five years in prison, he thought. There was no traffic in the opposite direction, and he turned abruptly, making an illegal U-turn in the middle of Euclid Avenue. The sports car behind him slowed, irritably, and the driver, a teenage girl, watched him with gaping alarm as he turned around and headed west again.

Six minutes.

By the time he arrived back at the intersection of Euclid and Old Oak, his hands were beginning to shake. Seven and a half minutes. He accelerated as he entered the concrete underpass beneath the railroad tracks, with its graffiti and wet, lime-encrusted walls, thinking he could make up a little time, but then, as if summoned by his anxiety, a patrol car pulled up behind him and he was forced to slow back down to the speed limit. Thirty-five miles an hour, and even the cop seemed a little impatient with it. The guy pulled up close, tailgating, and Troy could see the fatty, weight-lifter's face of Wallace Bean, one of the cops who, along with Kevin Onken and Ronnie Whitmire, had been his arresting officer on that night. Troy couldn't help but recall again the sound of Whitmire's pistol shot, and Bean shouting "Jesus Christ! Jesus Christ!" as Troy called Loomis's name and wept. Bean was perhaps the least loathsome of the three of them—he'd been a tight end on the football team when Troy was in high school, a large, dumb, friendly kid, the only one of the three of them who seemed to recognize that there was something wrong with breaking into a person's home and putting a bullet into the ceiling of his child's bedroom. "Your kid's okay, don't worry, don't worry," Bean had said as he put his large hand on Troy's head, helping him into the police car.

But still. The irony of Bean's appearance was a bit much for him to take at this particular, anxious moment, and when he saw the flashing yellow lights of a School Zone sign up ahead, he bit down hard on the inside of his cheek until he tasted blood. Here was South Elementary, where Loomis would be going if things had been different. SCHOOL ZONE: 20 MPH: SCHOOL ZONE, the sign said, and there was nothing he could do. Even though twenty miles per hour felt slower than walking, he let the speedometer sink down. Eight and a half minutes. He put on his turn signal at the corner of Old Oak and Deadwood Avenue, and Bean finally went around him, passing on the right. He drove past, not noticing Troy, focused on some mission or another that waited a bit farther south.

With Bean headed elsewhere, Troy sped down Deadwood. He had to take the risk, and he pressed down on the gas, faster and faster. Forty, fifty, sixty miles an hour. He passed the White Buffalo Trailer Court, where once he'd spent his childhood hours with Bruce and Michelle and baby Ray, he passed the familiar rows of ramshackle houses that edged the town. They were used to people speeding down Deadwood Avenue in cheap cars with broken mufflers, they didn't even look up as he passed. He swung around the turn of his own street, Gehrig, and fishtailed on the gravel of the unpaved road. Nine and a half minutes. He roared up his driveway and threw open the door of his car, not even pausing to slam it shut, fumbling with the house keys in his pockets. He sprinted through the gate and toward the back door, and when he saw Jonah standing there in his backyard, standing at the back door, his hands cupped around the window, trying to peer in, he didn't even have time to think about it.

He saw the color drain from Jonah's face as he approached, surprised and alarmed and stricken. "Oh," Jonah said. "Hey, I . . ." And he held up his hands as if Troy might be rushing forward to hit him.

But he didn't have time to consider it. Troy brushed past Jonah. "I'm in a big hurry," he grimaced, as his trembling fingers fitted the key into the back door. Jiggling wildly. He threw the door open and almost fell into the kitchen, toward the phone. He glanced at his watch, his fingers clumsy and shaking as he dialed the number.

Ten and a half minutes. He gasped into the phone. "This is 1578835. Checking in."

There was a long silence. And then a voice, male, stoned-sounding, said: "Okay. You're clear."

He didn't know how long he leaned against the wall, catching his breath. He felt light-headed, his heart still beating rapidly, and he thought ahead to the questions that Lisa Fix might ask him the next time they met. "Let's see," she would say. "Tuesday, October eighth. Why did it take you so long to get home? Almost eleven minutes." And there would have to be an excuse.

It was a few more minutes before he remembered Jonah. He looked over at the back door, still ajar, and kneaded his tired shoulders with his fingers. "Jonah!" he called. "Come on in! The door is open."

No answer.

With effort, he heaved himself away from the wall he had been melting into, and walked toward the screen door. "Jonah!" he called. "Come on in!"

But Jonah was nowhere in sight. Troy stared out into the empty backyard, frowning. The old swing hung limply from the branch of the tree.

"Hello?" Troy said. But no one was there.

18

October 10, 1996

They grew up together in Little Bow, South Dakota. Two brothers, Troy and Jonah. They ran through the bare, grassless backyard toward the railroad tracks, carrying sticks and yelling "Charge," yelling "Seize them!" like soldiers in a cartoon, and Troy, who was older, led the way. They swept their weapons down on a battalion of high weeds.

They sat at the kitchen table eating bologna sandwiches that their grandfather had made, and under their chairs, the dog Elizabeth lowered her muzzle thoughtfully onto her paws, hoping for food to fall. Troy ate silently for a while, moody; his eyes rested on Jonah. He could be bossy sometimes, even a bully, but Jonah knew that Troy would protect him.

"We should set up a fortress, don't you think?" Troy said—he was a soldier talking to his wise, bearded adviser—and Jonah nodded. "Yes," he said, and he remembered the clutter of plywood and two-by-fours that his grandfather had left behind the garage. They would spend the afternoon building, and when their mother came home she would call from the back door. She was tired after a day at work, but she wanted to talk to them. She pressed her lips against Troy's forehead, and then Jonah's, listening to their stories as Grandpa Joe and the dog came softly from the little back room into the kitchen.

And when they became adults they would be close, Jonah thought. There would be a quiet attachment between them, even though they took different paths. They would sit at the bar drinking beers together. Jonah would stand on Troy's doorstep, an armful of Christmas gifts for Loomis; they'd sit on the hood of Troy's car, watching Fourth of July fireworks, and later they might go camping together, or drive up to see Mount Rushmore, or Devil's Tower; if Jonah had a flat tire, he would naturally call Troy. "I need some help," he'd say, and Troy would make some wry joke. Then Troy would say: "Sure, bro. I'll be there in two minutes."

Was this corny? Clichéd?

Jonah wasn't sure. The truth was, he didn't really know how he might have felt in another life, in an alternate universe. He had seen movies and television shows, he'd read books, but he had very little sense of what daily, long-term friendship, brotherhood, might be like.

So far in his life he hadn't had much experience with relationships. He knew what it felt like to fail, he knew that somehow he'd made a mess of his friendship with Steve and Holiday. He knew what it was like to live alone, to sit in a silent apartment, or in a bar. He knew, from a few experiences, what a one-night stand felt like, what it was like to have anonymous sex. He knew what it was like to work with people, the way to get along with coworkers. He knew how to be invisible, the way he was in high school, speaking to no one, walking with his head down through the hallways. He knew how to live with his mother. But this didn't amount to much, he realized.

He spent a lot of time thinking about it. He sat cross-legged on the living room floor of his trailer, in front of the coffee table, writing down the names of everyone he'd ever known on notecards. He divided it into categories: aquaintances, bosses/landlords, coworkers, potential friends, relatives, lovers. It was like a game of solitaire. What is a relationship between two people? he thought. How is it accomplished? The sun came in through slats on the blinds. The trailer was full of small thick-bodied gray moths, Millers, they were called, clustered on the windowsills, beating their wings lethargically. He scooped them up by the handful and put them outside, where they fluttered in the dusty gravel that was his lawn.

He was thinking about his various failures. The mysterious ones most of all. Like, once, in Chicago, it was an older woman, a lady in her mid-forties, about his mother's age. Her name was Marie. She was wiry and athletic of body, and planted her fingers into the skin of Jonah's unscarred back like stakes as he pushed inside of her. He was pretty happy. He felt like he was figuring things out, as if he were on the verge of coming to some realization.

Marie was happy at first, too. They talked about books, about Saul Bellow, whom she had met once, and about pop music, about the local low-fi music scene. They talked about how the idea of what was beautiful changed from decade to decade. She told him that he was what she was looking for, that he was better than beautiful—she liked his eyes, their intensity, and his hair, which was blond and flat, and his face, which would have reminded her of a boy from a sixties beach movie. "But now it's something different altogether," she said, and leaned toward him. "I can't put my finger on it," she said, and reached out and touched his lips with her index finger.

But then, afterward, in the dark of Jonah's efficiency, she suddenly changed. He didn't know what had happened. She seemed sad and upset. She drew her knees up under the covers, and put her chin on them. "Oh," she said, by which he guessed she meant "What am I doing here?" Or "What have I done?"

"Are you okay?" Jonah said. He was thinking of his mother, who used to sit in this way, naked under the covers, drinking wine from a plastic tumbler and reading her books on unexplained mysteries. It occurred to him that this woman had a son who was gravely injured—killed, perhaps—and that she was thinking of him now. "Hey," Jonah said. "Don't be sad. It's okay."

"No," she said, with bitterness. "It's not 'okay.' It's actually something very different than 'okay.' "

All right, Jonah thought. What she was saying was probably true, and he waited for her to continue, but she didn't. "You can tell me if you want," he said at last, but she shook her head. "Sometimes it helps to talk about it," he said. "Is it about your son?"

"I don't have a *son*!" she said venomously, and when she looked at him a film of tear-water was thickening over her eyes and lashes.

"Jesus," she said. "What *are* you?"

He was silent for a moment, not really understanding her question. "I'm just a person," he said. "I'm not anything specific." It made him feel weird. He felt the shards of his life moving around, organizing and reorganizing themselves.

"Why do you think I have a son?" said this lady, who looked so much like Jonah's mom. Her eyes were wide and suspicious now, and she flinched out of bed when he tried to talk, leaning over the floor to pick up her clothes and press them against her breasts and crotch as if he had sneaked into her house while she was naked. She cradled her clothes as she backed into the bathroom and shut the door.

"What's wrong?" Jonah called to her, and he could hear her beyond the bathroom door, grunting and struggling into her clothes as he knocked politely. "Are you all right?" he called. But she wouldn't answer.

What are you? she asked, and he thought about it again.

At the restaurant in Chicago, he wasn't anything. Just a worker. He'd spent most of his time cutting vegetables, chopping. He was good at this—he could slice a mushroom into paper-thin pieces, reduce a head of broccoli into tiny flowerettes in seconds. The cuts on his fingers he barely noticed, and his coworkers sometimes thought this was funny, maybe because he was so scarred up. He thought something was probably wrong with his nerves, because most of the time he didn't even feel pain, and he'd sliced the ends off his fingers and it was only the blood that told him that he'd made a mistake. *"Primo,"* they called to him. "*Primo,* you are bleeding."

Most of the men he worked with in Chicago were Mexican, or from some Latin American country. They didn't ask any questions. They were always talking in Spanish and then looking at Jonah brightly and laughing. In some ways, Jonah thought, this was maybe for the best. He picked up a few things. He knew words like *cebolla* and *cuchillo* and *cabron,* and sometimes they would teach him phrases—like once they got him to say *"muchas panochas en America,"* and when he repeated it there was such an uproar of hilarity so that he knew it was probably obscene. But when he asked the line cook, Alphonso, what *panocha* meant, Alphonso was solemn. "It means 'sugar,' *Primo,*" he said. "Brown sugar."

Were they friends, Jonah and these men? He supposed. The night after he'd gotten the information from the PeopleSearch Agency, the night he'd found his brother, he wished he could tell them. He tried to think of the word for "brother" in Spanish. *Hermano.* But what was the word for "found"? What was the word for "adopted"? For "long-lost"? How did you say "I am going to be leaving soon"?

He didn't know. He smiled at them more than usual that night, trying to show them through his expression what he meant. Since he'd spent so much time with them, he imagined that they were close in a way, but most of the time he didn't really know what they were saying. He had thought about learning Spanish, but he decided that if he could speak their language they wouldn't like him as much anymore.

None of them seemed curious about his scars, though once a little dishwasher, a wiry, high-cheekboned Mayan-looking boy named Ernesto had pointed to them. He balled up his fists and made a soft "tok" with his tongue, miming fighting. Jonah shook his head. "No," he said.

Jonah showed him his teeth, tapping them.

"Dientes," Ernesto said.

"Woof," Jonah said, imitating a dog. "Arf, arf."

"Perro," Ernesto said.

Ernesto nodded solemnly, apparently understanding, though also wary. He reached out and ran his finger along the thick, pale raised skin that ran along Jonah's forearm. *"Perro?"* he said again, uncertainly, and Jonah nodded, flushed a bit, exhilarated. This was the first person he'd told the truth to since he'd come to Chicago, and the moment seemed fraught with danger. He had unbuttoned his shirt and showed Ernesto a little of his chest. "Ay," Ernesto said, and Jonah smiled at him, shrugging. He waited, not breathing, while Ernesto touched his skin. *"El lobo,"* Jonah said, which he knew was the Spanish word for wolf, and Ernesto chuckled, drawing away a little. "It's okay," Jonah told him, and Ernesto grinned. He puffed out his chest and drew an "X" over Jonah's bared skin with his finger, *swip, swip,* like

Zorro. "S'okay," he said, repeating, imitating as if Jonah were full of bravado. Jonah had thought that perhaps it was the beginning of a friendship.

But then a few days later, he went to work and found that Ernesto wasn't there anymore. When Jonah asked, Alphonso simply shrugged. Ernesto had been killed, Alphonso said—stabbed in a fight outside some bar in the Mexican area of town.

"Jesus," Jonah said, and he was aware of that feeling of velocity again. "He was just a kid, wasn't he? How old was he?"

"I don't know, *Primo,*" Alphonso said, and looked at Jonah heavily. "Old enough to die, I guess," he said, and showed Jonah the palms of his hands. It wasn't Jonah's fault, of course, that Ernesto was dead, but the way Alphonso looked at him left a film of guilt for the rest of the night. He was leaving. He thought of that woman, backing away from him. "What *are* you," she said. He didn't know.

And now, what? He found himself thinking about that moment in Troy's backyard, when Troy had driven up unexpectedly, just as Jonah was cupping his hand to peer in the back window.

When he saw Troy the next day, he'd been able to explain it away easily enough. "Sorry about . . . yesterday," he'd said. "I was just stopping by because I had a question about the schedule. I hope I didn't . . . disturb you."

And Troy had only shrugged. "Mm," Troy said, distractedly. "No big deal."

But still, it was troubling. He'd been so deeply in his own head, pacing along the circumference of Troy's house, touching the edges of the windowsills, pretending that he belonged there. It was *his* yard, *his* home, *his* child's swing hanging from the tree. *We'll clean it up and it will be pretty nice,* he was thinking, and then he'd turned to see Troy rushing forward.

His first intuition was that Troy was going to hit him. He imagined for a moment that Troy had found out somehow, and he pictured being knocked down and kicked repeatedly in the side and stomach. "Who do you think you are?" Troy would roar. "What *are* you?"

But instead Troy had brushed right past him. *I'm in a big hurry,* Troy said, as if to a stranger he'd just met, hardly looking at him, and in some ways that was worse than a blow. Jonah stood there in the yard for a moment as Troy disappeared into the house, and he could feel himself dissipating, the other lives he'd been imagining lifting away, foolish as balloons.

He was nothing. He remembered that woman, Marie, her face pinched as she said *I don't have a son*; he remembered Ernesto's gentle, uncomprehending eyes as Jonah struggled with basic words: *Perro . . . dientes . . .* He saw his mother staring at him dully, expelling smoke from her mouth when she came upon him babbling away to himself, and all of the various costumes of his imagination fell away. He could feel himself shrinking.

He saw himself as Troy had: an oddball stranger, a minor character, uninvited, unwelcome, standing for no good reason in his coworker's yard.

What are you doing here? Troy's expression had said, and he felt the weight of that question settle over him. He didn't know the answer.

In practical terms, his life in St. Bonaventure was not so different from his life in Chicago. The small trailer house he'd found in a place called Camelot Court was as dull and anonymous as the efficiency he'd rented from Mrs. Orlova. The other residents, consumed with the problems of work and family, with the mundane sufferings of unspectacular poverty, paid him little mind. He would hear them sometimes, screaming at their children or deeply involved in some love argument, but he rarely saw them. He kept to himself: watching TV, reading, trying to work things out in his mind.

When he finally left the trailer that day his head was so full of thoughts that it was almost surprising to see people. It was about two in the afternoon, and he was on his way to work, still sifting through his imaginary notecards, and he stopped short when he saw them. They were a group of teenage boys, sitting on the hood of an old Mustang in the gravel roadway that ran between the trailers. Right behind his car; they were blocking him in.

The four boys were passing a joint back and forth. Jonah paused on the wooden steps that led up to the screen door of his trailer while they eyed him, talking softly to one another. This wouldn't have bothered him so much, except they had a dog—a thickly muscled mongrel of some sort. Unleashed. It stood a few yards away from Jonah, the hair on its back pricked up in spikes, barking. Jonah stood steady, watching the animal. He couldn't bring himself to move or speak, and it was an effort not to simply retreat into his trailer.

Finally, one of the boys, the oldest of the four, seemed to take notice of Jonah. "Hey, man," the kid said, as if Jonah had just appeared. "How you doing?"

"Fine," Jonah said, flatly. The dog didn't move toward him, but in order to get to his car he would need to walk nearer to it. In Chicago he would cross the street when he saw a pet owner walking a tethered dog along the sidewalk, and he knew which parks to avoid.

"You new here?" the boy said, and his followers grinned, staring at Jonah expectantly. At twenty-five, his face was still too young to have any authority over them—even with the scar, people often mistook him for a teenager himself.

"Yes," Jonah said. "I just moved in." He glanced at the dog again, and the leader boy followed his gaze.

"Rosebud!" the kid said, firmly, and gave Jonah a sly half smile. "Don't worry," the kid said to Jonah. "She won't bite unless I tell her to." He clapped his hands, hard, and Jonah watched as the dog obediently sat down, running its tongue across its chops, its ears pricked up expectantly.

The boy turned back to Jonah and nodded, pleased with himself, proud owner of Rosebud. He didn't seem threatening, exactly. He was short, round-faced, wearing a muscle shirt. There was brownish black facial hair sprouting over his lip and on his chin, though this did not yet amount to a mustache or a goatee. His eyes seemed basically gentle, albeit very drugged, and he might have even seemed friendly if it wasn't for his dog.

"So what's your name?" the kid said, after he and Jonah had faced each other for a moment, and Jonah cleared his throat.

"Jonah," he said. The younger ones seemed to think this was funny for some reason, ribbing each other and chuckling, but their leader only observed Jonah, apparently earnest.

"Jinx," he said, and rubbed his hand over the thigh of his jeans before holding it out to shake. "I live over there, with my mom." He pointed in the direction of a series of long trailers, each with a small patch of grass and brightly colored lawn ornaments.

"Pleased to meet you," Jonah said, cordially, and the kid showed his small, gilt-edged teeth. Rosebud let out a thoughtful whine.

"So," Jinx said, and shifted from foot to foot, still grinning. He was very stoned, Jonah thought. They all were. Jonah kept his hands stiffly at his sides as the boy leaned forward, confidentially. "I have to ask you, man," the boy said. "What's with the, uh," and he made a quick swipe along his cheek to indicate Jonah's scar. "What's with the jack-o'-lantern effect? Are you a fighter?"

Jonah was silent for a moment, and the teens, lined up on the hood of the Mustang, stared at him curiously. He wasn't afraid of them. They were clumsy with drugs, and he felt fairly sure they posed little threat. He had discovered fairly early on in his junior high school years that he was stronger than most of the bullies, and more impervious to pain. The knowledge that he had the ability to hurt people had always been a steadying force when he faced encounters such as this, and he curled his hand around his car key, the sharp tip of the key protruding a little from between his ring and middle finger. The only thing he felt nervous about was the dog.

"I'm not a fighter," Jonah said, but he hardened his eyes, and Jinx took a small step back. Jonah knew very well how to make his expression scary—it was making it look normal that was the problem. He put out his thumb, deliberately, and traced along the ridge of the scar. "I'm not anything," he said, and he kept his eyes on Jinx as he stepped cautiously toward his car. Rosebud didn't move, though she growled low in her throat. He hoped they didn't see what an act of bravery it took, with the unleashed dog sitting there, to walk down the stairs, to open his car door. If he hadn't been almost late for work, he didn't think he could have managed it. He unrolled his window a few inches.

"Would you mind moving your car," he said, coolly, though his heart was beating very fast. "I can't quite get past you."

And Jinx made a kind of formal bow. "No problem, Jonah," he said, his eyes glinting.

When he arrived at the Stumble Inn that day, the shift change was already under way. Vivian was cooking, and Troy was tending bar, and Crystal was bustling about, doing various side work in preparation for the evening. Jonah had been surprised to learn that the four of them made up the entirety of the regular staff. There were two other employees, both part-time—a man named Chuck, who also worked as a city fireman and as a handyman, bartended the single Sunday shift, when the kitchen was closed; and an elderly, apparently alcoholic woman named Esther worked in the kitchen on Mondays. Jonah had met neither of these peripheral figures. He was scheduled to work five days a week—from three thirty P.M. to nine P.M. on Tuesdays, Wednesdays, and Thursdays, and from ten A.M. to two A.M. on Fridays and Saturdays—and he was already hopefully settling himself into a routine, with Troy and Vivian and Crystal as a kind of family around whom his daily life would begin to revolve. He liked, very much, the sense of a schedule solidifying, and it upset him that his encounter with the teenagers had disrupted it. He was flushed as he came in through the back door of the bar, even before Vivian said anything.

"You're getting close to late," Vivian said as he walked in, her voice grave and edged with pessimistic disappointment. She gazed at him as if she'd expected, all along, that he would screw up, and he waved his hands in exasperation.

"I apologize," he said. He saw Crystal and Troy turn to look at him, and he blushed. He had hoped, at the very least, to seem admirably dependable. A hard, earnest worker. He had always thought that if you were reliably good at your job, you could win anyone over, no matter what your appearance. He stood there awkwardly.

"I'm really sorry," he said, and cleared his throat. "I had teenager problems. A bunch of kids in my way." He smiled humorously, hoping that they would commiserate, but they didn't seem to understand.

"They were just sitting there in my driveway, blocking me in!" Jonah explained. "Some kid with a big ugly dog named Rosebud," Jonah said. "Ha! Do you think he's a fan of *Citizen Kane*?"

Jonah thought this was quite clever, but Vivian, and Crystal, and Troy all looked at him blankly.

"It's a movie," Jonah said. *"Citizen Kane."*

Vivian blinked, sternly. "Why don't you go downstairs and bring up a bucket of ice," she said, returning to her work, and Jonah felt a familiar weight of self-loathing settle over his shoulders. He shouldn't tell jokes. He shouldn't try to be gregarious. He was bad at both of these things, and he should know it by now.

It was quite busy for a while. After Vivian had left, after Troy had clocked out and hurried wordlessly out the door, the bar began to inexplicably fill up with patrons. Through the small order window he could see customers entering, leaning on the bar with their elbows, occupying the booths and tables. He could hear Crystal's musical, bell-like voice, greeting people and chatting with them and calling "order" to him. In his mind, the world irradiated outward—lifting above the roomful of townsfolk in their buzz of chatter, their beers and hamburgers; above the parking lot and the boarded-up facade of Zike's Roller Rink, above St. Bonaventure and the expanse of prairie that surrounded it, the dots of headlights on the roads that led away, the clusters of lights that represented the small cities in the distance—Denver, Cheyenne, Rapid City—the blurry scrim of clouds that held the atmosphere to the earth, the planet itself shrinking into an ellipsis, his own existence dwindling into something subatomic.

It helped to think of things this way. Enclosed in the box of the kitchen, in his dirty white apron and hair net and checked pants, sweat trickling out of the elastic of his paper cap and into his eyes, winding along the ridges of his scarred face, he felt vile. He brooded over the hot griddle and the stacks of prefab hamburgers, each separated by a tab of wax paper; the monotonous rituals of frying, lowering a handful of breaded, cheese-stuffed jalapeños into a vat of snapping oil. He was aware of his body as he crept into the bar area, glum as a prison worker, to refill the garnish bins with lime wedges and sliced circles of lemons; he was aware of his deeply bitten fingernails, his grimy hands lining slick dishes in racks, a fist around a scouring pad, scrubbing pots in his spare moments. This did not feel like starting his life over.

And then, without warning, the bar was empty. He looked at his watch—it was eleven o'clock and he heard Crystal calling after someone. "Thanks for stopping in!" she said, and her voice fell woodenly into the empty room. There was a moment of silence.

Then, after a moment, she turned to look at Jonah.

"Whew," she said, in a breezy, cheerfully friendly voice. "That was something else!" She grinned at him. With the bar empty, there was no one else to turn her warmth upon, and so suddenly he was the recipient: her able coworker, her comrade in arms. He was scouring the grill with a charcoal pad, and he peered out at her, blinking.

"Uh-huh," he said.

"You were great," she said. "I really think the food here is starting to get a reputation, because of you."

He put his head down, as if against a strong wind. "Uh-huh," he said.

"I'm serious," she said, and when he glanced back up, she was still looking at him. Her long blond hair hung straight, almost to her shoulder blades, and it was clear that she brushed and brushed it every morning. It caught the light and glowed, and he shifted uncomfortably at its brilliance. She was the type of girl who secretly imagined a man cherishing a lock of her hair, the type of girl who thought it was possible that the eyes could be windows upon the soul. There was a general tenderness, extending out to flowers and children and small animals and the elderly, and from there passing on to the rest of the world, to people like Jonah himself.

"How about a beer?" she said. "I'm going to pour myself one. And then we can finish up with the side work and get out of here."

He hesitated. "Sure," he said. He watched as she tilted a glass against the tap, and then he bent again to the griddle, scrubbing it hard. He looked up warily as she came into the kitchen with his glass of perfectly poured beer—golden liquid, topped with a soft head of white foam.

"Relax for a minute," she said, and caught his eye as he took the beer from her. "You're like a workhorse, Jonah! I haven't seen you take a break all night!"

"Thanks," Jonah said, and lifted the glass to his lips and drank. Crystal did the same, smiling as she tasted her beer in a way that made Jonah think of a missionary, sharing some exotic drink with a savage.

"So how is St. Bonaventure treating you, Jonah?" she said, after she'd taken a surprisingly long pull of her beer. "Are you settling in okay?"

Jonah shrugged. "Yeah," he said. "I'm doing all right."

"Despite the crazy teenagers and their mean dogs."

"Right," he said.

She downed the rest of the beer in a single long gulp. "Ahh," she said, and he watched as she went back out to fill her glass again. His own was still nearly full, and he took another sip.

"It must be an adjustment," she said brightly, as she came back in. "Moving here from Chicago! There's got to be a lot of culture shock involved!"

"A little," he said, and she smiled warmly again, as if this were a big admission on his part. He scratched at the last bit of blackness on the griddle, then took another sip of beer.

"But you like it here?" Crystal said.

"Yeah," said Jonah. He hesitated, took another sip of beer as Crystal drank deeply from hers. "It's all right," he said. "I think I like it."

"Do you?"

"I think so," he said, and reached over to turn off the fryalator. He glanced around the work area, to see if there was anything left unfinished. "Do you like it here?"

She shrugged, sipped again—she was half finished with her second beer. "I guess," she said. "I don't know. I mean, if I'd been driving down the interstate looking for someplace to settle, I don't know whether this would have been my first choice, but I'm here now. You get to know a place, and you're used to it. I like my house."

"That's good," Jonah said. He took a last drink of his beer, and Crystal held out her hand for his glass.

"Another?" she said, and when he hesitated, she smiled at him. "Why not?" she said, as if she was pretending to read his mind.

"I'm not a big drinker," he said, but she was already on her way

out to the bar, filling his glass again. She turned to look over her shoulder.

"Vivian told me about your accident," she said. "About your wife."

It was like a soft but dizzying blow to the head.

He felt himself flush, heat filling his cheeks and forehead. He thought he could recall what he'd said to Vivian: *I was in a car accident. It's not something I generally talk about. My wife— She was pregnant, and she died.* But had he said more than that? Had he, for example, given his wife a name, a background? He wasn't sure. He had known it was a mistake even as it came out of his mouth. *I don't like to talk about it,* he'd said, trying to backpeddle. *I shouldn't have said anything—if it could just stay . . . between us, I'd appreciate it.*

And he'd trusted Vivian, at that moment. Had believed her when she looked at him earnestly. *Oh, of course,* she'd said. *Just between us.* But now, as Crystal gazed at him, he could sense the ground beneath him softening, his feet sinking slowly. He knew his face was very red, and he was aware of that particular story, told on the spur of the moment, solidifying around him.

"Oh," he said hoarsely. He watched as Crystal walked again from around the bar and into the kitchen area. "That wasn't something . . . I . . . didn't want everyone to know about that," he said.

"I know," Crystal said. She smiled, melancholy, as she handed him another glass of beer. "I'm sorry," she said. "Vivian isn't very good at keeping secrets."

He swallowed, and brought the beer to his lips. "Oh," he said again, and he looked at Crystal. Maybe it was possible to change things, to undo the casual lie he'd told Vivian, to drag everything, at last, into the open. He wondered what would happen if he told her the truth—if he explained about Troy, and the adoption, and the PeopleSearch Agency. Maybe she would help him. But he wasn't certain. It might be that even now he was too deeply mired into the false person she thought he was.

"Does everyone know?" he said softly.

She looked at him.

"Jonah," she said. "You're living in a small town. It's not a place where you can keep to yourself."

He blinked.

"I'm sorry if I brought up something upsetting," Crystal said gently. "It's okay if you don't want to talk about it. People will understand."

As he trudged out into the parking lot, Jonah could feel the weight of the story roost on his shoulder—the velocity of the car rushing forward, the grille of the truck bearing down on him, the sound of his wife screaming. Poor Jonah, people would say. Starting his ruined life over in St. Bonaventure. Had Troy already heard as well? He stood there, staring at the old Festiva, trying to recalculate the history of his life. The air was chill, and a delicate, fern-shaped frost had branched across his windshield, though it turned to dew when he pressed his fingers to the glass.

It was nearly one o'clock in the morning, but he felt too worked up to return to his trailer, to sleep. He drove through the streets, and the October weather sent leaves raining down over him, swirling in the wind. He sat on the hood of his car outside Troy's house, watching as a Styrofoam cup ticked hollowly down the street, clop, clop, clop. Ghostly horse's hooves.

The house itself was dark, and the trees swayed back and forth in the autumn air, whispering. Troy, his brother, was asleep. Troy was sad and lonely also, but unlike Jonah he was a real person. He slept, dreaming of his solid life. His wife, his son. His job.

As for Jonah, he passed his flashlight through the tangled, gray-brown grass of Troy's backyard. Here was a plastic army man, kneeling, holding a bazooka. Here was a tree with a frayed rope hanging from a branch, like the memory of a noose. Here was a large stone in the middle of a flower bed, and a little rubber ball, bright orange. He felt like an archaeologist of Troy. If he studied long enough, he could take each of these small details and create something whole.

Why couldn't he do that for himself? Compared to most people, he barely existed—he was nothing, just a collection of random bits of history and memory he carried along, a series of shifting moods. A series of lies that he was forced to follow. It made him shudder: What was real, in his memory? He could picture his grandfather's stockinged feet, twitching as the old man reclined on the yellowed

sheets, watching television. He saw his mother leaning over him, flashlight in her hands, whispering, her voice slurred with drugs. He saw the baby, Henry, staring up at him, eyes utterly empty. He could picture the dog, Elizabeth, nudging her muzzle against his chest. But none of it fit together.

When he turned at last into the gravel roadways of Camelot Court, it was almost four, and he still felt tense and unnerved. He drove slowly. The tires crunched steadily against the gravel, and shadows emerged into his headlights as he approached, trembling echoes of dry weeds and branches and electrical poles, pinned suddenly in the middle of the road and then drawing back as he approached. A single leaf came twisting down and planted itself on the windshield in front of his face, like the palm of a hand pressed against the glass.

It startled him, and he put his foot on the brake abruptly. Up ahead, where the black shapes of a row of trailers were huddled, he could see a pair of red glowing spots moving toward him from out of the shadows. Eyes, reflecting his headlights. He could feel his heart freezing. Slowly, the figure of a dog slid out of the darkness into the glare of his headlights, sidling cautiously toward him, barking, its sharp-toothed mouth opening and closing against the air.

The sight of it made him panic. It was almost instinctual to press on the accelerator, as hard as he could. He could feel a scuttling, as if small insects were crawling over his skin. The dog held its ground for a moment, in a kind of wrestler stance, chest puffed out, head erect. At the last second, it tried to dodge away, but Jonah swerved as well.

There was a single scream, an exclamation of shrill, childish pain, and a soft thump as his tire passed over the body. He slammed on the brakes, then, his mouth quivering, threw the car into reverse, the tires spinning in the gravel, fishtailing. But his aim was surprisingly good. The back tire connected with the head, and he could feel the skull and snout collapse under the weight of the car, a small wet crunch.

He leaned his forehead on the steering wheel, not weeping but making a soft, deep, hitching sound in his throat that was almost the same thing. It took him a moment to calm himself, to feel his thoughts gathering out of the haze. And then to realize what he'd done, to remember the dog's name. He sat there silently, staring at the illuminated gravel road in front of him, watching as the wind forced a few ragged leaves and scraps of paper around and around in a solemn dancing ring.

19

July 27, 1974

Nora wakes in the middle of the night and Jonah is leaning over her, staring.

It takes her a second to even register where she is. She has been sleeping soundly, and at first is only aware of a vague unease. In her dream she is in a room in Mrs. Glass House, and she can see the single tree through the window, lit by moonlight. A shadow moves below—something heavy, like the shape of a desk or a dresser, but it's moving, sliding wetly along the floor like a snail would. And then she's aware, little by little, of the humid, sour smell of expelled breath against her face. Her eyes flutter open and his face is looming above her, his large unblinking eyes, his thin, almost skeletal head, like the head of a baby bird. It is almost a reflex to strike out; she doesn't even think. Her hand swings up and connects with the side of his face, knocking him onto the floor.

"Jesus!" she screams, and Gary, asleep beside her, flails his arms and legs wildly.

"What!" he shouts. "What!" swiveling his head in disoriented panic.

"Oh, my God," she says. The blow has knocked Jonah nearly across the room, and he is crumpled on the floor, motionless. "I hit him," she says to Gary, who is still blinking, dazed. "I was having a nightmare and I hit him."

She stands there, naked, in a daze herself, staring blankly at the small, shadowy, huddled form of the child. She takes a step, and then another, very slowly, toward it, and then she sees that it is beginning to stir. The child makes the small, throat-clearing noises that are his version of crying—little hitching grunts, an uncertain, somewhat froggy sound. Jonah hasn't wept since he was an infant, and now, at three, he rarely even makes his crying noises, even when he's hurt. It is one of the many things she finds uncanny, frightening, about him.

"Jonah," she says, and at last she brings herself to kneel beside him, to turn him over and put her arms around him.

"You hit me," Jonah says—not even accusingly, but in a soft, almost matter-of-fact voice, and Nora shudders. The side of his face is already swelling—he should be heaving with sobs.

"I'm sorry," she says, and rocks him a little. "I didn't mean to. You scared me."

And Jonah looks at her hard, his eyes wide and expectant. "I scared you," he repeats. "Why?"

"I didn't know it was you," she whispers. "I thought it was . . . something else." And Gary stands over them, watching as she slowly brushes Jonah's fine, weightless blond hair.

"Geez," Gary says. "You really socked him. What'd you do that for? The poor kid's going to have a black eye." She herself has begun to cry a little, and she looks up at him, a tear sliding along the bridge of her nose. She really didn't mean to hit him like that, she tells herself, so hard that she'd knocked him across the room. Not on purpose.

He won't leave her alone, that's part of the problem. He follows her everywhere, watching everything she does, staring silently and expectantly, focused, deeply fascinated by whatever mundane task she's performing—washing dishes, vacuuming, reading a magazine or a book. Now that he can climb out of his crib, it's impossible to get away from him, to get a moment's privacy. He won't watch television unless she sits there and watches it with him; he won't play with his toys unless he can bring them right under her feet, crawling his little plastic cars up her leg, walking his stuffed animals in a circle around her. She sits at the kitchen table, drinking coffee, feeling the soft taps as Jonah crouches below her, making the toys dance over her shoes.

He won't even take a nap. She has spanked him, over and over, for getting up when he's supposed to be sleeping, but he can't be persuaded. He will sneak out of bed, and after a short period of delicious aloneness, she will begin to sense him. He will be peering around the edge of the door frame, spying on her, or hidden somewhere—under a chair, or in a closet with the door open just enough that he can see.

"I've never seen a little boy who loves his mommy so much!" the neighbor, Arlene, had said. Arlene was a homely young housewife of about Nora's age, almost always in curlers, with a two-year-old girl and a four-year-old boy, and pregnant with another. For a while after Arlene had moved in, she would come over to drink coffee with Nora, to exchange innocuous and boring conversation. But Jonah wouldn't play with Arlene's children, and Nora could see that Arlene was as unnerved by Jonah as she was, despite her polite praise of Jonah's quiet vigilance. "He just can't take his eyes off you," Arlene said, giving a pinched smile that said *What's wrong with your child? He's abnormal.* And after a short period of shallow friendship, Arlene had found another mother down the block whom she liked better.

In the last few months, Nora has been trying more and more determined measures. The bedroom doors have push buttons that lock from the inside, rather than the out, and the doors open inward, so it isn't possible to wedge a chair against the doorknob to hold him in. One day, when it was sunny, she put him in the yard, and locked the door so he couldn't get back in. "Just play out there for a while," she had said. "Play with your toys in the grass." But he had only stood by the door, rattling the knob for a while, before he had begun to call to her. "Let me in! Mom! I can't get in!" Yelling loud enough that it threatened to bring Arlene or one of the other neighbors running to his rescue. Once, not long after that, she had locked herself in the bedroom. He had stood at the door for a long while, knocking and knocking. And then, after what seemed only a moment's silence, there had been a crash in the kitchen, the sound of shattering glass, and the steady "huh-huh-huh" of Jonah making his crying sound. She had to come out then, to find that he'd managed, somehow, to climb up on the counter and bring down an entire shelf of knick-knacks, beloved little things she'd saved over the years. Almost all of them destroyed.

She'd beaten him then. She'd turned him over her knee and brought one of Gary Gray's belts down on his buttocks, over and over, until she was afraid she'd leave marks on him. But the effect of this beating actually made things worse. For the next few days, and in fact for over a week, Jonah apologized at regular intervals. He would say, "I'm sorry I broke it, Mom. I'm sorry I broke it. I'm sorry I broke it." Apologizing sometimes two or three times in an hour. Finally, her nerves on edge, she had slapped him in the mouth.

"Stop apologizing!" she had cried. "I know you're sorry. Now stop! Stop! I can't stand it anymore."

She can't help thinking that Jonah is her punishment. That Jonah is what she deserves, a girl who gave her own baby away without even looking at it, who blithely relinquished a piece of herself, a part of her own body. This is her lost baby's revenge, this constant observation—as if Jonah knows by some instinct that she is untrustworthy, that she is an abandoner.

And she can't help but feel that Jonah is crafty beyond his years—calculating, even, for when Gary Gray comes home at night from work, he is much calmer. Much more like a normal toddler. He doesn't watch her in the same way, so that when she complains to Gary about her difficulties, Jonah shows no signs of his obsessive watching and following.

"He seems all right to me," Gary says. And then he looks at her steadily. "What about you?" he says. "Are you okay, honey?"

Even during the period when Jonah was apologizing over and over, Gary didn't see anything strange about it. "God!" he said, and laughed. "Poor kid! He's really conscientious, isn't he?"

And this is another punishment the world is meting out. In the beginning, when they'd first met and she was pregnant, Gary Gray had wanted to be Jonah's father. He'd offered—he'd been willing to have his name on the birth certificate, to make everything official. To marry her.

And she'd refused. She didn't really know what she'd been thinking, except that it was the kind of falsehood, the kind of hypocrisy, that reminded her of the Mrs. Glass House. Gary was *not* Jonah's father, and at the time a kind of possessiveness overcame her. She didn't want the baby to be named "Gray." She wanted him to be a Doyle—hers, only hers. It was this vanity that had driven her to make them write "Father Unknown" on Jonah's birth certificate. Many times she felt that if only the child's name were Jonah Gray, she might have saved herself, but Gary Gray didn't ask again in the years they lived together.

"You still love that guy, huh?" Gary had said when she'd turned down his offer, and she'd only shrugged, shaking her head.

"I don't even know his name," she said. It was an act of bravado that she knew Gary both loved and resented.

"You're crazy," he would say. "Crazy, crazy girl." And he meant this both as a criticism and as a declaration of love. The fact that she would turn him down, and yet still live with him, only made her more desirable. Elusive. Moody. A bit dangerous.

These days, she is aware that these attractions are beginning to fade, just as she is aware that her insistent ownership of her baby has faded. Jonah is not hers alone, and in fact, often it doesn't seem possible for him to have come out of her body. His corn- or silk hair, pallid skin, his sturdy, skinny, awkwardly unchildish body—it is always clear, when she and Gary and Jonah are out together, that he is not their son. Gary, part English and part Armenian, is thickly built, dark-haired, with a prominent nose and a dark, curly beard. She has copper-colored skin and long, straight black hair, thick eyebrows, an angular face.

As they all sit in the International House of Pancakes, it seems unlikely that they belong together. Jonah rolls on the seat beside her, pressing his feet against her thigh, singing softly to his hand. An old white woman observes them sternly. It is clear that Jonah is a Caucasian child, while Nora and Gary are "ethnic." Puerto Ricans? Arabs? Dark-skinned Jews? Nora can feel the woman trying to figure it out, her mouth pinched as she tries to decide. It reminds her of childhood, when people would observe her pink-skinned, Scotch/Irish father and her tan Sioux/German mother with distaste. But at least it was clear that she was their offspring. Jonah, on the other hand, seems like a cruel joke of science—that a man she barely remembers should have managed to implant his genes in Jonah so powerfully that her own are almost completely overshadowed. Here is another little punishment for her.

The morning after Jonah woke her in the middle of the night, he is much more subdued than usual, and it would almost be a blessing if she didn't feel so guilty. The side of his cheek where she slapped him is swollen so that his eye is almost squeezed shut, and nearly half his face is black and blue. It seems as if she can see the shadowy imprint of her hand in the shape of the bruise, a Rorschach of a hand. After breakfast she fills a dish towel with ice and has him hold it against his cheek, and he does this without protest. He leans over the kitchen table and watches as the melting ice drips from the cloth and pools on the table. "You are a nice lake," he says to the water, and gazes at her sadly when she wipes it away. But he has stopped staring at her—at least for the moment.

She would like to go somewhere, like she used to when Jonah was smaller. When he was an infant, they would take a bus to the el train, and from there they might go to a museum, or to a park along the lake, or a store that sold shells and postcards, wandering, while Gary was at work. It made her feel calmer, to lose herself in the throng of people on Michigan Avenue, to feel the city of Chicago spreading out around her, so that even if she walked along the sidewalks for years she would not be able to exhaust its possibilities.

But as Jonah has grown, it has become increasingly difficult to make such trips. He is now too heavy to comfortably carry for very long, and too big and restless for the stroller, which he will try to clamber out of while she is pushing it. And walking with him, even with his

hand clasped tightly in hers, is impossible. He always dawdles and tugs and resists when she tries to hurry him along. "Come on," she'll say, as he crouches stubbornly to look at an ant on the sidewalk that has captured his notice. "Come on!" she'll say, as he longs after the coins in the instrument box of a shaggy street saxophonist with frightening, filmy eyes, or strains to pick up a deflated orange balloon on the el-train platform, even as the train's doors are about to close. "Goddamnit, come on!" she finds herself snapping, pulling his arm sharply, and once, an elderly black man had reproached her. "Young woman, don't pull on that child's arm like that," he had said, in a soft, courtly southern voice, as if he were gently scolding a child himself. "You yank on him like that you going to hurt him." And she had blushed, she felt as if she would start crying.

"I'm sorry," she whispered, and the old man had observed her sternly, his hands folded over the crook of his cane as if it were a scepter.

"You need to pray for help," he said. "That's all we can do. Pray for help." And for the rest of the day, whatever small pleasures she might have gathered in downtown Chicago had been ruined by the man's sorrowful, judgmental eyes. It had been a long time before she tried to take Jonah anywhere after that.

And now, with his face so bruised, she doesn't dare leave the house. People will know, they will suspect, that she hit him. He might even tell on her, if some friendly stranger asks him. "Jonah," she says, and he looks up from a new puddle of ice water to stare at her. "Don't tell people I hit you," she says.

"Why?" Jonah says.

"Because," she says, "it will make me feel sad."

"Why?" Jonah says.

"Because it was an accident," she says. "You know that it was an accident, don't you?"

"Yes," he says.

"If you tell people that I hit you, I might have to go away forever," she said. "I might die."

And he looks at her, solemnly, his large eyes almost painful in their focused intensity. He doesn't say anything, but she thinks he understands.

Why does she always end up trapped? she wonders as she peers out the window at the narrow, West Chicago street, with its rows and rows of identical, tiny one-story houses, cheaply built "starter homes" that most of the residents will also finish in. She thinks of the place where she'd grown up, the miles of flatland surrounding her; she thinks of Mrs. Glass House, with its spike-tipped fence and locked doors. And now . . . what is she? A housewife to Gary Gray, who she isn't even married to. A prisoner to her child, who doesn't even resemble her. She puts her hand to the glass of the window and it is cool, almost permeable.

The first time she had tried to kill herself, she had intuited that there was no escape. She had seen, with sudden clarity, that her life was a series of boxes, a maze that she would run and run through and never find an exit, and she had thought, almost peacefully, *I don't want it. I don't want my life.*

The first time she had tried to kill herself she was twenty-two years old. She had been living with Gary for over a year, and Jonah was eleven months, asleep in his crib. She sat in the bathroom, seeing things very clearly. She saw the long, impossible tangle of her life spread out before her, the stretch of meaningless decades that led to her death, however old she would be, and she rejected it. The edges of her life became clear to her. She saw that it was a tunnel she would have to walk through. There were no crossroads, no turns she could make that would change things, and she sat there on the toilet, naked, writing carefully, in very small, beautiful letters, in a notebook, the water for her bath running very hot. She wrote a note for Gary, apologizing, and then another note for Jonah, telling him that she loved him, that she would always love him, etcetera. It was very poetic, and she cried for a while, silently, so Gary wouldn't hear her. He was watching TV, dozing in his reclining chair, as she pressed the razor blade to her wrist. She could see the blue veins, embedded, marbled under the surface of her skin, but they seemed very far down. She pressed the razor and it cut a little, drawing blood, and then she pressed harder. Blood began to trickle down her palm, and she submerged her arm in the warm water.

That was okay, but then to cut the other wrist was harder. Her wounded hand felt weak when she raised it out of the water, and blood trickled down her fingers, spattering the floor. She sawed feebly at her other wrist, and though she broke the skin she didn't seem to be capable of cutting through to the vein. Blood ran down her left hand, eddying through the water of the bath, smearing her palms and forearms and the razor itself. She was weeping distractedly, with frustration.

She couldn't do it. She remembers Gary startling up out of his easy chair, his gaping face as she'd stumbled out of the bathroom door into the hallway, naked, her hands raised above her head, blood running down her biceps and into her underarm. Blood everywhere. "Help me," she'd gasped, in her weakness. "I don't want to. I changed my mind." It could have been almost comic, she thought. The stupefied look on his face, her own ridiculous, childish cowardice. And then there had been the ambulance, the hospital.

There is so much to regret in this. In this memory, in this failure. She has tried very hard not to think of it, but the truth is that the wish to be dead hasn't left her, it has only become more distant and unattainable. She feels it move again, very slow, inside her, as she sits there in the kitchen with Jonah and his swollen face. She lifts her cigarette from the ashtray and it trembles as she tries to put it to her mouth, as if it is afraid of her.

And then, from the living room, a woman's voice speaks. "There are a lot of trees out there," the woman says, her voice uninflected, matter-of-fact. Her mother's voice, she thinks.

It is not the first time she has imagined hearing her mother's voice, but it has never been so clear, so real. She actually gets up and goes to the edge of the living room, half expecting to see, what? A ghost?

But there is nothing. Just the sad living room, with its sofa facing away from the window, toward the television. The lamp. The silent television itself. The end table piled with library books she hasn't been able to read—the words reconfiguring themselves into gibberish after a few paragraphs. No one is there, though she can feel something watching, listening.

She knows she has heard her mother's voice.

Her mother had been a young woman when she died, Nora realized now. Only thirty-six—a car accident, they said. But she comprehends her mother's message clearly. Out on the edge of the sandhills there were very few trees, but somehow her mother had managed to send a car directly into one, going perhaps seventy or eighty miles an hour. Her father said that she'd lost control of the car. Maybe she'd gotten distracted, or swerved to miss a dog. But Nora understands what her mother's message means. What she has always known in her heart.

There are a lot of trees out there, her mother had said, encouragingly.

This is perhaps the last thing she remembers clearly about her days in Chicago. That morning after she'd hit Jonah, that morning when her mother spoke to her. Years later, she will try to piece together what had happened to her—the entire month of August 1974 will have vanished, she won't know where. Once, she will even recklessly try to call Gary Gray, to ask him about it. What happened? But by that time, Gary will no longer be living in Chicago, and when she dials their old number an elderly woman will answer, who has never heard of Gary.

All that will be left to her will be the small fragments of images—a nest of wet, dappled lights, honking at her like cars; small objects—silverware, pencils, cigarettes—that leap away from her like tiny animals when she tries to touch them; that heavy shape, something inanimate like a desk or a couch, moving slowly in the dark house, the long, wet, dragging sound it made.

She will wake in a hospital in South Dakota, in Yankton. The South Dakota Human Services Center, it is called now, though she knew from childhood what it meant when people said someone got "shipped off to Yankton." The old Victorian building had once been known as the Dakota Hospital for the Insane, and that will be where she will reappear, as if materializing out of a mist. She will learn that this place is where her father had put her, when Gary Gray had given up on her and called him.

At last, on a day in late November, he will come to fetch her. To take her "home," back to the house she'd left years ago. She will forever after remember him standing there, his pale blue eyes deep with sorrow, holding Jonah by the hand.

"Come stay at home for a while, babygirl," he says softly, and she knows, looking at the two of them, her father and her child, that she will never get away. She will never, ever leave Little Bow again.

20

October 20, 1996

Here is the drug education class, week six: a junior high classroom, ten people, adults, slumped uncomfortably into desks that feel too small, the blackboard still chalked with Friday's seventh-grade social studies homework assignment. It's nine o'clock on a Sunday morning. Outdoors is a gray half-light that could be dawn or dusk, punctuated by a distracting wind that sends leaves and bits of paper into whirlwinds in the brick corners of the buildings, a dull wheeze of debris.

They sit as far apart from one another as possible. Eight men, two women, spread out in the room like dots on a map, with no roads in between. Troy bends his head, tracing his fingers along the words that some bored teenager had carved into the worn wood of the desktop—*Mr. Strunk Eats Own Bugers*—and it is followed by a series of hashmarks, apparently counting each time this act was witnessed. In the front of the room a plump man in a polo shirt and pleated slacks is talking about how he nearly lost his life due to cocaine addiction. He is wearing loafers with little tassels on them, and no socks. Troy runs his fingernail along the furrows of letters until his cuticles ache.

At least there is no one here he knows. That would be terrible—to have to sit here with one of his former customers, thinking that this was someone he had aided and abetted down their trail of addiction, someone he had wronged. But this ragged group isn't the kind of client pool that he drew from—they are much worse off than anyone he ever dealt with, and he is glad that he can slip into anonymity while he sits here. Just another sad victim of a *disease*, as they learn over and over. *Drug addiction is a disease.* An illness, a mental illness, that they are battling together.

He knows what they are talking about, of course. He has seen movies that portray the pain of withdrawal—heroin junkies strapped to beds and howling, alcoholics twitching with delirium seizures, speed freaks skeletal and soaked in their own sweat. He remembers how bad Bruce and Michelle had gotten, in those last years before they were arrested—dilated eyes, restless pacing, sudden outbursts of irritation, the expensive stereo equipment and coin collector morsels bought on a whim and then sold, abruptly. He remembers the hard time Carla had when she was pregnant with Loomis, how she had given up everything—all but the occasional beers or joint—and how quickly, after Loomis was born, she'd gone back to partying. It was as if those nine months of semi-sobriety had frightened her, as if she'd realized with a shock that she'd almost lost her true love. She returned to drinking and smoking pot, to weekend indulgence in crank or cocaine, with a ferocity that had at first excited him in its recklessness. She was so certain they could happily raise a child and still have a "good time," and Loomis himself had been so easy and undemanding—passing from person to person at a party, sleeping peacefully through loud music and laughter, as subdued as they were on hungover mornings—that at first he hadn't worried. She was so much fun, so sexy, that it wasn't until much later that he realized how much further into things she was than he. It wasn't until the very end that he found out that she was now more than occasionally smoking crack, that she was sleeping with some guy, an acquaintance of theirs, who ran a meth lab up in Barrytown.

He thinks of this again, as the plump former cokehead pauses, with a hitch in his voice. "I destroyed my life," the cokehead says, and Troy frowns. He had discovered, in those last years with Carla, that he didn't really have the stamina for addiction, and he is aware now, sitting here in the drug education class, that he has never personally been desperate for a fix in the way these people must be. It makes him feel like a fraud to be among them. When the speaker talks about "drug pushers," about "enablers," he lowers his head, blushing.

His is a different sort of addiction. Despite his self-justifications, despite the fact that his customers always seemed like normal people, he can't help but think that he also played on their vulnerabilities. He hadn't liked getting high half as much as he'd liked helping people to get high; he liked watching other people get out of control, and he'd liked this about Carla especially—he remembers betting people that she could drink them under the table, he remembers helping her score a hit of this or that drug that she wanted to try, he remembers those brief moments when an uncertainty would darken her expression and he would smile and shrug. *Why not? Go for it.* And he feels again that he deserves every bad thing that has happened to him.

Standing in the parking lot of the school, as they all drift to their cars after class, this thought lingers with him. *Drug Pusher,* he thinks, as he settles into the seat of his drug-money Corvette. He tries to reassure himself—he never hurt anyone, he thinks, but now a small wedge of doubt filters in, and he prods it. In the distance, beyond the bleachers of the football field, a motorcycle is buzzing along the street, and he wonders if this might be Ray, riding along on Troy's old motorcycle. "You might as well take it," Troy had told him, after he was arrested. "Get some use out of it. I won't be doing any biking for a while." He listens to the toothy, metallic buzz disappearing into the windy corridor of house-lined blocks, and then he puts his key into the ignition.

The last time he'd talked to Ray had been in early September. Ray had come by the house, fairly stoned, and he'd just let himself in, as he was used to doing. Troy was sitting in the living room, playing Tetris on an old Nintendo system that he'd plugged into the TV, when he'd heard Ray's voice from the darkened kitchen. "Troy!"—whispering loudly—"Hey, man! It's me!" And Troy came into the kitchen to find Ray bent over the sink, drinking water from the faucet.

"What are you doing?" Troy said, and Ray lifted his head from the stream of the tap.

"I'm thirsty," Ray said. He stood up, wobbling a little, leaning against the counter for balance, and his eyes crinkled into a cheerful, half-moon squint. "Hey," he said, affectionately.

"Hey," Troy said, and he cleared his throat, watching as Ray fumbled in his jacket pocket and brought out a joint.

"Don't light that," Troy said.

Ray hesitated, as if Troy were joking. Then he seemed to understand. "Oh shit!" he grinned. "I almost forgot. I'm like in the police zone here." He glanced up at the ceiling. "Do they have, like, cameras in here?"

"No," Troy said, and didn't smile. He folded his arms over his chest. No one would know Ray was here, probably—Ray wasn't under surveillance—but it still made him nervous. "So," he said, a bit stiffly. "What's up?"

"Aw, man," Ray said. "I just came by to visit, that's all. You look like shit." Troy was standing there in his boxer shorts, and Ray took a moment to appraise him, his eyes tracing grimly down as if to confirm his judgment, and at last resting on the parole anklet. He grimaced, as if looking at a deformity. "Oh, man," he said, softly. "This is horrible. They've got a machine attached to you, dude."

"Yeah," Troy said. "I know."

"Oh, man," Ray said. "Jesus Christ," and when he lifted his head his eyes had grown heavy and moist. "Troy," he said. "Can I give you a hug?"

Troy shrugged, then stood there, a bit rigid, as Ray wrapped his lanky, bench-pressed arms around his shoulders, squeezing tight. "I know I shouldn't be here," Ray said. "But I miss you. I miss you a lot, man.

"You've been on my mind a lot lately, you know?" Ray said. "That's what I've been wanting to tell you. You, like, raised me. After Dad went to jail and Mom married Merit, there wasn't anyone in the world I could count on except you." He stepped back, putting his fingertips to his eyes, rubbing them hard. "Jesus," he said. "This sucks! I can't believe it. I mean, you're like my best friend, man, and now . . . I mean, it's going to be years before we can party together again." And then he stood there for a moment, regaining himself. "I hate this government," he said. "This is like Nazi Germany. That they can put . . . some kind of dog collar on a human being!"

They stared at each other for a moment, and finally, Troy shrugged, uncertainly.

"It's not that bad," he said, at last. "It's not a big deal."

Ray looked at him doubtfully and shook his head, backing against the edge of the sink. His face pinched earnestly, and Troy found himself thinking of Ray as a child—Ray, the toddler he'd once baby-sat for, all those years ago, in Bruce and Michelle's trailer. He thought of that hopeful, yearning, worshipful gaze as Troy had read him a story. *Goodnight, Moon.*

"Look," Troy said. "It's not the end of the world. Maybe it's time for me to . . . I don't know. Move in a different direction."

"I hope you're right," Ray said. He hung his head for a time, in the way people do when they come to the end of a prayer, or a confession.

"I had another reason for coming here," he said. He lifted his eyes to Troy's face, and then carefully drew out a roll of paper money from his pocket. "I've been making a lot," he said. "I know that you think that the stripping stuff is ridiculous, but I've been making a lot of money. And . . ."

He paused for a moment, trying to find a man-to-man expression. "Actually, I actually have to tell you. I guess you probably figured that I took the money and . . . the rest of the shit . . . when the cops showed up. Me and Mike Hawk. We, like, jumped the fence, and ran out into the hills. Jesus! I don't think I've ever been so scared in my entire life. And then, you know, we had all these great drugs . . ."

"Let's not talk about that," Troy said, and his heart sank suddenly in a flutter of paranoia, as if the monitor on his anklet might be recording something. "Let's just drop the subject."

"Okay," Ray said, but he didn't seem to really understand. "Troy—man!" he said. "I'm not trying to fuck with you, but you have no idea how good this stuff is. It's amazing. I mean, I have to confess to you that I've just been selling it a little at a time, and kind of mixing it with some of the cheaper stuff that I can get from the connections that I have—and I'm being totally careful! But what I wanted to say was that I want to cut you in on it, because you know, it's really yours."

Troy didn't say anything for a long time. It was so obviously stupid that it seemed like a cruel joke, but Ray seemed unaware. He just stood there, cautiously offering Troy a wad of folded-over bills, and Troy had to resist the urge to slap the money out of Ray's hands. He imagined some melodramatic gesture, in a moment of adrenaline—snatching the money from Ray's hand and burning it, or stuffing it down the garbage disposal. But instead the two of them merely stood there facing each other.

"Ray," Troy said at last, "are you out of your mind? I'm on parole, man. I'm not even sure I'm going to be able to keep my kid. And you want to give me a down payment on some weed that you stole from me?"

"I didn't steal it!" Ray exclaimed. "I was doing you a favor! I mean, that's what I meant to do!"

"Well," Troy said, his voice rising sharply. "Do me another favor, and don't try to give me drug money. What are you thinking? Do you want us both to go to prison?" He stood there, red in the face, his teeth set, his muscles tightening. "Are you some kind of idiot?" he said.

Ray stared at him, wide-eyed, and then, abruptly, without warning, tears began leaking down his face. He closed one hand over the wad of money, and put the palm of the other over his face.

"I'm sorry," Ray said, and Troy felt himself shrinking, his arms folded, his hands tightening on the flesh of his upper arms. He was the one who should be sorry. *You, like, raised me,* Troy thought, flinching under the weight of Ray's sad eyes. They both stood there, looking at the floor. "I'm sorry," Ray said. "I'm really sorry."

That was the last time he talked to Ray. It's been a month and a half now, and as he spills from the junior high school parking lot onto the road toward home, he has half a mind to call Ray when he gets back. To apologize, maybe. To explain about drug pushers and enablers, to explain the mistakes he's made in his life. It wouldn't be illegal, he thinks. They can't stop him from talking to his own cousin. But he's also afraid. If Ray is selling drugs now, it might be a way for them to keep him from Loomis for even longer.

By the time he's back at home, he's feeling too depressed to call anyone. It's eleven o'clock on a Sunday morning, and all he wants to do is get back into bed. The weather is starting to get cold. He sits in the bedroom, takes off his shoes and socks, peels off his shirt. He turns on the little space heater, plugs in the electric blanket. He burrows under the covers, closing his eyes tight against the pale sunlight that slants in through the blinds. Sometimes he believes he's been instrumental in screwing up the lives of all the people he's loved—Ray, Carla, Loomis. Sometimes he thinks that if he could only trace the path of his life carefully enough, everything would become clear. The ways that he screwed up would make sense. He closes his eyes tightly. His life wasn't always a mistake, he thinks, and he breathes uncertainly for a while, trying to find a pathway into unconsciousness, into sleep.

But instead there are memories. Unfortunately. Prodding him. He follows a line from Ray, back through Carla, back through Bruce and Michelle and their trailer, back into all the old stuff. His mother, his father, his childhood, all the little details he hasn't thought about in years. Suddenly they are present, and he is aware of that distant recollection of contentment wafting over him as he closes his eyes.

He finds himself thinking of his old family—he thinks of climbing into bed between his parents on Sunday mornings, his mom and dad murmuring sleepily as he slipped under the covers at their feet and burrowed his way in between them. He thinks of sitting on the couch, watching TV, how his mother would put her arm around him and her leg over his father's lap, all of them tangled together under an afghan spread, or together in a tent, when they used to go camping, their three sleeping bags side by side.

They had all seemed so happy. He can remember those weekends at the lake so clearly—gathering wood for a fire, swimming, climbing onto his father out in the water, his bare feet slipping against his father's skin. Diving off his father's shoulders. At night, the three of them would wade along the edge of the shore, catching crawdads.

There was something, some magic, about the way the flashlight's beam made a bowl of light beneath the water, the way, under the beam, everything was clear and distinct—the bits of floating algae and minute water animals, the polished stones and sleepy minnows flashing silver, the crawdads sidling backward with their claws lifted like pistols. His parents were silhouettes against the slick, blue-black skin of the lake, and Troy was aware that the sky and the lake were both like deep water, depth upon depth.

At that moment, he had loved the world so much that it almost ached; he had loved his young mother and father with a kind of fierceness that he could feel in his muscles. His mother would enfold him in a towel, drying him, her nose brushing against his hair. Smelling him. His father, smiling, looking at the two of them, carefully setting another piece of wood on the fire, his face alit and noble and full of a stern, kingly pride.

Even now, after all these years, he still can't understand why they'd gotten divorced. For such moments to exist, and then to vanish seemed impossible, and he certainly couldn't fathom it when he was eleven, when he and his mother finally moved out of the house. Back then, he was certain that his parents would get back together eventually—how could it be that people who had experienced such happiness wouldn't want to return to it?

He remembers when he was thirteen, when his mother got married again, he still firmly believed that it was only a passing phase. His mother's new husband was a gentle, boring man named Terry Shoopman, a balding high school guidance counselor with a foreshortened, potbellied torso and incredibly long, spindly legs, and Troy couldn't imagine that it would last between them. He watched with skepticism as Terry moved in, ignoring his presence for the most part, weathering it.

A year later, when he was fourteen, Troy was still expecting things to go back to normal. Then Terry had gotten a job in Bismarck. Troy had refused to go, despite his mother's cajoling and promises. She wouldn't be able to stay away for long, he thought. He had moved back in with his father then, though the truth was he had begun to spend almost all his free hours at Bruce and Michelle's trailer, by that time smoking a lot of pot along with Bruce and Michelle and their parade of teenagers, while he waited for his mother to give up on Bismarck, to tire of Terry Shoopman and come to her senses. To come home.

He probably should have gone with her. Sometimes, thinking back, he is aware that he would have been better off. His father's drinking had grown quietly worse, more involved and ritualized, starting shortly after dinner and continuing, with steady determination, until he passed out. Meanwhile, Bruce and Michelle had begun to lose themselves to cocaine.

It wasn't until much later, not until after he'd been arrested and sober for several months, that he understood the sort of quiet, steady life that Terry had offered his mother. And he was aware that she had made a choice. She had let him go—had taken her own chance for happiness and comfort. He would have made her miserable, if she'd insisted that he come with her.

Back then, though, he thought she'd done him a favor to let him stay in St. Bonaventure, to let him settle into the life of a resourceful, unsupervised teenage boy. Back then he'd dreaded his visits to Bismarck, that anonymous bedroom they prepared for him: bed, dresser, desk, the pictures of sailboats on the walls, the books that some son of his mother and Terry might have read: *Treasure Island* and *The Flora and Fauna of North America* and *Jonathan Livingston Seagull*. At least they had cable TV.

Years later, when his father died—his heart finally, steadily poisoned by years of alcohol and cigarettes and self-pity—Troy probably should have gone back up to Bismarck with his mother. But he was twenty years old. He had started to date Carla. He told his mother that he was planning to go to college, or trade school, or maybe the military, but the truth was that he had taken over a large part of Bruce and Michelle's marijuana business—Bruce was in prison and Michelle was dating an odd, wealthy old man named Merit Wilkins, thirty years her senior, and moving to Arizona.

And then he'd married Carla. They lived on in his dad's old house, the house he'd grown up in, and there were wonderful, invigorating parties. Ray, aged fifteen, had run away from the place in Arizona where he'd lived with Michelle and Merit Wilkins, and he stayed with Troy and Carla, sleeping on the couch and irregularly attending high school in St. Bonaventure. It was another little family, Troy thought for a while, and shortly before Carla found out she was pregnant with Loomis, they even took a camping trip together, Troy and Carla and Ray. He'd made them wade around looking for crawdads with a flashlight.

But it wasn't real in the same way. Even after Loomis was born, it didn't feel as natural as it had when he himself was a little kid. His mother wasn't coming back—she couldn't come back now, of course—and when she, too, died, she hadn't yet had the chance to drive down to Nebraska to see Loomis. She'd only seen him in pictures.

They'd behaved badly at the funeral, he remembers. He and Carla and Ray, all of them stoned throughout the whole thing; the fourteen-month-old Loomis, solemn and intelligent even then, sat in the crook of Carla's arm as they toked up in the car outside the funeral home. The smell of marijuana must have wafted off them as they promenaded slowly past his mother's corpse in its casket, as they sat in the pew and listened to the preacher. He dully greeted a few of his old aunts and uncles, faces from his parents' long-gone parties, now scattered, now strangers. They went back to the house where his mother had lived out the last decade of her life with Terry Shoopman, and ate from relish trays of raw vegetables and dip, casseroles and cold fried chicken, pies and cakes. They sat together in a little cluster, he and Carla and Ray, talking about the idiotic things stoned people talk about, and when Terry Shoopman had come up and clutched Troy in a hug, he had seen Carla and Ray widening their eyes ironically from beyond Terry's shoulder. Terry had called Troy "son," and held Loomis tenderly.

"I still want to be a grandfather to this child," Terry had said, wet-eyed. "I hope you know that. I loved your mother very much. She was a very special lady."

For several years, Terry Shoopman had continued to send Loomis presents on his birthday and at Christmas. He had even called a few times. "Why don't you come up and visit me?" he'd said. "I'd love to see Loomis." And he had tried to remind Troy of the "fun" they'd once had, when Troy, as a teenager, used to spend Christmas or summer months with his mother and Terry in Bismarck. The truth was, Troy hardly remembered those times, he'd been so stoned; and after a while, after a few gentle rebuffs, Terry stopped calling, stopped sending cards and presents. Troy hoped that Terry had found another woman. Though he'd never wanted Terry as a stepfather, he didn't wish him ill.

His memory tunnels through these paths as he dozes under his mother's comforter, his mind a slow-moving dune. He opens his eyes long enough to see that it is after four in the afternoon, and then he is dreaming again, going over and over his own history. He can clearly see the places where he might have changed things, where he might have done a better job making his life, though most of those paths also lead away from Loomis's existence, and he can't bear that. Loomis, he thinks, is the one good thing he's done in his life.

As for the rest, he doesn't know. Can someone help him? He could call Michelle, in Arizona. She's forty-four now, she might have something wise to say, as she walks the golf courses with her wealthy husband; he could call Bruce, who is still in prison, denied parole after attacking another inmate; he could call Terry Shoopman, or one of the various relatives he once knew as a child—the aunts and uncles, the cousins he once played with on those long-ago childhood nights, to whom he hasn't spoken in years. But there is no real connection left, and he is aware that he is not even held to them by blood. He is the one who was adopted. His mother and father pulled him into their families, but now that they are dead, what remains? There is only Carla, who has left him; and Loomis, who has been taken away; and Ray, gone now, too, banished. *Get out, you moron,* he'd said.

He opens his eyes again, rubbing his bare feet against each other. God, God, God, he thinks, and lying there, he can picture his mother's body in the casket. She didn't really look like herself, and when Troy touched her hands they were as weightless as husks. They moved easily out of their folded position across her chest. He thought they'd be stiff, frozen into place, but in fact they were like dry branches and when he tried to press them back into their prayerful position they slipped farther astray. They hovered above each other as if they were trying to clasp something to her chest, and he had to ask the mortician for help. "I screwed up my mom's hands," he said, stoned out of his mind. "I'm sorry." He didn't cry for her until much later.

21

October 20, 1996

Even though it's almost sunset, Troy has to get out of bed to answer the doorbell. He hasn't been asleep, exactly, but he hasn't been quite willing to get up either. What is there to do, after all? Make coffee, this late in the day? Find something to eat? Watch TV? Continue to contemplate the unchangeable mistakes he's made?

But when the bell rings a second time, he finally slides himself out from under the covers.

He looks terrible, he knows—shirtless, barefoot, wearing only a pair of sweatpants, his eyes bleary with unsustained sleep, hair standing up in stiff tufts. He sees himself in the mirror that hangs by the doorway, tries to pat his hair down a bit as the doorbell bongs its three descending notes again. "Screw it," he whispers to his drawn, bleary face, and turns to throw open the front door.

It's Jonah—Jonah from work.

They both stand there, hesitantly. Jonah is holding a grocery bag in each hand. "Hey," he says, as if he is surprised that Troy has appeared at the door. "How's it going?" he says.

"Hey," Troy repeats, and then they are silent again. The chill wind ripples Jonah's hair and loose jacket as he stands there, and Troy crosses his arms tightly across his bare chest.

"I thought you might need some groceries," Jonah says at last.

"Some groceries?" Troy says. He tries to take this in, but can't quite gather what Jonah's getting at. It has the quality, he thinks, of some very dry-witted practical joke, and he feels himself wavering at the edge of a punch line. "You brought me food," he says. "From the supermarket."

"Yeah," Jonah says, and he gives the bags a little lift, to demonstrate. "I was going to, just, like, leave the bags on the . . . doorstep. But then I was worried that, you know, some animals or something would get into it. So."

"Okay . . ." Troy says, and raises his eyebrows. "And you're leaving food on my doorstep because . . . ?"

"Well," Jonah says, and looks helplessly down at the two bags as if he's handcuffed to them. "I wanted to make myself useful, I guess." Another gust of wind bursts across them, fierce, bending the heads of the trees and sending the leaves into a flutter of birdlike uproar and alarm.

"Dang," Troy says, flinching at the chill. "Listen, man, why don't you . . . Just come in, okay? Let me close this door before I freeze to death."

Jonah stands nervously in the living room while Troy slams the door shut on the weather. When Troy turns back to look at him he is red in the face, blushing noticeably, the long scar that runs from his eye to the edge of his mouth paler and more prominent.

"I hope I'm not . . . intruding," Jonah says. "I feel like this was a really stupid idea."

But Troy only shrugs. He finds a half-clean T-shirt draped over the couch and pulls it on with a shudder. The transition from the sleepy, overheated bedroom to the icy winds on the porch has left his mind and body in a little state of shock, and he peers at Jonah, slow-blinking. "So . . ." Troy says. "What's up?"

"I don't know," Jonah says, and then seems to consider. "I feel really stupid. It was just—I don't know, I was talking to Crystal. And she was saying how she was worried about you, and she didn't know how you were able to even do simple things like go out and get groceries with the . . . the house arrest. And so I was out in the supermarket, and, so. I bought some food. I mean, I thought it might help you."

They look at each other.

"Crystal's kind of a fricking busybody, don't you think?" Troy says.

"Well," Jonah says. "Not necessarily." He stands there, still holding the two sacks in a posture that seems both hopeful and resigned to failure. What do you do with such a person? Troy wonders. What do you say? He has heard the story of Jonah's life—from Crystal, of course—all about the car accident. Jonah and his wife, eight months pregnant, driving on the expressway in Chicago, on their way to a movie. The semi-truck, boxing them in and then suddenly veering out of control, the crunch of metal, the sound of the wife screaming. He had found himself picturing it vividly, and now looking at the scars on Jonah's hands, Troy can't help but think of these images again. Here is a guy whose life has been even worse than Troy's own, and it's hard to be rude to him.

"Well, anyways," Troy says, after a pause. "Come on in the kitchen. Let's see what you've got there."

They don't say anything as Jonah sets the bags on the kitchen table. Troy glances at the stack of dirty dishes in the sink, the visible balls of dust that have collected at the bottom of the kitchen counters, the unsent letter to Mrs. Keene still propped between the salt and pepper shakers on the table. Yes, he thinks. It is the house of someone whose life is falling apart, the sort of person you'd bring charity groceries to.

"I don't want to seem like a jerk, or anything," Jonah says.

"Don't worry about it," Troy says.

"I mean, I didn't know what you really needed, so I just thought . . ."

"I appreciate the gesture."

"I thought you might like some bread . . . and cheese . . . and some lunch meat . . . and maybe, like, a cantaloupe?"

"Okay," Troy says.

"I bought a six-pack of beer, but I don't know whether you can drink it."

"Not really," Troy says. "That's probably not a good idea."

"So . . . I also bought some soda? Coke?"

And Troy sighs, softly.

"Coke is great," he says. "That's fine."

They are sitting at the kitchen table, with the food laid out between them like some complicated puzzle. Troy finds glasses and some plates, and a jar of mayonnaise in the refrigerator, then sits down across from Jonah, both of them shyly quiet, concentrating on their work, as they make sandwiches. Troy pours a Coke over the ice in his glass, and Jonah opens a beer.

"You know," Troy says, "I know that Crystal means well, but I really wish that . . ."

"It's my fault," Jonah says. "I'm sorry. It was a really dumb thing to do."

"That's not what I meant."

"I understand what you mean," Jonah says. He smiles apologetically at his sandwich before biting it. "But I'm not doing it because of that. I . . . just wanted to be friendly. You seem like a cool guy. And . . . I don't have a very easy time getting to know people."

And Troy isn't sure what to say to this. "Okay," he says at last, watching as Jonah takes another cautious bite of bread. It's strange to be sitting here with someone, after all the time he's spent alone. Jonah is the first person who's been in Troy's kitchen since he kicked Ray out, a month and a half ago, and despite the guy's edginess, it's not a bad feeling. Troy has spent a lot of time at this kitchen table—laughing it up with his customers, playing cards with Ray, eating cereal with Loomis in the morning—and he can feel the remnants of these old comforts hovering in the back of his mind.

"So," Troy says, after the silence has extended for a while. "You're from Chicago, right?"

"Yes," Jonah says.

"Is that where you're from originally?"

"Um," Jonah says. "Sort of. More or less." He shifts a little, regarding his sandwich. "Actually," he says, "I spent part of my childhood in South Dakota. Just a little small town."

"Ah," Troy says. "So you're used to this kind of small-town shit."

"Kind of, I guess."

"It's not that bad, I suppose," Troy says. "You get used to people, and it's comfortable. Not as hectic as Chicago, I imagine. Personally, I've never been east of Omaha."

"Oh, really," Jonah says, and Troy notices how his expression seems to tighten, focusing. "Didn't you—" he says. "Did you ever want to? Travel around or anything?"

"Oh, I don't know," Troy says. "Maybe at one point, I guess. But, you know. I had a kid, and all my family is from around here, and all that. And now . . . well, you've heard the story from Crystal. I would've liked to go to college, I think."

Jonah gives him another sharpened look. "Oh, really?" he says. "To do what?"

"I don't know," Troy says. He shrugs bashfully, thinking of his conversation with Ray, months ago, the skeptical look on Ray's face. "I thought about something like . . . commercial art? I didn't get very far into considering it, to be honest." He clears his throat. "But I guess you've been to college, yourself. That's what Crystal the busybody says, anyway."

Jonah wrinkles his nose. "Oh," he says. "Not really. I just, I took a few classes, here and there. You know. Just basic liberal arts stuff—American lit, history, math. Nothing very . . . focused."

"Uh-huh," Troy says. He's impressed by the way Jonah says "liberal arts," so easily—as if they both understand exactly what that means. "Lit" means "literature," Troy thinks, and he likes the sound of it. *American lit. Liberal arts.* He tries to picture what it would be like to go to college in Chicago, but all he can think of is a postcard one of his former customers had sent him of the John Hancock Building, with the antennae sticking up from its roof like two horns.

"So," Troy says. "Do you think you'll ever go back?"

"To Chicago?"

"To college."

"Probably not," Jonah says. He looks down at his hand, and Troy watches as he traces the pad of a fingertip along the upraised furrow of a scar, a rivulet that runs from wrist to knuckle. "I don't think I really have the . . . aptitude for it. I like the learning part of it. It's just . . . you know, the tests, and going to classes all the time, and that stuff. And besides, the things I'm interested in aren't actually going to be worth anything. Prehistoric civilizations? Or film appreciation? Or theories of mathematics? That's the kind of stuff I liked, and it's not going to be something to put on a résumé."

"Yeah," Troy says. "But then again, who cares, so long as it's interesting to you? If you like learning about it, isn't that all that matters?"

"Well . . . it does cost a lot of money."

Troy sighs. He's curious, he guesses; there's something foreign and vaguely romantic about the idea of a classroom full of students and an old professor expounding on something like "film appreciation," or "prehistoric civilizations." He can imagine great, arcane swaths of knowledge that he's never even heard about. "Okay," he says. "Tell me one piece of totally useless information that you learned." He smiles, and when Jonah rolls his shoulders sheepishly, he reaches over and pours him a little more beer. "Come on," he says, "take a drink and tell me something, college guy. I'm interested."

"All right," Jonah says. He draws on the beer, and for a moment it seems that there is a glint in Jonah's gray, flickery eyes that makes Troy feel as if they met a long time ago. "Okay," he says, at last. "Here's one," and he intones as if reciting. "The Swedish mathematician Helge von Koch hypothesized that an infinitely long line surrounded a finite area."

"Huh," Troy says, and he chuckles a little, because it is totally incomprehensible. "Do you understand what you just said?"

"I guess so," Jonah says, and he gives a little shrug, shy but proud. There's that glint in his eye again, which makes Troy think of the way Loomis looks when he knows an answer to a hard question. "I mean," Jonah says, "it's easier if you see it on paper. It's kind of like, you know how in grade school you made those snowflakes out of construction paper? You fold the paper up into a four, or an eight, and then you start to make jagged edges around it. You can keep making it lacier and lacier, and if you had the right tools, microscopic tools or whatever, you could go on making it more and more intricate. It could go on forever, that's the thing, because things can get smaller into infinity. Like you cut down to a molecule. And then you cut that down into an atom. And then you cut the atom into the particles that are smaller than an atom. And so on. So if you stretch out the edges around the snowflake into a straight line, it would potentially go on into infinity. Therefore."

"I get it," Troy says, pleased. "An infinitely long line surrounds a finite area. I can see that, sort of. It's kind of like one of those puzzles. Like one of those mind benders. Optical illusions. Right?"

"A little," Jonah says. And then he's silent. "I mean, it's abstract. You can't actually see something that's infinite, so it's just a puzzle in your mind." There's something in his solemn, calmly satisfied expression that makes Troy think of Loomis again. "It's interesting, though," he says. "To me."

Troy can't help but feel empathy for the guy. Jonah's life could have been something different, he thinks, if it hadn't been for that car accident. He can picture Jonah's wife: She wouldn't have been very attractive, Troy imagines, probably fat, but sharp and serious in her thoughts, the total opposite of Carla, and he thinks that they would have had a girl, a beautiful child. And Jonah would have finished college, and even if there weren't specific, practical applications to what he studied, the degree itself would have taken him somewhere. Something with computers, maybe, or a job at a library. And they would have had a happy life. He can imagine them all living in Chicago—in an apartment of some kind, with a coffee shop nearby, and they would push their daughter's stroller through some large city park, while Jonah talked about film, or math, or something else like that, and his plump long-haired wife looked at him with gentle admiration.

All of this comes vividly into his mind as they sit there, he and Jonah. He peers down, tenderly, upon his image of Jonah's happy family—and then his thoughts alight briefly on his own childhood, on his own mother and father and him at the lake, and finally on the life he should have provided for Loomis, if he and Carla had been different people, if they'd been able to overcome themselves.

"So, Jonah," he says at last, and tries to pinch off this last image.

"Be honest with me, man. What are you doing in St. Bonaventure? I mean really?"

He is surprised, even a bit taken aback, by how quickly Jonah looks up at this question. Jonah's mouth tightens, and something behind his eyes seems to flash.

"What do you mean?" he says.

"I don't mean anything negative," Troy says. "It's just, what are you? Twenty-three years old?"

"Twenty-five."

"Same difference," Troy says. "All I'm saying is that you're not going to want to work as a cook at the Stumble Inn for the rest of your life, right?" Troy pauses, purses his lips. "Don't you think you could do better for yourself?"

"I don't know," Jonah says, and his voice is a little brittle. "I like cooking for the Stumble Inn." He glances toward the dirty dishes in the sink, toward the black itinerary open on the counter. "Do you think you could do better for *your*self?" he says, softly.

"Ha," Troy says. "Not anymore, man. Maybe if I was twenty-five again, I would do things differently."

He's quiet then, embarrassed by his own self-pity. Because, of course, why should it be any harder for Troy to start his life over? Jonah has just lost his pregnant wife, his face is a mess of scars, his parents, according to Crystal, are dead. If anything, Troy thinks, Jonah's life has been harder than his own, and he feels a guilt settle over him. For some reason he thinks of his mother in her coffin, the way her stiff hands had come undone, his stupid, stoned efforts to put them back into place. He grimaces.

"I'm sorry," he says, after a moment. "You should do whatever makes you happy. I mean, if cooking at the good old Stumble University is what you want to do, more power to you."

Jonah looks at him inscrutably. His fingers touch the crust of uneaten sandwich, and Troy is surprised to see that the guy's hands are trembling.

"I'm looking for someone," he says.

"Uh-huh," Troy says, tentatively. "That's good." For a second he's aware of some unplaceable buzz in the air. "That's what you should be doing, man. You know, I know a lot of women. If you want, I could—"

"I mean," Jonah says, and he makes a sort of squint. "I mean, someone specific."

Troy watches Jonah's expression shift. The unscarred side of his face shudders a little, like the hide of a horse that is trying to shiver away a fly. Jonah tilts his head, leaning forward, and his hands tighten and then resolve themselves.

"I think we're brothers," Jonah says.

"Ha," Troy says. He tries to smile but an uncomfortable stiffness has settled over him. Jonah is shivering. His teeth actually chatter.

"I mean, really," Jonah breathes. "Your mom. Your biological mom. She's my mom, too."

And Troy feels his uneasy smile slip away.

22

October 13, 1996

It was a Sunday when they first met. It was the week before Jonah got up the nerve to go to Troy's house with the groceries. The weather was beginning to turn, and the wind ran in streams over everything, all day long. Tumbleweeds clogged the fences on the edges of town.

He'd found the street without any problem. Here it was, just a block away from the park. *Foxglove Road.* No doubt it was a pleasant place to live, Jonah thought, a quiet, curving little cul-de-sac with houses made to resemble English cottages, or so he imagined, each with bright-colored trim on the windows and eaves, with neat, yellowing lawns and fading flower beds, small statues of gnomes or fawns or the Virgin Mary. More tumbleweeds.

Jonah was sitting in his car when the boy and his grandmother came out, but they didn't glance his way. They continued down the sidewalk, the grandmother carrying a book and an unopened umbrella, a heavy woman, moving slowly. The child ran along in front of her, dashing and then, after a while, skipping, though with a thoughtful and even serious look on his face, as if skipping was a means of meditation.

There were other children in the park but not many adults. Jonah settled down in the chilly grass near some bare bushes, out of notice, but not enough to seem like he was hiding. He put his hood up and pretended to be bored, pretended that one of the milling children was his, that he was just another dutiful father. No one paid any attention: A pair of mothers talked avidly, sitting on the swings; Loomis's grandmother sat on a bench and bent her head toward her book.

As for Loomis, he was involved in some game of pretend. The other children held no interest for him, and he walked along the line of the play area, past the slides and bouncy horses and the monkey bars, his hands clasped behind his back, looking at the ground. He would occasionally say something to himself aloud. Jonah glanced over to where the grandmother was sitting. She wasn't paying attention.

Loomis was small for his age, Jonah thought, not skinny but compact, broad-shouldered, like a miniature adult. His hair was dirty blond and straight, and he had a round, solemn face. Jonah watched as he bent down and picked up something from the wood-chip playground bed—a piece of plastic, a forgotten toy. The child examined it, frowning, mumbled to himself. Then he put it in his pocket. He was about thirty yards from where Jonah was sitting, but drawing closer.

Jonah felt in his own pockets. A throat drop, a crumpled receipt from the pharmacy, a nub of pencil. And then: Here was the little rubber ball he'd picked up in the grass behind Troy's house, a bright Day-Glo orange superball that was made to bounce hard and high.

He looked over again toward the grandmother, at the mothers on the swings. And then, very carefully, he tossed the ball. It curved up, pinged against the trunk of a tree, and fell to the ground a few feet from Loomis.

The child's head turned, alert. Jonah watched as Loomis's eyes alit on the ball, watched as he walked cautiously toward it, as if it were a small strange animal that had fallen from a tree, stunned. Loomis stared at it, stroked his chin thoughtfully, then reached down to scoop it up.

"Loomis," Jonah said, in a short, husky voice. He kept his eye on the grandmother, but she didn't look up from her book. So he said it again, "Loomis," and the boy lifted his head sharply. They saw each other: Loomis's eyes fixed on him, wary and curious, and Jonah lifted his hand. He showed Loomis his palm, five fingers spread out. Then, deliberately, he got up and moved farther along the edge of the bushes, out of sight of the grandmother and the other adults, and the other children. And out of Loomis's sight as well.

After a moment Jonah heard the crunch of leaves. He was sitting in the dirt, half-hidden under the branches of a square-cut evergreen, his head down, his face shadowed. Loomis rounded the corner and peered at him.

"Hello, Loomis," Jonah said. He was very still, his sweatshirt hood pulled up, his hands resting on his knees—motionless, but prepared to hurry off if someone should notice him.

"How do you know my name?" Loomis said. He stood there, his eyebrows furrowed, nose wrinkled a little, his hands at his side like a cowboy about to draw pistols. Ready to run away.

"I just know." He spoke as if he didn't care whether Loomis came closer or not. "What are you doing? Are you solving a mystery?"

"I'm on a quest," Loomis said. "I'm looking for fossils."

"That's interesting," Jonah said. "Have you found any?"

"Not yet." Loomis took a step forward, then hesitated. "Are you a friend of my dad's?"

"Sort of," Jonah said. He shrugged, holding very still. "I'm sort of on a quest myself, if you want to know the truth."

Loomis considered this.

"What kind of quest?" Loomis said, angling himself so that he could get a look at Jonah's face. His mouth grew smaller.

"I'm looking for my brother," Jonah said at last. Why not? He dipped his hooded face, aware that Loomis was staring hard, uncertainly, at his scars. He brought his hands together, moving them with a slow, gentle, underwater drift, folding his palms together. "My mother had a baby before I was born," he said softly. "But she had to give him away. And now I'm looking for him."

Loomis frowned. "Why did she have to give the baby away?"

"She just had to," Jonah said. "She didn't have any choice."

Loomis narrowed his eyes thoughtfully. "Hmm," he said, at last, and Jonah took a quick glance to where the grandmother was still reading. "That sounds sort of like Moses," Loomis said. "His mother put him in a basket and into the river. Doesn't that sound dangerous?"

"A little," Jonah said. Loomis was looking at him seriously, an odd, stern little boy, his body still not relaxed. "Everything is dangerous in a certain way. But, well . . ." He was trying to pay attention to all of the elements at once. Here was the grandmother; here were the other adults, the screaming children; the slide and swings and merry-go-round spinning on its turnstile; here were the cars passing on the road in the distance behind him; here were the erratic movements of autumn leaves and branches. He groped in his mind: "But . . ." he said, "sometimes you have to take a risk. She put the baby in the river because she didn't have any other choice."

"It just doesn't seem like a good idea to me," Loomis said. "Couldn't you give the baby to a friend? Why would you put it in the river?"

"I don't know," Jonah said. He was struck by the image of his mother in the garb of the ancient Israelites, bending over the reedy, red-clay banks of a stream, the current drawing quivering lines in the water. "I guess people do things they regret." He considered.

"I think your father is my brother," he said.

He was surprised at how easily he was able to say this. After all the hand-wringing he'd done since he first came to St. Bonaventure, he found that it came out of his mouth without any of the doubts and second-guessing he'd been grappling with. It was just a fact.

"Do you know my dad?" Loomis said.

"Your dad is my brother," Jonah said. "I'm your uncle."

He expected, somehow, that this would have a greater impact than it did. Everything in his life had been leading to this moment. He pictured Loomis's eyes widening, a sudden rush of emotion, but Loomis only blinked, looking at him skeptically.

"Do you know my uncle Ray?"

And Jonah was silent, his heart beating. "I can't really tell you too much about it right now," Jonah said. He paused, thoughtfully. "I'm not sure if I can trust you to keep a secret."

"Oh," Loomis said. He seemed briefly taken aback by this. Jonah said nothing, just looked, very seriously, into Loomis's face.

"You don't want to get your dad into trouble, do you?" Jonah said.

"I can keep a secret," Loomis said, defensively. He paused, and for the first time turned to look over his shoulder, toward his grandmother. "Are you really my uncle?" he said.

"Yes," Jonah said.

Loomis stared at him dubiously.

"You have a scar on your face," he said.

"I know," Jonah said. "A dog bit me. When I was a little boy, about your age."

"Oh," Loomis said, and he seemed impressed and curious. He might have even come closer, but then in the distance, the grandmother lifted her head at last and looked around, scanning the playground. Jonah began to step backward, away.

"I'll talk to you again, maybe," Jonah said. "But only if you can keep a secret." He craned his neck, while the leaves disengaged themselves from the branches overhead. "You know, if you tell your grandma you saw me, your dad will get in a lot of trouble."

"I won't tell," Loomis said, softly. His face was pinched, solemn with worry, and he followed Jonah for a few steps as he walked into the shrubs and foliage. A leaf fell, and then another one, and Loomis stood there silently.

"Loomis!" the old woman called, and then, hesitantly, Loomis turned and walked back toward where she was sitting.

23

November 1996

Winter has arrived early this year. Temperatures have fallen abruptly, the little lakes and streams are frozen, there are storms and high winds all over the Midwest. Snow is coming down in Chicago, where Steve and Holiday are asleep, back to back, while their son Henry, now a toddler, sits up and stares at the blinking neon that pulses distantly beyond the closed curtains of his room; flakes melt against the window as Mrs. Orlova folds her hands against her breasts and frowns, waiting for a teakettle to boil in the darkened kitchen of her apartment; snow accumulates over the ditch in Iowa where Nora's ashes have settled, and on the South Dakota reservation where Jonah's grandmother's sister, Leona, lives, and on the yellow house he grew up in, now occupied by an earnest young evangelical couple and their children; on the edge of Little Bow, in the graveyard, fat, wet clumps of snow alight on the simple gravestone of Jonah's grandfather: JOSEPH DOYLE 1910–1984.

It is snowing in St. Bonaventure, Nebraska, as well. Ray the stripper is standing barefoot in the living room of a bachelorette party, undoing his shirt to the beat of rap music that blares from his boom box, a chilly sweat trickling down his back; and Junie, the former Stumble

Inn cook, opens his eyes briefly and fingers the plastic IV drip that has been inserted into his arm. The boy Jinx sleeps in his trailer with his little brother beside him in the bed, as his mother laughs at something on television in the living room. Police Officer Kevin Onken is cruising sleepily down empty streets, his windshield wipers flapping a slow metronome beat beneath the soft hush of his car's heater, and he perks up for a moment as the car carrying Jonah drifts by. Onken pays attention, watches the bright red radar numbers tick across the console. But Jonah isn't speeding. He keeps both hands on the wheel as he drives up Flock Road, along the contour of the park. The roads are slick. Jonah is cautious.

Crystal is just prescient enough to wake when she hears Jonah's old, rattling Festiva pass her house; her mind works in associations, and the distinctive sound of that car has lodged just firmly enough that she thinks *Jonah?* before settling back into the cushion of the couch, where she has fallen asleep.

Still, the ghost of him crosses through her subconscious: the shy slinking of his conversations, the radar of unspoken thoughts he had beamed out, some winking spark she couldn't quite catch.

She had been surprised at how abruptly he'd quit his job at the Stumble Inn. He'd seemed to be settling in fairly well by her estimation. He seemed to respond to Troy in particular.

But then, for no reason, he didn't show up for work.

"It just really concerns me," she said to Troy that afternoon, thinking that he might have some insight. "I honestly thought he was fitting in. Didn't you?"

But Troy only shrugged, moodily, his face growing unresponsive.

"Did he say anything to you?" she asked. "I didn't think he seemed unhappy here."

"I don't know anything about it," Troy said, and bent his head down to his crossword.

Crystal looked at him, sharply. "You guys didn't have an argument or something, did you?" she said, and he was silent, hesitant enough to confirm some event—disagreement? personality clash?—in her mind.

"Oh, Troy," she said. "He was a nice guy. What happened?"

"Nothing happened," Troy said, but she could feel the untruthfulness seeping out from him. "I hardly knew the guy."

"But didn't you feel bad for him?" Crystal said.

"Sure," Troy said. "Of course I felt bad for him. I feel bad for a lot of people." And then he moved off, abruptly, his back tight, out onto the barroom floor to straighten the chairs.

Vivian heard through the grapevine that Jonah had been hired as a cook by The Gold Coin. "That little shit," Vivian said, and Crystal lowered her eyes. "If he wanted more money he could have asked for it," Vivian said. "I don't appreciate that kind of behavior. Being left in the lurch like that. I guess he thought he was too good for us."

"I don't know," Crystal said, neutrally.

"I have half a mind to drive out to that banty-assed trailer of his and give him a piece of my mind," Vivian said. "I did him a favor, hiring him on the spot like that. I'll tell you, it goes to show what people are like in the world these days."

"Well," Crystal said, gently, "who knows what really happened?"

But Vivian wasn't a very forgiving person. She liked loyalty, and that was nearly all she liked about people. She had managed, over the years, to secure Crystal and Troy; and old Junie, the now-dying cook she had hoped Jonah would replace. There had been others, of course, workers who had stayed on for months or even years, but she resented them all, just as she resented Jonah, the little liar. That first day that he hadn't shown up for work, she had called him, and he'd feigned being sick.

"Oh," he'd said, when he recognized her voice. "Vivian. I was just about to call you. I've got a fever." And she was aware of the way he suddenly tried to make his voice sound frail. "I'm sorry I didn't call. . . . It was just, it really knocked me out. I've been practically delirious. I lost track of the time."

"This puts me in a bad situation," she said. "I've got a menu posted. What am I supposed to do with it?"

"I know," Jonah said hoarsely. "I'm . . . really sorry."

The next day, he called to say that he quit. He didn't even have the decency to come by. He just left a message on the bar's answering machine.

"This is Jonah Doyle," he said. His voice came out, boxy and full of static. "I'm just calling because . . . I wanted to let you know. I don't think I'll be able to come to work anymore. I . . . well." And then there was a long pause. "I'm sorry," he said. "Thank you for the opportunity to work at the Stumble Inn. I really appreciate it."

Vivian pressed the button marked "erase," very hard. But after a few weeks had passed, she didn't think too much about him, though she'd still look forward to catching him in the supermarket or someplace and telling him off.

Quitting his job at the Stumble Inn was a show of faith, Jonah thought. A sacrifice. To quit like that, so abruptly; to cut himself off from the people, like Crystal and Vivian, that he and Troy had in common. He hoped that Troy appreciated the gesture.

But it was necessary. Even as he struggled to tell Troy the facts of the story, he realized that they would need to put some distance between them for a while. He said as much.

"Look," he said, "I know that . . . maybe I didn't exactly go about this in the right way, and it's a little hard to . . . get your mind around. I mean, I want to give you some space, just to . . . think things over."

And Troy had stared at him.

"I don't want you in my workplace," Troy said at last. "I just . . . don't want people gossiping about this adoption shit. It's like the kind of thing they'd put in the fucking newspaper . . . for human interest or something. It's just too weird for me, you know?"

"I agree completely," Jonah said. He nodded earnestly, using the same grim frown that Troy was wearing. "That seems best," he said. "I mean, I realize that my taking the job there in the first place was, uh, probably not the smartest idea, but . . ."

"I'm serious," Troy said. "I want you to quit. Tomorrow."

"I understand," Jonah said.

"And I don't want you to tell them either. About this . . . this . . .

adoption stuff." He paused, heavily. "The last thing I need is to have Vivian and Crystal all *titillated*."

"You're absolutely right," Jonah said.

Jonah thinks of this again as he drives along the edge of the park, and he can feel the blush rising in his cheeks. He can picture Troy's pained, flinching look. "Jesus," Troy had said. "Why didn't you just tell me? This is— It's kind of a creepy feeling. I mean, it's like being stalked or something."

"Well," Jonah said, "that's not what I meant." And Troy had put his palms over his face.

"Jesus," he said. "This is not something I need to deal with right now."

"I know," Jonah whispered. "I realize that. I'm . . . sorry."

Beyond his windshield, the snow is a powdery mist. It turns the trees and houses and signs into the grainy, blurry grays of television static. The sky seems to be pressing down, collapsing, settling over ground.

Jonah slows. The heat coming from the defroster smells vaguely of carbon monoxide, and fits over his mind like a stocking cap. He presses his foot against the brake and squeezes his eyes shut for a moment.

At first Troy didn't seem to believe what Jonah was saying.

"Look," Troy said, "I'm not into this whole adoption thing. As far as I'm concerned, once the woman signs the papers, that's the end of it. I mean, I had a mom and dad that I was happy with. That's it."

"Okay," Jonah said. "But listen, let's just settle it once and for all. I've got the papers in my car. Don't you at least want to look at them? I mean, they could be wrong."

And Troy was silent for a long time. He knitted his hands together, hardening his mouth.

"Okay," he sighed. "Okay, let's see what you've got."

Now, as the snow comes down, Troy can't help but look again at the materials that Jonah has given him. The original birth certificate:

Baby Boy Doyle, it says, and he blanches again as he traces through the columns. Mother: Nora Doyle. Occupation: High school student. Father: Unknown. Occupation: Unknown. He feels his chest tighten, despite himself. This is not what he wants, he thinks. At first he'd really thought that he wanted this sneak, Jonah, and his adoption search nonsense out of his life forever. But now he's not so sure. A heaviness fills his diaphragm, and he draws breath, lets it out in a long stream.

Nora Doyle, he thinks. He doesn't much like her, this woman who had given him away, but now that she's in his mind he can't get rid of her. In his imagination, Nora Doyle vaguely resembles Carla—one of those unpleasant psychological tricks that a person doesn't want to think about too hard. He'd like to see a picture of the woman, if only to erase this creepy association from his brain.

And, well, he *does* have questions. She has been only the vaguest outline in his head up until now, a generic silhouette, like the picture on a bathroom door that meant "women." He might have been happy for things to stay that way. But now, without his even wanting it, this person, this mother, has begun to develop weight and contours, materializing into something that's almost solid. As angry as he was with Jonah at first, he knows that he's going to break down and call him after all.

He leans his forehead against the glass of the window, taps his cigarette against the rim of an ashtray. He's sitting there, wearing sweatpants and a T-shirt, a prisoner, and after a moment he reaches down and digs his fingers into the skin around the belt of his parole anklet. It itches, and he scrapes his nails back and forth, distractedly.

It's not long after eleven at night, and Jonah parks a few blocks away from the house. A blast of wind hits his face when he gets out of the car, and he keeps his head down, pulling up the collar of his coat, aware of the snowflakes settling over his hair in a thin layer.

By now he has gotten used to Foxglove Road. He knows, in general, when people go to sleep, he knows who has barking dogs, who has garage lights with motion detectors, he knows the yards with the best trees and bushes to cover him, though in this storm it's doubtful that even someone watching out a window could see him as he moves quickly down the sidewalk and up the driveway that leads to the backyard. He is a dappled shadow, passing through the swirl of snow, his hands balled up in the pockets of his jacket, his shoulders hunched, soundless. But even on a clear night, he would be invisible, he thinks. He knows the puddles of shade, the easiest way to beat a quick retreat, the places where he can stand still and blend into the background.

He knows the circumference of Judy Keene's house. In front, the large window is the living room, and the other, smaller, is Judy's bedroom. Another window into Judy's bedroom faces the driveway. At the back of the house, there is the kitchen, and then the back door, and then Loomis's room.

He has been thinking about Troy's letter to Mrs. Keene. *I realize that there are many good reasons why you have been reluctant to allow Loomis to have contact with me,* Troy had written, and Jonah recalls that precise block-letter handwriting, like the calligraphy in the voice bubbles of a cartoon. It was an earnest, heartbreakingly careful script, Jonah thought, neatly aligned on a page from a legal pad. *Although I know I have made mistakes I only want what is best for him,* Troy had written, and Jonah thought of Troy bent over his crossword puzzle at the bar, the tip of his tongue caught between his teeth as he filled in the squares; he thought of Troy hunched down, washing beer glasses, his eyes far away. Now he understands what Troy was feeling.

He has found himself looking at the letter over and over. He took it without thinking really—he had noticed it sitting on the kitchen table the evening he'd brought the groceries to Troy's house, had noticed it was addressed to Judy Keene. He had picked it up curiously when Troy was in the bathroom, and then, when Troy came out, he crumpled it into his pocket—all he needed was for Troy to catch him snooping! He had almost forgotten about it, as events had unfolded that night, and in fact it wasn't until the next day that he'd remembered, when he discovered the envelope balled up in the front pocket of his pants.

He had been feeling a lot of despair that morning, as he unfolded the letter and spread it out on the coffee table in front of him. He'd made a mess of their first real meeting—*I think we're brothers:* God!

How stupid!—and even after he had shown Troy the PeopleSearch information, even after Troy seemed to believe him, there was a chilliness that Jonah was afraid they'd never get over. *This is not something I need to deal with right now,* Troy had said, and Jonah had felt his heart contracting.

"I know it seems weird," Jonah had said. "But it's something that means a lot to me. I've been wondering about you for my whole life. I know that probably doesn't make any sense."

And Troy had looked at him bleakly. "It makes sense," Troy said. "I just don't know whether I can deal with it right now. To tell you the truth, I don't really need any more complications in my life."

"I can imagine that it's a lot to take in," Jonah said, but it wasn't until that next day, with the letter unfolded in front of him, that he truly realized what Troy meant. *Please, Mrs. Keene, I am Loomis's father and I love him. Have mercy on me.*

Jonah recognized that kind of desperation perfectly, and sitting there in his trailer, with the pale morning light slanting in through the smeary windows of his trailer, it was almost as if Troy was sitting there beside him. Confiding. It was almost as if the letter had been meant for Jonah rather than Judy Keene. *Have mercy on me,* Troy said, and Jonah pictured himself reaching out and closing his hand over Troy's wrist.

"I know you may not believe this," Jonah imagined saying. "But I understand what you're talking about." He had lain his palm across the words on the letter. Could he say, "I really want to help you"? Could he say, "I want to be a brother to you"?

Probably not.

But he likes to think about it. Standing in the steadily ticking snow outside of Loomis's window, he can vaguely see the shape of the child lit by a dim night-light, Loomis under the covers in his bed, his sleeping head peeking out of the spaceship-patterned comforter. Jonah puts the pad of his fingertips against the glass, watching the flowers of snow crystals catch against his knuckles and turn to water. He's aware of the accumulation on his shoulders and hair, and he likes to think that at some level Loomis knows that his new uncle is watching over him.

Have mercy on me, he thinks, and he wishes that the glass could turn liquid beneath his touch, that his hand could pass through, that the walls and windows of the world would give way to him. Just for this one time.

24

June 4, 1997

At three in the afternoon, four hours after Judy first noticed that Loomis was missing, the trail dogs arrive. There are several police cars parked in front of her house, and two heavyset men stand on the sidewalk with their arms folded hard against their chests, talking to Kevin Onken.

Judy is sitting on the steps in front of her house, very still. She feels a drop of perspiration slip from her hair and along the back of her ear, leaving a slow, cool track behind it like a snail. She shudders, watching as a man with a Doberman pinscher crouches on his haunches to look the dog in the eye, to speak to it, stroking its muzzle. Some of the neighbors have come out to stand on their front steps as well, shading their eyes; the few that have come up to inquire have been turned away, but she is aware of a circle of watchfulness around her. She observes as the dog man presses one of Loomis's T-shirts to the Doberman's nose, whispering to it. The dog's ears lift into triangles, and its bobbed tail vibrates enthusiastically.

Soon she is going to get up and walk over to the men and ask for information. But right now she just needs to sit here for a moment.

Her arm has stopped working. She tries to lift it and nothing happens. She stares at her hand and wills her fingers to curl and grip. They don't. The arm rests on her knee, and she reaches out cautiously to prod it with her finger. There's no feeling in it.

She tries to assure herself that it's just stress, that it's some odd psychosomatic reaction to the situation. If it was a stroke or a heart attack, wouldn't it hurt?

If she tells someone, they will call an ambulance, she knows. She will find herself in an emergency room, tended by condescending nurses. Whatever is happening back at home—whether Loomis is found, or whether he is dead, or whether clues to his whereabouts are discovered—all of this will be kept from her as she is poked and attached to monitors, as she becomes a body that is being examined and cared for. They will turn her into a willful child—as a grammar school teacher, she knows all their tricks, all the things about her personality they will want to control and subdue.

What is happening? A thick, balding man walks past her, stepping around her and into her house without saying a word, without a simple "May I?" And then she hears him talking to someone on a walkie-talkie.

"I guess they're bringing the father over right now. They don't have any take on the whereabouts of the mother of the child," he says. She can see his slacks, some kind of brown cotton with an ironed crease down the leg, made by an old-fashioned wife, no doubt, or a dry cleaner.

"No, it was just the grandmother who was watching him," the man says, and glances at her without much interest. His shoes are black and shiny, slip-ons, with leather tassels hanging from the tongue.

"I don't know . . . I don't know . . ." the man says. His eyes turn sidelong at Judy, as if he is considering asking her a question. "No, they didn't get divorced," he says, and lowers his voice a little. He must believe that she is hard of hearing, or that she is too confused to realize what he's talking about. "It sounds like she just up and left," he says, in a judgmental voice that makes Judy stiffen. "Drug addict of some sort, apparently," he says, and makes a short, snorting "heh" sound, as if the person he is talking to has made a snide remark. "No," he says. "I don't think so. I'm looking at her right now. She's just sitting there on the step. She looks pretty out of it."

She wants to respond to this, to glare at this buffoon and let him know she can hear his spittley voice, but she is afraid that her voice will come out slurred, like a drunk's. She is staring at the unresponsive arm, thinking very hard at it. Her brain sends a signal to her index finger, to lift, just a little, and she imagines that she sees it shudder. But maybe not. For some reason, she thinks of that famous Israeli psychic from the seventies, who was said to be able to bend spoons with the power of his mind. She focuses all of her brain's energy on the finger, and she can feel her face growing red, the flesh of her cheeks quivering a little. *Go on,* she urges it gently, *Go on,* she thinks, but nothing happens. A watery tremor trickles through her, and she closes her eyes.

She is struck by the premonition that Carla is nearby. There is, somewhere at the edge of the yard, the hint of Carla's voice, and Judy thinks: *Oh!* Her mind clutches loosely at the sound, and she imagines that they have found Carla, or that Carla has simply appeared, joining the circle of men and dogs on the sidewalk, introducing herself, flirting. Judy can visualize Carla standing there with her hip cocked, drawing on a cigarette, her hard mouth and sly eyes. "Why do you always look at me that way?" Judy can imagine her saying, and there is the high, shimmering tine of insect music from the trees, the sense of something encroaching. A pattern of sun beats against her eyelids through the dappled branches.

She is aware of herself dividing. There is a reasonable self, floating above her perceptions, a practical mind that observes the sensual organism. She is aware of herself as muscle and fat wrapped in damp skin, aware of herself as a dry, yellow-tasting tongue, aware of the matrix of sounds that spreads out from the center point of her body, the interstate of blood moving, the grasping tendrils of the spirit, seeking purchase.

The reasonable self knows that nothing at all is happening. She is just an old fat lady, sitting on a stoop with her eyes closed. Carla is not here, and besides, even if by some miracle Carla suddenly arrives on the scene, even if Judy opens her eyes and Carla is staring at her from across the lawn, there will be only enmity between them. She has known for a long time now that there will be no resolution or last-minute deathbed reconciliation; she has known that their relationship is a closed casket, sealed and buried and irretrievable. It doesn't matter if she opens her eyes or not. Carla, her real daughter, won't be there.

And yet there is still the hint of a voice, still the thick flutter of illogic, and she finds herself picturing Carla not as she would be today, but Carla as she was, Carla, aged fourteen or fifteen, her hair teased and moussed, her makeup overdone, wearing a shimmering silver shirt and faux leather pants. A silly, reckless girl, Judy thinks, a girl without qualities, a girl who needs a stern hand. Her child, and yet so different from her that it seemed as if a mistake had been made.

"Do you know how much it hurts me when your teachers call to complain about your behavior?" Judy used to say. "Do you like humiliating me, is that it?" And when Carla had said nothing, Judy had continued, as if to herself. "It really makes me feel so depressed," she said. "A lot of these people are my colleagues, do you know that? People I work with, people I'm friends with, and then to have you behaving in such a way in their classroom! It's so disrespectful, Carla, and you know, I don't feel like you love me very much, when you act this way. If you really loved me, you wouldn't keep embarrassing me."

Carla used to cry a little, after these incidents. She would go to sleep with her stuffed animals encircled in her arms, a blanket pulled over her head. Quick to blame others. *I never did anything. It's not my fault. They're lying. They're trying to get me in trouble.* And then shortly afterward, there were the drugs, and the arguments about that, and the concealment of the drugs, and the drug rehab clinic that she'd finally decided on.

"Mom," Carla said, "please don't make me go." That was the last time Carla had called her Mom, Judy thinks. "I'll do better," Carla said. "I swear I'll listen to you from now on."

Judy can say nothing now. She just sits there on the stoop with her eyes closed, with her arm motionless, pressing her tongue between her teeth, remembering that drive to the clinic—Carla in the passenger seat, her face turned toward the window, occasionally making the small, froggy sounds of swallowed weeping. Judy had believed, at the time, that the treatments at the clinic would remove the drugs and the alcohol and the recalcitrant desire for them the way chemotherapy burned away a cancer. She believed that her daughter would be returned to her, whole and clean and grateful, and thinking this she had hardened herself to Carla's whimpering.

She never would have expected that her daughter would, instead, become worse. In rehab, Carla would meet a new friend, a girl who'd teach her easy pathways to new types of drugs; in rehab, Carla would stubbornly refuse to admit that she was "powerless" against addiction, and the therapist would call Judy in, and they would both sit there, explaining and insisting and steadily beating her with their words, until she admitted, at last, her eyes blazing and puffy with tears, that she was "powerless."

For a flash, Judy can feel Carla's fingers against her wrist, her flushed face against Judy's neck. She holds a three-year-old Carla in her lap, reading to her, singing to her. Television is limited, in their house, to educational programs. They drive all the way to Denver, to go to art museums, listening to tapes of classical music in the car. Her IQ was tested—well above average, not quite genius level but close.

"You can be anything you want," Judy said. "I just want you to be happy."

And Carla, perhaps age ten, had gazed at her suspiciously. Even then, Judy had known that things between them would end badly. "You're capable of so much," Judy said. "That's what I don't understand about you. Why do you enjoy sabotaging yourself?"

"Mrs. Keene?" someone says. "Are you all right?"

She doesn't say anything. *Admit that you are powerless,* Judy thinks, and even now it is not something she could bring herself to do. She *will* get up, she thinks. She *will* tell them that Loomis's disappearance has nothing to do with her daughter, or, for that matter, her worthless son-in-law, who they are discussing in the living room, just at the edge of her hearing. She *will* open her eyes, she thinks. And maybe Carla will be standing there.

"Mrs. Keene?" someone says again, and she tries to pull her eyelids open.

She grimaces: a terrible headache. She is touching her left tricep with her fingers, and when she lifts her eyelids the light hits her in a sharp, painful flash. She is aware that her eyes are beginning to leak tears, blurring her sight. The left eye appears to be blind. A large black dot grows over her vision like an iris, dilating and dilating, a thickness of spots, like a swarm of bees. She shuts the eye and it seems to go away.

She can feel her body listing, slipping into the empty air beyond her shoulder.

What if she's dying? she thinks.

What if she never knows the end of the story? She shudders, and her mind continues to lurch forward into the future, that simple expectation of time passing—another moment, and another moment. It seems impossible that it will abruptly cease. It seems impossible that you will never know what happens next, that the thread you've been following your whole life will just . . . cut off, like a book with the last pages torn out. That doesn't seem fair, she thinks.

PART THREE

PART THREE

25

June 1966

Despite herself, Nora can't help but imagine names for the baby. She likes boys' names—old-fashioned, heroic ones: Agamemnon, Pyrrhus, Octavion, Aristedes. She has been reading a book about the ancient heroes of Greece and Rome, and it makes her sad that people can't be given such names anymore.

Octavion Doyle, she thinks as she walks down to the cafeteria for supper. *Jupiter Doyle,* and she smiles vaguely to herself. *Zeus.*

She is aware of the other girls moving with her down the hallway but she doesn't acknowledge them. They are dressed as she is in cheap smocks, their old perms and hairdos now growing limp and fading; they smell of sleep and old cigarettes, and the acrid musk of their private parts.

She has watched the girls who have gone before her; she has seen how it works. They fade and fade, until at last they begin to go into labor, and then they are never seen again. She knows: They give birth to babies, babies that childless parents are already waiting for. And then, pregnant no longer, they are returned to their former lives, or to new lives in distant towns, where they can forget. She knows this is what happens, but it's becoming harder and harder for her to believe. Once they're gone, it feels as if they are dead.

As they close in on the cafeteria, her baby tells her that he is hungry. She puts her hand to her belly as he lolls, moving his limbs inside her; she feels the anxious urgency of his squirm, his eagerness, and she whispers under her breath: *shhh.* For a moment, he quiets, though he continues to send tingles of anticipation through her, eager for the food.

She can't say why, but she knows that it's a boy inside her. *Hector? Alexander? Theseus?* Whatever his name, he is a clearly masculine presence, and in some ways that is a comfort. She wouldn't want to have a girl, she thinks. There's too much trouble, too much sorrow that goes along with it.

She eats in silence at the end of the table, not even thinking about the food, really—a patty of meat in gravy, a side of canned green beans, a dollop of whipped potato, applesauce—she shovels it in, automatically, and the baby's urgency calms. At the other end of the table others are chatting, something about rock bands, but she sits there with her face lowered, steadily spooning the potato whip and applesauce into her mouth, making small involuntary sounds, muted sighs of satisfaction.

Across the table one of the newer girls regards Nora warily, with a reserved air of disapproval. Table manners, Nora thinks. She's been making sounds in her haste to get the baby satisfied, smacking and chewing and grunting: disgusting. She lifts her head long enough to give the new girl a direct, baleful stare. She watches as the girl twitters silently, unnerved, but she doesn't maintain eye contact. The new girl looks down at her own food deliberately, her lips pursed, and brings a small spoonful of applesauce to her mouth as if she is eating a pearl.

Nora doesn't care. She has given up on even the simple basics of social contact. After Maris vanished, after Dominique had gone into labor, after the baby itself had become her primary human connection, she didn't feel the need to engage in the empty rituals of greeting and polite time-passing. It seems pointless, she thinks. She can spend her time more fruitfully reading, or simply communing with the developing creature inside her—its movements, its pleasures and displeasures, the early rudiments of its thoughts traveling through her body. It says, *I'm hungry. I'm restless. I'm happy.* She can feel these things as clearly as if it had spoken to her directly.

Sometimes she will open her eyes at night and she will be aware that it is awake.

You wouldn't really give me away, would you? it thinks, curled up inside her, its limbs moving softly.

And she stares into the darkness.

Why are you so stubborn? it murmurs, plaintively.

She doesn't know the answer to such questions. Only a few months ago she would have wished this thing, this baby, out of existence without a second thought. She remembers punching herself in the belly; she remembers tasting bleach, which she had heard could induce a miscarriage; she remembers how adamant she'd been with her father, who'd argued with her, gently, sorrowful, befuddled. He thought she should get married, and he'd wept when she admitted that she hadn't told the baby's father. "Honey," he said, "that's not right. That's not right. Believe me, he'd want to know what's going on. You just have to give him the chance."

And she'd looked at him sternly. Didn't he get it? What would the future be for her? Married at age sixteen, two high school dropouts, stuck forever in Little Bow, South Dakota, everyone's lives ruined. She felt her teeth clench. Why would she choose that for herself? Why would she force anyone else to accept that life? *I want what's best for the baby,* she'd told her father, *and that's not having me for a mother.*

But now, sitting in Mrs. Bibb's office, less than a week before her due date, she is less certain. She watches as Mrs. Bibb looks at some papers on the desk, and then up, frowning.

"I've been concerned about you, Miss . . . Doyle," Mrs. Bibb says. Nora sits in the large wing-backed chair across from Bibb's desk, where once, long ago, Nora and her father had listened to Mrs. Bibb's recitation of the rules of residency. "There's been some concern about your comportment lately. Do you know what I mean by the word *comportment?*"

"Yes," Nora says. She lets a thick lock of her hair obscure one of her eyes like a patch, and lowers her head.

"You're a very bright girl," Mrs. Bibb says. "I've always known that. And I felt that I ought to talk to you, because these next few weeks are going to be extraordinarily difficult." She purses her mouth, folding her hands deliberately on the desk, left hand on top of right, so that her own, real golden wedding ring glints. "Your body is changing, Nora," Mrs. Bibb says. "You're going through a lot of physical changes that can also affect you . . . psychologically. And when that happens, very often girls will begin to have second thoughts."

"Well," Nora says.

But Mrs. Bibb clears her throat. "I wanted to say, Miss Doyle, that I admire your spirit very much. And I wanted to affirm once again that you are doing the right thing. I'm not at liberty to say much, but I can tell you that there are several very loving, childless couples who are waiting to give this child a real home. It's such an act of generosity, Miss Doyle. Such a gift for this child. But I know that it must be a struggle for you."

"Well," Nora says again, and her throat constricts. "What . . . what if I've changed my mind?"

Mrs. Bibb smiles, benignly. "You haven't changed your mind, Miss Doyle," she says. "You may be going through some changes in your body's chemistry, but that is natural, and it will pass, I can assure you. You'll be able to get on with your own life, and you'll have given this child you're carrying an opportunity that it simply couldn't have if it were being raised by an unwed teenager. We agreed on these points, I think, when you first came to the Mrs. Glass House. Didn't we?"

"Yes," Nora says at last, and the baby shifts reproachfully inside her.

Even though she has sworn to herself that she wouldn't, even though she continues to make a concerted effort, she has been thinking about the boy again.

Wayne. She lets his name pass through her mind, and his face comes trailing after, unbidden. Wayne. His dark curly hair; his long face, handsome for a farm kid—the prominent nose, the earnest brown eyes, the uncertain mouth—each detail emerging from the darkness like the smile of the Cheshire cat.

She hadn't thought that she was in love with him. Nevertheless, here he is again, a shadow leaning over her thoughts, a pang: Wayne Hill, sly-smiled wrestler boy who sat behind her in ninth-grade math. Younger than she was by almost nine months, not as tall as she was, unsophisticated. Why would she fall in love with Wayne Hill?

But she *was* in love with him, she thought. A little. At least it seemed so now, from this distance. Now, a hollow ache shudders through her as she thinks of him. It feels as if somehow he might have saved her, he might have saved her and their baby, if only she had told him.

She was not like her classmates, the other fifteen-year-old girls in her school who seemed to fall in love as if it were some sort of pastime, girls who spent hours and hours mooning over boys or photos of celebrities. She wasn't the type, she told herself. For one thing, she wasn't interested in the insular, clubby world of a small-town high school, with its after-school groups and cheerleaders and people "going steady"—all the fake rituals and social codes were vaguely repulsive to her; she preferred to remain outside such concerns, more interested in the lives of people she read about in books, more interested in art, in getting good grades, in the future—in which she might become an actress, or a painter, or a journalist. Each of these seemed like a real possibility, distanced from her only by hard work, and luck, and time. She had already begun to send away for information about various colleges, just so she could read their brochures and course catalogs.

Of course, she was outside of the world of high school whether she wanted it or not. Her life, her family, was too complicated—she and her father lived a few miles from town, and, since her mother's death, he was depressed; she took care of him, and even if she'd wanted to, she couldn't stay after school for the extracurricular activities. Her father came home from work and ate the supper she'd made for him. He was tired, and usually wanted only to drink his beers and sit in his room. He wasn't going to drive her into town for a football game, or a meeting of the Art Club, or to the movies where many of her peers went on their dates.

In any case, she wasn't entirely sure what boys she might have dated. She was the only person in their school who was mixed race, and she thought that this, too, put her outside of the main body of students. Indians and white people kept separate for the most part. They didn't date one another, certainly, and so, while boys of both races looked at her, appraised her, flirted sometimes, no one had ever asked her out. They weren't sure, she thought, what category she fit into.

The summer after she'd turned fifteen, the summer between ninth and tenth grade, she had persuaded her father to take her into town on his way to work so that she could go to the library, or the swimming pool. It was only one day a week. It was boring out in the country alone, and he hadn't objected too much to the idea. "Just stay out of trouble," he would always say, but he'd trusted her. "You're such a responsible girl, Nora. If it wasn't for you, I don't think I'd still be alive. That's the truth."

That was the summer she started seeing Wayne Hill. She knew who he was, of course. They'd had classes together, they even rode the same bus to and from school—Wayne lived on a farm a few miles beyond her house—but they'd never really spoken before. He was an athlete, somewhat of a smart aleck. The only thing that surprised her was that his name consistently appeared on the honor roll, along with hers.

And she was surprised, that day in June of 1965, to encounter him at the library. He didn't seem like the bookish type, but there he was, running his finger along the spines of books in the Fiction section, in the same concave of bookcases she was standing in. He looked at her curiously, and their eyes met for a moment before she glanced back to the shelves. After a minute, she was aware that he'd moved closer.

"You look like you could be dangerous," Wayne said, under his breath. "Did anyone ever tell you that? Like maybe you're a spy, or an assassin."

She didn't say anything for a moment. Then she shifted, irritably. "I just want to look at these books," she said, and he grinned at her, a wolfish grin, his lips jutting out a little, hearty and cocky and tinged at the edges with a hint of sadness.

"No problem," he said, and his eyes seemed to glint at her. "Have you ever read any Ray Bradbury?"

"No," she said, stiffly.

"You should," he said. And he reached down, right at the level below her waist, and pulled out a book. "Here," he said. "*A Medicine for Melancholy*. I bet you'll like it."

She hesitated for a moment, and then took it from him.

"I didn't mean anything negative when I said you looked like a spy," he said. "I just meant . . . you look like an interesting person. You look mysterious."

And she'd met his eyes, frowning. He was a compact, broad-shouldered, muscular boy. His eyes were a very strange pale, milky blue, like one of those Alaskan sled dogs.

For a few weeks they had met at the library, just to talk. Then they'd met at the swimming pool. Then they'd gone out, trailing their towels and street clothes, into the bushes just beyond the swimming pool fence. To kiss—to touch arms and brush their legs against each other—their skin still damp and warm and smelling of chlorine.

"I want to tell you something," he said. "I've been in love with you for a long time." And he laughed, beaming his grin at her. "Ever since we started riding the school bus together, I've been wanting to talk to you. You know? Every time you got on the bus, I would just get this . . . glow . . . in my heart. I know that sounds corny. You know, I meant it when I said you look mysterious. That's what I always thought."

In July he began walking to her house during the day. His family farm was six miles from the little yellow house where she and her father lived, and he would make excuses for his absence from chores that he was expected to perform. He would usually arrive in the early afternoon—trudging along the sides of gravel roads, crossing the long pasture behind her house.

Tuesday, Wednesday, Thursday. Her father was still at work, and she was home alone with the puppy, Elizabeth. Nora had been trying to train the dog, to teach it tricks. She would bark furiously when Wayne came up the driveway, but then when Nora snapped her fingers Elizabeth would sit. And after a few times, Elizabeth didn't bark anymore. She was used to Wayne.

He would sit there, stroking her fur. "She's a beautiful animal," Wayne said, and his eyes squinted as he smiled, cheerful half-moons. "You're lucky," he said. "I've never seen a dog like this."

And Nora had joined him in petting. "She's a Doberman pinscher. This man my father worked with gave her to him. They're very smart, supposedly. They're the smartest dogs—that's what the man told my father."

"Mm," Wayne said. They'd been petting the dog together, and their hands met as they ran down the sleek muscles of Elizabeth's back. The palm of Wayne's hand ran across her knuckles, over her wrist, up her forearm.

He looked at her. They kissed.

Before long they were in her bedroom, in her cheap, girlish four-poster, and Elizabeth the puppy was sitting anxiously outside the closed door.

That was the first time. It was not gross, like she imagined when she thought of her classmates and their activities. It was . . . something else. Like a part of her brain she hadn't known existed. Like discovering she could speak a foreign language that she had never heard before. She didn't know why she'd done it—she had been curious, she guessed, and whatever part of her was awakening, whatever part of her was impulsive and insane, caught hold suddenly. Her hand shivered as it made contact—a warm, pins-and-needles thrum, and Wayne Hill lifted his eyes to stare at her. Sharp blue eyes. She felt her hand underneath his shirt, brushing against his small, hard nipple, and he closed his eyes. "Hey," he said. His palms closed over her breasts, pressing against the cloth of her blouse.

The thing that surprised her the most was how easily she had become pregnant. In her mind, pregnancy had always seemed like a choice that people made, a switch that they might turn off and on. Birth control was a rumor that both of them had heard of, but they both believed the other things they'd heard as well—if she jumped up and down hard afterward, if she douched with Listerine, if she took a long hot bath that night—if she did that, if she didn't *want* to become pregnant, everything would be all right.

She must have become pregnant in late August or early September.

By then, school had started, and things had begun to cool between them. Not purposefully. It was just that they were both suddenly aware of the problems—of what people would say.

In gym, a Sioux girl named Elizabeth Tall had bumped hard against her shoulder.

"I hear you like that little white wrestler boy," she said, her eyes grim. "I guess you think you're too good for Indian guys, huh?"

And he must have gotten some version of the same thing, some ribbing from his peers on the wrestling team, because they didn't speak to each other in the hallway of the school.

In algebra, in late September, he passed her a note. It said: "We need to talk."

But they never did.

This is something she thinks about more and more frequently as she sits in her room in Mrs. Glass House, waiting for her labor to commence. She is frightened, a little, though the nurses have tried to reassure them. They have explained what will happen, have told them about contractions, and about water breaking, and they say that there are tranquilizers, pain medications; it won't hurt as much as they fear, they are told, and there is a slide show about a procedure called a spinal, in which women can be numbed from the waist down. They will still be able to push the baby out, but it won't hurt as much.

Even as she listens to this, she finds herself wondering about Wayne Hill. Did he suspect that she was pregnant? She imagines him talking to her father, standing at the doorway of the house, wanting to know where she is. *I love her,* Wayne says, *I demand to know where she has gone.* They argue at first, Wayne and her father, but finally they come to an agreement. *We've got to save her,* they say. She closes her eyes, picturing the two of them, Wayne and her father, on their way to Mrs. Glass House, on their way to her rescue.

Years later, when she was incarcerated in the South Dakota Human Services Center as a mental patient, a young psychologist named Dave McNulty told her that this fantasy was probably the first manifestation of her illness. She had laughed at him.

"Manifestation," she said, and her cigarette trembled as she brought it to her lips. It was funny. Physically, McNulty looked like a wimpy, brown-eyed version of Wayne himself, Wayne with longer, shaggier hair and a tweed jacket, leather-patch elbows.

"Let's talk about the birth," McNulty said. "Let's talk about how you felt."

"I don't remember anything," she said.

And she didn't. She had a vague notion of the nurse saying to her: "This is Thorazine. It's going to calm you down a little." She had a vague notion of signing papers, and then asking to see the baby.

"Oh, honey," the nurse said, "your baby is already gone. He's already with his new family. Don't you remember? You said you didn't want to look at him."

"Is that what I said?" Nora whispered, and the nurse noded.

"He's gone?" Nora said.

And the nurse just stared at her.

26

June 4, 1997

Loomis wakes and it's raining. He sees the droplets of water moving horizontally across the windshield, pulled unsteadily by the velocity, and he thinks of small fish moving through an aquarium tank, the aquarium that used to be in his father's house, with the mollies, and angelfish, and swordtails, and silver dollars. They have been driving for a long time, he thinks.

He is stretched out in the backseat of Jonah's car, covered by a blanket. It is okay not to wear a seat belt, Jonah had told him. He closes his eyes, and then opens them.

"Are we there yet?" he says, and he can see Jonah's eyes in the rearview mirror, glancing back at him.

"I don't think so," Jonah says.

Loomis rolls his shoulders, yawns. "Is it still a long time?" he says, and he watches for a moment as Jonah gazes out the windshield at the interstate, his face framed against the blur of passing telephone poles.

"Actually," Jonah says, "I think it might be a lot longer than I expected."

27

December 18, 1996

This is the day that Loomis turns six, and Troy can't stop thinking about it. He wakes up at four in the morning and sits in the living room, drinking coffee, listening to the radio, static-filled classic rock out of some faraway station in Denver. He wonders whether Loomis is going to have a birthday party. It is the last week before Christmas vacation, and perhaps the kindergarten teacher will lead the class in singing the birthday song to Loomis. Then Loomis will come home from school, and perhaps Judy will have decorated the house with streamers. Perhaps she will have baked a fancy cake in the shape of a dinosaur, or some other icon Loomis likes. Perhaps some of his friends from school will be invited over, to play games and watch Loomis open his presents. Troy imagines this; he doesn't know anything for sure.

He'd sent his own batch of presents to Judy's house three days ago. Mostly it was stuff that he'd ordered off the television: a special set of many-colored markers, and a set of books about animals, and a combination telescope-microscope, and some Batman figurines. He'd also sent a card he'd made himself: a grinning, cartoonish brontosaurus, with carefully inked letters that said: "Happy Birthday to Loomis. From: His Dad! With: Lots of Love!" He'd spent quite a few hours at the kitchen table working on that card, and as dawn light begins to filter in, he tries to decide whether Judy will give it to Loomis. He can imagine her just throwing it away. Maybe even tossing out the gifts, as well, before Loomis even sees them.

At eight in the morning, he dials Judy's number.

He has been very patient about this, he thinks. When she asked him not to call, back in August, she'd said that it was just "until Loomis got settled in." So he'd waited a month. But when he called in September, she'd been very curt with him. Loomis wasn't available to talk, she said. She would prefer it if he waited until she called him.

"Jesus Christ!" Troy said. "When is that going to be? It's been months since I talked to him," he said, and she'd given him a long silence.

"It will be when I'm ready," she said tightly, and the next day he'd gotten a call from his parole officer, Lisa Fix.

"Troy," Lisa Fix said. "Why are you harassing your mother-in-law on the phone?"

"I'm not," Troy said, but he felt himself blushing bitterly.

"Well," Lisa said, "I just got a complaint from her, and if you really want to end up off parole and in jail, this is a good way to go about it. You need to get a handle on yourself, my angry friend."

"What are you talking about?" Troy said. "I just called to try to talk to Loomis."

"That's not what she said," Lisa Fix said, evenly, in the voice of a woman who was used to being lied to. "She told me that you swore at her, and were threatening toward her, and I don't know or care what the actual truth of the conversation was. All I know is that this has absolutely got to stop. If you can't get some self-control, she's going to end up pressing charges against you, and then you'll never see that kid again."

Thinking of this, his hands shake when he hears her pick up the phone. It's risky, but he still can't believe that Judy would hate him that much. Surely, he thinks, she's not completely without a heart, and when she says "Hello," in her crisply friendly voice, he makes a conscious effort to sound as meek and gentle and repentant as he can.

"Hello, Mrs. Keene?" he says softly. "This is Troy. Troy Timmens." He hears her thin intake of breath and he squeezes his eyes shut, willing her not to hang up. "Mrs. Keene," he says, "I'm really, really sorry to bother you, and I'm not trying to disrespect your wishes or invade your privacy or anything. It's just that . . . I haven't heard from you in a while and I was really hoping that I might be able to wish Loomis a happy birthday. I really don't mean to harass you or anything. Honest to God. I just want to . . . open the lines of communication."

There is a long pause. He doesn't know what she is thinking, but he can sense that this is an unfriendly silence. The utter lack of sound is like a deep, toothy mouth that he is lowering his head into.

"So . . ." he says at last. "Did you get the presents? And the card?"

"Yes," her voice says.

"And . . . you will give them to him, won't you?"

He hears her throat clear, deliberately, and he can feel the hairs on the back of his neck prickle. She sighs. "No, I don't think so."

Her voice is firm and reasonable, reminding Troy of the years she'd spent teaching second-graders. "I want to be frank with you, Troy, and I'd like you to do me the courtesy of listening and trying to understand." She pauses for a moment, in the way a teacher might pause to underline a word on the blackboard. "Loomis doesn't need your gifts," she says. "Or your cards. Or your phone calls. He needs a stable life. He's happy in school, and he's a bright, thoughtful, caring child. The last thing he needs is to have you trying to bribe him with cheap toys and getting him all riled up."

Troy keeps his mouth shut, though he can feel the heat in his face. He is not crying, but his nose is running, and his chest feels tight and quivery when he tries to speak. "But . . ." he says, and then stops himself. He knows that it will do no good to argue with her, it will only make matters worse. He takes a breath.

"I understand what you're saying," he says, even as his hands tighten hard against each other. "But would it be possible for me to talk to him for one minute? Just to say 'happy birthday.' That's all." And he can feel his throat constricting. "I'm his father, Judy. I want to be a good father. I know you don't believe that, but if you'd just . . . give me a chance . . ."

"You want to be a good father," Judy repeats, and echoed by her, the words sound limp and pathetic. Troy stares out the kitchen window, where the tree swing is still hanging, encrusted, petrified with a layer of old snow and ice. What can he say?

"You're not a very reflective person, are you, Troy?" Judy says, very calmly and clearly, that neutral, therapist's tone that makes Troy flinch. "I don't know what your definition of being a good father is, but to my mind, you are the exact opposite of a good father. I would like you to think about the *facts*, Troy, the facts from my perspective. You sold drugs out of your home, while you had a child. You supplied drugs to my daughter, the mother of your child, who you knew was an addict. You opened your house to the very lowest scum of the earth, so they could purchase drugs, and these people wandered freely in and out of your house while your own vulnerable child was sleeping, or playing nearby, or maybe even watching while you and your cronies got high. Those are not the actions of a good father, Troy. I think you've gotten so used to charming people and maybe you've been lying to yourself for so long that you don't even know right from wrong anymore.

"But I do. I have a very firm grasp of right and wrong, young man, and this is something you need to hear. Do you know the most loving thing you could do for your son right now? Leave him alone." And then she repeats this forcefully, as if it is the answer to an important question. *"Leave him alone,"* she says. "Give your son a real gift, Troy. Show him real love. Don't make him miss you and yearn for you, because you know you will only ruin his life."

By the time he arrives in Lisa Fix's office, at one in the afternoon, Troy has calmed down somewhat. He even smiles at her, and she smiles back, adjusting the collar of her large yellow turtleneck as she types some things into her computer. It's a cold day. The parole office sits among a row of interconnected brick storefronts, directly across from the courthouse. A weathered cowboy is walking down the sidewalk and

Troy watches him pass, trudging with his hat pulled down over his face against the blast of snow sparks.

"So," Troy says, when Lisa finally turns to look at him. "Six months to go."

"Let's not get ahead of ourselves," she says, and she glances down into his journal, toying distractedly with her pen, clicking the retractable point of it slowly in and out. "You're doing fine, Troy, but let's do this a week at a time, okay?"

"It's my son's sixth birthday today," Troy says. "His grandmother won't even let me wish him happy birthday over the phone. Why don't you humor me? Give me something to look forward to."

She purses her lips, giving her pen another rueful click. "What do you want from me, Troy? I'm not here to predict the future. And I'm not here to humor you either."

"I just want to confirm the schedule of things," Troy says. He sighs, leaning his arm on her desk, his fingers brushing the little magnetic tube in which paper clips are imprisoned. "I just want to know— I mean, assuming that there are no glitches or fuckups on my part, or . . . *whatever*— She has to give Loomis back, doesn't she? That whole consent form that I signed for the probate court: Judy's guardianship of Loomis. It's temporary, right? Once I'm done with my parole, custody of Loomis reverts back to me, right?"

"Yes," Lisa says. "Technically, the custody would revert to you." Troy watches as she reclines back in her wheeled swivel chair, her eyes shifting, glancing out the window.

"Technically?" Troy says. "What do you mean by that?"

"Well," Lisa says. She looks at him for a long moment. Her round, freckled face grows solemn. "Listen," she says, finally. "I don't know whether I should tell you this or not. But you should probably talk to your lawyer."

And the look in her eyes sends the kind of thrum through him that he had felt, earlier that day, when Judy had said: *Leave him alone.*

"What do you mean?" Troy says.

"I mean that you should talk to your lawyer," Lisa says. "I'm not trying to get you riled up, Troy. But I think you should know. Your mother-in-law, Mrs. Keene, submitted a petition to the probate court to terminate your wife's parental rights. I just saw it yesterday. It's a pretty basic petition—nobody's been able to contact your wife for over six months, so it should be fairly easy to prove abandonment. I don't think Mrs. Keene will have a problem making her case."

Troy folds his hands together. Another person walks by the big window beyond Lisa Fix's desk, an elderly woman in a long wool coat and a pointed stocking cap. His hands are beginning to shake a little.

"And . . . ?" he said.

"And nothing," Lisa Fix says. "It's just— I think she has a good lawyer. I don't want to upset you, but if you think about it, once the mother's rights are terminated . . ."

"Then I would be the next hurdle, right?"

"I think it's a possibility," Lisa says. "But listen. I'm not telling you this to get you all worked up. Even if Mrs. Keene did petition against you, I don't think she could win. The law tends to favor biological parents. I'm telling you this because I think you need to be aware of it. What you need to do is keep your nose clean. Take your drug education class, do your community service, don't get into trouble. But if I were you, I would be prepared for the possibility that Mrs. Keene is going to challenge your custody."

Troy is quiet. He hunches his shoulders, staring down at the tile floor beneath his feet, his hands clasped tightly together. "Okay," he says at last. "Thank you."

As he drives back home he is aware again of that sense of entrapment he'd felt when the police had shown up at his door, all those months ago—that long, dreamlike pause where you imagine that there is still some way to escape. *Wait,* he thought. His hands were trembling as he clutched the steering wheel.

Do you know the most loving thing you could do for your son right now?

He could send his car swerving into a tree, he thinks. He could drive to Judy's house and strangle her. He could just keep on driving—cut off the parole anklet at the next intersection, head out to California, or Hawaii, or overseas—like Carla, disappearing into the vastness of the world.

You're not a very reflective person, are you, Troy?

No, he thinks as he turns down Deadwood Avenue. His windshield wipers tick insistently against the steady dots of melting snow that alight on the glass, asserting themselves briefly before being wiped clean.

Okay, he thinks. It is two-thirty in the afternoon, and he shudders as an old Guns and Roses song starts playing on the radio: a song that he and Carla had once liked, back before Loomis was born, and he almost starts to choke up.

Even before he turns into the driveway, he can see Jonah sitting there, perched on the hood of his old Festiva, right across the street from the house, waiting patiently. As he toggles the gear shift into park, he watches Jonah clamber off his car and stride up the driveway, and his muscles tighten. The old partying life he'd had with Carla falls away; the last chords of "Sweet Child o' Mine" cut off as he kills the engine.

"Hey," Jonah calls uncertainly. "Troy!" And Troy keeps on walking. He holds out his hand, like a traffic cop: *Stop. Keep your distance.* But Jonah shadows him as he walks toward the back door.

"Troy?" Jonah calls after him. "Troy?" And maybe he is so used to being ignored that he's oblivious, and Troy has too much ingrained midwestern politeness to simply keep walking. He turns to look over his shoulder, glowering, and Jonah widens his eyes.

"Hey," Jonah says. "I was, uh. I was just . . . stopping by? Like we talked about?"

Troy stands still for a moment, blinking. He remembers now that they'd made some kind of arrangement—"An appointment," Jonah had said. "Just to sit down and talk"—but it had completely slipped his mind. He thinks of excuses, pushes his hand through his hair. Though he has come to accept that the papers Jonah had given him are the truth, it's still a little hard to believe that this person is his brother. It's hard to know what to do with him. Where to put him on the list of things that need to be worried about.

"You know, Jonah," he says, "this is really bad timing."

And Jonah gives him a stricken look.

"Oh," Jonah says. "What's wrong?"

"Everything," Troy says. But this sounds melodramatic. "Nothing."

Their eyes meet. What is he supposed to do with the look on

Jonah's face, which reminds him of nothing so much as the abused kids he'd known in grade school—that expression they'd get if you'd pay attention to them, a bleak hopefulness opening briefly and then shutting. What is he supposed to do with the fact that for a brief flash he can see the sort of younger brother Jonah would have been? He can feel a kind of shadow life pull across him like a cloud scudding across the sun, and he can picture Jonah: a grubby and wiry-tough little kid, beloved of no one but fiercely loyal nevertheless, and he feels oddly guilty, aware of all the ways he would have broken that imaginary younger brother's heart.

"Nothing's wrong," he says quietly. It's already more complicated than he wants it to be, even as he turns to go into the house to make his phone call to the monitoring device people. He sighs as Jonah hesitantly follows after him, but he doesn't say anything more. He just picks up the phone and dials.

Despite everything, Jonah *has* been on his mind—or at least the idea of Jonah. His brother? His biological half brother? A stranger he shares some genes with? It has occurred to him that, besides Loomis, Jonah is the only other person he's met in his life who is biologically related to him, and he's not really sure what to think about it.

At first, he'd simply been angry. Discovering that Jonah had spent those first six weeks spying on him had bothered him more than he cared to admit. He was already feeling vulnerable, aware of his own body being constantly monitored, and thinking of those weeks that Jonah had worked alongside him at the Stumble Inn actually made his skin crawl—the uneasy, dreamlike awareness that someone he barely knew was hovering at the periphery of his life, gathering information, pretending to be someone he wasn't. It was scary.

But he also found himself regretting how mean he'd been. He recalled the way Jonah had flinched like someone who was used to being hit, nodding in agreement when Troy had said, *I don't want you in my workplace. I don't even know whether I want anything to do with you.* Afterward, thinking about it, it had seemed cruel. It had connected in his mind with the way Judy had treated him, and Lisa Fix and his lawyers. When Jonah had called him a few days later, he'd held the phone in his hands for a long time without speaking, listening to Jonah's hoarse explanations.

"It was a stupid thing to do," Jonah kept saying. "I know I was a coward about it. I know that now, but I just . . . chickened out, every time I wanted to tell you."

"Yeah," Troy had said. "Well, maybe that was the right instinct."

"I don't know," Jonah had said, and there was a sandpaper edge of emotion in his voice that made Troy's heart tighten. "I know this sounds stupid," Jonah said, "but it was like you were the last person in the world I had any connection to. And I didn't want to come all the way just to have you slam the door in my face. I wanted . . . I don't know. To get to know you a little. I know we're not *really* brothers, but . . . I got caught up with the idea of it. The idea of connection. I'm sorry that I wasn't, braver, about it."

And Troy wasn't sure what to say. What do you do with a statement like that? *The idea of a connection.*

"Well," Troy had said. It came to him that everything Jonah had loved was gone: his parents, wife, his unborn baby, the future he'd imagined for himself. "Well," Troy said, "we should talk about it."

He thinks of this all again as he recites his information to the parole service. *Jonah is my brother,* he thinks, gazing over to where Jonah is still standing in the doorway, in his cheap, puffy ski coat and blue stocking cap, his arms crossed over his chest. *My brother. Biological half brother.* And there is a kind of uncomfortable wonder to this fact.

"You're clear," the monitoring device guy says, and Troy slowly depresses the receiver. Jonah's eyes skim over the surface of Troy's face, even as he wavers in the doorway, keeping a respectful distance, his head cocked like a sad dog.

"It's okay," Troy says. "You might as well come on in."

Growing up as an only child, Troy used to have fantasies about having a brother. A little brother was what he always imagined—and in fact, back in the days when he was baby-sitting, he had come up with a game that Ray loved, in which they'd pretended to be siblings. Tim and Tom were their pretend names, and they made believe that Ray was only two years younger than Troy, instead of almost eight. It was a way to control Ray, he supposed, to keep him from wanting to play irritating kids' games or watch babyish movies that Troy disliked, but it also spoke to his own secret wish to have a cohort, a trusted follower in his adventures, someone to tease and argue with and hang out with.

He can't quite picture Jonah in that mode, exactly. Jonah would have been too much trouble, he imagines—and he has another guilty flash of that strange, fierce, large-eyed little brother he would have hurt and disappointed. Ray wasn't a good model, he thought. Ray had been too easy, too pliant, and in fact, he had probably done Ray a disservice, especially during Ray's teenaged years, when Ray was living with him and Carla. He'd let Ray do whatever he wanted, as if he was in his twenties, and had even encouraged him to drink beer and get high and drive without a license and basically join with impunity in the general hell-raising that he and Carla were engaged in. Ray could have used a real parent.

Still, he found himself wondering what Jonah would have been like if they'd been raised together. Would he have grown up so skittish and evasive, so spacey and unsocialized? Troy doesn't think so. He's not just a guy who had a tragedy with a car accident, Troy thinks. Whatever's wrong with him has been building up for years and years, and Troy can't help but feel that Jonah would have been better off if he'd been around to look out for him.

And maybe he himself would be different as well. Jonah wouldn't have been as malleable as Ray. It wouldn't have been a replay of the old Tim and Tom game—Jonah was much smarter, much more deeply involved with his own imagination, and maybe if they'd known each other earlier, Troy would have grown up to be, as Judy said, a more reflective person.

Of course, if they'd grown up together, they wouldn't be the same people at all. If and if and if— The little marks and scars they would have made on each other would have molded them in ways that were impossible to calculate. It's a little like that math puzzle Jonah had told him about: *an infinitely long line surrounds a finite area.* Fathomless.

"Do you want some coffee?" he says to Jonah, who has settled at the kitchen table.

"Well . . ." Jonah says.

"I'm going to have some myself, okay? So it's not a big decision. You want it or you don't want it. Whichever you choose is fine."

"Okay," Jonah says, and he holds his coat in his arms, fiddling with it. "I guess I don't want coffee, actually." His eyes widen and unwiden. "Is this a bad time?" he says. "I can come back later—"

"It's always a bad time," Troy says, and shrugs. How much does he want to say? "Listen," he says, and glances sharply at the phone. "I'm sorry I didn't turn out to be . . . what you were hoping for." He makes a laughing sound. "You drew some pretty unlucky cards when you came looking for me, didn't you?"

Jonah seems taken aback. "No!" he says, as if Troy has implied some bad intention. "Not at all." He purses his lips. "Is there anything I could do to help?" he says.

"You could kill me," Troy says. Then he shakes his head, disliking his own blithe sarcasm, his own self-pity, which he knows Jonah won't find funny. "Never mind," he says. "Nothing you can do, man. This is the hole I dug for myself, and I'll have to deal with it."

"Well," Jonah says, "even if it's something little. Like . . . going to the store for you . . . or whatever. There's probably something I could do."

"Not really," Troy says, and then they are both silent, listening as the coffee machine begins to gurgle and bubble.

"So how's things at work?" Troy says, and shifts his weight. "Ha! You know, someone mentioned the Gold Coin the other day and Vivian got all edgy about it. She's still pissed at you for jumping ship."

"Well," Jonah says. "I wish I was still at the Stumble Inn with you guys. I'm not very good at making friends with people."

"Mm," Troy says, and there is a twinge of guilt. "You're not missing anything," he says, and pours himself a cup of coffee from the still-filling pot, not caring that it spills a little. He sits down at the table, rests his forehead against the ham of his palm. He thinks again of his conversation with Lisa Fix. "Shit," he says, under his breath, and Jonah gazes at him cautiously.

"It's about Loomis, I guess," Jonah says, and Troy looks down. Is this the conversation he wants to be having?

"Sort of," Troy says. "Not really. It's not important."

"It's Loomis's birthday today, isn't it?"

And Troy looks up at him sharply. "How did you know that?"

Jonah shrugs. "You told me. Remember? We talked about all of this stuff. I just have a good memory for dates."

"Huh," Troy says, and it's another way in which they are completely different. Troy is aware again of the way in which Jonah soaks up information, that glint of gentle, steady computation in his eyes, which Troy had noticed when Jonah talked about his college classes, or when he talked about the details that he'd gathered about Troy himself—Troy had been amazed, and more than a little disconcerted, to look through the folders of court records and letters, certificates and credit reports, all annotated in Jonah's tiny cursive handwriting. He can picture Jonah alone in his trailer, transcribing their conversations into a little notebook or something. He's probably got shelves of notebooks, Troy thinks. He probably knows what he ate for breakfast three years ago on this day.

"That's right," Troy says at last. "It's his birthday. Six years old. Pretty amazing if you think about it. I mean, that's when you start to become a real person. You start getting, like, a *consciousness*, you know? You start getting this sense of yourself as a separate person in the world. I mean, your mind is more mature. You remember what it was like to be six years old, more than you remember being a toddler. And then after that, you're starting to become yourself. Your personality and brain. It's weird to think of that happening to a person you saw getting born."

"I guess," Jonah says, and watches as Troy sips coffee. Troy can see his expression moving through its shifts, the time-lapse-photography quality of a leaf, opening. "Did you get to talk to him?" Jonah says at last.

And Troy blushes. "No," he says. He shifts in his chair, grimaces, and he can't help but feel a little ashamed—a failure as a father, a man whose child would be better off without him, at least according to Judy. "That's actually a problem right now. I haven't been able to talk to him . . . for a while."

"Oh," Jonah says, and Troy watches as he processes this. "What are you going to do?" he says finally.

"I don't know," Troy says. "I don't think there's anything I can do, really. At least while I'm in this situation."

Jonah inclines his head, and his entwined fingers twitch lightly. Their eyes meet for a moment, and Troy is aware of . . . what? That odd, ambient sense of connection. He remembers the day Loomis was born, the moment when the nurse had lowered the swaddled infant into his arms, and it had struck him, suddenly, that Loomis was the first person he had ever met who was connected to him by blood, and now, as he looks at Jonah's eyes, he can feel a flutter of recognition in the pit of his stomach. That's the connection, he thinks. If Jonah and Loomis stood side by side, an observer would easily recognize that they were related. There are particularities of expression, something shared in the way their eyes flicker and then grow calm, a certain ruminative turn of the mouth. The resemblance is so clear for a moment that Troy feels a knot in his throat.

28

Winter 1997

Jonah drives around and around the edges of St. Bonaventure, but he can't seem to find a way out of his predicament. It has been this way always, he thinks—a long hallway, like the corridor of a motel or apartment building, and he winds his way along, checking the knobs, feeling his fingertips pulse with the dull electric current of all the people he might have been. He could have stayed on in Little Bow, working his way through the kitchen to a job as an orderly at the old folks' home. He could have tried to weather his way through Chicago—finishing college, maybe. Finding a career. Pursuing the tentative relationships that he'd made with more tenacity, maybe even *really* meeting a wife, having a family. He could have stuck it out at the Stumble Inn, too; he could have become friends with Troy, if not his brother; he could have been almost happy with Crystal and Vivian, making food for people. Almost.

But it is as if each possible life is just beyond his reach. He thinks of a fly against a windowpane, tapping steadily against a transparent barrier. He always gets to a certain point, he thinks, and then he fails.

And so it goes again: the worst one of all. He had the opportunity to make a real connection. He has shown bravery, has taken wild chances—is there anyone, he thinks, who would have taken such measures as he had to get close to Troy? Who else would have had such determination?

Yet he has let himself screw it up so easily. So stupidly. As many times as he goes over his life in his mind, he can't seem to find a way past the roadblocks that he has created for himself. He drives past the Discount Mart, with the great, dirty hills of snow plowed up in the corners of its parking lot. He drives to the edge of the interstate, to the truck stop with rows of sentient eighteen-wheelers lined up not far from the gas pumps. He drives along past country houses and sheds, posted at intervals along the rutted state highway, past winter fields and telephone lines hung with xylophones of icicles. White-faced Hereford cows alongside a fence, the snow accumulating on their backs. A blank billboard, with tatters of old advertising hanging from it in strips. He should be able to figure out a way to make this work, he thinks. He should be able to correct his mistakes somehow.

His biggest failures, he supposes, were the simple ones, the ones that shouldn't have caught him off guard. Like that day in November, when he'd brought in all the paperwork, and Troy had gotten to see his original birth certificate for the first time.

In the beginning, it seemed to be going well. Troy sat there reading the document over and over, and his hands actually shook as he turned the pages. Jonah watched as Troy's mouth tightened.

"Baby Boy Doyle," Troy said. He didn't look up for a long moment, and Jonah shifted, tense and respectful.

"I know it's kind of heavy," Jonah said, and cleared his throat. "It's a lot to take in at one time." He was trying to imagine what Troy might be thinking. Was he wondering about Nora, picturing his infant self as he was parted from her, his infant's eyes watching a blank ceiling unscrolling above him? Was he parsing the ways that his life might have been different? Did he feel, as Jonah sometimes did, the vast randomness of life spreading out in a long plain all around him?

But when Troy lifted his head, he was not overcome with emotion. He looked puzzled.

"Wait a minute," Troy said. "Why is your last name Doyle?"

"What do you mean?" Jonah said.

"I just mean . . . that's Nora's maiden name. I thought you said you had a father."

"Oh," Jonah said, and he could feel the blush spreading across his face, bane of liars.

"Actually," he said, and hesitated for a moment. "Well . . . my father's last name was Doyle, too. They weren't . . . related or anything. It's not that uncommon of a name. It just so happened that they were . . . lucky that way."

He smiled at Troy, who was looking at him with his forehead wrinkled—disbelieving?—Jonah couldn't be sure.

"Huh," Troy said. "Well, that was convenient, I guess."

"They used to joke about it," Jonah said. "That's . . . actually, that's how they met. He was getting her mail by mistake. His name was, um. Norwood. Norwood Doyle."

"*Nor*wood?"

"Yup," Jonah said, and he looked Troy in the eye, steadily, smiling, hopefully sincere. "It was some sort of family name. He hated it. He went by Woody."

It still bothered him that he'd saddled himself with this imaginary, spur-of-the-moment father with the goofy name. It was such a mistake, he thought, because now he had to spend time inventing stories about this man, Woody Doyle, whom Troy had inexplicably taken an interest in.

"What kind of a father was he?" Troy said, one day in December. "Did you like him?"

"Hmm," Jonah said. "Well, sure. Of course. He was a carpenter. Like my grandfather. He built me a tree house when I was . . . I don't know . . . about eight. He was a pretty quiet guy, though."

"What did he look like?" Troy asked.

"Like me, I guess," Jonah said. "I mean, without the—" and he gestured lightly toward the scars on his face. "You know. Kind of blondish-brown hair. Round face. The same sort of build, basically."

"It's too bad you don't have any pictures," Troy said, and Jonah stiffened inwardly.

This had been an issue between them, this lack of photographic evidence. It was the thing that Troy seemed to find hardest to believe, even though it was perhaps the most truthful thing Jonah had told him.

"You mean you don't have *any* pictures of your family?" Troy said, incredulously, and Jonah thought of the time, all those years ago, when he'd been clearing out the old yellow house outside of Little Bow, the auctioneer, Mr. Knotts, watching him as he tossed the photos into an extra-large garbage bag. *You should go through those,* Mr. Knotts had said. *People can be rash when they are in mourning.* And now, of course, he was sorry.

"I lost them . . . in a fire," he'd told Troy, and Troy raised his eyebrows.

"That's *weird,*" Troy said. "You mean there's no more pictures of them—period? I mean, there's got to be pictures of them somewhere. What about, like, other of your relatives? Or a high school yearbook?"

"Maybe," Jonah said doubtfully. "I wouldn't know how to get ahold of one."

And Troy had shrugged. "Well," he said, "you figured out how to find *me*. That's got to be harder than tracking down a few pictures!"

Troy didn't understand, Jonah thought. Troy had no idea how easy it was to disappear off the face of the earth, how easy it was for time to swallow you up. He thinks again of his mother's ashes, combining with the soil in a ditch somewhere in Iowa, shot through with the roots of small plants, which drew the nutrients from what remained of her body before dying themselves. Or his grandfather. More than fifteen years have passed since Joseph Doyle's death, and by now Jonah himself is perhaps the last living person on the planet who had loved the old man, who remembers his face clearly, who remembers the stories that he'd told about himself.

Maybe, Jonah sometimes thinks, he himself is fading out in the same way. He has spent so much of his adulthood wishing to be a different person, so many hours dreaming of exactly this sort of transformation. In the new self that he's portraying, Nora no longer walks through the rooms of the little house, muttering to herself, telling him that she wanted to die and then finding excuses not to; there is no Elizabeth, her bobbed tail tucked shyly between her legs; there isn't the sound of his grandfather's coughing phlegm into a handkerchief, there is no longer that morning when Jonah found him dead, his rigid fingers clutching the silky edging of an old blanket, pressing it to his half-open mouth.

There is hardly anything at all. His life is suddenly a large, empty house, with each vacant room waiting to be furnished. His made-up wife. His invented father. His pretend childhood.

He wonders if it is possible to unlie yourself.

Sitting in his trailer house, he tries to find a way to go back to the beginning, to that day in September when he'd arrived in St. Bonaventure, to do it over again. He draws diagrams in his notebooks, working backward, trying to fold up the expanding accordion of lies. February, January, December, November, October, September. He tries to walk himself through the dull dailiness of his new job at the Gold Coin Restaurant—burritos and chimichangas, tostadas and refried beans; through the days indoors, behind the shades, under a blanket on the couch, watching television, reading.

He finds himself driving a lot. Sitting in his car with the defroster on high, idling in the empty, snowy parking lot of Zike's Roller Rink, with its boarded-up windows. Puttering up into the hills behind Troy's house, where, months ago, he brought Rosebud, after he'd killed her.

The dog's body is concealed in a little alcove under a cliff of lichen-covered pumice rock, and he's not sure why he's drawn to check on it from time to time. Maybe he's just making sure it's still there—some kind of guilt or superstition pricking him. The body is almost skeletal now, crusted with snow, mummified, the skin pulled taut over bones, the lips shrinking back over the teeth in a kind of smile. Standing over the corpse with the wind and the dust of snow blowing up in whirlwinds, he thinks of that teenaged boy, Jinx, standing at his door. "I wonder if you've seen my dog," Jinx said, and he was no more than fourteen, though when they'd first met he'd seemed somehow threatening. Powerful with his group of stoned cronies. "I let her out last night, and she never came back."

And Jonah had looked at him, his forehead creasing, miming concern. "No," he said, and he was aware then that almost all of his life was a secret. The boy's eyes, undrugged, had an earnest, deerlike gentleness that reminded him a little of Troy, and Jonah had felt his heart blanch.

"Sorry," he said. "But . . . I'll keep my eyes open for her. I'm sure she'll . . . turn up."

December turned into January turned into February, and still Jonah would wake up at night and hear Jinx calling from the porch of his house.

"Rosebud," Jinx's voice would echo. His hands cupped around his mouth. "Rosebud! Rosebud!" And Jonah would press his face hard against his pillow.

Troy wanted to talk about the past, that was the worst part of it all. Troy wanted to hear stories about Grandpa Joe and the orphan train, about Joe and Lenore, their grandmother, who had died in a car accident before Troy or Jonah was born, and Jonah felt obliged to make up stories out of nothing. It was irritating that Troy was so interested in Lenore's relatives, the aunt Jonah had been to visit once, Aunt Leona, whose face Jonah could barely recall.

"Wow," Troy had said. "So we're part Indian. Part Sioux. That's really kind of cool."

Jonah sighed lightly. "I guess," he said.

And then he wanted to know about Nora. It was even harder to talk about her, since all the characteristics that Jonah most remembered about her were compromised by her imaginary marriage to the imaginary Woody Doyle. And it was even more difficult to talk about his own life, since he had to make up nearly everything. He had a Chicago childhood to invent, a house on the west side, with a pretend father and mother patched together out of projections: What would she have been like, if she'd been happy, if she'd been normal? What would he himself have been like? With that as his premise, he had to create an entirely new childhood, and from there, concoct a girl who would fall in love with him, and whom he would marry, and who would die in a car accident.

At first, this didn't seem so problematic. It was only when Troy began to talk about his own past, it was only when Jonah saw the photo albums that Troy kept, the stacks of pictures and mementos, each with a little anecdote or funny story attached, that he saw how thin and underdeveloped his own make-believe world was.

They looked at pictures a lot, at first. Dozens and dozens of Troy's "relatives"—the family he was adopted into. Here was Troy as a baby. Troy's adoptive mother and father, and Troy himself, aged about ten, outside a tent at a lakeside campground. Troy's cousins Bruce and Michelle, and their child, Ray, circa 1979. Troy's father, in an upholstered recliner, grinning, holding a beer. Troy and Carla and teenage Ray, sitting in the same kitchen that he and Troy now occupied. He looked at the photo, and Troy put his thumb across the bong that was prominently centered in the middle of the table. "Ignore that," Troy said, shrugging, flipping the page, and here was a collection of photos of Loomis as a baby. Even as a toddler, Loomis's eyes were recognizable: stern and serious and critical.

What could Jonah do in the face of such records? He had no such organized bank of history, nothing that tethered him to the facts of the world, not even something so small as a photo album.

Troy seemed so dauntingly grounded, so familiar with the story of his life, that Jonah found himself ashamed of the pitiful skeleton of his own.

He remembers the day of Loomis's sixth birthday, the way they'd sat there, looking at photo after photo of Loomis, the child's life mapped out year by year.

"You remember what it was like to be six?" Troy said.

"Yes," Jonah said. But he didn't know what else to say. "It's funny," Jonah said at last. "I'm not really sure if I remember anything correctly. About being a kid." He presses the inside of his lip against his teeth, trying to think. He should have stories about growing up in Chicago, about Woody and Nora Doyle, about the girl he'd married, but nothing came to him.

"I got bitten by a dog," Jonah said, and he could feel himself blushing as if this were a lie. "That's what I remember about being six. My mom's dog, Elizabeth. She was a . . . Doberman, and . . . she bit me pretty badly. I've always been kind of scared of dogs, ever since."

"Huh," Troy said. "Was that in Chicago?"

"In South Dakota," Jonah said. He could feel a pang against the surface of his eyes, a sharpness. "I had to go to the hospital."

"Wow," Troy said, and he seemed to muse on this, but not very sympathetically, Jonah thought. "We never really had pets," Troy continued. "I don't know why. My mom, I guess, didn't like the idea of having animals in the house." Then he smiled, as if remembering something fondly. "We had fish for a while," he said. "I really loved those fish."

"Ah," Jonah said. He hesitated. "I . . . like fish, too," he said.

He could have said it then. He could have said, "Look, Troy, I've been lying to you all along. I want to tell you the true story of my life." He even stood up for a moment, pushing his chair back from the kitchen table, sick of the single room that they seemed to have settled themselves into, sick of the weight of the false life that he kept on inventing. He stood there, helplessly. Each time he and Troy met, it felt as if he'd unraveled a little bit further from himself, from his true history. Each afternoon that they sat down at that kitchen table to talk, it felt like he was acting out a persona that was more false than the time before. It wouldn't be long, he thought, and he would be completely imaginary.

29

February 27, 1997

Troy has been thinking a lot about Nora lately. Despite everything, despite all the more pressing concerns, he finds her floating up from the back of his mind. *Nora Doyle,* he thinks as he trudges out the back door of the Stumble Inn, past the fat, unhappy Dumpster, pulling his stocking cap over his ears, the muddy slush of the parking lot beginning to solidify beneath his shoes as the little bit of sun sinks away. "You look a little pale," Crystal had told him as he was leaving. "Are you doing okay?" And he'd shrugged. "Just a cold," he said, and now, sitting in the car with the defrost on, he finds a crumpled piece of tissue and blows his nose grimly. Exhaust plumes thickly out from his muffler into the cold air, and he can imagine Nora, a teenaged girl five or six months pregnant with him, staring out a window of the Mrs. Glass House at the snow. He thinks of that long ago day when he was eleven, when Carla's friend Chrissy had talked to him about being adopted. *Don't you wonder about your mother?* Chrissy had said, and he recalls the small fissure that had opened up inside him at that moment, even though he'd tried to ignore it for years and years.

He has a vague image of her. A narrow face, Jonah had said, high cheekbones, dark eyes, a prominent nose. Long black hair, he thinks as he stands in his kitchen. "It was down to her waist when I was growing up," Jonah had told him, and Troy has a glimmer of her again, as if he has seen her before. The back of his neck quivers. He can see her face as she gazes out through her window, her mantle of dark hair, her features unclear through the layer of condensation on the glass. Would he have been moving inside her?

Probably not, he thinks, and he puts a pan of water on the stove to boil. He finds a package of powdered soup—yellow chicken-flavored dust, dehydrated noodles—and pours it into the pot, then changes from his work clothes into sweats while it heats. He looks in the medicine cabinet for some kind of cold remedy, and at last settles on a chewable grape antihistamine that he'd bought for Loomis sometime last year. He unrolls some toilet paper and blows his nose again.

She would have put her palms against the windowpane, he imagines. A sixteen-year-old girl. Water would have trickled down from the imprint of her hands.

The last few days have been pretty awful, and maybe that's what brings Nora into his mind. Monday had been the fifth anniversary of his mom's death, and he'd been surprised to find that it hadn't really gotten easier. The dull ache of grief opened up around him, exacerbated by his frustrating dealings with Jonah, by his worries about Loomis and custody. He'd learned that Judy had already, without any dramatic confrontation, managed to terminate Carla's parental rights, and he knew it was only a matter of time before a similar petition was leveled against him. He'd spent the better part of the day trying to reach his lawyer, Eric Schriffer, pressing the phone receiver to his ear as Nora and his mom and Carla circled through his mind in slow, lazy figure eights: dead, missing, lost. He listened to the soft, muddy bump as he was put on hold. Schriffer was "in a meeting," or "not in the office," or "on the other line."

They'd been friends once, Troy thought. They used to sit around and get stoned, and they'd had some pretty good talks, and even as he listened to tinny classical music being played for him through the phone lines, he could imagine confiding in Eric. He would tell him about Jonah and all the adoption stuff. He would tell him about the odd, elusive connections he could feel at the edge of his thoughts—his adoptive mom, and Carla, and Nora, these women he'd lost, pacing together in a wheel in his mind.

But when Eric finally picked up the phone, in the late afternoon, it was clear that they were friends no longer. He had only started to talk about the termination of Carla's parental rights when Schriffer cut him off.

"Listen, Troy," Schriffer said, in a bright, quick voice. "This is nothing to worry about. This is a fluke of your ex-wife's behavior that has nothing to do with you. I just got a report from your parole officer, and you're doing great. Even if she does present a petition, it will never in a million years make it to court. The law is on the side of the biological parent, man. You just need to take it easy and relax."

"Yeah," Troy said, and he could feel all of the things that he'd imagined telling Schriffer shriveling up. "Yeah, I understand, except—"

But Schriffer was already moving on. "It's really good talking to you, Troy," he said. "But I really have to get going. I'm sorry. It's really been hectic around here lately."

"Ah," Troy said. "Well then."

He paces through the house, drinking his soup from a coffee cup. He changes the sheets on his bed—the old king-size four-poster that had once belonged to his parents, and which he'd later shared with Carla. He checks on Loomis's room, the room that had once been Troy's as a child, and retapes some of the slumping drawings, loosened by the dry, forced-air heat. He sits down and sorts through some of his mom's things from the hall closet, her mementos and letters, her high school yearbook. Her jewelry box, where there is a little plastic baggie full of his own baby teeth, tucked alongside the earrings and necklaces. If he'd had a little alcohol in him, he might have even called Terry Shoopman, just to talk to someone who had known his mom, just to hear Shoopman bend his dull, steady high school guidance counselor voice to Troy's worries.

"You shouldn't feel guilty," Terry Shoopman would say. "Your mother always wanted you to find out more about your biological family. To tell you the truth, she was always a little troubled that you didn't show more interest in it when you were a child.

"It's true you've had a run of bad luck, Troy," Terry Shoopman would say. "But it seems silly to try to make these connections. Your wife, and your mother, and this woman Nora? They're all very different people. Surely you realize that."

"Yes," Troy would say. "That's true."

"I think you're spending too much time alone, young man," Terry Shoopman would say. "You need to get a grip on yourself."

"Yes," Troy says aloud, and curls his palm around the baggie of his baby teeth. He recalls what Jonah had said, a few weeks ago. They had been talking about Jonah's wife, Holiday, about the car accident, and Jonah had shrugged his shoulders abruptly.

"I really can't think about it anymore," Jonah said. "I need to move on." And then he'd looked at Troy plaintively, his eyes roving, scanning Troy's face. "You just . . . keep moving, right?" he said. "You're always . . . in the process of becoming a different person. Don't you think?"

"I guess," Troy said. He wasn't sure what to say to the strange, urgent conviction in Jonah's eyes.

There was so much that Jonah was evasive about, so many questions he skirted with general philosophical principles. He said that it was "hard to remember," that it was "not really that important," that there were "things he doesn't like to talk about."

"Jonah takes the Fifth Amendment once again," Troy would say, half joking, half irritated. "What is there to be so slippery about, man?"

"I'm just not that . . . interested in the past," Jonah had said, and lowered his head stubbornly. "I like to sort of . . . live in the present."

"Uh-huh," Troy said. "Well, for me the present kind of sucks, so we're a little bit at odds, don't you think?"

And Jonah had shrugged, moodily. "I'm telling you the truth," he said. "I just don't remember. I don't think about that stuff."

Nora was a particularly touchy subject for some reason, and Troy couldn't understand why. He knew there was something Jonah wasn't telling him. The silences grew longer when she slipped into the horizon of the conversation. Jonah's mouth grew small, reproachful, when

Troy asked a direct question. It was as if Jonah didn't quite recognize that Nora was what connected them, that Nora, at least biologically, was Troy's mother, too.

"Did she ever—" he had asked Jonah once. "Did she mention me, ever?"

And Jonah had shifted in his chair. "Well," he said. He brought his foot up and cradled it in his lap. "I think she thought about you," he said.

"What do you mean?"

"I don't know. It was just a feeling I got."

"But you knew," Troy said, after a moment. "You knew about me, that she'd given a baby up for adoption. She told you?"

"Well," Jonah said. "More or less." He cleared his throat. "You know," he said, "she didn't talk about anything personal with me. It was just like a . . . typical parent-child thing. Nothing special. I don't have any real insights or anything. You know? She cooked, and she kept the house clean, and she liked to read books. She liked art, I guess. She had lots of postcards of different paintings. And seashells. She collected seashells."

"Oh," Troy said. He watched as Jonah looked down at his hands. Unlike most people, Jonah tended to rest his hands with his palms facing up—maybe because of the scars that ran down his knuckles to his wrists—but it gave him an oddly religious quality. "You didn't like her very much," Troy said carefully, and Jonah glanced up, abruptly, startled.

"I didn't *dislike* her," Jonah said. His brow furrowed. His expression came near to annoyance, the closest that Troy had ever encountered. "We didn't always get along the best," Jonah said. "But she wasn't a bad person, exactly."

He had tried to be sensitive about Jonah's reluctance. He understood that there were things that were hard to talk about, and he had the vague notion that Jonah and Nora had some sort of falling-out, that there was some aspect that needed to be approached delicately. He even offered up his own adopted mother as an example, hoping that his stories about her would act as prompts to Jonah's recalcitrant memory.

Awkwardly, he had told Jonah the story of his mother's funeral—how stoned they'd been, how he'd undone the prayerful clasp of the corpse's nearly weightless branchlike hands. He had never told this anecdote to anyone before, but he gave it to Jonah, and they were both silent for a moment when he was done with it.

Troy shrugged, giving Jonah a sad, apologetic half smile. "It's fucked up," he said.

"A little," Jonah said. "Not— I don't think you did anything wrong, exactly."

"I don't know," Troy said. "I feel pretty guilty about it. I miss her." He waited, expectantly, but Jonah just sat there. His eyes shifted slightly, and he licked his lips.

"What was it like for you?" Troy said. "Was there a funeral for . . . Nora?"

Jonah seemed to freeze.

"Not really," he said. "Well, not in the traditional sense."

Troy raised his eyebrows expectantly.

"She was cremated," Jonah said. "So there wasn't a casket or anything. It was just . . . a quick thing."

"She died young," Troy said, after a moment. "I was thinking about that the other day. She was only, like, what? Forty-three?"

Jonah didn't say anything. Troy was aware of a whole map of memories moving through Jonah's brain, unspoken.

"She killed herself," Jonah said at last. "I don't really know why. But she, well," he said.

"Oh," Troy said.

"It was pills, basically," Jonah said. There was a long, ambient silence in the kitchen, and Jonah was motionless. Outside, the icicles that hung from the eaves cast reflected waves of light through the window, trembling yellow-gray shadows. "It was pretty straightforward. She took, like, a whole bottle full of pills, and then she died. I guess she was unhappy. I don't know."

It came as a blow, this information—this death.

Troy was surprised at how heavily it settled over him. This woman, this Nora, whose body he'd once inhabited, whose picture he'd never seen but whom he has put together from Jonah's hesitant descriptions. Suddenly she was a presence.

His mother.

Whatever he'd hoped for her crumbled a little.

"I'm sorry," he said softly, and hesitated. His hand felt shaky as he put it across his mouth, but Jonah's expression hardened.

"I probably shouldn't have told you that," Jonah said. "It's not like . . . something I dwell on. I'm not trying to make you feel sorry for me."

"I know," Troy said, and paused: a shudder. "But . . . I feel sorry for *her*, man. I mean, she killed herself! And you didn't tell me that?"

"I didn't want you to think she was a bad person," Jonah said, at last. "I didn't want you to think she was crazy."

"Jonah," Troy said. At that moment, there was something in Jonah's eyes that made Troy feel sad—a shifting, trapped look, the kind of expression you might have when you reached the dead end of a maze for the third or fourth time.

For a moment Troy half considered reaching across the table and touching the guy's hand. Okay, his brother. His mom had killed herself. His wife was dead. He was, Troy realized with sudden clarity, desperate.

"That's why you didn't keep any pictures, I guess," Troy said.

Troy goes through all of this in his mind as he sits there on the floor with his mother's jewelry box between his legs. It has been over two weeks since he last talked to Jonah, and it's weird. He's not sure whether Jonah will ever be back.

"I don't get it, Jonah," Troy had said. "Look, I thought the reason you decided to find me was . . . because she was our mother. I mean, if you can't be straight with me, what are you doing here? What's the point?"

"I don't know," Jonah said.

"What do you want from this, man?" Troy said. "I mean, let me ask you a question. What do you want from life?" And Jonah just shook his head, as if the question baffled him.

The house is dark now, and Troy doesn't bother to turn on the lights. He sits in Loomis's bedroom with the window open a little, breathing the freezing air, blowing smoke into it.

Here are the things that Troy wants from life: He wants to be a good father, to see Little Man grow up; he wishes he was the kind of dad who maintains the love of his son, over a period of years; he wants the adult Loomis to remember him fondly when he is dead. He wants to be the kind of man that Carla would want to come back to, sober and repentant, and if he can't have that, he wants to meet a beautiful, gentle girl he can make a home with. He wants great sex. He wants his old friends—Ray and Mike, Lonnie, all the guys he'd played cards with or got drunk with at the bar, the people who would sit out in the yard in the summer, the tiny bats dipping in the twilight above the branches, the stereo speakers sending stupid rock and roll into the yard, his bare feet in the grass. He wants to live next door to his parents. He wants them to be alive, still happily married and growing old together—and they would go on camping trips, his mom and dad, him and Carla, Loomis, maybe another kid or two not yet born. He wants to notice a piece of the world every day, something beautiful or funny or strange, that he can think about. He wants to be content most of the time.

He sighs. Across town Loomis is taking a bath, sitting with dignity among cloud peaks of bubbles, and maybe the time they spent together is already half like a dream; to the north, in Bismarck, Terry Shoopman watches a science program on public television, and a photo of Troy's mother is still centered on the surface right above the screen—Troy's mother and Shoopman on their wedding day; to the west, in Las Vegas or Reno, Carla runs her lighter under the glass of a pipe, her lower legs tangled in the sheets, a guy asleep beside her, and in a large house in Arizona, Ray's mother Michelle pours herself a glass of wine, stands in her kitchen, frowning as if she can feel someone thinking about her in the distance.

As for Jonah, Troy can't imagine what he's doing, what he's thinking. Maybe he's working at the Gold Coin, or sitting in his trailer, reading, solitary, an airtight wall between himself and his past. He remembers the blank look Jonah gave him. "I don't know," Jonah said at last. "I think . . . I guess . . ." Then he let out a kind of laugh. "I really don't know what I want," he said. "I really don't."

30

April and May 1997

When Jonah left St. Bonaventure, he didn't plan to come back. It was over, he decided. He'd made such a fool of himself—showing up drunk on Troy's doorstep, telling him, what? It didn't matter. It had been clear for a long time that things were never going to work out the way he wanted them to. Whatever hopes he'd had for Troy were gone now. He had screwed everything up again.

He packed only a few things before he left. He was very deliberate about it. Spartan, he thought, and liked the sound of the word. He laid all his clothes out on the bed: five T-shirts; three pairs of jeans; seven each of underwear and socks. These went into paper grocery bags, lined up in the trunk of the car. He put his cassette tapes into their little case and set them on the passenger seat. He put the envelopes with his money in the glove box, bundles of tens, twenties, fifties—everything he'd managed to save, plus what little was left of the original nest egg that he'd gotten from the sale of the house. He thought of that day, long ago, when he was clearing out his mother's belongings; he thought of the auctioneer, dressed like some old-fashioned Grand Ole Opry singer, shaking his head sorrowfully as Jonah stuffed trash bags full of photos and mementos. "Son, don't do anything you're going to regret."

There was a weird pleasure in it, though. That was what he realized. It reminded him of a time when he was a child, a day when he and his grandfather were trying to fly a kite in the stubble field out beyond their house. After a few failed attempts at getting the kite into the air, his grandfather remembered that a kite needed to have a tail. They searched around in the field for a while, looking for a bit of rag, and after a minute or two his grandfather said, "Oh, what the hell," and cut off a long strip from the bottom of his shirt—just like that!—with a pocket knife. Jonah recalled being a little shocked. "Oh, Grandpa," he said. "Don't do that!" But his grandfather just shrugged, and they knelt down in the dirt to work on the kite. He'd thought about that shirt for a long time afterward. He was impressed by the idea that adults could simply tear their own shirts on purpose, and there would be no repercussions. Later, he'd taken one of his own shirts out behind the house, cutting into it with a pair of his mother's scissors, frightened that someone would catch him but also exhilarated. He buried the ribbons of cloth in the garden, his face flushed, his shirt-murdering hands trembling.

He thought of this feeling again as he looked over his possessions: his victims. He had considered trying to hold a garage sale, but on second thought there was more satisfaction in sentencing this segment of his life to death. In thinking that there were still things in his life that he would live to regret losing. He stood with his arms folded in the living room of his trailer, considering, and then he began to stuff all the little flotsam that he'd cherished into garbage bags and cardboard boxes, filling containers one by one and hauling them out to the communal Dumpster in the alleyway behind the trailer court.

It felt good. He broke the base of a lamp against the metal side of the Dumpster. He slit open a bag of flour and let the contents slide in a curl of fog over some discarded shoes. He wavered only a few times before he befouled his well-thumbed old college textbooks and beloved paperback novels with the poured-out contents of his refrigerator—a bottle of ketchup, jar of pickles, cottage cheese, spaghetti sauce. Good-bye books. Good-bye term papers that he'd written when he was taking college classes. Good-bye stupid, desperate, self-pitying journals and diaries he'd been keeping. And finally, after a slight hesitation, good-bye packet of information that connected him to Troy, the photocopies of the birth certificate and court records. He crumpled these papers up very deliberately, shoving them into a two-ply plastic garbage bag full of household cleaning products that he'd bought when he first moved in. An electricity crackled across his fingers. Good, he thought, dragging bag after bag into the daylight, down the dirt path, to the alleyway. Good riddance.

It was a Saturday morning, and after a while the neighborhood kid, Jinx, came out to sit on the hood of a car. Still dogless, Jinx slouched back on his elbows, watching his baby brother playing in the dirt with matchbox cars, and when Jonah went past a third time, he lifted his head.

"Hey, Jonah," he said. "You throwing anything good away?" And Jonah smiled tightly.

"Not really," Jonah said, but on his next trip to the Dumpster he presented Jinx with a fairly new boom box that he'd bought at Discount Mart. "I was just going to get rid of this," he said. "Maybe you can find some use for it."

"Nice," Jinx said, mildly, and rubbed his hand over his incomplete mustache. "You moving out or something?"

"Something like that," Jonah said. He felt a small twinge of guilt, once again, for the death of the boy's dog. "I'm feeling the need to start my life over."

"Oh," Jinx said, "that's cool," and his grubby little brother gazed up at Jonah solemnly, crashing the fender of a matchbox car against Jonah's shoe.

"Yeah," Jonah said. He fingered the small framed photo in his pocket—the Polaroid snapshot of Troy and Loomis that Troy had given him. He'd thought about throwing this away, too, but now he thought he would keep it for just a while longer.

"Well," Jonah said, and held out his hand. "I guess this is good-bye."

Jinx smiled sleepily, regarding Jonah's extended palm for a moment, then at last inserting his damp teenaged hand into it.

"Good luck," Jinx said. "Have a nice life."

For a while Jonah wound his way along the interstate, stopping from time to time to glance at a road atlas. It was strange, he thought, to find the place he once lived, the towns he'd passed through, represented only as dots along great rivering roads. The maps showed the world spread outward from St. Bonaventure—from North Platte, from Omaha, from Chicago, from every center—spiderwebs, veins, nets that cast themselves across the open prairie. He recalled that day in the fall when he'd first driven to St. Bonaventure, when he'd stupidly imagined that his life was some kind of film—*the story begins,* he'd thought then. Now he wasn't sure what to think. *The story never ends? The story is pointless?*

Near the center of the state, he turned himself southward, past Red Cloud, where Willa Cather once lived, into a series of Kansas towns—Lebanon, Mankato, Belleville, Concordia—and into the larger world, which spread indeterminately outward. He could continue on this route, through Kansas, Oklahoma, Texas, all the way to Mexico City, or beyond, through Central and South America, to the tip of Antarctica. In between, there were many great cities, and millions of people, but that didn't comfort him very much. It didn't seem to matter really.

In Wichita he sat in a strip bar at the edge of the interstate, where a topless red-haired woman danced in high heels. He drank a gin and tonic, then rested in his car with his eyes closed. He traveled down I-35 through part of Oklahoma, stopping for gas in Broken Arrow. He ate a cheeseburger in Okmulgee. He crossed onto the Indian Nation Turnpike, on his way to Texarkana, before twining his way lengthwise across Louisiana to New Orleans, where he planned to live for a while.

But he hated it there. It was not the sort of place where you started over, he thought. On a block in the French Quarter, he watched a teenaged girl helping her friend throw up into a garbage can. A walking tour passed by, led by a man with a shock of black hair like a horse's tail, and curling stiletto fingernails, at least three inches long. The man was wearing a cape and a top hat, with dark makeup around his eyes, and he looked at Jonah's face suggestively as he passed, as if they were kin, as if Jonah was yet another curiosity he might point out to the docile people following behind him.

Jonah slept in his car that first week, trying to decide if he really wanted to rent a room. At night he sat with the map light on, reading the various brochures for attractions that were scattered across the city, listening to the radio and the street sounds. One night he woke up and a couple were having athletic sex while braced against his car. He sat there in the backseat, blinking, watching the man grin fiercely as he thrust himself against his partner, a woman bent double, with her face pressed against Jonah's hood. Jonah wasn't sure what to do. The man seemed to be looking directly at him, his gritted, gilt-edged teeth glinting under the streetlight, and Jonah didn't move. Did the man see him? Jonah wondered. He felt for a moment as if he were disappearing, ceasing to exist, and in the morning, he wasn't sure if it had really happened.

It reminded him a little of that March morning after his birthday, the stuff he'd been trying not to think about. He'd awakened on Troy's couch, and at first he didn't remember much of anything. Hungover. His head was too fuzzy, too painful, and when he tried to sit up he could feel his equilibrium swinging around him in a nauseated, wobbling circle. His shoes and socks were on the carpet, next to a plastic bucket that had been placed near his head. He sat up, rubbing his hands against his face, and it was then that a little flash of the night before came to him. He remembered the bottle of bourbon he'd purchased for his twenty-sixth birthday, and then showing up at Troy's back door. They were sitting at the kitchen table, as usual, but he didn't remember what exactly they'd said. All he knew was that he'd slipped up. Told more than he should. (*I don't have a wife. There wasn't any car accident.* He remembered that much for sure.) Called Troy names. (*If I had your life, I wouldn't have fucked it up as bad as you did.* Had he said that?)

What had he done? There were large, unpleasantly blank chunks throbbing in his memory, but it didn't matter what he'd actually said. It was clear to him even in his hungover state that the damage was irreversible. He picked up his shoes and socks and limped, barefoot, along the cold cement of Troy's driveway to his car.

For the next few days he slept. He unplugged the phone, didn't bother to go into work. He lay in the dim bedroom and tried to piece together the conversation they'd had. The alcohol had fragmented it into dozens upon dozens of tiny shards—some nearly clear, some blurry, some utterly dark. He could picture Troy's face, grim, silent, listening. Ultimately, he had no idea what he'd told Troy—how much of the truth, how many new lies he might have layered on top. But he knew that he'd ruined things.

For a few weeks he tried to imagine himself into New Orleans, but it seemed less and less probable—like a bad rerun of his first days in Chicago, without the eager, hopeful belief in the idea of becoming a different person. He didn't know what to do with himself. From a phone booth on Bourbon Street he called Steve and Holiday's number, and listened to Holiday's voice on the answering machine before hanging up. He called Crystal about an hour later from the same phone booth, listening sadly to her surprised, stiffening voice.

"Oh! Jonah," she said. "How nice of you to call!"

"I'm in New Orleans," he said, and Crystal exclaimed as if impressed.

"That must be exciting!"

"Yes," Jonah said. He could feel the people moving around him on the sidewalk as Crystal hesitated awkwardly. "How is everybody doing?" he said. "I've missed you guys."

"That's so sweet of you," she said. And he wavered there in the brittle politeness of her silence.

I don't have anywhere to go, he imagined himself saying. *I want to go home but I don't know where that is.* He winced at how pathetic it sounded, how self-pitying. What could she possibly say to that? What could she do to help him?

"So," he said at last. "How's Troy doing? He must be just about done with parole by now."

When he finally arrived in Little Bow, South Dakota, it was the middle of May. Over four years had passed since he was last in this, his hometown, but nothing much had changed. Main Street was still the same sad cluster of shops. The movie theater where he'd spent so much of his time was still there, and so was the high school, the football field, the clump of bushes beyond the chain-link fence where teenagers were still standing, furtively smoking cigarettes and joints.

A few miles outside of town, the little yellow house where he grew up was still there as well. He passed down the long gravel road where once the school bus would drop him off; here was the same metal mailbox with the red latch-flag that you could lift to tell the postman that outgoing mail was contained inside; here were the stubble field and prairie, here were the kitchen windows and the white door, the weeds beginning to grow in the flower beds on either side.

He sat there for a while, his car idling, and at last a woman came out of the house holding a baby against the crook of her hip. Another child, about three, a girl child in a purple smock, followed behind.

"Hello?" the woman said cautiously. She was a homely little woman, about Jonah's age, with short brown hair and a pointed, witchy nose. "May I help you?" she said. Her voice was gentle and musical.

Jonah rolled down the window. "I'm sorry," he said. "I'm not here to bother you. I used to live here once."

"Oh, really," the woman said, pleasantly. She glanced in the backseat of Jonah's car, where a stack of dirty clothes was covered by a blanket and pillow, and an old flashlight was wedged alongside a smattering of books and magazines. "Just passing through?" the woman said. She didn't seem to notice—or at least, she didn't respond to—the scars on Jonah's face. "Do you want to look inside? It's a little messy, but I'd be glad to show you."

At the edge of his vision, Jonah could see Elizabeth loping along the side of the house, her paw lifted because of a thorn. He could see the clothesline where his mother hung the wash, draped with billowing blankets.

"I know what it's like to want to come back to your old house," the woman said kindly. "I think about doing that myself. I grew up in Boise, and I know someday I'm going to do the same thing you are. I'll just park in the driveway and take a long look. I think that's an important thing to do."

"Yes," Jonah said. The little girl looked at him from behind her mother—a thin, hollow-eyed child, her blond hair lifting in the constant wind, her brow furrowed.

"We love this house," the woman said. "We're so happy here."

After a moment, Jonah returned her smile. "I'm glad," he said.

Later that same day he found his grandfather's headstone in the cemetery. There were some plastic flowers next to it, very old—the color in them had faded, and the plastic itself had become weathered and brittle. They were meant to resemble orchids, and he picked them up and put them under his arm. His grandmother's grave was alongside: Lenore, who died in a car accident when his mother was a girl. There should have been a gravestone for his mother, as well, he supposed. But of course there wasn't.

He'd been dreaming about her lately. He dreamed about her walking, the way she walked when she was taking Thorazine, the jerky, deliberate steps of someone who doubted the solidity of the ground in front of her. He could see her contracted eyes, the pupils about the size of the head of a pin. He remembered walking with her in the supermarket when he was a teenager, dreading the moment when she'd see an infant in a stroller and go into her routine, her old, bitter joke. *Oh look,* she'd say, *there's my baby!* and he'd flinch as she tottered forward, her once beautiful hair now stiff and unruly, cut in a shag style, her mouth small and dry and trying to make an exaggerated smile for the infant. Jonah stood there stiffly as the woman pushing the stroller recoiled at their approach. *There's my baby!* his mother crooned. *There's my baby!* His mother was only thirty-five but looked much older. Her body was wiry, monkeylike, with ropy arms and stumbly, stick legs, wearing clothes from the children's department at Sears, girly jeans and a pink T-shirt, and he sometimes thought that if he grabbed her wrist, her hand would come off and the thin fingers would curl and shrivel around his thumb.

He dreamed that she was leaning over him as he was sleeping, shining a flashlight into his eyes. He dreamed that she was singing to him, a song from one of her records, slow, terribly sad: *I wish I had a river I could skate away on,* she murmured, her alto voice throaty and thin in the darkness above his bed. The damp pads of her fingertips passed along his face, along the ridges of his scars, and when he groaned and tried to push her hands away, she winced, then smiled.

"Don't worry," she said. "I'll be gone soon enough. Then I won't bother you anymore."

"Good," he said, and when he tried to close his eyes again she bent down and kissed him firmly on the mouth.

"No one will ever love you again," she said softly, as if to herself. "You know that, don't you?"

And he squeezed his eyes shut, pressed his face to the pillow, just wanting to get back to sleep.

"Yes," he said.

And he supposed that it was true. He drove around town one more time, past the old folks' home where he'd once worked, past the Harmony Chicken Farm, where his mother had once spent her days, packing eggs, and in the late afternoon he even drove out onto the reservation. His grandmother's sister, Leona, would be in her middle seventies, he guessed—if she was still alive—and after a few passes down the rutted dirt roads, a few angry dogs snapping and chasing at his tires as he rolled through their territory, he found at last the boxy, prefab house his grandfather had once taken him to, years before. The bare, grassless yard was scattered with toys—a purple bike, a basketball, a naked Barbie, some plastic building material—and when he knocked at the screen door a Lakota boy a few years younger than he came to the door. The boy was wearing a white T-shirt and jeans, and his hair was cut very short, as if he might have been in the marines.

"Can I help you?" the boy said.

Jonah cleared his throat. "Well," he said. "Actually, I was looking for Leona Cook. I don't know whether she still lives here."

The boy was silent, his eyes passing over Jonah's face and body with a heavy, neutral look of appraisal. Behind him, Jonah could see a boy and a girl, aged about six or seven, sitting on a couch, watching television. He could hear the bloinks and xylophones of cartoons.

"What do you want her for?" the boy said.

"Well," Jonah said, "I guess she's my great-aunt. Her sister, Lenore, was my grandmother, and I just thought . . . well, I just . . ."

"She's not in very good shape," the boy said. "She had another stroke a few weeks ago." He didn't open the screen door.

"Are you her son?" Jonah said, and the boy blinked at him.

"Her grandson," he said, his voice uninflected.

"Well," Jonah said. "I guess that means I'm your cousin. Your . . . third cousin? Maybe. My name is Jonah."

"Oh," the boy said. He glanced down at Jonah's palm, which was extended as if to shake hands, the scrim of the screen door still between them.

"You know," the boy said. "It's probably not a good time. She can't really talk or nothing. She just sits there, you know? With her fingers moving? I don't think it would be good for her to have a stranger in the house." He peered uncertainly at Jonah, and of course he must have wondered about this pale blond guy with the scars on his face, claiming to be his cousin. Maybe, Jonah thought, Leona would confirm their relationship, but maybe she wouldn't remember him at all. Maybe, he thought, there was no one left alive who really knew who he was.

At last, he traced over the route he took, years before, along the edges of South Dakota, Nebraska, Iowa. Here was the old two-lane highway he'd traveled down once. He watched along the edges of the road the fence posts, the growing weeds, the barbed wire. He had to drive past, a few times, before he finally saw the place.

Miraculously, the urn was still there, upturned over a fence post, weathered and rusted, but still present. Four years had passed. Nothing remained of her body, of course.

He felt his hand against the gear shift, putting the car into park, and then he turned the key in the ignition and the idling car went dead. A weight settled over him. Even after all this time, it was still only the two of them, just as she had said.

He was a little past his twenty-second birthday when she died. He had been working at the old folks' home, washing dishes, and when he came into the house everything was silent.

"Mom?" he'd said. "Mom?" For years he had been rehearsing

the moment when he would come home and find her dead. His shoulders tensed; the skeletons of expectations began to erect themselves around him.

He'd pressed his hand against her door, and rattled the knob. "Mom?" he said, and for some reason he knew that it was real this time. He could feel her inside the room, the flick of a fishtail, a muscle spasm before the fish was cut open, its mouth closing on dry, useless air. He pressed open the door, and there she was, as he had pictured her so often: her nightgown pushed up past her thighs, her mouth ajar, her hands stiffened. He stood there in the doorway, pretty sure that she was dead.

"Mom . . . ?" he said, and his heart quickened. The radio was still going. Her eyes were open as an announcer gave the weather, introducing a song. Her body seemed to be stiff, and he was prepared to put his fingers on her eyelids and push them closed.

He never did find out how many pills she had taken, how many different poisons she'd consumed. There was probably an autopsy report, but he never saw it. All he remembered was that when the pads of his fingertips touched her eyes, to close them, she opened her mouth, and an emptiness poured out. Her lips tried to form words. She gagged, her throat muscles suddenly beginning to work. One eye fixed on him while the other drifted off.

He always told himself that there was nothing he could do at that point. The doctors were unsurprised by her death; they didn't seem surprised that he hadn't saved her, but she herself had widened her eyes. "Don't make me go," she whispered, and her fist closed around his pinkie finger, the way an infant will clasp whatever is pressed into its palm. "I don't want to go," she said, and pressed her damp mouth against the side of his face.

For a moment, sitting there along the road, he recalled what her fingers felt like as they clenched tight and then, step by step, became dead. It wasn't like in a movie. The grip pulsed for a while, squeezing and unsqueezing, but it didn't stop. It kept on for some time, spasmodically, long after his mother had stopped making sounds, stopped breathing. The last part of her that moved was her legs, kicking out suddenly. Her feet flexed, shoving off, as if she were in deep water, trying to make her way to the surface.

31

June 4, 1997

It was going to be a short ride, at first. They were going to spend a few hours together. But now Jonah isn't sure how far, exactly, he's gone. An hour, two hours? He watches the speedometer, he passes cars and is passed by them, though mostly he stays in the right-hand lane. He can feel his steering-wheel hands and accelerator feet merging with the movement of the car.

Landscapes pass but don't really impress themselves on his brain, sliding through his eyes and out the back of his head—the painted lines, the signs with their shining reflector strip lettering, the barren prairie sod divided by fences for no clear reason, jagged buttes rising up, clusters of shacks, occasional cow or tree, thunderstorm. Jonah can feel the road beneath him, a taut string that his wheels are riding on, and he tries to put his mind in order. They cross into Wyoming, and Loomis rises up from dozing and presses his cheek against the cool backseat window.

"Where are we now?" Loomis says, and Jonah curls his fingers. He can feel the body of the car more than he can feel his own body.

"We're outside of a town called Torrington," Jonah says. "I'm still looking for an interesting place for us to visit."

Loomis is silent, gazing out, blinking. Driving, he says, makes him tired.

"I'm thinking maybe we'll head south for a while," Jonah says. "That might be better."

Loomis considers this for a moment, his face stern with sleepiness. "Okay," he says.

It's probably early afternoon when they get off the interstate and onto the back roads. Loomis is sleeping again, and Jonah has settled into the unconscious posture of the long-distance driver, which is itself a kind of sleep, a kind of hypnosis.

It has begun to occur to him that, officially, he might be considered a kidnapper. Especially with those small-town, St. Bonaventure policemen. Especially with everything he has heard about Judy Keene. And he's becoming nervous. It doesn't yet seem that he has done anything criminal—Loomis isn't unhappy, he thinks, Loomis had come with him willingly. *Just for a ride, just for a day together.* But at the same time, as he looks out at the road, he can't help but worry about what might be happening back in St. Bonaventure. She might have called the police by now, he thinks, and he imagines a search party, focused at first on the immediate area but then tracking in ever-widening circles; authorities will begin to transmit information about a "missing child" to policemen in other towns and other states. Maybe he is exaggerating.

So far Loomis himself hasn't questioned anything, and maybe there's nothing to question. He was glad to see Jonah. Jonah had been away on a long trip, but he'd come back to St. Bonaventure just to visit Loomis. Just to see him one last time.

He isn't even sure when the idea of taking Loomis for a drive had occurred to him. Was it the moment when he arrived back in St. Bonaventure after his long trip? Was it when he found himself, that June morning, parking his newly purchased used car in the alleyway behind Judy's house? Was it the moment when the opportunity presented itself, the moment when he stood, hidden at the edge of Judy Keene's yard, watching as Loomis lifted up rocks along the fence to look for worms and insects, the child's face stolid and scientific as he bent down?

"Loomis," Jonah had whispered, when the child came close to the shadows of the lilac branches, and the boy had looked up, startled.

"What are you up to today?" Jonah had said, and tossed another dog treat into the neighbors' yard. By that time, after so many visits to Judy's house, the neighbor dog had come to know him, to see him as another food bringer, and though the animal made Jonah tense, he felt fairly secure. It was chained to a clothesline. It didn't bark, as it had the first few times.

"Hello," Loomis said.

"Hi," Jonah said. "I came back to visit you. I missed you."

"You did?" Loomis said, curiously.

"Yes, I did. I'm sorry I was gone for so long. I actually missed you a lot."

"It's been boring around here," Loomis said, and Jonah glanced in the direction of the house. He could hear the television turned up, a chorus of people singing some old-fashioned song—"June Is Busting Out All Over." Maybe that was the moment.

"Would you like to go for a little ride?" Jonah had said, without really thinking. "Maybe go on a picnic or something? I have something important I want to talk to you about."

"Oh, really?" Loomis had said, and then he'd given a little shrug. "Okay," he said, and when Jonah reached down, Loomis held his arms up with a kind of gentlemanly dignity, allowing Jonah to lift his body over the fence.

They trusted each other, Jonah thinks. It just seemed like the right thing to do, for both of them. *Let's spend a day together,* Jonah had said, and if Loomis had said no he would have accepted it without question.

But Loomis had wanted to come with him, he thinks. He observes in the rearview mirror as Loomis breathes experimentally on the rain-cooled window, then draws an *L* through the condensation with his finger. When Loomis glances up, Jonah smiles.

"Is it a lot longer?" Loomis says.

Jonah is still trying to formulate the scenario in his own mind. Where, exactly, are they going?

"I don't know yet," he says. His eyes focus on the car in front of him and he pinches his mouth tightly, considering. He can feel the tires revolving against the seamless highway, the river of wind parting before the car's prow, rushing in flapping pennants along its sides.

It is almost two when they stop in the small town of Straub, in between Wyoming and Colorado. Fuel and food. The gas station they pull into is part of a national chain, done up in bright, unpleasant yellows and oranges, the windows adorned with signs for beer and soda and cigarettes, the rows of gas pumps sheltered under a long aluminum canopy, high enough for a semi to rest comfortably beneath it. Jonah gets out and inserts the nozzle into his gas tank, compressing the trigger on the handle, watching the face of the pump as the dollars and cents and gallons begin to tumble upward, numbers rolling on an axis like the slots in a gambling machine. It had stopped raining quite a while back, but the air is green-smelling, full of pollen and stirred-up dust.

When he finishes pumping, he opens the back door and leans in. Loomis is awake, but bleary, his eyes still thick with sleep, the imprint of the car seat on one side of his face.

"Do you want a pop?" Jonah says, cheerfully.

But Loomis gives him a solemn look. "I'm not supposed to drink it," he says. "It's bad for my teeth."

"Oh really?" Jonah says, still smiling hopefully. "Wouldn't you like to try that red cherry kind?"

"No thank you."

"Okay," Jonah says. There is a minor deflation. "What about some juice? Or . . . chocolate milk, maybe?"

"Juice would be fine."

"And a snack?"

"Okay."

Inside, Jonah scopes the aisles. He finds a juicelike drink in the cooler, and picks out a variety of foodstuffs—some beef jerky for him, chips, a mass-produced pastry with cherry filling, peanuts, bright orange cheese-cracker squares with peanut butter spread in the middle, sunflower seeds, candy. A plush, cross-eyed toy dog that giggles and says "Do it again!" when you press its belly. A set of eight crayons and a coloring book with robots.

He sets all this on the counter, and the old man at the cash register watches him carefully, looking hard at Jonah's scars. Jonah is used to being watched carefully.

"How's it going?" Jonah says.

"Not bad," the man says. He appears to be in the late stages of alcoholism—gaunt, with nicotine-stained yellow-white hair and rosettes of blood vessels on his cheeks and nose. "Is this all for you today?"

"I also have the gas," Jonah says, and he glances out, looking at the numbers on each of the pumps. "On three, I think." He watches uncertainly as the man begins to ring up his items. "A little something to keep my kid entertained. I'm on vacation with my son."

"Is that right?" the old man says.

"Yes," Jonah says, "I think that's right," and the man fingers his purchases, turning them slowly to find the bar codes, touching the cash register buttons with his old, soft fingertips. Jonah thinks: *My wife died recently, and my son and I decided to take a trip for a while. Just to get a change of scenery, you know? Get our heads clear.*

"I haven't been in Colorado since I was a little kid myself," Jonah says, as the man rubs a candy bar vigorously across the electronic eye that reads the prices. "I was born here."

"Well," the old man says, "welcome home then." And Jonah smiles tightly even though the man isn't looking at him.

He tries to remember what his mother said about Colorado. Had they lived there together once? Or was that something that had happened to her before he was conceived? He tries to remember the various stories she'd told him—many of them lies, no doubt. As they cross back out onto the highway, Jonah lets her cross his mind, letting her out of the small compartment that he relegates her to on most days. Her bare feet walk across gray, mossy stones, those long toes gripping delicately, the nails painted red. He tries to get a good look at her expression, to guess at what she might be thinking, but her long hair droops around her face.

I think we'll always be lonely, you and I, she says softly, and he presses his teeth against the inside of his lip. That's not the direction he wants to travel.

"Hey," Jonah says to Loomis, who is gently dangling his legs over the edge of the backseat, who has cautiously taken a single bite of a cheese cracker. Loomis lifts his head, raising his eyebrows expectantly.

"How would you like to sleep in a tent?" Jonah says. "Does that sound like fun?"

Even now he's not sure how far he plans to go. He's not a kidnapper, he thinks, and in many ways he may even be doing Troy a favor. He remembers what Troy had said during one of those long conversations they'd had that past winter, when they were trying to become friends.

"I think I'm about to get fucked," Troy had said. "I think I'm going to lose my kid."

"How could they do that?" Jonah asked.

"These lawyers," Troy had said, "they can do whatever they want to a person like me."

"Oh," Jonah said, but he hadn't believed it then. He didn't realize it was true until later, when he'd talked to Crystal that one time.

"Oh, Jonah," she'd said, "things aren't going so well for Troy. I guess his mother-in-law is going to get custody of Loomis for a while. Even after he gets off parole. Isn't that terrible?"

"Yes," Jonah had said, holding on to the pay-phone receiver, which felt like a bone in his hand. He could picture the time he'd seen Judy and Loomis at the supermarket, how she'd had Loomis sitting in that uncomfortable child seat, with the humiliating strap of a sort of seat belt around Loomis's waist. Judy was fat but not jolly; her jaw had a squared-off, somewhat militaristic quality, and she seemed to be angry about something as she looked at the ingredients on a cereal box. Loomis was more subdued than Jonah had ever seen him, sitting there, staring at his palm, and he didn't look up though Jonah had liked the idea of their eyes meeting, of exchanging a secret wink.

He remembered what Troy had told him. "I know I've screwed up," Troy said. "But I love my son, you know? I do." And Jonah had nodded. He could imagine the three of them, driving south. A beach in Mexico. A tourist restaurant that he and Troy would open together. *Maybe we could just leave,* he thought, but he knew how Troy would respond. That ironic cock of the eyebrow, that grimace. As if the world beyond St. Bonaventure were some science-fiction planet.

The campground appears about an hour and a half later, eight miles off the highway, along the eastern side of the Rockies: LITTLE ICEBERG LAKE RECREATION AREA. PRIVATELY OWNED AND OPERATED. CAMPING, FISHING, CANOE RENTAL.

"This looks nice, doesn't it?" Jonah says, and Loomis peers over the lip of the window, his fingers brushing the nipple of the door lock, his eyes serious as they bump down a narrow, poorly maintained dirt road toward what appears to be an old outhouse that has been converted into a guard station.

When Jonah stops, a teenaged girl with short brown hair and a long, acne-ravaged chin comes out of the structure carrying a clipboard. She collects fifteen dollars and when Jonah asks for a "secluded" spot, she consults her clipboard grimly, directs him to Lot 23B. She hands him a photocopied, hand-drawn map, which shows a curving maze of roads lined with numbered boxes. She circles 23B.

Little Iceberg Lake is not a particularly popular destination apparently. It is four o'clock in the afternoon, but so far only four recreational vehicles are parked in the front lots, one of them so ancient and bedraggled that it might be haunted. Circles of rust dot its white, aluminum sides, and a tattered awning near the door is hung with limp wind chimes. Several of the windows are broken—repaired with duct tape and translucent plastic, or not repaired at all, shards of glass still hanging from the edges of the frame. Beyond it is a wooden hut—a set of bathrooms and showers and a pay telephone—and then a trail of tire ruts that leads into the evergreens. They pass a few campsites before reaching 23B: two motorcycle men, long-bearded tattooed gnomes sitting on stumps in front of a small bonfire; four college boys, unpacking a polished black Jeep; a family at a picnic table, all blondes of different sizes and genders, eating watermelon; a man and a woman—twins, perhaps—both with their hair plaited into braids, playing Frisbee in an open area. At the far end of this road, a post has been branded with the numbers and letters, *23B*, and Jonah pulls up beside it. There is a small picnic table, one leg manacled to the earth by a thick, rusted chain, and a campfire pit, encircled by a ring that appears to be a section of a sawed-off metal drum barrel. The ground is grassless, trampled bare.

"We'll pitch our tent here," Jonah says. "Then we can make a fire."

Things seem to be going well for a while. It is interesting to put the long, flexible tent poles together, and Loomis enjoys the patient project of threading them through the eyelets of canvas, the struggle to erect the frame, bending the poles until the canvas skin stretches taut across them, staking the hollow, flat-bottomed balloon of tent to the ground. He is involved in unrolling the sleeping bags inside the structure, pleased by the way the late-afternoon sun glows against the nylon membrane of canvas, the way the opening zips and unzips. It keeps both of them occupied and engaged, and then they drive to a small general store where they can buy marshmallows and hot dogs and ice.

"Are you having fun?" Jonah asks, as they turn back onto the road that leads to Little Iceberg Lake.

"Uh-huh," Loomis says, but he looks at Jonah guardedly. He is holding the paper bag containing the foodstuffs in his lap, very formally, as if bearing a religious icon. "Jonah," he says, at last. "Does my grandma know where we are?"

"Of course," Jonah says. "I called her when I was at the gas station, and she said it was okay. She said that she's glad you're getting a nice vacation. She said you should just relax and enjoy yourself."

"Oh," Loomis says. For a moment, his gray eyes cloud with concern, uncertainty.

"I have some important things to talk to you about," Jonah says.

"Oh," Loomis says.

"But first we have to look for wood. We have to find enough good, dry wood to keep a campfire going. Doesn't that seem like the best plan?"

"Yes," Loomis says. He shifts in his seat as they are driving, fingering the seat-belt strap.

They walk along the wooded area behind the tent, picking up sticks and bits of fallen brush. The evergreens slope down to a creek, which apparently feeds into Little Iceberg Lake, and they stroll along its banks in the twilight, listening to the soft, swallowing plunk of frogs as they flee into the water at noisy human footsteps. Jonah's arms are laden with dry wood, and Loomis wanders out in front, scoping the pathways. They look enough alike, Jonah thinks, that no one will question the fact that they are related. Actually, he thinks, they *could* be father and son. Loomis looks from side to side and when he sees a bit of fallen wood he strides toward it confidently.

"That looks like a good piece," Jonah says.

"I think so, too," Loomis says, and bends to pick it up.

Jonah will have to call Troy eventually. Troy will probably be freaked out about it, probably angry, but then he will see the logic of it. Even if they'd parted on bad terms, even if he thinks of Jonah as a liar and a sneak, he will have to recognize that Jonah has done a very loving thing. He has rescued Troy's son. Whatever else has happened between them, that will have to count for a lot.

They will come to an understanding, Jonah thinks. He'll explain it all. A few days, a week, and they'll all meet together.

All this comes to him dreamily, as if it's a fairy tale he read long ago, some movie he'd seen as a child on "The Wonderful World of Disney." He vaguely remembers the scene: a little boy and a young man standing with the kindling they've gathered, among the Ponderosa pines and their puzzle-piece bark, the crisp carpet of needles beneath their feet, light stabbing through the boughs in milky shafts. The boy and man face each other hesitantly.

"Loomis," Jonah says. He adjusts the bundle of wood he is carrying, first cradling it and then bracing it against his hip. Finally, he sets it down on the ground. "Listen," he says. "There are some things I want to discuss with you. I was talking with your grandma, and she, well, she was saying that it might be good if you stayed with me for a while. She's old, you know, and I think she needs a break for a little bit. Now that you're out of school for the summer and everything."

"Stay with you?" Loomis says, at last. "For how long?"

"Let's get a fire started," Jonah says, "and then we can talk about it. Okay?"

Building a fire is fun. Loomis is fascinated by the process—the biggest log in the center, surrounded by a tepee of branches, the twigs and bits of bark around the circumference. They spend a lot of time building this structure, and then Jonah hands him the box of matches.

"Just drop the matches around the edges, where the kindling is, okay?" Jonah says. He helps Loomis pull the match head along the flint paper on the side of the box, but when the flame sparks, Loomis flinches and drops the matchstick quickly as if it has snapped at him.

"That's all right," Jonah says, encouragingly. "It's good to be cautious. You don't want to get burned." Then he takes another matchstick from the box. "Go ahead. Just do it slowly this time, now that you know what's going to happen."

Loomis takes the match between his fingers, his brow furrowing, his tongue clenched lightly between his teeth in concentration, reminding Jonah for a moment of Troy bending over his crossword puzzles. "Okay," Jonah says, and Loomis surprises him with the neat, expert flick of his wrist. A hiss—and then Loomis is holding up the flame, his wide, astonished eyes catching the flicker of light. He grins.

"That's perfect!" Jonah says, and his breath hitches in his throat, at the purity of Loomis's pleasure. "Now put it on the kindling. That's right . . . get that little stuff burning." He hestitates for a moment, then rests his palm very lightly on Loomis's shoulder, a shudder of tenderness moving up his arm. "That's right," he murmurs. This is the closest he's ever felt to another person.

In the movie, the man and the boy had gone up into the mountains to have a serious talk. He remembers it clearly. The man had a beard and bright blue eyes and wore a flannel shirt. The boy was troubled, moody.

They saw a moose crossing a stream. They sat around a small fire in the darkness, and the man played his harmonica for a while.

Jonah thinks of this movie as they sit around the fire they have made together. Loomis is roasting a hot dog, proudly holding his long, sharpened sapling over the flames. Jonah hums a few notes, experimentally, then stops. He can't think of any songs, not really.

Instead, he finds his thoughts drifting toward his mother again, his mother on the day of his grandfather's funeral, how sane and sober she'd seemed. She'd put on makeup, and plaited her long hair into a single, tight braid that ran down her back. She'd worn a black dress, and Jonah wore black pants and one of his grandfather's button-up shirts, one of his grandfather's neckties, which she'd knotted for him. He can recall her fingers moving beneath his chin, the brush of her brisk knuckles against his throat. The gentle finality as the tie was cinched around his collar.

Later, back at the house, they'd sat at the kitchen table together, and she spoke to him as if they were equals, as if they were brother and sister, drinking wine in the late afternoon. She reached out and touched his cheek.

"He loved you a lot, you know," she said. And Jonah had watched as her eyes grew a film of water, as she looked past his face, out the window. "It's kind of dangerous, to be loved that much by somebody. It's hard to recover from it. It's not as if you're going to run across someone else who feels that intensely about you."

"I know," Jonah said, uncertainly, and she ran the pads of her fingers along the back of his hand, making a sigh that slid into his heart like a fishhook.

"Loomis," he says at last. The silence has been extending for a while by that point, the night pressing down on the little circle of fire. He recalls the bearded man in the movie, the way he took the harmonica from his mouth and sat solemnly for a while, watching orange flecks lifting off from the campfire and winking out in the braid of rising smoke. And then he remembers what the movie was about. He remembers what the man had said. *Son,* the man had said. I *have some bad news. Your father is dead.*

"Loomis," Jonah says, and clears his throat. He tries it out: "Son?"

But unlike the boy in the movie, Loomis doesn't lift his head. Instead, he focuses on the little stuffed dog, and presses it.

"Heh, heh, heh," the dog says. "Do it again."

Sparks rise with the smoke in little eddies above the flaming logs, and Jonah cannot really get a clear sense of Loomis's expression as the orange light shudders across the boy's face. *Heh heh heh,* the dog says. *Do it again.* And then a pause. *Heh heh heh. Do it again.* Jonah waits, trying to imagine the exact right words. But Loomis just keeps pressing the dog's stomach, over and over.

32

June 4, 1997

At first it had seemed ridiculous. The policemen—Kevin Onken and Wallace Bean, the same cops who had arrested him—standing there on his doorstep, shifting earnestly from foot to foot, embarrassed to inform him that his son seemed to be . . . lost.

"Lost?" he said, and he looked at them, puzzled. This was St. Bonaventure, Nebraska; it wasn't the kind of place where children can get lost for long. "What do you mean?" he said. "You mean he wandered off?" He flicked his eyes from one cop to the other, aware of the suspicious way they were regarding him. Gauging his reaction.

"Oh, I get it," he said. "You think he's here?" And he gazed bitterly at them. The first image that struck him was of Loomis running away from Judy's place—trekking slowly across the lawns and alleyways and parking lots of St. Bonaventure, making his way toward his dad's. They would find Loomis halfway between, and for a second he was almost happy. He would talk to his lawyer, telling him how this Custodial Parent who was supposedly more qualified than he was had been neglecting his child. He pictured a courtroom scene, with Loomis at the stand, telling the judge: "I wanted to get away from her. I wanted to live with my dad again."

Onken and Bean stared at him sternly.

"You guys want to come in and search the place?" Troy said, and stepped back, as if to invite them inside. "I'm sure Judy Keene tried to insinuate that I came over and . . . kidnapped him or something, but I've been here all day." He lifted his pant leg. "I've still got the monitor on, guys. You can check and see if I've left the house. He may be headed over here, for all I know, but it's not my fault if he wants to get away from that woman."

"Troy," Wallace Bean said, and shifted his hams. "Mr. Timmens," he corrected himself, and it was the shift into formality that sent a sudden prickle through Troy's mind. He watched the movement of Wallace's jaw beneath the skin.

"I think this might be turning into a serious situation," Wallace said.

He sat in the back of the police car, with his hands folded tightly in his lap. It was ridiculous, he told himself. St. Bonaventure wasn't the kind of place where some crazy comes along and snatches a child out of a backyard. It wasn't even the kind of place where you could wander that far—a twenty-minute walk in any direction would lead you to the edge of town, to the hills and fields and prairie that surrounded the town for miles upon miles. They had told him they'd brought in trail dogs, and the air in the back of the car had begun to feel thick. There was no handle on the inside of his door, no knob that would unroll the window.

"Loomis doesn't like dogs," he said, even though it seemed beside the point. "He'll just hide from them." He looked through the metal netting that separated him from the men in the front seat. "Look," he said, "maybe someone should be at my house. That's probably where he's going. He's probably just trying to work his way back home."

But they didn't say anything. He stared at their heads. The shaved, tapered hair, the inner tube folds of flesh that were stacked up on the back of Wallace's neck, and he suddenly remembered that horrible story, that kid who was killed—What was it? Ten years ago?—knocked in the head and dying of hypothermia in the basement freezer. Joshua Aiken. What a stupid way to die! But Loomis was a smart kid, Troy thought, and cautious. He wasn't going to fall down a well or get hit by a car or eat some poisonous berries or something.

Loomis was fine, he told himself. He wasn't the type of kid who would be lured into a car by some stranger. Troy breathed steadily through his nose, in and out. "This is ridiculous," he said aloud, flinching at the memory of an old dream: Loomis at the top of a tree, perched impossibly on a thin branch.

And then he thought: Jonah?

It had been almost three months since he and Jonah last talked. He even remembered the date—March 18—because it was, Jonah claimed, his birthday.

It was one of those late March days—neither winter nor spring, as if the seasons were fixed; the days muffled, melting into one another, the rain and snow mixing together.

Jonah appeared to be a little drunk. He wasn't quite stumbling, but when Troy let him into the kitchen he held up a bottle of bourbon, hesitating as he set it in the middle of the table, as if he were trying to center on some particular target.

"Hey," Troy said. He hadn't heard from Jonah in some weeks, and he wasn't sure what to make of this. He watched as Jonah sat down and took a little sip from the bottle. Without thinking too much about it, Troy went to the cabinet and drew out a highball glass. He picked up the bottle and poured three fingers of the bourbon into it, set it down in front of Jonah, who blinked at it, nonplussed.

"Thanks," Jonah said. He put his fingers around the glass, but didn't bring it to his mouth. "Guess what?" he said, his voice a little thick. "It's my birthday. Did you remember?"

"Well," Troy said. "Not really. I've had a lot on my mind, man." He cleared his throat, then warily settled down into the chair opposite, their old position since the beginning. "How old are you?" Troy said. "What? Like, twenty-six?"

"That's exactly on the money," Jonah said with strained cheerfulness. He took a sip of the liquor and shuddered at the taste. "Twenty-six," he said, hoarsely, then took another swallow. He was clearly not used to drinking such stuff, and Troy wasn't sure whether to intervene or let things play out. When Jonah set down his glass, a kind of moody, melancholy hostility emanated from his downcast face.

"Well," Troy said, "happy birthday, man. I guess I should have gotten you a card or something."

"Ha," Jonah said.

In retrospect, Troy thought he might have been more careful, more gentle. But he was used to seeing people drink. He had spent a large portion of his life as a bartender, a professional presiding over the drowning of sorrows, and this particular stage of things was quite familiar. Jonah was intoxicated—depending on his tolerance, depending on how quickly he had been consuming the alcohol, he'd probably imbibed anywhere between four and eight ounces of bourbon. Not a lot, in Troy's estimation, but enough so that Jonah was now on a cusp, and Troy understood his hesitation. Soon Jonah would lack control. A few more swallows and he would make a firm commitment to true drunkenness; certain kinds of mental regulation and inhibition would become elusive—straight lines of self-consciousness would become more and more difficult to walk down, heel to toe. By Troy's estimation, Jonah was about three gulps of eighty-proof liquor away from this altered state. *Okay,* Troy thought. This had been going on for too long, sitting across the table from each other in these circling conversations. It connected in his mind with the circumstances of his parole, the days and days alone in this house, the empty rooms, the television playing in the background. He lit a cigarette, folded his hands expectantly.

"Okay," Troy said, "so," he said, and carefully poured a little more into Jonah's glass. "So . . ." Troy said. "What's been happening? I haven't heard from you in a while."

"Not much, really," Jonah said, and then he sighed thickly with his lips, like a horse. "I guess I've been trying to figure out what I'm doing here."

"Uh-huh," Troy said, and gave him a small, ironic smile. "Tell me about it."

He felt a soft spasm of alarm, remembering this, sitting in the police car. He could picture the look that Jonah had given him, a kind of icy, endless gloom that he hadn't completely understood. Then he remembered

Crystal telling him—When? Back in May?—that Jonah had called her house, that Jonah had been asking about him. He wondered now what she had said. Had she told him that Judy had gained custody of Loomis? He would bet that she had.

"Wallace," he said now, speaking to the back of Bean's head as they traveled through the underpass toward Euclid. "Listen," he said. But then he realized that it was a very complicated thing to explain.

There's this guy who's kind of my half brother, he thought, and he could picture Jonah settling heavily into the kitchen chair across from him, the way they faced each other as they'd been doing for months, awkwardness emanating in thin, invisible waves. Except that now, without any apparent reason, Jonah had seemed so angry.

"I've been thinking about leaving town," Jonah said, as if this were something that would shock Troy, or make him feel guilty.

"Oh really," Troy said. "That doesn't seem like a bad idea. Back to Chicago?"

"Probably not," Jonah said. Troy observed as Jonah steeled himself to finish the last warm bit of whiskey in his glass. "Do you have any ice? I think maybe I'd like some ice in this."

Troy got up wordlessly and went to the freezer.

"I think . . . I think I just want to travel around for a while. I don't even know where." He paused as Troy dropped three ice cubes into his glass, observed as Troy poured another three fingers of bourbon over it. "There's nothing for me in Chicago," Jonah said. "I don't know whether there's anything for me anywhere."

"Hm," Troy said. He had known for a long time that it was best to remain neutral toward this kind of self-pity—a good bartender neither argued with it nor sympathized, but simply listened, simply asked noncommittal questions.

Jonah said that he might go to New Orleans, which had a lot of interesting history. Maybe he'd try Seattle, which he'd heard was a good city, and he'd never seen the Pacific Ocean. Maybe Arizona. Maybe he'd go back and visit Little Bow, South Dakota, where he grew up. "Make sure the graves are still there," he said. "Ha!"

Troy watched uncertainly as Jonah rolled the ham of his hand against his forehead. He was fairly drunk, in Troy's estimation, and the weight of his head slowly slid along the plain of his palm. "Listen, Jonah," Troy said. He thought for the first time in months about the letter that he'd tried to write to Judy, that pathetic, groveling letter, propped between the salt and pepper shakers on the table, along with the month's bills. For a moment, he half considered thrusting the letter into Jonah's hands, making him read it. *This is what it feels like to be really screwed,* he wanted to say. *This is what it feels like to be really trapped. At least you can drive away!*

But the letter wasn't there. He couldn't remember where he'd put it, and his face darkened. "Listen, man," he said. "I don't quite know what you want from me. I mean, let's say we're brothers. Half brothers. Whatever. What is this supposed to lead to? I've got a lot on my plate right now, if you haven't noticed, and you sit there like I'm *failing* you, or something. What do you want? Just tell me what you want."

He watched as Jonah shook the ice in his glass. Head down.

"I don't know," Jonah said. "I don't think it matters really. I think I'll always be lonely."

"What the fuck is that supposed to mean?"

And Jonah raised his eyes—a grim, bleary, furious glance that took Troy aback. "It's just something *our mom* used to tell me," he said, sharply, and then he let out a weird laugh. "You don't understand about her, you know."

"What?" Troy said.

"Oh, never mind," Jonah said. "People seem to think it's all either nature or nurture or some combination, but you know what? I think it's even worse than that. It's all . . . random. It's all chaos and luck and whether you're, like—" he cleared his throat. "Whether you're, like . . . stupid and cowlike, like *you*, or else you have some inkling of how deluded it all is."

Troy stared at him. *Cowlike.* "Don't be an asshole," he said. "You think I've had it so great? Well, I haven't, believe me."

But Jonah only bared his teeth. "You don't know," Jonah said, and his hand slurred in the air. "You don't have. Any. Fucking. Idea. You . . . You're just the baby in the basket. She always, our mother always used to say, *that's my baby*—and when I was little I always thought it was you, but it wasn't. It was just. Various babies. You were, like, I don't know, all *happy* somewhere else. I just wanted to change places with you, that's what I really wanted, if you want to know the truth. Because if I had your life . . . If I had your life, I wouldn't have fucked it up as bad as you did. I would have done better, you know? You had such a good chance and you just trashed it! I just wanted you . . . to be happy. That's all."

What do you say to that? Troy had wondered. If there was an understudy waiting in the wings to relive your life for you, could you doubt that they would improve on your performance? He kept his hands folded as Jonah took another drink of Jim Beam, as he drew a hiccupped breath.

"Listen," Troy said, softly. He couldn't help but feel sorry, he couldn't help but feel that Jonah was right. He had made a mess of his life. "Jonah, look, I . . ."

But Jonah's face remained in his hands. Was he crying? He shuddered when Troy touched his back, and stared up at Troy with wide eyes.

"I can't believe how bad I screwed this up," Jonah said, and his face twisted as if Troy had trapped him, as if Troy had finally, after hours of interrogation, broken his spirit. "You know, right?" Jonah whispered. "You figured it out, right? I never had a wife that died. I was never in a car accident. Our mom never got married to anybody. I'm not that person . . . I'm not anything."

It wasn't a shock, really. Everything he knew about Jonah seemed to settle and solidify. Of course he didn't have a wife, Troy thought. Of course he didn't have the kind of normal childhood he'd invented. He could sense the weeks that they'd spent together tighten and grow heavy in his mind. Of course he'd been lying the whole time, and there wasn't even any reason for it. Just fear, Troy thought, and, what, probably shame of his real life. He couldn't summon much outrage at the revelation. All he felt was a kind of dull, exhausted pity.

It was about four in the morning, and Jonah stumbled out the back door, tottered over the wet, muddy lawn. He grasped the tire swing and bent over, expelling a long, wet stream of vomit. His legs wavered for a moment, and then he sat down in a pile of melting snow.

"Jonah," Troy said. He stood there in the doorway, not sure how far the limits of his parole extended. Five yards, ten yards outside the house. He waded into the yard, trailing the electronic signals that his anklet might be emanating. He put his arms around Jonah, dispassionately, lifting him up. "Don't," Jonah whispered. "You win. Leave me alone." But Troy continued to pull his body across the yard, into the house: *You win, you win,* Jonah kept saying, even as his body grew slack.

Now, picturing this again, he could feel their lives locking into place, his and Jonah's.

"You guys," he said to the two policemen, "I think . . ."

But then he was silent. He could see the flashing lights of the ambulance parked in front of Judy's house as they turned onto Foxglove Road. Paramedics were running across the lawn, pushing a stretcher, and he could tell, even from a distance, that it was Judy.

"Oh Jesus, Jonah, don't do this," he whispered, but all he heard was Jonah murmuring.

You win.

You win.

33

June 5, 1997

A little bit after midnight, Loomis seems at last to be sound asleep. Jonah loosens his arms from around the child and slowly lowers him into the sleeping bag, letting his hand brush slowly across the soft cheek as Loomis makes a small, staccato whimper. "Shh," Jonah says. "Shhhhh," he whispers, as if he's letting the air out of himself.

He waits a while, until he is certain that Loomis is asleep, and then he steps outside of the tent to look at the fire. It hadn't gone as well as he'd hoped, and he still feels a little shaky, a little unnerved by how upset Loomis had become. He'd seemed to be taking it well at first, with the wood gathering and fire building, but then, as it grew later, Loomis had withdrawn more and more, and when Jonah had suggested that it was time for bed, his lip had quivered.

"I don't think I want to stay here," Loomis had said. "I'm not feeling very comfortable."

"Well," Jonah said, "we have to stay here at least for tonight. We're camping. I thought you said you'd like to sleep in a tent."

"I changed my mind," Loomis said, and Jonah's heart had quickened.

"You just have to try it out," he said.

"For how long?"

"Just a little while," Jonah said. "It's a vacation. Your grandma hasn't been feeling well lately, and so she asked me just to take you for a few days."

"I didn't even know that she knew you," Loomis said, frowning. "You said that I shouldn't tell her I was talking to you."

Jonah tried to smile. "I think you're a little confused," he said. "I mean, you know the situation with your dad, right?"

"My dad?"

"He got into trouble," Jonah breathed. "The truth is, Loomis, he and your grandma haven't been getting along very well, so I didn't want you to talk about me because I thought she would get mad about it. But the situation has changed. She needed someone to look after you, so I stepped in. At her request."

"Why can't I stay with my dad?"

Jonah sat there for a moment, nonplussed. "Loomis," he'd said at last, "he's still . . . having some problems. I don't want to worry you or anything, but your dad can't take care of you right now. He's in jail. That's why I'm here."

They looked at each other. At first it seemed okay—it was just a single tear, spilling over the edge of his eye, and Loomis wiped it away quickly. "I think I'm scared," Loomis said. And then, without warning, he began to weep.

Thinking of those sobs, Jonah still feels a little light-headed. He can't help but recall the sound of his mother's crying, the way his heart would tighten as he stood outside her door, his cheek pressed against the wall. It made you feel helpless.

He knows that he'll have to start making some big decisions soon, and he tosses a pinch of dirt into the fire, watching it spark.

They are surely looking for him by now. More than twelve hours have passed since he and Loomis drove past the St. Bonaventure city limits, and no doubt the police have been called. He guesses that probably everyone is very stirred up, though that wasn't his intention. He wonders if it is possible that he could even be arrested, even if he explained the circumstances, even though Loomis is his nephew by blood and they were just going on an outing. He imagines himself back in St. Bonaventure, in a courtroom, the judge ordering him to wear the same kind of monitor that Troy wears. Forced to sit in that old trailer, which would perhaps be a kind of justice.

He could still call Troy, he thinks. The fire is dying out, and he pokes at it with a stick, stirring the embers. There had been a pay phone near the entrance of the park, and he could walk down there, while Loomis was sleeping. He feels in his pocket: five quarters, three dimes, a few pennies. Maybe. He turns the end of his stick on the coals until the tip of it is orange. He looks at his watch, squinting, holding it close to his face. It's almost twelve-thirty.

Would Troy be in bed when the phone rang? He tries to project himself into that moment, to picture Troy rolling over to pick up the receiver—not fully asleep, surely, not with Loomis missing and all the worries that would be crawling like ants inside his head.

"Hello?" he would say, abruptly—Troy would no doubt be expecting bad news, and Jonah would have to pause.

"Troy," he would say at last. "It's Jonah."

Or maybe he would say, simply, "It's me."

He gets up and wanders toward the stake near their campsite, shuffling the road gravel beneath his feet.

"Troy," he thinks, hesitantly. "Hey, sorry to call so late. I figured you might be worried, so I just wanted to let you know that Loomis and I decided to go on a little trip together. I know I should have called sooner, but I didn't realize . . ."

No, no, he thinks. *Start over.*

"Troy, we need to talk," he says firmly. "I have Loomis here with me, and we've been talking some stuff over. He doesn't want to live with his grandma anymore, that's the thing. He wants to live with you and me. So we came up with this plan, you see . . ."

No, he thinks. Not right.

"Troy," he says, in a low voice, very calm and serious. "I'm just calling to let you know that Loomis is with me." And then he'll just have to cut Troy off, whatever he says. "Don't get upset. Just hear me out, okay? I need to know what you want me to do, because I think there are a lot of options that we might want to consider. But I really think . . ."

He takes a few steps down the gravel road, walking quickly into the darkness, aware of a hollow, fluttery feeling in his chest and legs. He looks over his shoulder at the hunched shadow of the tent where Loomis is sleeping, and then back toward the trail that leads to the pay phone. It's about half a mile, he guesses.

"I think I can help you," he says. "I know that you lost custody of Loomis, but if you just listen to me, if we just work together, we can all start over. I know it sounds crazy. I know that things haven't gone so well between us, and I know that I've lied to you in the past, but I swear to you that you can trust me. Just listen, okay?

"We'll let some time pass," he murmurs, in his mind. "Let's say about a month, or even two. Maybe they'll think your ex-wife took him. And then, when you're off your parole, we'll set up a meeting place. I think it should be in Mexico. Maybe near the beach, it'll be nice. I know you think you can't start over, but you can. We can both find some kind of job down there—I mean, there are bars and restaurants all over the world, and we're good at what we do. So we can just settle there for a while. You and Loomis and me. I know that it might sound outrageous, but maybe that's what you need. Maybe you just need to make a break. We can all start over, and there might be some snags at first but I think it will turn out okay."

He stands there in the middle of the road, two or three campsites down from his own, and there is only starlight, the galaxies hovering over him. Crickets. Cicadas. "It's better than just sitting there, and letting yourself get bulldozed over," he says. "You've gotten yourself into a situation now where you have to do something radical. It's like you're on a road, and you need to just pull over and . . . abandon the car. You just start walking away from the roads. Does that make sense?"

He waits for a moment, and finally, Troy sighs.

"How can I trust you, Jonah?" Troy murmurs at last. "Everything that comes out of your mouth is a lie. You lie when the truth would be easier."

And Jonah is silent for a while. *No, no,* he thinks. He listens to the steady churr of insects from the surrounding dark, to the even, rhythmic grinding of pebbles beneath the soles of his shoes. Over his shoulder, the fading campfire is barely visible in the distance.

"I realize," he says. "I've made some mistakes."

Then he starts over.

"Troy," he says. "It's me," he says, and Troy takes in a harsh breath through his teeth.

You scarfaced son-of-a-bitch, I'm going to kill you. The police are already looking for you and when they find you I hope they beat the holy shit out of you. You're going to go to prison for a long time.

"Troy," he says. "Listen, I knew you'd be angry but . . ."

Mexico? Troy says. *What is this, some kind of cheesy movie? Do you think you can just stroll across the border with a child you've kidnapped? And then what? Once you're in a new country you just call "olly-olly-oxen-free" and you're not a Class-A felon anymore? Do you think it's some sort of game to live the rest of your life as a fugitive?*

"Well," Jonah says. He looks around. The boughs of trees hang over him, observing, and a night creature—a frog or something—makes a deep, glottal, percussive sound.

And what is Loomis supposed to do when he grows up? What kind of life is he getting out of this plan of yours?

Jonah hesitates. *Start over,* he thinks again, but his mind gropes and finds nothing. What is he going to say? There is a long, unraveling space that he tumbles into.

He had imagined that the cluster of buildings with the pay phone was about a half mile away, but it seems as if he's been walking for a very long time. He holds his wristwatch up to his face, trying to make out the shapes of the hands on the numbers. He thinks of the flashlight, back in the tent next to Loomis, and wishes he'd brought it. It's very dark, and the moon doesn't seem to be anywhere in the sky.

Would the police really be looking for him specifically?

It sends a shiver through him, because he can imagine Troy's voice, he can imagine the policeman writing quickly with one of those short, eraserless pencils. "He's got a long, prominent scar along the left side of his face, from his eye, right across his cheek, all the way down to his throat. He's sort of a dirty blond, not quite six feet tall. Believe me, people will remember him if they see him."

He puts his hand to his chest, and he can feel his body vibrating as if there is a small motor inside him. What if he called Troy and the phone lines were bugged? What if Troy said, "Oh, yes, I think that's a good idea, I think we should meet," and all the while a policeman was standing there with a small machine hooked to Troy's phone, tracing the call? This is far-fetched, he tries to tell himself. Why would the police think Jonah had taken Loomis? Why would Troy, for that matter? They hadn't talked in months, and as far as Troy knew, Jonah was still in New Orleans, or someplace even farther.

But alone in the middle of the gravel road in the dark, he can't be certain of anything. Ahead, there is no sign of the buildings where he had seen the pay phone. Behind him, the campsite where Loomis is sleeping is no longer visible either. He scans the trees along the edge of the road, and can make out the glimmer of someone's campfire. The beam of a flashlight rattles against the treetops in the distance, then goes out. He can make out the sound of low voices from the shadows, someone still awake and talking, but he's not sure where they are.

Maybe he shouldn't call Troy, he thinks. Not tonight, at least. Maybe it should just be him and Loomis for a little while. A few days, a few weeks. He turns and begins walking back the way he came.

The campfire is almost completely out by the time he gets back. Only a few embers are pulsing out orange light through a crust of black ash, and he looks for his stick to stir them again. He doesn't know where he put it, and he feels a little sick as he casts around for it. It's as if his brain is actually moving around inside his skull as he tries to trace through the maze that he's somehow created for himself. He imagines sitting in a cafe in some Mexican village, drinking lemonade with Loomis, looking up as Troy comes through the doorway, his face solemn but respectful as he nods at Jonah, as Loomis leaps out of his seat. He imagines a nighttime roadblock, the cars ahead of him slowing, the cops running the beam of their flashlight along the body of his car, over his face, and he tries to twist the steering wheel, to accelerate. He imagines pulling up outside of Troy's house near dawn, opening the car door to let Loomis out.

Something rattles just beyond the edge of the campfire pit, and his thoughts stop. He can see the silhouette of a small child standing in the darkness.

"Loomis?" he whispers, but this child is shorter than Loomis. A toddler, he thinks, before he sees the yellow of its eyes.

A raccoon. It gazes at him as it stands there on its hind legs, its hands tucked close to its chest, and then it makes a slow, uncertain nod, bobbing its chin at him. Behind it, another one is backing tail-first out of the paper grocery bag where he and Loomis had left the remains of their supper—paper plates, half-eaten hot dogs, crumpled bag of chips. There are some other ones out there, too—four or five, he guesses. He can see their eyes.

"Shoo," he says hoarsely, but instead of approaching them, instead of waving his hands or stomping, he takes a step backward. That numb feeling, that stuff he doesn't think of, a mouth closing over his face. "Shh," he says.

None of them run away, though the one that backed out of the grocery bag stands up on its hind legs as well, holding the empty plastic wrapper that the hot dogs came in, nodding.

He puts his hand against the side of the tent, groping for the entryway. He thinks to retrieve the flashlight that he'd left there next to the sleeping bag that Loomis was curled into. He'll shine the beam of the flashlight on them, directly at them. That will chase them off, he thinks.

The opening of the tent is unzipped, and he crouches down with his eyes still on the raccoons, backing his way in. It's almost completely dark inside the little bubble of tent, and he runs his fingers along the edge of Loomis's sleeping bag, feeling for the flashlight, but it isn't there. *Damn,* he whispers, tracing his hands clumsily along the slick nylon floor of the tent, blind in the darkness. He doesn't want to wake Loomis up, and he takes extra care not to brush or bump against the child.

But when he puts his hand near Loomis's pillow, he draws in a sudden breath. Loomis's head isn't there, and when he presses his hand against the lump of sleeping bag, there's nothing but air inside it. No body. No Loomis. Disbelieving, he pats the sleeping bag harder and a tinny mechanical laugh rises up. "Heh heh heh," a voice says. "Do it again." He startles, lifting the bean-filled little toy by its string tail.

"Loomis?" he says. He turns in a circle around the tiny space, feeling around the circumference, clutching the sleeping bags, the pillows, as if Loomis were something tiny, like a key, that could be lost in the folds. Outside the tent, there is merely the soft, snuffling sound of the raccoons as they calmly go about their work.

34

June 5, 1997

Loomis has never been afraid of the dark, but in the woods it is harder to be brave. This is more dark than he's ever experienced, so he tries not to think too much about it. He holds his flashlight stiffly in front of him, pretending that the pool of light it casts is a dog he's walking. He likes this idea. A light-dog, he thinks, and it makes him feel a bit safer, even if it is make-believe.

He stops for a moment to look behind him, pointing the light at the bars of trees and tree shadows in his wake. The tent is somewhere back there in the distance, but he can't see it anymore, and he walks his pool of light around him in a circle. Twigs, pine needles, rocks. An empty can that says *Coors.* He listens intently to the steady, pulsing chirp of insects. He doesn't hear footsteps, though. He doesn't hear Jonah calling for him, and so he turns and continues walking, trying not to step on anything that makes a snap or rustle. There are plenty of people around somewhere nearby, he tells himself—he saw them as they drove to their campsite—but right now he only wants to put distance between himself and Jonah. If Jonah comes back and finds he's gone, Loomis imagines that he will try to catch him and make him sleep in that tent again.

He had slept for a little while, even though he was upset. Even though he'd started to cry, which is not something he likes to do. Some of the children in kindergarten cry over very small things, and Loomis doesn't really approve. But he hadn't been able to control his tears this time—he had been feeling very uncomfortable and nervous, and when Jonah said that he had telephoned Grandma Keene, he felt certain this was a lie. And then Jonah said that his dad was in jail. That was the thing that scared him the most.

At school, they teach you that Strangers, bad people, will sometimes pretend to be your friend. They might try to give you drugs, or pull you into their car and make you a prisoner. They might try to touch you in your private parts, and this is inappropriate. If this ever happens, they said, you should try to get away, and tell a grown-up that you trust, like a policeman or a teacher.

He is not really sure if Jonah is a stranger or not. All he really knows is that it is important for him to call his grandma, or his dad. He had woken up to the sound of the raccoons—five or six of them, bandits, tiptoeing and fingering through their campsite—and when he'd opened the zippered slit in their tent, he saw that Jonah had gone.

"Hello?" he said, and the raccoons ignored him, continuing their work disdainfully, as if they were aware that he was a child and they were adults. He held the flashlight in both hands, running it along the perimeter of the site. "Jonah?" he said. And when there was no answer, he hesitated for a moment.

Then he started walking.

He has been going forward for a while now when he pauses again. The forest is deep, he thinks, and it might be a long time before he can find a house. He thinks of fairy tales he has heard—*Hansel and Gretel, Little Red Riding Hood*—and though he's not afraid of talking wolves or witches, he wonders if there's any truth to those stories. Are there still woodsmen he could possibly encounter? Or are they extinct, like milkmen and cobblers? He pushes his light into the distance ahead of him, trying to see a pathway through the trees. He would like to meet a woodsman now, he thinks, and he imagines a man with a feather in his hat, a bow and a quiver of arrows swung over his shoulder, whistling along a path. He thinks about animals, too, about the book he had checked out of the library: *Wildlife of the Mountain States*. Colorado, he knows, is home to the lynx, an endangered species, and also to the black bear and the puma. The puma, also known as the cougar or mountain lion, crouches silently in the bushes or sometimes in trees when it is hunting. He can see the picture in the book, the tawny, large-eyed cat, and he can remember his grandma's voice as she read. "Movement, especially running, triggers prey instincts in mountain lions," and thinking of this he holds very still. He runs the beam of his flashlight along the boughs of pine trees above him, toward the star-lined lid of sky. He listens again for footsteps, for the sound of Jonah breathing. A gust of small insects passes across his face, alighting in his hair before he shakes them away.

He has been thinking a lot about his dad and mom. It has been a long time since they've spoken, but he thinks of them often. Dreams of them. Grandma Keene doesn't seem to know much about where they are. His mother, she says, had to go on a long trip, somewhere far away, and his father got into trouble. He can remember the night when the men, the police, came into his house, how he'd tried to hide under the bed as they pounded through the rooms. He can remember the bed-skirt pulling back, the man saying "Come out from under the bed, sir," and the thick hand closing around his ankle. "Come out from under the bed, sir," the man had bellowed, and when he'd cried out they'd fired a gun at him. He remembers the sound, vibrating against the walls, and the way he'd curled up and stiffened, his rigid body pulled along the dusty floor like a mop as they dragged him out.

"Oh, geez," said the man. "It's a kid." And he could hear his father crying. His dad crying. "It's okay, Loomis, it's okay," his dad said, and he'd kept his eyes squeezed tightly shut.

He'd known—his grandma had told him—that his dad had been arrested, and had to go away for a while.

But he wasn't in *jail*! Like a robber or a killer. He had known that Jonah wasn't telling the truth, but that was the lie that was the worst.

That was the lie that made him realize Jonah was trying to trick him, and a mixture of fear and outrage looped around in the pit of his stomach. Maybe Jonah wasn't his uncle after all, Loomis thought. He didn't want to be on vacation. He didn't want to sleep in a tent. He thought of that terrible and frightening movie, *The Wizard of Oz*, which he swore he would never watch again. He remembered the moment when the girl was locked in a castle, and she saw her grandmother in a crystal ball. "Dorothy!" the grandmother was shouting. "Dorothy! Where are you?" It was the most frightening thing he'd ever witnessed—that poor grandma, trapped inside the ball, blind and plaintively calling—and he thought of this as he and Jonah sat there by the fire. He knew, suddenly, he knew in his heart, that his own grandmother didn't know where he was. She was looking for him. He couldn't help himself then; he began to cry.

He stands there as these memories pass through his mind. Then, very faintly, he hears a voice in the distance. "Looooomis!" someone is calling, and he tightens his grip around the flashlight.

And despite what he knows about the pumas, he begins to run.

When he comes at last to the clearing, the voice has fallen away into the distance. The beam of the flashlight has been rattling in front of him, bouncing off the ground and the trunks of trees, careening through leaves and the shadowy mouths that sprang out after them, shapes bending and elongating and tilting themselves when the light struck them, and Loomis fell a few times, tripping over a root or a branch and then pulling himself up to run some more.

"Loomis!" the voice says in the distance. "Where are you?"

He stops when the trees open up onto the campsite. There is a fire there, still high and flickering, and a larger tent, a kind of A-frame construction with poles that hold up an awning. The people are sitting in lawn chairs next to the fire. A man and a woman, both with their hair plaited into braids, both of them blond and darkly tanned, their skin almost leathery. The man seems to be dozing, and the woman points her feet toward the fire, sleepily. She puts a little pipe to her mouth, and draws deeply on it. After a moment, a long, curling stream of smoke trails from her mouth and nose and drifts into the air.

Loomis hesitates at the edge of a tree, watching as the woman stares at the fire. Then her eyes settle on him. They look at each other, both of them blinking, considering, like a cat and bird staring at each other through the glass of a window. Loomis watches as she touches her fingers to one ear and then another, as if adjusting them.

"Randy," the woman says, and the man stirs uncertainly. "Open your eyes for a minute. I think I see a little boy standing over there."

For a moment, Randy doesn't open his eyes, and Loomis doesn't move. It would maybe be possible for him to melt back into the shadows, to slip behind a tree, but instead he just freezes.

"Hello," the woman says in a soft voice, such as you might use to speak to a rabbit wearing human clothes. She doesn't look exactly like his mother. His mother had never worn braids, he thinks, but he steps a little forward anyway. There is something about her face—the turn of her mouth, the way her eyelids droop in a dreamy, unconcerned, smiling way—that reminds him of his mom.

It has been one year and three months since he last saw her—he knows because he has kept a record of it in his mind—and sometimes he is afraid that he will forget what she looks like. But he remembers her very clearly right now, and he looks at the woman hesitantly.

"Hello," Loomis says, still holding his flashlight-dog firmly, making it heel beside him. "I'm trying to find a telephone," he says as politely as he can. "I need to call my grandmother and tell her where I am."

The two of them, the man and the woman, exchange glances, and Loomis sees the man widen his eyes with amusement at the woman. He knows that they think he's funny—adults often do—because he is small for his age but doesn't talk like a baby, because he has a good vocabulary, because he doesn't act spastic, like some of the kids at kindergarten.

"No telephone here, little guy," the man named Randy says, and grins. "Kinda late to be out wandering around by yourself, don't you think?"

Loomis doesn't say anything. He doesn't like this person very much; he reminds him a little of his uncle Ray, who always wants to swing Loomis on his shoulders or wrestle with him even though Loomis has told him that he doesn't like to roughhouse, who teases him and calls him Little Professor Man, as if it is a joke to want to know things about the world. This Randy is of the same sort, and Loomis turns his attention back to the woman.

"Can you tell me where I could find a telephone?" he says, hopefully. "I'm a little upset right now, and I really need to talk to my grandmother."

"You're upset?" the woman says, and chuckles, gently. "Oh, you poor thing. Where's your mom and dad, sweetie?"

"I don't know," Loomis says. "That's why I need to call my grandmother. I'm living with her, and she takes care of me for right now."

"Okay . . ." the lady says, doubtfully, and she and the man named Randy give one another that private, bemused look again. "Are you camping around here somewhere?" she says, and Loomis is silent. He is aware that if they take him back to Jonah, Jonah will tell them the same lies. He will not be allowed to call his grandmother.

"Do you think there's a day camp around here somewhere?" the woman says to Randy. "Boy Scouts or something?"

"Escaping the Boy Scouts," Randy says, and chortles. "On the run. A refugee. He makes his way toward freedom."

"Stop it," the woman says, but Loomis can tell that she thinks Randy is funny. But she is at least kindly when she looks at him again. "Where did you come from, sweetie? Are you camping with somebody? Are you with a group?"

"My address is 508 Foxglove Road, St. Bonaventure, Nebraska," Loomis says. "The phone number is . . ."

"Name, rank, and serial number," Randy says.

"Shut up, Randy," the woman says, wrinkling her forehead. She sits up and gestures for Loomis to come closer. But he doesn't move.

"You can sit over here," the woman says. "It's all right. What's your name, honey?"

"Loomis," he says, and shifts from foot to foot. "Loomis Timmens."

"Loomis," she says. "That's an interesting name."

"Thank you," he says. He takes a step toward her, then thinks better of it. She seems nice, but he doesn't quite trust Randy.

"Loomis," she says, and he watches her cautiously as she stands up. "How did you get here, in Colorado, if your home is in Nebraska?"

Loomis hesitates. He looks down at the faithful spot his flashlight's beam is casting. "Somebody brought me here," he says carefully. "But

I don't think he asked my grandma for permission, and that's why I want to call her. I'm afraid she might be worried about me."

"Oh, geez," the woman says, and her face darkens a little.

And then, not far away, the voice of Jonah drifts out of the trees. "Loooomis," he is calling, and Randy sits up, cupping a hand to his mouth.

"He's over here!" Randy bellows.

Loomis doesn't know what to do when he sees Jonah coming through the trees, into the circle of campfire light. He thinks that maybe he should try to run, but instead he just stands there, feeling mixed up—scared, but also oddly guilty at the sight of Jonah's stricken, concerned face. He has never tried to run away before, and a part of him can't help but feel that he has been a bad boy.

"Loomis!" Jonah says, and looks nervously from the man to the woman. "I'm so glad I found you! I was really worried about you. You shouldn't wander off like that—you could get lost!" He lets out a sigh, and shakes his head humorously at Randy. "Wow!" he says. "What a relief! Thank you guys for finding him."

"No problem," Randy says, proudly, as if he'd casually saved Loomis from drowning.

"He's a little upset," Jonah says, and he tries to smile but a shudder runs down his face and across his shoulders, so that the smile doesn't seem quite real. "I'm his uncle, and I guess . . . I didn't realize that he'd get so scared. I just thought he'd like to go camping, you know? To go on a little vacation. Because, well, he's had a very hard time. His parents are gone, and . . . and his grandma passed away a few days ago, so . . ."

Loomis feels these words hit him sharp, deliberate blows, like slaps. He takes a step backward, clutching the flashlight to his chest. "You're lying!" he says loudly. He can't believe that someone would lie in such a way, and his mouth trembles with outrage. "You took me here," he says. "And you didn't tell my grandma! And she's *worried* about me." He wipes his face, aware that they are all staring at him.

Jonah's hand trembles as he puts it up to his face, up to his scar. The man named Randy lifts an eyebrow, uncertainly, his eyes moving from Loomis to the woman. But she is staring at Loomis, as if trying to make a decision.

"He's confused," Jonah says, but his voice wavers. "It was quite a shock."

"You're lying," Loomis says again, and he gazes up at the woman, because he knows that she will see in his face that he's telling the truth. She will not believe Jonah, he thinks. She will help him find a telephone. He watches her mouth growing small as she thinks. The woods seem to freeze for a moment. The darkness settles over the small circle of firelight like a lid over a box.

35

December 18, 2002

Troy wakes up to a gray light that could be dawn or dusk or afternoon, a pale cloudy day outlining the edges of the window shade. He sits up. Today is Little Man's twelfth birthday, he thinks, and though he knows it's a fact he has a moment of uncertainty, a free-floating gust of Rip van Winkle time in which he can imagine his son, aged four or six, asleep in the next room, his cheeks still soft and peach-shaped, his face solemn, pressed against the pillow, dreaming hard. "Little Man," he thinks: an old nickname they haven't used in years and years, coming back to him out of the past. He rubs his hands over his eyes. Hard to believe that his child will soon be a teenager; hard to believe that they're still here, in this same old house that Troy had grown up in, that they've managed, after all, to stay together.

He opens the shade and looks out to where a light snow is falling and imagines that it is probably near the end of morning, the beginning of afternoon. He was up very late, and he pads blearily down the hall, glances into Loomis's room. Loomis—Loo, as he calls himself now—has left for school already, of course. The days of shaking him gently by the shoulder to wake him, the days of packing lunches and making breakfast are long gone, and though he'd never relished pulling himself out of bed after a late night at work, he does miss that morning ritual a little. These days, Loo is like a considerate roommate. He rises to his own alarm clock long before Troy is even aware of morning, and most often he's already asleep when Troy comes home at night, his homework stacked neatly on the kitchen table, the dishes washed, the clothes taken out of the dryer and folded. It makes Troy nervous to think of Loomis growing up, moving away, growing distant.

He stares at himself in the bathroom mirror. Though he is only thirty-six, his dark hair has already begun to show some gray.

He is not crazy about the way time moves forward. Thirty-six is not old, he knows, but five years, ten years, seems like less than it used to. Loomis is in middle school now, and in ten years he will have graduated from college. You ought to make the time precious, he thinks, and he is pleased to see that Loomis has opened the presents that he left out on the kitchen table the night before—some books, shirts and pants, a new watch. A laptop computer—he'd had to juggle the finances a little for that one—and he smiles, imagining the look on Loomis's face when he unwrapped it.

When he opens the front door to grab the newspaper he sees that the mail has already arrived. He is aware again of that shudder of timelessness, that sensation of being unmoored. He could be twenty-five, or fifty. He could wake and find that actually Loomis had disappeared long ago and never come back, nothing left but a computerized age-progression photo on a card that advertised missing children. He could wake up and find that he himself was only twelve years old, listening to the refrigerator open in the next room, listening to the hiss of carbonation as his father cracked open a morning beer. There is a little snow on the ground as Troy extends his hand out the front door and sinks it into the mailbox. December 18, 2002, he thinks. That's where I am.

And the dates on the letters confirm it. Here, look: a few bills, some junk mail, a Christmas card. He glances at the return address, then down to where his bare foot has left an imprint in the dusting of snow on the stoop.

He is halfway back across the living room when a voice calls out behind him.

"Troy!"

He is still sleepy enough, still deep enough in his head that it startles him badly. He whirls around, his hands coming up instinctively to shield his face, half expecting— What? An intruder? An attack? His eyes scope the room quickly before he locates the source of the voice: Here is Ray, sitting cross-legged on the floor behind the television.

"Jesus Christ!" Troy says. "What are you doing in my house?"

"Hey, Mr. Zombie Man," Ray says, and Troy slowly untenses. Ray is setting up a video game console, poking at some buttons on the controller. "You are really out of it, do you know that? I said hi and you strolled right past me like you were sleepwalking. What's the deal, man? Did you finally decide to start smoking weed again?"

Troy frowns. "No," he says, and he folds the Christmas card in half and puts it in his pocket. "I just woke up."

"You just woke up?" Ray exclaims. "Dude, it's one o'clock in the afternoon. What were you getting up to last night?"

"Nothing," Troy says. He shifts from foot to foot as Ray fiddles with some more buttons. The screen comes to life. There is the blast of heroic music, and a wrestling match announcer begins shouting.

"Geez," Ray says. "Look at this. This is fan-fucking-tastic. It's like the most realistic I've ever seen."

"Ray," Troy says, "what do you think you're doing?" But Ray doesn't look up. His eyes are focused on the screen as he starts up a game.

"It's a present," he says. "And not necessarily for you, my friend." Troy watches as Ray begins to flex and flinch along with the wrestlers he's controlling onscreen, his face hardening as the computerized action heats up.

"You didn't have to do that," he says, but Ray doesn't look up. "That's an expensive piece of equipment."

Ray only shrugs. He's not really that much different than he was when he was a teenager. He has a shaved head now, and a bristle of goatee, but his attitudes have remained the same, and even his body is as toned and neat as it had been when he was a stripper. He has never married, never even had a serious girlfriend. Looking at him, it would be hard to believe that he is a respectable business owner now, a member of the St. Bonaventure Commerce Association and the local Rotary Club.

"Look," Ray says. "I didn't buy it for you anyways, so don't worry about it." He glances up briefly, uncertainly, and their eyes meet. A myriad of things.

There has been some awkwardness between them lately. There have been more than a few times when they've had sharp words about the finances of the Stumble Inn, more than a few times when Troy has been made aware that he is, essentially, Ray's employee. "You're the manager," Ray used to say, when Ray first bought the bar from Vivian. "As far as I'm concerned, you run the place. Your decisions are my decisions." And mostly this had been true, but at the same time it was always clear that Ray was the *owner* of the bar. He was the owner, by this point, of four bars and one liquor store in St. Bonaventure and the surrounding towns. A local entrepreneur. They have never broached the subject of how much wealthier Ray was than Troy. No mention had ever been made of that valise full of drugs, which had been the original source of Ray's good fortune. It was clear that Ray was much shrewder with his income than Troy had ever been.

But even after all these years, Troy's social life still revolved around Ray and Loomis: a rock concert in Denver, a grade-school band concert in the tinny auditorium, a double date at a restaurant in which Ray and his girl played tag underneath the table, while Loo discussed species of birds with the woman Troy was supposed to be getting to know.

Troy watches as a tablet with the words GAME OVER hovers on the TV screen, and Ray smiles up at him sheepishly.

"Sit down," Ray says. "I challenge you to a battle, man."

Troy probably thinks too much about the past. He finds himself distracted by things he should have put out of his mind a long time ago—thinking about people like Lisa Fix, his old parole officer, whom he had dated for a couple of years after his release, before she'd left town for a job in Denver; or Vivian, who continues to sit regally at the same bar stool every night, Monday through Thursday, ever since her retirement. He can imagine how Ray would chide him: "What are you dwelling on that stuff for?" Ray would say. "How many years ago was that? Like, ten?" The truth is, he still thinks of these people almost every day—Judy Keene. Carla. Terry Shoopman. Jonah.

He lifts his head. Kick! Punch! Dodge! A couple of hours later, when Loomis gets home, Ray and he are still sitting there, and Troy hasn't won a single game.

Ray is the first to notice when Loomis walks in. "Hey, Birthday Guy!" Ray calls, and he holds out his hands dramatically toward the television screen. "Behold!" Ray says, and Troy smiles sheepishly, looking up from his seat on the floor into his son's face, as if Loomis is a grown-up and he is a small child.

"Hey," Loomis says, and he lets his eyes rest softly on Troy—as if to say "Are you doing okay, Dad?"—before he grins politely in Ray's direction. "Oh, my gosh," he says. "Uncle Ray, that's *really* cool. Thank you very much."

"You just have to remember that it's for you and not for your dad!" Ray says. "He's been sitting here playing all afternoon. I can't get him away from the thing."

"Uh-huh," Loomis says. He is reserved, as always, standing a little apart from them—still small for his age, though his shoulders are getting broader, his jawline is squaring off and becoming a man's. He waits there at the edge of the living room as Troy stands up. He allows Troy to hug him, to push back his messy bangs and plant a kiss on his forehead.

"Happy birthday," Troy says hoarsely, and Loomis accepts the fierceness of his father's affection with quiet dignity. He grunts a little, gasping good-naturedly as Troy squeezes him hard. "I love you, son," Troy whispers into his ear. "I love you so much."

After Ray is gone, a quiet settles over the house again. They sit at the kitchen table eating cake and ice cream, comfortable enough in each other's company. Happy enough, Troy thinks. He has tried hard to be a good father, and he knows that Loomis has made an effort to be a good son. They have had a solid life together, Troy thinks, though he wishes that they'd had a few more special moments, outside the routines of work and school, outside the rituals of watching television together and hiking out in the hills beyond the house. They don't argue about things. They seem to live their lives together smoothly.

Still, as they sit there at the table, Troy can't help but wish there was more time. He thinks about all the vacations they'd talked about and tentatively planned—to visit Washington, D.C., or Ireland, or South America—that they've never managed to afford. He thinks about the time he told Loomis he was thinking about taking some college correspondence courses, and Loomis had been so excited.

"We should just move someplace where there's a college," Loomis had said. "I wouldn't mind moving."

"Well," Troy said. "There's the money issue to consider. I can't just up and quit my job, right?"

And Loomis had shrugged. There was a deflation that Troy was aware of.

"I guess not," Loomis said, and Troy knew that he had said the wrong thing, that he had brushed against the edge of some different life that Loomis had fantasized about.

"You know, Loo," he'd said then. "I think it's a little late for me to become a different person."

And though Loomis had only been ten at the time, he'd made an irritable face. "Why do you have to be a different person to go to college?" Loomis had said. "Doesn't it sound like it would be fun?"

"Yeah," Troy said. "Sure." And he didn't meet Loomis's eyes. That was when their relationship started to change, he thought. When Loomis started to worry about him.

He had begun to be concerned about Troy's girlfriends. Suddenly, Loomis had recalled Lisa Fix and her pancake breakfasts, her stern help with grade-school math problems. "Whatever happened to her?" Loo said, and he had abruptly started to take an interest in the women that Troy went out with, even though no one serious emerged.

"Do you think you'll ever get married again?" Loomis had asked him once, trying to be casual, but it had taken him aback.

"I doubt it," Troy had said, as if it were a joke. "Who would I get married to?"

"I don't know," Loomis said. "One of these people you go on dates with, maybe."

"Any of them that you like in particular? Just give me a name and I'll propose."

"Oh, right," said Loomis, who had never liked to be teased. He turned his eyebrows downward, seriously. "What about Lisa Fix? She wanted to marry you, didn't she?"

"Ha," Troy said. "Did she tell you that?"

"No," Loomis said. "I just thought . . . you guys were together for a long time."

"I guess so. And we liked each other well enough. But, you know, I think Lisa Fix was interested in finding somebody a little more ambitious than I turned out to be." He considered for a moment, looking carefully into Loomis's eyes. "So what are you driving at, man?" he said, and ran his hand gently over the back of Loomis's hair. "You miss having a mom, I guess."

"Not really," Loomis said.

"Do you ever think about your mom? I know we don't talk about it much, and . . ."

"I don't know," Loomis said. "Not exactly."

"Oh," Troy said. He didn't think this was true, but what could he say? Over seven years have passed now since they last spoke to her, and still there was no word. Would it do any good to tell Loomis that he was fairly certain that she was still alive, that she was out there somewhere, in a new life? Would it do any good to tell Loomis that he still half expects the phone to ring, one of these years?

"You know you can talk to me about it, if you want," Troy had said, and Loomis glanced down at his fingers. "I mean, she's your mom. You've got to think about her sometimes, right?"

"I guess so," Loomis said. "I don't remember her that well. Besides," he said politely, "it's not like I want her to come back and live with us or something." And he paused for a moment, weighing his words. "I was just thinking that it might be good for *you* if you got married. I mean, I just want you to be happy, that's all."

And Troy had smiled, though Loomis's earnest, worried eyes made his heart hurt. "I am happy, son," he said softly. "I'm a very happy man."

He thinks of this all again as he watches Loomis stirring his ice cream, turning it into soft-serve. They have a good relationship, he thinks. They love each other. Loomis is doing very well in school. He seems content.

"So," Troy says, after a moment. "How was your day?"

"Fine," Loomis says. "How about you?"

"The usual," Troy says. "I slept until, like, one in the afternoon, and then Ray showed up, so . . ." He leans back in his chair, and then he remembers the Christmas card, still folded in the front pocket of his jeans. He puts his hand on it. "Actually," he says. "There was one thing." He smiles, awkwardly, and draws out the somewhat crumpled envelope. "Looks like we got a letter."

"Oh?" Loomis says.

"From Jonah Doyle."

Loomis says nothing. His eyes widen, then he looks down to his bowl and gives his ice cream another stir. This is another thing they don't talk about very much. They don't talk about what happened on the day that Jonah took Loomis to Colorado, the day Judy died. It's not something Loomis remembers very clearly, or at least that's what he says. Troy is aware that he has brought up another issue that might make Loo worry.

"Hm," Loomis says. "I thought he was in jail."

"No, no," Troy says. "He's been out for a while, actually. I told you that."

"No, you didn't. I don't remember you ever telling me that."

"Really?"

"I don't think so, Dad."

"Oh," Troy says. "Well, he's not in jail. He's been out for a little while now, I think. I could have sworn that I told you."

Loomis gives him one of his concerned, watchful looks. He has gotten Troy to cut his smoking down to almost nothing, and he has lately been taking note of Troy's bouts of insomnia. "You know," he has said, "sleep is really important for your health." And then: "Are you worried about something, Dad? What do you think about when you're up so late?" Now, looking at the card from Jonah, he pinches his mouth as if it might be another bad habit that Troy is acquiring.

"Why would he send us a Christmas card?" Loomis says. "That's kind of *weird*."

"I guess," Troy says. For Loomis, Jonah Doyle is a distant and somewhat unpleasant memory, little more.

"I want to go set up that laptop," Loomis says at last. "I have to tell you, that's the best present I've ever gotten in my life." He gives Troy another hug before he vanishes into his room.

Maybe it *is* weird, Troy thinks, as he sits there. Maybe his whole life is weird. He can imagine what Ray would have to say about it, or anyone in town for that matter. The event, as ultimately minor as it was, had caused quite a stir around St. Bonaventure, and people still referred to it as a "kidnapping." "That kidnapping that happened a few years back," people would say. It had been in the newspaper—even a small article in the *Omaha World Herald*—and folks in town had been pretty stirred up about it. Even now, customers at the bar would occasionally ask after Loomis— "How is he doing?" they would say, softly, as if he might still be suffering from the trauma. And Troy could only shrug. "He's fine," he would say, cheerfully. "Smart as a whip. Doing excellent in school. A really great kid."

He would listen as people expressed their outrage toward Jonah. "I hope they lock that guy up and throw away the key." Troy would nod.

What could he say? He seemed to be the only person in town shocked by the harshness of the sentence, the only person who'd blanched at the idea that Jonah should have been charged with felony murder for Judy's death, certainly the only one who had mixed feelings about the charge of criminal child enticement, which is what Jonah eventually pleaded guilty of, among other things. Even Jonah seemed to think that he deserved what he got.

Troy, on the other hand, didn't know what to think. There were too many things that he didn't quite understand, too many small, unexplained mysteries that had never been answered.

He had visited Jonah a few times in prison. There hadn't been a trial—since Jonah had pled guilty to all of the charges leveled against him—and this was another thing that Troy found inexplicably upsetting. It was as if Jonah was happy to go to jail, as if it were a fate that he had been waiting for, and he remembered sitting there at the table in the waiting room of the prison as Jonah shuffled in, wearing his gray prisoner outfit. Their eyes met, and Jonah seemed almost comfortable. He sat down across from Troy, and his gaze was steadier than it had ever been.

"Hello, brother," he said softly, and Troy felt a shudder go through him.

"Hello," Troy said. They sat there across from each other, and Troy tried to think of what to say.

"I guess you must be pretty mad at me," Jonah said at last, but there was an edge in his voice that suggested it was Jonah who was angry with Troy. "I was kind of surprised when you said you were coming to visit, you know? I mean, I really made a mess of everything."

"Yeah," Troy said. "In a way. But—I don't know—I suppose that I just wanted to talk some things over. There's a lot of stuff that we never really got . . . resolved, if you know what I mean."

"Like what?"

Troy shifted in his chair. The room they were sitting in was a small enclosed space, with glass windows on all sides. A guard stood outside the door with her arms folded, examining her fingernails distractedly, glancing occasionally to where they sat at the gray metal table. He sighed. What *did* he want, after all? He was aware once again of that feeling of having disappointed Jonah. *If I had had your life,* he thought.

"I don't know," Troy said at last. "I suppose I thought I'd get the real story. I mean, not just about Loomis but about . . . our mom, and everything. I'd like to get the real story about you, too."

"So would I," Jonah said, and smiled a little, a kind of private joke that eluded Troy completely. He had no idea what Jonah was thinking.

"I don't know, Troy," Jonah said. "I guess I had this idea that if I found you and put all these pieces together I could sort of solve the past—like it was a puzzle, you know? It's just that now I've kind of realized that it really isn't going to help me at all."

"Well," Troy said, and he sat there, puzzling, trying to find some coherence in what Jonah had said. "I guess I just don't get it, Jonah. I mean, I don't even understand what you're doing here. You didn't even try to defend yourself or explain yourself, and I guess that troubles me. Even if you were trying to kidnap Loomis, which I don't think you were, why didn't you just run away when you got caught? You just sat there with Loomis and those two people and waited for the police to come. That doesn't make any sense to me."

And Jonah had only shrugged. "I was depressed," he said. "I really didn't intend . . ." he said, and then he stopped as if checking himself. "I don't know what I intended, actually. It was just that—I didn't have a lot of energy left." He looked down at the table for a moment.

"You know," he said. "I don't really think I can explain myself to you, Troy. I'm sorry."

Perhaps that should have been enough. Does it matter that he'll never know what really happened?

He's not sure—but he nevertheless has found himself going over the small mysteries of his life—following rumors he hears from time to time about Carla's whereabouts, talking to detectives in Vegas and Lake Tahoe, sorting through the little scraps of information he has gathered about his biological family. It's become a kind of hobby, trying to put things together, these empty blocks in his life like squares in a crossword that he can't complete.

They keep him occupied, these projects. They are the sort of things that keep him up late at night—"worries," Loomis calls them, but Troy finds it interesting, and he's even had some successes over the years. He knows, for example, a little bit of the truth of his biological family. He has seen the grave in Little Bow, South Dakota, where Joseph Doyle was buried, and he has read the obituaries and death certificates. He has a copy of the article from the *Little Bow News*: "Boy Attacked by Family Dog," which he had taken along with him the last time he'd visited Jonah in jail.

They had maintained a cordial if distant relationship up until then. Mostly, Jonah would send him short, oddly formal letters, usually talking about the books that he was reading. He had gotten a job in the prison library and seemed very pleased about it. "I'm in the process of really learning a lot about myself," he had written, and he signed his letters: "All the Best to You and Yours."

But when Troy had shown him the Xerox of the article from the Little Bow newspaper, he had grown silent for a long time. He turned his hands over, palms up, and stared at Troy.

"I think I told you about that once," he said, coldly.

"You did?" Troy said. "I don't think so."

"It's not something I really want to talk about," Jonah said, and a few days later Troy had received a short letter in the mail.

"I'd like to take some time away from our relationship," Jonah had written.

It has been almost four years since that last letter, and after Loomis has disappeared into his room, Troy sits for a while in his easy chair in front of the television with the sound muted, turning the Christmas card over in his hands. The return address is printed on the back in Jonah's tiny, neat cursive: 2210 Hickory Street, Kingston, Jamaica, which seems as if it could be a joke. Troy had been a big Bob Marley fan, back in the day; Troy and Carla and Ray used to fantasize about living in Jamaica. But it seems to be serious. He turns the card over, and there is a Jamaican postmark over a Jamaican stamp.

And when he opens the letter he sees that it's not a Christmas card after all. It's just an ordinary card, a photo of a gnarled tree and a beach and a sunset—a scene from Jamaica, he guesses—and when he opens it he finds an old Polaroid: a picture of him and Loomis from years ago, the two of them standing in the backyard, Troy bent down on his haunches with Little Man beside him, his arm thrown around his father's shoulder. Loomis looks to be about five, and though the color has washed out a little, though there are some smudges along the edges, the two of them look brilliantly happy. He turns the photo over, then looks at the small block of carefully inked letters in the center of the card.

Dear Troy,

I have settled here in Jamaica for a while, perhaps permanently. I am doing graduate work at University in Information Science though I also am seriously considering the possibility of pursuing Medicine.

I found this photo while cleaning out some old files and notes and thought that you should have it back. I have changed a lot over the years but I am still not very good about saving pictures.

I hope you are well.
My Best to You and Yours,

Jonah

He sits there for a while, reading it over a few times, aware of a vague discouragement settling over him. What had he been expecting, after all? Some kind of confession? An explanation? A reconciliation? No, he thinks, and it occurs to him that all Jonah had wanted was evidence that his unhappy life wasn't his own fault—*If* he'd had a different mother. *If* he'd grown up in a different place—some kind of proof that he was unlucky, which was not what Troy could give him.

Still, despite everything, Troy can't help but feel that he's luckier than Jonah understands. I'm a lucky man, he would tell Jonah.

Lucky. He was a man who'd almost lost the person he loved most in the world, but he got another chance. The most amazing thing in the world. Don't worry about me, he wants to tell Loomis. I got you back. The best thing that could ever happen to me has already happened.

36

March 18, 1971

When the second baby comes, Nora is better prepared. She is in a hospital in Chicago, and no one is planning to take her baby away. She is safe. The doctor is a gentle, balding man who wears a clownish bow tie and calls her "Mrs. Gray." She has a house, and even a little room where they will put the new arrival, the crib they assembled together a few weeks ago, the tiny blankets and stuffed animals and rubber-nippled bottles lined up on a shelf. She isn't alone. Gary is sitting outside in the waiting room, nervously smiling at the mounted television, and even though he isn't the biological father, he will protect her because he loves her.

This is almost the way it is supposed to be.

Through most of her pregnancy she has been able to focus her thoughts on this new baby; she has been able to project herself into a happy future, to slide into the brightness of it as if she herself is being born, the elements slowly unblurring like a developing photo: child, husband, house, tree, mother. She promises herself that she is capable of having a happy life. She promises this new baby that it will be fine, it will be fine, she will be careful. She will steer their lives as neatly as she can.

But once the contractions start, she finds herself losing hold of the path that she has been trying to follow. It seems that she is shrinking: her fingers growing shorter, pulling back into her knuckles like a turtle's head into its shell; her hands withdrawing into her wrists, her wrists withdrawing into her shoulders, her entire body slowly gathering itself toward a central point. A shimmering nurse orbits along her line of sight, and she squeezes her eyes shut, pulling a stream of breath through her teeth. A force gathers at her middle and grips.

She had thought that she didn't remember anything about that first birth, but she remembers these pains clearly. Hard to believe they'd ever left her, and for a moment she is back in that hospital, back in the Mrs. Glass House, giving birth to a baby she will never see. *I've changed my mind,* she thinks. She remembers whispering it, *I've changed my mind, I've changed my mind,* pressing her head from side to side against her pillow, even as they wait at the edge of the room to take her child away.

She is crying a little, and the nurse's hand appears above her face to run a cloth across her forehead and eyes.

There is still a little space between the contractions. They are far enough apart that she can cling, briefly, to the single line that she's been following: the future, the new baby, the house, the tree. But it's hard to stay on track. Even as she dozes fitfully, even as the nurse's hand touches her wrist, adjusts a tube.

It's hard to believe that this is how it's done. That this is how we get here into the world, by accident or design, the microscopic pieces of ourselves borne by fluids and blood and growing into a tiny kingdom of cells inside someone else's body. It seems so difficult to become alive. So improbable.

Something cold is pressed between her lips, and her mouth works soundlessly. How can it be possible? she wonders. How can you come to understand your life when even the beginning is so complicated: a single cell imprinted with the color of your eyes and the shape of your face, the pattern on your palm and the moods that will shadow you through your life. How can you be alive when every choice you make breaks the world into a thousand filaments, each careless step branching into long tributaries of alternate lives, shuddering outward and outward like sheet lightning.

For a moment, she can feel it. She can sense herself dividing, multiplying, splitting into particles. She can feel the baby inside her, and the absence of the baby. She can sense the child that she had given away, lingering curiously over her, even as its physical body sleeps dreamlessly in a warm bed, in a pretty house at the edge of the sea. She thinks again of that house in the Winslow Homer painting, that landscape that had struck her so suddenly when she'd seen it: *Oh, that's where my baby lives,* she thought.

The child would be four years old now, almost five, and in the second before the next contraction she walks up the path toward that house. Wayne Hill is sitting in the grass with their child—a girl? No, a boy. A sturdy little guy with dark hair and Wayne's blue eyes, who waves when he sees her. Wayne and their son are sitting there eating Popsicles, and Wayne grins playfully, his mouth blue from the food coloring. He's wearing his navy uniform, and she lifts her hand, swinging her knapsack full of books. She works part-time in a small library. She takes courses at the college when they can afford it. But they are happy, and he sometimes tells her how grateful he was that she trusted him. He tells his buddies about the day he'd rescued her from the Mrs. Glass House, how brave she'd been, in the middle of a snowstorm, five months pregnant and climbing over the fence where his car was waiting.

And then her body clenches again, and for some reason she finds herself thinking of a memory from her childhood. That balloon, she thinks, squeezing her eyes shut. That yellow balloon her father had bought her at the fair when she was six. *Babygirl,* he said, *this is for you, because you're special,* and he tied the string around her wrist. She had never seen a helium balloon before, had never known that something could float like that, like magic.

She was standing in the yard when the knot around her wrist had unloosened. She remembers it clearly—the balloon, unmoored, lifting up. She'd clutched for the string but missed, and it kept rising and rising, shrinking, listlessly disappearing into clear expanse of sky.

She couldn't believe, back then, that things could be lost forever, that they could be irretrievable. She stood out there in the yard for most of the afternoon, shouting at the sky, commanding it, stomping her foot.

"Come back!" she called, and held her arms up, pleading. "Come back! Come back! Come back!"

She just wants a second chance, she thinks. She just wants to be able to think a moment before she takes another step into her life, to pause and trace along the edges of the people that she might become, but already they are putting a plastic mask over her face, already they are talking to her about breathing and bearing down, and she doesn't know what she wants yet. She doesn't know.

Thanks due: Noah Lukeman, Dan Smetanka, Elisabeth Dyssegaard, Steve Lattimore, Tom Barbash, Sheri Mount, Gilly Hailparn, Marie Coolman, Martha Collins, Sylvia Watanabe, Michael Byers, John Martin, Brian Bouldrey, Peggy McNally, Scott McNulty, Heather Bentoske.